S0-BAY-381

THE
BEDFORD
READER

THE
— BEDFORD —
READER

EDITED BY

X. J. Kennedy & Dorothy M. Kennedy

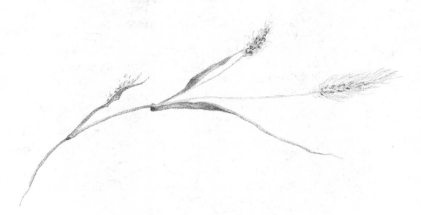

A Bedford Book

ST. MARTIN'S PRESS • NEW YORK

Library of Congress Catalog Card Number: 81-48531
Copyright © 1982 by St. Martin's Press, Inc.
All Rights Reserved.
Manufactured in the United States of America.
5432
fedcba
For information, write St. Martin's Press, Inc.,
175 Fifth Avenue, New York, N.Y. 10010

ISBN: 0-312-07117-5

Typography: Anna Post
Cover design: Steve Snider
Cover photography: Arthur Furst

• ACKNOWLEDGMENTS •

Maya Angelou, "Champion of the World." From *I Know Why the Caged Bird Sings,* by Maya Angelou. Copyright © 1969 by Maya Angelou. Reprinted by permission of Random House, Inc.

Russell Baker, "Work in Corporate America." Copyright © 1972 by Russell Baker. Reprinted by permission of the Harold Matson Company, Inc.

William F. Buckley, Jr., "Why Don't We Complain?" Reprinted by permission of Wallace & Sheil Agency, Inc. Copyright © 1960, 1963 by William F. Buckley, Jr. First published in *Esquire.*

Bruce Catton, "Grant and Lee: A Study in Contrasts." From *The American Story,* ed. Earl Schenck Miers, © 1956 by Broadcast Music, Inc. Used by permission of the copyright holder.

Alistair Cooke, "Justice Holmes and the Doffed Bikini." From *The Americans,* by Alistair Cooke. Copyright © 1979 by Alistair Cooke. Reprinted by permission of Alfred A. Knopf, Inc.

Malcolm Cowley, "Vices and Pleasures: The View from 80." An excerpt from *The View from 80* by Malcolm Cowley. Copyright © 1976, 1978, 1980 by Malcolm Cowley. Reprinted by permission of Viking Penguin Inc.

John Crompton, "The Magnitude of the Spider's Task." From *The Life of the Spider* by John Crompton, published by Collins, Publishers. Reprinted by permission of the publisher.

Acknowledgments and copyrights continue at the back of the book on pages 586–588, which constitute an extension of the copyright page.

FOR INSTRUCTORS

Old wood burns brightest, declares a proverb. In *The Bedford Reader*, we have tried to gather and stack much that has aged well. Among the fifty-four short essays in the book, some will be familiar: perhaps Thurber's "University Days," Catton's "Grant and Lee," Mitford's "Behind the Formaldehyde Curtain" and others—trustworthy, seasoned material in handy lengths. Like most composition readers, the book is arranged rhetorically. Surely our explanations of rhetorical matters and terms are as unoriginal as can be. What then is new? the owner of a shelfload of other textbooks may want to know.

In a vital way, we believe, this book is different. It moves beyond supplying model essays for close study; it tries to demonstrate how a work of effective writing is written—not in theory, but in fact. It even shows you eight professional writers toiling at student assignments—thinking over their subjects, planning, writing and revising, sometimes crumpling up what they have written and beginning anew. Besides writing essays especially for *The Bedford Reader*, they have added candid accounts of their essay-writing experiences.

Most of the essays, however, are by well-known authors. We have tried for a readable blend of classic and contemporary essays on topics a student will care about. We admitted no essay we did not enjoy reading and would not want to teach. When torn between including one essay and another, we chose the one in which a rhetorical method was clearly central. In the first forty-eight essays, the student will meet the four conventional modes of discourse: narration, description, the traditional methods of exposition, and argument. Six additional essays will show that a writer may employ more than one method in a single essay. Five of the six (all but the essay by Susan Allen Toth) contain argumentation and may be particularly useful to the instructor who wishes to stress persuasive writing.

· METHOD, PROCESS, AND STRATEGY ·

At the start of each chapter, we try to explain matters as simply as possible, and to avoid that style of textbookese in which writers wax more loftily abstract the more fervently they urge the student to use examples.

Our explanations are divided into three parts: (1) *The Method*, in which we define, illustrate, and set forth the usefulness of narration, description, the various expository methods, or argument; (2) *The Process*, in which we explain step by step how to use the method—which may involve prewriting, outlining, revising, trying out an essay on a friend, or any other work necessary; and (3) a paragraph-length example, in which we illustrate each method. Following each paragraph is a comment telling how we wrote it and, sometimes, why we didn't write it differently. To lend these examples interest and consistency, we focus all the paragraphs on the same subject: television.

The paragraph examples and comments illustrate more than a method. They are meant to demonstrate *strategy*—whatever writers may do in seeking to write effectively. Though strategy may include the pursuit of a method, it may also include defining one's purpose clearly, adjusting one's diction or tone to the needs of an audience, organizing thoughts, arranging examples in a particular order, working over sentence structure, and indeed, doing anything else a writer needs to do in writing well.

• HOW THIS BOOK WORKS •

Throughout the book, we have tried to arrange things from simplest to most complicated. In each chapter, the essays follow a sequence from easiest and most immediately engaging to most challenging. (The commissioned essays stand last in each chapter, however, so that you can find them easily.) In a similar way, we have arranged the chapters in what we believe to be a straight line from relatively simpler methods of writing to more complex. Because life has already prepared most students to write a first-person memoir or anecdote, the book opens with narration. Description follows, on the theory that students can then be asked to write a sensory report of a person, a place, or a thing. Next come the methods of exposition: from example (basic and continually useful) to analogy (most difficult and useful just once in a while).

Last in line are two forms of writing that call into play all the other methods students have learned. Definition (explained in Chapter 9), generally considered a method of exposition, often invites the writer to use description, comparison, classification, or any other method. Argument (discussed in Chapter 10), also seizes on whatever method or methods it requires. Either chapter, or both, may be helpful in reviewing any of the preceding chapters. If, however, you don't see eye to eye with us, or you wish to take up these matters in a different order, nothing will hinder you. If you care to teach not by rhetorical modes but by subjects or themes, see the list *Essays Arranged by Subject* at the back of the book.

After each essay (except the six essays for further reading), we offer three groups of questions and some suggested writing topics. *Questions on Meaning and Purpose* focus on content; *Ques-*

tions on Writing Strategy *point* not only to the method shown in a chapter, but also to audience, organization, transitions, and many another matter of concern. Questions on Language and Vocabulary *include*, besides diction and figures of speech, some attention to words that may give some students trouble. In writing questions we first asked ourselves: Exactly what in this essay matters? What can a student learn? Since the same elements are not equally important in each essay, we made no attempt to tailor each group of questions to a fixed length. When we felt that more questions were needed, we asked them. Questions frequently refer the student to a glossary, *Useful Terms*. This glossary contains not only short definitions, but often, too, words of advice. Besides the *Suggestions for Writing* that follow each essay, more general writing topics will be found at the end of each chapter.

· THE COMMISSIONED ESSAYS AND ·
· POSTSCRIPTS ON PROCESS ·

While firmly believing in acquainting students with the work of Jonathan Swift and other immortals, we trust that the book's eight commissioned essays will seem to them easier to emulate than "A Modest Proposal." As in a usual classroom situation, our professional writers were asked to rely mainly on a certain rhetorical method. Essays were commissioned for all seven methods of exposition and for argument. Each writer was given a deadline and a length. In completing their assignments, our professionals ran into problems that the student will find familiar. After every commissioned essay, in a *Postscript on Process*, each writer details the experience of writing the essay and overcoming its difficulties. If, after reading these postscripts, students take away nothing else, they will see that writing is hard, demanding work—even for professionals.

For a writing assignment, you may want to ask your students, too, to write both an essay and a Postscript on Process. For further suggestions on using the commissioned essays and postscripts, please see *Instructor's Manual to Accompany* The Bedford Reader.

• ACKNOWLEDGMENTS •

Richard S. Beal, former director of composition and associate dean of Boston University, and Sylvan Barnet, chairman of the English Department at Tufts University, read over our work not once but twice, added many suggestions, repeatedly clarified our thinking, and kept us from going astray. For its conception and fulfillment the book is most deeply indebted to Charles H. Christensen, publisher of Bedford Books. Deep thanks go also to Joan Feinberg, assistant publisher, and to Jane Aaron, Patrice Boyer, Jeff Denham, Sue Dunham, Doug Goransson, Anna Post, and Steve Snider. At St. Martin's Press, Tom Broadbent, Marcia Cohen, Marilyn Moller, Richard Steins, Lynne Williams, and Ellen Wynn gave generous support. Bill and Joan Jacobs discovered the postscript to Orwell. In providing Bedford Books with a replica of the Bedford (Massachusetts) flag, flown at the battle of Concord, Albert F. Puzzo and Roger Thurrell of the present-day Bedford Minutemen lent inspiration. Somehow the banner's motto *Vince Aut Morire* (win or die) seemed to fit, though we were fighting only the Battle of Division and Classification. We remain grateful to former students at Ohio University, the University of Michigan, the University of North Carolina (Greensboro), and Tufts University for countless friendly skirmishes over their themes.

• FOR THE RECORD •

The name of this book and its publisher comes from Bedford Street, an old London address of Macmillan, the parent company of St. Martin's Press. That it also draws on the name of the town where we live is pure coincidence. Still, for us, the title of *The Bedford Reader* may be the book's best example of words rich in connotations. In it faraway mingles with nearby. We begin to suspect what Henry Thoreau must have felt, hearing on a Sunday morning the sound of the Bedford bells that, from across a distance of seven miles, shook the waters of his pond and "conversed with every leaf and needle."

X. J. Kennedy and Dorothy M. Kennedy
Bedford, Massachusetts

CONTENTS

xi

5 PROCESS ANALYSIS: Explaining Step By Step 175

8 CAUSE AND EFFECT: Asking Why   327

The effect of this radical plan, claims its author, will be virtually
to eliminate drug addiction in the United States. Is it worth a
try?

The brilliant "biology watcher" who wrote *The Medusa and the
Snail* sheds light upon what causes warts. But what cures this
common malady? Science or magic?

Merely to face a page of trigonometry strikes terror into the
hearts of some men and many women. A probe into the origins
of this fear suggests a connection between sex roles and math
performance.

Suddenly, on the evening of October 30, 1938, people all over
the United States began weeping, praying, making frantic calls
to the police, and evacuating their homes. Why?

More and more would-be parents are willing to adopt children
handicapped physically or mentally, or past babyhood. Once,

such children would have been regarded as untouchables. What
has worked this change?

POSTSCRIPT ON PROCESS:
Leaving Some Things Out   373
Resisting the temptation to veer off on tangents, Traugot began
with an outline—but refused to be enslaved by it.

9   DEFINITION: Establishing a Boundary   377

Helping a child to understand what a parent does for a living, a
humorist views today's business world with an irreverent eye.

How much are you worth? Exactly ninety-seven cents, in terms
of your chemical constituents. Questioning this cheap appraisal
of the human body, a biophysicist returns to an earlier, magnificent definition.

Naked, trying for a head-to-toe suntan, a young woman on a
public beach defies convention. What shall we say is "indecency," after all?

Writing is closely akin to thinking. Clarify one and you clarify the other, asserts a great opponent of smokescreens, fog, and murk in English prose.

Three Contemporary Essays

Although in her candid survey of Ames, Iowa, in the 1950s the writer reveals things once whispered around town, she depicts a more innocent way of life that—well, what do you think? Has it disappeared?

Recalling both pleasures and pains of his boyhood, a Hispanic American writer reflects upon what language has meant to him and to his family. His views of bilingual education may provoke controversy.

Wooden-headedness, rampant among those who govern, results when passions frustrate the intelligence. Those who govern wisely are the exception. Will they always be so?

FOR STUDENTS

Why Read? Why Write?
Why Not Phone?

In recent years, many prophets have forecast the doom of the written word. Soon, they have argued, books and magazines will become museum pieces. Newspapers will be found only in attics. The mails will be replaced by a computer terminal in every home.

Although the prophets have been making such forecasts for three decades, their vision is far from realized. Books remain more easily portable than computer terminals and television sets—cheaper, too, and in need of less upkeep and energy. The newspaper reader continues to obtain far more information in much less time than the viewer of the six o'clock news. Russell Baker, in a light-hearted essay on corporate business in America (Chapter 9), finds that most business is still conducted with the aid of paper. A letter or memorandum leaves no doubt about what its writer is after. It is a permanent record of thought, and it lies on its recipient's desk, expecting that something will be done about it.

The day may come when we will all throw away our pens and typewriters, to compose on the glowing screens of word-processors and transmit paragraphs over cables; still, it is doubt-ful that the basic methods of writing will completely change. Whether on paper or on screens, we will need to arrange our thoughts in a clear order. We will still have to explain them to others plainly and forcefully.

That is why, in almost any career or profession you may enter, you will be expected to read continually, and also to write. This book assumes that reading and writing are a unity. Deepen your mastery of one and you deepen your mastery of the other. The experience of carefully reading an excellent writer, noticing not only what the writer has to say but also the quality of its saying, rubs off (if you are patient and perceptive) on your own writing, too.

In *The Bedford Reader*, we hope you will find a few essays you will enjoy and care to remember. The essays illustrate ten methods of writing that writers often use in thinking about their subjects and in shaping what they write. These methods aren't parlor (or classroom) games; they are practical ways of saying what you have to say. To begin with, of course, you have to have something worth saying. Discovering such a subject may call for preliminary reading, conversation, and thought.

Besides introducing you to many of the finest writers of the past (if you haven't met them before), this book includes eight essays by contemporary American writers—all professionals—who were specially commissioned to write for it. Each writer was given a choice of subjects, a method, a length, and a deadline—just as you may be given in your composition course. After each of these commissioned essays you will find a *Postscript on Process*, an account of the writer's experience in carrying out an assign-ment. The writers tell various things: how they began to write, how they revised, what problems they met, what solutions they worked out. From what they say, you will see that you aren't the only one who ever finds writing difficult.

In reading any essay in this book, read first for whatever interest or pleasure the essay may offer. Then, if you like, try answering the questions that follow it. If need be, you will want to look back over the essay and reread it in whole or in part. Some of our questions refer you to a glossary at the back of the book, *Useful Terms*. It contains words you may find helpful in discussing both the essays in this book and the essays you write. This glossary will give you more than just brief definitions. It is there to offer you further information and support.

Effective writing is a matter of caring about what you say. Good writers always think and feel first, slowly revolving a subject in mind before they begin, trying to relate it to their own lives. Good writers believe their own words. That is why readers believe them, too.

THE
BEDFORD
READER

NARRATION

Telling a Story

· THE METHOD ·

"What happened?" you ask a friend who sports a luminous black eye. Unless he merely grunts, "A golf ball," he may answer you with a narrative — a story, true or fictional.

"OK," he sighs, "you know The Tenth Round? That night-club down by the docks that smells of formaldehyde? Last night I heard they were giving away $500 to anybody who could stand up for three minutes against this karate expert, the Masked Samurai. And so . . . "

You lean forward. At least, you lean forward *if* you love a story. Most of us do, particularly if the story tells us of people in action or in conflict, and if it is told briskly, vividly, and with insight into the human heart. *Narration*, or storytelling, is therefore a powerful method by which to engage and hold the attention of listeners — readers as well. A little of its tremendous power flows to the public speaker who starts off with a joke, even a stale joke ("A funny thing happened to me on my way over here . . . "), and to the preacher who at the beginning of a sermon tells of some funny or touching incident he has observed. In its opening paragraph, an article in a popular magazine ("Vampires Live Today!") will give us a brief, arresting narrative: perhaps the case history of a car dealer who noticed, one moonlit night, his incisors strangely lengthening.

At least a hundred times a year, you probably resort to narration, not always for the purpose of telling an entertaining story, but usually to illustrate an idea, to report information, to argue, and to persuade. That is, although a narrative can run from the beginning of an essay to the end, more often in your writing (as in your speaking) a narrative is only a part of what you have to say. It is there because it serves a larger purpose. In truth, because narration is such an effective way to put across your ideas, the ability to tell a compelling story — on paper, as well as in conversation — may be one of the most useful skills you can acquire.

The term *narrative* takes in abundant territory. A narrative may be short or long; factual or imagined; as artless as a tale told in a locker room, or as artful as a novel by Henry James. A narrative may instruct and inform, or simply divert and regale. It may set forth some point or message, or it may be as devoid of significance as a comic yarn, or a horror tale whose sole aim is to curdle your blood. In *The Bedford Reader*, our concern is not with fiction (a branch of imaginative literature), but with narration as the recital of the actual. (If, however, you care to study narration in fiction, read novels: *Pride and Prejudice, David Copperfield, War and Peace, Anna Karenina, Madame Bovary, Huckleberry Finn*, or some other classic suggested by your instructor. Not only do such works exhibit masterly and imaginative storytelling, but they are also a great way to spend rainy nights.)

A novel is a narrative, but a narrative doesn't have to be long. Sometimes an essay will include several brief stories. See, for instance, William F. Buckley's argument "Why Don't We Complain?" (page 443) and Susan Allen Toth's memoir of growing up in Ames, Iowa, "Nothing Happened" (page 507). A type of brief story often used to illustrate a point is the *anecdote*, a short, entertaining account of a single incident. Sometimes told of famous persons, anecdotes add color and life to history, biography, autobiography, and every issue of *People* magazine. Besides being fun to read, an anecdote can be deeply revealing. W. Jackson Bate, in his biography of Samuel Johnson, traces the growth of the great eighteenth-century critic and scholar's ideas, and, with the aid of anecdotes, he shows that his subject was human and lovable. As Bate tells us, Dr. Johnson, a portly and imposing gentleman of fifty-five, had walked with some friends to the crest of a hill, where the great man,

> delighted by its steepness, said he wanted to "take a roll down." They tried to stop him. But he said he "had not had a roll for a long time," and taking out of his pockets his keys, a pencil, a purse, and other objects, lay down parallel at the edge of the hill, and rolled down its full length, "turning himself over and over till he came to the bottom."

However small the event it relates, this anecdote is memorable — for one reason, because of its attention to detail: the exact list of the contents of Johnson's pockets. In such a brief story, a superhuman figure comes down to human size. In one stroke, Bate reveals an essential part of Johnson: his boisterous, hearty, and boyish sense of fun.

An anecdote may be used to explain a point. Asked why he had appointed to a cabinet post Josephus Daniels, the harshest critic of his policies, President Woodrow Wilson replied with an anecdote of an old woman he knew. On spying a strange man urinating through her picket fence into her flower garden, she invited the offender into her yard because, as she explained to him, "I'd a whole lot rather have you inside pissing out than have you outside pissing in." By telling this story, a rude *analogy* (see Chapter 7 for more examples), Wilson made clear his situation in regard to his political enemy more succinctly and pointedly than if he had given a more abstract explanation. As a statesman, Woodrow Wilson may have had his flaws; but as an illustrative storyteller, he is surely among the less forgettable United States presidents. Although usually brief, an anecdote sometimes will go on for pages. In fact, James Anthony Froude's

account of the beheading of Mary, Queen of Scots (in this chapter), is an extended anecdote that reveals the character of the
queen, though it is much more detailed than most anecdotes.

• THE PROCESS •

So far, we have been concerned with a few of the uses of
narration: to explain, to persuade, to supply information, to illustrate a point. Now let us look at the structure of an effective
story and exactly how you go about telling one.

Before you begin to write, you need to decide which of the
two chief strategies of narration will best suit your particular
story: to tell it by *scene* or to tell it by *summary*. When you tell a
story in a scene, or in scenes, you remember (or visualize) each
of its events as vividly and precisely as if you were there — as
though it were a scene in a film or play and the reader its audience. This is the strategy of all fine novels and short stories,
and of much excellent nonfiction as well. You portray people,
not merely mention them; you recall dialogue, or faithfully invent it. You may also use *description* (a method to be discussed
in the next chapter). For example of scene-drawing, see James
Anthony Froude's "The Execution of Queen Mary," on page
28. So vivid is Froude's account that, even though the historian
wrote it three centuries after the fact, it seems that of an
eyewitness. Froude helps us visualize in detail a highly dramatic
tableau, a complicated one with a large cast of characters.
Sometimes, however, a scene may be drawn in only two or
three sentences. This is the brevity we find in W. Jackson Bate's
glimpse of the hill-rolling Johnson. Unlike Froude, Bate is not
trying to weave a whole tapestry of detail, but apparently is trying to show, in one brief and simple event, a trait of his hero's
character.

To tell a story by the method of summary, you relate its
events in condensed form: you do *not* depict people and their
surroundings in great detail, but strive to record the essentials
smoothly and continuously. This is the method of narration
that most of us employ in most of the stories we tell, for it requires less time and fewer words. A story told by summary may

be as skillfully written and effective, however, as a story told in scenes. In his scientific fable "But a Watch in the Night" (page 304), James C. Rettie, by the method of summary, covers in a few pages a colossal span of time: the history of the earth for the past 757 million years. In the limited room at his disposal, Rettie cannot stop to draw the scene of the execution of Mary, Queen of Scots, for in his imaginary movie, the event of her death is relatively brief. Although nothing in Rettie's essay is treated in great detail, the effect is nonetheless spellbinding.

Whether scene or summary will prove a better method for your story depends on how many events you have to tell and how thoroughly you want to tell them; your purpose in writing will also affect your choice. An encyclopedia article narrating the events in the life of a famous person is usually written in summary form, for its aim is to supply information concisely. A book-length biography of the same person, however, will probably include at least a few scenes, because the writer seeks to depict the subject thoroughly and to render a whole life alive. To be sure, both methods of narration may occur in the same story. Often, summary will be a valuable strategy for the writer who wishes to pass briskly from one scene to the next or to hurry by some less important events. If you were writing, for instance, an account of a man's fiendish passion for horse racing, and you didn't want to dwell on the other facts of his life, you could introduce a later scene with this brief summary: "Seven years went by, and after being twice married and once divorced, Lars found himself again back at Hialeah."

After you choose your narrative method, you will need to select your *point of view*, the angle of vision from which the story will be told. Do you want to relate the events yourself, in the first person? This is usually the natural way to tell a story in which you were the central character or a participant. Or do you not need to involve yourself? Then, you may want to write in the third person, maintaining the distance of an outsider. Obviously, Froude cannot say, "I watched the queen kneel down"; he must write as a third-person observer in reconstructing the scene from historical evidence. Also in this chapter, Maya Angelou, James Herriot, and James Thurber supply memoirs written in the first person, which better enables them to report their feelings and to position themselves in the midst of their experiences. An omniscient narrator, one who is all-knowing, can see into the minds of the characters. Do you want to be such a narrator and reveal thought, or remain objective? Sometimes it is effective to get inside minds, and sometimes it is effective merely to be an outside reporter. Note how much Woodrow Wilson's anecdote would *lose* by going into its characters' thoughts: "The old woman was angry and embarrassed at seeing the stranger. . . ." Or: "The man himself thought her outburst the most ludicrous thing he had ever heard." Obviously the storyteller's purpose in telling the anecdote is to make a point, not to explore psychology.

In planning your story, you might organize all the events in chronological order — unless you can see a better method of organization. Chronological order, although it is simplest for a writer to follow, may not always be the most effective arrangement. Perhaps you will seize your reader's attention more firmly if you begin *in medias res* (Latin, "in the middle of things"), opening with a highly dramatic event — even though it happened late in the story. If you do so, perhaps you will want to return to earlier events by means of a *flashback*, or a scene relived in memory. In writing a news story, a reporter often begins with the end of the story, placing the main event in the *lead*, or opening paragraph. Dramatically, this may be the weakest possible method of telling a story; but to provide entertainment is not the main purpose of a good reporter — it is to tell quickly what happened. (On the other hand, a writer whose purpose is to entertain, such as a fiction writer, usually saves the main event for last to keep the reader in enjoyable suspense for as long as possible.)

Good storytellers know what to emphasize. Whether or not they are trying for drama, they will not fall into a boring drone: "And then I went down to the club, and I had a few beers, and I noticed this sign, GO 3 MINUTES WITH THE MASKED SAMURAI, WIN $500, so I went and got knocked out, and then I had a pizza, and then I went home." In this bare-bones, lazily connected kind of summary, the narrator reduces all the events to equal unimportance. A more adept storyteller would dwell on the big fight itself and omit the pizza. (The beers, however, might well be essential. Perhaps they were what caused the narrator to take on the Samurai.)

In a story Mark Twain liked to tell, a woman's ghost returns to claim her golden arm, which her greedy husband had un-screwed from her corpse. Twain used to end his story by sud-denly shrieking *"YOU got it!"* at a member of the audience and enjoying the sound of the victim's surprised yell. That final punctuating shriek may be a technique that will work only in oral storytelling, and yet, like Twain, most storytellers like to end with a bang if they can. The final impact, however, need not be so obvious. As Maya Angelou demonstrates in her story in this chapter, you can achieve impact just by leading to a point. In an effective written narrative, a writer usually hits the main events of a story especially hard, often saving the best punch (or the best karate chop) for the very end.

· NARRATION IN A PARAGRAPH ·

Oozing menace from beyond the stars or from the deeps, televised horror powerfully stimulates a child's already frisky imagination. As parents know, a "Creature Double Feature" has an impact that lasts long after the click of the OFF but-ton. Recently a neighbor reported the strange case of her eight-year-old. Discovered late at night in the game room watching *The Exorcist*, the girl was promptly sent to bed. An hour later, her parents could hear her chanting something in the darkness of her bedroom. On tiptoe, they stole to her door to listen. The creak of springs told them that their daughter was swaying rhythmically to and fro and the smell of acrid smoke warned them that something was burning. At once, they shoved open the door to find the room flickering with shadows cast by a lighted candle. Their daughter was sit-ting up in bed, rocking back and forth as she intoned over and over, "Fiend in human form . . . Fiend in human form . . . " This case may be unique; still, it seems likely that similar events take place each night all over the screenwatching world.

Comment. This paragraph puts an anecdote to work to support a thesis statement: the claim, in the second sentence, that for children the impact of TV horror goes on and on. The story relates a small, ordinary, but disquieting experience taken from the writer's conversation with friends. A bit of suspense is introduced, and the reader's curiosity is whetted, when the parents steal to the bedroom door to learn why the child isn't asleep. The crisis — the dramatic high moment in the story when our curiosity is about to be gratified — is a sensory detail: the smell of smoke. At the end of the paragraph, the writer stresses the importance of these events by suggesting that they are probably universal. In a way, he harks back to his central idea, reminding us of his reason for telling the story. Narration, as you can see, is a method for dramatizing your ideas.

· Maya Angelou ·

MAYA ANGELOU was born Marguerita Johnson in St. Louis in 1928. After an unpleasantly eventful youth by her account ("from a broken family, raped at eight, unwed mother at sixteen"), she went on to join a dance company, star in an off-Broadway play (*The Blacks*), write three books of poetry, produce a series on Africa for PBS-TV, serve as a coordinator for the Southern Christian Leadership Conference at the request of Martin Luther King, Jr., and accept three honorary doctorates. She is best known, however, for the four books of her searching, frank, and joyful autobiography — beginning with *I Know Why the Caged Bird Sings* (1970), which she adapted for television, through her most recent volume, *The Heart of a Woman* (1981).

Champion of the World

"Champion of the World" is the nineteenth chapter from *I Know Why the Caged Bird Sings*; the title is a phrase taken from it. Remembering her childhood, the writer tells how she and her older brother, Bailey, grew up in a town in Arkansas. The center of their lives was grandmother and Uncle Willie's store, a gathering place for the black community. On the night when this story takes place, Joe Louis, the "Brown Bomber" and the hero of his people, defends his heavyweight title against a white contender.

The last inch of space was filled, yet people continued to wedge themselves along the walls of the Store. Uncle Willie had turned the radio up to its last notch so that youngsters on the porch wouldn't miss a word. Women sat on kitchen chairs, dining-room chairs, stools and upturned wooden boxes. Small children and babies perched on every lap available and men leaned on the shelves or on each other. 1

The apprehensive mood was shot through with shafts of gaiety, as a black sky is streaked with lightning. 2

9

"I ain't worried 'bout this fight. Joe's gonna whip that   3
cracker like it's open season."

"He gone whip him till that white boy call him Momma."   4

At last the talking was finished and the string-along songs   5
about razor blades were over and the fight began.

"A quick jab to the head." In the Store the crowd grunted.   6
"A left to the head and a right and another left." One of the
listeners cackled like a hen and was quieted.

"They're in a clinch, Louis is trying to fight his way out."   7

Some bitter comedian on the porch said, "That white man   8
don't mind hugging that niggah now, I betcha."

"The referee is moving in to break them up, but Louis final-   9
ly pushed the contender away and it's an uppercut to the chin.
The contender is hanging on, now he's backing away. Louis
catches him with a short left to the jaw."

A tide of murmuring assent poured out the doors and into   10
the yard.

"Another left and another left. Louis is saving that mighty   11
right . . . " The mutter in the Store had grown into a baby roar
and it was pierced by the clang of a bell and the announcer's
"That's the bell for round three, ladies and gentlemen."

As I pushed my way into the Store I wondered if the an-   12
nouncer gave any thought to the fact that he was addressing as
"ladies and gentlemen" all the Negroes around the world who
sat sweating and praying, glued to their "master's voice."[1]

There were only a few calls for R. C. Colas, Dr. Peppers,   13
and Hires root beer. The real festivities would begin after the
fight. Then even the old Christian ladies who taught their children and tried themselves to practice turning the other cheek
would buy soft drinks, and if the Brown Bomber's victory was a
particularly bloody one they would order peanut patties and
Baby Ruths also.

Bailey and I laid the coins on top of the cash register. Uncle   14
Willie didn't allow us to ring up sales during a fight. It was too

---

[1]"His master's voice," accompanied by a picture of a little dog listening to
a phonograph, was a familiar advertising slogan. (The picture still appears on
RCA Victor records.)

noisy and might shake up the atmosphere. When the gong rang
for the next round we pushed through the near-sacred quiet to
the herd of children outside.

"He's got Louis against the ropes and now it's a left to the   15
body and a right to the ribs. Another right to the body, it looks
like it was low. . . . Yes, ladies and gentlemen, the referee is
signaling but the contender keeps raining the blows on Louis.
It's another to the body, and it looks like Louis is going down."

My race groaned. It was our people falling. It was another   16
lynching, yet another Black man hanging on a tree. One more
woman ambushed and raped. A Black boy whipped and
maimed. It was hounds on the trail of a man running through
slimy swamps. It was a white woman slapping her maid for being forgetful.

The men in the Store stood away from the walls and at at-   17
tention. Women greedily clutched the babes on their laps while
on the porch the shufflings and smiles, flirtings and pinching of
a few minutes before were gone. This might be the end of the
world. If Joe lost we were back in slavery and beyond help. It
would all be true, the accusations that we were lower types of
human beings. Only a little higher than apes. True that we were
stupid and ugly and lazy and dirty and, unlucky and worst of
all, that God Himself hated us and ordained us to be hewers of
wood and drawers of water, forever and ever, world without
end.

We didn't breathe. We didn't hope. We waited.   18

"He's off the ropes, ladies and gentlemen. He's moving   19
towards the center of the ring." There was no time to be relieved. The worst might still happen.

"And now it looks like Joe is mad. He's caught Carnera   20
with a left hook to the head and a right to the head. It's a left
jab to the body and another left to the head. There's a left cross
and a right to the head. The contender's right eye is bleeding
and he can't seem to keep his block up. Louis is penetrating
every block. The referee is moving in, but Louis sends a left to
the body and it's an uppercut to the chin and the contender is
dropping. He's on the canvas, ladies and gentlemen."

Babies slid to the floor as women stood up and men leaned   21
toward the radio.

"Here's the referee. He's counting. One, two, three, four,   22
five, six, seven . . . Is the contender trying to get up again?"
All the men in the store shouted, "NO."   23
" — eight, nine, ten." There were a few sounds from the au-   24
dience, but they seemed to be holding themselves in against tremendous pressure.

"The fight is all over, ladies and gentlemen. Let's get the   25
microphone over to the referee . . . Here he is. He's got the
Brown Bomber's hand, he's holding it up . . . Here he is . . ."

Then the voice, husky and familiar, came to wash over us —   26
"The winnah, and still heavyweight champeen of the
world . . . Joe Louis."

Champion of the world. A Black boy. Some Black mother's   27
son. He was the strongest man in the world. People drank Coca-
Colas like ambrosia and ate candy bars like Christmas. Some of
the men went behind the Store and poured white lightning in
their soft-drink bottles, and a few of the bigger boys followed
them. Those who were not chased away came back blowing
their breath in front of themselves like proud smokers.

It would take an hour or more before the people would leave   28
the Store and head for home. Those who lived too far had made
arrangements to stay in town. It wouldn't do for a Black man
and his family to be caught on a lonely country road on a night
when Joe Louis had proved that we were the strongest people in
the world.

• QUESTIONS ON MEANING AND PURPOSE •

1. What do you take to be the author's purpose in telling this story?
   (See *Purpose* in Useful Terms.)
2. What connection does Angelou make between the outcome of the
   fight and the pride of the black race? To what degree do you think
   the author's view is shared by the others in the Store listening to
   the broadcast?
3. To what extent are the statements in paragraphs 16 and 17 to be
   taken literally? What purpose do they serve in Angelou's narrative?

4. Primo Carnera was probably *not* the Brown Bomber's opponent on the night Maya Angelou recalls. Louis fought Carnera only once, on June 25, 1935, and it was not a title match; Angelou would have been no more than seven years old at the time. Does the author's apparent error detract from her story?

• QUESTIONS ON WRITING STRATEGY •

1. What details in the opening paragraphs indicate that an event of crucial importance is about to take place?
2. How does Angelou build up suspense in her account of the fight? At what point were you able to predict the winner?
3. Comment on the irony in Angelou's final paragraph. (See *Irony* in Useful Terms.)
4. How many stories does "Champion of the World" contain? What are they?

• QUESTIONS ON LANGUAGE •
• AND VOCABULARY •

1. Explain what the author means by "string-along songs about razor blades" (paragraph 5).
2. How does Angelou's use of nonstandard English contribute to her narrative? (See *Nonstandard English* under *Diction* in Useful Terms.)

• SUGGESTIONS FOR WRITING •

1. In a brief essay, write about the progress and outcome of a recent sporting event and your reaction to the outcome. Include enough illustrative detail to bring the contest to life.
2. Write an essay based on some childhood experience of your own, still vivid in your memory.

· James Herriot ·

JAMES HERRIOT, born James Alfred Wight in 1916 in Scotland, attended Glasgow Veterinary College and established a practice in Yorkshire, England, when he was in his twenties. Not until he was over fifty, though, did he publish *All Creatures Great and Small* (1972), the first account of his early days as a Yorkshire veterinarian. The book and its successors, *All Things Bright and Beautiful* (1974), *All Things Wise and Wonderful* (1977) and *The Lord God Made Them All* (1981) have to date sold over eleven million copies. Herriot has also published a tour book, *James Herriot's Yorkshire* (1979), produced with photographer Derry Brabbs. The author still writes and practices veterinary medicine in Yorkshire.

Just Like Bernard Shaw

Herriot's love of animals, his quiet sense of humor, and his keen appreciation for the colorful Yorkshire neighbors who enliven his memoirs have made his books popular with readers everywhere. "Just Like Bernard Shaw" (Herriot's phrase) is the twenty-third chapter of *The Lord God Made Them All* (1981). In this anecdote, proving that the events that inspire a good story don't have to be earth-shaking, the veterinarian wryly details one family's reaction to the news that playwright Bernard Shaw has suffered a mishap.

It was in 1950 that one of my heroes, George Bernard Shaw, broke his leg while pruning apple trees in his garden. By a coincidence I had been reading some of the prefaces that same week, revelling in the unique wit of the man and enjoying the feeling I always had with Shaw — that I was in contact with a mind whose horizons stretched far beyond those of the other literary figures of the day, and most other days.

I was shocked when I read about the calamity, and there was no doubt the national press shared my feelings. Banner headlines pushed grave affairs of state off the front pages, and for weeks bulletins were published for the benefit of an anxious

1

2

public. It was right that this should be, and I agreed with all the phrases that rolled off the journalists' typewriters. "Literary genius . . . " "Inspired musical critic who sailed fearlessly against the tide of public opinion . . . " "Most revered playwright of our age . . . "

It was just about then that the Caslings' calf broke its leg, too, and I was called to set it. The Casling farm was one of a group of homesteads set high on the heathery Yorkshire moors. They were isolated places and often difficult to find. To reach some of them you had to descend into gloomy, garlic-smelling gills and climb up the other side; with others there was no proper road, just a clay path through the heather, and it came as a surprise to find farm buildings at the end of it.

Caslings' place didn't fall into either of these categories. It was perched on the moor top, with a fine disregard for the elements. The only concession was a clump of hardy trees that had been planted to the west of the farm to give shelter from the prevailing wind, and the way those trees bent uniformly towards the stones of house and barns was testimony to the fact that the wind hardly ever stopped blowing.

Mr. Casling and his two big sons slouched towards me as I got out of the car. The farmer was the sort of man you would expect to find in a place like this, his sixty-year-old face purpled and roughened by the weather, wide, bony shoulders pushing against the ragged material of his jacket. His sons, Alan and Harold, were in their thirties and resembled their father in almost every detail, even to the way they walked, hands deep in pockets, heads thrust forward, heavy boots trailing over the cobbles. Also, they didn't smile. They were good chaps, all of them, in fact, a nice family, but they weren't smilers.

"Now, Mr. Herriot." Mr. Casling peered at me under the frayed peak of his cap and came to the point without preamble. "Calf's in t'field."

"Oh, right," I said. "Could you bring me a bucket of water, please? Just about lukewarm."

At a nod from his father, Harold made wordlessly for the kitchen and returned within minutes with a much-dented receptacle.

I tested the water with a finger. "Just right. That's fine."   9

We set off through a gate with two stringy little sheepdogs   10
slinking at our heels, and the wind met us with savage joy, swirl-
ing over the rolling bare miles of that high plateau, chill and
threatening to the old and weak, fresh and sweet to the young
and strong.

About a score of calves was running with their mothers on a   11
long rectangle of green cut from the surrounding heather. It was
easy to pick out my patient, although, when the herd took off at
the sight of us, it was surprising how fast he could run with his
dangling hind leg.

At a few barked commands from Mr. Casling, the dogs   12
darted among the cattle, snapping at heels, baring their teeth at
defiant horns till they had singled out cow and calf. They stood
guard then till the young men rushed in and bore the little animal to the ground.

I felt the injured limb over with a tinge of regret. I was sure I   13
could put him right, but I would have preferred a foreleg.
Radius and ulna healed so beautifully. But in this case the
crepitus was midway along the tibia, which was more tricky.

However, I was thankful it was not the femur. That would   14
have been a problem, indeed.

My patient was expertly immobilized, held flat on the sparse   15
turf by Harold at the head, Alan at the tail and their father in
the middle. One of a country vet's difficulties is that he often
has to do vital work on a patient that won't keep still, but those
three pairs of huge hands held the shaggy creature as in a vise.

As I dipped my plaster bandages in the water and began to   16
apply them to the fracture, I noticed that our heads were very
close together. It was a very small calf — about a month old —
and at times the three human faces were almost in contact. And
yet nobody spoke.

Veterinary work passes blithely by when there is good con-   17
versation, and it is a positive delight when you are lucky enough
to have one of those dry Yorkshire raconteurs among your help-
ers. At times I have had to lay down my scalpel and laugh my
fill before I was able to continue. But here all was silence.

The wind whistled, and once I heard the plaintive cry of a 18
curlew, but the group around that prostrate animal might have
been Trappist monks. I began to feel embarrassed. It wasn't a
difficult job; I didn't need a hundred percent concentration.
With all my heart I wished somebody would say something.

Then, like a glorious flash of inspiration, I remembered the 19
recent clamor in the newspapers. I could start things off, at
least.

"Just like Bernard Shaw, eh?" I said with a light laugh. 20

The silence remained impenetrable, and for about half a 21
minute it seemed that I was going to receive no reply.

Then Mr. Casling cleared his throat. " 'oo?" he inquired. 22

"Bernard Shaw, George Bernard Shaw, you know. He's 23
broken his leg, too." I was trying not to gabble.

The silence descended again, and I had a strong feeling that 24
I had better leave it that way. I got on with my job, dousing the
white cast with water and smoothing it over while the plaster
worked its way under my fingernails.

It was Harold who came in next. "Does 'e live about 'ere?" 25

"No . . . no . . . not really." I decided to put on one more 26
layer of bandage, wishing fervently that I had never started this
topic.

I was tipping the bandage from the tin when Alan chipped 27
in.

"Darrowby feller, is 'e?" 28

Things were becoming more difficult. "No," I replied airily. 29
"I believe he spends most of his time in London."

"London!" The conversation, such as it was, had been car- 30
ried on without any movement of the heads, but now the three
faces jerked up towards me with undisguised astonishment and
the three voices spoke as one.

After the initial shock had worn off the men looked down 31
at the calf again, and I was hoping that the subject was dead
when Mr. Casling muttered from the corner of his mouth. "He
won't be in t' farmin' line, then?"

"Well, no . . . he writes plays." I didn't say anything about 32
Shaw's intuitive recognition of Wagner as a great composer. I

could see by the flitting side glances that I was in deep enough, already.

"We'll just give the plaster time to dry," I said. I sat back on   33
the springy turf as the silence descended again.

After a few minutes I tapped a finger along the length of the   34
white cast. It was as hard as stone. I got to my feet. "Right, you
can let him go now."

The calf bounded up and trotted away with his mother as   35
though nothing had happened to him. With the support of the
plaster his lameness was vastly diminished, and I smiled. It was
always a nice sight.

"I'll take it off in a month," I said, but there was no further   36
talk as we made our way over the field towards the gate.

Still, I knew very well what the remarks would be over the   37
farmhouse dinner table. "Queer lad, that vitnery. Kept on
about some friend of his in London broke his leg."

"Aye. Kept on just like the man knows us."   38

"Aye. Queer lad."   39

And my last feeling as I drove away was not just that all   40
fame is relative but that I would take care in future not to start
talking about somebody who doesn't live about 'ere.

• QUESTIONS ON MEANING AND PURPOSE •

1. What prompts Herriot to start talking to the three farmers about Shaw's broken leg?
2. What is the veterinarian's attitude toward Mr. Casling and his sons?
3. What purpose other than to entertain do you find in "Just Like Bernard Shaw"? (See *Purpose* in Useful Terms.)

• QUESTIONS ON WRITING STRATEGY •

1. How does Herriot firmly establish that George Bernard Shaw's broken leg was of concern to people throughout England? Of what importance is this fact to the author's story?
2. What do the snatches of dialogue (and dialect) contribute to this account? (See *Dialect* under *Diction* in Useful Terms.)

3. What is the tone of Herriot's anecdote? (See *Tone* in Useful Terms.)

• QUESTIONS ON LANGUAGE •
• AND VOCABULARY •

1. Acquaint yourself with the definitions of the following medical terms in Herriot's account: radius, ulna, crepitus, tibia (paragraph 13); femur (14).
2. What does the author mean when he says, in the final paragraph, that "all fame is relative"?
3. Why do you suppose Herriot chooses to fall into Yorkshire speech in his narrative's closing word?

• SUGGESTIONS FOR WRITING •

1. Sum up, in a paragraph or two, the reasons for the communication gap between the veterinarian and the Caslings.
2. Based on your own experience, write an anecdote about an encounter that did not proceed smoothly: an interview, a blind date, a business transaction, a reunion, or whatever else strikes you as a likely possibility. Include enough vivid detail so that your reader will be moved to agonize along with you.

· James Thurber ·

JAMES THURBER (1894–1961), a native of Columbus, Ohio, made himself immortal with his humorous stories of shy, bumbling men (such as "The Secret Life of Walter Mitty") and his cartoons of men, women, and dogs that look as though he had drawn them with his foot. (In fact, Thurber suffered from weak eyesight and had to draw his cartoons in crayon on sheets of paper two or three feet wide.) As Thurber aged and approached blindness, he drew less and less, and wrote more and more. His first book, written with his friend E. B. White, is a takeoff on self-help manuals, *Is Sex Necessary?* (1929); his later prose includes *My Life and Hard Times* (1933), from which "University Days" is taken; *The Thirteen Clocks*, a fable for children (1950); and *The Years with Ross* (1959), a memoir of his years on the staff of *The New Yorker*.

University Days

Ohio State University in World War I may seem remote from your own present situation, but see if you don't agree that this story of campus frustration is as fresh as the day it was first composed. Notice how, with beautiful brevity, Thurber draws a scene, introduces bits of revealing dialogue, and shifts briskly from one scene to another.

I passed all the other courses that I took at my university, but I could never pass botany. This was because all botany students had to spend several hours a week in a laboratory looking through a microscope at plant cells, and I could never see through a microscope. I never once saw a cell through a microscope. This used to enrage my instructor. He would wander around the laboratory pleased with the progress all the students were making in drawing the involved and, so I am told, interesting structure of flower cells, until he came to me. I would just be standing there. "I can't see anything," I would say. He would begin patiently enough, explaining how anybody can see through a microscope, but he would always end up in a fury, claiming that I could *too* see through a microscope but just pretended that I couldn't. "It takes away from the beauty of flowers anyway," I used to tell him. "We are not concerned with beauty in this course," he would say. "We are concerned solely with what I may call the *mechanics* of flars." "Well," I'd say, "I can't see anything." "Try it just once again," he'd say, and I would put my eye to the microscope and see nothing at all, except now and again a nebulous milky substance — a phenomenon of maladjustment. You were supposed to see a vivid, restless clockwork of sharply defined plant cells. "I see what looks like a lot of milk," I would tell him. This, he claimed, was the result of my not having adjusted the microscope properly, so he would readjust it for me, or rather, for himself. And I would look again and see milk.

I finally took a deferred pass, as they called it, and waited a year and tried again. (You had to pass one of the biological sciences or you couldn't graduate.) The professor had come back from vacation brown as a berry, bright-eyed, and eager to explain cell-structure again to his classes. "Well," he said to me, cheerily, when we met in the first laboratory hour of the semester, "we're going to see cells this time, aren't we?" "Yes, sir," I said. Students to right of me and to left of me and in front of me were seeing cells; what's more, they were quietly drawing pictures of them in their notebooks. Of course, I didn't see anything.

"We'll try it," the professor said to me, grimly, "with every adjustment of the microscope known to man. As God is my witness, I'll arrange this glass so that you see cells through it or I'll give up teaching. In twenty-two years of botany, I — " He cut off abruptly for he was beginning to quiver all over, like Lionel Barrymore,[1] and he genuinely wished to hold onto his temper; his scenes with me had taken a great deal out of him.

So we tried it with every adjustment of the microscope known to man. With only one of them did I see anything but blackness or the familiar lacteal opacity, and that time I saw, to my pleasure and amazement, a variegated constellation of

[1] A noted American stage, radio, and screen actor (1878–1954).

flecks, specks, and dots. These I hastily drew. The instructor, noting my activity, came back from an adjoining desk, a smile on his lips and his eyebrows high in hope. He looked at my cell drawing. "What's that?" he demanded, with a hint of a squeal in his voice. "That's what I saw," I said. "You didn't, you didn't, you *didn't!*" he screamed, losing control of his temper instantly, and he bent over and squinted into the microscope. His head snapped up. "That's your eye!" he shouted. "You've fixed the lens so that it reflects! You've drawn your eye!"

Another course that I didn't like, but somehow managed to   5 pass, was economics. I went to that class straight from the botany class, which didn't help me any in understanding either subject. I used to get them mixed up. But not as mixed up as another student in my economics class who came there direct from a physics laboratory. He was a tackle on the football team, named Bolenciecwcz. At that time Ohio State University had one of the best football teams in the country, and Bolenciecwcz was one of its outstanding stars. In order to be eligible to play it was necessary for him to keep up in his studies, a very difficult matter, for while he was not dumber than an ox he was not any smarter. Most of his professors were lenient and helped him along. None gave him more hints in answering questions or asked him simpler ones than the economics professor, a thin, timid man named Bassum. One day when we were on the subject of transportation and distribution, it came Bolenciecwcz's turn to answer a question. "Name one means of transportation," the professor said to him. No light came into the big tackle's eyes. "Just any means of transportation," said the professor. Bolenciecwcz sat staring at him. "That is," pursued the professor, "any medium, agency, or method of going from one place to another." Bolenciecwcz had the look of a man who is being led into a trap. "You may choose among steam, horse-drawn, or electrically propelled vehicles," said the instructor. "I might suggest the one which we commonly take in making long journeys across land." There was a profound silence in which everybody stirred uneasily, including Bolenciecwcz and Mr. Bassum. Mr. Bassum abruptly broke this silence in an amazing manner. "Choo-choo-choo," he said, in a low voice, and turned instantly scarlet. He glanced appealingly around the room. All of us, of course, shared Mr. Bassum's desire that Bolenciecwcz should stay abreast of the class in economics, for the Illinois game, one of the hardest and most important of the season, was only a week off. "Toot, toot, too-toooooot!" some student with a deep voice moaned, and we all looked encouragingly at Bolenciecwcz. Somebody else gave a fine imitation of a locomotive letting off steam. Mr. Bassum himself rounded off the little show. "Ding, dong, ding, dong," he said, hopefully. Bolenciecwcz was staring at the floor now, trying to think, his great brow furrowed, his huge hands rubbing together, his face red.

"How did you come to college this year, Mr. Bolenciecwcz?" 6
asked the professor. "*Chuffa* chuffa, *chuffa* chuffa."

"M'father sent me," said the football player. 7

"What on?" asked Bassum. 8

"I git an 'lowance," said the tackle, in a low, husky voice, 9
obviously embarrassed.

"No, no," said Bassum. "Name a means of transportation. 10
What did you *ride* here on?"

"Train," said Bolenciecwcz. 11

"Quite right," said the professor. "Now, Mr. Nugent, will 12
you tell us — "

If I went through anguish in botany and economics — for 13
different reasons — gymnasium work was even worse. I don't even like to think about it. They wouldn't let you play games or join in the exercises with your glasses on and I couldn't see with mine off. I bumped into professors, horizontal bars, agricultural students, and swinging iron rings. Not being able to see, I could take it but I couldn't dish it out. Also, in order to pass gymnasium (and you had to pass it to graduate) you had to learn to swim if you didn't know how. I didn't like the swimming pool, I didn't like swimming, and I didn't like the swimming instructor, and after all these years I still don't. I never swam but I passed my gym work anyway, by having another student give my gymnasium number (978) and swim across the pool in my place. He was a quiet, amiable blonde youth, number 473, and he would have seen through a microscope for me if we could have got away with it, but we couldn't get away with it. Another thing I didn't like about gymnasium work was that they made you strip the day you registered. It is impossible for me to be happy when

I am stripped and being asked a lot of questions. Still, I did better than a lanky agricultural student who was cross-examined
just before I was. They asked each student what college he was
in — that is, whether Arts, Engineering, Commerce, or Agriculture. "What college are you in?" the instructor snapped at
the youth in front of me. "Ohio State University," he said
promptly.

It wasn't that agricultural student but it was another a   14
whole lot like him who decided to take up journalism, possibly
on the ground that when farming went to hell he could fall back
on newspaper work. He didn't realize, of course, that that
would be very much like falling back full-length on a kit of
carpenter's tools. Haskins didn't seem cut out for journalism,
being too embarrassed to talk to anybody and unable to use a
typewriter, but the editor of the college paper assigned him to
the cow barns, the sheep house, the horse pavilion, and the animal husbandry department generally. This was a genuinely big
"beat," for it took up five times as much ground and got ten
times as great a legislative appropriation as the College of
Liberal Arts. The agricultural student knew animals, but nevertheless his stories were dull and colorlessly written. He took all
afternoon on each of them, on account of having to hunt for
each letter on the typewriter. Once in a while he had to ask
somebody to help him hunt. "C" and "L," in particular, were
hard letters for him to find. His editor finally got pretty much
annoyed at the farmer-journalist because his pieces were so un-
interesting. "See here, Haskins," he snapped at him one day,
"why is it we never have anything hot from you on the horse
pavilion? Here we have two hundred head of horses on this
campus — more than any other university in the Western Conference except Purdue — and yet you never get any real low-
down on them. Now shoot over to the horse barns and dig up
something lively." Haskins shambled out and came back in
about an hour; he said he had something. "Well, start it off
snappily," said the editor. "Something people will read."
Haskins set to work and in a couple of hours brought a sheet of
typewritten paper to the desk; it was a two-hundred-word story
about some disease that had broken out among the horses. Its
opening sentence was simple but arresting. It read: "Who has

noticed the sores on the tops of the horses in the animal husbandry building?"

Ohio State was a land grant university and therefore two
years of military drill was compulsory. We drilled with old
Springfield rifles and studied the tactics of the Civil War even
though the World War was going on at the time. At 11 o'clock
each morning thousands of freshmen and sophomores used to
deploy over the campus, moodily creeping up on the old chemistry building. It was good training for the kind of warfare that
was waged at Shiloh but it had no connection with what was
going on in Europe. Some people used to think there was German money behind it, but they didn't dare say so or they would
have been thrown in jail as German spies. It was a period of
muddy thought and marked, I believe, the decline of higher education in the Middle West.

As a soldier I was never any good at all. Most of the cadets
were glumly indifferent soldiers, but I was no good at all. Once
General Littlefield, who was commandant of the cadet corps,
popped up in front of me during regimental drill and snapped,
"You are the main trouble with this university!" I think he
meant that my type was the main trouble with the university
but he may have meant me individually. I was mediocre at drill,
certainly — that is, until my senior year. By that time I had
drilled longer than anybody else in the Western Conference,
having failed at military at the end of each preceding year so
that I had to do it all over again. I was the only senior still in
uniform. The uniform which, when new, had made me look
like an interurban railway conductor, now that it had become
faded and too tight made me look like Bert Williams in his
bellboy act.[2] This had a definitely bad effect on my morale.
Even so, I had become by sheer practice little short of wonderful
at squad maneuvers.

One day General Littlefield picked our company out of the
whole regiment and tried to get it mixed up by putting it
through one movement after another as fast as we could execute
them: squads right, squads left, squads on right into line, squads

---

[2]A popular vaudeville and silent-screen comedian of the time, Williams in
one routine played a hotel porter in a shrunken suit.

right about, squads left front into line, etc. In about three minutes one hundred and nine men were marching in one direction and I was marching away from them at an angle of forty degrees, all alone. "Company, halt!" shouted General Littlefield. "That man is the only man who has it right!" I was made a corporal for my achievement.

The next day General Littlefield summoned me to his office. He was swatting flies when I went in. I was silent and he was silent too, for a long time, I don't think he remembered me or why he had sent for me, but he didn't want to admit it. He swatted some more flies, keeping his eyes on them narrowly before he let go with the swatter. "Button up your coat!" he snapped. Looking back on it now I can see that he meant me although he was looking at a fly, but I just stood there. Another fly came to rest on a paper in front of the general and began rubbing its hind legs together. The general lifted the swatter cautiously. I moved restlessly and the fly flew away. "You startled him!" barked General Littlefield, looking at me severely. I said I was sorry. "That won't help the situation!" snapped the General, with cold military logic. I didn't see what I could do except offer to chase some more flies toward his desk, but I didn't say anything. He stared out the window at the faraway figures of co-eds crossing the campus toward the library. Finally, he told me I could go. So I went. He either didn't know which cadet I was or else he forgot what he wanted to see me about. It may have been that he wished to apologize for having called me the main trouble with the university; or maybe he had decided to compliment me on my brilliant drilling of the day before and then at the last minute decided not to. I don't know. I don't think about it much any more.

18

---

1. In what light does Thurber portray himself in "University Days"? Is his self-portrait sympathetic?
2. Are Bolenciecwcz and Haskins stereotypes? Discuss.

3. To what extent does Thurber sacrifice believability for humorous effect? What is his main purpose? (See *Purpose* in Useful Terms.)

• QUESTIONS ON WRITING STRATEGY •

1. How do Thurber's opening, his transitions, and his final sentence contribute to the humor of his essay? See *Introductions, Transitions,* and *Conclusions* in Useful Terms.)
2. Criticize the opening sentence of the story Haskins writes about horse disease (quoted in paragraph 14).
3. Thurber does not explain in "University Days" how he ever did fulfill his biological sciences requirement for graduation. Is this an important omission? Explain.
4. Do you find any support in Thurber's essay for the view that he is genuinely critical of certain absurdities in college education?

• QUESTIONS ON LANGUAGE •
• AND VOCABULARY •

1. Be sure to know what the following words mean: nebulous (paragraph 1); lacteal opacity, variegated (4).
2. Analyze how Thurber's word choices heighten the irony in the following phrases: "like falling back full-length on a kit of carpenter's tools" (paragraph 14); "a genuinely big 'beat' " (14); "the decline of higher education in the Middle West" (15). (See *Irony* in Useful Terms.)
3. What is a land grant university (paragraph 15)?

• SUGGESTIONS FOR WRITING •

1. How does Thurber's picture of campus life during the days of World War I compare with campus life today? What has changed? What has stayed the same? Develop your ideas in a brief essay.
2. Write an essay called "High School Days" in which, with a light touch, you recount two or three anecdotes from your own experience, educational or otherwise.

· James Anthony Froude ·

JAMES ANTHONY FROUDE (1818–1894) — pronounce his name *Frood* — was a celebrated English historian. A best-seller in its day, his chief work, the *History of England from 1529 to the Death of Elizabeth*, published in twelve volumes between 1856 and 1870, makes history as colorful and engrossing as a good Victorian novel. Froude was named Regius Professor of Modern History at Oxford only two years before his death, it having taken a while for his work to be seen as not merely popular, but also respectable.

The Execution of Queen Mary

Today we read Froude not for reliable history, but for his ability to make the past seem immediate and alive. Although sometimes highhanded with his sources, imagining details that he could not know, Froude has a cinematographer's eye for a scene and a brisk, vigorous, and dramatic sense of storytelling. "The Execution of Queen Mary" (editors' title) is taken from chapter 34 of the closing volume of Froude's *History*. In its entirety, this twelve-volume work chronicles the struggle of England to break away from the Church of Rome, an institution the biased historian apparently disliked. One of his central villains, therefore, is the proud and passionate Mary, last Roman Catholic ruler of Scotland. Not without reason, Froude blames her for conspiring with the Earl of Bothwell to blow up the house of her husband. The alleged plot worked, and, three months after her sudden widowing, Mary wed Bothwell. This rashness proved a blunder; indignant Scots forced the queen to abdicate. Mary took refuge in England under the protection of her cousin, Queen Elizabeth (who, being the daughter of Henry VIII, founder of the Church of England, was a staunch Protestant). In custody, Mary was accused of plotting against Elizabeth. She was tried and found guilty. Our story begins on an afternoon in 1587, as two of Mary's judges call on the exiled queen in her chambers at Fotheringay Castle, where she is a prisoner.

Briefly, solemnly, and sternly they delivered their awful message. They informed her that they had received a commission under the great seal to see her executed, and she was told that she must prepare to suffer on the following morning.

She was dreadfully agitated. For a moment she refused to believe them. Then, as the truth forced itself upon her, tossing her head in disdain and struggling to control herself, she called her physician and began to speak to him of money that was owed to her in France. At last it seeems that she broke down altogether, and they left her with fear either that she would destroy herself in the night, or that she would refuse to come to the scaffold, and that it might be necessary to drag her there by violence.

The end had come. She had long professed to expect it, but the clearest expectation is not certainty. The scene for which she had affected to prepare she was to encounter in its dread reality, and all her busy schemes, her dreams of vengeance, her visions of a revolution, with herself ascending out of the convulsion and seating herself on her rival's throne — all were gone. She had played deep, and the dice had gone against her.

Yet in death, if she encountered it bravely, victory was still possible. Could she but sustain to the last the character of a calumniated suppliant accepting heroically for God's sake and her creed's the concluding stroke of a long series of wrongs, she might stir a tempest of indignation which, if it could not save herself, might at least overwhelm her enemy. Persisting, as she persisted to the last, in denying all knowledge of Babington,[1] it would be affectation to credit her with a genuine feeling of religion; but the imperfection of her motive exalts the greatness of her fortitude. To an impassioned believer, death is comparatively easy.

Her chaplain was lodged in a separate part of the castle. The Commissioners, who were as anxious that her execution should wear its real character as she was herself determined to convert

---

[1]Anthony Babington, Roman Catholic attendant at Mary's court, put to death for plotting to free Mary.

it into a martyrdom, refused, perhaps unwisely, to allow him access to her, and offered her again the assistance of an Anglican Dean. They gave her an advantage over them which she did not fail to use. She would not let the Dean come near her. She sent a note to the chaplain telling him that she had meant to receive the sacrament, but as it might not be she must content herself with a general confession. She bade him watch through the night and pray for her. In the morning when she was brought out she might perhaps see him, and receive his blessing on her knees. She supped cheerfully, giving her last meal with her attendants a character of sacred parting; afterwards she drew aside her apothecary, M. Gorion, and asked him if she might depend upon his fidelity: when he satisfied her that she might trust him, she said she had a letter and two diamonds which she wished to send to Mendoza.[2] He undertook to melt some drug and conceal them in it where they would never be looked for, and promised to deliver them faithfully. One of the jewels was for Mendoza himself; the other and the largest was for Philip.[3] It was to be a sign that she was dying for the truth, and was meant also to bespeak his care for her friends and servants. Every one of them so far as she was able, without forgetting a name, she commended to his liberality. Arundel, Paget, Morgan, the Archbishop of Glasgow, Westmoreland, Throgmorton, the Bishop of Ross, her two secretaries, the ladies who had shared the trials of her imprisonment, she remembered them all, and specified the sums which she desired Philip to bestow on them. And as Mary Stuart then and throughout her life never lacked gratitude to those who had been true to her, so then as always she remembered her enemies. There was no cant about her, no unreal talk of forgiveness of injuries. She bade Gorion tell Philip it was her last prayer that he should persevere, notwithstanding her death, in the invasion of England. It was God's quarrel, she said, and worthy of his greatness: and as soon as he had conquered it, she desired him not to for-

[2]Mary's friend, the former Spanish ambassador to England. Thinking him a spy for the Jesuits, Elizabeth had sent him packing.
[3]King Philip II of Spain.

get how she had been treated by Cecil, and Leicester, and Walsingham; by Lord Huntingdon, who had ill-used her fifteen years before at Tutbury; by Sir Amyas Paulet, and Secretary Wade.[4]

Her last night was a busy one. As she said herself, there was much to be done and the time was short. A few lines to the King of France were dated two hours after midnight. They were to insist for the last time that she was innocent of conspiracy, that she was dying for religion, and for having asserted her right to the crown; and to beg that out of the sum which he owed her, her servants' wages might be paid, and masses provided for her soul. After this she slept for three or four hours, and then rose and with the most elaborate care prepared to encounter the end.

At eight in the morning the Provost-marshal knocked at the outer door which communicated with her suite of apartments. It was locked and no one answered, and he went back in some trepidation lest the fears might prove true which had been entertained the preceding evening. On his returning with the Sheriff, however, a few minutes later, the door was open, and they were confronted with the tall majestic figure of Mary Stuart standing there before them in splendor. The plain gray dress had been exchanged for a robe of black satin; her jacket was of black satin also, looped and slashed and trimmed with velvet. Her false hair was arranged studiously with a coif, and over her head and falling down over her back was a white veil of delicate lawn. A crucifix of gold hung from her neck. In her hand she held a crucifix of ivory, and a number of jeweled Paternosters were attached to her girdle. Led by two of Paulet's gentlemen, the Sheriff walking before her, she passed to the chamber of presence in which she had been tried, where Shrewsbury, Kent, Paulet, Drury, and others were waiting to re-

[4]Enemies whom Mary blamed for her conviction and death sentence. William Cecil and Sir Francis Walsingham had organized forces of secret police to detect plots against England; the Earl of Huntingdon and Sir Amyas Paulet had served as Mary's jailers; the Earl of Leicester had resisted Elizabeth's suggestion that he become Mary's husband; Sir William Wade had seized Mary's private papers.

ceive her. Andrew Melville, Sir Robert's brother,[5] who had
been master of her household, was kneeling in tears. "Melville,
she said, "you should rather rejoice than weep that the end of
my troubles is come. Tell my friends I die a true Catholic. Commend me to my son. Tell him I have done nothing to prejudice
his kingdom of Scotland, and so, good Melville, farewell." She
kissed him, and turning asked for her chaplain Du Preau. He
was not present. There had been a fear of some religious melodrama which it was thought well to avoid. Her ladies, who had
attempted to follow her, had been kept back also. She could not
afford to leave the account of her death to be reported by
enemies and Puritans, and she required assistance for the scene
which she meditated. Missing them, she asked the reason for
their absence, and said she wished them to see her die. Kent
said he feared they might scream or faint, or attempt perhaps to
dip their handkerchiefs in her blood. She undertook that they
should be quiet and obedient. "The Queen," she said, "would
never deny so slight a request;" and when Kent still hesitated,
she added with tears, "You know I am cousin to your Queen, of
the blood of Henry VII, a married Queen of France, and
anointed Queen of Scotland."

It was impossible to refuse. She was allowed to take six of   8
her own people with her, and select them herself. She chose her
physician Burgoyne, Andrew Melville, the apothecary Gorion,
and her surgeon, with two ladies, Elizabeth Kennedy and
Curle's young wife Barbara Mowbray, whose child she had bap-
tized.

"Allons donc," she then said — "Let us go," and passing out   9
attended by the Earls, and leaning on the arm of an officer of
the guard, she descended the great staircase to the hall. The
news had spread far through the country. Thousands of people
were collected outside the walls. About three hundred knights
and gentlemen of the country had been admitted to witness the
execution. The tables and forms had been removed, and a great

---

[5]Baron Robert Melville, counselor to Elizabeth, had pleaded with the
queen to spare Mary's life.

wood fire was blazing in the chimney. At the upper end of the hall, above the fireplace, but near it, stood the scaffold, twelve feet square and two feet and a half high. It was covered with black cloth; a low rail ran round it covered with black cloth also, and the Sheriff's guard of halberdiers were ranged on the floor below on the four sides to keep off the crowd. On the scaffold was the block, black like the rest; a square black cushion was placed behind it, and behind the cushion a black chair; on the right were two other chairs for the Earls. The axe leant against the rail, and two masked figures stood like mutes on either side at the back. The Queen of Scots as she swept in seemed as if coming to take a part in some solemn pageant. Not a muscle of her face could be seen to quiver; she ascended the scaffold with absolute composure, looking round her smiling, and sat down. Shrewsbury and Kent followed and took their places, the Sheriff stood at her left hand, and Beale[6] then mounted a platform and read the warrant aloud.

In all the assembly Mary Stuart appeared the person least interested in the words which were consigning her to death.   10

"Madam," said Lord Shrewsbury to her, when the reading was ended, "you hear what we are commanded to do."   11

"You will do your duty," she answered, and rose as if to kneel and pray.   12

The Dean of Peterborough, Dr. Fletcher, approached the rail. "Madam," he began, with a low obeisance, "the Queen's most excellent Majesty"; "Madam, the Queen's most excellent Majesty"—thrice he commenced his sentence, wanting words to pursue it. When he repeated the words a fourth time, she cut him short.   13

"Mr. Dean," she said, "I am a Catholic, and must die a Catholic. It is useless to attempt to move me, and your prayers will avail me but little."   14

"Change your opinion, Madam," he cried, his tongue being loosed at last; "repent of your sins, settle your faith in Christ, by him to be saved."   15

---

[6]Robert Beale, secretary to Mary's enemy Sir Francis Walsingham.

"Trouble not yourself further, Mr. Dean," she answered; "I   16
am settled in my own faith, for which I mean to shed my
blood."

"I am sorry, Madam," said Shrewsbury, "to see you so ad-   17
dicted to Popery."

"That image of Christ you hold there," said Kent, "will not   18
profit you if he be not engraved in your heart."

She did not reply, and turning her back on Fletcher, knelt   19
for her own devotions.

He had been evidently instructed to impair the Catholic   20
complexion of the scene, and the Queen of Scots was determined that he should not succeed. When she knelt he commenced an extempore prayer in which the assembly joined. As
his voice sounded out in the hall she raised her own, reciting
with powerful deep-chested tones the penitential Psalms in
Latin, introducing English sentences at intervals, that the audience might know what she was saying, and praying with
especial distinctness for her Holy Father the Pope.

From time to time, with conspicuous vehemence, she struck   21
the crucifix against her bosom and then, as the Dean gave up
the struggle, leaving her Latin, she prayed in English wholly,
still clear and loud. She prayed for the Church which she had
been ready to betray, for her son, whom she had disinherited,
for the Queen whom she had endeavored to murder. She
prayed God to avert his wrath from England, that England
which she had sent a last message to Philip to beseech him to invade. She forgave her enemies, whom she had invited Philip not
to forget, and then, praying to the saints to intercede for her
with Christ, and kissing the crucifix and crossing her own
breast, "Even as thy arms, O Jesus," she cried, "were spread
upon the cross, so receive me into thy mercy and forgive my
sins."

With these words she rose; the black mutes stepped for-   22
ward, and in the usual form begged her forgiveness.

"I forgive you," she said, "for now I hope you shall end all   23
my troubles." They offered their help in arranging her dress.
"Truly, my lords," she said with a smile to the Earls, "I never
had such grooms waiting on me before." Her ladies were al-

lowed to come up upon the scaffold to assist her; for the work to be done was considerable, and had been prepared with no common thought.

She laid her crucifix on her chair. The chief executioner   24
took it as a perquisite, but was ordered instantly to lay it down. The lawn veil was lifted carefully off, not to disturb the hair, and was hung upon the rail. The black robe was next removed. Below it was a petticoat of crimson velvet. The black jacket followed, and under the jacket was a body of crimson satin. One of her ladies handed her a pair of crimson sleeves, with which she hastily covered her arms; and thus she stood on the black scaffold with the black figures all around her, blood-red from head to foot.

Her reasons for adopting so extraordinary a costume must   25
be left to conjecture. It is only certain that it must have been carefully studied, and that the pictorial effect must have been appalling.

The women, whose firmness had hitherto borne the trial,   26
began now to give way, spasmodic sobs bursting from them which they could not check. "*Ne criez vous,*" she said, "*J'ai promis pour vous.*"[7] Struggling bravely, they crossed their breasts again and again, she crossing them in turn and bidding them pray for her. Then she knelt on the cushion. Barbara Mowbray bound her eyes with a handkerchief. "*Adieu,*" she said, smiling for the last time and waving her hand to them, "*Adieu, au revoir.*" They stepped back from off the scaffold and left her alone. On her knees she repeated the Psalm, *In te, Domine, confido,* "In thee, O Lord, have I put my trust." Her shoulders being exposed, two scars became visible, one on either side, and the Earls being now a little behind her, Kent pointed to them with his white wand and looked inquiringly at his companion. Shrewsbury whispered that they were the remains of two abscesses from which she had suffered while living with him at Sheffield.[8]

---

[7]"Do not cry; I have promised on your behalf that you will not."
[8]George Talbot, Earl of Shrewsbury, had been charged by Queen Elizabeth with keeping Mary in his custody.

When the psalm was finished she felt for the block, and lay- 27
ing down her head muttered: "*In manus, Domine tuas, commendo
animam meam.*"9 The hard wood seemed to hurt her, for she
placed her hands under her neck. The executioners gently removed them, lest they should deaden the blow, and then one of
them holding her slightly, the other raised the axe and struck.
The scene had been too trying even for the practiced headsman
of the Tower. His arm wandered. The blow fell on the knot of
the handkerchief, and scarcely broke the skin. She neither
spoke nor moved. He struck again, this time effectively. The
head hung by a shred of skin, which he divided without with-
drawing the axe; and at once a metamorphosis was witnessed,
strange as was ever wrought by wand of fabled enchanter. The
coif fell off and the false plaits. The labored illusion vanished.
The lady who had knelt before the block was in the maturity of
grace and loveliness. The executioner, when he raised the head,
as usual, to show it to the crowd, exposed the withered features
of a grizzled, wrinkled old woman.

· QUESTIONS ON MEANING AND PURPOSE ·

1. Describe the character of Mary, Queen of Scots, as you
   understand it from Froude's account.
2. How does the fact that Mary is a Roman Catholic pose a
   particular threat to her cousin Queen Elizabeth?
3. How deep and sincere, according to the historian, is Mary's faith?
   (Suggestion: See paragraph 4, and try putting Froude's comments
   into your own words. Is there irony in the remark, "To an impassioned believer, death is comparatively easy"?)
4. By what methods does Mary try to use her public death for
   propaganda? How do the forces of Queen Elizabeth attempt to
   thwart Mary's intentions?
5. Does Froude intend us to admire Mary's fortitude as she kneels to
   receive the headsman's blow?

9"Into thy Hands, O Lord, I commend my spirit." (See Luke 23:46.)

6. What do you understand by the writer's statement in the last paragraph, "and at once a metamorphosis was witnessed, strange as was ever wrought by wand of fabled enchanter"? Is he saying that Mary was transformed into a magnificent legend, or that she was revealed to have worn a disguise?

• QUESTIONS ON WRITING STRATEGY •

1. Closely inspect those passages in which Froude details Mary's appearance and costume on the morning of her death. Notice the remark in paragraph 24: "And thus she stood on the black scaffold with the black figures all around her, blood-red from head to foot." What do these details contribute to Froude's narrative?
2. In paragraphs 3 and 4, Froude lets on that he knows the very thoughts that raced through Mary's head. Do you approve of this technique in the writing of history? How is it valuable to a story-teller?
3. In taking this story from Volume XII of Froude's *History of England*, we decided to cut it short. In the original, Froude goes on to detail the mopping-up operation after the execution as follows:

> Orders had been given that everything which she had worn should be immediately destroyed, that no relics should be carried off to work imaginary miracles. Sentinels stood at the doors who allowed no one to pass out without permission; and after the first pause, the earls still keeping their places, the body was stripped. It then appeared that a favorite lapdog had followed its mistress unperceived, and was concealed under her clothes; when discovered it gave a short cry and seated itself between the head and the neck, from which the blood was still flowing. It was carried away and carefully washed, and then beads, Paternosters, handkerchief—each particle of dress which the blood had touched, with the cloth on the block and on the scaffold, was burned in the hall fire in the presence of the crowd. The scaffold itself was next removed; a brief account of the execution was drawn up, with which Henry Talbot, Lord Shrewsbury's son, was sent to London, and then everyone was dismissed. Silence settled down on Fotheringay, and the last scene of the life of Mary Stuart, in which tragedy and melodrama were so strangely intermingled, was over.

Now, the discovery of a dog concealed on a decapitated body is a surprising detail; still we thought that the sudden
transformation of a queen into a hag was a more powerful
ending. Which ending do you prefer? Why do you believe it
makes for a better story?

• QUESTIONS ON LANGUAGE •
• AND VOCABULARY •

1. In giving details of the appearance of Mary and her guards,
   Froude uses certain words no longer familiar. In paragraph 7, for
   instance, we find *coif* (a close-fitting skullcap) and *lawn* (linen).
   Paternosters is still a familiar word, but here it refers to every
   eleventh bead of a rosary: the one at which the Lord's Prayer is
   said. Mary's girdle isn't a modern "foundation garment," but a
   ribbon or belt. In paragraph 9, *halberdiers* are guards carrying
   halberds: spearlike weapons with long handles and pointed steel
   heads. What does your knowing the meaning of these words add
   to your ability to visualize Froude's scenes? (See *Archaisms* under
   Diction in Useful Terms.)
2. With the aid of your dictionary, define the following words as
   Froude uses them: calumniated, suppliant (paragraph 4); Anglican, apothecary, cant, persevere (5); conspiracy (6); meditated,
   trepidation, melodrama, Puritans (7); mutes, composure (9); obeisance (13); complexion, extempore, penitential (20); vehemence,
   intercede (21); perquisite (24); conjecture (25); spasmodic, abscesses (26); metamorphosis, fabled, plaits (27).

• SUGGESTIONS FOR WRITING •

1. Froude has been called "the last of the great amateur historians,"
   meaning that, unlike most professional historians today, he wrote
   history with more flair than fidelity, more literary art than
   methodical research. In a paragraph or a brief essay, attack or defend Froude's procedures. Make it clear to your reader whether
   you are judging Froude as a historian or as a storyteller.
2. With "The Execution of Queen Mary" freshly in mind, read H. L.
   Mencken's essay on capital punishment, "The Penalty of Death,"
   in Chapter 10. Then write a short essay in answer to this question: What evidence does Froude provide that shows Mencken to
   be right (or wrong)? (See *Evidence* in Useful Terms.)

3. Barbara W. Tuchman in her "An Inquiry into the Persistence of Unwisdom in Government" (Essays for Further Reading) says, "A problem that strikes one in the study of history, regardless of period, is why man makes a poorer performance of government than of almost any other human activity." Pretend for the moment that you are James Anthony Froude and, without obliging yourself to imitate Froude's style (unless you feel sure you can do so), write a comment on Tuchman's thesis statement. If you wish, you may begin, "The reasons for man's incompetence in ruling are not difficult to discover. As we learn from the pathetic history of Mary, Queen of Scots, they account for woman's incompetence in ruling, too."

· ADDITIONAL WRITING TOPICS ·

NARRATION

Write a narrative with one of the following as your subjects. It may be (as your instructor may advise) either a first-person memoir, or a story written in the third person, observing the experience of someone else. Decide before you begin whether you are writing (1) an anecdote; (2) an essay consisting mainly of a single narrative; or (3) an essay that includes more than one story.

1. A memorable experience from your early life.
2. A lesson you learned the hard way.
3. A trip into unfamiliar territory.
4. An embarrassing moment that taught you something.
5. A brush with death.
6. A monumental misunderstanding.
7. An accident.
8. An unexpected encounter.
9. A story about a famous person, or someone close to you.
10. A conflict or contest.
11. An assassination attempt.
12. A historic event of significance.

· 2 ·

DESCRIPTION

Writing with Your Senses

· THE METHOD ·

Like narration, description is a familiar method of expression, already a working part of you. In any talk-fest with friends, you probably do your share of describing. You depict in words someone you've met, probably by describing her clothes, the look on her face, the way she walks. You describe somewhere you've been, something you admire, something you just can't abide. In a diary or in a letter to a friend, you describe your college (cast concrete buildings, crowded walks, pigeons rattling their wings); or perhaps you describe your brand-new second-hand car, from the snakelike glitter of its hubcaps to the odd antiques in its trunk, bequeathed by its previous owner. You hardly can live a day without describing something or hearing something described. Small wonder that, in written discourse, description is almost as indispensable as paper.

Description reports the testimony of your senses. It invites your readers to imagine that they too not only see, but perhaps also hear, taste, smell, and touch the very subject you describe Usually, you write a description for either of two purposes: (1) to convey information without bias or emotion; or (2) to impress your reader with whatever the subject you describe makes you feel.

In writing with the first purpose in mind, you write what may be called an *objective* (or *impartial*, or *functional*) description. You describe your subject so clearly and exactly that your reader will understand it, or recognize it, and you leave your emotions out of it. Technical or scientific descriptive writing is usually objective: a manual detailing the parts of an internal combustion engine, a biologist's report of a previously unknown species of frog. You write this kind of description in sending a friend directions for finding your house ("Look for the green shutters on the windows and a new garbage can at the front door"). Although in a personal letter describing your house, you might very well become emotionally involved with it (and call it, perhaps, a "fleabag"), to convey your feelings about it is not your purpose in writing an objective description. You are trying to make it easily recognized.

The other type of descriptive writing may be called *subjective* (or *emotional*, or *impressionistic*) description. This is the kind included in a magazine advertisement for a new car. It's what you write in your letter to a friend setting forth what your college is like (whether you are pleased or displeased with it). In this kind of description, you may use biases and personal feelings — in fact, they are essential. Let us consider a splendid example: a subjective description of a storm at sea. Charles Dickens, in his memoir *American Notes*, conveys his passenger's-eye view of an Atlantic steamship on a morning when the ocean is wild:

> Imagine the ship herself, with every pulse and artery of her huge body swollen and bursting . . . sworn to go on or die. Imagine the wind howling, the sea roaring, the rain beating; all in furious array against her. Picture the sky both dark and wild, and the clouds in fearful sympathy with the waves,

making another ocean in the air. Add to all this the clattering on deck and down below; the tread of hurried feet; the loud hoarse shouts of seamen; the gurgling in and out of water through the scuppers; with every now and then the striking of a heavy sea upon the planks above, with the deep, dead, heavy sound of thunder heard within a vault; and there is the head wind of that January morning.

I say nothing of what may be called the domestic noises of the ship; such as the breaking of glass and crockery, the tumbling down of stewards, the gambols, overhead, of loose casks and truant dozens of bottled porter, and the very remarkable and far from exhilarating sounds raised in their various staterooms by the seventy passengers who were too ill to get up to breakfast.

Notice how many *sounds* are included in this primarily ear-minded description. We can infer how Dickens feels about the storm. It is a terrifying event that reduces the interior of the vessel to chaos; and yet the writer (in hearing the loose barrels and beer bottles merrily *gambol*, in finding humor in the seasick passengers' plight) apparently delights in it. Writing subjectively, he intrudes his feelings. Think of what a starkly different description of the very same storm the captain might set down — *objectively* — in the ship's log: "At 0600 hours, watch reported a wind from due north of 70 knots. Whitecaps were noticed, in height two ells above the bow. Below deck, much gear was reported adrift, and ten casks of ale were broken and their staves strewn about. Mr. Liam Jones, chief steward, suffered a compound fracture of the left leg . . . ." But Dickens, not content simply to record information, strives to ensure that the mind's eye is dazzled and the mind's ear is regaled.

Description is a method of writing usually found in the company of other methods. Often, for instance, it will enliven narration and make the persons in the story and the setting unmistakably clear. Writing an argument in his essay "Why Don't We Complain?", William F. Buckley begins with a description of eighty suffering commuters perspiring in an overheated train; the description makes the argument more powerful. Often, description will help a writer in examining the effects of a flood, or in comparing and contrasting two towns. Keep the method of

description in mind when you come to try expository and argumentative writing.

· THE PROCESS ·

Before you begin to write a description, go look at your subject. If that is not possible, your next best course is to spend a
few minutes imagining your subject until, in your mind's eye,
you can see it in detail. Understand your purpose in writing.
Ask yourself what features of your subject you will need to mention in order to fulfill this purpose. If, for example, you plan to
write a subjective description of an old house, emphasizing its
spooky atmosphere, you may want to mention its squeaking
bats and shadowy hallways, rather than its busy swimming pool
and the disco music that issues from indoors.

As a whole, your description should convey one dominant
impression. (The swimming pool and the disco music might be
useful details in a description meant to convey the impression
that the house is full of merriment.) Perhaps there will be many
details to notice; and you will want to arrange them so that
your reader can see which ones matter most. In his subjective
description of the storm at sea, Charles Dickens carefully sorts
out the pandemonium for us. He groups miscellaneous sounds
into two classes: those of the sea and the sailors, and the
"domestic noises" of the ship's passengers, their smashing dishes
and rolling bottles, and the crashing of stewards who wait on
them. An effective description often will reveal some such clear
principle of organization.

You can organize a description in any of several ways. Some
writers, as they describe something, make a carefully planned
inspection tour of its details, moving spatially (from left to right,
from near to far, from top to bottom, from center to periphery),
or perhaps moving from prominent objects to tiny ones, from
dull to bright, from commonplace to extraordinary — or vice
versa. The plan you choose is the one that best fulfills your purpose. If you were to describe, for instance, a chapel in the middle of a desert, you might begin with the details of the lonely
terrain. Then, as if approaching the chapel with the aid of a
zoom lens, you might detail its exterior and then go on inside.

That might be a workable method to write a description, *if* your purpose were to emphasize the sense that the chapel is an island of beauty and warmth in the midst of desolation. Say, however, that your purpose was quite different: to emphasize the interior design of the chapel. You might then begin your description inside the structure, perhaps with its most prominent feature, the stained glass windows. You might mention the surrounding desert later in your description, but only incidentally. An effective description makes a definite impression. The writer arranges details so that the reader is firmly left with the feeling the writer intends to convey.

Whichever method you follow in arranging details, stick with a single method all the way through your description. Don't start out describing a group of cats by going from old cats to kittens, then switching in the middle of your description and lining up the cats according to color. If your arrangement would cause any difficulty for the reader, then you need to rearrange your details. If a writer, in describing a pet shop, should skip about wildly from clerks to cats to customers to catfood to customers to catfood to clerks, then the reader may quickly be lost. Instead, the writer might group clerks together with customers, and cats together with catfood (or in some other clear order). But suppose (the writer might protest) it's a wildly confused pet shop I'm trying to describe? No matter — the writer nevertheless has to write in an orderly manner, if the reader is to understand. Dickens describes a scene of shipboard chaos, yet his prose is orderly.

There are writers, of course, who just go ahead and write, arranging the features of a description in whatever sequence they pop into mind. Such writers trust their unconscious minds to do the organizing. They may work from only the sketchiest of outlines, or none at all, but probably — if their work is to be readable — they have to rewrite and rewrite, crossing out any detail that, on rereading, doesn't fit. This carefree procedure sometimes produces results, but, in general, the essay that you plan is the easier kind to write.

Feel no grim duty to include every perceptible detail. To do so would only invite chaos — or perhaps, for the reader, mere tedium. Pick out the features that most matter. One revealing, hard-to-forget detail (such as Dickens' truant porter-bottles) is, like a single masterly brush stroke, worth a whole coat of dull paint. In selecting or discarding details, ask, What am I out to accomplish? What main impression of my subject am I trying to give?

Luckily, to write a memorable description, you don't need a storm at sea or any other awe-inspiring subject. As E. B. White demonstrates in his essay in this chapter, "Once More to the Lake," you can write about a summer cabin on a lake as effectively as you can write about a tornado. Although we tend to think of description as referring to a single object, you can describe an abstraction or a general type. You can, for instance, describe a new style of dress, or the identifying features of Italian sports cars, or a typical turnpike food-and-fuel plaza. Here is humorist S. J. Perelman using metaphor to convey the garish brightness of a certain low-rent furnished house. Notice how he makes clear the abstract spirit of the place: "After a few days, I could have sworn that our faces began to take on the hue of Kodachromes, and even the dog, an animal used to bizarre surroundings, developed a strange, off-register look, as if he were badly printed in overlapping colors."[1] The subject of a description may even be as intangible as a disease, or an interior sensation — as Joan Didion shows us in her feelingful essay on migraine, "In Bed."

When you, too, write an effective description, you'll convey your sensory experience as exactly as possible. Find vigorous, specific words, and you will enable your reader to behold with the mind's eye — and to feel with the mind's fingertips.

· DESCRIPTION IN A PARAGRAPH ·

At 2:59 this Monday afternoon, a thick hush settles like cigarette smoke inside the sweat-scented TV room of Harris Hall. First to arrive, freshman Lee Ann squashes down into the catbird seat in front of the screen. Soon she is flanked by roommates Lisa and Kate, silent, their mouths straight lines,

[1]"The Marx Brothers," *The Last Laugh* (New York: Simon and Schuster, 1981), p. 152.

their upturned faces lit by the nervous flicker of a detergent ad. To the left and right of the couch, Pete and Anse crouch on the floor, leaning forward like runners awaiting a starting gun. Behind them, stiff standees line up at attention. Farther back still, English majors and jocks compete for an unobstructed view. Fresh from class, shirttail flapping, arm crooking a bundle of books, Dave barges into the room demanding, "Has it started? Has it started yet?" He is shushed. Somebody shushes a popped-open can of Dr. Pepper whose fizz is distractingly loud. What do these students so intently look forward to — the announcement of World War III? A chord of music climbs and the screen dissolves to a title: *General Hospital.*

Comment: Although in the end the anticipated mind-blower turns out to be merely an installment of a gripping soap opera, the purpose of this description is to build one definite impression: that something vital is about to arrive. Details are selected accordingly: *thick hush, nervous flicker,* people jostling one another for a better view. The watchers are portrayed as tense and expectant, their mouths straight lines, their faces upturned, the men on the floor crouching forward. The chief appeal is to our visual imaginations, but a few details address the ears of the mind (the fizz of a can of soda, people saying *Shhh-h-h!*) and the nose of the mind (*sweat-scented*) besides.

In organizing this description, the writer's scrutiny moves outward from the television screen: first to the students immediately in front of it, then to those on either side, next to the second row, then to the third, and finally to the last anxious arrival. By this arrangement, the writer presents the details to the reader in a natural order. The main impression is enforced, since the TV screen is the center for all eyes.

· Joan Didion ·

JOAN DIDION was born in Sacramento, California in 1934 and was graduated from the University of California, Berkeley, in 1956. Didion has written three novels, *Run River* (1963), *Play It As It Lays* (1971), and *A Book of Common Prayer* (1977); and first collected her essays in *Slouching Towards Bethlehem*, (1969). She has worked as a feature editor for *Vogue*, a columnist for the *Saturday Evening Post*, and a contributing editor for the *National Review*. Recently she coauthored the screenplay for the film *True Confessions* with her husband John Gregory Dunne.

In Bed

"In Bed," an essay from Joan Didion's most recent collection, *The White Album* (1979), describes migraine headaches in general and her own in particular. She demonstrates without a doubt that feelings, as well as people, places, and things, are fit subjects for description. Any migraine victim will acknowledge that the author knows whereof she speaks. Even nonsufferers are likely to wince under the spell of Didion's vivid, sensuous prose.

Three, four, sometimes five times a month, I spend the day in bed with a migraine headache, insensible to the world around me. Almost every day of every month, between these attacks, I feel the sudden irrational irritation and flush of blood into the cerebral arteries which tell me that migraine is on its way, and I take certain drugs to avert its arrival. If I did not take the drugs, I would be able to function perhaps one day in four. The physiological error called migraine is, in brief, central to the given of my life. When I was 15, 16, even 25, I used to think that I could rid myself of this error by simply denying it, character over chemistry. "Do you have headaches *sometimes? frequently? never?*" the application forms would demand. "Check one."

Wary of the trap, wanting whatever it was that the successful circumnavigation of that particular form could bring (a job, a scholarship, the respect of mankind and the grace of God), I would check one. "*Sometimes,*" I would lie. That in fact I spent one or two days a week almost unconscious with pain seemed a shameful secret, evidence not merely of some chemical inferiority but of all my bad attitudes, unpleasant tempers, wrongthink.

For I had no brain tumor, no eyestrain, no high blood pressure, nothing wrong with me at all: I simply had migraine headaches, and migraine headaches were, as everyone who did not have them knew, imaginary. I fought migraine then, ignored the warnings it sent, went to school and later to work in spite of it, sat through lectures in Middle English and presentations to advertisers with involuntary tears running down the right side of my face, threw up in washrooms, stumbled home by instinct, emptied ice trays onto my bed and tried to freeze the pain in my right temple, wished only for a neurosurgeon who would do a lobotomy on house call, and cursed my imagination.

It was a long time before I began thinking mechanistically enough to accept migraine for what it was: something with which I would be living, the way some people live with diabetes. Migraine is something more than the fancy of a neurotic imagination. It is an essentially hereditary complex of symptoms, the most frequently noted but by no means the most unpleasant of which is a vascular headache of blinding severity, suffered by a surprising number of women, a fair number of men (Thomas Jefferson had migraine, and so did Ulysses S. Grant, the day he accepted Lee's surrender), and by some unfortunate children as young as two years old. (I had my first when I was eight. It came on during a fire drill at the Columbia School in Colorado Springs, Colorado. I was taken first home and then to the infirmary at Peterson Field, where my father was stationed. The Air Corps doctor prescribed an enema.) Almost anything can trigger a specific attack of migraine: stress, allergy, fatigue, an abrupt change in barometric pressure, a contretemps over a parking ticket. A flashing light. A fire drill. One inherits, of course, only the predisposition. In other words I spent yesterday in bed with a headache not merely because of my bad attitudes, unpleasant tempers and wrongthink, but because both my grandmothers had migraine, my father has migraine and my mother has migraine.

No one knows precisely what it is that is inherited. The 4 chemistry of migraine, however, seems to have some connection with the nerve hormone named serotonin, which is naturally present in the brain. The amount of serotonin in the blood falls sharply at the onset of migraine, and one migraine drug, methysergide, or Sansert, seems to have some effect on serotonin. Methysergide is a derivative of lysergic acid (in fact Sandoz Pharmaceuticals first synthesized LSD-25 while looking for a migraine cure), and its use is hemmed about with so many contraindications and side effects that most doctors prescribe it only in the most incapacitating cases. Methysergide, when it is prescribed, is taken daily, as a preventive; another preventive which works for some people is old-fashioned ergotamine tartrate, which helps to constrict the swelling blood vessels during the "aura," the period which in most cases precedes the actual headache.

Once an attack is under way, however, no drug touches it. 5 Migraine gives some people mild hallucinations, temporarily blinds others, shows up not only as a headache but as a gastrointestinal disturbance, a painful sensitivity to all sensory stimuli, an abrupt overpowering fatigue, a strokelike aphasia, and a crippling inability to make even the most routine connections. When I am in a migraine aura (for some people the aura lasts fifteen minutes, for others several hours), I will drive through red lights, lose the house keys, spill whatever I am holding, lose the ability to focus my eyes or frame coherent sentences, and generally give the appearance of being on drugs, or drunk. The actual headache, when it comes, brings with it chills, sweating, nausea, a debility that seems to stretch the very limits of endurance. That no one dies of migraine seems, to someone deep into an attack, an ambiguous blessing.

My husband also has migraine, which is unfortunate for 6 him but fortunate for me: perhaps nothing so tends to prolong an attack as the accusing eye of someone who has never had a headache. "Why not take a couple of aspirin," the unafflicted will say from the doorway, or "I'd have a headache, too, spend-

ing a beautiful day like this inside with all the shades drawn."
All of us who have migraine suffer not only from the attacks
themselves but from this common conviction that we are per-
versely refusing to cure ourselves by taking a couple of aspirin,
that we are making ourselves sick, that we "bring it on
ourselves." And in the most immediate sense, the sense of why
we have a headache this Tuesday and not last Thursday, of
course we often do. There certainly is what doctors call a
"migraine personality," and that personality tends to be ambitious, inward, intolerant of error, rather rigidly organized,
perfectionist. "You don't look like a migraine personality," a
doctor once said to me. "Your hair's messy. But I suppose you're
a compulsive housekeeper." Actually my house is kept even
more negligently than my hair, but the doctor was right nonetheless: perfectionism can also take the form of spending most of
a week writing and rewriting and not writing a single
paragraph.

But not all perfectionists have migraine, and not all mi-   7
grainous people have migraine personalities. We do not escape
heredity. I have tried in most of the available ways to escape my
own migrainous heredity (at one point I learned to give myself
two daily injections of histamine with a hypodermic needle,
even though the needle so frightened me that I had to close my
eyes when I did it), but I still have migraine. And I have learned
now to live with it, learned when to expect it, how to outwit it,
even how to regard it,when it does come, as more friend than
lodger. We have reached a certain understanding, my migraine
and I. It never comes when I am in real trouble. Tell me that my
house is burned down, my husband has left me, that there is
gunfighting in the streets and panic in the banks, and I will not
respond by getting a headache. It comes instead when I am
fighting not an open but a guerrilla war with my own life, during weeks of small household confusions, lost laundry, unhappy
help, canceled appointments, on days when the telephone rings
too much and I get no work done and the wind is coming up.
On days like that my friend comes uninvited.

And once it comes, now that I am wise in its ways, I no   8
longer fight it. I lie down and let it happen. At first every small
apprehension is magnified, every anxiety a pounding terror.

Then the pain comes, and I concentrate only on that. Right there is the usefulness of migraine, there in that imposed yoga, the concentration on the pain. For when the pain recedes, ten or twelve hours later, everything goes with it, all the hidden resentments, all the vain anxieties. The migraine has acted as a circuit breaker, and the fuses have emerged intact. There is a pleasant convalescent euphoria. I open the windows and feel the air, eat gratefully, sleep well. I notice the particular nature of a flower in a glass on the stair landing. I count my blessings.

· QUESTIONS ON MEANING AND PURPOSE ·

1. According to the author, how do migraines differ from ordinary headaches? What are their distinctive traits?
2. What once made Didion ashamed to admit that she suffered from migraines?
3. While imparting facts about migraine, what does Didion simultaneously reveal about her own personality?
4. Sum up in your own words the tremendous experience that Didion describes in the final paragraph.

· QUESTIONS ON WRITING STRATEGY ·

1. Didion's essay draws upon both subjective personal experience and objective medical knowledge. How does she signal her transitions from impressionistic to impartial description, and from impartial back to impressionistic? (See *Transitions* in Useful Terms.)
2. Point to a few examples of sensuous detail in Didion's writing. What do such images contribute to her essay's effect? (See *Image* in Useful Terms.)
3. In paragraph 2 when Didion declares that she "wished only for a neurosurgeon who would do a lobotomy on house call," do you take her literally? What do you make of her remark in paragraph 5: "That no one dies of migraine seems, to someone deep into an attack, an ambiguous blessing"? (See *Hyperbole* under *Figures of Speech* in Useful Terms.)
4. What similarity do you find between the subject of "In Bed" and

that of Lewis Thomas's "On Warts" (page 337)? What differences
do you find between the two authors' treatments of their subjects?

· QUESTIONS ON LANGUAGE ·
· AND VOCABULARY ·

1. Consult a dictionary if you need help in defining the following:
   vascular, contretemps, predisposition (paragraph 3); synthesized,
   contraindications (4); aphasia, aura (5).
2. Speaking in paragraph 1 of the *circumnavigation* of an application
   form, Didion employs a metaphor. In paragraph 7 she introduces
   another: a *guerrilla war*. In paragraph 8 she uses a simile: "The
   migraine has acted as a circuit breaker." Comment on the aptness
   of these figures of speech. (See *Figures of Speech* in Useful Terms.)
3. In the title of Didion's essay, what arrests you? Is this title a
   shameless teaser, a curiosity-rousing phrase that has nothing to do
   with the essay, or does it fit?

· SUGGESTIONS FOR WRITING ·

1. Write a paragraph in which, by means of impartial description,
   you familiarize your reader with an illness you know intimately. (If
   you have never had such an illness, pick an unwelcome mood you
   know: the blues, for instance, or an irresistible desire to giggle during a solemn ceremony.)
2. Then write, on the same subject, a second paragraph: this time,
   an impressionistic description of the same malady or mood.

· J. Frank Dobie ·

JAMES FRANK DOBIE (1888–1964) was born on a Texas ranch
and was graduated from Southwestern University. An author
and a professor at the University of Texas, he was also a
renowned collector of folk tales and Texas lore. Among his
best-known books are *The Longhorns* (1941) and *Tales of Old-
Time Texas* (1955).

My Horse Buck

"My Horse Buck" first appeared in *The Atlantic Monthly* in
1952. In addition to describing his favorite horse in loving
detail in this essay, Dobie muses about people he has known,
both those he has come to value less as he grows older and
those whose friendship has withstood the test of time. In
1977, "My Horse Buck" was chosen for inclusion in *119 Years
of The Atlantic*, a collection of the best articles ever printed in
the magazine.

All the old-time range men of validity whom I have known   1
remember horses with affection and respect as a part of the best
of themselves. After their knees have begun to stiffen, most men
realize that they have been disappointed in themselves, in other
men, in achievement, in love, in most of whatever they expected out of life: but a man who has had a good horse in his
life — a horse beyond the play world — will remember him as a
certitude, like a calm mother, a lovely lake, or a gracious tree,
amid all the flickering vanishments.

I remember Buck. He was raised on our ranch and was   2
about half Spanish. He was a bright bay with a blaze in his face
and stockings on his forefeet. He could hardly have weighed
when fat over 850 pounds and was about 14 hands high. A
Mexican broke him when he was three years old. From then on,
nobody but me rode him, even after I left for college. He had a

fine barrel and chest and was very fast for short distances but did not have the endurance of some other horses, straight Spaniards, in our remuda. What he lacked in toughness, he made up in intelligence, especially cow sense, loyalty, understanding, and generosity.

As a colt he had been bitten by a rattlesnake on the right ankle just above the hoof; a hard, hairless scab marked the place as long as he lived. He traveled through the world listening for the warning rattle. A kind of weed in the Southwest bears seeds that when ripe rattle in their pods a good deal like the sound made by a rattlesnake. Many a time when my spur or stirrup set these seeds a-rattling, Buck's suddenness in jumping all but left me seated in the air. I don't recall his smelling rattlesnakes, but he could smell afar off the rotten flesh of a yearling or any other cow brute afflicted with screwworms. He understood that I was hunting these animals in order to drive them to a pen and doctor them. In hot weather they take refuge in high weeds and thick brush. When he smelled one, he would point to it with his ears and turn towards it. A dog trained for hunting out wormy cases could not have been more helpful.

Once a sullen cow that had been roped raked him in the breast with the tip of a horn. After that experience, he was wariness personified around anything roped, but he never, like some horses that have been hooked, shied away from an animal he was after. He knew and loved his business too well for that. He did not love it when, at the rate of less than a mile an hour, he was driving the thirsty, hot, tired, slobbering drag end of a herd, animals stopping behind every bush or without any bush, turning aside the moment they were free of a driver. When sufficiently exasperated, Buck would go for a halting cow with mouth open and grab her just forward of the tail bone if she did not move on. Work like this may be humiliating to a gallant young cowboy and an eager cow horse; it is never pictured as a part of the romance of the range, but it is very necessary. It helps a cowboy to graduate into a cowman. A too high-strung horse without cow sense, which includes cow patience, will go to pieces at it just as he will go to pieces in running or cutting cattle.

Buck had the rein to make the proverbial "turn on a two-bit piece and give back fifteen cents in change." One hot summer while we were gathering steers on leased grass about twelve miles from home, I galled his side with a tight cinch. I hated to keep on riding him with the galled side, but was obliged to on account of a shortage of horses. As I saddled up in camp one day after dinner, I left the cinch so loose that a hand might have been laid between it and Buck's belly. We had to ride about a mile before going through a wire gap into the pasture where some snaky steers ran. As we rode along, a vaquero called my attention to the loose cinch.   5

"I will tighten it when we get to the gap," I said.   6

"*Cuidado* (have care) and don't forget," he said.   7

At the gap, which he got down to open, I saw him look at me. I decided to wait until we struck something before tightening the girth. Two minutes later my father yelled and we saw a little bunch of steers high-tailing it through scattered mesquites for a thicket along a creek beyond. I forgot all about the cinch. Buck was easily the fastest horse ridden by the four or five men in our "cow crowd." He left like a cry of joy to get around the steers.   8

As we headed them, they turned to the left at an acute angle, and Buck turned at an angle considerably more acute. Sometimes he turned so quickly that the *tapadera* (toe-fender) of my stirrup raked the ground on the inside of the turn. This time when he doubled back, running full speed, the loose saddle naturally turned on him. As my left hip hit the ground, I saw stars. One foot was still in a stirrup and the saddle was under Buck's belly. I suppose that I instinctively pulled on the reins, but I believe that Buck would have stopped had he not been bridled. His stop was instantaneous; he did not drag me on the ground at all. He had provocation to go on, too, for in coming over his side and back, the spur on my right foot had raked him. He never needed spurs. I wore them on him just to be in fashion.   9

Sometimes in running through brush, Buck seemed to read my mind — or maybe I was reading his. He was better in the brush than I was. In brush work, man and horse must dodge,   10 turn, go over bushes and under limbs, absolutely in accord, rider yielding to the instinct and judgment of the horse as much as horse yields to his.

Buck did not have to be staked. If I left a dragrope on him,   11
he would stay close to camp, at noon or through the night. He was no paragon. Many men have ridden and remembered hardier horses. He was not proud, but carried himself in a very trim manner. He did the best he could, willingly and generous- ly, and he had a good heart. His chemistry mixed with mine. He was good company. I loved to hear him drink water, he was so hearty in swallowing, and then, after he was full, to watch him lip the water's surface and drip big drops back into it.

Sometimes after we had watered and, passing on, had come   12
to good grass near shade, I'd unsaddle and turn him loose to graze. Then I'd lie down on the saddle and, while the blanket dried, listen to his energetic cropping and watch the buzzards sail and the Gulf clouds float. Buck would blow out his breath once in a while, presumably to clear his nostrils but also, it seemed to me, to express contentment.

He never asked me to stop, unless it was to stale, and never,   13
like some gentle saddle horses, interrupted his step to grab a mouthful of grass; but if I stopped with slackened rein to watch cattle, or maybe just to gaze over the flow of hills to the horizon, he'd reach down and begin cutting grass. He knew that was all right with me, though a person's seat on a grazing horse is not nearly so comfortable as on one with upright head. Occasional- ly I washed the sweat off his back and favored him in other ways, but nobody in our part of the country pampered cow horses with sugar or other delicacy.

While riding Buck in boyhood and early youth, I fell in love   14
with four or five girls but told only one. She was right in con- sidering the matter a joke and thereby did me one of the biggest favors of my life. All those rose-lipped maidens and all the light- foot lads with whom I ran in those days have little meaning for me now. They never had much in comparison with numerous people I have known since. Buck, however, always in associa- tion with the plot of earth over which I rode him, increases in meaning. To remember him is a joy and a tonic.

· QUESTIONS ON MEANING AND PURPOSE ·

1. What qualities did Dobie's horse Buck possess that gave him a permanent place in the author's memory?
2. From Dobie's essay, what do you learn about the everyday life of a cowboy? About Dobie himself?

· QUESTIONS ON WRITING STRATEGY ·

1. How does Dobie avoid sentimentality in his description of the horse he loved? (See *Sentimentality* in Useful Terms.)
2. Examine paragraph 13. Are the descriptive details arranged according to some principle of order, or do they seem to have been recorded as they flowed from Dobie's memory?
3. How appropriate is Dobie's tone to the content of his essay? (See *Tone* in Useful Terms.)

· QUESTIONS ON LANGUAGE ·
· AND VOCABULARY ·

1. What does Dobie mean in paragraph 2 when he describes Buck as having "a blaze in his face and stockings on his forefeet"? (See *Dead Metaphor* in Useful Terms under *Figures of Speech*.)
2. Find the meanings of these words derived from Spanish: remuda (paragraph 2); vaquero (5); mesquite (8). Define the following words as well: galled, cinch (5); girth (8); paragon (11); cropping (12); stale (13).

· SUGGESTIONS FOR WRITING ·

1. Write a brief paper in which you explain the kind of "chemistry" Dobie mentions in paragraph 11. Use examples to make the concept come alive.
2. Describe a favorite pet, or other animal of your acquaintance, trying to explain its effect upon your life. If the animal had faults or idiosyncrasies, strike a fair balance in your description between these and the traits that made it lovable. (A light tone, rather than a solemn one, may be appropriate. See *Tone* in Useful Terms.)

· Mark Twain ·

MARK TWAIN (1835–1910), born Samuel Langhorne Clemens, grew up in Hannibal, Missouri, the town his books made famous. In the course of his life, the brilliant creator of Huck Finn and Tom Sawyer was a steamboat pilot, a newspaperman, a gold miner, a world traveler, a writer, and a lecturer. Full of contradictions, Twain was a humorist whose view of life grew more and more bitter as he grew old. His reputation as one of America's finest writers is firmly established. Ernest Hemingway said that American literature "begins with *Huckleberry Finn*."

S–t–e–a–m–boat a–comin'!

"S–t–e–a–m–boat a–comin'!" (Twain's phrase) is excerpted from an early chapter of the autobiographical *Life on the Mississippi* (1883). Included in *Life on the Mississippi* is an account of the author's successful effort to become a steamboat pilot. With this knowledge, you can read Twain's description well aware that his early enthusiasm for the glamour of steamboat life was more than a passing fancy.

When I was a boy, there was but one permanent ambition among my comrades in our village[1] on the west bank of the Mississippi River. That was, to be a steamboatman. We had transient ambitions of other sorts, but they were only transient. When a circus came and went, it left us all burning to become clowns; the first negro minstrel show that ever came to our section left us all suffering to try that kind of life; now and then we had a hope that, if we lived and were good, God would permit us to be pirates. These ambitions faded out, each in its turn; but the ambition to be a steamboatman always remained.

[1]Hannibal, Missouri.

59

Once a day a cheap, gaudy packet arrived upward from St.   2
Louis, and another downward from Keokuk. Before these
events, the day was glorious with expectancy; after them, the
day was a dead and empty thing. Not only the boys, but the
whole village, felt this. After all these years I can picture that
old time to myself now, just as it was then: the white town
drowsing in the sunshine of a summer's morning; the streets
empty, or pretty nearly so; one or two clerks sitting in front of
the Water Street stores, with their splint-bottomed chairs tilted
back against the walls, chins on breasts, hats slouched over
their faces, asleep — with shingle-shavings enough around to
show what broke them down; a sow and a litter of pigs loafing
along the sidewalk, doing a good business in watermelon rinds
and seeds; two or three lonely little freight piles scattered about
the "levee"; a pile of "skids" on the slope of the stone-paved
wharf, and the fragrant town drunkard asleep in the shadow of
them; two or three wood flats at the head of the wharf, but nobody to listen to the peaceful lapping of the wavelets against
them; the great Mississippi, the majestic, the magnificent Mississippi, rolling its mile-wide tide along, shining in the sun; the
dense forest away on the other side; the "point" above the
town, and the "point" below, bounding the river-glimpse and
turning it into a sort of sea, and withal a very still and brilliant
and lonely one. Presently a film of dark smoke appears above
one of those remote "points"; instantly a negro drayman,
famous for his quick eye and prodigious voice, lifts up the cry,
"S–t–e–a–m–boat a–comin'!" and the scene changes! The town
drunkard stirs, the clerks wake up, a furious clatter of drays
follows, every house and store pours out a human contribution,
and all in a twinkling the dead town is alive and moving. Drays,
carts, men, boys, all go hurrying from many quarters to a common center, the wharf. Assembled there, the people fasten their
eyes upon the coming boat as upon a wonder they are seeing for
the first time. And the boat *is* rather a handsome sight, too. She
is long and sharp and trim and pretty; she has two tall, fancy-
topped chimneys, with a gilded device of some kind swung between them; a fanciful pilot-house, all glass and "gingerbread,"
perched on top of the "texas" deck behind them; the paddle-
boxes are gorgeous with a picture or with gilded rays above the

boat's name; the boiler-deck, the hurricane-deck, and the texas deck are fenced and ornamented with clean white railings; there is a flag gallantly flying from the jack-staff; the furnace doors are open and the fires glaring bravely; the upper decks are black with passengers; the captain stands by the big bell, calm, imposing, the envy of all; great volumes of the blackest smoke are rolling and tumbling out of the chimneys — a husbanded grandeur created with a bit of pitch-pine just before arriving at a town; the crew are grouped on the forecastle; the broad stage is run far out over the port bow, and an envied deck-hand stands picturesquely on the end of it with a coil of rope in his hand; the pent steam is screaming through the gauge-cocks; the captain lifts his hand, a bell rings, the wheels stop; then they turn back, churning the water to foam, and the steamer is at rest. Then such a scramble as there is to get aboard, and to get ashore, and to take in freight and to discharge freight, all at one and the same time; and such a yelling and cursing as the mates facilitate it all with! Ten minutes later the steamer is under way again, with no flag on the jack-staff and no black smoke issuing from the chimneys. After ten more minutes the town is dead again, and the town drunkard asleep by the skids once more.

· QUESTIONS ON MEANING AND PURPOSE ·

1. What do you learn from Twain's essay about life in Hannibal, Missouri, in the early part of the nineteenth century?
2. How does the author's description of the steamboat's arrival account for the fact that, for the young Twain and his comrades, "the ambition to be a steamboatman always remained"?
3. What seems to you Twain's central purpose in writing this description? (See *Purpose* in Useful Terms.)

· QUESTIONS ON WRITING STRATEGY ·

1. How does Twain organize the details in his description?
2. At what point in his essay does Twain switch from past to present tense? What is the effect of this shift?

3. What evidence of Twain's famous sense of humor do you find?
4. If paragraph 1 were omitted, would this essay be stronger or weaker? Discuss.
5. What transitions give Twain's long second paragraph coherence? (See *Transitions* and *Coherence* in Useful Terms.)

· QUESTIONS ON LANGUAGE ·
· AND VOCABULARY ·

1. Define the following: levee, point, gingerbread, texas deck, skids, drays. Consult your dictionary if you need help.
2. Paraphrase Twain's reference to the smoke pouring out of the steamboat chimney as "a husbanded grandeur created with a bit of pitch-pine just before arriving at a town." (See *Paraphrase* in Useful Terms.)
3. Pick out those words or phrases in which Twain expresses himself most colorfully. What images does he give us? (See *Image* in Useful Terms.)

· SUGGESTIONS FOR WRITING ·

1. Relying on Twain's description of life in nineteenth-century Hannibal, Missouri, zero in on two or three of the major differences between "then" and "now" in a brief essay.
2. Describe a memorable scene from your childhood. Include language that appeals to the senses.

· E. B. White ·

ELWYN BROOKS WHITE, born in 1899, lives on a farm in North Brooklin, Maine. From there he keeps an eye on the rest of the country. From 1926 until lately, he was a regular contributor to *The New Yorker*, and his essays, editorials, anonymous features for "The Talk of the Town," and fillers helped build the magazine a reputation for wit and good writing. If as a child you read *Charlotte's Web* (1952), you have met E.B. White before. His *Letters* were collected in 1976 and his *Essays* in 1977. On July 4, 1963, President Kennedy named White in the first group of Americans to receive the Presidential Medal for Freedom, with a citation that called him "an essayist whose concise comment on men and places has revealed to yet another age the vigor of the English sentence."

Once More to the Lake

"The essayist," says White in a foreword to his *Essays*, "is a self-liberated man, sustained by the childish belief that everything he thinks about, everything that happens to him, is of general interest." In White's case this belief is soundly justified. Perhaps if a duller writer had written "Once More to the Lake," or an essay by that title, we wouldn't much care about it, for at first its subject seems as personal, flat, and ordinary as a letter home. White's loving and exact description, however, brings this lakeside camp to life for us. In the end, the writer arrives at an awareness that shocks him — shocks us, too, by a familiar sensory detail in the last line.

August 1941

One summer, along about 1904, my father rented a camp on a lake in Maine and took us all there for the month of August. We all got ringworm from some kittens and had to rub

1

Pond's Extract on our arms and legs night and morning, and my father rolled over in a canoe with all his clothes on; but outside of that the vacation was a success and from then on none of us ever thought there was any place in the world like that lake in Maine. We returned summer after summer — always on August 1 for one month. I have since become a salt-water man, but sometimes in summer there are days when the restlessness of the tides and the fearful cold of the sea water and the incessant wind that blows across the afternoon and into the evening make me wish for the placidity of a lake in the woods. A few weeks ago this feeling got so strong I bought myself a couple of bass hooks and a spinner and returned to the lake where we used to go, for a week's fishing and to revisit old haunts.

I took along my son, who had never had any fresh water up   2
his nose and who had seen lily pads only from train windows. On the journey over to the lake I began to wonder what it would be like. I wondered how time would have marred this unique, this holy spot — the coves and streams, the hills that the sun set behind, the camps and the paths behind the camps. I was sure that the tarred road would have found it out, and I wondered in what other ways it would be desolated. It is strange how much you can remember about places like that once you allow your mind to return into the grooves that lead back. You remember one thing, and that suddenly reminds you of another thing. I guess I remembered clearest of all the early mornings, when the lake was cool and motionless, remembered how the bedroom smelled of the lumber it was made of and of the wet woods whose scent entered through the screen. The partitions in the camp were thin and did not extend clear to the top of the rooms, and as I was always the first up I would dress softly so as not to wake the others, and sneak out into the sweet outdoors and start out in the canoe, keeping close along the shore in the long shadows of the pines. I remembered being very careful never to rub my paddle against the gunwale for fear of disturbing the stillness of the cathedral.

The lake had never been what you would call a wild lake.   3
There were cottages sprinkled around the shores, and it was in farming country although the shores of the lake were quite

heavily wooded. Some of the cottages were owned by nearby farmers, and you would live at the shore and eat your meals at the farmhouse. That's what our family did. But although it wasn't wild, it was a fairly large and undisturbed lake and there were places in it that, to a child at least, seemed infinitely remote and primeval.

I was right about the tar: it led to within half a mile of the shore. But when I got back there, with my boy, and we settled into a camp near a farmhouse and into the kind of summertime I had known, I could tell that it was going to be pretty much the same as it had been before — I knew it, lying in bed the first morning smelling the bedroom and hearing the boy sneak quietly out and go off along the shore in a boat. I began to sustain the illusion that he was I, and therefore, by simple transposition, that I was my father. This sensation persisted, kept cropping up all the time we were there. It was not an entirely new feeling, but in this setting it grew much stronger. I seemed to be living a dual existence. I would be in the middle of some simple act, I would be picking up a bait box or laying down a table fork, or I would be saying something and suddenly it would be not I but my father who was saying the words or making the gesture. It gave me a creepy sensation.

We went fishing the first morning. I felt the same damp moss covering the worms in the bait can, and saw the dragonfly alight on the tip of my rod as it hovered a few inches from the surface of the water. It was the arrival of this fly that convinced me beyond any doubt that everything was as it always had been, that the years were a mirage and that there had been no years. The small waves were the same, chucking the rowboat under the chin as we fished at anchor, and the boat was the same boat, the same color green and the ribs broken in the same places, and under the floorboards the same fresh water leavings and débris — the dead helgramite, the wisps of moss, the rusty discarded fishhook, the dried blood from yesterday's catch. We stared silently at the tips of our rods, at the dragonflies that came and went. I lowered the tip of mine into the water, tentatively, pensively dislodging the fly, which darted two feet away, poised, darted two feet back, and came to rest again a lit-

4

5

tle farther up the rod. There had been no years between the
ducking of this dragonfly and the other one — the one that was
part of memory. I looked at the boy, who was silently watching
his fly, and it was my hands that held his rod, my eyes watching. I felt dizzy and didn't know which rod I was at the end of.

We caught two bass, hauling them in briskly as though they   6
were mackerel, pulling them over the side of the boat in a busi-
nesslike manner without any landing net, and stunning them
with a blow on the back of the head. When we got back for a
swim before lunch, the lake was exactly where we had left it, the
same number of inches from the dock, and there was only the
merest suggestion of a breeze. This seemed an utterly enchanted
sea, this lake you could leave to its own devices for a few hours
and come back to, and find that it had not stirred, this constant
and trustworthy body of water. In the shallows, the dark, water-
soaked sticks and twigs, smooth and old, were undulating in
clusters on the bottom against the clean ribbed sand, and the
track of the mussel was plain. A school of minnows swam by,
each minnow with its small individual shadow, doubling the attendance, so clear and sharp in the sunlight. Some of the other
campers were in swimming, along the shore, one of them with a
cake of soap, and the water felt thin and clear and unsubstan-
tial. Over the years there had been this person with the cake of
soap, this cultist, and here he was. There had been no years.

Up to the farmhouse to dinner through the teeming dusty   7
field, the road under our sneakers was only a two-track road.
The middle track was missing, the one with the marks of the
hooves and the splotches of dried, flaky manure. There had
always been three tracks to choose from in choosing which
track to walk in; now the choice was narrowed down to two.
For a moment I missed terribly the middle alternative. But the
way led past the tennis court, and something about the way it
lay there in the sun reassured me; the tape had loosened along
the backline, the alleys were green with plantains and other
weeds, and the net (installed in June and removed in September) sagged in the dry noon, and the whole place steamed with
midday heat and hunger and emptiness. There was a choice of

pie for dessert, and one was blueberry and one was apple, and the waitresses were the same country girls, there having been no passage of time, only the illusion of it as in a dropped curtain — the waitresses were still fifteen; their hair had been washed, that was the only difference — they had been to the movies and seen the pretty girls with the clean hair.

Summertime, oh, summertime, pattern of life indelible with fade-proof lake, the wood unshatterable, the pasture with the sweetfern and the juniper forever and ever, summer without end; this was the background, and the life along the shore was the design, the cottages with their innocent and tranquil design, their tiny docks with the flagpole and the American flag floating against the white clouds in the blue sky, the little paths over the roots of the trees leading from camp to camp and the paths leading back to the outhouses and the can of lime for sprinkling, and at the souvenir counters at the store the miniature birchbark canoes and the postcards that showed things looking a little better than they looked. This was the American family at play, escaping the city heat, wondering whether the newcomers in the camp at the head of the cove were "common" or "nice," wondering whether it was true that the people who drove up for Sunday dinner at the farmhouse were turned away because there wasn't enough chicken.

It seemed to me, as I kept remembering all this, that those times and those summers had been infinitely precious and worth saving. There had been jollity and peace and goodness. The arriving (at the beginning of August) had been so big a business in itself, at the railway station the farm wagon drawn up, the first smell of the pine-laden air, the first glimpse of the smiling farmer, and the great importance of the trunks and your father's enormous authority in such matters, and the feel of the wagon under you for the long ten-mile haul, and at the top of the last long hill catching the first view of the lake after eleven months of not seeing this cherished body of water. The shouts and cries of the other campers when they saw you, and the trunks to be unpacked, to give up their rich burden. (Arriving was less exciting nowadays, when you sneaked up in your car

and parked it under a tree near the camp and took out the bags
and in five minutes it was all over, no fuss, no loud wonderful
fuss about trunks.)

Peace and goodness and jollity. The only thing that was   10
wrong now, really, was the sound of the place, an unfamiliar
nervous sound of the outboard motors. This was the note that
jarred, the one thing that would sometimes break the illusion
and set the years moving. In those other summertimes all motors were inboard; and when they were at a little distance, the
noise they made was a sedative, an ingredient of summer sleep.
They were one-cylinder and two-cylinder engines, and some
were make-and-break and some were jump-spark, but they all
made a sleepy sound across the lake. The one-lungers throbbed
and fluttered, and the twin-cylinder ones purred and purred,
and that was a quiet sound, too. But now the campers all had
outboards. In the daytime, in the hot mornings, these motors
made a petulant, irritable sound; at night in the still evening
when the afterglow lit the water, they whined about one's ears
like mosquitoes. My boy loved our rented outboard, and his
great desire was to achieve single-handed mastery over it, and
authority, and he soon learned the trick of choking it a little
(but not too much), and the adjustment of the needle valve.
Watching him I would remember the things you could do with
the old one-cylinder engine with the heavy flywheel, how you
could have it eating out of your hand if you got really close to it
spiritually. Motorboats in those days didn't have clutches, and
you would make a landing by shutting off the motor at the
proper time and coasting in with a dead rudder. But there was a
way of reversing them, if you learned the trick, by cutting the
switch and putting it on again exactly on the final dying revolution of the flywheel, so that it would kick back against com-
pression and begin reversing. Approaching a dock in a strong
following breeze, it was difficult to slow up sufficiently by the ordinary coasting method, and if a boy felt he had complete
mastery over his motor, he was tempted to keep it running
beyond its time and then reverse it a few feet from the dock. It
took a cool nerve, because if you threw the switch a twentieth of

a second too soon you would catch the flywheel when it still had speed enough to go up past center, and the boat would leap ahead, charging bull-fashion at the dock.

We had a good week at the camp. The bass were biting well   11 and the sun shone endlessly, day after day. We would be tired at night and lie down in the accumulated heat of the little bedrooms after the long hot day and the breeze would stir almost imperceptibly outside and the smell of the swamp drift in through the rusty screens. Sleep would come easily and in the morning the red squirrel would be on the roof, tapping out his gay routine. I kept remembering everything, lying in bed in the mornings — the small steamboat that had a long rounded stern like the lip of a Ubangi, and how quietly she ran on the moonlight sails, when the older boys played their mandolins and the girls sang and we ate doughnuts dipped in sugar, and how sweet the music was on the water in the shining night, and what it had felt like to think about girls then. After breakfast we would go up to the store and the things were in the same place — the minnows in a bottle, the plugs and spinners disarranged and pawed over by the youngsters from the boys' camp, the Fig Newtons and the Beeman's gum. Outside, the road was tarred and cars stood in front of the store. Inside, all was just as it had always been, except there was more Coca-Cola and not so much Moxie and root beer and birch beer and sarsaparilla. We would walk out with the bottle of pop apiece and sometimes the pop would backfire up our noses and hurt. We explored the streams, quietly, where the turtles slid off the sunny logs and dug their way into the soft bottom; and we lay on the town wharf and fed worms to the tame bass. Everywhere we went I had trouble making out which was I, the one walking at my side, the one walking in my pants.

One afternoon while we were at that lake a thunderstorm   12 came up. It was like the revival of an old melodrama that I had seen long ago with childish awe. The second-act climax of the drama of the electrical disturbance over a lake in America had not changed in any important respect. This was the big scene, still the big scene. The whole thing was so familiar, the first feeling of oppression and heat and a general air around camp of not wanting to go very far away. In midafternoon (it was all the same) a curious darkening of the sky, and a lull in everything that had made life tick; and then the way the boats suddenly swung the other way at their moorings with the coming of a breeze out of the new quarter, and the premonitory rumble. Then the kettle drum, then the snare, then the bass drum and cymbals, then crackling light against the dark, and the gods grinning and licking their chops in the hills. Afterward the calm, the rain steadily rustling in the calm lake, the return of light and hope and spirits, and the campers running out in joy and relief to go swimming in the rain, their bright cries perpetuating the deathless joke about how they were getting simply drenched, and the children screaming with delight at the new sensation of bathing in the rain, and the joke about getting drenched linking the generations in a strong indestructible chain. And the comedian who waded in carrying an umbrella.

When the others went swimming my son said he was going in, too. He pulled his dripping trunks from the line where they had hung all through the shower and wrung them out. Languidly, and with no thought of going in, I watched him, his hard little body, skinny and bare, saw him wince slightly as he pulled up around his vitals the small, soggy, icy garment. As he buckled the swollen belt, suddenly my groin felt the chill of death.

• QUESTIONS ON MEANING AND PURPOSE •

1. When E. B. White takes his son to the summer place he himself had loved as a child, what changes does he find there? What things have stayed the same?

2. How do you account for the distortions that creep into the author's sense of time?

3. What does the discussion of inboard and outboard motors (paragraph 10) have to do with the author's divided sense of time?

4. What do you take to be White's main purpose in this essay? At what point do you become aware of it? (See *Purpose* in Useful Terms.)

• QUESTIONS ON WRITING STRATEGY •

1. To what degree does White make us aware of the impression that this trip to the lake makes upon his son?
2. In paragraph 4, the author first introduces his confused feeling that he has gone back in time to his own childhood, an idea that he repeats and expands throughout his account. What purpose do the repetitions serve?
3. Try to describe the impact of the essay's final paragraph. By what means is it achieved?
4. To what extent is this essay written to appeal to any but middle-aged readers? Is it comprehensible to anyone whose vacations were never spent at a Maine summer cottage?

• QUESTIONS ON LANGUAGE •
• AND VOCABULARY •

1. Be sure you know the meanings of the following words: incessant, placidity (paragraph 1); gunwale (2); primeval (3); transposition (4); helgramite (5); undulating, cultist (6); indelible, tranquil (8); petulant (10); imperceptibly (11); premonitory (12); languidly (13).
2. Comment on White's diction in his reference to the lake as "this unique, this holy spot" (paragraph 2). (See *Diction* in Useful Terms.)
3. Explain what White is describing in the sentence that begins, "Then the kettle drum . . . " (paragraph 12). Where else does the author use metaphors (See *Metaphor* under *Figures of Speech* in Useful Terms.)

• SUGGESTIONS FOR WRITING •

1. In a descriptive paragraph, try to appeal to each of your reader's five senses.
2. Describe in a brief essay a place you loved as a child. Or, if you have ever returned to a favorite old haunt, describe the experience. Was it pleasant or painful — or both? What, exactly, made it so?

· ADDITIONAL WRITING TOPICS ·

DESCRIPTION

1. This is an in-class writing experiment. Describe another person in the room so clearly and unmistakably that when you read your description aloud, your subject will be recognized. (Be objective. No insulting descriptions, please!)

2. Write four paragraphs describing one subject from *each* of the following categories. It will be up to you to make the general subject refer to a particular person, place, thing, or event, feeling or abstraction. Write at least one paragraph as an *objective* description and at least one as a *subjective* description. (Identify your method in each case, so that your instructor can see how well you carry it out.)

Person

a. A friend or roommate.
b. A typical high school student.
c. One of your parents.
d. An elderly person you know.
e. A prominent politician.
f. A historic figure.

Place

a. A classroom.
b. A college campus.
c. A vacation spot.
d. A hospital emergency room.
e. A snow scene.
f. A forest.

Thing or Event

a. A dentist's drill.
b. A foggy day.
c. A season of the year.
d. A walk on the beach or in the snow.
e. An auction.
f. A block party.
g. A fire or a drowning.

h. A day at the fair.
i. A birthday celebration.
j. A dramatic performance.

Feeling or Abstraction

a. The symptoms of an illness.
b. Love.
c. Rage.
d. Fear.
e. Frustration.
f. Patriotism.
g. Success.
h. Justice.

3

EXAMPLE

Pointing to Instances

· THE METHOD ·

"There are many women runners of distinction," a writer begins, and quickly goes on, "among them Jacqueline Gareau, Jan Merrill, Allison Roe, Grete Waitz. . . ."

You have just seen examples at work. An example (from the Latin *exemplum*: "one thing selected from among many") is an instance that reveals a whole type. By selecting an example, a writer shows the nature or character of the group from which it is taken. In a written essay, an example will often serve to illustrate a general statement. For example, here is film critic Pauline Kael, making a point about the work of a veteran actor, Cary Grant:

> The romantic male stars aren't necessarily sexually aggressive. Henry Fonda wasn't; neither was James Stewart, or,

later, Marcello Mastroianni. The foursquare Clark Gable, with his bold, open challenge to women, was more the exception than the rule, and Gable wasn't romantic, like Grant. Gable got down to brass tacks; his advances were basic, his unspoken question was "Well, sister, what do you say?" If she said no, she was failing what might almost be nature's test. She'd become overcivilized, afraid of her instincts — afraid of being a woman. There was a violent, primal appeal in Gable's sex scenes: it was all out front — in the way he looked at her, man to woman. Cary Grant doesn't challenge a woman that way. (When he tried, as the frontiersman in *The Howards of Virginia*, he looked thick and stupid.)[1]

Kael might have allowed the opening sentence of her paragraph — the topic sentence — to remain a vague generalization. Instead, she follows it immediately with the names of three male movie stars who gently charm, not sexually challenge, their women audiences. Then, to show the style of acting she *doesn't* mean, she gives the example of Clark Gable. Her main purpose (in her paragraph, and in fact, in her whole essay) is to set forth the style of Cary Grant. That is why she adds an example of a film in which, when Grant tried to play a sexually aggressive character, he failed miserably. By all of these examples, Kael not only explains and supports her generalization, she lends life to it.

The method of giving examples — of illustrating what you're saying with a "for instance" — is not merely helpful to practically all kinds of writing, it is indispensable. Bad writers — those who bore us, or lose us completely — often have an ample supply of ideas; their trouble is that they never pull their ideas down out of the clouds by using specific illustrations. A dull writer, for instance, might declare, "The true romantic film star is a man of gentle style"; but, instead of giving examples, the writer might go on, "Romantic film stars are thus striking a nonaggressive blow for the dignity of womankind," or something, thus adding still another large, unillustrated idea. Specific examples are *needed* elements in good prose. Not only do

---

[1] "The Man from Dream City," in *When the Lights Go Down* (New York: Holt, Rinehart and Winston, 1980), p. 4.

Example **77**

they make your ideas understandable, but they also engage your reader's interest and concern. (The previous paragraphs have tried — by giving examples from Pauline Kael and from "a dull writer" — to illustrate this point.)

Although examples may be given as briefly and numerously as in the sentence about women runners of distinction (which simply lists names), examples also may be extended, treated at some length and in ample detail. In a funny and incisive essay in this chapter, Andrew Ward portrays a run-down gas station, with its unlovable owner and its mean watchdog. Ward offers the portrait as an example of a type of American business that is rapidly vanishing, and he spends most of his essay in developing this example — and in making his point unforgettable.

In illustrating a point, how many examples do you need to give? As many as it takes to make your point clear. One is enough for Ward, who details a typical, old-fashioned gas station of a kind that most readers will recognize. (His essay, incidentally, goes on to make a second point with a second example.) But for Alvin Toffler, in another essay in Chapter 9, a whole array of brief examples seems needed to show the extent of a certain phenomenon (which Toffler calls "the de-massified media") — something that most of us haven't recognized before. In your own writing, when giving examples, you may find the methods of *narration* (Chapter 1) and *description* (Chapter 2) particularly useful. Sometimes an example takes the form of a brief story, anecdote, or case history. Sometimes it embodies a vivid description of a person, place, or thing.

• THE PROCESS •

Where do you find examples? In anything you know — or care to learn. Start close to home. You can seek examples in your own immediate knowledge or experience. Assigned an elephant-sized subject that you think you know nothing about — moral and ethical dilemmas, for instance — rummage your memory, and you may discover that you are an expert on it. In what moral and ethical dilemmas have you ever found yourself? Having to decide whether to defy a parent's instructions to return with the car by midnight because, out of the goodness of your heart, you felt obliged to drive a drunken friend home? Being tempted to pilfer from the jelly-jar of a small boy's Kool-Aid stand when you needed a quarter for a bus? No doubt you can supply your own examples. It is the method — exemplifying — that matters. To bring some huge and ethereal concept down to earth may just set your expository faculties galloping over the plains of your own life to the sound of "hi-yo, Silver!" For different examples, you can explore your conversations with others, your studies, and the storehouse of information you have gathered from books, newspapers, magazines, radio and TV, and from popular hearsay: proverbs and sayings, bits of wisdom you've heard voiced in your family, folklore, popular song.

Now and again, you may feel an irresistible temptation to make up an example out of thin air. This procedure is risky, but can work wonderfully — if, that is, you have a wonder-working imagination. When Henry David Thoreau, in *Walden*, attacks Americans' smug pride in the achievements of nineteenth-century science and industry, he wants to illustrate that kind of invention or discovery "which distracts our attention from serious things." And so he makes up an example — far-fetched, but one that drives straight to his point:

> We are eager to tunnel under the Atlantic and bring the Old World some weeks nearer to the New; but perchance the first news that will leak through into the broad, flapping American ear will be that the Princess Adelaide has the whooping cough.

This example (especially the phrase about the American ear) bespeaks genius; but, of course, not every writer can be a Thoreau — or needs to be. A hypothetical example may well be better than no example at all; yet, as a rule, an actual illustration taken from fact or experience is likely to carry more weight. Suppose you have to write about the benefits — any benefits — that recent science has conferred upon the nation. You might imagine one such benefit: the prospect of one day being able to vacation in outer space and drift about in free fall like a soap bubble. That imagined benefit would be all right, but it is ob-

Example **79**

viously a conjecture that you dreamed up without going to the library. Do a little digging in recent books and magazines (for the latter, with the aid of the *Readers' Guide to Periodical Literature*). Your reader will feel better informed to be told that science — specifically, the NASA space program — has produced useful inventions. You add:

> Among these are the smoke detector, originally developed as Skylab equipment; the inflatable air bag to protect drivers and pilots, designed to cushion astronauts in splashdowns; a walking chair that enables paraplegics to mount stairs and travel over uneven ground, derived from the moonwalkers' surface buggy; the technique of cryosurgery, and the removal of cancerous tissue by fast freezing.

By using specific examples like these, you render the idea of "benefits to society" more concrete and more definite. Such examples are not prettifications of your essay; they are necessary if you are to hold your readers' attention and convince them that you are worth listening to. When John Lempesis cites some of the consequences of drunken driving (in his essay in Chapter 10), he might have given a vague, hypothetical example. He might have imagined some typical young person who, after a car accident, was psychologically damaged. Instead, he tells us the story of a real person — Gail — who, never quite recovering from a car crash, has to drop out of school because she is unable to concentrate. In his essay, facts not only interest us, they also lend the argument authority. (There is, however, a special kind of hypothetical example that you sometimes may find useful: analogy, dealt with in Chapter 7.)

Lazy writers think, "Oh well, I can't come up with any example here — I'll just leave it to the reader to find one." The flaw in this assumption is that the reader may be as lazy as the writer. As a result, a perfectly good idea may be left suspended in the stratosphere. S. I. Hayakawa tells the story of a professor who, in teaching a philosophy course, spent a whole semester on the theory of beauty. When students asked him for a few examples of beautiful paintings, symphonies, or works of nature, he refused, saying, "We are interested in principles, not in particulars." The professor himself may well have been interested in principles, but it is a safe bet that his classroom resounded with snores. In written exposition, it is undoubtedly the particulars — the pertinent examples — that keep a reader awake and having a good time, and taking in the principles besides.

• EXAMPLE IN A PARAGRAPH •

A television sitcom may claim to take place in Fargo, or Seattle, or Buies Creek, and yet it will homogenize its locale, removing any local characteristics. Consider, for instance, how *Mork and Mindy* transforms Boulder, Colorado, into Anywhere, U.S.A. Though people in this spectacularly situated town live in the blue shade of the Rockies, neither Mindy nor Mork ever visits Estes Park, and no stranger complains of high altitude. When, for a season, the program introduced scenes in a local restaurant, was the restaurant a Colorado steakhouse? Was it one of Boulder's beloved chili emporia? No, it was a New York deli. Still more faceless and all-American is the Wisconsin of *Happy Days* and its spinoff *Laverne and Shirley*. At no time has any patron of Arnold's high school hangout been heard to order a bratwurst. Arthur Fonzarelli, apparently, is an old-time Brooklyn motorcycle fancier, accent and all. Like no known Milwaukee is the one in the old *Laverne and Shirley* series. Supposedly typical Milwaukee working women, the two main characters were name DeFazio and Feeney. Now, to be sure, Italian-Americans and Irish-Americans can be found in Milwaukee, with some difficulty; but, had the scriptsmiths been true to the ethnic composition of the city, they probably would have christened the pair Schmidt and Kosnowski. Our heroines were always shown working in a brewery, and they went bowling now and then; but did viewers in Milwaukee never think it odd that no one on the show ever visited Mitchell Park, lolled on the lakefront, voted the Socialist ticket, bought creampuffs at the Wisconsin State Fair, or read the *Journal* and the *Sentinel?* Certainly it was no surprise when, in a new season, the two beer-cappers quit their jobs and swelled the migration to the Sunbelt, leaving the Milwaukee of their past to exist only in reruns. At last report, they were working

Example **81**

in Hollywood — or some town called by that name. In truth,
it may be Hollywood, Louisiana, or a never-never isle midway
between Brooklyn and Byzantium.

Comment. This writer's opening statement — the thesis
sentence — might have been harder to grasp without examples.
By referring in detail to three situation comedies, the writer illustrates a creative liberty to be noticed in TV shows: that of
wiping away all distinctive local features and lifestyles from
wherever the show is supposed to take place. The three programs might have just been mentioned by name as examples of
sitcoms that all-Americanize their locales. Mere mentions,
though, probably would be less interesting, and, hence, less effective. To ask *why* TV comedies homogenize their settings and
to guess at an answer would call for another paragraph — one
that might be written by the method of cause and effect (dealt
with in Chapter 8), rather than by the method of example.

· Roger Rosenblatt ·

ROGER ROSENBLATT, born in 1940, took his Ph.D. at Harvard and served from 1970 to 1973 as director of the expository writing program there. Deciding to leave the academic world, he moved to Washington, D.C., where he became literary editor of *The New Republic* and a columnist and member of the editorial board of the Washington *Post*. Now a senior writer for *Time* magazine, he has written one book of literary criticism, *Black Fiction* (1974).

Oops! How's That Again?

For the past years *Time* has been printing a weekly essay, always on a large and significant general subject. "Oops! How's That Again?" a contribution to this series, appeared in 1981. Rosenblatt, despite a space limit imposed on him, manages to enrich his discussion with memorable examples; and although, as befits its subject, the tone of his essay is humorous, Rosenblatt is concerned with the psychological causes of bloopers. The essay is funny, but it is much more.

"That is not what I meant at all. That is not it, at all."
— T. S. Eliot, *The Love Song of J. Alfred Prufrock*

At a royal luncheon in Glasgow last month, Businessman   1
Peter Balfour turned to the just-engaged Prince Charles and wished him long life and conjugal happiness with Lady Jane. The effect of the sentiment was compromised both by the fact that the Prince's betrothed is Lady Diana (Spencer) and that Lady Jane (Wellesley) is one of his former flames. "I feel a perfect fool," said Balfour, who was unnecessarily contrite. Slips of the tongue occur all the time. In Chicago recently, Governor James Thompson was introduced as "the mayor of Illinois," which was a step down from the time he was introduced as "the Governor of the United States." Not all such fluffs are so easy to take,

82

however. During the primaries, Nancy Reagan telephoned her husband as her audience listened in, to say how delighted she was to be looking at all "the beautiful white people." And France's Prime Minister Raymond Barre, who has a reputation for putting his *pied* in his *bouche*, described last October's bombing of a Paris synagogue as "this odious attack that was aimed at Jews and that struck at innocent Frenchmen" — a crack that not only implied Jews were neither innocent nor French but also suggested that the attack would have been less odious had it been more limited.

One hesitates to call Barre sinister, but the fact is that verbal errors can have a devastating effect on those who hear them and on those who make them as well. Jimmy Carter never fully recovered from his reference to Polish lusts for the future in a mistranslated speech in 1977, nor was Chicago's Mayor Daley ever quite the same after assuring the public that "the policeman isn't there to create disorder, the policeman is there to preserve disorder." Dwight Eisenhower, John Kennedy, Spiro Agnew, Gerald Ford, all made terrible gaffes, with Ford perhaps making the most unusual ("Whenever I can I always watch the Detroit Tigers on radio"). Yet this is no modern phenomenon. The term *faux pas* goes back at least as far as the seventeenth century, having originally referred to a woman's lapse from virtue. Not that women lapse more than men in this regard. Even Marie Antoinette's fatal remark about cake and the public, if true, was due to poor translation.

In fact, mistranslation accounts for a great share of verbal errors. The slogan "Come Alive with Pepsi" failed understandably in German when it was translated: "Come Alive out of the Grave with Pepsi." Elsewhere it was translated with more precision: "Pepsi Brings Your Ancestors Back from the Grave." In 1965, prior to a reception for Queen Elizabeth II outside Bonn, Germany's President Heinrich Lübke, attempting an English translation of *"Gleich geht es los"* (It will soon begin), told the Queen: "Equal goes it loose." The Queen took the news well, but no better than the President of India, who was greeted at an airport in 1962 by Lübke, who, intending to ask, "How are you?" instead said: "Who are you?" To which his guest answered responsibly: "I am the President of India."

The most prodigious collector of modern slips was Kermit   4
Schafer, whose "blooper" records of mistakes made on radio
and television consisted largely of toilet jokes, but were nonetheless a great hit in the 1950s. Schafer was an avid self-pro-
moter and something of a blooper himself, but he did have an
ear for such things as the introduction by Radio Announcer
Harry von Zell of President "Hoobert Heever," as well as the
interesting message: "This portion of *Women on the Run* is
brought to you by Phillips' Milk of Magnesia." Bloopers are the
lowlife of verbal error, but spoonerisms are a different fettle of
kitsch. In the early 1900s the Rev. William Archibald Spooner
caused a stir at New College, Oxford, with his famous spoonerisms, most of which were either deliberate or apocryphal. But a
real one — his giving out a hymn in chapel as "Kinquering
Kongs Their Titles Take" — is said to have brought down the
house of worship, and to have kicked off the genre. After that,
spoonerisms got quite elaborate. Spooner once reportedly
chided a student: "You have hissed all my mystery lectures. In
fact, you have tasted the whole worm, and must leave by the
first town drain."

Such missteps, while often howlingly funny to ignorami like   5
us, are deadly serious concerns to psychologists and linguists.
Victoria Fromkin of the linguistics department at U.C.L.A. regards slips of the tongue as clues to how the brain stores and ar-
ticulates language. She believes that thought is placed by the
brain into a grammatical framework before it is expressed —
this in spite of the fact that she works with college students. A
grammatical framework was part of Walter Annenberg's trouble
when, as the newly appointed U.S. Ambassador to Britain, he
was asked by the Queen how he was settling in to his London
residence. Annenberg admitted to "some discomfiture as a result of a need for elements of refurbishing." Either he was over-
whelmed by the circumstance or he was losing his mind.

When you get to that sort of error, you are nearing a   6
psychological abyss. It was Freud who first removed the element
of accident from language with his explanation of "slips," but
lately others have extended his theories. Psychiatrist Richard

Yazmajian, for example, suggests that there are some incorrect words that exist in associative chains with the correct ones for which they are substituted, implying a kind of "dream pair" of elements in the speaker's psyche. The nun who poured tea for the Irish bishop and asked, "How many lords, my lump?" might therefore have been asking a profound theological question.

On another front, Psychoanalyst Ludwig Eidelberg made   7
Freud's work seem childishly simple when he suggested that a slip of the tongue involves the entire network of id, ego and superego. He offers the case of the young man who entered a restaurant with his girlfriend and ordered a room instead of a table. You probably think that you understand that error. But just listen to Eidelberg: "All the wishes connected with the word 'room' represented a countercathexis mobilized as a defense. The world 'table' had to be omitted, because it would have been used for infantile gratification of a repressed oral, aggressive and scopophilic wish connected with identification with the preoedipal mother." Clearly, this is no laughing matter.

Why then do we hoot at these mistakes? For one thing, it   8
may be that we simply find conventional discourse so predictable and boring that any deviation comes as a delightful relief. In his deeply unfunny *Essay on Laughter* the philosopher Henri Bergson theorized that the act of laughter is caused by any interruption of normal human fluidity or momentum (a pie in the face, a mask, a pun). Slips of the tongue, therefore, are like slips on banana peels; we crave their occurrence if only to break the monotonies. The monotonies run to substance. When that announcer introduced Hoobert Heever, he may also have been saying that the nation had had enough of Herbert Hoover.

Then too there is the element of pure meanness in such   9
laughter, both the meanness of enjoyment in watching an embarrassed misspeaker's eyes roll upward as if in prayer — his hue turn magenta, his hands like homing larks fluttering to his mouth — and the mean joy of discovering his hidden base motives and critical intent. At the 1980 Democratic National Convention, Jimmy Carter took a lot of heat for referring to Hubert Humphrey as Hubert Horatio Hornblower because it was in-

stantly recognized that Carter thought Humphrey a windbag. David Hartman of *Good Morning America* left little doubt about his feelings for a sponsor when he announced: "We'll be right back after this word from General Fools." At a conference in Berlin in 1954, France's Foreign Minister Georges Bidault was hailed as "that fine little French tiger, Georges Bidet," thus belittling the tiger by the tail. When we laugh at such stuff, it is the harsh and bitter laugh, the laugh at the disclosure of inner condemning truth.

Yet there is also a more kindly laugh that occurs when a   10 blunderer does not reveal his worst inner thoughts, but his most charitable or optimistic. Gerald Ford's famous error in the 1976 presidential debate, in which he said that Poland was not under Soviet domination, for instance. In a way, that turned out to contain a grain of truth, thanks to Lech Walesa and the strikes; in any case it was a nice thing to wish. As was U.N. Ambassador Warren Austin's suggestion in 1948 that Jews and Arabs resolve their differences "in a true Christian spirit." Similarly, Nebraska's former Senator Kenneth Wherry might have been thinking dreamily when, in an hour-long speech on a country in Southeast Asia, he referred throughout to "Indigo-China." One has to be in the mood for such a speech.

Of course, the most interesting laugh is the one elicited by   11 the truly bizarre mistake, because such a mistake seems to disclose a whole new world of logic and possibility, a deranged double for the life that is. What Lewis Carroll displayed through the looking glass, verbal error also often displays by conjuring up ideas so supremely nutty that the laughter it evokes is sublime. The idea that Pepsi might actually bring one back from the grave encourages an entirely new view of experience. In such a view it is perfectly possible to lust after the Polish future, to watch the Tigers on the radio, to say "Equal goes it loose" with resounding clarity.

Still, beyond all this is another laugh entirely, that neither   12 condemns, praises, ridicules nor conspires, but sees into the essential nature of a slip of the tongue and consequently sympathizes. After all, most human endeavor results in a slip of the something — the best-laid plans gone suddenly haywire by natural blunder: the chair, cake or painting that turns out not ex-actly as one imagined; the kiss or party that falls flat; the life that is not quite what one had in mind. Nothing is ever as dreamed.

So we laugh at each other, perfect fools all, flustered by the   13
mistake of our mortality.

• QUESTIONS ON MEANING AND PURPOSE •

1. In which paragraphs of Rosenblatt's essay do you find any of these purposes: to illustrate different kinds of verbal errors, to probe why they happen, to explain why we laugh at them, or simply to entertain us? Which seems Rosenblatt's main purpose?
2. Quote the famous remark by Marie Antoinette to which Rosenblatt refers in paragraph 2.
3. What explanations does Rosenblatt advance for the human tendency to make verbal errors? Is the reader meant to regard all of the theories with equal seriousness?
4. What relationship does Rosenblatt discover between verbal errors and the work of Lewis Carroll?
5. What examples of verbal error (public blunders, memorable mistranslations, "bloopers," spoonerisms) have you heard or read about recently? When you cite one that seems particularly revealing, take a guess at its possible cause.

• QUESTIONS ON WRITING STRATEGY •

1. What is the topic sentence in paragraph 2? (See *Topic Sentence* in Useful Terms.) In illustrating this general statement, how many examples does Rosenblatt give? Where does he draw them from?
2. Into what groups has Rosenblatt organized his numerous examples of verbal missteps?
3. What effect does the author achieve by using the first person plural in his concluding sentence? (See *Conclusions* in Useful Terms.)
4. Recall the fact that this essay first appeared in *Time*, a news magazine whose audience largely consists of people in business and in the professions (medicine, law, teaching, media, technology). Why would you expect such readers to find verbal errors a subject of personal interest?

· QUESTIONS ON LANGUAGE ·
· AND VOCABULARY ·

1. Rosenblatt occasionally uses French words. Be sure you know the meanings of *pied, bouche* (paragraph 1), and *faux pas* (2); and you will more fully appreciate the humor in paragraph 9 if you know what a *bidet* is.
2. Look up *bar sinister* in the dictionary. Then explain Rosenblatt's play on words when he says, "One hesitates to call Barre sinister. . . . " (paragraph 2).
3. From examples that the author gives in paragraph 4, explain what a *spoonerism* is. What is *kitsch?*

· SUGGESTIONS FOR WRITING ·

1. If you have ever had the experience of putting your *pied* in your *bouche*, recount it and its consequences. You might, as an alternative, tell how this fate befell someone else.
2. Examine some other variety of verbal behavior for which you can collect enough examples. (Some possibilities: nicknames, sportswriters' colorful figures of speech, coined words, slang, the invented names of fast foods, the special vocabulary of a subculture such as runners or poker players, dialect and regional speech.) Like Rosenblatt, give examples and then try to account for the phenomenon they exemplify.

· Andrew Ward ·

ANDREW WARD, born in 1946, now lives in Connecticut and is a contributing editor for *The Atlantic Monthly*. He attended Oberlin College and the Rhode Island School of Design. Ward has published two collections of his work, *Fits and Starts: The Premature Memoirs of Andrew Ward* (1978) and *Bits and Pieces* (1980). He continues to write — humorously.

They Also Wait Who Stand and Serve Themselves

"They Also Wait Who Stand and Serve Themselves" was first published in the *Atlantic*. Detailing in two extended examples a gas station as it was and as it is, the essay seems to prove that, with the passage of time, a bad scene can be counted upon to worsen. There is more here, though, than simple nostalgia for a vanishing institution.

Anyone interested in the future of American commerce should take a drive sometime to my neighborhood gas station. Not that it is or ever was much of a place to visit. Even when I first moved here, five years ago, it was shabby and forlorn: not at all like the garden spots they used to feature in the commercials, where trim, manicured men with cultivated voices tipped their visors at your window and asked what they could do for you.

Sal, the owner, was a stocky man who wore undersized, popped-button shirts, sagging trousers, and oil-spattered work shoes with broken laces. "Gas stinks" was his motto, and every gallon he pumped into his customers' cars seemed to take something out of him. "Pumping gas is for morons," he liked to say, leaning indelibly against my rear window and watching the digits fly on the pump register. "One of these days I'm gonna dump this place on a Puerto Rican, move to Florida, and get into something nice, like hero sandwiches."

He had a nameless, walleyed assistant who wore a studded 3
denim jacket and, with his rag and squeegee, left a milky film on
my windshield as my tank was filling. There was a fume-crazed,
patchy German shepherd, which Sal kept chained to the air
pump, and if you followed Sal into his cluttered, overheated office next to the service bays, you ran a gauntlet of hangers-on,
many of them Sal's brothers and nephews, who spent their time
debating the merits of the driving directions he gave the bewildered travelers who turned into his station for help.

"I don't know," one of them would say, pulling a bag of 4
potato chips off the snack rack, "I think I would have put 'em
onto 91, gotten 'em off at Willow, and then — bango! —
straight through to Hamden."

Sal guarded the rest room key jealously and handed it out 5
with reluctance, as if something in your request had betrayed
some dismal aberration. The rest room was accessible only
through a little closet littered with tires, fan belts, and cases of
oil cans. Inside, the bulb was busted and there were never any
towels, so you had to dry your hands on toilet paper — if Sal
wasn't out of toilet paper, too.

The soda machine never worked for anyone except Sal, 6
who, when complaints were lodged, would give it a contemptuous kick as he trudged by, dislodging warm cans of grape soda
which, when their pop-tops were flipped, gave off a fine purple
spray. There was, besides the snack rack in the office, a machine
that dispensed peanuts on behalf of the Sons of Garibaldi. The
metal shelves along the cinderblock wall were sparsely stocked
with cans of cooling system cleaner, windshield de-icer, an-
tifreeze, and boxed head lamps and oil filters. Over the battered
yellow wiper case, below the Coca Cola clock, and half hidden
by a calendar from a janitorial supply concern, hung a little
brass plaque from the oil company, awarded in recognition of
Salvatore A. Castallano's ten-year business association.

I wish for the sake of nostalgia that I could say Sal was a 7
craftsman, but I can't. I'm not even sure he was an honest man.
I suspect that when business was slow he may have cheated me,
but I never knew for sure because I don't know anything about
cars. If I brought my Volvo in because it was behaving strangely, I knew that as far as Sal was concerned it could never be a

simple matter of tightening a bolt or re-attaching a hose. "Jesus," he'd wearily exclaim after a look under the hood. "Mr. Ward, we got problems." I usually let it go at that and simply asked him when he thought he could have it repaired, because if I pressed him for details he would get all worked up. "Look, if you don't want to take my word for it, you can go someplace else. I mean, it's a free country, you know? You got spalding on your caps, which means your dexadrometer isn't charging, and pretty soon you're gonna have hairlines in your flushing drums. You get hairlines in your flushing drums and you might as well forget it. You're driving junk."

I don't know what Sal's relationship was with the oil com- 8
pany. I suppose it was pretty distant. He was never what they call a "participating dealer." He never gave away steak knives or NFL tumblers or stuffed animals with his fill-ups, and never got around to taping company posters on his windows. The map rack was always empty, and the company emblem, which was supposed to rotate thirty feet above the station, had broken down long before I first laid eyes on it, and had frozen at an angle that made it hard to read from the highway.

If, outside of television, there was ever such a thing as an oil 9
company service station inspector, he must have been appalled by the grudging service, the mad dog, the sepulchral john. When there was supposed to have been an oil shortage a few years ago, Sal's was one of the first stations to run out of gas. And several months ago, during the holiday season, the company squeezed him out for good.

I don't know whether Sal is now happily sprinkling olive oil 10
over salami subs somewhere along the Sun Belt. I only know that one bleak January afternoon I turned into his station to find him gone. At first, as I idled by the no-lead pump, I thought the station had been shut down completely. Plywood had been nailed over the service bays, Sal's name had been painted out above the office door, and all that was left of his dog was a length of chain dangling from the air-pump's vacant mast.

But when I got out of the car I spotted someone sitting in 11
the office with his boots up on the counter, and at last caught sight of the "Self-Service Only" signs posted by the pumps. Now, I've always striven for a degree of self-sufficiency. I fix my

own leaky faucets and I never let the bellboy carry my bags. But I discovered as I squinted at the instructional sticker by the nozzle that there are limits to my desire for independence. Perhaps it was the bewilderment with which I approach anything having to do with the internal combustion engine; perhaps it was my conviction that fossil fuels are hazardous; perhaps it was the expectation of service, the sense of helplessness, that twenty years of oil company advertising had engendered, but I didn't want to pump my own gas.

A mongrel rain began to fall upon the oil-slicked tarmac as I   12
followed the directions spelled out next to the nozzle. But somehow I got them wrong. When I pulled the trigger on the nozzle, no gas gushed into my fuel tank, no digits flew on the gauge.

"Hey, buddy," a voice sounded out of a bell-shaped speaker   13
overhead. "Flick the switch."

I turned toward the office and saw someone with Wild Bill   14
Hickok hair leaning over a microphone.

"Right. Thanks," I answered, and turned to find the switch.   15
There wasn't one. There was a bolt that looked a little like a switch, but it wouldn't flick.

"The switch," the voice crackled in the rain. "Flick the   16
switch."

I waved back as if I'd finally understood, but I still couldn't   17
figure out what he was talking about. In desperation, I stuck the nozzle back into my fuel tank and pulled the trigger. Nothing.

In the office I could see that the man was now angrily pull-   18
ing on a slicker. "What the hell's the matter with you?" he asked, storming by me. "All you gotta do is flick the switch."

"I couldn't find the switch," I told him.   19

"Well, what do you call this?" he wanted to know, pointing   20
to a little lever near the pump register.

"A lever," I told him.   21

"Christ," he muttered, flicking the little lever. The digits on   22
the register suddenly formed neat rows of zeros. "All right, it's set. Now you can serve yourself," the long-haired man said, ducking back to the office.

As the gas gushed into my fuel tank and the fumes rose to   23
my nostrils, I thought for a moment about my last visit to

Sal's. It hadn't been any picnic: Sal claimed to have found something wrong with my punting brackets, the German shepherd snapped at my heels as I walked by, and nobody had change for my ten. But the transaction had dimension to it: I picked up some tips about color antennas, entered into the geographical debate in the office, and bought a can of windshield wiper solvent (to fill the gap in my change). Sal's station had been a dime a dozen, but it occurred to me, as the nozzle began to balk and shudder in my hand, that gas stations of its kind were going the way of the village smithy and the corner grocer.

I got a glob of grease on my glove as I hung the nozzle back   24
on the pump, and it took more than a minute to satisfy myself
that I had replaced the gas cap properly. I tried to whip up a feeling of accomplishment as I headed for the office, but I could not forget Sal's dictum: Pumping gas is for morons.

The door to the office was locked, but a sign directed me to   25
a stainless steel teller's drawer which had been installed in the
plate glass of the front window. I stood waiting for a while with
my money in hand, but the long-haired man sat inside with his
back to me, so at last I reached up and hesitantly knocked on
the glass with my glove.

The man didn't hear me or had decided, in retaliation for   26
our semantic disagreement, to ignore me for a while. I reached
up to knock again, but noticed that my glove had left a greasy
smear on the window. Ever my mother's son, I reflexively
reached into my pocket for my handkerchief and was about to
wipe the grease away when it hit me: at last the oil industry had
me where it wanted me — standing in the rain and washing its
windshield.

· QUESTIONS ON MEANING AND PURPOSE ·

1. What makes this essay something more than simple nostalgia?
   What mixture of feelings toward Sal's gas station does Ward express?

2. For what reason does Ward prefer the gas station of the past over what it has become?

3. How would you characterize the author's relationship with the oil industry?

4. What is the central purpose of this essay: to describe two methods of running a gas station, or to show through two extended examples a certain profound change? Exactly what in the essay indicates its purpose? (See *Purpose* in Useful Terms.)

• QUESTIONS ON WRITING STRATEGY •

1. In what parts of this essay does the writer make particularly good use of the method of description (explained in Chapter 2)?

2. How effectively do the essay's two extended examples illustrate Ward's thesis? (See *Thesis* in Useful Terms.)

3. Where in his essay does Ward use irony? (See *Irony* in Useful Terms.)

4. Of what advantage is it to the writer that his audience is familiar with gas stations? Where does the essay tell you things you already know? Where does it tell you something you might not have realized before? (See *Audience* in Useful Terms.)

• QUESTIONS ON LANGUAGE •
• AND VOCABULARY •

1. Figure out, from context or from the dictionary, the meanings of the following: walleyed, ran a gauntlet (paragraph 3); reluctance, aberration, accessible (5); contemptuous (6); sepulchral (9); retaliation, semantic (26).

2. What do you make of the words in Sal's diagnosis (paragraph 8): "spalding on your caps," "your dexadrometer isn't charging," "hairlines in your flushing drums"? Is Sal feeding the author a line of double talk, or is Ward showing his audience how the language of auto mechanics sounded to him?

3. What is a *mongrel rain* (paragraph 12)? Is *mongrel* an effective modifier here? Why, or why not?

4. Draw on your knowledge of the Old West to explain *Wild Bill Hickok hair* (paragraph 14).

5. The title of Ward's essay is an allusion to a sonnet by the English poet John Milton, beginning "When I consider how my light is spent," and ending with the insight that those who serve God passively (like Milton, who was blind and could no longer take an

active role in the Puritan cause) "also serve who only stand and wait." How does this allusion serve Ward? (See *Allusion* in Useful Terms.)

· SUGGESTIONS FOR WRITING ·

1. In a light-hearted essay, agree or disagree with Ward's insight that "progress" is not necessarily synonymous with improvement.
2. Try to describe in a brief essay some familiar institution of contemporary life: supermarkets, drive-in movies, game arcades, or whatever else interests you. Be sure to include at least one extended example.
3. Discuss in an essay full of examples: To what extent does the current trend toward depersonalization in retailing extend beyond gas stations?

· Dina Ingber ·

DINA INGBER, born in 1948, has a B.A. in anthropology from Brooklyn College and an M.A. in journalism from Penn State. She is a freelance writer whose work has appeared in *Us, Celebrity, Cosmopolitan,* and in *Science Digest,* where "Computer Addicts" was first published in 1981. While living in Israel for three years, she worked on the *Jerusalem Post.* Ingber's recent writing has dealt mainly with science and health.

Computer Addicts

"Computer Addicts" examines some of the casualties of a new craze that is sweeping the land. While most "hackers" develop a take-it-or-leave-it attitude toward their consoles, there are some who, like alcoholics or compulsive gamblers, become slaves to their habit. Day and night, they tap away at computer keyboards, devising ever more intricate programs and games. Can they — should they — be cured?

It is 3 A.M. Everything on the university campus seems 1
ghostlike in the quiet, misty darkness — everything except the computer center. Here, twenty students, rumpled and bleary-eyed, sit transfixed at their consoles, tapping away on the terminal keys. With eyes glued to the video screen, they tap on for hours. For the rest of the world, it might be the middle of the night, but here time does not exist. As in the gambling casinos of Las Vegas, there are no windows or clocks. This is a world unto itself. Like gamblers, these young computer "hackers" are pursuing a kind of compulsion, a drive so consuming it overshadows nearly every other part of their lives and forms the focal point of their existence. They are compulsive computer programmers. Some of these students have been at the console for thirty hours or more without a break for meals or sleep.

Some have fallen asleep on sofas and lounge chairs in the computer center, trying to catch a few winks but loath to get too far away from their beloved machines.

Most of these students don't have to be at the computer center in the middle of the night. They aren't working on assignments. They are there because they want to be — they are irresistibly drawn there.

And they are not alone. There are hackers at computer centers all across the country. In their extreme form, they focus on nothing else. They flunk out of school and lose contact with friends; they might have difficulty finding jobs, choosing instead to wander from one computer center to another, latching on to other hacker groups. They may even forgo personal hygiene.

"I remember one hacker. We literally had to carry him off his chair to feed him and put him to sleep. We really feared for his health," says a computer-science professor at MIT.

Of course, such extreme cases are very rare. But modified versions are common. There are thousands of them — at universities, high schools, even on the elementary school level — wherever young people have access to computers. One computer-science teacher spoke of his three-year-old daughter who already likes to play endlessly with his home computer.

What do they do at the computer at all hours of the day or night? They design and play complex games; they delve into the computer's memory bank for obscure tidbits of information; like ham radio operators, they communicate with hackers in other areas who are plugged into the same system. They even do their everyday chores by computer, typing term papers and getting neat printouts. One hacker takes his terminal home with him every school vacation so he can keep in touch with other hackers. And at Stanford University, even the candy machine is hooked up to a computer, programmed by the students to dispense candy on credit to those who know the password.

At the high-school level, students have been known to break into the computer room after school and spend hours decoding other systems. By breaking the code, they can cut into other programs, discovering the computerized grading system of their school or making mischievous (and often costly) changes to other people's programs.

Computer-science teachers are now more aware of the implications of this hacker phenomenon and are on the lookout for potential hackers and cases of computer addiction that are already severe. They know that the case of the hackers is not just the story of one person's relationship with a machine. It is the story of a *society's* relationship to the so-called thinking machines, which are becoming almost ubiquitous.

Many feel we are now on the verge of a computer revolution that will change our lives as drastically as the invention of the printing press and the Industrial Revolution changed society in the past. By the most conservative estimates, one out of three American homes will have computers or terminals within the next five to ten years. Electronic toys and games, which came on the market in 1976, already comprise a more than half-billion-dollar business. And though 300,000 Americans now work full time programming computers, at least another 1.2 million will be needed by 1990. Many of them are likely to come from today's young hackers.

The computer hackers who hang out at university and high-school computer centers are, for the most part, very bright students. They are good at problem solving and usually good in mathematics and technical subjects. And they are almost always male.

There is a strong camaraderie and sense of belonging among hackers. They have their own subculture, with the usual in jokes and even a whole vocabulary based on computer terminology (there is even a hacker's dictionary). But to outsiders, they are a strange breed. In high schools, the hackers are called nerds or the brain trust. They spend most of their free time in the computer room and don't socialize much. And many have trouble with interpersonal relationships.

Bob Shaw, a 15-year-old high-school student, is a case in point. Bob was temporarily pulled off the computers at school when he began failing his other courses. But instead of hitting the books, he continues to sulk outside the computer center, peering longingly through the glass door at the consoles within.

Pale and drawn, his brown hair unkempt, Bob speaks only 13
in monosyllables, avoiding eye contact. In answer to questions
about friends, hobbies, school, he merely shrugs or mumbles a
few words aimed at his sneakered feet. But when the conversation turns to the subject of computers, he brightens — and
blurts out a few full sentences about the computer he's building
and the projects he plans.

"Apparently there is a class of people who would rather use 14
the computer than watch TV, go bowling, or even go out on a
date," says Ralph Gorin, Director of Computer Facilities at
Stanford University. "They find that the computer has a large
number of desirable properties. It's not terribly demanding, and
it does what it's told, which is much nicer than human beings. I
mean, when was the last time someone did what you told him
to do?"

"People are afraid inside," explains Lizzy, a 16-year-old 15
high-school computer-science student. "Sometimes it's easier to
be a friend to a computer that won't make fun of you. It's easier
than the pressures of a peer group."

"The computer will never insult you," says another 16
youngster.

"Everyone has problems socially to some degree, and the 17
computer can act as just another escape mechanism," Gorin explains. "The youngster feels like 'I just can't stand it anymore,'
so he runs down to the computer room. The computer doesn't
care what time it is or what you look like or what you may have
been doing lately. The computer doesn't scold you or talk
back."

Are the hackers just a group of social outcasts who hook up 18
with machines because they can't make it with people? That
would probably be a gross exaggeration — and yet, "Most
hackers do have problems adjusting socially," admits J.Q.
Johnson, a graduate student at Stanford. "Perhaps because they
don't have much social life, they spend more time at the computer center."

Joel Bion, a sophomore at Stanford, explains how he got 19
hooked: "I've been working with computers since I was eight. I
grew up in Minnesota and I didn't have many friends. I wasn't

into sports and couldn't participate in gym class because I had asthma. Then I found a computer terminal at school. I bought some books and taught myself. Pretty soon I was spending a few hours on it every day. Then I was there during vacations. Sure, I lost some friends, but when I first started I was so fascinated. Here was a field I could really feel superior in. I had a giant program, and I kept adding and adding to it. And I could use the computer to talk to people all over the state. I thought that was great social interaction. But, of course, it wasn't, because I never came into face-to-face contact."

Joel managed to break his addiction after a few years and is now a peer counselor at Stanford. But his lack of interpersonal relationships during the hacker period is common, and this problem has led Stanford psychologist Dr. Philip Zimbardo to take a closer look at the hacker phenomenon.   20

Hackers at Stanford have what is known as an electronic bulletin board that allows them to send each other messages on the computer. What struck Zimbardo was that the programmers could be sitting right next to each other at adjacent consoles, but rather than talking directly, they communicated via computer.   21

Zimbardo also noticed that the messages left on the bulletin board lacked emotion, and the thoughts were expressed in formulalike terms similar to programming language. "It could be," says Zimbardo, "that people who become hackers already have social deficiencies and becoming a hacker is a way of copping out of having intimate relationships.   22

"I've known some hackers whose addiction to playing with the computer and thinking exclusively in terms of information transmission makes it impossible for them to relate to anyone who's not a hacker," Zimbardo continues. "The danger is that they can come to think about people in much the same way that they think about computers. Computers are always consistent, so they begin to expect that consistency from people, which by virtue of human nature is not possible or even desirable."   23

Zimbardo describes the case of a computer student who was working with him on a special assignment. The student interacted with excessive formality. He couldn't deal with small talk,   24 and all his conversations were task-oriented: "You will do this. This must be done." He gave commands rather than making requests or suggestions. And he couldn't deal with the "fickleness" of human nature. All this, according to Zimbardo, was a reflection of the way the student interacted with the computer. Ultimately the student was dismissed because of his inability to get along with others.

"In some extreme cases, hackers exhibit elements of paranoia, because people can't be trusted the way computers can," says Zimbardo. "When people don't do just what he orders them to do, the hacker begins to perceive hostile motives and personal antagonism."   25

It would be absurd to label all hackers paranoid or even deviant. But it would also be naive to shrug off the hacker phenomenon as meaningless.   26

Perhaps this attachment to a machine could be viewed as just another side of man, the technological animal, who has always been obsessed with tools, machines, gadgets and gimmicks.   27

"There used to be a time when the term *hacker* referred to someone who was just enthusiastic about computers. It wasn't pejorative. Some people feel that way about cars or music to some degree," says Ralph Gorin.   28

Certainly the outstanding members of any creative field — the Picassos and the Beethovens — spent extraordinary amounts of time at their craft and were considered somewhat odd. And as Gorin points out, the computer, by its very nature, has an even stronger pull.   29

"Computers are attractive because, to a higher degree than any other object, they are interesting and malleable."   30

Interesting and malleable: two key words if you want to understand the hacker's addiction and the increasing allure of the computer for all segments of our society.   31

The computer can be almost as interesting as a human being. Like people, it is interactive. When you ask it a question, it gives you an answer. And because it stores great quantities of information, it can often answer more questions, more accurately, than human friends.   32

This interaction has led some to attribute human char- 33
acteristics to the machine. Such anthropomorphizing of inanimate objects is not unusual. Ships, trains and planes, for example, are often given human names.

But humanizing the computer seems much more natural 34
because the machine does appear to "think" and "talk" like a
person. As a result, some students form strong emotional attachments to their computers. "Some kids probably think the
computer 'likes' them," says George Truscott, a math and computer teacher in Palo Alto, California.

Hackers are not the only ones interacting with the com- 35
puter on a personal level. The amazing powers of the machine
have enticed even the most sophisticated scientists into wondering just how human it can become. The newly developing science of artificial intelligence aims at programming the computer
to think, reason and react in much the same way that people
do. Computers can diagnose a patient's ailments and recommend treatments. They can mimic the dialogue of a psychother-
apist or the reasoning of a lawyer.

If computers can replace our most admired humans, the 36
professionals, then why shouldn't the hackers feel close to them
and invest emotional energy in them? After all, the computer
seems to have unlimited potential. Already, with today's technology, tens of thousands of words can be stored on a tiny
silicon chip measuring less than a centimeter square and a
millimeter thick. And any item of information on the chip can
be called up and displayed on a TV screen in a fraction of a second. So the computer user has access to worlds of information
within reach, literally, of his fingertips. And the computer can
rearrange that information and interrelate facts or draw conclusions at the programmer's command. It is, as Gorin points out,
extremely malleable.

By programming a computer, a youngster can create a 37
world of his own. That is, he feeds a set of rules in, and it acts
according to those rules only. It is bent to the will of the programmer.

A favorite hacker pastime is playing computer games; these 38
are not the games you see in pinball parlors but much more
complex versions that hackers invent.

At Stanford, for example, hackers stay up into the wee 39 hours playing Adventure. The object is to find various pieces of treasure hidden in different parts of a cave. To do this, you must instruct the computer (that is, type instructions into the console) as to what direction to take (north, south, east, west, up, down, jump, run, etc.). After each command, the computer describes the area you have reached and what lies around you. You encounter obstacles along the way — snakes, dragons, darkness, slimy pits — but you also encounter magical objects that can help you overcome the obstacles.

"With a computer, the possibilities are limited only by your 40 imagination," Gorin explains. "You can be a spaceship pilot, a great explorer or a treasure hunter. It can lead you into the world of fantasy all of your own making."

Joseph Weizenbaum, professor of computer science at MIT, 41 thinks that the sense of power over the machine ultimately corrupts the hacker and makes him into a not-very-desirable sort of programmer. The hackers are so involved with designing their program, making it more and more complex and bending it to their will, that they don't bother trying to make it understandable to other users. They rarely keep records of their programs for the benefit of others, and they rarely take time to understand why a problem occurred.

Computer-science teachers say they can usually pick out the 42 prospective hackers in their courses because these students make their homework assignments more complex than they need to be. Rather than using the simplest and most direct method, they take joy in adding extra steps just to prove their ingenuity.

But perhaps those hackers know something that we don't 43 about the shape of things to come. "That hacker who had to be literally dragged off his chair at MIT is now a multimillionaire of the computer industry," says MIT professor Michael Dertouzos. "And two former hackers became the founders of the highly successful Apple home-computer company."

When seen in this light, the hacker phenomenon may not 44 be so strange after all. If, as many psychiatrists say, play is really the basis for all human activity, then the hacker games are really the preparation for future developments.

Sherry Turkle, a professor of sociology at MIT, has for years   45
been studying the way computers fit into people's lives. She
points out that the computer, because it seems to us to be so
"intelligent," so "capable," so . . . "human," affects the way we
think about ourselves and our ideas about what we are. She
says that computers and computer toys already play an important role in children's efforts to develop an identity by allowing
them to test ideas about what is alive and what is not.

"The youngsters can form as many subtle nuances and tex-   46
tured relationships with the computers as they can with people," Turkle points out.

Computers are not just becoming more and more a part of   47
our world. To a great degree, they *are* our world. It is therefore
not unlikely that our relationship with them will become as subjective as that of the hackers. So perhaps hackers are, after all,
harbingers of the world to come.

• QUESTIONS ON MEANING AND PURPOSE •

1. Ingber implies certain similarities between computer enthusiasts
   and compulsive gamblers. List those similarities and point to any
   important differences between the two.
2. What details in Ingber's essay help you understand the hacker's
   fascination with computers?
3. What dangers lurk in the tendency of some students to "form
   strong emotional attachments to their computers"?
4. Ingber suggests in her last sentence that "perhaps hackers are,
   after all, harbingers of the world to come." On what evidence
   does she base this conclusion?
5. Which of the following do you find Ingber doing: describing a
   trend, finding reasons for it, entertaining her audience, warning
   them, or reassuring them? Which of these purposes seems upper-
   most?

• QUESTIONS ON WRITING STRATEGY •

1. Ingber begins her essay not with a thesis statement but with a
   description of a computer center at 3 A.M. How does this introduction contribute to the essay's effectiveness?

2. Taken by themselves, what do the examples of Bob Shaw (paragraphs 12 and 13), Joel Bion (19), and Dr. Zimbardo's student (24) seem to indicate? By what examples in the essay does the writer add positive features to her portrait of the hackers?
3. Does Ingber seem prejudiced against the hackers or impartial toward them? What is the tone of her essay? (See *Tone* in Useful Terms.)
4. If "Computer Addicts" is typical of the contents of *Science Digest*, how would you describe the audience of that magazine? What amount of specialized or technical knowledge seems expected of a *Science Digest* reader?
5. If Ingber were to rewrite "Computer Addicts," addressing herself only to an audience of college students, what changes in her essay might result?

• QUESTIONS ON LANGUAGE •
• AND VOCABULARY •

1. *Hacker* is a slang word with more than one meaning. Define the word as it is used in this essay.
2. Look up the following words in the dictionary: ubiquitous (paragraph 8); camaraderie, subculture (11); monosyllables (13); paranoia (25); pejorative (28); anthropomorphizing (33); nuances (46).
3. Despite the availability of synonyms, Ingber uses the word *malleable* three times (in paragraphs 30, 31, and 36) to describe computers. What is the effect of these repetitions?

• SUGGESTIONS FOR WRITING •

1. In an essay, describe an encounter between a computer and you, or someone you know. (Perhaps you have learned the hard way that computers can make monumental errors!)
2. Write a paper in which you use examples to help you explain some other aspect of contemporary life that deeply interests you. Consider, for instance, some other way in which science or technology has drastically altered our jobs, schooling, life styles, or use of leisure time.

· Malcolm Cowley ·

MALCOLM COWLEY, born in 1898, has had a long and distinguished career as translator, critic, poet, lecturer, editor, and literary historian. He has served as visiting professor of English at many universities and as literary editor of *The New Republic* (1930–40). Cowley has written, among other books, *Exile's Return* (1934), *The Literary Situation* (1954), and *Blue Juanita: Collected Poems* (1964). Crowned with honors, he now works and, apparently, grows old gracefully at home in Connecticut.

Vices and Pleasures:
The View from 80

With serene good humor, the author of "Vices and Pleasures: The View from 80" (editors' title) looks at old age and discovers that, while it has its disadvantages, life's closing chapter also offers compensations to those who can appreciate them. Though the work of an octogenarian, Cowley's writing is frank, fresh, and full of pertinent examples. This essay is the beginning of Cowley's book *The View from Eighty* (1981).

Even before he or she is 80, the aging person may undergo   1
another identity crisis like that of adolescence. Perhaps there
had also been a middle-aged crisis, the male or the female meno-
pause, but for the rest of adult life he had taken himself for
granted, with his capabilities and failings. Now, when he looks
in the mirror, he asks himself, "Is this really me?" — or he
avoids the mirror out of distress at what it reveals, those bags
and wrinkles. In his new makeup he is called upon to play a new
role in a play that must be improvised. André Gide, that long-
lived man of letters, wrote in his journal, "My heart has remained so young that I have the continual feeling of playing a
part, the part of the 70-year-old that I certainly am; and the in-

firmities and weaknesses that remind me of my age act like a prompter, reminding me of my lines when I tend to stray. Then, like the good actor I want to be, I go back into my role, and I pride myself on playing it well."

In his new role the old person will find that he is tempted by new vices, that he receives new compensations (not so widely known), and that he may possibly achieve new virtues. Chief among these is the heroic or merely obstinate refusal to surrender in the face of time. One admires the ships that go down with all flags flying and the captain on the bridge.

Among the vices of age are avarice, untidiness, and vanity, which last takes the form of a craving to be loved or simply admired. Avarice is the worst of those three. Why do so many old persons, men and women alike, insist on hoarding money when they have no prospect of using it and even when they have no heirs? They eat the cheapest food, buy no clothes, and live in a single room when they could afford better lodging. It may be that they regard money as a form of power; there is a comfort in watching it accumulate while other powers are dwindling away. How often we read of an old person found dead in a hovel, on a mattress partly stuffed with bankbooks and stock certificates! The bankbook syndrome, we call it in our family, which has never succumbed.

Untidiness we call the Langley Collyer syndrome. To explain, Langley Collyer was a former concert pianist who lived alone with his 70-year-old brother in a brownstone house on upper Fifth Avenue. The once fashionable neighborhood had become part of Harlem. Homer, the brother, had been an admiralty lawyer, but was now blind and partly paralyzed; Langley played for him and fed him on buns and oranges, which he thought would restore Homer's sight. He never threw away a daily paper because Homer, he said, might want to read them all. He saved other things as well and the house became filled with rubbish from roof to basement. The halls were lined on both sides with bundled newspapers, leaving narrow passageways in which Langley had devised booby traps to catch intruders.

On March 21, 1947, some unnamed person telephoned the police to report that there was a dead body in the Collyer house. The police broke down the front door and found the hall impassable, then they hoisted a ladder to a second-story window. Behind it Homer was lying on the floor in a bathrobe; he had starved to death. Langley had disappeared. After some delay, the police broke into the basement, chopped a hole in the roof, and began throwing junk out of the house, top and bottom. It was 18 days before they found Langley's body, gnawed by rats. Caught in one of his own booby traps, he had died in a hallway just outside Homer's door. By that time the police had collected, and the Department of Sanitation had hauled away, 120 tons of rubbish, including besides the newspapers, 14 grand pianos and the parts of a dismantled Model T Ford.

Why do so many old people accumulate junk, not on the scale of Langley Collyer, but still in a dismaying fashion? Their tables are piled high with it, their bureau drawers are stuffed with it, their closet rods bend with the weight of clothes not worn for years. I suppose that the piling up is partly from lethargy and partly from the feeling that everything once useful, including their own bodies, should be preserved. Others, though not so many, have such a fear of becoming Langley Collyers that they strive to be painfully neat. Every tool they own is in its place, though it will never be used again; every scrap of paper is filed away in alphabetical order. At last their immoderate neatness becomes another vice of age, if a milder one.

The vanity of older people is an easier weakness to explain, and to condone. With less to look forward to, they yearn for recognition of what they have been: the reigning beauty, the athlete, the soldier, the scholar. It is the beauties who have the hardest time. A portrait of themselves at twenty hangs on the wall, and they try to resemble it by making an extravagant use of creams, powders, and dyes. Being young at heart, they think they are merely revealing their essential persons. The athletes find shelves for their silver trophies, which are polished once a year. Perhaps a letter sweater lies wrapped in a bureau drawer. I remember one evening when a no-longer athlete had guests for dinner and tried to find his sweater. "Oh, that old thing," his wife said. "The moths got into it and I threw it away." The athlete sulked and his guests went home early.

Often the yearning to be recognized appears in conversa- 8
tion as an innocent boast. Thus, a distinguished physician,
retired at 94, remarks casually that a disease was named after
him. A former judge bursts into chuckles as he repeats bright
things that he said on the bench. Aging scholars complain in
letters (or one of them does), "As I approach 70 I'm becoming
avid of honors, and such things — medals, honorary degrees,
etc. — are only passed around among academics on a *quid pro
quo* basis (one hood capping another)." Or they say querulously, "Bill Underwood has ten honorary doctorates and I have
only three. Why didn't they elect me to . . . ?" and they mention the name of some learned society. That search for honors is
a harmless passion, though it may lead to jealousies and defor-
mations of character, as with Robert Frost in his later years.
Still, honors cost little. Why shouldn't the very old have more
than their share of them?

To be admired and praised, especially by the young, is an 9
autumnal pleasure enjoyed by the lucky ones (who are not always the most deserving). "What is more charming," Cicero
observes in his famous essay *De Senectute*, "than an old age surrounded by the enthusiasm of youth! . . . Attentions which
seem trivial and conventional are marks of honor — the morning call, being sought after, precedence, having people rise for
you, being escorted to and from the forum. . . . What pleasures
of the body can be compared to the prerogatives of influence?"
But there are also pleasures of the body, or the mind, that are
enjoyed by a greater number of older persons.

Those pleasures include some that younger people find hard 10
to appreciate. One of them is simply sitting still, like a snake on
a sun-warmed stone, with a delicious feeling of indolence that
was seldom attained in earlier years. A leaf flutters down; a
cloud moves by inches across the horizon. At such moments the
older person, completely relaxed, has become a part of nature —
and a living part, with blood coursing through his veins. The
future does not exist for him. He thinks, if he thinks at all, that
life for younger persons is still a battle royal of each against
each, but that now he has nothing more to win or lose. He is
not so much above as outside the battle, as if he had assumed
the uniform of some small neutral country, perhaps Liechten-

stein or Andorra. From a distance he notes that some of the combatants, men or women, are jostling ahead — but why do they fight so hard when the most they can hope for is a longer obituary? He can watch the scrounging and gouging, he can hear the shouts of exultation, the moans of the gravely wounded, and meanwhile he feels secure; nobody will attack him from ambush.

Age has other physical compensations besides the nirvana   11
of dozing in the sun. A few of the simplest needs become a pleasure to satisfy. When an old woman in a nursing home was asked what she really liked to do, she answered in one word: "Eat." She might have been speaking for many of her fellows. Meals in a nursing home, however badly cooked, serve as climactic moments of the day. The physical essence of the pensioners is being renewed at an appointed hour; now they can go back to meditating or to watching TV while looking forward to the next meal. They can also look forward to sleep, which has become a definite pleasure, not the mere interruption it once had been.

Here I am thinking of old persons under nursing care.   12
Others ferociously guard their independence, and some of them suffer less than one might expect from being lonely and impoverished. They can be rejoiced by visits and meetings, but they also have company inside their heads. Some of them are busiest when their hands are still. What passes through the minds of many is a stream of persons, images, phrases, and familiar tunes. For some that stream has continued since childhood, but now it is deeper; it is their present and their past combined. At times they conduct silent dialogues with a vanished friend, and these are less tiring — often more rewarding — than spoken conversations. If inner resources are lacking, old persons living alone may seek comfort and a kind of companionship in the bottle. I should judge from the gossip of various neighborhoods that the outer suburbs from Boston to San Diego are full of secretly alcoholic widows. One of those widows, an old friend, was moved from her apartment into a retirement home. She left behind her a closet in which the floor was covered wall to wall with whiskey bottles. "Oh, those empty bottles!" she explained. "They were left by a former tenant."

Not whiskey or cooking sherry but simply giving up is the   13
greatest temptation of age. It is something different from a
stoical acceptance of infirmities, which is something to be admired. At 63, when he first recognized that his powers were failing, Emerson wrote one of his best poems, "Terminus":

> It is time to be old,
> To take in sail: —
> The god of bounds,
> Who sets to seas a shore,
> Came to me in his fatal rounds,
> And said: "No more!
> No farther shoot
> Thy broad ambitious branches, and thy root.
> Fancy departs: no more invent;
> Contract thy firmament
> To compass of a tent."

Emerson lived in good health to the age of 79. Within his   14
narrowed firmament, he continued working until his memory
failed; then he consented to having younger editors and collab-
orators. The givers-up see no reason for working. Sometimes
they lie in bed all day when moving about would still be possible, if difficult. I had a friend, a distinguished poet, who sur-
rendered in that fashion. The doctors tried to stir him to action,
but he refused to leave his room. Another friend, once a successful artist, stopped painting when his eyes began to fail. His
doctor made the mistake of telling him that he suffered from a
fatal disease. He then lost interest in everything except the
splendid Rolls-Royce, acquired in his prosperous days, that
stood in the garage. Daily he wiped the dust from its hood. He
couldn't drive it on the road any longer, but he used to sit in the
driver's seat, start the motor, then back the Rolls out of the
garage and drive it in again, back twenty feet and forward twenty feet; that was his only distraction.

I haven't the right to blame those who surrender, not being   15
able to put myself inside their minds or bodies. Often they must
have compelling reasons, physical or moral. Not only do they
suffer from a variety of ailments, but also they are made to feel
that they no longer have a function in the community. Their
families and neighbors don't ask them for advice, don't really

listen when they speak, don't call on them for efforts. One notes that there are not a few recoveries from apparent senility when that situation changes. If it doesn't change, old persons may decide that efforts are useless. I sympathize with their problems, but the men and women I envy are those who accept old age as a series of challenges.

For such persons, every new infirmity is an enemy to be out-witted, an obstacle to be overcome by force of will. They enjoy each little victory over themselves, and sometimes they win a major success. Renoir was one of them. He continued painting, and magnificently, for years after he was crippled by arthritis; the brush had to be strapped to his arm. "You don't need your hand to paint," he said. Goya was another of the unvan-quished. At 72 he retired as an official painter of the Spanish court and decided to work only for himself. His later years were those of the famous "black paintings" in which he let his im-agination run (and also of the lithographs, then a new tech-nique). At 78 he escaped a reign of terror in Spain by fleeing to Bordeaux. He was deaf and his eyes were failing; in order to work he had to wear several pairs of spectacles, one over another, and then use a magnifying glass; but he was producing splendid work in a totally new style. At 80 he drew an ancient man propped on two sticks, with a mass of white hair and beard hiding his face and with the inscription "I am still learning." 16

Giovanni Papini said when he was nearly blind, "I prefer martyrdom to imbecility." After writing sixty books, including his famous *Life of Christ*, he was at work on two huge projects when he was stricken with a form of muscular atrophy. He lost the use of his left leg, then of his fingers, so that he couldn't hold a pen. The two big books, though never to be finished, moved forward slowly by dictation; that in itself was a triumph. Toward the end, when his voice had become incomprehensible, he spelled out a word, tapping on the table to indicate letters of the alphabet. One hopes never to be faced with the need for such heroic measures. 17

"Eighty years old!" the great Catholic poet Paul Claudel wrote in his journal. "No eyes left, no ears, no teeth, no legs, no wind! And when all is said and done, how astonishingly well one does without them!" 18

· QUESTIONS ON MEANING AND PURPOSE ·

1. According to Cowley, what causes the "identity crisis" that aging people are likely to undergo?
2. List the vices, the compensations, and the virtues the author says many old people have in common.
3. Which virtue of old age does Cowley regard as the most admirable? Which temptation of old age seems to him the most prevalent?
4. "Cowley's purpose is simply to claim that all the sugar is in the bottom of the cup." How accurate is this remark? In a sentence, how would *you* sum up Cowley's apparent purpose in writing?

· QUESTIONS ON WRITING STRATEGY ·

1. What do Cowley's illustrative examples contribute to his insights about old people? In particular, what point is made by the quotation from Emerson's poem "Terminus"?
2. What examples does Cowley take from his own experience? Upon what other sources of examples does he draw?
3. Where in his essay does the author capitalize on the fact that he is himself an old man? To what extent does his age heighten his credibility?
4. What rhetorical questions does Cowley pose in paragraphs 1, 8, 9, and 10? What do they contribute? (See *Rhetorical Question* in Useful Terms.)
5. Take a close look at paragraph 16. In what sentence or sentences do you find the main idea? What two examples serve to illustrate it?
6. In the next paragraph (17), the example of Giovanni Papini seems to illustrate the same general truth; for what possible reason does Cowley make it a separate paragraph?
7. What final effect does Cowley achieve by his quotation from Paul Claudel? From the essay as a whole, do you have the sense that Cowley approves or disapproves of Claudel's observation?

· QUESTIONS ON LANGUAGE ·
· AND VOCABULARY ·

1. Consult your dictionary for definitions of these words: succumbed (paragraph 3); lethargy (6); querulously (8); precedence, preroga-

tives (9); indolence (10); nirvana, climactic (11); stoical (13); firmament (14); unvanquished (16); atrophy (17).

2. Cowley says of the aging person, "In his new makeup he is called
   upon to play a new role in a play that must be improvised" (paragraph 1). What is his "new makeup"? What is the "play that must
   be improvised"?

· SUGGESTIONS FOR WRITING ·

1. In your own essay, concoct a recipe for growing old gracefully.
2. Using examples to illustrate, as Cowley does, write an essay about
   the virtues, vices, and compensations of people your own age.

· Ilene Kantrov ·

ILENE KANTROV, born in 1950, has had a busy career as a writer, teacher and editor. From 1974 to 1977 she taught freshman writing at Tufts University, where she received her doctorate. More recently she served as senior staff editor for the biographical encyclopedia *Notable American Women*, a publication of Radcliffe College; and she is currently a writer and consultant for the Education Development Center. A freelance writer, she has written book reviews for *Equal Times*, *New Age*, and *Second Wave*.

Women's Business

In "Women's Business," Ilene Kantrov paints a portrait of Lydia E. Pinkham, then goes on to tell about other business-women who followed in Lydia's footsteps. In their pursuit of success, these female entrepreneurs were not always, it seems, ladies first.

The face of the kindly matron beamed from the pages of 1
newspapers and magazines across the country. The advertising copy promised relief from "falling of the womb and all female weaknesses," touting the product as "the greatest remedy in the world." The year was 1879, and the product was an unproven home remedy called Lydia E. Pinkham's Vegetable Compound. Lydia Pinkham, the woman whose countenance graced the periodical pages, developed the advertising campaign that traded on her benign image.

Pinkham brought to her marketing effort the passionate 2
social activism characteristic of many women of her era. Convinced that she offered more than a mere product, she used her advertising to champion women's rights, temperance, and fiscal reform. One of her cleverest marketing techniques was a Department of Advice. Encouraging women to bypass male physicians to seek guidance from another woman, she dispensed

practical suggestions about diet, exercise, and hygiene, along with endorsements of her own medicine.

Yet Pinkham did not hesitate to exploit traditional feminine   3
fears — and feminine stereotypes — to market her product. She printed testimonials from women reporting cures not only for a range of physical symptoms, but also for infertility, "nervousness," "hysteria," and even marital discord. According to one early newspaper ad, the murder of a Connecticut clergyman by his wife, whose insanity was "brought on by 16 years of suffering with Female Complaints," could have been prevented by timely administration of the Compound to the afflicted woman.

As a result of such bold marketing, the company that   4
Pinkham had founded with her sons earned $200,000 in 1881. Lydia Pinkham herself became something of a folk heroine — the subject of popular songs, jokes, and bawdy verse.

Pinkham's introduction of feminine packaging to capitalist   5
enterprise earned her a special place in the annals of American business as well as women's history. It also set a pattern for women entrepreneurs in the following century. The handful of women who emulated Pinkham's success likewise followed her in importing traditional feminine roles into the masculine world of commerce. When feminine ideals collided with the realities of the marketplace, however, the businesswoman often bested the lady.

Like Pinkham, her successors consciously exploited their   6
images as women to promote their products. In some cases, the image was that of glamorous socialite: arch-rivals Helena Rubinstein and Elizabeth Arden competed not only in selling cosmetics but also in luring publicity by their marriages to European aristocrats. More often the image cultivated was that of mother or grandmother: following Pinkham in this mold, for example, were Margaret Rudkin, founder of Pepperidge Farm, Inc., and Jennie Grossinger, who ran a resort hotel in upstate New York renowned for its food and entertainment. Grossinger managed to remain the solicitous Jewish grandmother in the eyes of her customers long after she had hired a public relations man and Grossinger's Hotel began serving 150,000 guests a year.

Women's businesses tended to grow out of traditional   7
women's skills and catered mainly to women. Lydia Pinkham
had collected and administered folk remedies to her family for
years before the collapse of her husband's real estate business
led her to begin marketing herbal preparations for "female complaints." Margaret Rudkin, faced with a comparable need to
supplement her husband's income, also looked close to home.
She reportedly baked her first loaf of additive-free whole wheat
bread as part of a special diet for an asthmatic son, and secured
her first order from her neighborhood grocer in 1937.

To transform a home craft into a thriving business, these   8
female capitalists joined a canny sense of women's tastes with
the audacity of a gambler in creating and marketing innovations designed to shape those tastes. In 1909 Elizabeth Arden
introduced her first line of makeup, not then widely considered
respectable, as "facial treatments." As the beauty market began
to expand in the 1920s she kept several steps ahead of demand:
introducing, for example, such exotic and vaguely medicinal
concoctions as Sensation salve, Arden gland cream, and the
Vienna Youth Mask. Applications of the Youth Mask, constructed of papier-mâché and tinfoil, required the customer to
be hooked up to a diathermy machine, which applied heat via
electric current. Arden assured the women who submitted to
the treatment — and paid dearly for the privilege — that they
were restoring dead skin tissue.

In addition to skin care and cosmetics, Elizabeth Arden   9
salons eventually added hairstyling, ready-made and custom
clothes, and advice on nutrition and exercise. Arden herself
practiced and advocated yoga, adapting the exercises for the
women who frequented her salons and Maine health spa. Competing salon proprietor Helena Rubinstein published a book expounding the benefits of eating raw foods and sold her customers on the diet. In promoting the idea that a beauty salon
could provide women with the means to "remake" themselves,
inside and out, both women manifested the conviction
of American businesswomen from Lydia Pinkham on that
they were providing other women with something more than a
product.

Few of them matched Pinkham in the degree to which she   10
merged her marketing effort with a crusade for economic and
social change. But other American women entrepreneurs combined an equally shrewd eye for profit with a passionate belief in
their products' social or moral efficacy. Gertrude Muller, who
invented the "toidey seat" in 1924 and parlayed it into an entire
line of child care products, in 1930 began enclosing in the
packages pamphlets she wrote about child raising. Her products, and the literature that accompanied them, embodied a
progressive philosophy of child rearing, and one of her booklets
was widely distributed by doctors and used by home economics
instructors. Of course, none of this free publicity hurt business.

A black female capitalist, Annie Turnbo-Malone also cast   11
herself in the role of social activist. Her business was founded at
the turn of the century on a hairdressing preparation that, like
Lydia Pinkham's Vegetable Compound, was of questionable efficacy. But, again like Pinkham, she developed an innovative
marketing strategy — a network of franchised sales agents —
and used it both to earn big money and to promote her causes.
Turnbo-Malone established a school for training agents in her
"poro" system of hairdressing, named it Poro College, and
advertised it as a vehicle for the uplift of her race and a passport
to economic independence for women. Her literature also
branched out beyond hair care to advocate the benefits of good
hygiene, thrift, and other homely virtues.

Turnbo-Malone and her sister capitalists genuinely believed   12
in the beneficence of their products and services. If not all of
them proclaimed themselves, as Lydia Pinkham did, "Saviour of
her Sex," several of them acted the part. And a number turned
their profits into good works: Turnbo-Malone, Helena Rubinstein, and Jennie Grossinger, for example, were noted philanthropists as well as executives. They contributed lavishly to
hospitals, schools, and cultural organizations.

Though they aimed to serve as well as to sell, however,   13
these businesswomen frequently put profit ahead of altruism.
Their advertising claims were often extravagant, even mislead-
ing. And when regulatory agencies such as the FDA and FTC
began to crack down on questionable business practices, female
entrepreneurs were as likely to be cited as their male counter-

parts. Helena Rubinstein, for instance, was forced by the FDA to withdraw some of the medicinal claims she made for her products.

The latent conflict between the profit motive and the social   14
service ethic of female entrepreneurs is perhaps best exemplified once again by Lydia Pinkham: a passionate temperance advocate who had no qualms about selling a product that contained sufficient alcohol to make it 40 proof. "Grandma," backed by the Women's Christian Temperance Union, was selling booze.

• QUESTIONS ON MEANING AND PURPOSE •

1. Which of Lydia E. Pinkham's business methods did later women capitalists adopt for their own enterprises? In what ways did they depart from Pinkham's model?
2. How did the businesswomen the writer introduces in her essay differ from their male counterparts? In what ways did they resemble male entrepreneurs of their day?
3. How would you expect a militant feminist to react to this essay? Are any of the writer's general statements debatable?

• QUESTIONS ON WRITING STRATEGY •

1. What is the thesis of this essay? (See *Thesis* in Useful Terms.) In what paragraph is it stated?
2. Would the essay have been more effective if its thesis had been placed in the introductory paragraph? By beginning and ending with the example of Lydia E. Pinkham, what does Kantrov gain?

• QUESTIONS ON LANGUAGE •
• AND VOCABULARY •

1. Be sure you can define the following words: canny, audacity (paragraph 8); expounding (9); efficacy, parlayed (10); innovative (11); beneficence, philanthropists (12); latent (14).
2. What does the writer's use of the slang word *booze* contribute to the essay's conclusion? (See *Slang* under *Diction* in Useful Terms.)

· SUGGESTIONS FOR WRITING ·

1. In a brief essay, give an example of one contemporary woman who has succeeded in business. Detail the extent to which she has emulated Lydia E. Pinkham; also her departures from Pinkham's methods.
2. Write an essay giving examples of products on the market today that, like Lydia E. Pinkham's Vegetable Compound, feature someone's name or image. Describe the real or fictitious person associated with each product and explain the person's appeal.

Showing Vague Words
No Mercy

Some writers relish the process of working over a paragraph again and again, until words convey their message with clarity and elegance. Others find revision a painful exercise. Almost all professional writers agree, however, that a paragraph thoughtfully revised is a paragraph inevitably strengthened. Ilene Kantrov shows how she moved from the first version to the finished version of her thesis statement.

It was as a teacher of composition and an editor that I learned the valuable lesson I now apply to all my writing: have no mercy on yourself. I found I could hardly insist that my students "get things right" or justify the changes I'd made in the manuscripts I edited unless I was equally ruthless in evaluating my own writing. 1

It's still not easy for me to turn a cold critical eye on my own prose. After all, I protest, "those are *my* words," and I hate to admit they're less than ideal. Besides, as I read them over, their very familiarity lulls me into approval. 2

But ultimately I find that the satisfaction of "getting it right" is worth the agony of stepping into the uncongenial role of self-editor. 3

Consider the first draft of my thesis statement. The final version appears in the fifth paragraph of my essay. 4

In the century that followed the first sales of Lydia E. Pinkham's Vegetable Compound in 1875, the handful of women entrepreneurs who emulated Pinkham's success frequently emulated her style of doing business as well.

It's certainly harmless, and not badly written, but it does not set the stage for what is to come. What *about* Pinkham's "style of doing business" did they emulate?

So back to the typewriter, and out with the second version: 5

> Lydia Pinkham is surely a special case in the annals of American business as well as women's history. Yet the ingredients that contributed to the phenomenal success of Pinkham's enterprise set a pattern for women entrepreneurs in the following century. The handful of women who emulated Pinkham's success likewise followed her in turning the limitations of traditional feminine stereotypes and roles to their benefit in the masculine world of commerce. In the process, they created an often effective, if sometimes uneasy, alliance between feminine ideals and the realities of the marketplace.

This paragraph has more substance. But, mustering as much detachment as I could, I had to acknowledge several problems: It's still too vague, the last two sentences are unwieldy, and the language isn't very lively. Let's look at it sentence by sentence.

The first sentence puts too much stress on Pinkham's   6
uniqueness, contradicting the idea, stated in the following sentences, that she established a pattern. The final version of this sentence, while acknowledging Pinkham's specialness, connects it to the aspect of her business that set the pattern: "Pinkham's introduction of feminine packaging to capitalist enterprise earned her a special place in the annals of American business as well as women's history." The revision also zeroes in, from the start, on the tension between "feminine" and "capitalist."

The second sentence suffers from the same vagueness as the   7
original draft, requiring the following sentences to explain it. Once I had revised the first sentence, defining the "ingredients," I was able to pare down this second sentence significantly: "It also set a pattern for women entrepreneurs in the following century."

Next to be sacrificed was the wordy and rather dull middle   8
portion of the third sentence: "followed her in turning the limitations of traditional feminine stereotypes and roles to their benefit." By substituting "importing traditional feminine roles," I not only built on the metaphorical "world of commerce," but also made the entire sentence far more compact: "The handful of women who emulated Pinkham's success likewise followed

her in importing traditional feminine roles into the masculine world of commerce."

Turning to the last sentence, I had to admit it was awkwardly broken up and lacked sharpness. In revising, I came up with the active verb "collided" and the contrast between "businesswoman" and "lady": "When feminine ideals collided with the realities of the marketplace, however, the businesswoman often bested the lady." This version also points directly to the conflict between profit and ideals that the essay concludes with.

Notice that, having held the whip over myself, I've made two kinds of changes: refining the message, and tightening and enlivening the language. It takes care, it takes a fresh "ear" (having some time away from a draft and reading out loud help), and it takes a willingness to stand up to your own weak, lazy, too easily satisfied self. But self-editing is a lot like dieting: it hurts now, but it makes you feel — and look — a lot better later.

Select one of the following general statements, or set forth a general statement of your own that one of these inspires. Making it your central idea (or thesis), maintain it in an essay full of examples. Draw your examples from your reading, your studies, your conversation, or your own experience.

1. People one comes to admire don't always at first seem likable.
2. Fashions this year are loonier than ever before.
3. Bad habits are necessary to the nation's economy.
4. Each family has its distinctive life style.
5. Certain song lyrics, closely inspected, will prove obscene.
6. Scientists are human. (To decide: In your essay, what will *human* mean?)
7. Comic books are going to the dogs.
8. At some point in life, most people triumph over crushing difficulties.
9. Churchgoers aren't perfect.
10. TV commercials suggest: Buy this product and your love life will improve like crazy.
11. Home cooking can't win over fast food.
12. Ordinary lives sometimes give rise to legends.
13. Some people I know are born winners (or losers).
14. Books can change our lives.
15. Certain machines *do* have personalities.
16. Some road signs lead drivers astray.

4

COMPARISON
AND CONTRAST

Setting Things Side by Side

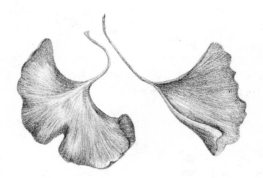

· THE DUAL METHOD ·

Should we pass laws to regulate pornography, or just let pornography run wild? Which team do you place your money on, the Dolphins or the Colts? To go to school full-time or part-time: what are the rewards and drawbacks of each way of life? How do the Republican and the Democratic platforms stack up against each other? How is the work of Picasso like or unlike that of Matisse? These are questions that may be addressed by the dual method of *comparison and contrast*. In comparing, you point to similarities; in contrasting, to differences. Together, the two strategies use one subject to explain or clarify another by setting the two side by side.

With the aid of this dual method, you can show why you prefer one thing to another, one course of action to another, one idea to another. In an argument in which you support one of two possible choices, a careful and detailed comparison and contrast of the choices may be extremely convincing. In writing a good expository essay by the dual method, you demonstrate that you understand your subjects thoroughly. That is why, on exams that call for essay answers, often you will be asked to compare and contrast. Sometimes the examiner will come right out and say,"Compare and contrast nineteenth-century methods of treating drug addiction with those of the present day." Sometimes, however, comparison and contrast won't even be mentioned by name; instead, the examiner will ask, "What resemblances and differences do you find between John Updike's short story 'A & P' and the Grimm fairy tale 'Godfather Death'?" Or, "Evaluate the relative desirability of holding a franchise as against going into business as an independent proprietor." But those — as you realize when you begin to plan your reply — are just other ways of asking you to compare and contrast.

In practice, the two methods are usually inseparable. A little reflection will show you why you need both. Say you intend to write a portrait-in-words of two people. No two people are in every respect exactly the same, or entirely dissimilar. Simply to compare them, or to contrast them, would not be true to life. To set them side by side and portray them accurately, you must consider both similarities and differences.

A good essay in comparing and contrasting serves a purpose. Most of the time, the writer of such an essay has one of two purposes in mind:

1. *The purpose of evaluating, or judging between two things.* In daily life, this is often the reason we compare and contrast two possibilities: which college course to elect, which movie to see, which luncheon special to take — chipped beef over green noodles or fried smelt on a bun? Our thinking on a matter such as the last is quick and informal: "Hmmmm, the smelt *looks* better. Red beef, green noodles — ugh, what a sight! Smelt has bones, but the beef is rubbery. Still, I don't like the smell of that smelt. I'll go for the beef (or maybe just grab a hamburger after class)."

In essays, too, a writer, by comparing points, decides which of two things is more admirable: "Organic Gardening, Yes; Gardening with Chemical Fertilizers, No!" — or "Skydiving Versus the Safe, Sane Life." In writing, as in thinking, you need to consider the main features of both subjects, the positive features and the negative, and to choose the subject whose positive features more clearly predominate.

2. *The purpose of showing each of two subjects distinctly by considering both side by side.* Writing with such a purpose, the writer doesn't necessarily find one of the subjects better than the other. In "The Black and White Truth About Basketball" in this chapter, Jeff Greenfield details two styles of playing the game; and his conclusion is not that either black or white basketball is the more beautiful, but that the two styles can complement each other on the same court. In some essays, however, one of the subjects may appear much more central than the other. When William Ouchi, in his essay in this chapter, compares and contrasts Japanese workers with American workers, he is explaining the Japanese attitude toward holding a job, not the American attitude, with which his readers, presumably, are already familiar. Ouchi therefore devotes more space to the Japanese, not because he is partial but because he is explaining the Japanese to his fellow Americans.

• THE PROCESS •

The first step in planning to compare and contrast anything is to select subjects that will display a clear basis for comparison. In other words, you have to pick out two subjects that obviously have enough in common to be worth comparing and contrasting. You'll have the best luck if you choose two of a kind: two California wines, two mystery writers, two schools of political thought. You can't readily compare and contrast, say, bowling in America with teacher-training in Sweden, because the basis for comparison isn't apparent.

Whether your purpose in writing your essay is to judge between two subjects or to make their natures unmistakably clear, you'll need to show your reader a valid reason for bringing the two together. From the very title of his essay "Grant and Lee," Bruce Catton leads us to expect insights into the Civil War and the characters of its two commanders. But if you were to meet an essay called "General Grant and Mick Jagger," you would find it hard to see any real basis for comparison. Although the writer might wax ingenious and claim, "Like Grant, Mick has posed a definite threat to Nashville," the ingenuity would soon wear thin and the yoking together of general and rock star would fall apart.

The basis for comparison has to be carefully limited. You would be quixotic to try to compare and contrast the Soviet way of life with the American way of life in 500 words; you probably couldn't include all the important similarities and differences. In a brief paper, you would be wise to select a single point: to show, for instance, how day care centers in Russia and the United States are both alike and dissimilar.

Students occasionally groan when asked to compare and contrast things; but, in fact, this method isn't difficult. You have only to plan your paper carefully in advance, make an outline (either in your head or on paper), and then follow it. Here are two usual ways to compare and contrast:

1. Set forth all your facts about Subject A, then do the same for Subject B. Next, sum up their similarities and differences. In your conclusion, state what you think you have shown. This procedure works for a short paper of a couple of paragraphs, but for a longer one, it has a built-in disadvantage. Readers need to remember all the facts so that when they come to the summary, they can follow it. If the essay is long and lists many facts, this procedure may present the reader with unnecessary difficulty.

2. Usually more workable in writing a long paper than the first method, a different method is to compare and contrast as you go. You consider one point at a time, taking up your two subjects alternately. In this way, you continually bring the subjects together, perhaps in every paragraph. Your outline might look like this:

TITLE: "Jed and Jake: Two Bluegrass Banjo-pickers"

PURPOSE: To show the distinct identities of the two musicians

INTRODUCTION: Who are Jed and Jake?

1. *Training*
   Jed: studied under Scruggs
   Jake: studied under Segovia

2. *Choice of material*
   Jed: traditional
   Jake: innovative

3. *Technical dexterity*
   Jed: highly skilled
   Jake: highly skilled

4. *Playing style*
   Jed: likes to show off
   Jake: keeps work simple

5. *On-stage manner*
   Jed: theatrical
   Jake: cool and reserved

CONCLUSION

And your conclusion might be: Although similar in degree of skill, the two differ greatly in aims and in personalities. Jed is better suited to the Grand Ol' Opry; Jake, to a concert hall. Now that would be a more extensive outline than you would need for a very brief (say, 250-word) essay; but it might be fine for an essay of seven substantial paragraphs. (If you were writing only 250 words, you might not need any formal outline at all. You might just say your say about Jed, then do the same for Jake, briefly sum up the differences and similarities between the two and then conclude.) Another way to organize a longer paper would be to group together all the similarities and then group together all the differences. No matter how you group your points, they have to balance; you can't discuss, for example, Jed's on-stage manner without discussing Jake's too. If you have nothing to say about Jake's on-stage manner, then you might as well omit the point.

As you write, an outline will help you to see the shape of your paper, and to keep your procedure in mind. A sure-fire flunking paper is the kind that proposes to compare and contrast two subjects and then proceeds to discuss quite different elements in each: Jed's playing style and Jake's choice of material, Jed's fondness for smelt on a bun and Jake's hobby of antique car collecting. The writer of such a paper doesn't compare and contrast the two musicians at all, but provides two quite separate discussions.

By the way, the dual method of comparison and contrast works most efficiently for a pair of subjects. If you want to write about *three* banjo-pickers, it will probably be easiest first to consider Jed and Jake, then Jake and Josh, then Josh and Jed. (As you can see, the more items you have to compare and contrast, the greater the complexity of the outline you will need and the greater the complexity of your task.)

In writing an essay of this variety, you may find an outline proves to be your firmest friend, but don't be the simple tool of your outline. Few essays are more boring to read than the long comparison-and-contrast written mechanically. The reader comes to feel like a weary spectator at a tennis match, whose head has to swivel from side to side: now Jed, now back to Jake; now Jed again, now back to Jake again. . . . No law decrees that an outline has to be followed in absolutely lock-step order, nor that a list of similarities and a list of differences must be of the same length, nor that if you spend fifty words discussing Jed's banjo-picking skill, you are obliged to give Jake his fifty, too. Your essay, remember, doesn't need to be as symmetrical as a pair of salt and pepper shakers. What is your outline but a simple means to organize your account of a complicated reality? As you write, keep casting your thoughts upon a living, particular world — not twisting and squeezing that world into a rigid scheme, but moving through it with open senses, being patient and faithful and exact in your telling of it.

· COMPARISON AND CONTRAST ·
· IN A PARAGRAPH ·

To behold, on aged and defective 16-millimeter film, the original production of Paddy Chayevsky's written-for-television *Marty*, makes strikingly clear the differences between televised drama in 1953 and televised drama today. For one thing, television currently has no series like the Goodyear

Playhouse, which first showed Chayevsky's famous drama. Each week it brought before its mass audience a new, complete, and original hour-long play. Although *Marty* later was adapted for a Hollywood movie, it generated no spinoffs or sequels. Nowadays, a television playwright is usually limited to another episode in the lives of characters whom the viewers already know. For another thing, *Marty* features no tire-squealing car chase, no T-shirt doffing or bodice ripping, no *Dallas*-like mansion with fountains of champagne. Instead, it shows us simply and realistically the beginning of love between a heavyset butcher and a mousy-haired high-school teacher: both of them single and aging, lonely and shy, accustomed to wearing the label "dog" and never going out twice with the same person. A Goodyear Playhouse production, moreover, had to be enacted within a single studio. Unlike the writer of today, Chayevsky couldn't order a crew to film outdoor scenes on location. And so, in scenes that last up to five minutes — a time that a present-day viewer, used to fast action and ten-second takes, might find interminable — the camera dwells upon the faces of two motionless characters. We watch Marty and his pal Angie, a fellow bachelor, seated at a table, deciding how to spend Saturday night ("What do you want to do?" — "I dunno, what do *you* want to do?"). Oddly, the effect is spellbinding. Because of the tiny dimensions of the sets, long panning shots are impossible, and, to enliven static scenes, the actors have to project themselves with vigor. Like the finest actors on television today, Rod Steiger, as Marty, exploits every on-screen moment. In 1953, television plays went out over the airwaves live. Today, thanks to videotape, there is no such threat of error, bloopers, or blown lines; but the effect of canned drama is a chill slickness. By technical standards of today, *Marty* is primitive. In a way, though, televised drama in the 1980s has even stricter confines. Back in 1953, televised drama gazes intently upon the faces of two people, yet, when spendidly done, as in *Marty*, it probes souls. With few exceptions, televised drama today shows us a larger world — only to nail a box around it.

Comment. The writer of this closely-knit paragraph is spelling out the differences between televised drama of today and drama of television's so-called Golden Age. In discussing the latter, he confines himself to *Marty*, a particularly outstanding example. That both eras of television have actors who vigorously exploit their moments on screen is the only similarity he notices. In building the paragraph, the writer followed an outline that looked like this:

1. *Today:* no series of new plays, just specials
   Then: Goodyear Playhouse, showcase for playwrights
2. *Today:* appeal of familiar characters
   Then: appeal of story
3. *Today:* violence, sex, luxury
   Then: simple realism
4. *Today:* outdoor scenes filmed on location
   Then: a few sets inside one studio
5. *Today:* brief fast-moving scenes
   Then: long lingering static scenes
6. *Today:* good acting
   Then: good acting
7. *Today:* everything videotaped in advance
   Then: plays done live
8. *Conclusion:*   TV drama today shows a smaller world.

In fulfilling this outline, the writer didn't proceed in a rigid, mechanical alternation of *Today* and *Then*, but took each point in whatever order came naturally. This is a long outline, as a paragraph so full and meaty required, and it might have sufficed for a whole essay had the writer wanted to develop his comparison at greater length with the aid of other examples.

· Jeff Greenfield ·

JEFF GREENFIELD, born in 1943, was graduated from Yale University School of Law; and he became a sportswriter, a humorist and (at present) a media commentator for CBS-TV. Earlier in his career, he served as a staff aide and writer of speeches for both John V. Lindsay, former mayor of New York City, and the late Attorney General Robert F. Kennedy. His books include *A Populist Manifesto* (1972), *Where Have You Gone, Joe DiMaggio?* (1973), *The World's Greatest Team* (a history of the Boston Celtics; 1976), and *Television: The First 50 Years* (1977).

The Black and White Truth about Basketball

When Jeff Greenfield's survey of "black" and "white" basketball, subtitled "A Skin-Deep Theory of Style," was first published in *Esquire* magazine in 1975, it provoked immediate interest and controversy. For *The Bedford Reader*, Greenfield revised his essay and brought it up to date. (His thesis remains essentially unchanged.)

The dominance of black athletes over professional basketball is beyond dispute. Two thirds of the players are black, and the number would be greater were it not for the continuing practice of picking white bench warmers for the sake of balance. The Most Valuable Player award of the National Basketball Association has gone to blacks for eighteen of the last twenty-one years. In the 1979–80 season, eight of the top ten were black. The NBA was the first pro sports league of any stature to hire a black coach (Bill Russell of the Celtics) and the first black general manager (Wayne Embry of the Bucks). What discrimination remains — lack of opportunity for lucrative benefits such as speaking engagements and product endorsements — has more to do with society than with basketball.

This dominance reflects a natural inheritance; basketball is   2
a pastime of the urban poor. The current generation of black
athletes are heirs to a tradition half a century old: in a neighborhood without the money for bats, gloves, hockey sticks, tennis
rackets, or shoulder pads, basketball is accessible. "Once it was
the game of the Irish and Italian Catholics in Rockaway and the
Jews on Fordham Road in the Bronx," writes David Wolf in his
brilliant book, *Foul!* "It was recreation, status, and a way out."
But now the ethnic names are changed; instead of Red
Holzmans, Red Auerbachs, and McGuire bothers, there are
Julius Ervings and Darryl Dawkins and Kareem Abdul-Jabbars.
And professional basketball is a sport with a national television
contract and million-dollar salaries.

But the mark on basketball of today's players can be   3
measured by more than money or visibility. It is a question of
style. For there is a clear difference between "black" and
"white" styles of play that is as clear as the difference between
155th Street at Eighth Avenue and Crystal City, Missouri.
Most simply (remembering we are talking about culture, not
chromosomes), "black" basketball is the use of superb athletic
skill to adapt to the limits of space imposed by the game.
"White" ball is the pulverization of that space by sheer intensity.

It takes a conscious effort to realize how constricted the   4
space is on a basketball court. Place a regulation court (ninety-
four by fifty feet) on a football field, and it will reach from the
back of the end zone to the twenty-one-yard line; its width will
cover less than a third of the field. On a baseball diamond, a
basketball court will reach from home plate to just beyond first
base. Compared to its principal indoor rival, ice hockey, basketball covers about one-fourth the playing area. And during the
normal flow of the game, most of the action takes place on
about the third of the court nearest the basket. It is in this
dollhouse space that ten men, each of them half a foot taller
than the average man, come together to battle each other.

There is, thus, no room; basketball is a struggle for the edge: 5
the half step with which to cut around the defender for a lay-up,
the half second of freedom with which to release a jump shot,

the instant a head turns allowing a pass to a teammate breaking for the basket. It is an arena for the subtlest of skills: the head fake, the shoulder fake, the shift of body weight to the right and the sudden cut to the left. Deception is crucial to success; and to young men who have learned early and painfully that life is a battle for survival, basketball is one of the few games in which the weapon of deception is a legitimate rule and not the source of trouble.

If there is, then, the need to compete in a crowd, to battle   6
for the edge, then the surest strategy is to develop the *unexpected*; to develop a shot that is simply and fundamentally different from the usual methods of putting the ball in the basket. Drive to the hoop, but go under it and come up the other side; hold the ball at waist level and shoot from there instead of bringing the ball up to eye level; leap into the air and fall away from the basket instead of toward it. All these tactics take maximum advantage of the crowding on a court; they also stamp uniqueness on young men who may feel it nowhere else.

"For many young men in the slums," David Wolf writes,   7
"the school yard is the only place they can feel true pride in what they do, where they can move free of inhibitions and where they can, by being spectacular, rise for the moment against the drabness and anonymity of their lives. Thus, when a player develops extraordinary 'school yard' moves and shots . . . [they] become his measure as a man."

So the moves that begin as tactics for scoring soon become   8
calling cards. You don't just lay the ball in for an uncontested basket; you take the ball in both hands, leap as high as you can, and slam the ball through the hoop. When you jump in the air, fake a shot, bring the ball back to your body, and throw up a shot, all without coming back down, you have proven your worth in uncontestable fashion.

This liquid grace is an integral part of "black" ball, almost   9
exclusively the province of the playground player. Some white stars like Bob Cousy, Billy Cunningham, Doug Collins, and Paul Westphal had it: the body control, the moves to the basket, the free-ranging mobility. They also had the surface ease that is integral to the "black" style; an incorporation of the

ethic of mean streets — to "make it" is not just to have wealth, but to have it without strain. Whatever the muscles and organs are doing, the face of the "black" star almost never shows it. George Gervin of the San Antonio Spurs can drive to the basket with two men on him, pull up, turn around, and hit a basket without the least flicker of emotion. The Knicks' former great Walt Frazier, flamboyant in dress, cars, and companions, displayed nothing but a quickly raised fist after scoring a particularly important basket. (Interestingly, the black coaches in the NBA exhibit far less emotion on the bench than their white counterparts; Al Attles and K. C. Jones are statuelike compared with Jack Ramsey or Dick Motta.)

If there is a single trait that characterizes "black" ball it is   10
leaping agility. Bob Cousy, ex-Celtic great and former pro coach, says that "when coaches get together, one is sure to say, 'I've got the one black kid in the country who can't jump.' When coaches see a white boy who can jump or who moves with extraordinary quickness, they say, 'He should have been born black, he's that good.' "

Don Nelson, former Celtic and coach of the Milwaukee   11
Bucks, recalls that in 1970, Dave Cowens, then a relatively unknown Florida State graduate, prepared for his rookie season by playing in the Rucker League, an outdoor Harlem competition that pits pros against playground stars and college kids. So ferocious was Cowens' leaping power, Nelson says, that "when the summer was over, everyone wanted to know who the white son of a bitch was who could jump so high." That's another way to overcome a crowd around the basket — just go over it.

Speed, mobility, quickness, acceleration, "the moves" — all   12
of these are catch-phrases that surround the "black" playground style of play. So does the most racially tinged of attributes, "rhythm." Yet rhythm is what the black stars themselves talk about; feeling the flow of the game, finding the tempo of the dribble, the step, the shot. It is an instinctive quality, one that has led to difficulty between systematic coaches and free-form players. "Cats from the street have their own rhythm when they play," said college dropout Bill Spivey, onetime New York high-school star. "It's not a matter of somebody setting you up

and you shooting. You *feel* the shot. When a coach holds you back, you lose the feel and it isn't fun anymore."

Connie Hawkins, the legendary Brooklyn playground star, said of Laker coach Bill Sharman's methodical style of teaching, "He's systematic to the point where it begins to be a little too much. It's such an action-reaction type of game that when you have to do everything the same way, I think you lose something." 13

There is another kind of basketball that has grown up in America. It is not played on asphalt playgrounds with a crowd of kids competing for the court; it is played on macadam driveways by one boy with a ball and a backboard nailed over the garage; it is played in Midwestern gyms and on Southern dirt courts. It is a mechanical, precise development of skills (when Don Nelson was an Iowa farm boy his incentive to make his shots was that an errant rebound would land in the middle of chicken droppings), without frills, without flow, but with effectiveness. It is "white" basketball: jagged, sweaty, stumbling, intense. A "black" player overcomes an obstacle with finesse and body control; a "white" player reacts by outrunning or outpowering the obstacle. 14

By this definition, the Boston Celtics are a classically "white" team. The Celtics almost never use a player with dazzling moves; that would probably make Red Auerbach swallow his cigar. Instead, the Celtics wear you down with execution, with constant running, with the same play run again and again. The rebound triggers the fast break, with everyone racing downcourt; the ball goes to Larry Bird, who pulls up and takes the jump shot, or who fakes the shot and passes off to the man following, the "trailer," who has the momentum to go inside for a relatively easy shot. 15

Perhaps the most classically "white" position is that of the quick forward, one without great moves to the basket, without highly developed shots, without the height and mobility for rebounding effectiveness. What does he do? He runs. He runs from the opening jump to the last horn. He runs up and down the court, from base line to base line, back and forth under the basket, looking for the opening, for the pass, for the chance to 16 take a quick step and the high-percentage shot. To watch San Antonio's Mark Olberding, a player without speed or moves, is to wonder what he is doing in the NBA — until you see him swing free and throw up a shot that, without demanding any apparent skill, somehow goes in the basket more frequently than the shots of any of his teammates. And to have watched Boston Celtic immortal John Havlicek is to have seen "white" ball at its best.

Havlicek stands in dramatic contrast to Julius Erving of the   17
Philadelphia 76ers. Erving has the capacity to make legends come true; leaping from the foul line and slam-dunking the ball on his way down; going up for a lay-up, pulling the ball to his body and throwing under and up the other side of the rim, defying gravity and probability with moves and jumps. Havlicek looked like the living embodiment of his small-town Ohio background. He would bring the ball downcourt, weaving left, then right, looking for the path. He would swing the ball to a teammate, cut behind a pick, take the pass and release the shot in a flicker of time. It looked plain, unvarnished. But there are not half a dozen players in the league who can see such possibilities for a free shot, then get that shot off as quickly and efficiently as Havlicek.

To former pro Jim McMillian, a black with "white" at-   18
tributes, himself a quick forward, "it's a matter of environment. Julius Erving grew up in a different environment from Havlicek — John came from a very small town in Ohio. There everything was done the easy way, the shortest distance between two points. It's nothing fancy, very few times will he go one-on-one; he hits the lay-up, hits the jump shot, makes the free throw, and after the game you look up and you say, 'How did he hurt us that much?' "

"White" ball, then, is the basketball of patience and   19
method. "Black" ball is the basketball of electric self-expression. One player has all the time in the world to perfect his skills, the other a need to prove himself. These are slippery categories, because a poor boy who is black can play "white" and a white boy of middle-class parents can play "black." Jamaal Wilkes and Paul Westphal are athletes who seem to defy these categories.

And what makes basketball the most intriguing of sports is how these styles do not necessarily clash; how the punishing intensity of "white" players and the dazzling moves of the "blacks" can fit together, a fusion of cultures that seems more and more difficult in the world beyond the out-of-bounds line.

• QUESTIONS ON MEANING AND PURPOSE •

1. According to Greenfield, how did black athletes come to dominate professional basketball?
2. What differences does the author discern between "black" and "white" styles of play? How do exponents of the two styles differ in showing emotion?
3. How does Greenfield account for these differences? Sum up in your own words the author's point about school yards (paragraph 7) and his point about macadam driveways, gyms, and dirt courts (paragraph 14). Explain "the ethic of mean streets" (paragraph 9).
4. Does Greenfield stereotype black and white players? Where in his essay does he admit that there are players who don't fit neatly into his two categories?
5. Do you agree with the author's observations about playing style? Can you think of any evidence to the contrary? (See *Evidence* in Useful Terms.)

• QUESTIONS ON WRITING STRATEGY •

1. How much do we have to know about professional basketball to appreciate Greenfield's essay? Is it written only for basketball fans, or for a general audience? (See *Audience* in Useful Terms).
2. In what passage in his essay does Greenfield begin comparing and contrasting? What has been the function of the paragraphs that have come before this passage?
3. In paragraph 4 the author compares a basketball court to a football field, a baseball diamond, and an ice hockey arena. What is the basis for his comparison?
4. Note that this essay does not follow a single method of comparison and contrast. After setting "black" and "white" stars

side by side (paragraph 9), Greenfield considers the two styles one at a time in paragraphs 10 through 17. Does this change of methods weaken his essay, or is it in any way justified?

5. Revising his essay for *The Bedford Reader*, Greenfield changed many of his examples. In paragraph 2, for instance, the Julius Ervings, Darryl Dawkins, and Kareem Abdul-Jabbars were, in the 1975 version of the essay, "Earl Monroes and Connie Hawkins and Nate Archibalds." In paragraph 9, George Gervin of the San Antonio Spurs replaced Bob McAdoo of the Buffalo Braves. In 15, Larry Bird was substituted for John Havlicek. In 16, San Antonio's Mark Olberding was originally "Boston's Don Nelson"; and in the same paragraph, Havlicek is now dubbed a *Boston Celtic immortal*. Why did Greenfield make these and other similar changes? How do they make the essay more effective?

· QUESTIONS ON LANGUAGE ·
· AND VOCABULARY ·

1. Consult the dictionary if you need help in defining the following words: lucrative (paragraph 1); ethnic (2); pulverization (3); constricted (4); inhibitions, anonymity (7); uncontestable (8); flamboyant (9); errant, finesse (14); execution (15); embodiment (17).

2. Talk to someone who knows basketball if you need help in understanding the head fake, the shoulder fake (paragraph 5); fast break, jump shot, "trailer" (15); high-percentage shot (16); a pick (17). What kind of diction do you find in these instances? (See *Diction* in Useful Terms.)

3. When Greenfield says, "We are talking about culture, not chromosomes" (paragraph 3), how would you expect him to define these terms?

4. Explain the author's reference to the word *rhythm* as "the most racially tinged of attributes" (paragraph 12).

· SUGGESTIONS FOR WRITING ·

1. In a paragraph or two, discuss how well you think Jeff Greenfield has surmounted the difficulties facing any writer who makes generalizations about people.

2. Compare and contrast college basketball and professional basketball (or, for a narrower subject, a college team and a pro team).

3. Write a brief essay in which you compare and contrast the styles of any two athletes who play the same game.
4. Compare and contrast the styles of two people in the same line of work, showing how their work is affected by their different personalities. You might take, for instance, two singers, two taxidrivers, two bank tellers, two evangelists, two teachers, or two symphony orchestra conductors.

· William Ouchi ·

WILLIAM OUCHI, born in 1943, earned an M.B.A. from Stanford University and a doctorate in business administration from the University of Chicago. A professor in the Graduate School of Management at U.C.L.A. and a prominent business consultant, he is the author of *Theory Z: How American Business Can Meet the Japanese Challenge* (1981).

Japanese and American Workers: Two Casts of Mind

"Japanese and American Workers: Two Casts of Mind" (editors' title) is excerpted from *Theory Z*. In the book, comparing Japanese collectivism with American individualism, Ouchi traces the influence of both traditions on industrial productivity. His thesis is that, with sensitive regard for cultural differences, the best of both worlds can be combined in one excellent system.

Collective Values

Perhaps the most difficult aspect of the Japanese for   1
Westerners to comprehend is the strong orientation to collective values, particularly a collective sense of responsibility. Let me illustrate with an anecdote about a visit to a new factory in Japan owned and operated by an American electronics company. The American company, a particularly creative firm, frequently attracts attention within the business community for its novel approaches to planning, organizational design, and management systems. As a consequence of this corporate style, the parent company determined to make a thorough study of Japa-

142

nese workers and to design a plant that would combine the best of East and West. In their study they discovered that Japanese firms almost never make use of individual work incentives, such as piecework or even individual performance appraisal tied to salary increases. They concluded that rewarding individual achievement and individual ability is always a good thing.

In the final assembly area of their new plant long lines of young Japanese women wired together electronic products on a piece-rate system: the more you wired, the more you got paid. About two months after opening, the head foreladies approached the plant manager. "Honorable plant manager," they said humbly as they bowed, "we are embarrassed to be so forward, but we must speak to you because all of the girls have threatened to quit work this Friday." (To have this happen, of course, would be a great disaster for all concerned.) "Why," they wanted to know, "can't our plant have the same compensation system as other Japanese companies? When you hire a new girl, her starting wage should be fixed by her age. An eighteen-year-old should be paid more than a sixteen-year-old. Every year on her birthday, she should receive an automatic increase in pay. The idea that any one of us can be more productive than another must be wrong, because none of us in final assembly could make a thing unless all of the other people in the plant had done their jobs right first. To single one person out as being more productive is wrong and is also personally humiliating to us." The company changed its compensation system to the Japanese model.

Another American company in Japan had installed a suggestion system much as we have in the United States. Individual workers were encouraged to place suggestions to improve productivity into special boxes. For an accepted idea the individual received a bonus amounting to some fraction of the productivity savings realized from his or her suggestion. After a period of six months, not a single suggestion had been submitted. The American managers were puzzled. They had heard many stories of the inventiveness, the commitment, and the loyalty of Japanese workers, yet not one suggestion to improve productivity had appeared.

The managers approached some of the workers and asked   4
why the suggestion system had not been used. The answer: "No
one can come up with a work improvement idea alone. We
work together, and any ideas that one of us may have are actually developed by watching others and talking to others. If
one of us was singled out for being responsible for such an idea,
it would embarrass all of us." The company changed to a group
suggestion system, in which workers collectively submitted suggestions. Bonuses were paid to groups which would save bonus
money until the end of the year for a party at a restaurant or, if
there was enough money, for family vacations together. The
suggestions and productivity improvements rained down on the
plant.

One can interpret these examples in two quite different   5
ways. Perhaps the Japanese commitment to collective values is
an anachronism that does not fit with modern industrialism but
brings economic success despite that collectivism. Collectivism
seems to be inimical to the kind of maverick creativity exemplified in Benjamin Franklin, Thomas Edison, and John D.
Rockefeller. Collectivism does not seem to provide the individual incentive to excel which has made a great success of
American enterprise. Entirely apart from its economic effects,
collectivism implies a loss of individuality, a loss of the freedom
to be different, to hold fundamentally different values from
others.

The second interpretation of the examples is that the   6
Japanese collectivism is economically efficient. It causes people
to work well together and to encourage one another to better efforts. Industrial life requires interdependence of one person on
another. But a less obvious but far-reaching implication of the
Japanese collectivism for economic performance has to do with
accountability.

In the Japanese mind, collectivism is neither a corporate or   7
individual goal to strive for nor a slogan to pursue. Rather, the
nature of things operates so that nothing of consequence occurs
as a result of individual effort. Everything important in life happens as a result of teamwork or collective effort. Therefore, to
attempt to assign individual credit or blame to results is un-

founded. A Japanese professor of accounting, a brilliant scholar trained at Carnegie-Mellon University who teaches now in Tokyo, remarked that the status of accounting systems in Japanese industry is primitive compared to those in the United States. Profit centers, transfer prices, and computerized information systems are barely known even in the largest Japanese companies, whereas they are a commonplace in even small United States organizations. Though not at all surprised at the difference in accounting systems, I was not at all sure that the Japanese were primitive. In fact, I thought their system a good deal more efficient than ours.

Most American companies have basically two accounting systems. One system summarizes the overall financial state to inform stockholders, bankers, and other outsiders. That system is not of interest here. The other system, called the managerial or cost accounting system, exists for an entirely different reason. It measures in detail all of the particulars of transactions between departments, divisions, and key individuals in the organization, for the purpose of untangling the interdependencies between people. When, for example, two departments share one truck for deliveries, the cost accounting system charges each department for part of the cost of maintaining the truck and driver, so that at the end of the year, the performance of each department can be individually assessed, and the better department's manager can receive a larger raise. Of course, all of this information processing costs money, and furthermore may lead to arguments between the departments over whether the costs charged to each are fair.

In a Japanese company a short-run assessment of individual performance is not wanted, so the company can save the considerable expense of collecting and processing all of that information. Companies still keep track of which department uses a truck how often and for what purposes, but like-minded people can interpret some simple numbers for themselves and adjust their behavior accordingly. Those insisting upon clear and precise measurement for the purpose of advancing individual interests must have an elaborate information system. Industrial life, however, is essentially integrated and interdependent. No one builds an automobile alone, no one carries through a banking transaction alone. In a sense the Japanese value of collectivism fits naturally into an industrial setting, whereas the Western individualism provides constant conflicts. The image that comes to mind is of Chaplin's silent film "Modern Times" in which the apparently insignificant hero played by Chaplin successfully fights against the unfeeling machinery of industry. Modern industrial life can be aggravating, even hostile, or natural: all depends on the fit between our culture and our technology.

A Difference of Tradition

The *shinkansen* or "bullet train" speeds across the rural areas   10
of Japan giving a quick view of cluster after cluster of farmhouses surrounded by rice paddies. This particular pattern did not develop purely by chance, but as a consequence of the technology peculiar to the growing of rice, the staple of the Japanese diet. The growing of rice requires the construction and maintenance of an irrigation system, something that takes many hands to build. More importantly, the planting and the harvesting of rice can only be done efficiently with the cooperation of twenty or more people. The "bottom line" is that a single family working alone cannot produce enough rice to survive, but a dozen families working together can produce a surplus. Thus the Japanese have had to develop the capacity to work together in harmony, no matter what the forces of disagreement or social disintegration, in order to survive.

Japan is a nation built entirely on the tips of giant, sub-   11
oceanic volcanoes. Little of the land is flat and suitable for agriculture. Terraced hillsides make use of every available square foot of arable land. Small homes built very close together further conserve the land. Japan also suffers from natural disasters such as earthquakes and hurricanes. Traditionally homes are made of light construction materials, so a house falling down during a disaster will not crush its occupants and also can be quickly and inexpensively rebuilt. During the feudal period until the Meiji restoration of 1868, each feudal lord sought to

restrain his subjects from moving from one village to the next for fear that a neighboring lord might amass enough peasants with which to produce a large agricultural surplus, hire an army and pose a threat. Apparently bridges were not commonly built across rivers and streams until the late nineteenth century, since bridges increased mobility between villages.

Taken all together, this characteristic style of living paints the picture of a nation of people who are homogeneous with respect to race, history, language, religion, and culture. For centuries and generations these people have lived in the same village next door to the same neighbors. Living in close proximity and in dwellings which gave very little privacy, the Japanese survived through their capacity to work together in harmony. In this situation, it was inevitable that the one most central social value which emerged, the one value without which the society could not continue, was that an individual does not matter. 12

To the Western soul this is a chilling picture of society. Subordinating individual tastes to the harmony of the group and knowing that individual needs can never take precedence over the interests of all is repellent to the Western citizen. But a frequent theme of Western philosophers and sociologists is that individual freedom exists only when people willingly subordinate their self-interests to the social interest. A society composed entirely of self-interested individuals is a society in which each person is at war with the other, a society which has no freedom. This issue, constantly at the heart of understanding society, comes up in every century, and in every society, whether the writer be Plato, Hobbes, or B. F. Skinner. The question of understanding which contemporary institutions lie at the heart of the conflict between automatism and totalitarianism remains. In some ages, the kinship group, the central social institution, mediated between these opposing forces to preserve the balance in which freedom was realized; in other times the church or the government was most critical. Perhaps our present age puts the work organization as the central institution. 13

In order to complete the comparison of Japanese and American living situations, consider flight over the United States. Looking out of the window high over the state of Kansas, we see 14 a pattern of a single farmhouse surrounded by fields, followed by another single homestead surrounded by fields. In the early 1800s in the state of Kansas there were no automobiles. Your nearest neighbor was perhaps two miles distant; the winters were long, and the snow was deep. Inevitably, the central social values were self-reliance and independence. Those were the realities of that place and age that children had to learn to value.

The key to the industrial revolution was discovering that   15
non-human forms of energy substituted for human forms could increase the wealth of a nation beyond anyone's wildest dreams. But there was a catch. To realize this great wealth, non-human energy needed huge complexes called factories with hundreds, even thousands of workers collected into one factory. Moreover, several factories in one central place made the generation of energy more efficient. Almost overnight, the Western world was transformed from a rural and agricultural country to an urban and industrial state. Our technological advance seems to no longer fit our social structure: in a sense, the Japanese can better cope with modern industrialism. While Americans still busily protect our rather extreme form of individualism, the Japanese hold their individualism in check and emphasize cooperation.

· QUESTIONS ON MEANING AND PURPOSE ·

1. What reasons does Ouchi give for the Japanese workers' discomfort with the piece-rate system?
2. According to Ouchi, what changes did the American plant managers have to make in their suggestion system before the Japanese workers would accept it?
3. Explain the differences the author has observed between Japanese and American systems of accounting.
4. Sum up Ouchi's view of Japanese collectivism and American individualism as natural outgrowths of each country's history and tradition.

5. Do you think the Japanese approach to work would succeed in the American factory system? Why or why not?

· QUESTIONS ON WRITING STRATEGY ·

1. How does Ouchi use narration in his comparison of Japanese and American business methods? To what extent does the author make use of description and example?
2. What is the tone of Ouchi's essay? (See *Tone* in Useful Terms.) How appropriate is the author's tone to his subject?
3. To what extent does the evidence Ouchi introduces into his essay justify his conclusion?
4. Exactly what in this essay indicates the writer's probable audience? What can you infer about the probable interests, general knowledge, and level of education of his readers?

· QUESTIONS ON LANGUAGE ·
· AND VOCABULARY ·

1. Examine Ouchi's use of *accountability* in paragraph 6, and *accounting* in paragraphs 7 and 8. Explain the subtle difference in meaning between the two words.
2. Define the following words, referring to your dictionary if necessary: orientation, collective, incentives (paragraph 1); anachronism, inimical, maverick (5); implication (6); arable (11); homogeneous, proximity, inevitable (12); precedence, repellent (13).
3. What does Ouchi mean by these *isms*: collectivism, industrialism (paragraph 5); automatism, totalitarianism (13)?

· SUGGESTIONS FOR WRITING ·

1. Marshaling evidence of your own, write a paragraph in which you maintain that American individualism is better preparation for industrialized living than is Japanese collectivism. (Remember, offer evidence — no Fourth of July oratory, please.)
2. Choose any task: harvesting apples, assembling a wardrobe, organizing a term paper, finding a job, obtaining a neighbor's cooperation. In a brief essay, compare and contrast two approaches to the task and decide which one is better. Give evidence to support your conclusion.

· Bruce Catton ·

BRUCE CATTON (1899–1978) was a Michigan-born newspaper-man who became one of America's leading historians of the Civil War. His book *A Stillness at Appomattox* (1953) earned him both the Pulitzer Prize for the writing of history and the National Book Award. In addition, Catton's many works include *Mr. Lincoln's Army* (1951), *The Hallowed Ground* (1956), *Waiting for the Morning Train: An American Boyhood* (1972), and *Gettysburg: The Final Fury* (1974).

Grant and Lee:
A Study in Contrasts

"Grant and Lee: A Study in Contrasts" first appeared in *The American Story*, a book of essays written by eminent historians. In his discussion of the two great Civil War generals, Catton contrasts not only two very different men, but the conflicting traditions they represented. Catton's essay builds toward the conclusion that, in one outstanding way, the two leaders were more than a little alike.

When Ulysses S. Grant and Robert E. Lee met in the parlor   1
of a modest house at Appomattox Court House, Virginia, on April 9, 1865 to work out the terms for the surrender of Lee's Army of Northern Virginia, a great chapter in American life came to a close, and a great new chapter began.

These men were bringing the Civil War to its virtual finish.   2
To be sure, other armies had yet to surrender, and for a few days the fugitive Confederate government would struggle desperately and vainly, trying to find some way to go on living now that its chief support was gone. But in effect it was all over when Grant and Lee signed the papers. And the little room where they wrote out the terms was the scene of one of the poignant, dramatic contrasts in American history.

They were two strong men, these oddly different generals,   3
and they represented the strengths of two conflicting currents
that, through them, had come into final collision.

Back of Robert E. Lee was the notion that the old aristo-   4
cratic concept might somehow survive and be dominant in
American life.

Lee was tidewater Virginia, and in his background were   5
family, culture, and tradition . . . the age of chivalry trans-
planted to a New World which was making its own legends and
its own myths. He embodied a way of life that had come down
through the age of knighthood and the English country squire.
America was a land that was beginning all over again, dedicated
to nothing much more complicated than the rather hazy belief
that all men had equal rights, and should have an equal chance
in the world. In such a land Lee stood for the feeling that it was
somehow of advantage to human society to have a pronounced
inequality in the social structure. There should be a leisure
class, backed by ownership of land; in turn, society itself should
be keyed to the land as the chief source of wealth and influence.
It would bring forth (according to this ideal) a class of men with
a strong sense of obligation to the community; men who lived
not to gain advantage for themselves, but to meet the solemn
obligations which had been laid on them by the very fact that
they were privileged. From them the country would get its leadership; to them it could look for the higher values — of thought,
of conduct, of personal deportment — to give it strength and
virtue.

Lee embodied the noblest elements of this aristocratic ideal.   6
Through him, the landed nobility justified itself. For four years,
the Southern states had fought a desperate war to uphold the
ideals for which Lee stood. In the end, it almost seemed as if the
Confederacy fought for Lee; as if he himself was the Confederacy . . . the best thing that the way of life for which the
Confederacy stood could ever have to offer. He had passed into
legend before Appomattox. Thousands of tired, underfed, poorly clothed Confederate soldiers, long-since past the simple enthusiasm of the early days of the struggle, somehow considered
Lee the symbol of everything for which they had been willing to

die. But they could not quite put this feeling into words. If the Lost Cause, sanctified by so much heroism and so many deaths, had a living justification, its justification was General Lee.

Grant, the son of a tanner on the Western frontier, was everything Lee was not. He had come up the hard way, and embodied nothing in particular except the eternal toughness and sinewy fiber of the men who grew up beyond the mountains. He was one of a body of men who owed reverence and obeisance to no one, who were self-reliant to a fault, who cared hardly anything for the past but who had a sharp eye for the future. 7

These frontier men were the precise opposites of the tidewater aristocrats. Back of them, in the great surge that had taken people over the Alleghenies and into the opening Western country, there was a deep, implicit dissatisfaction with a past that had settled into grooves. They stood for democracy, not from any reasoned conclusion about the proper ordering of human society, but simply because they had grown up in the middle of democracy and knew how it worked. Their society might have privileges, but they would be privileges each man had won for himself. Forms and patterns meant nothing. No man was born to anything, except perhaps to a chance to show how far he could rise. Life was competition. 8

Yet along with this feeling had come a deep sense of belonging to a national community. The Westerner who developed a farm, opened a shop or set up in business as a trader, could hope to prosper only as his own community prospered — and his community ran from the Atlantic to the Pacific and from Canada down to Mexico. If the land was settled, with towns and highways and accessible markets, he could better himself. He saw his fate in terms of the nation's own destiny. As its horizons expanded, so did his. He had, in other words, an acute dollars-and-cents stake in the continued growth and development of his country. 9

And that, perhaps, is where the contrast between Grant and Lee becomes most striking. The Virginia aristocrat, inevitably, saw himself in relation to his own region. He lived in a static society which could endure almost anything except change. Instinctively, his first loyalty would go to the locality in 10 which that society existed. He would fight to the limit of endurance to defend it, because in defending it he was defending everything that gave his own life its deepest meaning.

The Westerner, on the other hand, would fight with an   11
equal tenacity for the broader concept of society. He fought so because everything he lived by was tied to growth, expansion, and a constantly widening horizon. What he lived by would survive or fall with the nation itself. He could not possibly stand by unmoved in the face of an attempt to destroy the Union. He would combat it with everything he had, because he could only see it as an effort to cut the ground out from under his feet.

So Grant and Lee were in complete contrast, representing   12
two diametrically opposed elements in American life. Grant was the modern man emerging; beyond him, ready to come on the stage, was the great age of steel and machinery, of crowded cities and a restless, burgeoning vitality. Lee might have ridden down from the old age of chivalry, lance in hand, silken banner fluttering over his head. Each man was the perfect champion of his cause, drawing both his strengths and his weaknesses from the people he led.

Yet it was not all contrast, after all. Different as they were —   13
in background, in personality, in underlying aspiration — these two great soldiers had much in common. Under everything else, they were marvelous fighters. Furthermore, their fighting qualities were really very much alike.

Each man had, to begin with, the great virtue of utter   14
tenacity and fidelity. Grant fought his way down the Mississippi Valley in spite of acute personal discouragement and profound military handicaps. Lee hung on in the trenches at Petersburg after hope itself had died. In each man there was an indomitable quality . . . the born fighter's refusal to give up as long as he can still remain on his feet and lift his two fists.

Daring and resourcefulness they had, too; the ability to   15
think faster and move faster than the enemy. These were the qualities which gave Lee the dazzling campaigns of Second Manassas and Chancellorsville and won Vicksburg for Grant.

Lastly, and perhaps greatest of all, there was the ability, at   16
the end, to turn quickly from war to peace once the fighting was

over. Out of the way these two men behaved at Appomattox came the possibility of a peace of reconciliation. It was a possibility not wholly realized, in the years to come, but which did, in the end, help the two sections to become one nation again . . . after a war whose bitterness might have seemed to make such a reunion wholly impossible. No part of either man's life became him more than the part he played in their brief meeting in the McLean house at Appomattox. Their behavior there put all succeeding generations of Americans in their debt. Two great Americans, Grant and Lee — very different, yet under everything very much alike. Their encounter at Appomattox was one of the great moments of American history.

• QUESTIONS ON MEANING AND PURPOSE •

1. What is Bruce Catton's purpose in writing: to describe the meeting of two generals in a famous moment in history; to explain how the two men stood for opposing social forces in America; or to show how the two differed in personality?

2. Summarize the background and the way of life that produced Robert E. Lee; then do the same for Ulysses S. Grant. According to Catton, what ideals did each man represent?

3. In the historian's view, what essential traits did the two men have in common? Which trait does Catton think most important of all? For what reason?

4. How does this essay help you understand why Grant and Lee were such determined fighters?

5. Although slavery, along with other issues, helped precipitate the Civil War, Catton in this particular essay does not deal with it. If he had recalled the facts of slavery, would he have destroyed his thesis that Lee had a "strong sense of obligation to the community"? (*What* community?)

• QUESTIONS ON WRITING STRATEGY •

1. From the content of this essay, and from knowing where it first appeared, what can you infer about Catton's original audience?

At what places in his essay does the writer expect of his readers a great familiarity with United States history?

2. What effect does the writer achieve by setting both his introduction and his conclusion in Appomattox? (See *Introductions* and *Conclusions* in Useful Terms.)

3. For what reasons does Catton contrast the two generals *before* he compares them? Suppose he had reversed his outline, and had dealt first with Grant and Lee's mutual resemblances. Why would his essay have been less effective?

4. Pencil in hand, draw a single line down the margin of every paragraph in which you find the method of contrast. Then draw a *double* line next to every paragraph in which you find the method of comparison. How much space does Catton devote to each method? Why didn't he give comparison and contrast equal time?

5. Closely read the first sentence of every paragraph and underline each word or phrase in it that serves as a transition. Then review your underlinings. How coherent do you find this essay? (See *Transitions* and *Coherence* in Useful Terms.)

6. What is the tone of this essay — that is, what is the writer's attitude toward his two subjects? (See *Tone* in Useful Terms.) Is Catton poking fun at Lee in imagining the Confederate general as a knight of the Middle Ages, "lance in hand, silken banner fluttering over his head" (paragraph 12)?

7. Does Catton's treatment of the two generals as symbols obscure the reader's sense of them as individuals? (Lee, at least, is called a symbol in paragraph 6.) Discuss this question, keeping in mind what you decided to be Catton's purpose in writing his essay.

· QUESTIONS ON LANGUAGE ·
· AND VOCABULARY ·

1. In his opening paragraph, Catton uses a metaphor: American life is a book containing chapters. Find other figures of speech in his essay. (See *Figures of Speech* in Useful Terms.) What do they contribute?

2. Look up *poignant* in the dictionary. Why is it such a fitting word in paragraph 2? Why wouldn't *touching*, *sad*, or *teary* have been as good?

3. What information do you glean from the sentence, "Lee was tidewater Virginia" (paragraph 5)?

4. Define *aristocratic* as Catton uses it in paragraphs 4 and 6.

5. Define obeisance (paragraph 7); indomitable (14).

• SUGGESTIONS FOR WRITING •

1. Compare and contrast two other figures of American history with whom you are familiar: Franklin D. Roosevelt and John F. Kennedy, Lincoln and Douglas, or Susan B. Anthony and Elizabeth Cady Stanton — to suggest only a few.

2. In a brief essay full of specific examples, discuss: Do the "two diametrically opposed elements in American life" (as Catton calls them) still exist in the country today? Are there still any "landed nobility"?

3. In your thinking and your attitudes, whom do you more closely resemble — Grant or Lee? Compare and contrast your outlook with that of one famous American or the other. (A serious tone for this topic isn't required.)

· A. M. Rosenthal ·

ABRAHAM MICHAEL ROSENTHAL, born in Ontario, Canada, in 1922, came to the United States in 1926 and was naturalized in 1951. Now the executive editor of the *New York Times*, he is the author of *38 Witnesses* (1964). His articles have appeared in *The New York Times Magazine, Saturday Evening Post, Colliers,* and *Foreign Affairs.*

No News from Auschwitz

"No News from Auschwitz" was first published in the *New York Times* on August 31, 1958, when Rosenthal was a correspondent assigned to Warsaw, Poland. At the time, mention of the holocaust had practically disappeared from American newspapers and periodicals — as though Hitler's murder of six million Jews seemed too horrendous to recall. Rosenthal's article served in 1958 as a powerful reminder. It still does.

BRZEZINKA, POLAND — The most terrible thing of all, somehow, was that at Brzezinka the sun was bright and warm, the rows of graceful poplars were lovely to look upon and on the grass near the gates children played.   1

It all seemed frighteningly wrong, as in a nightmare, that at Brzezinka the sun should ever shine or that there should be light and greenness and the sound of young laughter. It would be fitting if at Brzezinka the sun never shone and the grass withered, because this is a place of unutterable terror.   2

And yet, every day, from all over the world, people come to Brzezinka, quite possibly the most grisly tourist center on earth. They come for a variety of reasons — to see if it could really have been true, to remind themselves not to forget, to pay homage to the dead by the simple act of looking upon their place of suffering.   3

Brzezinka is a couple of miles from the better-known southern Polish town of Oswiecim. Oswiecim has about 12,000   4 inhabitants, is situated about 171 miles from Warsaw and lies in a damp, marshy area at the eastern end of the pass called the Moravian Gate. Brzezinka and Oswiecim together formed part of that minutely organized factory of torture and death that the Nazis called Konzentrationslager Auschwitz.

By now, fourteen years after the last batch of prisoners was   5
herded naked into the gas chambers by dogs and guards, the story of Auschwitz has been told a great many times. Some of the inmates have written of those memories of which sane men cannot conceive. Rudolf Franz Ferdinand Hoess, the superintendent of the camp, before he was executed wrote his detailed memoirs of mass exterminations and the experiments on living bodies. Four million people died here, the Poles say.

And so there is no news to report about Auschwitz. There is   6
merely the compulsion to write something about it, a compulsion that grows out of a restless feeling that to have visited Auschwitz and then turned away without having said or written anything would somehow be a most grievous act of discourtesy to those who died here.

Brzezinka and Oswiecim are very quiet places now; the   7
screams can no longer be heard. The tourist walks silently, quickly at first to get it over with and then, as his mind peoples the barracks and the chambers and the dungeons and flogging posts, he walks draggingly. The guide does not say much either, because there is nothing much for him to say after he has pointed.

For every visitor, there is one particular bit of horror that   8
he knows he will never forget. For some it is seeing the rebuilt gas chamber at Oswiecim and being told that this is the "small one." For others it is the fact that at Brzezinka, in the ruins of the gas chambers and the crematoria the Germans blew up when they retreated, there are daisies growing.

There are visitors who gaze blankly at the gas chambers and   9
the furnaces because their minds simply cannot encompass them, but stand shivering before the great mounds of human hair behind the plate-glass window or the piles of babies' shoes or the brick cells where men sentenced to death by suffocation were walled up.

One visitor opened his mouth in a silent scream simply at   10
the sight of boxes — great stretches of three-tiered wooden
boxes in the women's barracks. They were about six feet wide,
about three feet high, and into them from five to ten prisoners
were shoved for the night. The guide walks quickly through the
barracks. Nothing more to see here.

A brick building where sterilization experiments were car-   11
ried out on women prisoners. The guide tries the door — it's
locked. The visitor is grateful that he does not have to go in,
and then flushes with shame.

A long corridor where rows of faces stare from the walls.   12
Thousands of pictures, the photographs of prisoners. They are
all dead now, the men and women who stood before the cameras, and they all knew they were to die.

They all stare blank-faced, but one picture, in the middle of   13
a row, seizes the eye and wrenches the mind. A girl, 22 years
old, plumply pretty, blond. She is smiling gently, as at a sweet,
treasured thought. What was the thought that passed through
her young mind and is now her memorial on the wall of the
dead at Auschwitz?

Into the suffocation dungeons the visitor is taken for a mo-   14
ment and feels himself strangling. Another visitor goes in, stum-
bles out and crosses herself. There is no place to pray at Auschwitz.

The visitors look pleadingly at each other and say to the   15
guide, "Enough."

There is nothing new to report about Auschwitz. It was a   16
sunny day and the trees were green and at the gates the children
played.

• QUESTIONS ON MEANING AND PURPOSE •

1. What reason does Rosenthal give for having written this essay?
2. What do the responses of his fellow tourists contribute to your
   understanding of the author's own reactions?

3. If Rosenthal had gone into greater detail about each of the horrors his pilgrimage revealed, do you think his essay would have been stronger or weaker? Explain.

· QUESTIONS ON WRITING STRATEGY ·

1. Comment on Rosenthal's choice of a title.
2. In paragraph 6, the author writes, "And so there is no news to report about Auschwitz"; and he begins paragraph 16 by declaring, "There is nothing new to report about Auschwitz." What do these two echoes of the title lend to the essay's impact?
3. On what aspect of the contrast between past and present does Rosenthal focus his attention? By what means does he emphasize the contrast? (See *Emphasis* in Useful Terms).

· QUESTIONS ON LANGUAGE ·
· AND VOCABULARY ·

1. Comment on Rosenthal's choice of words in his assertion that sunshine, light, greenness, and young laughter seem "wrong." With what justification can daisies growing in the ruins be called "horrible"?
2. Explain the author's use of the word *shame* in paragraph 11.

· SUGGESTIONS FOR WRITING ·

1. In a brief essay convey your personal responses to some historic site you have visited or to a moving historic event you have read about. To help the reader share your reactions, include precise, carefully chosen details in your writing rather than merely venting your feelings in a general way. Show what you felt through your description of what you saw or read.
2. Choose an old building in your town, a park, a ghost town, a converted schoolhouse, or any other place with a past. Write an essay in which you compare and contrast the place as it is now and as it once was.

· Joseph C. Goodman ·

JOSEPH C. GOODMAN, born in 1943, was graduated from Rutgers University in 1964. After taking a master's degree in creative writing from Johns Hopkins, he taught from 1967 to 1971 at Coppin State College in Baltimore and at the University of Maryland. Then he devoted himself to fiction, holding a writing fellowship at the Fine Arts Work Center in Provincetown, Massachusetts, in 1973–74. In the late 1970s he returned to graduate study at Tufts. His stories and criticism have appeared in leading publications including *Fiction*, *The New York Times*, and *Transatlantic Review*. At present he is Director of Public Relations for Wheelock College.

Shouts and Whispers: Academic Life in the Sixties and Today

The 1960s are usually remembered as a decade of protest and revolution on American college campuses: a more violent, exciting, and troubling time than either students or teachers more recently have known. As Goodman recalls those years, however, the early 1960s and the late 1960s were sharply different. In this highly individual memoir, he compares and contrasts the two ends of the decade; he then compares and contrasts the later end, the era of protest, with college as most of us know it today.

I am often mistaken for someone who went to college during the late 1960s. People take one look at me or hear me speak just a few words and they take for granted that I was a campus revolutionary or — if I wasn't one myself — that I spent a great deal of time in the company of those who were.

Friends a few years younger than I am make the same mistake. When they reminisce about their first student strike, march on Washington, or puff of marijuana, I am almost always included with a knowing wink or smile. When they grow wistful about the sense of solidarity they shared, I receive affectionate cuffs on the shoulder. And when they recount the real and the apocryphal stories of their college days — a roommate beating the draft by making eyes at an Army psychiatrist, a classmate shouting down a professor who said that art ought not to be political, a couple celebrating moving in together by sharing their first LSD trip — they often turn to me expectantly, awaiting my own contribution.

I am sorely tempted. They have not misjudged my values or 3 been wrong in thinking that I look back longingly upon academic life during that time. But the truth is — and I hope this admission will not disappoint too many of my friends — that I had already shaken my university president's hand and accepted my bachelor's degree from him by the time they started demanding he resign.

I was a student in the sixties. My undergraduate career 4 began, neatly enough, in 1960. But what was commonplace on campus between John Kennedy's election and Lyndon Johnson's was soon swept away during the second half of the decade in a flood of political, social, and cultural change. I was glad to be carried along in the current, to add my own dammed-up ideas and feelings to it, because by then I was full of bitterness about my own undergraduate experience. I was convinced that during the course of those four years I had suffered greatly in the hands of tyrannical professors, reactionary deans, and a system that worked to stifle creativity and erase individual differences.

Was it really that bad? From my current perspective, the 5 answer has to be no, probably not. But there were certainly differences, some of them extreme, between the university I attended and the one attended by young men and women just a few years later.

For one thing, my own education was conducted as politely 6 as a luncheon in the Ritz. My professors always addressed me as Mr. Goodman, and in return, I always placed Professor or Mister before their last names. In my senior year, I was at once flattered and flabbergasted when my advisor called me by my first name at a sherry party he threw for English majors who were about to graduate. Of course, I did not respond by calling him by his first name. I would sooner have called him Mac or Pal or Sport. I remained respectfully silent in the face of his startling gesture, hurrying away as soon as possible to find out if any of my classmates had received a similar benediction.

Professors and students dealt with each other at a distance that was a gap at best, a chasm at worst. My instructors were parental figures whose favor I tried to win, or they were antagonists whom I tried to outwit. In the classroom, we circled each other as warily as wrestlers, lacking both sympathy for and understanding of each other.

A similar restraint and sense of isolation characterized other campus relationships. There were women enrolled in my university, but *their* campus was on the other side of town where they attended their own classes, lived in their own dormitories, and navigated their own passages into adulthood. Fraternization was not unheard of, but it took place only before curfew, which, if I remember correctly, was 11 P.M. on weekdays and 1 A.M. on Fridays and Saturdays.

Choice — the privilege of choosing when we wished to go out or come in, what we wished to study, even how we wished to think — was an occasional luxury rather than a desired necessity. For the first two years, our course of study was prescribed, down to the last credit. We were expected to accept and uphold a whole range of conventions, from applauding at the conclusion of lectures to joining fraternities to writing about literary characters in the present tense. When it came to choosing a major, our options were both specific and limited. I heard (and believed) the story of the junior who was told at registration that there were no more spaces left for engineering majors. Panic-stricken, he gained an appointment with a dean who asked him if there weren't something else he wanted to be — a political scientist, perhaps, or possibly a teacher of French.

The dean who served up these alternatives might well have been the same one who, in my own junior year, suggested that I join the Navy. He made his suggestion not long after I received my third summons to appear in his office to explain why I had cut another Italian class. It was common knowledge that the dean had commanded a mine-sweeper in World War II, and my declaration that I would rather stay home and write short stories than attend Italian class must have struck him as a refusal to man my battle station. He promptly wrote a letter to my parents in which he wondered if I wouldn't be better educated at sea than in New Brunswick, New Jersey. "There is nothing wrong with growing up," the dean allowed, "but I question whether college is the place to do it." College, it seemed, was the place to continue doing pretty much what I had been doing most of my life: following the orders, urgings, and suggestions of my parents and others their age. For my four years of effort, I would gain improved intellectual skills. Maturity, self-knowledge, and creative development were best gained elsewhere.

I resented this notion and carried my resentment with me as   11
I graduated from college, breezed through a master's degree program in creative writing, and emerged as an instructor of English at a branch campus of a large southern university. Even if time had stood still, I would have tried to live down the restrictions and inadequacies of my college experience, tried to become the instructor I had never had as an undergraduate. But history preempted me. U. S. military assistance to South Vietnam turned into a massive assault against North Vietnam, and a subsequent shock wave rocked all our institutions, colleges and universities especially. The teach-in was invented, the Gulf of Tonkin Resolution was written, and the word "peacenik" was coined. I had just begun contemplating my move toward the mountain when it got up, strolled over to where I was standing, and fell on me.

While my recollections of my undergraduate and graduate   12
careers are in the form of a series of vignettes, like scenes in a long play, my memories of the years that followed — the late sixties and early seventies — are not nearly so orderly. Like the era itself, they are a blur of motion and color, a motion picture that seems different each time I watch it.

I cannot remember, for example, exactly when I first   13
became aware of unshaven male faces and uncurled female hair,

of blue jeans and surplus Army fatigue jackets, of Jimi Hendrix and Bob Dylan. But by the time these things attracted my conscious attention, I had already let my own beard grow, proudly patched the knees of my jeans, and taken to humming "The Times, They Are a-Changin' " in the shower. Nor can I recall exactly when I first heard that half the dormitories on campus housed both men and women and that students were allowed to petition the faculty if they wished to design their own interdisciplinary major. Overnight, it seemed, students had discovered their common concerns and the strength of their numbers. Classrooms were nearly empty when the student government scheduled a debate between members of the Students for a Democratic Society and of the Reserve Officer Training Corps. Hallways, lounges, and lawns became the sites of impromptu seminars on subjects ranging from the invasion of Cambodia to university policy on birth control. Prohibitions — whether against cohabitation, cutting class, or criticizing the President of the United States — seemed empty of meaning in the context of the Mai Lai massacre, the Watergate break-in, and the fall of Saigon. Perhaps the change was gradual, but it did not feel that way. It felt as if all at once the quiet groves of academe had come alive with sounds as raucous as Dixieland jazz and as impassioned as a family quarrel.

The genteel politeness of my undergraduate days gave way 14 to a candor so unrestrained that the distinction between life outside the university and within it was often blurred and sometimes erased. More than once, in the midst of teaching a creative writing class, I found myself imagining one of my old professors passing the open door. Would he have recognized what he heard as the poems and stories of young men and women determined to express their newly discovered consciousness, or would he have wondered why students were being asked to read from personal diaries and transcriptions of street-corner conversations?

That same professor would have been puzzled, I'm sure, by 15 my own classroom methods. At some point — perhaps my second year of teaching — I stopped taking attendance and started conducting the classroom discussion from a seat in the midst of my students. And it was probably at about this time that I began to introduce myself to my classes as Joe, explaining that I was more comfortable with first names because titles such as "Mister," "Miss," and "Professor" were like signs on doorways that required a visitor to knock before entering.

Just a few years before, my instructors had spoken mostly in commands. Now, as a large segment of the American population began questioning national priorities and preferences, I addressed my students more and more often with questions. "What do you think?" became a kind of punctuation mark that I could not resist using. What do you think — I wanted to know — about this poem, novel, image, rule of composition, reading assignment, test question, grade? What do you think about the draft, poverty, fame, religion? What do you think we ought to do at the election polls in November or in our class next Wednesday?

Of course, the question was thrown back at me many times. Discussions begun in class ended only when we had spilled out into a local hangout where, amid juke-box noise and beery laughter, our urgent voices finally seemed out of place. In the quiet aftermath of those arguments, it was easy to become friends with my students, to talk about hometowns, and families, the movies we had seen recently, what we planned to do this summer.

It is clear to me now, as it was not then, that my efforts to link arms with my students on campus and off were not only expressions of my belief in an egalitarian ideal, but also responses to their expectations of me. The growing public demand that as a nation we should examine our motives, admit our faults, and transcend our self-interest translated easily into a personal credo, and college students were among the first people to make this connection. They turned almost at once to their professors to ask for the same behavior they were asking of themselves.

I had accepted my professors' right to teach whatever they wanted in whatever way they wished much as I had accepted the fact that other people were rich. I resented the difference, sometimes suffered because of it, but never considered demanding that it be changed. Now, a teacher could be called upon to be not only rational and humane, but also sympathetic to the needs and preferences of his or her students. My brightest and most committed students let me know that they expected of me at least an ally, and perhaps more. They learned to publish their own course evaluations, to gain seats on standing faculty committees, and to speak their minds openly so that none of us, no matter how cleverly we tried, could claim ignorance of their feelings and thoughts.

I knew what mattered to my students, knew that they would challenge my assignments, question the fairness of my tests, and ask why I wasn't joining them to protest the arrival of a Marine Corps recruiting team on campus. Students had gained more control over their educations and enlarged their choices in many areas of their lives — that much was obvious. But what was less obvious was that in the process of challenging us, their teachers, they also granted us similar freedoms. In a revelatory moment, I realized that as a student I had never granted my professors the range of choices that my current students routinely granted me.

This recognition, that all of us in the academic community could now shape the educational process according to our evolving needs and preferences, helped me put down the urge to right the wrongs of my undergraduate career. I had come to understand the restraints that had held back both instructors and students in the past, and I felt certain that the future offered almost limitless possibility. This sense of possibility was undoubtedly a factor in my decision, after three years of teaching, to take time off and devote myself entirely to writing.

My sojourn lasted into the mid-1970s, when I returned to the university as instinctively as a homing pigeon. By then, the war in Vietnam was over, and our country was not so obviously divided into two camps. I looked forward to less troubled times on campus, for it seemed to me that in the absence of strife we could devote more of our energy to the educational revolution just begun.

During my first months back, I felt a bit dislocated and strained, but I explained these feelings away by reminding myself that I needed time to readjust to the rhythm of academic life. My discomfort lasted longer than it should have, though. Much of the time I felt like part of a drawing in a child's playbook. "What's wrong with this picture?" the caption asks, and close examination reveals a woman with her hat on upside down, a half-moon where the sun should be, a street sign that says GO instead of STOP.

It was true that students still had a voice in governing their institution, that faculty members were still trying to develop innovative and interesting courses, that trustees were still expected to consider ethical as well as fiscal issues. But something was missing, some quality that I had taken so much for granted in the past that I could not name or define it now. Perhaps it was the old refusal to comply, for now both students and faculty seemed more eager to accede to each other's wishes. Or perhaps it was any obvious visible sign of academic solidarity. With the passing of marches, demonstrations, and rallies, we were all less bold and less demanding. Or was it the old freedom from preoccupation with financial security? Faculty members, no longer certain of finding work in their profession, and students, paying increasingly higher tuition fees, seemed to be worrying in unison about the future.
24

I have not yet been able to arrive at a single answer, though recently I came close. I was walking away from my first class of the fall semester, trying to recall some of the names and faces of my new students, when it suddenly dawned on me what my first words had been. "Good morning, I'm Mr. Goodman."
25

• QUESTIONS ON MEANING AND PURPOSE •

1. In his opening sentence, the writer declares himself "often mistaken for someone who went to college during the 1960s." But then, in paragraph 4, he tells us that, indeed, he *was* a student in that decade. Does he contradict himself? Explain.
2. Sum up the chronology of the essay. In what years was Goodman a student? A teacher for the first time? When did he last return to academic life?

3. What main differences (or similarities) does the writer find between the college of his own student years and college during the Vietnam War? Between the latter and college today?
4. In his conclusion, what does Goodman consider in trying to account for the changed climate of the college campus today?
5. What do you think is Goodman's main purpose in this essay: to explain a change in our society, to record the history of his times, or to record his own personal history?

• QUESTIONS ON WRITING STRATEGY •

1. How does Goodman's brief history of his days as a student (paragraphs 4 through 10) prepare us to understand his welcoming the changes brought about during the Vietnam War?
2. What particular examples help to clarify and enliven this essay? Comment on the effectiveness of Goodman's imagining, in paragraph 14, one of his old professors passing his classroom door.
3. Does Goodman offer any value judgments? Is he arguing in favor of a classroom of the past (of the early 1960s or later 1960s) over the classroom of today?

• QUESTIONS ON LANGUAGE •
• AND VOCABULARY •

1. With the aid of your instructor, your fellow students, or an up-to-date encyclopedia, explain Goodman's allusions to recent history: especially Gulf of Tonkin Resolution, "peacenik," (paragraph 11); Students for a Democratic Society and Mai Lai massacre (13). (See *Allusion* in Useful Terms.)
2. Define apocryphal (paragraph 2), reactionary (4), benediction (6), fraternization (8), preempted (11), vignettes (12), genteel (14), egalitarian, credo (18).
3. Explain the metaphor in paragraph 23: the writer's feeling himself part of a drawing in a child's puzzle book. (See *Metaphor* under *Figures of Speech* in Useful Terms.)

• SUGGESTIONS FOR WRITING •

1. In a long paragraph, compare and contrast your own view with Goodman's view of college life today.

2. From your knowledge of recent history, from the experiences of friends and family, from the film *Hair*, or from any other sources, set forth in an essay your picture of the 1960s. Center your essay, as Goodman does, on young people: their opinions, life styles, responses to the Vietnam War. Obviously you can't sum up a whole decade in less than a volume; and so, confine yourself to a few main points, illustrating each with facts and examples.

Discovering What to Say

Sometimes in the middle of writing an essay, a writer will find that his carefully chosen subject is changing in front of his eyes. This experience may dismay him; and yet, as Joseph C. Goodman discovered, the original subject may have been only a preliminary to what, instead, the writer truly wishes to say.

I have often found that rewriting is not just a means of refining awkward sentences and focusing aimless paragraphs. It is also a means of discovering what I really want to say. This was the case in writing "Shouts and Whispers." I began by trying to write about a general subject in a supposedly objective way, and I ended up writing about myself in a decidedly personal way. The change took place only after I had begun putting words down on paper, and to whatever extent this essay succeeds, it does so because I was able to use the writing process itself to narrow my subject and adjust my point of view.

When I began the essay, I hoped to discuss the lack of understanding that often characterizes the relationship between students and teachers. I wanted to describe how each comes to see the other as an antagonist, and I even had a notion that I might be able to offer some suggestions for ameliorating this situation.

From the start I was uneasy making the psychological pronouncements that were the main points of my argument. With each generalization that I wrote — "students are encouraged to regard their teachers as surrogate parents," "instructors frequently suffer from performance anxiety," "students become hostile when asked to compete for a limited number of good grades" — I felt more and more uncomfortable. I was not speaking in my own voice, but in that of an imaginary expert.

Writing in this unfamiliar voice, I found that I was straining to choose each word. I completed paragraphs with a sense of physical relief, as if I had just carried a load of bricks up several flights of stairs, and I rarely left my desk without thinking that I would eventually have to redo whatever I had just written.

As I continued to struggle, I became aware of the fact that I 5 was having much less trouble developing examples and illustrations based on personal experience. When I began to narrate or explain my own experience in the classroom, I no longer labored over vocabulary and syntax, but moved easily from sentence to sentence, actually curious about what might appear next on the page.

It was not just the voice I was writing in that made me uncomfortable, but the subject I was writing about as well. As I 6 recollected and described what had happened to me as a college student and teacher, I realized that these experiences had been inextricably linked to the surrounding cultural, social, and political climate. Although there was a significant difference between taking a class and teaching one, there was an equally vivid contrast between being on campus during the early 1960s and being there during the later 1960s and early 1970s.

I decided to begin the essay again, this time sure that I 7 wanted to write more specifically about my own educational journey through the 1960s and 1970s. I had written nearly a complete essay by the time I decided to change my topic and point of view, but the early effort had yielded what all writers constantly hope to find and seldom do — a fresh idea.

1. In an essay replete with examples, compare and contrast any of the following pairs:

   Women and men as consumers.

   The styles of two runners.

   The personality of a dog and the personality of a cat.

   Alexander Hamilton and Thomas Jefferson: their opposing views of central government.

   The humor of two short narratives: James Herriot's "Just Like Bernard Shaw" and James Thurber's "University Days" (see Chapter 1).

   How city dwellers and country dwellers spend their leisure time.

   The jobs people dream of and the jobs they take.

   The presentation styles of two television news commentators.

2. In writing an essay on one of the following general subjects, by the method of comparison and contrast, your first step will be to select a basis for comparison. In dealing with two cities, for instance, you might consider the efforts to renovate their downtown areas, their styles of architecture, their relative habitability, or their responses to crime. Depending on whether your purpose were serious or otherwise, you might compare and contrast Republicans and Democrats in their attitudes toward labor unions, or consider adherents of the two parties as drinkers, or dressers.

   Two cities.

   Republicans and Democrats.

   Two buildings.

   Two football teams.

   German-made cars and Detroit-made cars.

   Two methods of farming.

   Two horror movies.

   Red wine and white wine.

   High school and college.

   Train travel and plane travel.

   Television when you were a child and television today.

· 5 ·

PROCESS ANALYSIS
Explaining Step by Step

· THE METHOD ·

A chemist working for a soft-drink firm is handed a six-pack of a competitor's product: Orange Quench. "Find out what this bellywash is," he is told. First, perhaps, he smells the stuff and tastes it. Then he boils a sample, examines the powdery residue, and tests for sugar and acid. At last, he draws up a list of the mysterious drink's ingredients: water, corn syrup, citric acid, sodium benzoate, coloring. Methodically, the chemist has performed an analysis. The nature of Orange Quench stands revealed.

Analysis, also called *division*, is the separation of something into its parts, the better to understand it. An action, or a series of actions, may be analyzed, too. Writing a report to his boss, the soft-drink chemist might tell how he went about learning the ingredients of Orange Quench. Perhaps, if the company wanted to imitate the competitor's product, he might provide instructions for making something just like Orange Quench out of the same ingredients. Writing with either of those purposes, the chemist would be using the method of *process analysis*: explaining step by step how something is done or how to do something.

Like any type of analysis, process analysis divides a subject into its components. It divides a continuous action into stages. Processes much larger and more involved than the making of Orange Quench also may be analyzed. When a news commentator tells about an armed revolution in a small republic, she may point out how the fighting began and how it spread, how the capital city was surrounded, how the national television station was seized, how the former president was taken prisoner, and how a general was proclaimed the new president. Exactly what does the commentator do? She takes a complicated event and divides it into parts. She explains what happened first, second, third, and finally. Others, to be sure, may analyze the event differently, but the commentator gives us one good interpretation of what took place, and of how it came about.

Because it is useful in explaining what is complicated, process analysis is a favorite method of news commentators — and of scientists who explain how atoms behave when split, or how to go about splitting them. The method, however, may be useful to anybody. Two kinds of process analysis are very familiar to you. The first (or *directive*) kind tells a reader how to do something, or make something. You meet it when you read a set of instructions for assembling newly purchased stereo components, or follow the directions to a stereo store ("Turn right at the blinker and follow Patriot Boulevard for 2.4 miles. . . . "). The second (or *informative*) kind of process analysis tells us how something is done, or how it takes place. This is the kind we often read out of curiosity. Such an essay may tell of events beyond our control: how the Grand Canyon was formed, how lions hunt, how a fertilized egg develops into a child. In this chapter, you will find examples of both kinds of process analysis — both the "how to" and the "how." In an entertaining directive, Jim Villas tells you how to make sublime fried chicken, and he writes as if he expects you to haul out your iron skillet and follow his advice. Jessica Mitford, in a spellbinding informative essay, explains how corpses are embalmed; but clearly, she doesn't expect you to rush down to your basement and give her instructions a try.

Sometimes the method is used very imaginatively. Foreseeing that the sun eventually will cool, the earth shrink, the oceans freeze, and all life perish, an astronomer who cannot possibly behold the end of the world nevertheless can write a process analysis of it. An exercise in learned guesswork, such an essay divides a vast and almost inconceivable event into stages that, taken one at a time, become clearer and more readily imaginable.

Whether it is useful or useless (but fun to imagine), a good essay in process analysis holds a certain fascination. Leaf through a current issue of a newsstand magazine, and you will find that process analysis abounds in it. You may meet, for instance, articles telling you how to tenderize cuts of meat, sew homemade designer jeans, lose fat, cut hair, play the money markets, arouse a bored mate, and program a computer. Less practical, but not necessarily less interesting, are the informative articles: how brain surgeons work, how diamonds are formed, how big cities combat crime, how a film star maintains homes on four continents. Readers, it seems, have an unslakable thirst for process analysis. On a recent list of the week's fifteen best-selling nonfiction books, we find eleven titles offering process analysis. Most are "how to" books. Topping the list is a work of advice on how to grow slim, by a Hollywood guru of self-denial; nearly as popular is a volume with larger concerns: how to live, eat, exercise, and think aggressively. Other titles promise to tell us how to negotiate with people, live alone happily, and cook gourmet dinners in thirty minutes. One confides *How to Make Love to a Man*. With *The Art of Japanese Management* in hand, we will be able to run our own McDonald's franchises on Zen principles. There is even *Miss Piggy's Guide to Life*, a spoof on more uplifting books of directives. Least earthbound is Carl Sagan's *Cosmos*, a work that purports to explain how the universe has evolved into what it is today. Evidently, if anything will still make an American crack a book, it is a step-by-step explanation of how something — even a universe — has been successful.

· THE PROCESS ·

Here are suggestions for writing an effective process analysis of your own. (In fact, what you are about to read is itself a process analysis.)

1. Have the process you are about to analyze clearly in mind. Think it through. This preliminary run-through will make the task of writing far easier, whether your process analysis be the directive or the informative kind.

2. If you are giving a set of detailed instructions, ask yourself: Are there any preparatory steps a reader ought to take? If there are, list them. (These might include: "Remove the packing from the components," or, "First, lay out three eggs, one pound of Sheboygan bratwurst. . . . ")

3. List the steps or stages in the process. Try setting them down in chronological order, one at a time — if this is possible. Some processes, however, do not happen in an orderly time sequence, but occur all at once. If, for instance, you are writing an account of an earthquake, what do you mention first? Cracks in the ground? Falling houses? Bursting water mains? Toppling trees? Mangled cars? Casualties? (Here is a subject for which the method of *classification*, to be discussed in Chapter 6, may come to your aid. You might sort out apparently simultaneous events into categories: injury to people; damage to homes, to land, to public property.)

4. Now glance back over your list, making sure you haven't omitted anything or instructed your reader to take the steps in the wrong order. Sometimes a stage of a process may contain a number of smaller stages. Make sure none has been left out. If any seems particularly tricky or complicated, underline it on your list to remind yourself when you write your essay to slow down and detail it with extra care.

5. Ask yourself, Will I use any specialized or technical terms? If you will, be sure to define them. You'll sympathize with your reader if you have ever tried to work a Hong Kong-made short-wave radio that comes with an instruction booklet written in translatorese, full of unexplained technical jargon; or if you have ever tried to assemble a plastic tricycle according to a directive that reads, "Position sleeve casing on wheel center in fork with shaft in tong groove, and gently but forcibly tap in medium pal nut head. . . ."

6. Use time-markers. That is, indicate *when* one stage of a process stops and the next begins. By doing so, you will greatly aid your reader in following you. Here, for example, is a paragraph of plain medical prose that makes good use of helpful time-markers. (In this passage, the time-markers are the words in *italics*.)

> In the human, *thirty-six hours after* the egg is fertilized, a two-cell egg appears. A twelve-cell development takes place *in seventy-two hours*. The egg is still round and has increased little in diameter. In this respect it is like a real estate development. *At first* a road bisects the whole area; *then* a cross road divides it into quarters, and *later* other roads divide it into eighths and twelfths. This happens without the taking of any more land, simply by subdivision of the original tract. *On the third or fourth day*, the egg passes from the Fallopian tube into the uterus. *By the fifth day* the original single large cell has subdivided into sixty small cells and floats about the slitlike uterine cavity *a day or two longer*, *then* adheres to the cavity's inner lining. *By the twelfth day* the human egg is already firmly implanted. Impregnation is *now* completed, *as yet* unbeknown to the woman. *At present*, she has not even had time to miss her first menstrual period, and other symptoms of pregnancy are *still several days distant*.[1]

Brief as these time-markers are, they define each stage of the human egg's journey. Note how the writer, after declaring in the second sentence that the egg forms twelve cells, backtracks

---

[1]Adapted from *Pregnancy and Birth* by Alan F. Guttmacher, M.D. (New York: New American Library, 1970).

for a moment and retraces the process by which the egg has subdivided, comparing it (by a brief analogy) to a piece of real
estate. (For more examples of analogy, see Chapter 7.) By showing your reader how one event follows another, time-markers
serve as transitions. Vary them so that they won't seem mechanical. If you can, avoid the monotonous repetition of a fixed
phrase (*In the fourteenth stage . . . , In the fifteenth stage . . .*). Even
boring time-markers, though, are better than none at all. As in
any chronological narrative, words and phrases such as *in the
beginning, first, second, next, after that, three seconds later, at the
same time*, and *finally* can help a process to move smoothly in
the telling and lodge firmly in the reader's mind. (Don't feel that
you have to mention *everything* that happens, though; mention
only the important points in the sequence.)

7. When you begin writing a first draft, state your analysis
in generous detail, even at the risk of being wordy. When you
revise, it will be easier to delete than to amplify.

8. Finally, when your essay is finished, reread it carefully. If
it is a simple *directive* ("How to Eat an Ice Cream Cone Without
Dribbling"), ask a friend to try it out. See if somebody else can
follow your instructions without difficulty. If you have written
an *informative* process analysis ("How the Dinosaurs Perished"),
however, ask others to read your essay and tell you whether the
process unfolds as clearly in their minds as it does in yours.

• PROCESS ANALYSIS IN A PARAGRAPH •

Everyone has heard of the Nielsen ratings, but how many
people know how the A. C. Nielsen Company learns which
television programs are the most popular with American
viewers? Arnold Becker explains in "The Network Ratings
Business" (written for Judy Fireman's *TV Book*) just how the
process works. First, a meter is installed in each of about 1200
households chosen by Nielsen as representative samples. In
each sample household, the meter registers whenever the television set is turned on and to what channel the dial is tuned.
In the middle of every night, a computer automatically dials a
phone number connected to each meter, and the meter transfers into the computer the data it has gathered. The computer

records which channels are switched on and at what times in all the sample households. With this information in hand, Nielsen matches the computer data with each network's daily schedule of programs. He is then able to tell the networks exactly how many households in the sample are tuned in to each TV show. The process is beautifully simple. What Becker fails to mention is that the rating system, ingenious though it may be, is not entirely foolproof. So far, Nielsen's computers are incapable of recording one crucial fact: Is the turned-on TV set in each sample household playing to an audience — or merely to an empty room?

Comment. Briefly and straightforwardly, this writer sums up four principal steps by which the Nielsen Company samples the habits of TV viewers. Time-markers indicate the stages: (1) *First*; (2) *In the middle of every night*; (3) *With this information in hand*; and (4) *then*. Note how valuable that last *then* is in the paragraph, indicating that Nielsen has at last arrived at a result. The two concluding sentences aren't strictly part of the process analysis; still, they seem essential in that they point to crucial facts that this whole efficient, computerized process actually leaves out. Incidentally, rather than wrestling repeatedly with some awkward phrase ("The A. C. Nielsen Company," "The Nielsen surveyors"), the writer elected simply to say Nielsen — as though one man were doing all the surveying. (That isn't the case, but her meaning is clear.) This paragraph illustrates the kind of writing you often do in a research paper: summing up in your own words, and in a shorter space, evidence found in a book.

· Jim Villas ·

JIM VILLAS was born in 1938 in Charlotte, North Carolina. After teaching comparative literature and romance languages at the universities of Missouri and North Carolina, Rutgers, and Hunter College, he switched careers on discovering that, as he puts it, "My stomach was more important than my brain." For the past decade he has served as food and wine editor for *Town & Country* magazine, and he also writes for *Esquire, Cuisine, Bon Appetit, Gourmet,* and *Travel & Leisure.* Although he travels throughout the world, eating and drinking, Villas prides himself on maintaining a nearly constant weight of 175 pounds. At this writing, he is working on a book to be called *American Taste.*

Fried Chicken

This fiery process analysis has haunted us ever since we read it in a book of essays on American subjects, *Mom, the Flag, and Apple Pie* (1976), compiled by the editors of *Esquire,* the magazine in which it first appeared. Recipes aren't customarily written with much passion and energy, but "Fried Chicken" is; and the essay shows that even down-to-earth directives can be fascinating, provided a writer deeply cares what he is talking about and expects us to care, too. Villas tells us that he learned his skill with a skillet from "an incredible fried chicken maker," his mother. After you read his mouthwatering advice, we trust you will never again want to settle for dried-up pullet with "about as much flavor as tennis balls."

When it comes to fried chicken, let's not beat around the   1
bush for one second. To know about fried chicken you have to have been weaned and reared on it in the South. Period. The French know absolutely nothing about it, and Julia Child and James Beard very little. Craig Claiborne knows plenty.[1] He's

---

[1]Three cookbook authors and cooking experts: Child is the "French Chef" of public television; Beard, a lecturer and newspaper columnist; Claiborne, food editor of the *New York Times.*

from Mississippi. And to set the record straight before bringing on regional and possible national holocaust over the correct preparation of this classic dish, let me emphasize and reemphasize the fact that I'm a Southerner, born, bred, and chicken-fried for all times. Now, I don't know exactly why we Southerners love and eat at least ten times more fried chicken than anyone else, but we do and always have and always will. Maybe we have a hidden craw in our throats or oversize pulley bones or ... oh, I don't know what we have, and it doesn't matter. What does matter is that we take our fried chicken very seriously, having singled it out years ago as not only the most important staple worthy of heated and complex debate but also as the dish that non-Southerners have never really had any knack for. Others just plain down don't *understand* fried chicken, and, to tell the truth, there're lots of Southerners who don't know as much as they think they know. Naturally everybody everywhere in the country is convinced he or she can cook or identify great fried chicken as well as any ornery reb (including all the fancy cookbook writers), but the truth remains that once you've eaten real chicken fried by an expert chicken fryer in the South there are simply no grounds for contest.

As far as I'm concerned, all debate over how to prepare fried chicken has ended forever, for recently I fried up exactly twenty-one and a half chickens (or 215 pieces) using every imaginable technique, piece of equipment, and type of oil for the sole purpose of establishing once and for all the right way to fix great fried chicken. In a minute I'll tell you what's wrong with most of the Kentucky-fried, Maryland-fried, oven-fried, deep-fried, creole-fried, and all those other classified varieties of Southern-fried chicken people like to go on about. But first *my* chicken, which I call simply Fried Chicken and which I guarantee will start you lapping:

Equipment (no substitutes):
A sharp chef's or butcher's knife 12 to 13 in. long
A large wooden cutting board
A small stockpot half filled with water (for chicken soup)
A large glass salad bowl
A heavy 12-in. cast-iron skillet with lid

Long-handled tweezer tongs
1 roll paper towels
2 brown paper bags
1 empty coffee can
A serving platter
A wire whisk
A home fire extinguisher

Ingredients (to serve 4):   4
3 cups whole milk
½ fresh lemon
1½ lbs. (3 cups) top-quality shortening
4 tbsp. rendered bacon grease
1 whole freshly killed 3½- to 4-lb. chicken
1½ cups plus 2 tbsp. flour
3 tsp. salt
Freshly ground black pepper

To Prepare Chicken for Frying. Remove giblets and drop in   5
stockpot with neck. (This is for a good chicken soup to be eaten
at another time.) Cut off and pull out any undesirable fat at
neck and tail. Placing whole chicken in center of cutting board
(breast-side up, neck toward you), grab leg on left firmly, pull
outward and down toward board, and begin slashing down
through skin toward thigh joint, keeping knife close to thigh.
Crack back thigh joint as far as possible, find joint with fingers,
then cut straight through to remove (taking care not to pull skin
from breast). Turn bird around and repeat procedure on other
thigh. To separate thigh from leg, grasp one end in each hand,
pull against tension of joint, find joint, and sever. Follow same
procedure to remove wings. Cut off wing tips and add to
stockpot.

To remove pulley bone (or wishbone to non-Southerners),   6
find protruding knob toward neck end of breast, trace with fingers to locate small indentation just forward of knob, slash
horizontally downward across indentation, then begin cutting
carefully away from indentation and downward toward neck till
forked pulley-bone piece is fully severed. Turn chicken backside

up, locate two hidden small pinbones on either side below neck toward middle of back, and cut through skin to expose ends of bones. Put two fingers of each hand into neck cavity and separate breast from back by pulling forcefully till the two pry apart. (If necessary, sever stubborn tendons and skin with knife.) Cut back in half, reserving lower portion (tail end) for frying, and tossing upper portion (rib cage) into stockpot. Place breast skinside down, ram tip of knife down through center cartilage, and cut breast in half.

(**Hint:** Level cutting edge of knife along cartilage, then slam blade through with heel of hand.) 7

Rinse the ten pieces of chicken thoroughly under cold running water, dry with paper towels, and salt and pepper lightly. Pour milk into bowl, squeeze lemon into milk, add chicken to soak, cover, and refrigerate at least two hours and preferably overnight. 8

To Fry Chicken. Remove chicken from refrigerator and allow to return to room temperature (about 70°). While melting the pound and a half of shortening over high heat to measure ½ inch in skillet, pour flour, remaining salt and pepper to taste into paper bag. Remove dark pieces of chicken from milk, drain each momentarily over bowl, drop in paper bag, shake vigorously to coat, and add bacon grease to skillet. When small bubbles appear on surface, reduce heat slightly. Remove dark pieces of chicken from bag one by one, shake off excess flour, and, using tongs, lower gently into fat, skin-side down. Quickly repeat all procedures with white pieces; reserve milk, arrange chicken in skillet so it cooks evenly, reduce heat to medium, and cover. Fry exactly 17 minutes. Lower heat, turn pieces with tongs and fry 17 minutes longer uncovered. With paper towels wipe grease continuously from exposed surfaces as it spatters. Chicken should be almost mahogany brown. 9

Drain thoroughly on second brown paper bag, transfer to serving platter *without* reheating in oven, and serve hot or at room temperature with any of the following items: mashed potatoes and cream gravy, potato salad, green beans, turnip greens, sliced homegrown tomatoes, stewed okra, fresh corn 10 bread, iced tea, beer, homemade peach ice cream, or water-melon.

To Make Cream Gravy. Discard in coffee can all but one   11
tablespoon fat from skillet, making sure not to pour off brown
drippings. Over high heat, add two remaining tablespoons flour
to fat and stir constantly with wire whisk till roux browns.
Gradually pour 1¾ cups reserved milk from bowl and continue
stirring till gravy comes to a boil, thickens slightly, and is
smooth. Reduce heat, simmer two minutes, and check salt and
pepper seasoning. Serve in gravy boat.

Now, that's the right way, the only way, to deal with fried   12
chicken. Crisp, juicy on the inside, full of flavor, not greasy and
sloppy, fabulous. Of course one reason my recipe works so well
is it's full of important subtleties that are rarely indicated in
cookbooks but that help to make the difference between impeccable fried chicken and all the junk served up everywhere today.
And just to illustrate this point, I cite a recipe for "Perfect Fried
Chicken" that recently appeared in *Ladies' Home Journal.*

> 1. Rinse cut-up 2½- to 3 lb. broiler-fryer and pat dry.
> 2. Pour 1 in. vegetable oil in skillet, heat to 375°. Com-
> bine ½ cup flour, 2 tsp salt, dash of pepper in a bag. Coat a
> few pieces at a time.
> 3. Preheat oven to 250°. Place paper towels in shallow
> baking pan.
> 4. Fry thighs and drumsticks, turning occasionally, for 12
> minutes until golden. Pierce with fork to see if juices run clear.
> Remove to baking pan and place in heated oven. Fry remain-
> ing pieces for 7 or 8 minutes. Serves four.

Snap! That's it. A real quicky. Fast fried chicken that prom-   13
ises to be perfect. Bull! It tastes like hell, and if you don't believe
me, try it yourself. The pitfalls of the recipe are staggering but
typical. First of all, nobody in his right mind fries a skinny two-
and-a-half-pound chicken for four people, not unless everyone's
on some absurd diet or enjoys sucking bones. Second, the recipe
takes for granted you're going to buy a plastic-wrapped chicken
that's been so hacked and splintered by a meat cleaver that

blood from the bones saturates the package. What help is offered if the chicken you happen to have on hand is whole or only partially cut up? Third, what type of skillet, and what size, for heaven's sake? If the pan's too light the chicken will burn on the bottom, and if you pour one full inch of oil in an eight-inch skillet, you'll end up with deep-fried chicken. And as for sticking forks in seared chicken to release those delicious juices, or putting fried chicken in the oven to get it disgustingly soggy, or serving a half-raw thick breast that's cooked only seven or eight minutes — well, I refuse to get overheated.

Without question the most important secret to any great 14
fried chicken is the quality of the chicken itself, and without question most of the three billion pullets marketed annually in the U.S. have about as much flavor as tennis balls. But, after all, what can you expect of battery birds whose feet never touch the dirty filthy earth, whose diet includes weight-building fats, fish flours, and factory-fresh chemicals, and whose life expectancy is a pitiful seven weeks? Tastelessness, that's what, the same disgraceful tastelessness that characterizes the eggs we're forced to consume. How many people in this country remember the rich flavor of a good old barnyard chicken, a nearly extinct species that pecked around the yard for a good fifteen weeks, digested plenty of barley-and-milk mash, bran, grain, and beer, got big and fat, and never sent one solitary soul to the hospital with contamination? I remember, believe you me, and how I pity the millions who, blissfully unconscious of what they missed and sadly addicted to the chicken passed out by Colonel Sanders, will never taste a truly luscious piece of fried chicken unless they're first shown how to get their hands on a real chicken. Of course, what you see in supermarkets are technically real chickens fit for consumption, but anyone who's sunk teeth into a gorgeous, plump barnyard variety (not to mention an inimitable French *poularde de Bresse*[2]) would agree that to compare the scrawny, bland, mass-produced bird with the one God intended us to eat is something more than ludicrous.

[2]A pullet from Bresse, a part of France whose poultry is "rightly considered the best in France," according to the French food encyclopedia *Larousse Gastronomique.*

I originally intended to tell you how to raise, kill, draw, and   15
prepare your own chickens. Then I came to my senses and faced
the reality that unless you were brought up wringing chickens'
necks, bleeding them, searching for the craws where food is
stored, and pulling out their innards with your hands — well, it
can be a pretty nauseating mess that makes you gag if you're not
used to it. Besides, there's really no need to slaughter your own
chickens, not, that is, if you're willing to take time and make
the effort to locate either a good chicken raiser who feeds and
exercises his chickens properly (on terra firma) or a reliable merchant who gets his chickens fresh from the farm. They do exist,
still, be their number ever so dwindling. If you live in a rural
area, simply get to know a farmer who raises chickens, start
buying eggs from him and then tell him you'll pay him any
amount to kill and prepare for you a nice 3½- to 4-pound pullet.
He will, and probably with pride. If you're in a large city, the
fastest method is to study the Yellow Pages of the phone book,
search under "Poultry — Retail" for the words "Fresh poultry
and eggs" or "Custom poultry" or "Strictly kosher poultry,"
and proceed from there.

Now, if you think I take my fried chicken a little too serious-   16
ly, you haven't seen anything till you attend the National
Chicken Cooking Contest held annually in early summer at different locations thoughout the country. Created in 1949, the
festival has a Poultry Princess; vintage motorcar displays; a flea
market; a ten-feet-by-eight-inch skillet that fries up seven and a
half tons of chicken; ten thousand chicken-loving contestants
cooking for cash prizes amounting to over $25,000; and big-
name judges who are chosen from among the nation's top newspaper, magazine, and television food editors. It's a big to-do. Of
course, I personally have no intention whatsoever of ever entering any chicken contest that's not made up exclusively of
Southerners, and of course you understand my principle. This,
however, should not necessarily affect your now going to the
National and showing the multitudes what real fried chicken is
all about. A few years back, a young lady irreverently dipped
some chicken in oil flavored with soy sauce, rolled it in crushed
chow mein noodles, fried it up, and walked away with top

honors and a few grand for her Cock-a-Noodle-Do. Without doubt she was a sweetheart of a gal, but you know, the people who judged that fried chicken need help.

· QUESTIONS ON MEANING AND PURPOSE ·

1. In "Fried Chicken" Jim Villas analyzes not one but at least three processes. What are they?
2. What is the basic premise of this essay? (See *Premise* in Useful Terms.)
3. What does the author tell you about himself? Does it convince you that he is an expert on his subject?
4. Identify the targets of the author's ire and explain why he rails against each one.
5. What parts of the essay fulfill the author's main purpose? What do the other parts contribute to the essay's effectiveness?

· QUESTIONS ON WRITING STRATEGY ·

1. In what ways does the writing in this essay differ from conventional cookbook writing?
2. Describe the author's tone. (See *Tone* in Useful Terms.) Is it likely to offend anyone in his audience? Why, or why not?
3. Is Villas's informal writing style appropriate to his subject? (See *Style* in Useful Terms.)
4. For what general point that Villas has previously stated does the *Ladies' Home Journal* recipe (paragraph 12) serve as an example? In stating his objections to the magazine's recipe, what order does he follow?
5. Do you think Villas would make changes in this essay if he were to present it to the National Poultry Growers Association? To the product development group of a fried chicken chain?

· QUESTIONS ON LANGUAGE ·
· AND VOCABULARY ·

1. How many examples of colorful language can you find in "Fried Chicken"? Exactly what makes them colorful? What colloquial ex-

pressions does Villas use? (See *Colloquial Expressions* in Useful Terms.)

2. Be sure you know what the following words mean: cartilage (paragraph 6); roux (11); inimitable, ludicrous (14); craws, terra firma (15).

3. What does "impeccable" (paragraph 12) mean? In the phrase "impeccable fried chicken," do you find a pun?

• SUGGESTIONS FOR WRITING •

1. In a paragraph or two, challenge the superiority of Jim Villas's fried chicken with your own favorite as cooked by yourself, a relative or friend, or even Colonel Sanders.

2. If you don't like fried chicken, write an essay in which you tell how to prepare some other food (ribs, tacos, lasagna, tofu, or whatever) — or even how to make a good cup of coffee.

3. Write a process analysis in which you demonstrate both the wrong way and the right way to perform a given task.

· Larry L. King ·

LARRY L. KING was born in Texas in 1929. He has been Professor of Journalism at Princeton and a contributor to *New Times*, *The Texas Observer*, *Texas Monthly*, and *Harper's*. King is the author of seven books including *Confessions of a White Racist* (1971) and *The Lost Frontier* (1973); however, he is perhaps best known as coauthor of the hit Broadway play, *The Best Little Whorehouse in Texas*.

Shoot-out
with Amarillo Slim

Larry L. King included "Shoot-out with Amarillo Slim" in his collection of essays, *Of Outlaws, Con Men, Whores, Politicians, and Other Artists* (1980). "I've always seemed to gravitate toward rascals, clowns, and pirates simply because they provide more entertaining shows," he says in the introduction to his book. This essay entertains as promised, while also carefully analyzing two processes.

The grapevine had it that thirty-four men, putting up $10,000 each, would convene in Benny Binion's Horseshoe Casino in Las Vegas to settle the world poker championship and thereby make the winner temporarily rich.

Among the high rollers would be Amarillo Slim Preston, who had the reputation of beating people at their own game. My game was dominoes. I began to fantasize about giving Amarillo Slim a chance to beat me. Never mind that he once had defeated a Ping-Pong ace while playing him with a Coke bottle or that he'd trimmed Minnesota Fats at pool while employing a broomstick as a cue. I could think of no such flashy tricks available to him in a domino game, unless he wished to play me blindfolded. In which case I would merrily tattoo him and take his money.

I first played dominoes on the kitchen table in my father's   3
Texas farmhouse before reaching school age. By age nine or ten
I could beat or hold my own against most adults and had graduated to contests staged in feedstores, icehouses, cotton gins, and
crossroads domino parlors. My father delighted in introducing
me to unsuspecting farmers, ranchers, or rural merchants and
then observing their embarrassment as they got whipped by a
fuzzless kid.

As a teenager I hustled domino games in pool halls and beer   4
joints, rarely failing to relieve oil-field workers of their hard-
earned cash. In the Army, while others sought their victims in
crap games or at the poker tables, I prospered from those who
fancied themselves good domino players. In later life I had written articles on the art of dominoes and, indeed, had been asked
to write a book about it. I recite all this so you will know that
Amarillo Slim would not be getting his hooks into any innocent
rookie should he accept my challenge.

A few words here about the game itself. It is played with   5
twenty-eight rectangular blocks known as dominoes, or rocks.
The face of each is divided in two, each half containing mark-
ings similar to a pair of dice — except that some are blank. The
twenty-eight dominoes represent all possible combinations from
double blank to double six.

In two-handed dominoes, the players draw for the right to   6
start the game, known as the down. After the dominoes are re-
shuffled, each player draws seven; the remaining fourteen rocks
go into the boneyard to await the unwary, unlucky, or inatten-
tive player.

Any domino may be played on the down, but subsequent   7
play is restricted: Players must follow suit by matching the pips,
or spots, on the exposed ends of the dominoes. Rocks are placed
end to end, except for doubles, which are set down at right
angles to the main line of dominoes. The first double played
becomes the spinner and may be developed in all four directions.

Players may score in three ways: (1) After each play, the   8
number of spots on all open ends is added; if the sum is divisible
by five, the player last playing scores the total; (2) when a player
puts down his last rock with a triumphant "Domino!" he scores

the value of the spots in his opponent's hand; (3) should the game be "blocked" — that is, if neither opponent can play — the one caught with the fewer points adds to his score the points his opponent has been stuck with, to the nearest complement of five.

The basic strategy is simple: Score, keep your opponent   9
from scoring, block his plays and make him draw from the boneyard, and then domino on him. The first player to score 250 points is the winner.

Dominoes is an easy game to learn and a difficult one to   10
master. Any kid can grasp its fundamentals. After that, progress is largely determined by the player's ability to recall what has been played and what is out, by his understanding of the mathematical probabilities, and by his being able to read what his opponent is trying to do. The luck of the draw plays a part in any given game, sure. But over the long haul, what might be called personality skills are more important than luck. These cannot be taught, but develop out of each player's inner core and chemistry. Either you got 'em or you ain't. My successful record as a domino player satisfied me that I had 'em, and I wondered if Amarillo Slim did. So I tracked the fabled gamesman down in Las Vegas to find out and to see if I could compete with the legendary gambler. In short, I wanted to know if I could play with the Big Boys.

"How many spots in a deck of dominoes?" Amarillo Slim   11
asked.

"Er-rah," I said. "You mean total spots? In the whole deck?"   12
Amarillo Slim pushed his considerable cowboy hat to the back of his head, further elongating his weathered and bony face, and nodded.

I took a swig of beer to cover my frantic mental arithmetic.   13
It was a question that never had occurred to me.[1] Slim patiently waited while dozens of big-time gamblers, participants in or witnesses to the World Series of Poker, milled about in the

---

[1]It should have. It would be vital to rapid calculation if one wondered whether to "block" the game. Since the odds rarely would be that close, I'd never bothered.

flashy Horseshoe Casino. "Well," I ultimately said with great
certainty, "I'm not exactly sure."

Amarillo Slim Preston shook his head, as if somebody had   14
told him his favorite dog had died, and the sorrow was just too
much to bear. His eyes said, *What is this poor fool doing challenging me to play dominoes for money when he don't know his elbow
from Pike's Peak?*

Slim said, "I'm tied up in this big poker game right now, pal;   15
but I ain't catchin' the cards, and my stake's so small it looks
like a elephant stepped on it. Soon as I'm out of it, I'll be happy
to accommodate you."

After he'd been eliminated from the high-stakes world   16
championship tournament (which, on another occasion, he had
won), we agreed to meet the following morning at eleven. We
would play three games for $50 each, though Slim made it clear
he probably would show more profit pitching pennies than in
playing dominoes for such a paltry sum. "I'm a fair country
domino player," he admitted, "but I'm not any world's expert.
You wouldn't be hustlin' ol' Slim, would you?" I think I thought
I told the truth when I denied it.

I had a few drinks to celebrate my opportunity and mentally   17
calculated that a twenty-eight-piece set of dominoes contained
exactly 172 spots. When I recalculated to corroborate this scientific fact, I got exactly 169. And then 166. Using pencil and
paper and rechecking four times, I became convinced the correct answer was 165. Exactly. Yes. *Seven-and-eight are fifteen,
carry the one. . . .*

Then I realized what I had been doing and said to myself: 18
*Don't let Amarillo Slim psych you out. Why, he's trying to play the
Coke-bottle-and-broomstick trick on you! It doesn't matter how many
spots are in the deck. He's trying to get you to occupy your mind with
extraneous matters. Forget it.* One hour after I'd completely and
totally forgotten it, I thought: *Hell, he probably doesn't know the
answer. He didn't give it, did he?* Then I calculated the spots three
more times: 165, yep. But it didn't make any difference.
Couldn't possibly have any bearing on the game. . . .

I was in the Horseshoe Casino at the appointed hour.   19
Amarillo Slim was not. I searched the poker pits, the blackjack

tables, the roulette-wheel crowds; among the rows of clickety-clacking slot machines; in the bars and restaurants. No Slim. I inquired of his whereabouts among gamblers, dealers, security guards, and perplexed tourists. I telephoned Slim's room three times and had him paged twice in two other casinos. No Slim. Sitting at the bar nearest the poker pits and reminding myself not to drink excessively, I pep-talked my soul: *You're good. You haven't been beaten in years. Remember to play your hand and not to worry about his. Don't listen to his jabber, because you know he's a talker. Concentrate.*

In the midst of my tenth or eleventh drink I spotted the big   21
cowboy hat. Under it stood Amarillo Slim, more than six feet tall and exactly two hours late. *Shoot-out time!* "Slim!" I cheer-fully cried. He gave me a vague wave and a who-are-you look and continued to talk with one of his cronies. Could he have *forgotten* so important a match?

"Oh, yeah, pal," he said when reminded. "You got a deck of   22
dominoes with you?" When I said I did not, Slim looked in-credulous. "You *don't!*" he exclaimed. You never would have suspected that the night before, he had assured me the house would provide a deck.

"Well, pal," Slim said a trifle sadly. "No matter how good   23
you are, I kinda doubt you can beat me without a deck."

"I'll go get one," I volunteered, eagerly plunging out of the   24
casino onto the sunny and garish sidewalks of Las Vegas, dodg-ing among the crowds of people who looked as if maybe God had run out of good clay when it came their turn and had made them from Silly Putty. As I visited my fourth novelty shop ("Naw, sir, we don't get many calls for dominoes no more"), it suddenly occurred to me that Amarillo Slim had his opponent running errands for him. Here I was rushing around, getting all sweaty and hot, while spending $10 besides, in order that Slim Preston might have an opportunity to take fifteen times that amount from me. *No, forget that! It's defeatist thinking! Keep your cool!*

When I returned to the Horseshoe, Slim was playing in a   25
pickup poker game. I caught his eye and held up the domino deck. Amarillo Slim looked at me — no, *through* me — as if he'd never seen such a sight in his life and then raked in a pot of

chips big enough to choke a longhorn steer. After I'd waved the dominoes four or five times, faint recognition dawned in his eyes. "Oh, yeah, pal," he called. "Just wait there for me."

I waited. And waited. And waited some more. By now I was doing a slow burn. *Okay for you, Slim, you shitass. When I finally corner your stalling ass, it belongs to the gypsies, pal!* A lot of Walter Mitty stuff began roistering in my head. I would so crush Amarillo Slim that he would retire from gaming for all time, publicly apologizing for his ineptitude. Meanwhile, however, I had time to eat a bowl of chili, whomp up on a friend in a practice game — 250 to 95 — and count the number of spots in the deck again. No doubt about it: 165.

Fully four hours after the appointed time, Amarillo Slim approached his challenger. He was tucking away a large roll of bills newly accepted from two amateur poker players, who, now wiser and lighter, began to sneak away as if guilty of large crimes. *Play him tough,* I instructed myself. *Don't give him anything. He's just another ol' Texas boy, like you. He's just a little skinnier, that's all.*

"You bring your photographer?" Slim asked.

"Uh, beg pardon?"

"I thought you said this was gonna be in *Sport* magazine," he said. "You mean you didn't bring a photographer?"

"I forgot," I said, before realizing I'd made absolutely no promise of a photographer.

Slim grunted and sat down at the table. So as to reestablish authority, I said, "Here are the ground rules. Fifty bucks per game. Two hundred fifty points wins a game. You play the seven dominoes you draw, no matter how many doubles." Slim gave me a who-don't-know-that look.

I poured the new deck onto the table. Slim bent over the dominoes and said, "Whut the *hail?*"

"Beg pardon?"

"Is this here a *deuce?*" he demanded of a rock he held before his eyes. Squinting like Mr. Magoo.

"Yeah. Sure."

"Damnedest-lookin' deuce *I* ever saw," Slim proclaimed. "All the deuces look like that, pal?" I decided not to answer.

Though the deuces in this particular deck were a shade peculiar in appearance, they were not enough different from the norm to make a federal case. Which Amarillo Slim now was doing. "Pal," he said, "I'm in a whole heap of trouble. I can't tell these funny-lookin' deuces from the aces. Why, you can wet in this hat if I can tell 'em apart."

Slim's lament began to attract a sizable crowd of professional gamblers and the merely curious. Among those pressing close to the table was a huge, grinning fat man called Texas Dolly, Doyle Brunson, who had reason enough to grin, having the previous evening won $340,000 playing poker. *The winnah and new world champ-een!* I suddenly was very aware of where I was, and who Amarillo Slim was, and that he'd been winning big stakes around the globe while I had been taking lunch money away from oil-field grunts and Pfcs. *If you're not nervous,* whispered a small inner voice, *then why are your hands shaking?* It was something like being the rookie deep back waiting to receive the opening kickoff in the Super Bowl, I imagine. And Vince Lombardi was coaching the other side.

I had decided on a conservative strategy for the first few hands, much as a football team might carefully probe the opposition's defense with basic fundamentals rather than quickly go for the long bomb. I would take any count available to me, no matter how small, rather than scheme to send Slim to the boneyard. If you send a skilled opponent to the boneyard too early, and he gets enough dominoes, he has more options and more scoring rocks available. So I would wait until the major scoring rocks had been played before going for the jugular; would settle for the field goal on my first possession. Grunt gains.

I won the down — coin toss? — and played the double five, at once scoring 10 and establishing the spinner. Fine; I'd run the kickoff back to my own 47; I held three other fives and figured to prosper from that spinner. Sure enough, I scored 25 points before Slim got on the board. Slim countered with combinations of sixes and fours, all the time mumbling how he couldn't tell aces from deuces "and here we are playin' for the whole kit and kaboodle." *Don't listen to him. Play your hand.* Every time I played a deuce — and often when I didn't — Slim said, "Is that thang a deuce, pal?" At the end of the first hand I led him, 40–25. I'd kicked my field goal.

In the second go-round I again was blessed with fives. Slim, however, was equally blessed with blanks. We traded large counts; I was reminded of a baseball game in which neither side could get anybody out. I'd make 10 and Slim would make 15; then he would make 15 and I would make 20. We each scored 65 points, so that after two hands I was up 105 to 90; Slim, of course, chattered incessantly about the funny-lookin' deuces I'd rung in on him.   41

The third hand was tense and low-scoring, each of us waiting for the other fellow to make a major mistake. Nobody did. We only made 15 points each; the game now stood 120 to 105; I silently congratulated myself on having not yet fallen behind for a single moment.   42

After the fourth hand I was certain that I had him. He pulled within 5 points early; but then I turned treys on him, and he had none. He went to the boneyard twice and got nothing that helped him. I dominoed on him for 30 points and now led, 195 to 155. *Duck soup. I got him. How's it feel, pal?*   43

Now Slim was rattling and jabbering like monkeys climbing chains. I resolved to shut him out. *Keep track of what's played and what's out. You're playing good dominoes. But you'll blow it if you permit him to break your concentration.*   44

Having discovered that I preferred to play rapid-fire dominoes, Amarillo Slim now began to slow the pace. Though surely he had not read it, he was utilizing a technique I had recommended: "Should your opponent prefer to play quickly, slow the game. Conversely, should *he* slow it, then you should give a wham-bam-thankee-ma'am response. Once you rob your opponent of his preferred pace, you control the tempo — and he who controls the tempo usually will control the game."   45

Slim edged up on me, nickeling and diming me to death; I began to feel like a team that had tried to freeze the ball too early and had lost its momentum, its . . . yes . . . *tempo!* My lead had dwindled to 15 points when it suddenly became clear why   46 he'd made such a fuss about the funny-lookin' deuces. I'd turned it all fours on him, and he had none. He was drawing from the boneyard, hunting for a four, when he suddenly exposed a domino in his hand and, peering at it as if he might qualify for aid to the blind, innocently asked, "Is that thang a deuce, pal?" I was astonished; clearly, it was not. Nor were the next three or four dominoes he deliberately exposed to my view.

By now the gamblers were hoo-hawing and laughing. The cardinal rule of dominoes, the very *first* rule — its being a game dependent on the calculating of odds and based upon the memory of what's been played and what has not — is that you never, but *never*, reveal anything of your hand to your opponent. Amarillo Slim was, in effect, playing me with an open hand! It was an insult of the magnitude a street fighter offers when he slaps another rather than hits him with a clenched fist. Such gestures say, *I can take you whenever I want you. You probably got to squat to pee.*

With the gamblers' laughter crashing about my reddening ears, I offered a good-sport grin as false and empty as an old maid's dream. There was a reason my face felt frozen somewhere between a grimace and a death mask: I now hated the bastard.

"Hey, pal," Slim said, "I'll make you a side bet of five hundred dollars that I can name the three rocks remainin' in the boneyard."

"No side bets," I said. "Play the game."

"Give you two to one," he offered.

"No, no. Dammit, play dominoes!"

By now it was all the old gamblers could do not to dance, so they settled for snickering, tee-heeing, and nudging each other with happy elbows. Without having any idea, then or now, of how it happened, I suddenly was behind by 20 points. You might say Slim had broken my concentration.

Slim then played a deuce, did an exaggerated double take, and said, "Whoee, kiss me sweet, damn if that wasn't a *deuce* and I didn't know I had any! Hell, pal, you'd of won that five hundred dollars side bet 'cause I was *sure* there was a deuce in that boneyard. And here I was lookin' at it all the time!" The gamblers enjoyed new spasms of mirth while I wondered if Nevada imposed the death penalty for mass murder.

Going into what proved to be the first game's final hand, I led by 10 points — 245 to 235. How, I don't know.   55

"All you need's a nickel," Slim said. "I'll give you two to one and bet on you to win."   56

"No," I said, "No, no. . . . "   57

I searched my hand and the board but could find no com-   58
bination that would make the decisive 5 points. It just wasn't there. *Play it close to the vest. You don't have any fives and only one blank and, therefore, no repeater rocks should he make a nickel or a dime. Play small dominoes. Nothing that'll let him get 15. Try for a combination of twos and threes so you can make that damn 5 playing defense. Since you don't have any counting rocks, he must have a pisspot full. Stop the long bomb! Intercept!*

I played the six-three, the three-outward; there was a blank   59
at the other end of the board.

Slim said, "Uh-oh. What you thought was cookin' ain't on   60
the fire. Now, pal, I'll bet you three to two that *I* win."

"No," I said. "No, no. . . . "   61

While I tried to calculate what obvious blunder I'd made   62
that so dramatically had changed the odds, Amarillo Slim played the blank six. Now there was a six at one end and a three at the other and — *oh, outhouse mouse! I didn't have another six!* So I couldn't cut the six off. I didn't have a four, so I couldn't play on the spinner, which was the double four. The only three I had was the double three. And if I played it — and I had no choice, the rules said I *had* to play it; it was the only play I had — there would be 12 points on the board. And should Slim have the four-three and play it on the spinner, he'd make 15 and win. I cursed the gods for having given me a handful of sorry aces and funny-lookin' deuces and little else, in a hand where I would have been the prohibitive favorite given even minimal fives or blanks.

I put down the double trey, as the rules required. Sure   63
enough, Slim played his four-three on the spinner and made the 15 points that did me in. I sat there feeling like the guy who'd

had a three-lap lead in the Indianapolis 500 and then, fifty yards from the finish line, burned out his motor and died. *Five lousy points!*

"Hail, I just got lucky," Slim said. "You know, pal, if you'd taken that two to one bet on yourself, I'd owe you money. And that game could have went either way. . . . " 64

Round two. One of Slim's big-time gambler buddies stepped close to him and said, "Okay, you've had your fun, but you cut it a little close. Now settle down and play dominoes." Slim winked at him. 65

Amarillo Slim played no more open hands, though he resorted to physical tricks: holding a half dozen rocks easily in his big left hand (*you* try it); shuffling his own dominoes while I tried to concentrate on my next play; dropping a domino and permitting it to bounce a shade too long before snatching it back to say, "You didn't see that one, did you, pal?" *Now why,* I wondered, *did he want me to see that one?* 66

While the second game was still nip-and-tuck, tied at 130, Slim so loudly and frequently dreaded my "slappin' me with that ace-five" that I feared a trap. Did he truly fear the ace-five or . . . *no!* He wanted me to play it! Sure! He was using double-think on me! I paused so long, looking for the trap, that Slim said, "Ain't it your play, pal?" I ignored him continuing to look for the trap. *Just because you don't see it doesn't mean it isn't there.* 67

So, naturally, I did not play the ace-five. I would not have played it with a gun at my head. Instead, I played the ace-four. And no sooner had done so than I realized, sickeningly, that I'd made my biggest goof since agreeing to the match. Now I was left with the ace-five as the lone rock in my hand, while neither aces nor fives were available to be played on. I would be forced to visit the boneyard. Even worse, there *was* a four available on the board; had I played my ace-five and held onto four — *the last available in the suit, which meant that Slim could not possibly have cut it off* — then I would have guaranteed myself a cinch "Domino" and would have caught Slim with about 50 points in his hand. *Oh, you jackass!* My perceptions were arriving a flash 68 late; it was like a victim flying through the air while realizing that if he'd taken one half step to the right, the truck wouldn't have hit him.

I had flat let Slim talk me out of playing that damned ace-five, had been conned and flummoxed and sent off on a wild-goose chase looking for a trap that didn't exist. This had blinded me to what *was* there. I had reacted as a rank amateur, making the kind of blunder I had always relied on my kitchen-table opponents to make. 69

Amarillo Slim flashed a private grin that said, *We know who's gonna win now, don't we, pal? You dropped more than you can pick up, and it's all over.* It very shortly was. Slim dominoed on me for a crushing 55-point profit, making my blunder one of more than 100 points, considering what I properly should have extracted from him, and handily accounting for more than the margin by which he ultimately won: 250 to 165. 70

By now my game was in shambles. I worried not about winning that third game, or even hanging tough, for my pride and poise had deserted me and sneaked off to hide. I was concerned, instead, with not additionally making an ass of myself through the use of more sophomoric blunders. I imagined that the on-looking gamblers were rolling their eyes and giggling and perhaps whispering that I should take up paper dolls. Consequently, I played the last game as if blind, airless, and in a hurry to catch a bus. Slim won, 250 to 190, to complete his sweep. Don't ask me how, if you're talking about the play by play. 71

I counted out seven $20 bills and a lone ten-spot to Amarillo Slim, who scooped them off the table with a practiced hand while offering the other in tardy fellowship. "Pal," he said, "I really and truly enjoyed it." 72

I showed him the teeth through which I was lying and said, "Me, too, pal." Then I leaned in and said softly, only for his ears, "Slim, there are a hundred sixty-five spots in a deck of dominoes." Slim grinned and winked. 73

As a friend and I tried to leave the gambling arena by an invisible path, one of the chuckling leather-lunged old gamblers called out, "What did you boys beat ol' Slim out of?" 74

"About thirty minutes," I said. 75

• QUESTIONS ON MEANING AND PURPOSE •

1. What two processes does King analyze in "Shoot-out with Amarillo Slim"? Which is the directive kind of process analysis? Which is the informative kind? Where in the essay does his explanation of each one begin?
2. In paragraphs 3 and 4, what does King disclose about his own background? For what purpose does his essay give this information?
3. Amarillo Slim employs at least six winning strategies in his first game of dominoes with the author. Identify them.
4. In paragraph 21, King mentions being in "the midst of my tenth or eleventh drink." What purpose is served by including this offhand remark?

• QUESTIONS ON WRITING STRATEGY •

1. How does King organize his process analysis in paragraphs 5 through 9? Briefly sum up the point he makes in each paragraph.
2. Point to effective examples of time-markers in this essay. (Time-markers are discussed on page 179).
3. How does King build suspense in his account of the first domino game? At what point in the essay do you know who will win? On what evidence do you base your conviction? (See *Suspense* in Useful Terms.)
4. What examples of irony do you find in paragraphs 4, 10, 16, and 45? (See *Irony* in Useful Terms.)

• QUESTIONS ON LANGUAGE •
• AND VOCABULARY •

1. What is the meaning of the word "temporarily" in the first sentence? What is a "considerable" cowboy hat (paragraph 12)? What does King mean by "Walter Mitty stuff" (paragraph 26)?
2. A "grunt" is a lineman's helper or other manual worker. What does the author mean, at the end of paragraph 39, by "grunt gains"?
3. What does King's occasional use of direct quotation contribute to his essay?

4. Consult the dictionary if you don't know the meanings of the following: extraneous (paragraph 18); roistering, ineptitude (26); jugular (39); incessantly (41); prohibitive (62); sophomoric (71).
5. Point to the similes and metaphors related to football, baseball, and auto racing in paragraphs 38, 39, 40, 41, 46, and 63. (See *Figures of Speech* in Useful Terms.) What function do they serve?

• SUGGESTIONS FOR WRITING •

1. Write a brief explanation of how to play a game you know well. Set forth its rules, its object, any winning strategies you know, and explain its appeal to you.
2. Write an account of a personal experience that had an outcome you didn't expect. At the end, answer the reader's unspoken question: What did you learn from it?
3. Have you ever been outwitted by a shrewd gambler, con artist or hyper-salesman? If so, write an account of the process by which you were deceived.

· Jessica Mitford ·

JESSICA MITFORD was born in Batsford Mansion, England, in 1917, the daughter of Lord and Lady Redesdale. In her autobiography, *Daughters and Rebels* (1960), she tells how she received a genteel schooling at home, then as a young woman left England for America and became a naturalized citizen. She also has become one of her adopted country's most distinguished muckrakers. Exposing with her typewriter what she regards as corruption, abuse, and absurdity in our society, she has written *The American Way of Death* (1963); *Kind and Unusual Punishment: The Prison Business* (1973); and *Poison Penmanship* (1979), a collection of her articles from *The Atlantic, Harper's,* and other periodicals. She has recently published a second volume of her autobiography, *A Fine Old Madness* (1977).

Behind the Formaldehyde Curtain

The most famous (or notorious) thing Jessica Mitford has written is *The American Way of Death*. The following essay is a self-contained selection from it. In the book, Mitford criticizes the mortuary profession; and when her work landed on best-seller lists, the author was the subject of bitter attacks from funeral directors all over North America. To finish reading the essay, you will need a stable stomach as well as an awareness of Mitford's outrageous sense of humor. "Behind the Formaldehyde Curtain" is a clear, painstaking process analysis, written with masterly style.

The drama begins to unfold with the arrival of the corpse at   1
the mortuary.

Alas, poor Yorick! How surprised he would be to see how   2
his counterpart of today is whisked off to a funeral parlor and is
in short order sprayed, sliced, pierced, pickled, trussed,
trimmed, creamed, waxed, painted, rouged and neatly dressed

— transformed from a common corpse into a Beautiful Memory Picture. This process is known in the trade as embalming and restorative art, and is so universally employed in the United States and Canada that the funeral director does it routinely, without consulting corpse or kin. He regards as eccentric those few who are hardy enough to suggest that it might be dispensed with. Yet no law requires embalming, no religious doctrine commends it, nor is it dictated by considerations of health, sanitation, or even of personal daintiness. In no part of the world but in Northern America is it widely used. The purpose of embalming is to make the corpse presentable for viewing in a suitably costly container; and here too the funeral director routinely, without first consulting the family, prepares the body for public display.

Is all this legal? The processes to which a dead body may be   3
subjected are after all to some extent circumscribed by law. In most states, for instance, the signature of next of kin must be obtained before an autopsy may be performed, before the deceased may be cremated, before the body may be turned over to a medical school for research purposes; or such provision must be made in the decedent's will. In the case of embalming, no such permission is required nor is it ever sought. A textbook, *The Principles and Practices of Embalming*, comments on this: "There is some question regarding the legality of much that is done within the preparation room." The author points out that it would be most unusual for a responsible member of a bereaved family to instruct the mortician, in so many words, to "*embalm*" the body of a deceased relative. The very term "embalming" is so seldom used that the mortician must rely upon custom in the matter. The author concludes that unless the family specifies otherwise, the act of entrusting the body to the care of a funeral establishment carries with it an implied permission to go ahead and embalm.

Embalming is indeed a most extraordinary procedure, and   4
one must wonder at the docility of Americans who each year pay hundreds of millions of dollars for its perpetuation, blissfully ignorant of what it is all about, what is done, how it is done. Not one in ten thousand has any idea of what actually takes

place. Books on the subject are extremely hard to come by. They are not to be found in most libraries or bookshops.

In an era when huge television audiences watch surgical 5 operations in the comfort of their living rooms, when, thanks to the animated cartoon, the geography of the digestive system has become familiar territory even to the nursery school set, in a land where the satisfaction of curiosity about almost all matters is a national pastime, the secrecy surrounding embalming can, surely, hardly be attributed to the inherent gruesomeness of the subject. Custom in this regard has within this century suffered a complete reversal. In the early days of American embalming, when it was performed in the home of the deceased, it was almost mandatory for some relative to stay by the embalmer's side and witness the procedure. Today, family members who might wish to be in attendance would certainly be dissuaded by the funeral director. All others, except apprentices, are excluded by law from the preparation room.

A close look at what does actually take place may explain in 6 large measure the undertaker's intractable reticence concerning a procedure that has become his major *raison d'être*. Is it possible he fears that public information about embalming might lead patrons to wonder if they really want this service? If the funeral men are loath to discuss the subject outside the trade, the reader may, understandably, be equally loath to go on reading at this point. For those who have the stomach for it, let us part the formaldehyde curtain. . . .

The body is first laid out in the undertaker's morgue — or 7 rather, Mr. Jones is reposing in the preparation room — to be readied to bid the world farewell.

The preparation room in any of the better funeral establish- 8 ments has the tiled and sterile look of a surgery, and indeed the embalmer-restorative artist who does his chores there is beginning to adopt the term "dermasurgeon" (appropriately corrupted by some mortician-writers as "demi-surgeon") to describe his calling. His equipment, consisting of scalpels, scissors, augers, forceps, clamps, needles, pumps, tubes, bowls and basins, is crudely imitative of the surgeon's, as is his technique, acquired in a nine- or twelve-month post-high-school course in an embalming school. He is supplied by an advanced chemical industry with a bewildering array of fluids, sprays, pastes, oils, powders, creams, to fix or soften tissue, shrink or distend it as needed, dry it here, restore the moisture there. There are cosmetics, waxes and paints to fill and cover features, even plaster of Paris to replace entire limbs. There are ingenious aids to prop and stabilize the cadaver: a Vari-Pose Head Rest, the Edwards Arm and Hand Positioner, the Repose Block (to support the shoulders during the embalming), and the Throop Foot Positioner, which resembles an old-fashioned stocks.

Mr. John H. Eckels, president of the Eckels College of Mortuary Science, thus describes the first part of the embalming procedure: "In the hands of a skilled practitioner, this work may be done in a comparatively short time and without mutilating the body other than by slight incision — so slight that it scarcely would cause serious inconvenience if made upon a living person. It is necessary to remove the blood, and doing this not only helps in the disinfecting, but removes the principal cause of disfigurements due to discoloration."   9

Another textbook discusses the all-important time element: "The earlier this is done, the better, for every hour that elapses between death and embalming will add to the problems and complications encountered. . . . " Just how soon should one get going on the embalming? The author tells us, "On the basis of such scanty information made available to this profession through its rudimentary and haphazard system of technical research, we must conclude that the best results are to be obtained if the subject is embalmed before life is completely extinct — that is, before cellular death has occurred. In the average case, this would mean within an hour after somatic death." For those who feel that there is something a little rudimentary, not to say haphazard, about this advice, a comforting thought is offered by another writer. Speaking of fears entertained in early days of premature burial, he points out, "One of the effects of embalming by chemical injection, however, has been to dispel fears of live burial." How true; once the blood is removed, chances of live burial are indeed remote.   10

To return to Mr. Jones, the blood is drained out through the veins and replaced by embalming fluid pumped in through   11 the arteries. As noted in *The Principles and Practices of Embalming,* "every operator has a favorite injection and drainage point — a fact which becomes a handicap only if he fails or refuses to forsake his favorites when conditions demand it." Typical favorites are the carotid artery, femoral artery, jugular vein, subclavian vein. There are various choices of embalming fluid. If Flextone is used, it will produce a "mild, flexible rigidity. The skin retains a velvety softness, the tissues are rubbery and pliable. Ideal for women and children." It may be blended with B. and G. Products Company's Lyf-Lyk tint, which is guaranteed to reproduce "nature's own skin texture . . . the velvety appearance of living tissue." Suntone comes in three separate tints: Suntan; Special Cosmetic Tint, a pink shade "especially indicated for young female subjects"; and Regular Cosmetic Tint, moderately pink.

About three to six gallons of a dyed and perfumed solution   12
of formaldehyde, glycerin, borax, phenol, alcohol and water is soon circulating through Mr. Jones, whose mouth has been sewn together with a "needle directed upward between the upper lip and gum and brought out through the left nostril," with the corners raised slightly "for a more pleasant expression." If he should be bucktoothed, his teeth are cleaned with Bon Ami and coated with colorless nail polish. His eyes, meanwhile, are closed with flesh-tinted eye caps and eye cement.

The next step is to have at Mr. Jones with a thing called a   13
trocar. This is a long, hollow needle attached to a tube. It is jabbed into the abdomen, poked around the entrails and chest cavity, the contents of which are pumped out and replaced with "cavity fluid." This done, and the hole in the abdomen sewn up, Mr. Jones's face is heavily creamed (to protect the skin from burns which may be caused by leakage of the chemicals), and he is covered with a sheet and left unmolested for a while. But not for long — there is more, much more, in store for him. He has been embalmed, but not yet restored, and the best time to start the restorative work is eight to ten hours after embalming, when the tissues have become firm and dry.

The object of all this attention to the corpse, it must be   14
remembered, is to make it presentable for viewing in an attitude of healthy repose. "Our customs require the presentation of our

dead in the semblance of normality . . . unmarred by the ravages of illness, disease or mutilation," says Mr. J. Sheridan
Mayer in his *Restorative Art*. This is rather a large order since
few people die in the full bloom of health, unravaged by illness
and unmarked by some disfigurement. The funeral industry is
equal to the challenge: "In some cases the gruesome appearance
of a mutilated or disease-ridden subject may be quite discouraging. The task of restoration may seem impossible and shake the
confidence of the embalmer. This is the time for intestinal fortitude and determination. Once the formative work is begun
and affected tissues are cleaned or removed, all doubts of success
vanish. It is surprising and gratifying to discover the results
which may be obtained."

The embalmer, having allowed an appropriate interval to   15
elapse, returns to the attack, but now he brings into play the
skill and equipment of sculptor and cosmetician. Is a hand missing? Casting one in plaster of Paris is a simple matter. "For
replacement purposes, only a cast of the back of the hand is necessary; this is within the ability of the average operator and is
quite adequate." If a lip or two, a nose or an ear should be missing, the embalmer has at hand a variety of restorative waxes
with which to model replacements. Pores and skin texture are
simulated by stippling with a little brush, and over this cosmetics are laid on. Head off? Decapitation cases are rather routinely
handled. Ragged edges are trimmed, and head joined to torso
with a series of splints, wires and sutures. It is a good idea to
have a little something at the neck — a scarf or a high collar —
when time for viewing comes. Swollen mouth? Cut out tissue as
needed from inside the lips. If too much is removed, the surface
contour can easily be restored by padding with cotton. Swollen
necks and cheeks are reduced by removing tissue through vertical incisions made down each side of the neck. "When the
deceased is casketed, the pillow will hide the suture incisions . . .
as an extra precaution against leakage, the suture may be
painted with liquid sealer."

The opposite condition is more likely to present itself — that   16
of emaciation. His hypodermic syringe now loaded with massage cream, the embalmer seeks out and fills the hollowed and

sunken areas by injection. In this procedure the backs of the hands and fingers and the under-chin area should not be neglected.

Positioning the lips is a problem that recurrently challenges the ingenuity of the embalmer. Closed too tightly, they tend to give a stern, even disapproving expression. Ideally, embalmers feel, the lips should give the impression of being ever so slightly parted, the upper lip protruding slightly for a more youthful appearance. This takes some engineering, however, as the lips tend to drift apart. Lip drift can sometimes be remedied by pushing one or two straight pins through the inner margin of the lower lip and then inserting them between the two front upper teeth. If Mr. Jones happens to have no teeth, the pins can just as easily be anchored in his Armstrong Face Former and Denture Replacer. Another method to maintain lip closure is to dislocate the lower jaw, which is then held in its new position by a wire run through holes which have been drilled through the upper and lower jaws at the midline. As the French are fond of saying, *il faut souffrir pour être belle.*[1]

If Mr. Jones has died of jaundice, the embalming fluid will very likely turn him green. Does this deter the embalmer? Not if he has intestinal fortitude. Masking pastes and cosmetics are heavily laid on, burial garments and casket interiors are color-correlated with particular care, and Jones is displayed beneath rose-colored lights. Friends will say "How *well* he looks." Death by carbon monoxide, on the other hand, can be rather a good thing from the embalmer's viewpoint: "One advantage is the fact that this type of discoloration is an exaggerated form of a natural pink coloration." This is nice because the healthy glow is already present and needs but little attention.

The patching and filling completed, Mr. Jones is now shaved, washed and dressed. Cream-based cosmetic, available in pink, flesh, suntan, brunette and blond, is applied to his hands and face, his hair is shampooed and combed (and, in the case of Mrs. Jones, set), his hands manicured. For the horny-handed son of toil special care must be taken; cream should be

[1]You have to suffer to be beautiful.

applied to remove ingrained grime, and the nails cleaned. "If he were not in the habit of having them manicured in life, trimming and shaping is advised for better appearance — never questioned by kin."

Jones is now ready for casketing (this is the present partici-   20
ple of the verb "to casket"). In this operation his right shoulder should be depressed slightly "to turn the body a bit to the right and soften the appearance of lying flat on the back." Positioning the hands is a matter of importance, and special rubber positioning blocks may be used. The hands should be cupped slightly for a more lifelike, relaxed apearance. Proper placement of the body requires a delicate sense of balance. It should lie as high as possible in the casket, yet not so high that the lid, when lowered, will hit the nose. On the other hand, we are cautioned, placing the body too low "creates the impression that the body is in a box."

Jones is next wheeled into the appointed slumber room   21
where a few last touches may be added — his favorite pipe placed in his hand or, if he was a great reader, a book propped into position. (In the case of little Master Jones a Teddy bear may be clutched.) Here he will hold open house for a few days, visiting hours 10 A.M. to 9 P.M.

All now being in readiness, the funeral director calls a staff   22
conference to make sure that each assistant knows his precise duties. Mr. Wilber Kriege writes: "This makes your staff feel that they are a part of the team, with a definite assignment that must be properly carried out if the whole plan is to succeed. You never heard of a football coach who failed to talk to his entire team before they go on the field. They have drilled on the plays they are to execute for hours and days, and yet the successful coach knows the importance of making even the bench-warming third-string substitute feel that he is important if the game is to be won." The winning of *this* game is predicated upon glass-smooth handling of the logistics. The funeral director has notified the pallbearers whose names were furnished by the family, has arranged for the presence of clergyman, organist, and soloist, has provided transportation for everybody, has organized and listed the flowers sent by friends. In *Psychology of Funeral Service* Mr. Edward A. Martin points out: "He may not

always do as much as the family thinks he is doing, but it is his helpful guidance that they appreciate in knowing they are proceeding as they should. . . . The important thing is how well his services can be used to make the family believe they are giving unlimited expression to their own sentiment."

The religious service may be held in a church or in the chapel of the funeral home; the funeral director vastly prefers the latter arrangement, for not only is it more convenient for him but it affords him the opportunity to show off his beautiful facilities to the gathered mourners. After the clergyman has had his say, the mourners queue up to file past the casket for a last look at the deceased. The family is *never* asked whether they want an open-casket ceremony; in the absence of their instruction to the contrary, this is taken for granted. Consequently well over 90 per cent of all American funerals feature the open casket — a custom unknown in other parts of the world. Foreigners are astonished by it. An English woman living in San Francisco described her reaction in a letter to the writer: 23

> I myself have attended only one funeral here — that of an elderly fellow worker of mine. After the service I could not understand why everyone was walking towards the coffin (sorry, I mean casket), but thought I had better follow the crowd. It shook me rigid to get there and find the casket open and poor old Oscar lying there in his brown tweed suit, wearing a suntan makeup and just the wrong shade of lipstick. If I had not been extremely fond of the old boy, I have a horrible feeling that I might have giggled. Then and there I decided that I could never face another American funeral — even dead.

The casket (which has been resting throughout the service on a Classic Beauty Ultra Metal Casket Bier) is now transferred by a hydraulically operated device called Porto-Lift to a balloon-tired, Glide Easy casket carriage which will wheel it to yet another conveyance, the Cadillac Funeral Coach. This may be lavender, cream, light green — anything but black. Interiors, of course, are color-correlated, "for the man who cannot stop short of perfection." 24

At graveside, the casket is lowered into the earth. This office, once the prerogative of friends of the deceased, is now per- 25 formed by a patented mechanical lowering device. A "Lifetime Green" artificial grass mat is at the ready to conceal the sere earth, and overhead, to conceal the sky, is a portable Steril Chapel Tent ("resists the intense heat and humidity of summer and the terrific storms of winter . . . available in Silver Grey, Rose or Evergreen"). Now is the time for the ritual scattering of earth over the coffin, as the solemn words "earth to earth, ashes to ashes, dust to dust" are pronounced by the officiating cleric. This can today be accomplished "with a mere flick of the wrist with the Gordon Leak-Proof Earth Dispenser. No grasping of a handful of dirt, no soiled fingers. Simple, dignified, beautiful, reverent! The modern way!" The Gordon Earth Dispenser (at $5) is of nickel-plated brass construction. It is not only "attractive to the eye and long wearing"; it is also "one of the 'tools' for building better public relations" if presented as "an appropriate non-commercial gift" to the clergyman. It is shaped something like a saltshaker.

Untouched by human hand, the coffin and the earth are now united.   26

It is in the function of directing the participants through this maze of gadgetry that the funeral director has assigned to himself his relatively new role of "grief therapist." He has relieved the family of every detail, he has revamped the corpse to look like a living doll, he has arranged for it to nap for a few days in a slumber room, he has put on a well-oiled performance in which the concept of *death* has played no part whatsoever — unless it was inconsiderately mentioned by the clergyman who conducted the religious service. He has done everything in his power to make the funeral a real pleasure for everybody concerned. He and his team have given their all to score an upset victory over death.   27

· QUESTIONS ON MEANING AND PURPOSE ·

1. What was your emotional response to this essay? Can you analyze your feelings?

2. To what does the author attribute the secrecy that surrounds the process of embalming?
3. What, according to Mitford, is the mortician's purpose? What common obstacles to fulfilling it must be surmounted?
4. What do you understand from Mitford's remark in paragraph 10, on dispelling fears of live burial: "How true; once the blood is removed chances of live burial are indeed remote"?
5. Do you find any implied purpose in this essay? Does Mitford seem primarily out to rake muck, or does she offer any positive suggestions to Americans?

• QUESTIONS ON WRITING STRATEGY •

1. What is Mitford's tone? (See *Tone* in Useful Terms.) In her opening two paragraphs, exactly what shows her attitude toward her subject?
2. Why do you think Mitford goes into so much grisly detail? How does it serve her purpose?
3. What is the effect of calling the body Mr. Jones (or Master Jones)?
4. Paragraph by paragraph, what time-markers does the author employ? (If you need a refresher on this point, see the discussion of time-markers on page 179.)
5. Into what stages has the author divided the embalming process?
6. To whom does Mitford address her process analysis? How do you know she isn't writing for an audience of professional morticians?
7. Consider one of the quotations from the journals and textbooks of professionals and explain how it serves the author's general purpose.
8. Of what value to the essay is the letter from the English woman in San Francisco (paragraph 23)?

• QUESTIONS ON LANGUAGE •
• AND VOCABULARY •

1. Explain the allusion to Yorick in paragraph 2. (See *Allusion* in Useful Terms.)
2. What irony do you find in Mitford's statement in paragraph 7, "The body is first laid out in the morgue — or rather, Mr. Jones is reposing in the preparation room"? Pick out any other words or phrases in the essay that seem ironic. (See *Irony* in Useful Terms.) Comment especially on those you find in the essay's last two sentences.

3. Why is it useful to Mitford's purpose that she cites the brand names of morticians' equipment and supplies (the Edwards Arm and Hand Positioner, Lyf-Lyk Tint)? List all the brand names in the essay that are memorable.

4. Define counterpart (paragraph 2); circumscribed, autopsy, cremated, decedent, bereaved (3); docility, perpetuation (4); inherent, mandatory (5); intractable, reticence, *raison d'etre*, formaldehyde (6); "dermasurgeon," augers, forceps, distend, stocks (8); somatic (10); carotid artery, femoral artery, jugular vein, subclavian vein, pliable (11); glycerin, borax, phenol, bucktoothed (12); trocar, entrails (13); stippling, suture (15); emaciation (16); jaundice (18); predicated (22); queue (23); hydraulically (24); cleric (25); therapist (27).

• SUGGESTIONS FOR WRITING •

1. Defend the ritual of the American funeral, or of the mortician's profession, against Mitford's sarcastic attack.

2. Compare and contrast the custom of embalming the corpse for display, as described by Mitford, with a possible alternative way of dealing with the dead.

3. With the aid of the *Readers' Guide to Periodical Literature*, find information about the recent phenomenon of quick-freezing the dead. Set forth this process, including its hoped-for result of reviving the corpses in the far future.

4. Analyze some other process whose operations may not be familiar to everyone. (Have you ever held a job, or helped out in a family business, that has taken you behind the scenes? How is fast food prepared? How are cars serviced? How is a baby sat? How is a house constructed?) Detail it step by step in an essay that includes time-markers.

· Don Ethan Miller ·

DON ETHAN MILLER, born in 1947, has been studying martial arts for the past twenty years, and for the past decade has taught T'ai Chi, self-defense, and stress reduction at places including hospitals, Dartmouth and Emerson Colleges, Clark University, and the Joy of Movement Center in Boston. The author of *Body Mind: The Whole Person Health Book*, Miller is a frequent contributor to *The Atlantic*, *Vogue*, and *The Village Voice*. *The Book of Jargon: An Essential Guide to the Inside Languages of Today* is to be published in 1982.

How the Bare Hand Passes Through the Bricks

"How the Bare Hand Passes Through the Bricks" (editors' title) has been adapted from an essay by Don Ethan Miller that appeared in *The Atlantic* in September 1980. In it, Miller offers a fascinating glimpse into a mystery he began to fathom only after years of training. (Warning: Without such years of training, don't try to break bricks!) In the first part of his essay, Miller tells of a frustrating experience that we need to know to appreciate the second part — a process analysis.

In the summer of 1967, I was enrolled as an exchange student from Dartmouth at the University of Leningrad, USSR. One evening, at a talent show presented by the foreign students, I gave a karate demonstration to a large audience of Russian students, professors, and invited friends. I had been studying karate in the States for several years and was fairly proficient at it, though some distance from the black belt level I was to attain three years later. After demonstrating the classic *kata*, or choreographed forms, and delivering a brief dissertation on the art, the climax of my act was to break a brick with my bare hand — a skill I had acquired a year before, and had repeated dozens of times.

My Russian friends proudly produced a construction brick 2
easily twice the size and three times the weight of the baked red
bricks I was accustomed to splitting back home. Undaunted, I
set it precisely to bridge the space between a pair of similar
bricks laid parallel on the stage floor. I knelt, and held one end
of the brick slightly off the base with my left hand. Rising slightly from my kneeling position, I inhaled, raised my right hand in
a short arc up to shoulder level, and then, yelling sharply,
brought my clenched fist down with the full force of my body
behind it, tightening all my muscles just at the moment of impact to transmit the force into the stone. Nothing happened. I
felt a dull pain in the base of my hand, and the shock wave of
the blow traveled back up my arm and shoulder. No matter;
this sometimes happens if the blow is not exactly right. I immediately reset the oversize brick and struck down again, quickly, absolutely as hard as I could. But again, it merely smacked
into the base brick and stopped.

I struck again and again, ten or fifteen violent, staccato 3
blows with my right hand, until the flesh broke and the blood
spurted out into the audience. Then I switched to my uninjured
left hand, hammering down with every particle of strength I
possessed: the brick remained indestructible. I was angry,
charged, determined; my adrenaline was flowing; I was hitting
the thing hard enough, it seemed, to go through steel. But the
Russian brick could not be broken.

After a long time, and only when both my hands were 4
smashed and bloody, and my friends in the wings urged me to
let the rest of the show continue, did I finally give up. I said
something by way of apology to the audience, walked off stage,
changed out of my karate uniform into my street clothes, and
walked alone and sullen into the Leningrad night air.

Across the street from the university hall was a construction 5
site, and there, barely visible in the half-light from a distant
streetlamp, lay a large pile of the very same bricks. I crossed the
street and picked one up. Slowly I turned it over in my battered
hands and then angrily hurled it to the ground — where it broke
on the edge of another brick! I knelt down, grabbed another
brick, and half hit, half threw it against two others from close

range; this one broke as well. I gathered up an armful of fresh bricks and hurried back inside the auditorium. Over the objections of several performers, I strode onstage and briskly set up the bricks. "Watch this," I said to the audience, in English. I inhaled, raised my fist, and struck downward with a confident yell. The brick didn't break!

I immediately hit it again: nothing. Two or three more shots in as many seconds, and I realized that to break the brick in this manner was truly impossible. Bewildered and humiliated after this new defeat, I sat back on my heels and closed my eyes — more to avoid looking out at the audience than anything else. I took a deep breath and relaxed my muscles. I forgot about the brick. I forgot the pain in my hands. White clouds drifted across a purple sky within my mental field of vision. I was aware of the wind of my own breathing. In a few seconds I had almost completely forgotten where I was and what I was "supposed" to be doing.

Just at that moment I opened my eyes, gently cradled the brick with my left hand, and — without tension, without haste, without any real effort — came down smoothly with my right hand, which *passed right through the brick*, without any sensation of impact.

I had, in fact, broken the brick with my hand, but the feeling was much more that it had "parted" in response to the completely new kind of action I had generated. I held up the two halves of the severed brick for the audience to see, but they had already seen and were on their feet, clapping and cheering wildly. The Russians are a people who know a lot about suffering and transcendence, and though I'm sure they had no idea of the particulars of my breakthrough, they recognized a victory of the spirit over insensate matter. I felt sure it was this victory, rather than the feat itself, that they were applauding.

There *are* ways to make the magic work, with some consistency. I have learned, over the course of my twenty-year odyssey through the martial arts, that the capacity of the human mind to coordinate and focus physiological energy is infinitely greater than the standard assumptions of biology and physics would lead us to believe. I have become convinced that there is something, a spirit or vital force, which the Japanese call *ki* and the Chinese *ch'i*, which is universal in origin yet manifest uniquely in every living creature; which can be cultivated and increased through certain types of practice. And, since that first night in Leningrad, I have acquired a reliable method for entering that particular state of effortless accomplishment.

Thus, when I now approach a stack of three two-inch cinder blocks to attempt a breaking feat, I do not set myself to "try hard," or to summon up all my strength. Instead I relax, sinking my awareness into my belly and legs, feeling my connection with the ground. I breathe deeply, mentally directing the breath through my torso, legs, and arms. I imagine a line of force coming up from the ground through my legs, down one arm, and out through an acupuncture point at the base of my palm, through the stone slabs, and down again into the ground, penetrating to the center of the earth. I do not focus any attention on the objects to be broken. Although when I am lifting or holding them in a normal state of consciousness the blocks seem tremendously dense, heavy, and hard, in the course of my one- or two-minute preparation their reality seems to change, as indeed the reality of the whole situation changes. I am no longer a thirty-two-year-old American writer in basketball sneakers doing strange breathing exercises in his suburban back yard in front of a pile of red patio blocks: I am a spiritual traveler, making the necessary preparations for a journey to a different world.

I know that I am in the other "zone" by certain signs: my breathing takes on a deep, raspy, unearthly tone; my vision changes, such that tiny pebbles on the ground appear huge, like asteroids; my body feels denser, yet at the same time light and free of tension. I feel that what I am doing is extremely important, that the attention of the entire universe is focused upon me. When I make my final approach to the bricks, if I regard them at all they seem light, airy, and friendly; they do not have the insistent inner drive in them that I do.

I do not hit the bricks; I do not break them. Rather, I take a deep breath, hold it for half a second, then *release* suddenly but smoothly, focusing on the energy line and allowing my arm to express it. My palm passes right through the place where the blocks were, but they have apparently parted just before I get there, and there is no sensation of impact, no shock wave, no pain. Whoever is watching usually applauds and congratulates me, but in the zone there is nothing to be congratulated for and it seems silly. One is merely surprised to realize how easy such things are if one is in the correct body–mind state. Gradually, one comes out of it, one tries to explain, but the essence of it is beyond the reach of words. Hours later, what remains is not the sense of destructive power but the feeling of attunement with universal forces, of identification with the mysterious but very real power of life itself. Passing through the bricks is only a way of entering another realm.

The real value of martial arts study, in other words, has 13 nothing to do with physical feats such as brick-breaking; in fact, it is not even primarily concerned with fighting. In our modern technologized society, it would be easier to buy a gun, or carry a can of mace. Their real value lies in what the martial arts tell us about ourselves: that we can be much more than we are now; that we have no need of fear; and that our capacities for energy, awareness, courage, and compassion are far greater than we have been led to believe. They tell us that all our personal limits — and by extension, our destructive social and historical patterns — can be transcended. Beginning with the next breath, drawn deeply.

• QUESTIONS ON MEANING AND PURPOSE •

1. What went wrong during Miller's demonstration for the Russian students in 1967? How do you account for his ultimate success on that occasion?
2. Describe the author's view of the relationship between mind and body.
3. In what way does "reality" change for Miller during the process?

4. Of what value to Miller is his ability to break bricks with his hand?

· QUESTIONS ON WRITING STRATEGY ·

1. What are the steps in the process by which Miller breaks bricks?
2. What special difficulties confront an author who sets out to analyze, as Miller does, a skill that took twenty years to master?
3. If Miller had written his essay for fellow martial artists instead of for *Atlantic* readers, what would you expect him to have discussed in greater detail?

· QUESTIONS ON LANGUAGE ·
· AND VOCABULARY ·

1. Look up the definitions of the following words if you are not familiar with them: proficient, choreographed, dissertation (paragraph 1); undaunted (2); staccato, indestructible, adrenaline (3); transcendence, insensate (8); odyssey, manifest (9); acupuncture (10); asteroids (11); attunement (12); transcended (13).
2. With what aspect of his subject does Miller deal in paragraphs 10 and 11? How do you account for the fact that, in an essay largely devoid of figurative language, it is these two paragraphs that contain simile, metaphor, and personification? (See *Figures of Speech* in Useful Terms.)

· SUGGESTIONS FOR WRITING ·

1. In a paragraph or two, recount how you succeeded at some task on your second try.
2. Write an essay in which you explain step by step how to learn a difficult physical skill: pitching a fastball, eating with chopsticks, swimming the butterfly stroke, manipulating a hang glider, or any other feat you care to analyze.

· Patrice Boyer ·

PATRICE BOYER was born in 1951. She earned a B. A. from the University of Pennsylvania in 1973 and an M. A. from the University of Manchester (England) in 1974. She has worked as a developmental editor of college textbooks and, more recently, as an account executive for a public relations firm.

How to Hype Hot Dogs

"How to Hype Hot Dogs" shows you how the P. R. people went about refurbishing the lowly hot dog's tarnished image. What Boyer's essay reveals about the fine art of media manipulation ensures that, when you bite into your next hot dog, you'll know the reason why.

The hot dog has an image problem. In an age of Perrier and granola, daily jogging and aerobic dance, it stands accused of sinning against nutrition and health. The U. S. government cited the hot dog as an offender in bad school-lunch planning. Consumer groups listed it among the "terrible ten" foods and even called it the "missile of death." 1

With all the negative publicity, consumers naturally stopped eating so many hot dogs. And after three consecutive years of declining sales, the hot dog makers and their suppliers began to panic. It was time, they decided, to put out a little publicity of their own. 2

More hot dog advertisements were not the answer. Advertising speaks only for a particular brand and can deliver only the simplest of messages: kids love hot dogs, they're convenient, they're economical. The hot dog association, however, had more complex nutritional issues to address for the entire industry: Hot dogs contain saturated fat, to be sure, but so does steak. They contain salt, but you don't salt hot dogs. And the sodium nitrite used to preserve them does not, as was once 3

223

maintained, cause cancer, whereas it does allow us to take them on picnics without worrying about spoilage.

What was needed was a varied approach that would convey   4
these complex but complementary messages to a wide and diverse audience. What was needed was a subtle approach that would attract people's attention without seeming to be prompted by the vested interest of a commercial sponsor. What was needed was a public relations campaign.

Agencies specializing in public relations, or P. R. for short,   5
take on clients that need to convey a persuasive message indirectly — not through paid advertising but by making it so interesting that newspaper editors and television producers will want to deliver it themselves. The idea — and it works — is that the public will see a disinterested party such as a food writer or a talk-show host as objective and thus convincing.

When the hot dog association approached a big public rela-   6
tions agency, the agency welcomed the job. It could stage a full-scale national promotion featuring hot dogs in general rather than a specific brand. And all it had to do, really, was to convince people that what they already liked was good for them. The way the public relations people leaped to the hot dog's aid illustrates in part how P. R. functions.

The first step was to create a comprehensive plan. Not   7
unlike an army's battle strategists, the P. R. people needed to know where to position their artillery, whom to aim it at, and when to fire. They started by consulting a study of the people who consume the 19 billion hot dogs eaten in America every year. Then they engaged in some brainstorming to outline the elements of the campaign:

The objective: Sell more hot dogs.

The message: Hot dogs are wholesome and nutritious.

The audiences: Those who buy (consumers) and those who influence buying (opinion leaders).

The strategies: Obtain unassailable data on hot dog nutrition, use nutrition experts to deliver those data to opinion leaders, and use attractive spokespeople to deliver a simplified version of the data to consumers.

The war was on to defuse the hot dog's enemies. The P. R. 8
people sent fact sheets on hot dog ingredients, technology, and
nutrition to opinion leaders — consumerists, heads of university
nutrition departments, and government agencies. Then they
began to take advantage of the close relation between themselves and the communications media, especially newspapers
and television. The P. R. people rely on the media to broadcast
their message, but the media also benefit, for the information
they receive makes their job of finding and reporting the news
that much easier. As a first step in involving the media, the P. R.
people sent newspaper food editors a kit containing hot dog
facts, photographs, and recipes. Many welcomed the information and printed it for over 3 million pairs of hungry eyes. But
other editors remained skeptical. Bigger artillery had to be
brought up.

Nothing commands greater respect than a major computer 9
study, particularly when its architects and interpreters are a nutrition authority and a prestigious university like Michigan
State. Into the computer went an analysis of every mouthful of
food consumed for seven days by families who ate hot dogs. Out
came lists of macronutrients and percentages of daily requirements — in short, scientific proof that hot dogs contribute
to the diet.

The P. R. people had to reach two audiences with their new 10
information — one expert, the other not — and for that they
needed two types of spokesperson. The nutrition authority in
charge of the computer study handled the heavies. He took his
show, "Hot Dog U," on the road, reaching opinion leaders
through seminars, scholarly papers, and an occasional television appearance.

For the less sophisticated audience, the P. R. people loosed 11
their imaginations. Why not have sports "hotdoggers," star
athletes with flash and style, deliver the nutrition message to
consumers? Not only would the fans respect the opinions of
their heroes, but they would also associate hot dogs with strong,
healthy bodies.

Thus was born the All-American Hotdogger Team. The 12
P. R. people talked it up to the media people, and before long

San Diegoans, Denverites, and Detroiters were waking to the sight of tennis sensation Andrea Jaeger cooking hot dogs on the local morning talk show or first-baseman Pete Rose declaring his support for the all-American food. Sports pages of large-circulation newspapers began running articles on basketball comedian Meadowlark Lemon's preference for hot dogs at sporting events and soccer whiz Ricky Davis's subsistence on hot dogs while in training. The P. R. agency bought the athletes' time, of course, but the 50 million television viewers and newspaper readers didn't know that. Instead, they heard a welcome message about a favorite food from credible sources.

At this stage the P. R. people also intensified their blitz of 13
newspaper food editors by researching, writing, and producing articles for the newspapers to use as their own. One article presented a full-color page of photographs and recipes for a hot dog do-it-yourself party. Adapting the salad bar concept to hot dogs, the article suggested over thirty toppings for a hot dog buffet, many reflecting regional preferences such as New York's stewed onions and California's sprouts and avocados. Since few newspapers can afford to produce their own color photographs, most of the food editors used the free materials, sending forth the message of hot dog fun and nutrition to another 6 million people. Another prepared article featured photographs and quotations from celebrities on how they top their hot dogs: Zsa Zsa Gabor with mustard, Jose Greco with garlic, and Gary Coleman with the works. Rarely would a newspaper writer have the time for this kind of research — or the perseverance to endure the countless slamming phones.

Besides sending their spokespeople and information kits to 14
the media, the P. R. people also staged events designed to attract media attention. Perhaps the most spectacular was the presentation of the Mile-Long Hot Dog (actually, a mile of hot dog links) at a ragtime festival in St. Louis, along the banks of the Mississippi. Capitalizing on the connection between America's native music and America's native food (the hot dog was introduced in St. Louis in 1907), the P. R. people shot a short newsfilm as the links were unwound against a background of riverboats and

old-time music. Several television stations sent their Action-Cam units for live coverage on the 6 o'clock news. In addition, the newsfilm went to other television news departments as filler material and was subsequently broadcast to 19 million viewers.

The P. R. people don't know precisely how many people have taken their message to the dinner table. Because public relations does not buy editorial space or broadcast time, it loses some control over the content of its message and where and when it appears, if it appears at all. (Some of the sports hotdoggers forgot to mention hot dogs on their television appearances.) What public relations loses in control, however, it gains in credibility. It's safe to say that some former enemies have been silenced or even converted. And consumers now have their own ammunition to defend their taste preferences. But the next time you see a television newsclip of a hot dog eating contest or read a recipe for butterflied hot dogs, you'll know that the war is still going on.

15

• QUESTIONS ON MEANING AND PURPOSE •

1. According to Boyer, in what specific ways are the media useful to the people hyping hot dogs?
2. Does Boyer's essay raise any questions in your mind about the ethical implications of hyping hot dogs? About the role of P. R. in contemporary life?
3. In a sentence, how would you sum up Boyer's main purpose in writing this essay?

• QUESTIONS ON WRITING STRATEGY •

1. What function do the first four paragraphs of Boyer's essay perform? What is the function of any good introduction? (See *Introduction* in Useful Terms.)
2. What does the writer's use of the third person rather than the first person point of view contribute to the tone of her essay? (See *Point of View* and *Tone* in Useful Terms.)

· QUESTIONS ON LANGUAGE ·
· AND VOCABULARY ·

1. Comment on the writer's use of the phrase "image problem" in the first paragraph. Who or what was responsible for the fact that hot dogs had a bad image?
2. What distinction does Boyer draw between public relations and advertising?

· SUGGESTIONS FOR WRITING ·

1. Write a paragraph in which you enumerate the steps you would take if you were organizing an election campaign for a friend, or were selling a product you had invented.
2. People, as well as products, develop images and image problems. Citing examples from your reading or your experience, comment in a brief essay on the process by which a person acquires his image. (Entertainers, politicians, jet setters, and professional athletes offer perhaps the easiest examples.)

POSTSCRIPT ON PROCESS

Aiming for an Audience

Sometimes a writer knows so much about a subject that she must choose with care which details to use in her essay. Equally important is the necessity of avoiding jargon that the reading audience will not understand, as Patrice Boyer discovered when she began to analyze the hot dog P. R. campaign.

Reaching my audience was my main concern in writing this 1 essay. I had to take a complicated process and make its steps intelligible to readers who knew nothing about it. That meant identifying the most prominent points and explaining the steps with familiar language and the right amount of detail.

Thinking the essay through was as difficult as writing it. I 2 wanted to explain the main steps in the general process of a public relations campaign using the hot dog campaign to illustrate each step. But what were the steps? After an entire year managing the hot dog P. R. campaign, I was a walking reference book on hot dogs and had a storehouse of anecdotes about the campaign. I knew the profiles of heavy, moderate, and light hot dog consumers, the names and circulations of every newspaper that ran my articles, and the problems involved in transporting a mile-long hot dog from Chicago to St. Louis. I knew trivia but not theory, not the general concepts underlying public relations. I had to sort the elements of the hot dog campaign into groups in order to arrive at some basic P. R. concepts: it can help sell products, it does so through third-party endorsement, it relies on the media, it differs from advertising in significant ways.

Once I had the theory, the steps fell into place; but now *I* 3 had to fill in details. Again, that meant focusing on my audience. Since I was writing for people with little or no knowledge of public relations, I had to avoid jargon and include only information that would advance the step-by-step analysis.

Avoiding jargon required that I keep clear of the shorthand   4
I used with my coworkers: "The bookers can't get a TV in At-lanta for the media rep. The pitch letters didn't work, so I'm putting out a press and photo call." Though efficient in the of-fice, such language would do little for people with no experience in the field. It had to be recast, and the few terms that were un-avoidable — like "opinion leaders" — had to be defined.

Similarly, I had to keep explanations straightforward. Most   5
of my explanations were much too involved the first time around because I knew so much more about the subject than I needed to communicate. I had to check myself frequently. Rath-er than trying to rattle off the entire essay, I wrote it in small sections. Each day I'd write several paragraphs and put my work away. The next day I'd read the work of the day before, chang-ing what seemed unnecessarily involved or simply unnecessary.

In this manner I plodded along. If it sounds less than in-   6
spired, it was. I discovered, however, that logical development comes before all else in process analysis. What I sacrificed in in-teresting but irrelevant anecdotes (the TV crews showed up be-fore the mile-long hot dog was tied together; Pete Rose eats two hot dogs in one bun), I gained in clarity of explanation. And since that was my goal, I finished my final revision and celebrated with a chili dog.

· ADDITIONAL WRITING TOPICS ·
PROCESS ANALYSIS

1. Write a *directive* process analysis (a "how to" essay) in which, drawing on your own knowledge, you instruct someone in doing or making something. Divide the process into steps and be sure to detail each step thoroughly. Some possible subjects (any of which may be modified or narrowed with the approval of your instructor):

    How to enlist people's confidence
    How to bake bread
    How to meditate
    How to teach a child to swim
    How to select a science fiction novel
    How to make money playing football pools
    How to drive a car
    How to prepare yourself to take an intelligence test
    How to catch fish
    How to tell a fish story
    How to compose a photograph
    How to judge cattle
    How to buy a used motorcycle
    How to enjoy an opera
    How to organize your own rock group
    How to eat an artichoke
    How to groom a horse
    How to bellydance
    How to make a movie
    How to build (or fly) kites
    How to start lifting weights
    How to aid a person who is choking
    How to behave on a first date
    How to be happy

    Or, if you don't like any of those topics, what else do you know that others might care to learn from you?

2. Step by step, working in chronological order, write a careful *informative* analysis of any one of the following processes. (This is

not to be a "how to" essay, but an essay that explains how something happens.) Make use of description wherever necessary, and be sure to include frequent time-markers. If one of these topics should give you a better idea for a paper, discuss your choice of subject with your instructor.

How a student is processed during orientation or registration
How you found living quarters
How you decided what to major in
How a professional umpire (or an insurance underwriter, or some other professional) does his or her job
How an amplifier works
How a political candidate runs for office
How a fire company responds to a fire
How birds teach their young (or some other process in the natural world: how sharks feed, how a snake swallows an egg)
How the Appalachian Trail was blazed
How a Rubik's cube functions (or how it drives people crazy)
How policemen control crowds
How people usually make up their minds when shopping for new cars (or new clothes)
How an idea has come to be accepted

3. Write a directive process analysis in which you use a light tone. Although you do not take your subject in deadly earnest, your humor will probably be effective only if you take the method of process analysis seriously. Make clear each stage of the process and explain it in sufficient detail.

How to get through the month of November (or March)
How to flunk out of college swiftly and efficiently
How to sleep through a class with open eyes
How to outwit a pinball machine
How to choose a mate
How to pass through a solid wall without making a hole in it (See Don Ethan Miller's essay in this chapter for suggestions.)

· 6 ·

DIVISION AND
CLASSIFICATION

Slicing into Parts, Sorting into Kinds

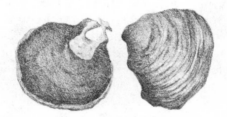

· THE METHODS ·

If you have read the previous chapter about process analysis, you'll recall that *division* (also called *analysis*) is the separation of something into its parts. It is the method by which a chemist breaks down an unfamiliar substance into its components; and as a method in writing, *division* is often used to explain some action or operation. A writer may divide such a subject into its chronological stages: telling us step by step how a fertilized human egg grows, or how the Nielsen Company determines the popularity of a TV show, or how a professional gambler goes about psyching out an opponent.

Think of the method of division, then, as an instrument ready to use and gleaming in your hand. With its aid, you can slice up a large and complicated subject into smaller parts that

233

you more easily can deal with — and that your reader more readily can grasp. At this point, kindly underline the following two sentences, because they're essential. You can apply the method of division not only to processes, but also to other subjects. In so doing, you take a thing and — much as you do with a process — separate it into its component parts. If, for example, your subject were fried chicken (the end result, not the process of cooking that Jim Villas recounts in his essay on page 182), you could divide it into breast, thighs, wings, drumsticks, and the part that goes over the fence last; and you could write an essay discussing each part and its respective merits. In their guidebook *New York on $20 a Day*, Joan Hamburg and Norma Ketay divide the city into sections: Midtown East, Midtown West, Pennsylvania Station and Chelsea, Little Italy, and so on. In reality, New York is not a distinctly different place from one street to the next; but by dividing New York into neighborhoods, the writers have organized their book in a way that will help the reader-tourist more easily take in the city's complicated geography.

Useful for tangible things such as chicken and cities, the method of division may suit a more abstract subject as well. In "I Want a Wife," an essay in this chapter, Judy Syfers divides the role of a wife into its various functions or services. In an essay called "Teacher," Robert Francis divides the knowledge of poetry he imparts to his class into six pie sections. The first slice is what he told his students that they knew already.

> The second slice is what I told them that they could have found out just as well or better from books. What, for instance, is a sestina?
> The third slice is what I told them that they refused to accept. I could see it on their faces, and later I saw the evidence in their writing.
> The fourth slice is what I told them that they were willing to accept and may have thought they accepted but couldn't accept since they couldn't fully understand. This also I saw in their faces and in their work. Here, no doubt, I was mostly to blame.
> The fifth slice is what I told them that they discounted as whimsey or something simply to fill up time. After all, I was being paid to talk.

> The sixth slice is what I didn't tell them, for I didn't try to
> tell them all I knew. Deliberately I kept back something—a
> few professional secrets, a magic formula or two.[1]

There are always multiple ways to divide a subject, just as there
are many ways to slice a pie. Francis could have divided his
knowledge of poetry into knowledge of English poetry, knowledge of American poetry, and so forth; or the writers of the
New York guidebook could have divided the city into historic
landmarks, centers of entertainment, shopping districts, and so
on. (Incidentally, Robert Francis's account of slicing his pie is
also an *analogy*, a method of illustrating a difficult idea in simple
terms. See Chapter 7 for more examples.)

The twin to division is the method of *classification*, the sorting out of things into categories. The method of classification is
familiar to us from everyday life. Preparing to can peaches, we
might begin by classifying the peaches on hand into three
groups: firm, soft, and rotten. In classification, your subject is a
number of things. Say, for instance, you're going to write an
essay explaining that people have widely different sleep habits.
Your subject is people as sleepers; and you might classify them
into late sleepers, mid-morning sleepers, and early risers.

Like division, classification is done for a purpose. In the case
of the peaches, we would sort them out in order to see which to
can at once, which to can later, and which to throw away. Writers, too, classify things for reasons. In their guide to New York,
Hamburg and Ketay arrange their discussion of the city's low-
priced hotels into categories: Rooms for Singles and Students,
Rooms for Families, Rooms for Servicemen, and Rooms for
General Occupancy. Their purpose is to match up the visitor
with a suitable kind of room. Their subject, remember, is multiple: hundreds of hotels. This is how you can tell classification
from division. In division, your subject is a *single* thing: one pie,
one city. If you were applying the method of division to a peach,
you might take a knife and separate your subject into skin, a pit,
and two halves. The essay you could write about a certain peach
by the method of division might interest a botanist, a farmer, or

---

[1] *Pot Shots at Poetry* (Ann Arbor: University of Michigan Press, 1980).

a cannery owner. Writing an essay by the method of division, you might divide a certain hotel into its component parts: lobby, rooms, coffeeshop, restaurant, bar, ballroom, kitchen, laundry, parking garage, and offices.

Just as you can divide a pie in many ways, you can classify a subject according to many principles. A different New York guidebook might classify hotels according to price: grand luxury class, luxury class, commercial class, budget class, fleabag, and flophouse. The purpose of this classification would be to match visitors to hotels befitting their pocketbooks. The principle you use in classifying things depends upon your purpose. A linguist might write an essay classifying the languages of the world according to their origins (Romance languages, Germanic languages, Coptic languages . . .), but a student battling with a college language requirement might write a humorous essay classifying them into three groups: hard to learn, harder to learn, and unlearnable. (Either way of sorting languages would be classification and not division, because the subject would be many languages, not one language. You could, of course, write an essay *dividing* the English language into British English, North American English, Australian English, and so on — *if* your purpose were to show regional varieties of English around the world.)

The simplest method of classification is *binary (or two-part) classification*, in which you sort things out into (1) those with a certain distinguishing feature and (2) those without it. You might classify a group of people, for example, into smokers and nonsmokers, blind people and sighted, runners and nonrunners, believers and nonbelievers. Binary classification is most useful when your subject is easily divisible into positive and negative categories.

Classification is a method particularly favored by writers who evaluate things. In a survey of current movies, a newspaper critic might classify the films into categories: "Don't Miss," "Worth Seeing," "So-So," and "Never Mind." This kind of classifying is the usual method of the magazine *Consumer Reports* in its comments on different brands of stereo speakers or canned tuna. Products are sorted into groups (excellent, good, fair, poor, and not acceptable), and the merits of each are discussed by the method of description. (Of a frozen pot pie: "Bottom crust gummy, meat spongy when chewed, with nondescript old-poultry and stale-flour flavor.")

As the writer of an anonymous jingle reminds us,

> Big fleas have little fleas, and these
> Have littler fleas to bite 'em,
> And these have fleas, and these have fleas,
> And on *ad infinitum.*

In being faithful to reality, you will sometimes find that you have to slice parts into smaller parts, or sort out the members of categories into subcategories. Writing about the varieties of English spoken around the world, a writer could subclassify them into regional dialects: breaking North American English into British Columbian English, Southern Appalachian English, and so on. To be more exact, a guidebook to New York might subdivide Midtown West into the Bryant Park area, Times Square, and the West Side.

As readers, we all enjoy watching a writer cleverly sort things out into categories, or break things into their elements; for we love to see whether the writer's classifications or divisions are familiar to us. This may account for the appeal of popular magazine articles such as "The Seven Common Garden Varieties of Moocher" and "The Five Most Embarrassing Social Blunders" or "The Eleven Components of a Kiss" (an essay in division).

Simple as division and classification are, both methods help us make sense of complex realities. Both separate a subject into smaller, more comprehensible units. Division takes one thing for its subject and answers the question, What are its parts? Classification, on the other hand, takes two or more things for its subject and answers the question, Into what groups or families can these be sorted? Both methods make large ideas more easily graspable, for both writer and reader.

• THE PROCESS •

In writing by either division or classification, having an outline at your elbow is a help. When dividing a subject into

parts, you'll want to make sure you don't omit any. When classifying the members of a group into various pigeonholes, you'll
probably need to glance at your outline from time to time, to
keep your pigeonholes straight.

In writing her brief essay "I Want a Wife," Judy Syfers must
have needed an outline to work out the different activities of a
wife carefully before she began, so that she clearly knew where
to draw her distinctions between them. Making a valid division
is chiefly a matter of giving your subject thought, but for the
division to seem useful and convincing to your reader, it will
have to refer to the world of the senses. The method requires
not only cogitation, but open eyes and a willingness to provide
examples and evidence.

In a workable classification, make sure that the categories
you choose don't overlap. If you were writing a survey of popular magazines for adults and you were sorting your subject into
categories that included women's magazines and sports magazines, you might soon run into trouble. Into which category
would you place *Women's Sports*? The trouble is that both
categories take in the same item. To avoid this problem, you'll
need to reorganize your classification on a different principle.
You might sort out the magazines by their audiences: magazines
for women, magazines for men, magazines for women and men.
Or you might group them according to subject matter: sports
magazines, literary magazines, astrology magazines, fashion
magazines, TV fan magazines, trade journals, and so on.
Women's Sports would fit into either of those classification
schemes.

Things may be classified into categories that reveal truth, or
into categories that don't tell us a damned thing. To sort out ten
U.S. cities according to their relative freedom from air pollu-
tion, or their cost of living, or the degree of progress they have
made in civil rights might prove highly informative and useful.
Such a classification might even tell us where we'd want to live.
But to sort out the cities according to a superficial feature such
as the relative size of their cat and dog populations wouldn't interest anyone, probably, except a veterinarian looking for a job.
Let your reader in on the basis for classification that you
choose, and explain why you have chosen it.

When you draw up a scheme of classification, be sure you include all essential categories. Omitting an important category can weaken the effect of your essay, no matter how well-written it is. It would be a major oversight, for example, if you were to classify the student body of a state university according to religious affiliations and not include a category for the numerous nonaffiliated. Your reader might wonder if your sloppiness in forgetting a category extended to your thinking about the topic as well.

For both division and classification, show your reader *why* you went to all the work of dividing or classifying, anyway, and what you have learned by it. In making your division or classification did you come to any conclusion? If so, state it. ("After dividing San Francisco into neighborhoods, and then classifying the neighborhoods, I feel sure that Minneapolis is the place for me after all.")

· DIVISION AND CLASSIFICATION ·
· IN TWO PARAGRAPHS ·

A canned laugh, whatever its style, is made up of three elements. The first is intensity, for a laugh machine can deliver a product of any desired volume, whether mild, medium, or ear-splitting. Duration is the second ingredient, for a laugh may be short, medium, or long. By jiggling keys, the machine-operator supplies a third ingredient: a fixed number of laughers. Any number is on tap, from a handful of titterers to a roaring throng. Should a producer desire a laugh from one sex or another, these may be subdivided into women or men. When Robin Williams accidentally reveals his polka-dotted boxer shorts on the *Mork and Mindy* show, the shrill merriment of women will predominate. Mindy's ripped dress, however, will be greeted with the guffaws of men. At the dubbing session, furiously working his keys and tromping his footpedals, the machine-operator blends his ingredients like a maestro weaving a symphony out of brass, woodwinds, percussion, and strings.

Though the machine will supply thirty-two different styles of laughter, most laughs fall into one of five reliable types. There is the *titter*, a light vocal laugh with which an imaginary audience responds to a comedian's least wriggle or grimace. Some producers rely heavily on the *chuckle*, a deeper, more chesty response. Most profound of all, the *bellylaugh* is summoned to acclaim broader jokes and sexual innuendoes. When provided at full level of sound and in longest duration, the bellylaugh becomes the Big Boffola. There is also the *wild howl* or *screamer*, an extreme response used not more than three times per show, lest it seem fake. These are crowd laughs, and yet the machine also offers the *freaky laugh*, the piercing, eccentric screech of a solitary kook. With it, a producer affirms that even a canned audience may include one thorny individualist.

Comment. The laugh machine, as you may have gathered, is used to fill a moment of silence in the soundtrack of a comedy program. Most televised comedies, even some that boast they have live audiences, rely on it. According to rumor (for its exact workings are a secret), the machine contains a bank of thirty-two tapes, which the operator turns on singly or in combination. In these two paragraphs, the writer first proceeded by the method of division, taking a single subject — a machine-made laugh — and breaking it into its components. The second paragraph groups laughs into five categories. Like anything else written by the method of classification, the paragraph takes as its subject a *number* of things, which it then sorts out.

· Judy Syfers ·

JUDY SYFERS, born in 1937 in San Francisco, where she now lives, earned a B.F.A. in painting from the University of Iowa in 1962. Drawn into political action by her work in the feminist movement, she went to Cuba in 1973, where she studied class relationships as a way of understanding change in a society. "I am not a 'writer,'" Syfers declares, "but really am a disenfranchised (and fired) housewife, now secretary. I have published other articles in various types of publications (one on abortion, one on union organizing, for instance) and have written for, edited, and produced a newsletter for school paraprofessionals in San Francisco."

I Want a Wife

"I Want a Wife" first appeared in the December 1971 issue of *Ms.* magazine. It has since become one of the best-known manifestoes in popular feminist writing, and it has been reprinted widely. In her essay, Syfers trenchantly divides the work of a wife into five parts, explains each part, and comes to an inescapable conclusion.

I belong to that classification of people known as wives. I am 1 A Wife. And, not altogether incidentally, I am a mother.

Not too long ago a male friend of mine appeared on the 2 scene fresh from a recent divorce. He had one child, who is, of course, with his ex-wife. He is looking for another wife. As I thought about him while I was ironing one evening, it suddenly occurred to me that I, too, would like to have a wife. Why do I want a wife?

I would like to go back to school so that I can become 3 economically independent, support myself, and, if need be, support those dependent upon me. I want a wife who will work and send me to school. And while I am going to school I want a wife to take care of my children. I want a wife to keep track of the children's doctor and dentist appointments. And to keep track of mine, too. I want a wife to make sure my children eat properly and are kept clean. I want a wife who will wash the children's clothes and keep them mended. I want a wife who is a good nurturant attendant to my children, who arranges for their schooling, makes sure that they have an adequate social life with their peers, takes them to the park, the zoo, etc. I want a wife who takes care of the children when they are sick, a wife who arranges to be around when the children need special care, because, of course, I cannot miss classes at school. My wife must arrange to lose time at work and not lose the job. It may mean a small cut in my wife's income from time to time, but I guess I can tolerate that. Needless to say, my wife will arrange and pay for the care of the children while my wife is working.

I want a wife who will take care of *my* physical needs. I want   4
a wife who will keep my house clean. A wife who will pick up after my children, a wife who will pick up after me. I want a wife who will keep my clothes clean, ironed, mended, replaced when need be, and who will see to it that my personal things are kept in their proper place so that I can find what I need the minute I need it. I want a wife who cooks the meals, a wife who is a *good* cook. I want a wife who will plan the menus, do the necessary grocery shopping, prepare the meals, serve them pleasantly, and then do the cleaning up while I do my studying. I want a wife who will care for me when I am sick and sympathize with my pain and loss of time from school. I want a wife to go along when our family takes a vacation so that someone can continue to care for me and my children when I need a rest and change of scene.

I want a wife who will not bother me with rambling com-   5
plaints about a wife's duties. But I want a wife who will listen to me when I feel the need to explain a rather difficult point I have come across in my course of studies. And I want a wife who will type my papers for me when I have written them.

I want a wife who will take care of the details of my social   6
life. When my wife and I are invited out by my friends, I want a wife who will take care of the babysitting arrangements. When I meet people at school that I like and want to entertain, I want a wife who will have the house clean, will prepare a special meal, serve it to me and my friends, and not interrupt when I talk about things that interest me and my friends. I want a wife who

will have arranged that the children are fed and ready for bed before my guests arrive so that the children do not bother us. I want a wife who takes care of the needs of my guests so that they feel comfortable, who makes sure that they have an ashtray, that they are passed the hors d'oeuvres, that they are offered a second helping of the food, that their wine glasses are replenished when necessary, that their coffee is served to them as they like it. And I want a wife who knows that sometimes I need a night out by myself.

I want a wife who is sensitive to my sexual needs, a wife who makes love passionately and eagerly when I feel like it, a wife who makes sure that I am satisfied. And, of course, I want a wife who will not demand sexual attention when I am not in the mood for it. I want a wife who assumes the complete responsibility for birth control, because I do not want more children. I want a wife who will remain sexually faithful to me so that I do not have to clutter up my intellectual life with jealousies. And I want a wife who understands that *my* sexual needs may entail more than strict adherence to monogamy. I must, after all, be able to relate to people as fully as possible.

If, by chance, I find another person more suitable as a wife than the wife I already have, I want the liberty to replace my present wife with another one. Naturally, I will expect a fresh, new life; my wife will take the children and be solely responsible for them so that I am left free.

When I am through with school and have a job, I want my wife to quit working and remain at home so that my wife can more fully and completely take care of a wife's duties.

My God, who *wouldn't* want a wife?

• QUESTIONS ON MEANING AND PURPOSE •

1. Sum up the duties of a wife as Judy Syfers sees them.
2. To what inequities in the roles traditionally assigned to men and to women does "I Want a Wife" call attention?
3. What is the thesis of this essay? (See *Thesis* in Useful Terms.) Is it stated or implied?
4. Is Syfers unfair to men?

• QUESTIONS ON WRITING STRATEGY •

1. What effect does Syfers obtain with the title "I Want a Wife"? (See *Effect* in Useful Terms.)
2. What purpose is served by the first two paragraphs?
3. What is the tone of this essay? (See *Tone* in Useful Terms.)
4. How do you explain the fact that Syfers never uses the pronoun "she" to refer to a wife? Does this make her prose unnecessarily awkward?
5. In what order or sequence does the author arrange her paragraphs? (To see it, try rearranging them.)
6. Knowing that this essay was first published in *Ms.* magazine in 1971, what can you guess about its intended readers? Does "I Want a Wife" strike a college audience today as revolutionary?
7. In her first sentence, Syfers says she belongs "to that classification of people known as wives"; but she develops her essay by division. In what way would the essay be different if the author had used classification?

• QUESTIONS ON LANGUAGE •
• AND VOCABULARY •

1. What is achieved by the author's frequent repetition of the phrase, "I want a wife"?
2. Be sure you know how to define the following words as Syfers uses them: nurturant (paragraph 3), replenished (6); adherence, monogamy (7).
3. In general, how would you describe the diction of this essay? (See *Diction* in Useful Terms.) How well does it suit the essay's intended audience?

• SUGGESTIONS FOR WRITING •

1. Write a brief essay entitled "I Want a Husband" in which, using examples as Syfers does, you enumerate the stereotyped roles traditionally assigned to men in our society.
2. Classify types of husbands, or types of wives.
3. Imagining that you want to employ someone to do a specific job, divide the task into two or three parts. Then, guided by your divisions, write an accurate job description in essay form.

· Ruth B. Purtilo and Christine K. Cassel ·

RUTH B. PURTILO and CHRISTINE K. CASSEL are the coauthors of *Ethical Dimensions in the Health Professions* (1981), a textbook for physicians, nurses, and other health care professionals. Dr. Purtilo, born in 1942, is at present Associate Professor of Health Care Ethics and Humanistic Studies at Massachusetts General Hospital in Boston. Dr. Cassel, born in 1945, is currently Instructor in Medicine in the University of Oregon Health Science Center and Fellow in Geriatrics at Portland Veterans' Administration Hospital.

Hateful Patients:
The Gomer, the Gork,
and the Crock

In reading the following essay, be aware that it was not written for a general audience; it is, however, interesting to us all. A self-contained section of Dr. Purtilo and Dr. Cassel's textbook, the case history of Eddy Underhill and the authors' remarks on "hateful patients" are designed to provoke thought about medical ethics. The purpose of the entire book, according to its preface, "is to prepare students for situations they will face in their professional lives that have an ethical component or dimension. . . . To fulfill our purpose we have presented ethical theory in language that anyone can understand and have balanced it with examples illustrating how the theory is applicable to the everyday experiences of health professionals."

When Eddy Underhill was admitted to the Veterans'   1
Hospital again, no one was surprised. He was well-known to the staff in the emergency room and to most of the ward personnel who had been there for any length of time, and none of them were glad to see him. Eddy lived in a furnished room in the skid

row section of town, where his veteran's pension was enough to
cover his rent plus enough alcohol to keep him drunk almost all
the time. Occasionally he would spend money on food, but
never if it meant going without booze.

This time he was admitted with impending delirium 2
tremens (DT's), a life-threatening condition resulting from alcohol withdrawal. Often such admissions would occur toward the
end of the month when his money ran out and scavenging
could not net him enough money to keep him drinking. (Other
times he was admitted for pneumonia, contracted after spending a winter night unconscious in the gutter, or bleeding from
esophageal varices, or trauma, from falling on the street or being beat up by thugs.)

Jesse Sampson, a young chaplain who had recently begun 3
working at the Veterans' Hospital, began visiting Eddy after his
acute withdrawal symptoms had subsided. Eddy had some degree of brain damage from his chronic alcohol abuse but was
garrulous and enjoyed "shooting the breeze" with this young
man who came to see him every day. Chaplain Sampson was
very different from the doctors and nurses at the hospital, who
spent as little time as possible with Eddy. The chaplain would
sit down in a chair next to the bed as if he were not in a hurry to
be somewhere else. He would ask Eddy questions about himself
and his life as if he really cared about the answers. Eddy told
Jesse that booze was his only real friend, that his life was lonely,
but seemed warmer and more convivial when he was drunk. He
had no family. His friends were the other people on skid row.
He had no ambitions. Life was hard, and pretty senseless, and
he just wanted to get through it as easily as he could. He ap-
preciated being brought to the hospital when he was in really
bad shape. There it was warm, and he got decent food, but most
of the people treated him with thinly veiled disgust. This often
made him angry. "I'm a gomer, you know. They hate my kind,
but they can't come right out and say so, so they try to ignore
me. They wish I would die, and sometime I will. Would serve
'em right. But they won't care; they'll just keep on goin' about
their prissy and proud ways. They think they are so good-

hearted, but they don't know what it's like to live on the street. To be alone with your only friend, the bottle. It's my life and I got a right to do what I want. I served my time in the war, and I got a right to be in this hospital — to come in here and get dried out and get a little food. I'm an old man. I got a right."

Jesse knew the doctors and nurses considered him naive and 4 foolish to be spending so much time with a worthless derelict — a gomer. He harbored no illusions that he could convince Eddy to stop drinking. He had seen his father struggle with alcoholism and knew the awful power of that addiction, knew the strong desire for life that was necessary for an alcoholic to go straight. Eddy had no such desire for life. He tolerated life, and demanded his share of respect from the hospital staff, and became angry when he didn't get it. But he knew the booze would kill him sooner or later, and he didn't much care.

For Jesse, it was enough to spend time with Eddy while he 5 was in the hospital, listen to his stories, and treat him with a little human decency. He had time to do this. The medical staff did not have the time but, more important, they did not have the interest. They resented Eddy for taking up their time and valuable hospital resources which might be used for a more "worthwhile" member of society.

Why are their feelings towards Eddy so strong? Why is it so 6 difficult for a health professional to act with respect toward Eddy? Why is he a gomer? Why is Jesse able to feel and express more compassion than the other members of the staff?

Outside our professional lives there are many people whom 7 we may not like. Similarly, there are patients encountered by health professionals who are not likable. Personality differences often account for such dislike, both in and out of professional life. But somehow it is unseemly to have antagonistic feelings toward patients, because it is part of the role of those in the helping professions to act with compassion and charity toward all who are in need of help. This is an important aspect of professionalism. Acting with compassion and charity can be accomplished without necessarily feeling personal affection for patients; but to do this it is helpful to understand the source of one's animosity toward certain patients, so that unrecognized assumptions and the feelings they engender are not allowed to govern one's professional behavior.

There are many kinds of patients who are difficult to like. 8
The "gomer" is just one of these. Other commonly used derogatory words referring to patients are "gork" and "crock." There are many others which vary from place to place and from specialty to specialty, but let us examine these in greater detail to understand the general phenomenon of the "undesirable patient."

A "gomer" is typically an older man who is both dirty and 9
debilitated. He is often a chronic alcoholic. A derelict or down-and-outer, the gomer subsists on public funds of some kind. He has an extensive history of multiple admissions to the hospital. He has real organic disease, which is usually related to poor personal hygiene, to inadequate nutrition, and to self-destructive habits such as alcohol or drug abuse and smoking.

A "gork" may start out as a "gomer" but is a much sicker 10
person. A gork is a patient who is moribund or unresponsive, generally having suffered irreversible brain damage of one sort or another. He or she is often also referred to as a "vegetable."

A "crock" is someone who has many complaints for which 11
no organic basis can be found. Such persons are often suspected of being hypochondriacs or malingerers. (A hypochondriac is a person who genuinely believes that he or she has organic disease, but whose symptoms can be traced to neurotic personality problems. A malingerer, on the other hand, is a person who intentionally deceives the health professional to obtain secondary gain, such as disability payments or time off from work.)

Although personal likes and dislikes are often individual 12
and idiosyncratic, the widespread use of these terms by health professionals suggests that there are certain general categories of patients who are disliked or, at least, considered undesirable by most professionals. If we examine some of the attributes shared by these patients more closely, and include in our examination the kind of interaction they usually have with the health care world, perhaps we can gain a better understanding of the source of these negative attitudes.

As with most . . . ethical issues . . . the problem of the 13
"hateful patient"[1] has dimensions related not only to those involved in any specific situation, but also to institutional and
social structures. Attributes of "hateful" patients have been
shown to be related to the following:

Low Social Class: Most health professionals come from 14
middle-class cultural backgrounds. This is especially true of physicians, but it is also relevant to other health professionals.
"Gomers" such as Eddy Underhill show us a side of life which is
unpleasant and unfamiliar. If we cannot understand a person's
way of life, or cultural context, it is difficult to relate to him. His
very existence challenges the materialistic values of the middle
class, and is therefore psychologically threatening. "Why
doesn't he get a job?" we might ask. Or, "Doesn't he care what
people think about him?" As one physician has pointed out,
"Even when the physician has genuine concern for the economically disadvantaged, he may, because of his own background,
unwittingly regard the extremely poor as 'different,' with a
flavor of inferiority included in the difference."

Physical Conditions Engendering Disgust Or Fear: Certain 15
aspects of physical illness are abhorrent to many people. Bodily
filth or infestation is only one example; for instance, an old man
with a maggot-infested ulcer on his leg is likely to be shunned.
This category also includes chronic disfiguring or disabling
diseases. An amputee, a patient with a grossly disfiguring
tumor, and a burn patient missing his ears or nose all confront
us with the reality of the fragility of the human body. We do not
like to be reminded that our existence depends in some fundamental way on flesh and bones, and our notions of normality

---

[1]These patients have usually been referred to as "undesirable" or "problem patients" or some other relatively benign euphemism. The recent appearance of the term "hateful patient" in the medical literature met with some
controversy, but has had the beneficial effect of urging health professionals to
confront their negative feelings about some patients more candidly. In doing
so they are then able to acknowledge that this is a real problem in patient
care, and address ways of improving the situation.

are narrowly defined. For most people physical attractiveness is a very important part of a sense of self-worth. We want to feel that other people like us, and our culture places a great deal of importance on physical attributes. This is one reason why our society has ignored many problems of the aged, because by ignoring them we can ignore the reality that we ourselves will one day become old and possibly infirm or disabled.

Uncooperativeness: The medical model of health care re- 16
quires that the patient be in a position of ignorance, and that in most cases he follow the orders of the health professional unquestioningly. Patients may consciously or unconsciously challenge this model in many ways. Those who engage in self-destructive behavior are frustrating to the health professional because their behavior indicates that they implicitly reject the advice and therefore the precepts of health and well-being. They are uncooperative because they do things to their bodies which effectively prevent a health professional from curing them. A health professional cannot feel any gratification from curing people whose behavior makes them sick again.

In response to this frustration, a large body of medical 17
literature addressing the problem of "noncompliance" has grown up in recent years. "Noncompliance" means that the patient, for one reason or another, does not cooperate with the health professional's program of treatment.

Chronic and terminal diseases are similarly threatening and 18
frustrating. These patients are "uncooperative" because they don't get well. We cannot act out our fantasies of being heroes in white uniforms if the patient can't or won't get well. Hypochondriacs fit into this category, too, even though they may not be physically ill, because no matter what is done for them they never give the satisfaction of being grateful for efforts on their behalf or acknowledging that treatments have helped them. For most people in the health professions feeling useful is one of the important satisfactions of the work, and the uncooperative patient denies those caring for him the chance to feel that satisfaction. It is frustrating to work so hard, apparently to no avail.

Psychological Dysfunction: In order to succeed in the health 19
professions, a person must have a certain amount of emotional
stability, for the training is difficult and the work itself can be
emotionally stressful. Persons with mental or emotional disorders are threatening to one's self-image in much the same way
as is the patient with physical disability. To feel compassion or
empathy for another person we must in some way identify a
common humanity shared between us. It is extremely difficult
to identify in this way with a psychotic, demented, or sociopathic patient. Feeling compassion for a neurotic, manipulative,
or suicidal patient is almost as difficult. Often alcoholism and
drug abuse are also expressions of emotional disorders. It is easy
to see psychological disorders as manifestations of a weak or
deficient character and to *blame the victim* for his or her disability. Professionals trained in psychiatric treatment generally have
a better understanding of these kinds of problems and are more
able to act compassionately toward such patients. When an
emotional problem manifests itself as a physical complaint,
health professionals trained to deal with "real" physical illness
may react with impatience and contempt. Consequently we call
patients with psychosomatic disorders "crocks" and thereby
deny the validity of their need for our help.

For professionals in emotionally stressful situations (work- 20
ing with any of the patients we have described as "undesirable"
is emotionally stressful) it is necessary to develop some defense
mechanisms to continue working. Labeling patients with derogatory words such as "gomer" or "gork" or "crock" is a way to
maintain a distance from them and to solidify the in-group of
the health professionals. It makes the difficult patients objects of
grim humor and thus mitigates some of the frustration of dealing with them. It is a way of saying, "This patient is just one of a
type, and everybody has the same problem with these *types*."
However, it strips the patient of his individuality; this is the
essence of the destructiveness of such labeling, for it thereby
strips him of his personhood. Thus labeled, the patient can no
longer claim the respect owed to a *person*. It was this lack of re-

spect that made Eddy so angry. Although health professionals would almost never call a patient "gomer" to his face, or in front of his family, the patient can sense the lack of respect in how he is being treated.

Jesse Sampson seemed to perceive Eddy Underhill as a *person* and therefore was better able to respect him and have compassion for him. Eddy's life history was unfortunate and depressing, perhaps, but it was his own, and Jesse honored that. Eddy had a philosophy to live by and had feelings about the way he was treated by other people. In labeling someone a "gomer" or a "crock" one effectively establishes barriers to respect and compassion for this human being, in addition to achieving a distancing from the unlikable individual, and for that reason alone such practices should be avoided.   21

What enabled Jesse to avoid the pitfalls of the depersonalized type of distancing that results from labeling? Perhaps one reason that Jesse was able to befriend Eddy is that a chaplain's job is, in some ways, to become a friend. The chaplain ministers to the person; he is not expected to clean up the patient, draw blood, or administer treatments. (This is not to say that all chaplains are better able to help so-called problem patients, but they do have certain advantages in that respect.) A chaplain does not have to deal with certain aspects of the patient's uncooperative or noncompliant behavior that are most apparent during treatment or hygiene. The chaplain does have an emotional investment in helping to improve a patient's condition since it affects that patient's overall well-being. It may be easier for a chaplain to keep sight of the big picture than it is for those health professionals who see the value of their work only in the successful treatment of certain physical disorders.   22

• QUESTIONS ON MEANING AND PURPOSE •

1. What differences do Purtilo and Cassel observe between the ways Eddy Underhill is treated by the hospital chaplain and by the medical staff? How do the authors account for the differences?

2. According to the authors, how does the middle-class background of most health professionals influence their attitude toward "gomers"?

3. What reasons do Purtilo and Cassel suggest for the negative responses engendered by disfigured, uncooperative, or emotionally and mentally impaired patients?

4. In addition to classifying and characterizing certain kinds of "hateful" patients, Purtilo and Cassel make a plea to their readers. What is the substance of their plea?

• QUESTIONS ON WRITING STRATEGY •

1. In what respects might the content and terminology of this essay be different if the writers had been addressing a general audience instead of prospective medical professionals?

2. What does the example of Eddy Underhill contribute to the essay's effect upon the reader? (See *Effect* in Useful Terms.)

3. By what steps in paragraphs 7 and 8 do the authors make the transition between the story of Eddy and the rest of the essay? (See *Transitions* in Useful Terms.)

• QUESTIONS ON LANGUAGE •
• AND VOCABULARY •

1. What are the connotations of gomer, gork, and crock? (See *Connotation and Denotation* in Useful Terms.)

2. How do you account for the fact that such terms are unfamiliar to most laymen? What induces health professionals to use these appellations?

3. Consult a dictionary if you need help defining the following words: delirium tremens, esophageal varices (paragraph 2); garrulous, convivial (3); animosity (7); moribund (10); idiosyncratic (12); abhorrent (15); implicitly (16); sociopathic, psychosomatic (19); mitigates (20).

• SUGGESTIONS FOR WRITING •

1. Imagine that you are a medical professional dealing with a "gomer," a "gork," or a "crock." In the form of a letter to a friend, detail as vividly as you can the events, emotions, and frustrations you believe this experience would entail.

2. Pretend you are a hateful patient. From Eddy Underhill's point of view, explain and try to justify your situation in a few paragraphs. (See *Point of View* in Useful Terms.)

3. From the point of view of someone who oversees or cares for others (for instance, a camp counselor, a nursing home aide, or a playground supervisor), classify the people in your charge.

4. Every job has its unrewarding aspects. Write a paper about a job familiar to you in which you classify the difficulties faced by anyone trying to do that job. Remember that classification entails more than just making a list.

· Gail Sheehy ·

GAIL SHEEHY was born in 1937. She earned her B.S. degree from the University of Vermont in 1958 and was a fellow in Columbia University's Journalism School in 1970. A contributor to *The New York Times Magazine, Esquire, McCall's, Ms., Cosmopolitan, Rolling Stone,* and other magazines, she has also written several books: *Lovesounds* (1970), *Speed Is of the Essence* (1971), *Panthermania* (1971), *Hustling* (1973), *Passages* (1976), and *Pathfinders* (1981). She is a contributing editor for *New York* magazine.

Predictable Crises
of Adulthood

"Predictable Crises of Adulthood" is adapted from the second chapter of the best-selling *Passages*. In it, Gail Sheehy identifies and describes six predictable stages that people pass through between the ages of eighteen and fifty. Not everyone, of course, goes through the stages at the prescribed time; but see whether any of these crises are familiar to you.

We are not unlike a particularly hardy crustacean. The 1 lobster grows by developing and shedding a series of hard, protective shells. Each time it expands from within, the confining shell must be sloughed off. It is left exposed and vulnerable until, in time, a new covering grows to replace the old.

With each passage from one stage of human growth to the 2 next we, too, must shed a protective structure. We are left exposed and vulnerable — but also yeasty and embryonic again, capable of stretching in ways we hadn't known before. These sheddings may take several years or more. Coming out of each passage, though, we enter a longer and more stable period in which we can expect relative tranquility and a sense of equilibrium regained. . . .

As we shall see, each person engages the steps of develop-   3
ment in his or her own characteristic *step-style*. Some people
never complete the whole sequence. And none of us "solves"
with one step — by jumping out of the parental home into a job
or marriage, for example — the problems in separating from the
caregivers of childhood. Nor do we "achieve" autonomy once
and for all by converting our dreams into concrete goals, even
when we attain those goals. The central issues or tasks of one
period are never fully completed, tied up, and cast aside. But
when they lose their primacy and the current life structure has
served its purpose, we are ready to move on to the next period.

Can one catch up? What might look to others like   4
listlessness, contrariness, a maddening refusal to face up to an
obvious task may be a person's own unique detour that will
bring him out later on the other side. Developmental gains won
can later be lost — and rewon. It's plausible, though it can't be
proven, that the mastery of one set of tasks fortifies us for the
next period and the next set of challenges. But it's important
not to think too mechanistically. Machines work by units. The
bureaucracy (supposedly) works step by step. Human beings,
thank God, have an individual inner dynamic that can never
be precisely coded.

Although I have indicated the ages when Americans are   5
likely to go through each stage, and the differences between
men and women where they are striking, do not take the ages
too seriously. The stages are the thing, and most particularly
the sequence.

Here is the briefest outline of the developmental ladder.   6

Pulling Up Roots

Before 18, the motto is loud and clear: "I have to get away   7
from my parents." But the words are seldom connected to action. Generally still safely part of our families, even if away at
school, we feel our autonomy to be subject to erosion from moment to moment.

After 18, we begin Pulling Up Roots in earnest. College,   8
military service, and short-term travels are all customary vehi-

cles our society provides for the first round trips between family and a base of one's own. In the attempt to separate our view of the world from our family's view, despite vigorous protestations to the contrary — "I know exactly what I want!" — we cast about for any beliefs we can call our own. And in the process of testing those beliefs we are often drawn to fads, preferably those most mysterious and inaccessible to our parents.

Whatever tentative memberships we try out in the world, the fear haunts us that we are really kids who cannot take care of ourselves. We cover that fear with acts of defiance and mimicked confidence. For allies to replace our parents, we turn to our contemporaries. They become conspirators. So long as their perspective meshes with our own, they are able to substitute for the sanctuary of the family. But that doesn't last very long. And the instant they diverge from the shaky ideals of "our group," they are seen as betrayers. Rebounds to the family are common between the ages of 18 and 22.

9

The tasks of this passage are to locate ourselves in a peer group role, a sex role, an anticipated occupation, an ideology or world view. As a result, we gather the impetus to leave home physically and the identity to *begin* leaving home emotionally.

10

Even as one part of us seeks to be an individual, another part longs to restore the safety and comfort of merging with another. Thus one of the most popular myths of this passage is: We can piggyback our development by attaching to a Stronger One. But people who marry during this time often prolong financial and emotional ties to the family and relatives that impede them from becoming self-sufficient.

11

A stormy passage through the Pulling Up Roots years will probably facilitate the normal progression of the adult life cycle. If one doesn't have an identity crisis at this point, it will erupt during a later transition, when the penalties may be harder to bear.

12

The Trying Twenties

The Trying Twenties confront us with the question of how to take hold in the adult world. Our focus shifts from the in-

13

terior turmoils of late adolescence — "Who am I?" "What is truth?" — and we become almost totally preoccupied with working out the externals. "How do I put my aspirations into effect?" "What is the best way to start?" "Where do I go?" "Who can help me?" "How did *you* do it?"

In this period, which is longer and more stable compared with the passage that leads to it, the tasks are as enormous as they are exhilarating: To shape a Dream, that vision of ourselves which will generate energy, aliveness, and hope. To prepare for a lifework. To find a mentor if possible. And to form the capacity for intimacy, without losing in the process whatever consistency of self we have thus far mustered. The first test structure must be erected around the life we choose to try.   14

Doing what we "should" is the most pervasive theme of the twenties. The "shoulds" are largely defined by family models, the press of the culture, or the prejudices of our peers. If the prevailing cultural instructions are that one should get married and settle down behind one's own door, a nuclear family is born. If instead the peers insist that one should do one's own thing, the 25-year-old is likely to harness himself onto a Harley-Davidson and burn up Route 66 in the commitment to have no commitments.

One of the terrifying aspects of the twenties is the inner conviction that the choices we make are irrevocable. It is largely a false fear. Change is quite possible, and some alteration of our original choices is probably inevitable.   16

Two impulses, as always, are at work. One is to build a firm, safe structure for the future by making strong commitments, to "be set." Yet people who slip into a ready-made form without much self-examination are likely to find themselves *locked in*.   17

The other urge is to explore and experiment, keeping any structure tentative and therefore easily reversible. Taken to the extreme, these are people who skip from one trial job and one limited personal encounter to another, spending their twenties in the *transient* state.   18

Although the choices of our twenties are not irrevocable, they do set in motion a Life Pattern. Some of us follow the lock-   19 in pattern, others the transient pattern, the wunderkind pattern, the caregiver pattern, and there are a number of others. Such patterns strongly influence the particular questions raised for each person during each passage. . . .

Buoyed by powerful illusions and belief in the power of the   20
will, we commonly insist in our twenties that what we have chosen to do is the one true course in life. Our backs go up at the merest hint that we are like our parents, that two decades of parental training might be reflected in our current actions and attitudes.

"Not me," is the motto, "I'm different."   21

Catch-30

Impatient with devoting ourselves to the "shoulds," a new   22
vitality springs from within as we approach 30. Men and women alike speak of feeling too narrow and restricted. They blame all sorts of things, but what the restrictions boil down to are the outgrowth of career and personal choices of the twenties. They may have been choices perfectly suited to that stage. But now the fit feels different. Some inner aspect that was left out is striving to be taken into account. Important new choices must be made, and commitments altered or deepened. The work involves great change, turmoil, and often crisis — a simultaneous feeling of rock bottom and the urge to bust out.

One common response is the tearing up of the life we spent   23
most of our twenties putting together. It may mean striking out on a secondary road toward a new vision or converting a dream of "running for president" into a more realistic goal. The single person feels a push to find a partner. The woman who was previously content at home with children chafes to venture into the world. The childless couple reconsiders children. And almost everyone who is married, especially those married for seven years, feels a discontent.

If the discontent doesn't lead to a divorce, it will, or should,   24
call for a serious review of the marriage and of each partner's aspirations in their Catch-30 condition. The gist of that condi-

tion was expressed by a 29-year-old associate with a Wall Street law firm:

"I'm considering leaving the firm. I've been there four years   25
now; I'm getting good feedback, but I have no clients of my own. I feel weak. If I wait much longer, it will be too late, too close to that fateful time of decision on whether or not to become a partner. I'm success-oriented. But the concept of being 55 years old and stuck in a monotonous job drives me wild. It drives me crazy now, just a little bit. I'd say that 85 percent of the time I thoroughly enjoy my work. But when I get a screwball case, I come away from court saying, 'What am I doing here?' It's a *visceral* reaction that I'm wasting my time. I'm trying to find some way to make a social contribution or a slot in city government. I keep saying, 'There's something more.' "

Besides the push to broaden himself professionally, there is   26
a wish to expand his personal life. He wants two or three more children. "The concept of a home has become very meaningful to me, a place to get away from troubles and relax. I love my son in a way I could not have anticipated. I never could live alone."

Consumed with the work of making his own critical life-   27
steering decisions, he demonstrates the essential shift at this age: an absolute requirement to be more self-concerned. The self has new value now that his competency has been proved.

His wife is struggling with her own age-30 priorities. She   28
wants to go to law school, but he wants more children. If she is going to stay home, she wants him to make more time for the family instead of taking on even wider professional commitments. His view of the bind, of what he would most like from his wife, is this:

"I'd like not to be bothered. It sounds cruel, but I'd like not   29
to have to worry about what she's going to do next week. Which is why I've told her several times that I think she should do something. Go back to school and get a degree in social work or geography or whatever. Hopefully that would fulfill her, and then I wouldn't have to worry about her line of problems. I want her to be decisive about herself."

The trouble with his advice to his wife is that it comes out of   30
concern with *his* convenience, rather than with *her* develop-

ment. She quickly picks up on this lack of goodwill: He is trying to dispose of her. At the same time, he refuses her the same latitude to be "selfish" in making an independent decision to broaden her own horizons. Both perceive a lack of mutuality. And that is what Catch-30 is all about for the couple.

Rooting and Extending

Life becomes less provisional, more rational and orderly in   31
the early thirties. We begin to settle down in the full sense. Most of us begin putting down roots and sending out new shoots. People buy houses and become very earnest about climbing career ladders. Men in particular concern themselves with "making it." Satisfaction with marriage generally goes downhill in the thirties (for those who have remained together) compared with the highly valued, vision-supporting marriage of the twenties. This coincides with the couple's reduced social life outside the family and the in-turned focus on raising their children.

The Deadline Decade

In the middle of the thirties we come upon a crossroads. We   32
have reached the halfway mark. Yet even as we are reaching our prime, we begin to see there is a place where it finishes. Time starts to squeeze.

The loss of youth, the faltering of physical powers we have   33
always taken for granted, the fading purpose of stereotyped roles by which we have thus far identified ourselves, the spiritual dilemma of having no absolute answers — any or all of these shocks can give this passage the character of crisis. Such thoughts usher in a decade between 35 and 45 that can be called the Deadline Decade. It is a time of both danger and opportunity. All of us have the chance to rework the narrow identity by which we defined ourselves in the first half of life. And those of us who make the most of the opportunity will have a full-out authenticity crisis.

To come through this authenticity crisis, we must reex-   34
amine our purposes and reevaluate how to spend our resources

from now on. "Why am I doing all this? What do I really believe in?" No matter what we have been doing, there will be parts of ourselves that have been suppressed and now need to find expression. "Bad" feelings will demand acknowledgment along with the good.

It is frightening to step off onto the treacherous footbridge. 35 leading to the second half of life. We can't take everything with us on this journey through uncertainty. Along the way, we discover that we are alone. We no longer have to ask permission because we are the providers of our own safety. We must learn to give ourselves permission. We stumble upon feminine or masculine aspects of our natures that up to this time have usually been masked. There is grieving to be done because an old self is dying. By taking in our suppressed and even our unwanted parts, we prepare at the gut level for the reintegration of an identity that is ours and ours alone — not some artificial form put together to please the culture or our mates. It is a dark passage at the beginning. But by disassembling ourselves, we can glimpse the light and gather our parts into a renewal.

Women sense this inner crossroads earlier than men do. 36 The time pinch often prompts a woman to stop and take an all-points survey at age 35. Whatever options she has already played out, she feels a "my last chance" urgency to review those options she has set aside and those that aging and biology will close off in the *now foreseeable* future. For all her qualms and confusion about where to start looking for a new future, she usually enjoys an exhilaration of release. Assertiveness begins rising. There are so many firsts ahead.

Men, too, feel the time push in the mid-thirties. Most men 37 respond by pressing down harder on the career accelerator. It's "my last chance" to pull away from the pack. It is no longer enough to be the loyal junior executive, the promising young novelist, the lawyer who does a little *pro bono* work on the side. He wants now to become part of top management, to be recognized as an established writer, or an active politician with his own legislative program. With some chagrin, he discovers that he has been too anxious to please and too vulnerable to criticism. He wants to put together his own ship.

During this period of intense concentration on external ad- [38] vancement, it is common for men to be unaware of the more difficult, gut issues that are propelling them forward. The survey that was neglected at 35 becomes a crucible at 40. Whatever rung of achievement he has reached, the man of 40 usually feels stale, restless, burdened, and unappreciated. He worries about his health. He wonders, "Is this all there is?" He may make a series of departures from well-established lifelong base lines, including marriage. More and more men are seeking second careers in midlife. Some become self-destructive. And many men in their forties experience a major shift of emphasis away from pouring all their energies into their own advancement. A more tender, feeling side comes into play. They become interested in developing an ethical self.

Renewal or Resignation

Somewhere in the mid-forties, equilibrium is regained. A [39] new stability is achieved, which may be more or less satisfying.

If one has refused to budge through the midlife transition, [40] the sense of staleness will calcify into resignation. One by one, the safety and supports will be withdrawn from the person who is standing still. Parents will become children; children will become strangers; a mate will grow away or go away; the career will become just a job — and each of these events will be felt as an abandonment. The crisis will probably emerge again around 50. And although its wallop will be greater, the jolt may be just what is needed to prod the resigned middle-ager toward seeking revitalization.

On the other hand . . . [41]

If we have confronted ourselves in the middle passage and [42] found a renewal of purpose around which we are eager to build a more authentic life structure, these may well be the best years. Personal happiness takes a sharp turn upward for partners who can now accept the fact: "I cannot expect *anyone* to fully understand me." Parents can be forgiven for the burdens of our childhood. Children can be let go without leaving us in collapsed silence. At 50, there is a new warmth and mellowing. Friends become more important than ever, but so does privacy. Since it is so often proclaimed by people past midlife, the motto of this stage might be "No more bullshit."

· QUESTIONS ON MEANING AND PURPOSE ·

1. In your own words, describe each of Sheehy's six predictable stages of adult life.
2. According to the author, what happens to people who fail to experience a given stage of growth at the usual time?
3. How would you characterize Sheehy's attitude toward growth and change in adult life?
4. For what purpose does Sheehy employ the method of division? How does it serve her readers, too?

· QUESTIONS ON WRITING STRATEGY ·

1. How apt, do you think, is the opening metaphor: the comparison between a lobster periodically shedding its shell and a person entering each new phase of growth? (See *Figures of Speech* in Useful Terms.)
2. What, if anything, does the author gain by writing her essay in the first person plural? (See *Person* in Useful Terms.)
3. What difficulties go along with making generalizations about human beings? To what extent does Sheehy surmount these difficulties?
4. How much knowledge of psychology does Sheehy expect of her audience?

· QUESTIONS ON LANGUAGE ·
· AND VOCABULARY ·

1. Consult your dictionary if you need help in defining the following words: crustacean (paragraph 1); embryonic, tranquility, equilibrium (2); autonomy, primacy (3); plausible (4); inaccessible (8); sanctuary (9); impetus (10); exhilarating, mentor (14); pervasive (15); irrevocable (16); tentative (18); wunderkind (19); visceral (25);

mutuality (30); dilemma (33); *pro bono*, chagrin, vulnerable (37); crucible (38); calcify (40).
2. What is a "nuclear family" (paragraph 15)?
3. The author coins a few phrases of her own. Refer to the context in which they appear to help you define the following: *step-style* (paragraph 3); Stronger One (11); *locked in* (17); Catch-30 (24); authenticity crisis (33).

• SUGGESTIONS FOR WRITING •

1. From your experience, observation, or reading, test the accuracy of one of Gail Sheehy's accounts of a typical period of crisis.
2. Inspired by Sheehy's division of life after eighteen into phases, look back on your own earlier life or that of a younger person you know, and detail a series of phases in it. Invent names for the phases.

· Desmond Morris ·

DESMOND MORRIS was born in Wiltshire, England in 1928 and earned a B.S. degree in zoology from Birmingham University and a Ph.D. degree from Oxford. From 1956 to 1959 he made animal behavior films at the London Zoo, then became curator of mammals for the Zoological Society in 1959. Increasingly, his interest in animal behavior led him toward an interest in human behavior. He now holds a Research Fellowship at Oxford. The author of more than fifty scientific papers and a dozen books, he has most recently written *The Naked Ape* (1967), *The Human Zoo* (1970), *Intimate Behavior* (1972), and *Manwatching* (1977).

Salutation Displays

When Desmond Morris observes two people greeting each other, he notices many more subtle exchanges between them than most people do. Not a step, a shrug, an eyebrow lift, or a flutter escapes his keen awareness. In "Salutation Displays," a chapter from *Manwatching*, the author classifies and names all the greeting displays that come into play when people meet. Note whether, by matching your own behavior or that of your friends with the author's observations, you have ever proven Morris right.

A Salutation Display demonstrates that we wish people   1
well, or, at the very least, that we wish them no harm. It transmits signals of friendliness or the absence of hostility. It does this at peak moments — when people are arriving on the scene, departing from it, or dramatically changing their social role. We salute their comings, their goings and their transformations, and we do it with rituals of greeting, farewell and celebration.

Whenever two friends meet after a long separation, they go   2
through a special Greeting Ritual. During the first moments of the reunion they amplify their friendly signals to super-friendly

signals. They smile and touch, often embrace and kiss, and generally behave more intimately and expansively than usual. They do this because they have to make up for lost time — lost friendship time. While they have been apart it has been impossible for them to send the hundreds of small, minute-by-minute friendly signals to each other that their relationship requires, and they have, so to speak, built up a backlog of these signals.

This backlog amounts to a gestural debt that must be repaid   3
without delay, as an assurance that the bond of friendship has not waned but has survived the passage of time spent apart — hence the gushing ceremonies of the reunion scene, which must try to pay off this debt in a single outburst of activity.

Once the Greeting Ritual is over, the old relationship be-   4
tween the friends is now re-established and they can continue with their amicable interactions as before. Eventually, if they have to part for another long spell, there will be a Separation Ritual in which the super-friendly signals will once again be displayed. This time they have the function of leaving both partners with a powerful dose of befriendedness, to last them throught the isolated times to come.

In a similar way, if people undergo a major change in social   5
role, we again offer them a massive outpouring of friendliness, because we are simultaneously saying farewell to their old self and greeting their new self. We do this when boy and girl become man and wife, when man and wife become father and mother, when prince becomes king, when candidate becomes president, and when competitor becomes champion.

We have many formal procedures for celebrating these occa-   6
sions, both the physical arrivals and departures and the symbolic comings and goings of the social transformations. We celebrate birthdays, christenings, comings-of-age, weddings, coronations, anniversaries, inaugurations, presentations, and retirements. We give house-warmings, welcoming parties, farewell dinners, and funerals. In all these cases we are, in essence, performing Salutation Displays.

The grander the occasion, the more rigid and institutional   7
are the procedures. But even our more modest, private, two-person rituals follow distinct sets of rules. We seem to be almost

incapable of beginning or ending any kind of encounter without performing some type of salutation. This is even true when we write a letter to someone. We begin with "Dear Mr. Smith" and end "Yours faithfully," and the rules of salutation are so compelling that we do this even when Mr. Smith is far from dear to us and we have little faith in him.

Similarly we shake hands with unwelcome guests and express regret at their departure, although we are glad to see the back of them. All the more reason, then, that our genuine greetings and farewells should be excessively demonstrative. 8

Social greetings that are planned and anticipated have a distinctive structure and fall into four separate phases: 9

1. The Inconvenience Display. To show the strength of our friendliness, we "put ourselves out" to varying degrees. We demonstrate that we are taking trouble. For both host and guest, this may mean "dressing up." For the guest it may mean a long journey. For the host it also entails a bodily shift from the center of his home territory. The stronger the greeting, the greater the inconvenience. The Head of State drives to the airport to meet the important arrival. The brother drives to the airport to greet his sister returning from abroad. This is the maximum form of bodily displacement that a host can offer. From this extreme there is a declining scale of inconvenience, as the distance traveled by the host decreases. He may only go as far as the local station or bus depot. Or he may move no farther than his front drive, emerging from his front door after watching through the window for the moment of arrival. Or he may wait for the bell to ring and then only displace himself as far as his doorway or front hall. Or he may allow a child or servant to answer the door and remain in his room, the very center of his territory, awaiting the guest who is then ushered into his presence. The minimal Inconvenience Display he can offer is to stand up when the guest enters the room, displacing himself vertically but not horizontally. Only if he remains seated as the guest enters and approaches him, can he be said to be totally omitting Phase One of a planned social greeting. Such omissions are extremely rare today and some degree of voluntary in- 10

convenience is nearly always demonstrated. If, because of some accident or delay, it is unavoidably omitted, there are profuse apologies for its absence when the meeting finally takes place.

At the time of farewell, the Inconvenience Display is 11 repeated in much the same form. "You know your own way out" is the lowest level of expression here. Beyond that, there is an increasing displacement from territorial base, with the usual social level being "I will see you to the door." A slightly more intense form involves going outside the house and waiting there until the departing figures have vanished from sight. And so on, with the full expression being an accompaniment to the station or airport.

2. The Distant Display. The main moment of greeting is 12 when body contact is made, but before this comes the moment of first sighting. As soon as host and guest have identified each other, they signify this fact with a recognition response. Doorstep meetings tend to curtail this phase, because contact can be made almost immediately the door is opened, but in most other greeting situations the Distance Display is prominently demonstrated. It consists of six visual elements: (1) the Smile; (2) the Eyebrow Flash; (3) the Head Tilt; (4) the Hail; (5) the Wave; and (6) the Intention Embrace.

The first three of these almost always occur, and they are 13 performed simultaneously. At the moment of recognition, the head tilts back, the eyebrows arch up, and the face breaks into a large smile. The Head Tilt and the Eyebrow Flash may be very brief. They are elements of surprise. Combined with the smile, they signal a "pleasant surprise" at seeing the friend. This basic pattern may or may not be augmented by an arm movement. The simplest such action is the Hail — the raising of one hand. A more intense version, typical of long-distance greetings, is the Wave, and a still more intense expression is the Intention Embrace, in which the arms are stretched out towards the friend, as if the greeter cannot wait to perform the contact-embrace that is about to take place. A flamboyant specialty sometimes added is the Thrown or Blown Kiss, again anticipating the contact to come.

As before, the same actions are repeated during the farewell 14
Separation Ritual, but with Intention Embraces less likely and
Thrown or Blown Kisses more likely.

Of these Distant Displays, the Smile, Head Tilt, and 15
Eyebrow Flash appear to be worldwide. They have been observed in remote native tribes that had never previously encountered white men. The raising of an arm in some form of
Hail or Wave salute is also extremely widespread. The exact
form of the arm movement may vary from culture to culture,
but the existence of *some* kind of arm action appears to be global
for mankind. The action seems to stem, like the Intention Embrace, from an urge to reach out and touch the other person. In
the Hail, the arm is raised up rather than reached out, because
this makes it more conspicuous from a distance, but the movement is essentially a stylized version of touching the distant
friend. More "historical" explanations, such as that the hand is
raised to show it is empty of weapons or that it is thrust up to
mime the action of offering the owner's sword, and therefore his
allegiance, may be true in certain specific contexts, but the action is too widespread and too general for this interpretation to
stand for all cases of Hailing.

The Wave takes three main forms: the Vertical Wave, the 16
Hidden-palm Wave, and the Lateral Wave. In the Vertical
Wave, the palm faces the friend and the hand moves repeatedly
up and down. This appears to be the "primitive" form of waving. In origin, it seems to be a vacuum patting action, the hand
patting the friend's body at a distance, again in anticipation of
the friendly embrace to come. The Hidden-palm Wave, seen
mainly in Italy, is also a patting action, but with the hand moving repeatedly towards the waver himself. To non-Italians, this
looks rather like beckoning, but it is basically another form of
vacuum embracing. The Lateral Wave, common all over the
world, consists of showing the palm to the friend and then moving it rhythmically from side to side. This appears to be an improved form of the other waves. The modification is essentially
one of increasing the visibility and conspicuousness of the patting action. In turning it into a lateral movement, it loses its embracing quality, but gains dramatically in visual impact from a

distance. It can be further exaggerated by extending it to full arm-waving, or even double-arm-waving.

3. The Close Display. As soon as the Distant Display has been performed, there is an approach interval and then the key moment of actual body contact. At full intensity this consists of a total embrace, bringing both arms around the friend's body, with frontal trunk contact and head contact. There is much hugging, squeezing, patting, cheek-pressing, and kissing. This may be followed by intense eye contact at close range, cheek-clasping, mouth-kissing, hair-stroking, laughing, even weeping, and, of course, continued smiling.

From this uninhibited display, there is a whole range of body-contacts of decreasing strength, right down to the formal handshake. The precise intensity will depend on: (1) the depth of the prior relationship; (2) the length of the separation; (3) the privacy of the greeting context; (4) the local, cultural display-rules and traditions; and (5) the changes that have taken place during the separation.

Most of these conditions are obvious enough, but the last deserves comment. If the friend is known to have been through some major emotional experience — an ordeal such as imprisonment, illness, or disaster, or a great success such as an award, a victory, or an honor — there will be a much more intense greeting and stronger embracing. This is because the Salutation Display is simultaneously a greeting and a celebration and is, in effect, double-strength.

Different cultures have formalized the close greeting performance in different ways. In all cases, the basis of the display is the full embrace, but when this is simplified, different parts of it are retained in different places. In some cultures, the head-to-head element becomes nose-rubbing, cheek-mouthing, or face-pressing. In others, there is a stylized mutual cheek-kiss, with the lips stopping short of contact. In others again, there is kissing between men — in France and Russia, for example — while in many cultures, male-to-male kissing is omitted as supposedly effeminate.

While these cultural variations are, of course, of interest, they should not be allowed to obscure the fact that they are all

17

18

19

20

21

variations on a basic theme — the body embrace. This is the fundamental, global, human contact action, the one we all know as babies, infants, and growing children, and to which we return whenever the rules permit and we wish to demonstrate feelings of attachment for another individual.

4. The "Grooming" Display. Following the initial body con-   22
tacts, we move into the final stage of the greeting ceremony, which is similar to the social grooming performances of monkeys and apes. We do not pick at one another's fur, but instead we display "Grooming Talk" — inane comments that mean very little in themselves, but which demonstrate vocally our pleasure at the meeting. "How are you?" "How nice of you to come," "Did you have a good journey?" "You are looking so well," "Let me take your coat," and so on. The answers are barely heard. All that is important is to pay compliments and to receive them. To show concern and to show pleasure. The precise verbal content and the intelligence of the questions is almost irrelevant. This Grooming Display is sometimes augmented by helping with clothing, taking off coats, and generally fussing with creature comforts. On occasion there is an additional Gift Display on the part of the guest, who brings some small offering as a further, material form of salutation.

After the Grooming Display is over, the friends leave the   23
special site of the greeting and move on to resume their old, familiar, social interactions. The Salutation Display is complete and has performed its important task.

By contrast, unplanned greetings are far less elaborate.   24
When we see a friend in the street, or somewhere away from home, we give the typical Distant Display — a smile and a wave — and perhaps no more. Or we approach and add a Close Display, usually a rather abbreviated embrace, but more usually a mere handshake. As we part, we again display, often turning for a final Distant Signal, as we move off.

Introductory Greetings take yet another form. If we are   25
meeting someone for the first time, we omit the Distant Display, simply because we are not recognizing an old friend. We do, however, offer a minor form of Close Display, nearly always a handshake, and we smile at the new acquaintance and offer him

a Grooming Display of friendly chatter and concern. We treat him, in fact, as though he were a friend already, not a close one but a friend none the less, and in so doing we bring him into our orbit and initiate a social relationship with him.

As a species of primate, we are remarkably rich in greetings and farewells. Other primates do show some simple greeting rituals, but we exceed them all, and we also show farewell displays which they seem to lack entirely. Looking back into our ancestry, there seems to have been a good reason for this development. Most primates move around in a fairly close-knit group. Occasionally, they may drift apart and then, on reuniting, will give small gestures of greeting. But they rarely part deliberately, in a purposeful way, so they have no use for Separation Displays. Early man established himself as a hunting species, with the male hunting group leaving for a specific purpose at a specific time, and then returning to the home base with the kill. For millions of years, therefore, we have needed Salutation Displays, both in the form of farewells, as the group split up in its major division-of-labor, and in the form of greetings, when they came together again. And the importance of success or failure on the hunt meant that these were not trivial, but vital moments in the communal life of the primeval tribe. Little wonder that today we are such a salutatory species.

• QUESTIONS ON MEANING AND PURPOSE •

1. How many kinds of Salutation Displays does Morris introduce? Of these, which one does he analyze the most thoroughly?
2. Name and describe Morris's four categories of anticipated social greetings. According to the author, how do unplanned social greetings differ from planned ones?
3. How does Morris account for the fact that human Salutation Displays are more numerous and elaborate than those of other primates?
4. How accurately do Morris's descriptions of the various Salutation Displays reflect the behavior of people in your own social group?
5. Sum up what you believe to be the purpose of the Morris's essay.

• QUESTIONS ON WRITING STRATEGY •

1. Where in his essay does Morris not only classify, but also divide?
2. In paragraph 16, what does the author subclassify into smaller groups?
3. By what method does Morris define each of the terms he uses in his discussion? (See Chapter 9, Definition.)
4. Is Morris addressing trained scientists like himself, or general readers? What in the essay indicates his intended audience?

• QUESTIONS ON LANGUAGE •
• AND VOCABULARY •

1. Be sure you know the meanings of the following words as Morris uses them: amicable (paragraph 4); institutionalized (7); flamboyant (13); allegiance (15); vacuum (16); stylized (20); primeval (26).
2. To what extent is Morris justified in beginning so many of his words and phrases with capital letters?

• SUGGESTIONS FOR WRITING •

1. For a working knowledge of how Morris has organized and classified a wealth of material, make a formal outline of his essay.
2. Describe a formal ritual common to our culture — such as a christening, a bar mitzvah, a confirmation, a wedding, a going-away party, a funeral — as if you were explaining it to someone from another planet.
3. In an essay, classify the body language you'd see in class, on a bus, at a mixer, or at a campus restaurant.

BRENDAN BOYD, born in 1945, has written two books, *The Great American Baseball Card Book* (1973) and *And a Player to Be Named Later*, to be published in 1982. Having worked as a comic-strip writer, a rock-music columnist for the *Los Angeles Times* and a racetrack groom, Boyd is now a trade book editor and writes a syndicated financial column called "Investor's Notebook."

Packaged News

Well aware that the show must go on, the writer of "Packaged News" aims a satiric shaft at the seven o'clock news on TV. With tongue in cheek, Boyd classifies his favorites among the stories he insists TV audiences can count on seeing — even on a day with absolutely no newsworthy events.

> Good evening, ladies and gentlemen. Welcome to *The Seven o'Clock News.*
> Nothing happened today.
> Goodnight.

That's the way television *should* handle the four out of seven days every week when current events go into suspended animation. But don't hang by your rabbit ears waiting for it to happen. Because the television news, contrary to FCC disclaimers, is not really the news at all. It's just another way for the networks to sell Efferdent, and for corporate America to unwind after its collective tough day at the office.

Thus, on those not-so-infrequent days when the Pope has not been shot, Afghanistan has not been invaded, and no member of the British Royal Family has needlessly disgraced himself, the networks still carry out their contractual obligation, if not necessarily their duty, to report the news, even though there's no news to report. They dust off their file of canned headlines, change a few names, and settle in to perpetuate the requisite delusion that something really did happen today .

Of course, the day will come when absolutely nothing hap-   3
pens. And on that day we'll all be subjected to the ultimate in
televised monotony: *The Seven o'Clock News with Absolutely
Nothing New About It Whatsoever*. As always, the events of this
numbingly uneventful day will be sorted into the usual predictable categories.

World Update

This first class of story is intended to make viewers feel that   4
because an event has limitless scale it also has limitless importance. Television newscasters like to distract us from the
vacuousness of their stories by impressing us with the amount of
ground these stories cover.

Soviet Leader Brezhnev Rumored Ill. This is the perfect lead   5
item for a slow news day. It's both potentially earthshaking and
completely irrefutable. It replaces that perennial favorite, *Mao
Rumored Dead*, which passed into blessed obsolescence several
years back when the Chinese leader actually died. If Brezhnev
has not been looking particularly feeble lately, some other Iron
Curtain codger's name may safely be substituted. And in a
pinch, a more generalized notion about totalitarians will suffice
— say, *Kremlin Shake-up Hinted.*

846 Perish in Indian Train Mishap. Or *267 Killed as Mexican*   6
Bus Plunges off Mountain. Or *536 Die in Burmese Ferry Crash*. In
all Third World disasters the volume of the victimization is
meant to compensate for our physical and emotional distance
from the event. But no matter how many Africans starve to
death in any given famine, television doesn't really consider it
news unless Frank Sinatra didn't punch a photographer that
day. The New York tabloids are rumored to use a formula in
determining space allocations for such stories. *800 Dead in Boliv-
ian Earthquake*, for example, is said to equal 6 *Felled by Ptomaine
at Staten Island Clambake.*

Troops Mass Along Nepalese Border. Troops are always mass-   7
ing somewhere. That's what troops do. And their massing is
always supposed to mean something ominous, although usually
it doesn't. Notice that we never see a follow-up story about
troops *disbanding* along the Nepalese border.

SALT Talks Winding Down. For ten years the only thing we   8
knew about the SALT talks was that they were about to re-
open. Now that we've finally figured out what the SALT talks
are supposed to be, they seem always to be winding down. To
establish the proper tedious mood, this story should be followed
by one of the following diplomatic grace notes: *NATO Maneuvers Begin. Rumblings in SEATO.* Or *Bilateral Trade Agreements
Signal New ERA in U.S.-New Zealand Friendship.*

Christian Democrats Score Gains in Belgium. There are 627   9
political parties in Europe. All but nine have the word Christian or Democrat in their names. And they're always scoring
gains.

U.N. General Assembly Convenes. This is a portentous oc-   10
currence which everyone in the world thinks he or she should
care about, but which nobody actually does.

U.S.-Cuba Thaw Seen Possible. This is the obligatory hopeful   11
note in East-West relations. It alternates with pictorial essays of
visiting American plumbers teaching mainland Chinese apprentices how to steam-clean a grease trap.

Cyprus After Makarios. Another in the always popular   12
series, "Incredibly Shallow Profiles of Enigmatic Dictators." A
personal favorite has always been *Souvanna Phouma, Cambodia's
Neutralist Playboy,* although I must admit a lingering fondness
for the now obsolete *Ethiopian Ruler Haile Selassie Marks 87th
Birthday by Buying New Summerweight Uniform.*

Pope Urges World Leaders to Seek Peace. But notice he never   13
says exactly *how.*

National Update

The second class of story is intended to make viewers feel   14
that because something is happening *near* them it is somehow
relevant *to* them. And let's face it, there is something more compelling about even the most banal range of events if the boredom they engender has a distinctly local flavor.

Former Senator Eugene McCarthy Mulling Third Party Try.   15
Ah, the sixties. They provide the networks with an endless
source of thirty-second filmclips on how Joan Baez has mel-

lowed, Jane Fonda hasn't, and Dick Gregory remains the world's skinniest nudge.

Conspiracy Theorists Hint New Oswald Evidence. Mention of   16
President Kennedy's assassin is frequently linked in a two-cushion shot with news that there are *Fresh Indications James Earl Ray Acted Alone in King Killing.*

47 Percent Favor Easing of Marijuana Laws. And the other 53   17
percent are too stoned to care. Polls are a favorite ploy for slow news days. Who, after all, can fail to attach at least marginal significance to a finding such as "72 percent of Americans believe that asparagus turns urine green, whereas a surprising 38 percent feel that getting in an eight-item supermarket express line with nine items should be punishable by death."

Kennedy Family Marks Anniversary of First Congressional Victory. Every day of the year is some sort of anniversary for the   18
Kennedys. No anchorman worth his capped teeth would let one slide by without paying perfunctory homage to "three decades of heartbreak."

Switch to Metric System Poses Problems. Or, "Is Celsius a   19
Communist plot to bore us to death?"

Ex-Nixon Crony Robert Vesco Linked to New Illegalities. Just   20
as every corporation in the United States is destined to be bought by ITT, every white-collar crime committed in the free world during the past fifteen years will eventually be linked to Robert Vesco.

Parents Unite to Fight Pornography in School Libraries. No   21
doubt they're up in arms against *Huckleberry Finn,* the underwear section of the Sears catalog, and the Manhattan Yellow Pages.

Business and Finance

The third class of story is meant to appeal to *the* primal in-   22
terest of every potential viewer — money. Economics is the ultimate mystery. And television broadcasters do nothing to allay our bewilderment with their nightly recalculations of our shrinking worth.

Housing Starts Decline 23 Percent. Housing starts, domestic car sales, and American exports have declined every month for the past twenty years. How far down, pray tell, is down? [23]

Prime Rate Rises ¼ Percent. All together now, class, what is the prime rate? That's right. It's the rate the nation's banks charge their most credit-worthy customers. And why did the Dow Jones Industrial Average go down yesterday? That's right. Profit taking. And why is it going up today? That's right. Bargain hunting. One of the more comforting characteristics of television news is that, having told us any salient fact about a given situation, it can safely be counted on to tell us that fact, and only that fact, over and over again. [24]

Human Interest, Human Horror

Television newscasters have always depended on the misfortune of strangers. These stories are meant to appeal to the kind of people who slow down on the highway to get a good look at a car wreck. That is to say — all of us. [25]

Cancer Linked to Banana Daiquiris. This one comes from television news's extensive "Life Causes Death" file. [26]

Detroit Man Goes Berserk, Turns Rifle on Crowd. He was unquestionably a quiet, neat, well-mannered man whom neighbors say would be the last person you'd ever expect to do such a thing. [27]

National Guard, Boy Scouts Scour Woods for Missing Toddler. Aside to Gloria Steinem: Why aren't the Girl Scouts ever called out on such occasions? [28]

Sidelights

Plus, if time permits (and unfortunately it always seems to) we can count on a quick hopscotching of headlines drawn from all of the preceding categories. These stories are too important sounding to ignore but too familiar to devote more than thirty seconds to. [29]

G.M. Recalls Every Car It Made Last Year
New Bomber Hits Cost Overruns

Guam Accelerates Drive for Statehood
Teamster Insurgents Press Leadership for Reforms
All-Volunteer Army Seen Foundering
Recluse Found Starved to Death With $3 Million Stuffed in Mattress
Postal Service to Seek Rate Increases
First Thompsons Gazelle in 27 Years Born in Captivity
Seven Tie for First-Round Lead in Greater Greensboro Open

Parting Inspirational Feature

This final story is meant to send the now ossified viewers away either laughing, shaking their heads, or feeling grateful that none of the awful things that happened that day happened to them.

Nation's Oldest Living Man Observes 116th Birthday. Every slow news day can use an uplifting senior citizen feature to top it off. There are only three possibilities here. The first involves either a visit to a rest home by a third-tier celebrity like Corbett Monica or Deborah Raffin, or a mass golden-ager outing to some heinously inappropriate setting (*150 Elders Enjoy Day at New Jersey Drag Speedway*). The second is a courage-in-the-face-of-adversity story such as *Despite Beatings, Blindness, Bankruptcy, Widowed Iron Lung Inhabitant Counts Blessings.* (I demand a recount.) The third, and most popular alternative, chronicles a birthday party for a senior citizen who, having achieved a particularly ill-advised longevity, is then required to state his prescription for long life. This recipe usually consists of equal parts smoking, drinking, and womanizing. But it makes no mention whatsoever of watching the seven o'clock news.

• QUESTIONS ON MEANING •

1. Lurking within Brendan Boyd's humor can be found several serious criticisms of televised news. Which of Boyd's thrusts seem most on target?

2. Comment on the writer's assertion in paragraph 1 that "the television news . . . is not really the news at all."
3. In your own words, how would you sum up Boyd's thesis in this essay? (See *Thesis* in Useful Terms.)

• QUESTIONS ON WRITING STRATEGY •

1. In sorting out the nonevents of the day into categories (World Update; National Update; Business and Finance; Human Interest; Human Horror; Sidelights; and Parting Inspirational Feature), does Boyd invent the categories, or only the names for them?
2. What is the effect of the essay's concluding sentence? (See *Conclusion* in Useful Terms.)
3. How effective do you find Boyd's satire? (See *Satire* in Useful Terms.)

• QUESTIONS ON LANGUAGE •
• AND VOCABULARY •

1. Be sure you know what Boyd means by the following: perpetuate, requisite (paragraph 2); vacuousness (4); irrefutable, obsolescence, codger (5); portentous (10); obligatory (11); banal, engender (14); nudge (15); ploy (17); perfunctory (18); allay (22); salient (24); ossified (30).
2. In paragraph 1, Boyd remarks that on some days current events "go into suspended animation." He adds, "But don't hang by your rabbit ears. . . ." Point to other phrases that contribute to the humor of Boyd's essay.

• SUGGESTIONS FOR WRITING •

1. Instead of classifying, as Boyd does, explain in a paragraph how an evening of network TV is typically *divided*.
2. In an informal, humorous essay, classify TV commercials. Invent names for each of your categories.
3. With familiar types of TV programs in mind (game show, detective thriller, interview show), make up several new types that, you predict, television producers will soon invent. Supply examples of possible new programs for each category.

4. Selecting one kind of television show now on the air (situation comedy, for instance), think of all the examples with which you are best acquainted. Then, in a short essay, classify them into smaller categories, to which you assign names. Situation comedy, for instance, might include "the bright young couple comedy," "the big family comedy," "the people at work comedy," and others.

Repackaging the News

Brendan Boyd tells how, faced by a great number of examples illustrating the point he wanted to make, he was able to wrestle his material into shape. Before beginning to write, he built a serviceable framework for his satire by classifying the examples into categories that readers can recognize.

The best things to write about are things you've experienced yourself. That way you both *know* and *feel* your subject. I usually find the things I write about under my nose, or rather they find me.

I was hired to write this piece, just as you, or any other student, might be assigned to write a paper. I was assigned a rhetorical pattern — classification. I was given a length range of 1000 to 1500 words. I was allowed to choose my own subject.

I originally thought of writing about rock musicians. But I soon discovered that every musician I wanted to write about was a world unto himself and thus resistant to clear-cut classification. Then one night I was watching television when it suddenly occurred to me that the television news is basically the same every night. Here was a topic that lent itself to classification; for I could analyze what made the news so repetitive, what kinds of stories came up again and again.

Before I began classifying, though, I thought some more about the topic. It was a particularly good one for me not only because I experienced it daily as a television viewer but also because I felt strongly about it. If nothing else, the news is supposed to be new. Yet the same things keep happening over and over again, and television, in the interests of selling advertising, keeps pretending they're new and sensational. This annoys me, and annoyance is a perfect point from which to begin writing about anything. If you're annoyed with something, you care about it. And if you care about it, you have a very good chance of making others care about it as well in your writing, provided you don't let your caring get in the way of your writing. It was to avoid this possibility that I chose a humorous style for this piece. You can often do more damage to something that annoys you by making fun of it than you can by ranting and raving about it. And you keep your readers' attention better, too.

In classifying television news, I wanted to depict its sameness graphically by organizing the recurrent stories into patterns of predictability. To arrive at the patterns, I first listed all the stories that turned up repeatedly on television. In reading over the completed list I noted that many items were related, such as disasters in Third World nations, or assassination conspiracy theories, or public-opinion poll results.

If you too have yawned through reports of these same non-happenings, then maybe these categories will make sense to you.

1. Write an essay by the method of division, in which you analyze one of the following subjects. In breaking your subject into its component parts, explain or describe each part in some detail; try to indicate how each part functions, or how it contributes to the whole. If you have to subdivide any parts into smaller ones, go ahead, but clearly indicate to your reader what you are doing.

   A day
   A year
   A paycheck
   A sonnet
   A short story, a play, or a dramatic film
   The government of your community
   The human brain
   A bookstore (or other place of business)
   A farm
   Chinese cooking
   The Bible
   A band or orchestra
   A hospital
   The public school system of your town or city

2. Write an essay by the method of classification, in which you sort out the following subjects into categories. Make clear your purpose in classifying things, and the basis of your classification. This essay shouldn't turn out to be a disconnected list, but should break down the subject into groups. You may find it helpful to make up a name for each group, or otherwise clearly identify it.

The records you own	Comic strips
Families	Movie monsters
Sports cars	Skiers
Penal institutions	Sports announcers
Stand-up comedians	Singers
Present-day styles of marriage	Bad habits
Vacations	Inconsiderate people
College students today	Radio stations
Paperback novels	

· 7 ·

ANALOGY

Drawing a Parallel

· THE METHOD ·

The photography instructor is perspiring. He is trying to explain the workings of a typical camera to people who barely know how to pop a film cartridge into an Instamatic. "Let me give you an analogy," he offers — and from that moment, the faces of his class start coming alive. They understand him. What helps is his *analogy*: a point-by-point comparison that explains something unknown in terms of something familiar.

"Like the pupil in the human eye," the instructor begins, "the aperture of a camera — that's the opening in front — is adjustable. It contracts or it widens, letting in a lesser or a greater amount of light. The film in the camera is like the retina at the back of the eye — it receives an image. . . ." And the instructor continues, taking up one point at a time, working out the similarities between camera and eye.

To make clear his explanation, the instructor uses an analogy often found in basic manuals of photography. The inner workings of a Konica FS-1 may be mysterious to a beginning student of photography, but the parts of the eye are familiar to anyone who has looked in a mirror, or has had to draw and label the parts of the eye in sixth grade. Not every time you write an essay, but once in a while, analogy will be a wonderfully useful method. With its help you can explain a subject that is complicated, unfamiliar, or intangible. You can put it into terms as concrete and understandable as nuts and nutcrackers.

If the photography instructor had said, "The human eye is a kind of camera," he would have stated a *metaphor*. As you may recall from having read any poetry, a metaphor is a figure of speech that declares one thing to be another — even though it isn't, in a strictly literal sense — for the purpose of making us aware of similarity. "Hope," says the poet Emily Dickinson, "is the thing with feathers / That perches in the soul" — thus pointing to the similarity between a feeling and a bird (also between the human soul and a tree that birds light in). By its very nature, an analogy is a kind of extended metaphor: *extended*, because it is usually lengthy and touches on a number of similarities. Here is an example. In August 1981, after *Voyager II* transmitted to Earth its spectacular pictures of Saturn, NASA scientists held a news briefing. They wanted to explain to the public the difficulty of what they had achieved. They realized, however, that most people have no clear idea of the distance from Earth to Saturn, nor of the complexities of space navigation; and so they used an analogy. To bring *Voyager II* within close range of Saturn, they explained, was analogous to sinking a putt from 500 miles away. Extending the metaphor, one scientist added, "Of course, you should allow the golfer to run alongside the ball and make trajectory corrections by blowing on it."[1] A listener can immediately grasp the point: such a feat is colossally hard.

Writers of scientific books and articles are particularly fond of analogy because they need to explain matters that the reader

---

[1]Quoted by Robert Cooke in a news story, "Voyager Sends a Surprise Package," *Boston Globe*, August 27, 1981.

without technical training may find difficult. But the method is a favorite, too, of preachers and philosophers, because it can serve to make things beyond the experience of our senses vivid and graspable. We see this happening in one of the most famous passages in medieval literature. It is an analogy given by the eighth-century English historian Bede, who tells how in the year 627 King Edwin of Northumbria summoned a council to decide whether to accept the strange new religion of Christianity. Said one counselor:

> Your Majesty, when we compare the present life of man on earth with that time of which we have no knowledge, it seems to me like the swift flight of a single sparrow through the banqueting-hall where you are sitting at dinner on a winter's day with your thanes and counselors. In the midst there is a comforting fire to warm the hall; outside, the storms of winter rain or snow are raging. This sparrow flies swiftly in through one door of the hall, and out through another. While he is inside, he is safe from the winter storms; but after a few moments of comfort, he vanishes from sight into the wintry world from which he came. Even so, man appears on earth for a little while; but of what went before this life or of what follows, we know nothing. Therefore, if this new teaching has brought any more certain knowledge, it seems only right that we should follow it.[2]

Why, after twelve centuries, has this analogy remained unforgotten? Our minds cannot grasp infinite time, and we hardly can comprehend humankind's relation to it. But we can readily visualize a winter's snow and rain and a sparrow's flight through a banquet hall.

Like a poet, who also discovers metaphors, the writer who draws an analogy gives pleasure to the reader by comparing things that may not have seemed comparable. In setting forth vigorous, concrete, and familiar examples, an analogy may strike us with force. For this reason, it is sometimes used by a writer who wishes to sway and arouse an audience, to engrave a message in memory. In his celebrated speech, "I Have a Dream,"

---

[2] *A History of the English Church and People*, trans. Leo Sherley-Price, rev. R. E. Latham (Baltimore: Penguin Books, 1968), p.127.

Martin Luther King, Jr., draws a remarkable analogy to express the anger and disappointment of American blacks that, one hundred years after Lincoln's Emancipation Proclamation, their full freedom has yet to be achieved. "It is obvious today," declares Dr. King, "that America has defaulted on this promissory note"; and he compares the founding fathers' written guarantee — of the rights of life, liberty, and the pursuit of happiness — to a bad check returned for insufficient funds. Yet his speech ends on a different note, and with a different analogy. He prays that the "jangling discords of our nation" will become in time a "symphony of brotherhood." (For the entire speech, see Chapter 10.)

Dr. King does not pretend to set forth a logical argument. There may be logic in his poetic words, but his purpose is to rouse his listeners and inspire them to fight on. Sometimes, however, you find the method of analogy used in an argument that pretends to be carefully reasoned, but really isn't logical at all. (For more about this misuse of analogy, see *Argument from Analogy* under *Logical Fallacies* in Useful Terms.)

Sometimes, an analogy provides a hypothetical example that clearly *illustrates* an idea that might be hard to grasp if explained by another method. Few of us can readily imagine what life would be like if we had been blind, deaf, and mute since early childhood. This was the condition in which Helen Keller — later famous as an author, a lecturer, and an educator — found herself at the age of seven. With a splendid analogy, she explains what her life was like, and what it was like to receive her first communication from her teacher, Anne Sullivan:

> Have you ever been at sea in a dense fog, when it seemed as if a tangible white darkness shut you in, and the great ship, tense and anxious, groped her way toward the shore with plummet and sounding line, and you waited with beating heart for something to happen? I was like that ship before my education began, only I was without compass or sounding line, and had no way of knowing how near the harbor was. "Light! give me light!" was the wordless cry of my soul, and the light of love shone on me in that very hour.[3]

[3]*The Story of My Life* (New York: Doubleday, 1903), p. 84.

By touching the palm of the child's hand, Anne Sullivan had taught her to spell out words. Helen Keller's almost unimaginable loneliness as a child, and the joy of her liberation, could hardly be better expressed. With the powerful aid of analogy, she renders her former situation at once clear, and forever memorable.

• THE PROCESS •

When you set forth a subject that you believe will be unfamiliar to your readers, then analogy may come to your aid. In explaining some special knowledge, the method is most likely to be valuable. Did you ever play some unusual sport? Are you expert in a particular skill, or knowledgeable in some hobby? Did you ever travel to some place your readers may not have visited? Have you ever learned the workings of some specialized machine (a mechanical potato-peeler, say, or an automatic pinsetter)? Have you had any experience that most people haven't? Is your family background, perhaps, unusual? You may then have a subject that will be made clearer by the method of analogy.

With subject in hand, then consider: exactly what will your analogy be? A bright idea has to dawn on you. If none *does* dawn, then it's far better to write your essay by some other method than to contrive a laborious, forced analogy. "Death is a dollar bill," one writer began — but the analogy that followed seemed a counterfeit. Remember: An effective analogy points to real similarities, not manufactured ones. (The author of the dollar bill essay went on: "Death is a cold condition, like cold, hard cash. . . ."—inflating an already weak currency.)

An analogy likens its subject to something more familiar than itself — as space navigation is likened to a game of golf. Your subject may be an abstraction or a feeling, but in analogy you can't use another abstraction or feeling to explain it. Were a scientist, for instance, to liken the steering of *Voyager II* to the charting of a person's spiritual course through life, the result might be a fascinating essay, but it wouldn't explain the steering of the spacecraft. (If the scientist's main *subject* were the charting of a spiritual course, and if he were writing for an audience of technicians to whom the steering of *Voyager II* was familiar, then indeed, he could write an analogy.)

There's one more preliminary test of your idea. Like all good metaphors, an analogy sets forth a writer's fresh discovery. The reader ought to think, "Look at that! Those two things are a lot alike! Who would have thought so?" (You, the writer — that's who.) That is why the analogy of a camera to the human eye (if you haven't heard it before) is striking; and why Bede's comparison of a life to the flight of a sparrow through a warm room is effective. You could write an essay likening toothpaste to bar soap, and remark that both make suds and float dirt away; but the result would probably put the reader to sleep, and anyhow, it wouldn't be an analogy. Both things would be simple and familiar, and too similar. You wouldn't be using one to explain the other. Dissimilarity, as well as similarity, has to be present to make a metaphor. And so, before you write, make sure that your subject and what you explain it with are noticeably *unlike* each other.

You now have your bright idea. Next you make a brief outline, listing your subject, what you'll use to explain it, and their similarities. Most analogies begin by likening the two, then go on to work through the similarities one point at a time. Never mind the differences. If your analogy is to form only a part of your essay, then later, perhaps, you will want to mention the differences — but wait until you have completed your analogy.

At last, with your outline before you, you are ready to write. As you work, visualize your subject (*if* it can be visualized — Bede's subject, the brevity of life, can't). Be sure to hold in your mind's eye the thing with which you explain your subject. Try for the most exact, concrete words you can find. An effective analogy is definite. It makes something swing wide, as a key unlocks a door.

• ANALOGY IN A PARAGRAPH •

Fred Silverman ran a network's TV schedule with all the self-assurance of a man writing menus for a truck stop. You could find him, as a rule, in the kitchen — for he insisted on tasting the cooking. If the woof of a dog didn't sound right in a cartoon, the producer had to be told how a dog barks. Like the proprietor of a diner who had to watch how much salt and pepper went into everything, Silverman worried and fussed, first as head programmer for CBS and then for ABC (the once sleepy joint that his menus transformed into the busiest, shiniest eatery around), later as president of NBC. Silverman worried according to a principle: "In putting together a schedule, the first thing you have to do is maintain a certain audience level." That meant ratings. With a universal bill of fare, Silverman set out to please all comers: truckers, teen-agers, families with kids, retirees. He happened to like what they liked, and it wasn't pheasant under glass. He noted which items moved and which didn't. He'd cancel an exotic *Pink Lady* show (featuring two Japanese singers, sensations in their country, but duds here) the way the menu-man might cross out a slow-selling sukiyaki. Was a situation comedy unappealing to the Nielsen appetite? In went a dash of adolescent sex, like A-1 sauce sloshed on the baconburger. People wanted to know what they were eating; they wanted none of this overly subtle stuff. In a police drama, the ingredients had to be recognizable types: cops, robbers, good guys, nasties, tall heroes, feminine flames. In the soap opera whose plot had become too complicated, out went two excess characters, like the stringbeans and the tomatoes yanked from the recipe for beef stew. It was Silverman who introduced block programming: the method of scheduling popular shows in a sequence, which the viewers consumed in a lump — like the Tuesday night $2.79 soup–spaghetti–salad combination. For the whole decade of the seventies, more successfully than any competitor's, Silverman's menus gave the people what they wanted. But somehow, the customers drifted. Suddenly the kitchen lights went out.

Comment. How the chief programmer of a television network decides what shows reach the screen (and survive) is a process with which most of us aren't familiar. The writer of this analogy set out to offer a rough sense of it. He decided to concentrate on the methods of Fred Silverman, probably the most famous of programmers, the man who had the deepest effect on prime-time viewing in the 1970s. Silverman's successful touch was the marvel of his competitors and peers in the television industry. To try to explain it, the writer drew insights from Sally Bedell's book *Up the Tube: Prime-Time TV and the Silverman Years* (New York: Viking Press, 1981), a detailed history of Silverman's career. (When NBC ratings dropped in the spring of 1981, Silverman was replaced as the network's president.) At first, the writer was going to compare Silverman to a cook, but the comparison seemed less accurate than to compare him to a menu writer who kept taking part in the cooking. In a paragraph, only a few points about Silverman's methods could be included; and so, before he began, the writer jotted them down in this simple outline form:

> Silverman (1) involved himself in production.
> (2) tried to please a mass audience.
> (3) shared tastes of that audience.
> (4) cancelled what didn't prove popular.
> (5) kept programs simple, characters typical.
> (6) introduced block programming.

The next step was to find what corresponded to these activities in a restaurant. The writer added to each point of his outline another comparable activity:

> (1) superintended use of salt and pepper.
> (2) tried to please truckers, teen-agers, families.
> (3) shunned pheasant under glass.
> (4) crossed out an item too exotic.
> (5) simplified beef stew recipe.
> (6) offered a combination special.

Following this enlarged outline, he wrote the paragraph. (It had to be rewritten three times before he liked it.) As this example demonstrates, an analogy likens its subject to a concrete term or terms—to things as definite as salt and pepper.

· Luke ·

LUKE, author of the third Gospel of the New Testament, was the son of Christian parents, by birth either a Roman or a Syrian. He is thought to be the "beloved physician" befriended by Paul and to have traveled with Paul in Macedonia, spreading the Christian faith. Many scholars believe that Luke also wrote the Acts of the Apostles from diaries he kept on these journeys. A well-educated man, he displays in his writings a knowledge of books, painting, and medicine — also, as Michael Fixler observes in his edition of *The Mentor Bible*, "a receptive eye for all that is festive and joyful."

Three Gospels

Writing in Greek, perhaps late in the first century, Luke in his Gospel recounts the life of Jesus and quotes the words of Jesus, presumably drawing from recent tradition and from the reports of eyewitnesses. In Luke 15:1–32 we find three parables, or brief narratives that teach lessons. They are the stories of the lost sheep, the lost silver, and the prodigal son.

Another time, the tax-gatherers and other bad characters were all crowding in to listen to him; and the Pharisees and the doctors of the law began grumbling among themselves: "This fellow," they said, "welcomes sinners and eats with them." He answered them with this parable: "If one of you has a hundred sheep and loses one of them, does he not leave the ninety-nine in the open pasture and go after the missing one until he has found it? How delighted he is then! He lifts it on to his shoulders, and home he goes to call his friends and neighbors together. 'Rejoice with me!' he cries. 'I have found my lost sheep.' In the same way, I tell you, there will be greater joy in heaven over one sinner who repents than over ninety-nine righteous people who do not need to repent.

"Or again, if a woman has ten silver pieces and loses one of them, does she not light the lamp, sweep out the house, and look in every corner till she has found it? And when she has, she calls her friends and neighbors together, and says, 'Rejoice with me! I have found the piece that I lost.' In the same way, I tell you, there is joy among the angels of God over one sinner who repents." 2

Again he said: "There was once a man who had two sons; and the younger said to his father, 'Father, give me my share of the property.' So he divided his estate between them. A few days later the younger son turned the whole of his share into cash and left home for a distant country, where he squandered it in reckless living. He had spent it all, when a severe famine fell upon that country and he began to feel the pinch. So he went and attached himself to one of the local landowners, who sent him on to his farm to mind the pigs. He would have been glad to fill his belly with the pods that the pigs were eating; and no one gave him anything. Then he came to his senses and said, 'How many of my father's paid servants have more food than they can eat, and here am I, starving to death! I will set off and go to my father, and say to him, "Father, I have sinned, against God and against you; I am no longer fit to be called your son; treat me as one of your paid servants."' So he set out for his father's house. But while he was still a long way off his father saw him, and his heart went out to him. He ran to meet him, flung his arms round him, and kissed him. The son said, 'Father, I have sinned, against God and against you; I am no longer fit to be called your son.' But the father said to his servants, 'Quick! fetch a robe, my best one, and put it on him; put a ring on his finger and shoes on his feet. Bring the fatted calf and kill it, and let us have a feast to celebrate the day. For this son of mine was dead and has come back to life; he was lost and is found.' And the festivities began. 3

"Now the elder son was out on the farm; and on his way back, as he approached the house, he heard music and dancing. He called one of the servants and asked what it meant. The servant told him, 'Your brother has come home, and your father 4 has killed the fatted calf because he has him back safe and sound.' But he was angry and refused to go in. His father came out and pleaded with him; but he retorted, 'You know how I have slaved for you all these years; I never once disobeyed your orders; and you never gave me so much as a kid, for a feast with my friends. But now that this son of yours turns up, after running through your money with his women, you kill the fatted calf for him.' 'My boy,' said the father, 'you are always with me, and everything I have is yours. How could we help celebrating this happy day? Your brother here was dead and has come back to life, was lost and is found.' "

• QUESTIONS ON MEANING AND PURPOSE •

1. In each parable, what is the subject of the analogy? To what is it likened?
2. How do the parables answer the taunt of the Pharisees and the doctors of the law?
3. What do you understand to be the purpose of all three parables?

• QUESTIONS ON WRITING STRATEGY •

1. In the story of the prodigal son, what is the implied message? In seeing it, how are you helped by the fact that this parable stands last in a series of three?
2. What kind of person is the elder son? How does the inclusion of this character make the story all the more memorable?
3. For what audience were these parables originally intended? What is their audience today?

• QUESTIONS ON LANGUAGE •
• AND VOCABULARY •

1. Who were the Pharisees?
2. This translation of the Gospel of Luke is taken from *The New English Bible: New Testament* (1961). Compare its language with

that of the Authorized, or King James Version (1611) in the first parable:

> 1 Then drew near unto him all the publicans and sinners for to hear him.

> 2 And the Pharisees and scribes murmured, saying, This man receiveth sinners, and eateth with them.

> 3 And he spake this parable unto them, saying,

> 4 What man of you, having a hundred sheep, if he lose one of them, doth not leave the ninety and nine in the wilderness, and go after that which is lost, until he find it?

> 5 And when he hath found it, he layeth it on his shoulders, rejoicing.

> 6 And when he cometh home, he calleth together his friends and neighbors, saying unto them, Rejoice with me; for I have found my sheep which was lost.

> 7 I say unto you, that likewise joy shall be in heaven over one sinner that repenteth, more than over ninety and nine just persons, which need no repentance.

What differences do you find in comparing and contrasting the two translations? What grounds can you find for preferring one version to the other?

• SUGGESTION FOR WRITING •

Write a modern parable, setting forth a message (either stated or clearly implied), and using the method of analogy.

· John Crompton ·

JOHN CROMPTON was born in England in 1893 and attended the University of Manchester. On the eve of World War I he went to Rhodesia to serve in the mounted police, and there became fascinated by the insect life of Africa. Returning to England, he deepened his studies, and became known as a naturalist with the appearance of his popular studies: *The Life of the Spider* (1950), *Ways of the Ant* (1954), *The Hunting Wasp* (1955), *The Living Sea* (1957), *A Hive of Bees* (1958), and *Snake Lore* (1964). That Crompton has written of insects, reptiles, and sea creatures with the verve of a novelist is no accident. Under another name, he has written nine novels of mystery and adventure.

The Magnitude
of the Spider's Task

Crompton makes his subject absorbing to us, as zoologist Alexander Petrunkevitch notes in his preface to *The Life of the Spider* (1950). It is rare, says Petrunkevitch, when "the ability to present a scientific subject in an easily understandable and highly entertaining manner is coupled with extensive knowledge, while at the same time the flight of fancy is not allowed to get out of bounds and remains under the control of reasoning." This is an excellent description of the following analogy, from the book's opening chapter. Crompton begins by telling how he first came to admire the work of Aranea, the outdoor spider who makes the familiar "orb web" with the cartwheel pattern. The skillful dance of the spider in weaving its web kept him fascinated for hours. In this analogy, he tries to make us understand Aranea's feat — and to communicate his own sense of wonder.

To give an idea of the magnitude of the spider's task I am go- 1
ing to set a man the same task, or rather the bare beginning of

the same task. If this is being anthropomorphic then it is equally anthropomorphic to photograph an insect with a man's hand behind it so that you may judge the insect's size, or pose beside a salmon one has caught. If man's capabilities or defects help us to gauge the capabilities or defects of animals and make the picture clearer we *ought* to use him as a measure. I am always doing it. I cannot help it. For instance, if I hear that some outer frameworks of Aranea webs are (as some are) ten feet across I automatically ask myself what that represents, and this I do not really know until I have worked out how wide it would be if made by a man on the same scale. Taking the spider at half an inch in length and the man at five feet, I find that it would represent 400 yards for creatures of our size. With behavior I use the same gauge. It is an unreliable gauge but it is the only gauge a man can use. Furthermore every one of us is an anthropomorphist. We could not understand one thing another animal does, however simple, without translating it — unconsciously — into our own sensations.

The first thing to be built in Aranea's web is the framework. This takes the form of a four-sided figure or, more rarely, a triangle. We will select St. Paul's Cathedral and Ludgate Hill[1] for the sight of the web the man will make. He will be seen in due course climbing up to the roof of a Ludgate Hill building. He is a good climber by the way, though he cannot climb anything precipitous unless he finds footholds — and he is an expert tight-rope walker. About his person are coils of rope ready to be payed out. He ties the end of his rope to one of the chimneys and clambers down again into the street and as soon as he has reached ground level proceeds at a run towards the cathedral, paying out rope as he goes. Still paying out rope he climbs the great edifice until he reaches the dome and here he hauls in the slack until the rope is taut, and fastens it somewhere at the top of the cathedral. In almost no time at all he has run down the other side of St. Paul's and climbed to the top of a shop away

2

[1]This selection is purely arbitrary. The American reader might get a better idea if he selected a street corner familiar to him.

down the street. Here he finds another chimney and again hauls in his rope and makes fast.

We are being very kind to this man. We are letting him make the simplest of web foundations, the triangle. So all he has to do now is to clamber over obstructions and climb to his original chimney, pulling in and making fast the rope from across the way. He has been using stout rope because this is the framework of his web and with luck will last him a long time. But even so, one thickness is not enough; he goes (tight-rope walking) round his triangle twice more, joining on rope and making it of treble thickness, which for such a small affair he judges sufficient. That same day, he will have to decide in what quarter he desires to take up residence and will probably fix on some apartment in Holborn.[2] He will insist of course on a telephone but he will install it himself. He will run a wire from his web to his bedroom and even when asleep the slightest vibration will inform him if a visitor has arrived.

The man has made the bare framework but has not started the snare. For the snare he will need a lot more expertness and agility than he has shown so far, ten times as much rope and several drums of glue. So we will, I think, dismiss him. He has served his purpose; we have an idea now of the vast scale of the web-weaving spider's work. No wonder it has to run.

• QUESTIONS ON MEANING AND PURPOSE •

1. Where in this essay does the writer announce his purpose?
2. How does Crompton defend his desire to view the animal world in human terms and to measure it by human measurements?
3. Explain what the writer means by the spider's "apartment" and its "telephone" (paragraph 3).
4. What part of the web is the "snare"?

[2]Or any other place about a mile away.

5. What does this analogy make clear to you that you didn't realize before?

• QUESTIONS ON WRITING STRATEGIES •

1. How does Crompton's opening paragraph prepare the reader to accept the rest of the discussion?
2. At what points does the writer place special emphasis on the great difficulties that a web-weaving man would have to surmount? (See *Emphasis* in Useful Terms.)
3. How does the method of process analysis also contribute to Crompton's explanation? Into what steps does the writer divide the human spider's task? (See Chapter 5, Process Analysis.)
4. At what moments in Crompton's essay do you sense that the writer is being ironic: that there is a discrepancy between his exact instructions to a would-be spider and his sense that the whole idea of trying to be a spider is preposterous? (See *Irony* in Useful Terms.)
5. Crompton wrote his book for an English audience familiar with the landmarks of London. How does he try to help the American reader?
6. What difficulties might Crompton's human spider meet that the writer doesn't even mention? Why doesn't the analogy include every conceivable difficulty?

• QUESTIONS ON LANGUAGE •
• AND VOCABULARY •

1. Define "anthropomorphic" and "anthropomorphist" (paragraph 1). Why is an understanding of these words essential to reading Crompton's discussion?
2. Be sure you also know the meanings of the following words: magnitude, gauge (paragraph 1); precipitous, edifice (2); treble (3); snare, agility (4).
3. What is the value of the allusions to St. Paul's Cathedral, Ludgate Hill, and Holborn? If you were transferring Crompton's human spider to an American city you know well, what places or landmarks might you allude to instead?
4. How much technical diction do you find in "The Magnitude of the Spider's Task"? (See *Diction* in Useful Terms.) Comment on the appropriateness of the writer's diction for his intended audience.

· SUGGESTIONS FOR WRITING ·

1. Comment in a paragraph on the efforts of Crompton's human spider, writing from a spider's point of view. Of course, you will have to be an anthropomorphist, and give the spider a human mind and the ability to write English prose. (See *Point of View* in Useful Terms.)

2. Write a coherent analogy likening the behavior of a human and that of an insect — or likening that of a human and that of some bird, fish, or mammal. (See *Coherence* in Useful Terms.)

· James C. Rettie ·

JAMES C. RETTIE is a man of mystery. Less is known about him than we know about Luke, and he is remembered as the author of a single acclaimed work: the following essay, often reprinted in textbooks and anthologies. Rettie wrote it in 1948 while working at an experimental station of the National Forest Service in Upper Darby, Pennsylvania. Then he completely disappeared, and so did all his traces.

"But a Watch in the Night": A Scientific Fable

In writing his essay, Rettie apparently drew some of his ideas from a U.S. Government pamphlet, "To Hold This Soil," prepared by the Department of Agriculture. In it, we are given a relatively matter-of-fact account of soil erosion. But Rettie had a flash of genius, and converted the pamphlet's statistics into a remarkable analogy, couched in a science fiction narrative.

Out beyond our solar system there is a planet called Copernicus. It came into existence some four or five billion years before the birth of our Earth. In due course of time it became inhabited by a race of intelligent men.

About 750 million years ago the Copernicans had developed the motion picture machine to a point well in advance of the stage that we have reached. Most of the cameras that we now use in motion picture work are geared to take twenty-four pictures per second on a continuous strip of film. When such film is run through a projector, it throws a series of images on the screen and these change with a rapidity that gives the visual impression of normal movement. If a motion is too swift for the human eye to see it in detail, it can be captured and artificially slowed down by means of the slow-motion camera. This one is geared to take many more shots per second — ninety-six or even more than that. When the slow motion film is projected at the normal speed of twenty-four pictures per second, we can see just how the jumping horse goes over a hurdle.

What about motion that is too slow to be seen by the human eye? That problem has been solved by the use of the time-lapse camera. In this one, the shutter is geared to take only one shot per second, or one per minute, or even one per hour — depending upon the kind of movement that is being photographed. When the time-lapse film is projected at the normal speed of twenty-four pictures per second, it is possible to see a bean sprout growing up out of the ground. Time-lapse films are useful in the study of many types of motion too slow to be observed by the unaided, human eye.

The Copernicans, it seems, had time-lapse cameras some 757 million years ago and they also had superpowered telescopes that gave them a clear view of what was happening upon this Earth. They decided to make a film record of the life history of Earth and to make it on the scale of one picture per year. The photography has been in progress during the last 757 million years.

In the near future, a Copernican interstellar expedition will arrive upon our Earth and bring with it a copy of the time-lapse film. Arrangements will be made for showing the entire film in one continuous run. This will begin at midnight of New Year's eve and continue day and night without a single stop until midnight of December 31. The rate of projection will be twenty-four pictures per second. Time on the screen will thus seem to move at the rate of twenty-four years per second; 1440 years per minute; 86,400 years per hour; approximately two million years per day; and sixty-two million years per month. The normal lifespan of individual man will occupy about three seconds. The full period of Earth history that will be unfolded on the screen (some 757 million years) will extend from what the geologists call Pre-Cambrian times up to the present. This will, by no means, cover the full time-span of the Earth's geological history but it will embrace the period since the advent of living organisms.

During the months of January, February, and March the picture will be desolate and dreary. The shape of the land masses and the oceans will bear little or no resemblance to those that we know. The violence of geological erosion will be much in evidence. Rains will pour down on the land and promptly go booming down to the seas. There will be no clear streams anywhere except where the rains fall upon hard rock. Everywhere on the steeper ground the stream channels will be filled with boulders hurled down by rushing waters. Raging torrents and dry stream beds will keep alternating in quick succession. High mountains will seem to melt like so much butter in the sun. The shifting of land into the seas, later to be thrust up as new mountains, will be going on at a grand scale.   6

Early in April there will be some indication of the presence of single-celled living organisms in some of the warmer and sheltered coastal waters. By the end of the month it will be noticed that some of these organisms have become multicellular. A few of them, including the Trilobites, will be encased in hard shells.   7

Toward the end of May, the first vertebrates will appear, but they will still be aquatic creatures. In June about 60 per cent of the land area that we know as North America will be under water. One broad channel will occupy the space where the Rocky Mountains now stand. Great deposits of limestone will be forming under some of the shallower seas. Oil and gas deposits will be in process of formation — also under shallow seas. On land there will still be no sign of vegetation. Erosion will be rampant, tearing loose particles and chunks of rock and grinding them into sand and silt to be spewed out by the streams into bays and estuaries.   8

About the middle of July the first land plants will appear and take up the tremendous job of soil building. Slowly, very slowly, the mat of vegetation will spread, always battling for its life against the power of erosion. Almost foot by foot, the plant life will advance, lacing down with its root structures whatever pulverized rock material it can find. Leaves and stems will be   9 giving added protection against the loss of the soil foothold. The increasing vegetation will pave the way for the land animals that will live upon it.

Early in August the seas will be teeming with fish. This will be what geologists call the Devonian period. Some of the races of these fish will be breathing by means of lung tissue instead of through gill tissues. Before the month is over, some of the lung fish will go ashore and take on a crude lizard-like appearance. Here are the first amphibians.

In early September the insects will put in their appearance. Some will look like huge dragonflies and will have a wing spread of 24 inches. Large portions of the land masses will now be covered with heavy vegetation that will include the primitive spore-propagating trees. Layer upon layer of this plant growth will build up, later to appear as the coal deposits. About the middle of this month, there will be evidence of the first seed-bearing plants and the first reptiles. Heretofore, the land animals will have been amphibians that could reproduce their kind only by depositing a soft egg mass in quiet waters. The reptiles will be shown to be freed from the aquatic bond because they can reproduce by means of a shelled egg in which the embryo and its nurturing liquids are sealed and thus protected from destructive evaporation. Before September is over, the first dinosaurs will be seen — creatures destined to dominate the animal realm for about 140 million years and then to disappear.

In October there will be series of mountain uplifts along what is now the eastern coast of the United States. A creature with feathered limbs — half bird and half reptile in appearance — will take itself into the air. Some small and rather unpretentious animals will be seen to bring forth their young in a form that is a miniature replica of the parents and to feed these young on milk secreted by mammary glands in the female parent. The emergence of this mammalian form of animal life will be recognized as one of the great events in geologic time. October will also witness the high water mark of the dinosaurs — creatures ranging in size from that of the modern goat to monsters like Brontosaurus that weighed some 40 tons. Most of them will be placid vegetarians, but a few will be hideous-

10

11

12

looking carnivores, like Allosaurus and Tyrannosaurus. Some of the herbivorous dinosaurs will be clad in bony armor for protection against their flesh-eating comrades.

November will bring pictures of a sea extending from the   13
Gulf of Mexico to the Arctic in space now occupied by the
Rocky Mountains. A few of the reptiles will take to the air on
bat-like wings. One of these, called Pteranodon, will have a
wingspread of 15 feet. There will be a rapid development of the
modern flowering plants, modern trees, and modern insects.
The dinosaurs will disappear. Toward the end of the month
there will be a tremendous land disturbance in which the Rocky
Mountains will rise out of the sea to assume a dominating place
in the North American landscape.

As the picture runs on into December it will show the mam-   14
mals in command of the animal life. Seed-bearing trees and
grasses will have covered most of the land with a heavy mantle
of vegetation. Only the areas newly thrust up from the sea will
be barren. Most of the streams will be crystal clear. The turmoil
of geologic erosion will be confined to localized areas. About
December 25 will begin the cutting of the Grand Canyon of the
Colorado River. Grinding down through layer after layer of
sedimentary strata, this stream will finally expose deposits laid
down in Pre-Cambrian times. Thus in the walls of that canyon
will appear geological formations dating from recent times to
the period when the Earth had no living organisms upon it.

The picture will run on through the latter days of December   15
and even up to its final day with still no sign of mankind. The
spectators will become alarmed in the fear that man has somehow been left out. But not so; sometime about noon on December 31 (one million years ago) will appear a stooped, massive
creature of man-like proportions. This will be Pithecanthropus,
the Java ape man. For tools and weapons he will have nothing
but crude stone and wooden clubs. His children will live a precarious existence threatened on the one side by hostile animals
and on the other by tremendous climatic changes. Ice sheets —
in places 4000 feet deep — will form in the northern parts of
North America and Eurasia. Four times this glacial ice will push
southward to cover half the continents. With each advance the
plant and animal life will be swept under or pushed southward.

With each recession of the ice, life will struggle to reestablish itself in the wake of the retreating glaciers. The woolly mammoth, the musk ox, and the caribou all will fight to maintain themselves near the ice line. Sometimes they will be caught and put into cold storage — skin, flesh, blood, bones and all.

The picture will run on through supper time with still very little evidence of man's presence on the Earth. It will be about 11 o'clock when Neanderthal man appears. Another half hour will go by before the appearance of Cro-Magnon man living in caves and painting crude animal pictures on the walls of his dwelling. Fifteen minutes more will bring Neolithic man, knowing how to chip stone and thus produce sharp cutting edges for spears and tools. In a few minutes more it will appear that man has domesticated the dog, the sheep and, possibly, other animals. He will then begin the use of milk. He will also learn the arts of basket weaving and the making of pottery and dugout canoes.   16

The dawn of civilization will not come until about five or six minutes before the end of the picture. The story of the Egyptians, the Babylonians, the Greeks, and the Romans will unroll during the fourth, the third and the second minute before the end. At 58 minutes and 43 seconds past 11:00 P.M. (just 1 minute and 17 seconds before the end) will come the beginning of the Christian era. Columbus will discover the new world 20 seconds before the end. The Declaration of Independence will be signed just 7 seconds before the final curtain comes down.   17

In those few moments of geologic time will be the story of all that has happened since we became a nation. And what a story it will be! A human swarm will sweep across the face of the continent and take it away from the . . . red men. They will change it far more radically than it has ever been changed before in a comparable time. The great virgin forests will be seen going down before ax and fire. The soil, covered for eons by its protective mantle of trees and grasses, will be laid bare to the ravages of water and wind erosion. Streams that had been flowing clear will, once again, take up a load of silt and push it toward the seas. Humus and mineral salts, both vital elements of productive soil, will be seen to vanish at a terrifying rate. The railroads and highways and cities that will spring up may divert atten-   18

tion, but they cannot cover up the blight of man's recent activities. In great sections of Asia, it will be seen that man must
utilize cow dung and every scrap of available straw or grass for
fuel to cook his food. The forests that once provided wood for
this purpose will be gone without a trace. The use of these agricultural wastes for fuel, in place of returning them to the land,
will be leading to increasing soil impoverishment. Here and
there will be seen a dust storm darkening the landscape over an
area a thousand miles across. Man-creatures will be shown
counting their wealth in terms of bits of printed paper representing other bits of a scarce but comparatively useless yellow
metal that is kept buried in strong vaults. Meanwhile, the soil,
the only real wealth that can keep mankind alive on the face of
this Earth is savagely being cut loose from its ancient moorings
and washed into the seven seas.

We have just arrived upon this Earth. How long will we   19
stay?

• QUESTIONS ON MEANING AND PURPOSE •

1. What is the subject of Rettie's analogy? To what does he liken it?
2. For what purpose does the writer include this analogy: to give us a
   sense of the vast extent of time, to show us how humankind
   would appear to alien beings, to demonstrate how much has gone
   into the growth and development of the earth and living things,
   or what?
3. Sum up the purpose of the essay as a whole. What is Rettie's *thesis*?
   (See *Thesis* in Useful Terms.)
4. Why does the writer end with a rhetorical question? What answer
   does he expect us to supply? (See *Rhetorical Question* in Useful
   Terms.)

• QUESTIONS ON WRITING STRATEGY •

1. Do you have any trouble in accepting Rettie's notion of a movie
   whose screening takes a year? What commonplace, practical ob-

jections to such a movie occur to you? Is Rettie's analogy silly, or does it serve him well?

2. What is the writer's point of view? How does the inclusion of the Copernicans help establish it? (See *Point of View* in Useful Terms.)

3. If Rettie had been asked to omit his analogy, what paragraphs would he have had to cut? Could his essay survive without the analogy? What would be lost?

4. What other environmental problems might Rettie have mentioned in his conclusion? Why doesn't he discuss such problems? (Suggestion: What would this have done to his plot summary of the movie?)

5. What kinds of transitions are most numerous at the start of paragraphs? Why are they essential in this essay? (See *Transitions* in Useful Terms.)

6. In what section of the essay does the method of process analysis appear? Into what main stages does the writer divide the history of the earth?

7. Can Rettie, in his conclusion, be accused of sentimentality? (See *Sentimentality* in Useful Terms.)

· QUESTIONS ON LANGUAGE ·
· AND VOCABULARY ·

1. The title of Rettie's essay is an allusion to Psalms 90:4 in the King James Version of the Bible: "For a thousand years in Thy sight are but as yesterday when it is past, and as a watch in the night." Can you explain this quotation? What light does it cast upon the essay? (See *Allusion* in Useful Terms.)

2. What is the value of the essay's subtitle "A Scientific Fable"? What is a fable?

3. What terms from the vocabulary of science (*Pre-Cambrian*, for example) occur in this essay? Is Rettie writing for an audience of trained specialists? Do you think he could have done without such terms?

4. Make sure the following words and phrases are part of your vocabulary: hurdle (paragraph 2); time-lapse camera (3); interstellar, geological, advent (5); desolate, erosion, torrents (6); multicellular (7); vertebrates, rampant, aquatic, spewed, estuaries (8); pulverized (9); spore-propagating, reptiles, amphibians, realm (11); unpretentious, replica, mammary, mammalian, carnivores, herbivorous (12); mantle, sedimentary (14); precarious, Eurasia,

recession (15); domesticated (16); eons, silt, humus, impoverishment, moorings (18).

· SUGGESTIONS FOR WRITING ·

1. In a paragraph or two, respond to Rettie's essay, and give reasons for your reaction.
2. Write an essay in which you discuss the effects on the environment of some human activity: for instance, manufacturing; the disposal of chemical wastes; the production of nuclear energy; the commercial taking of seals, whales, or other wild animals. Decide whether to take an objective or a subjective attitude toward your material. (See *Objective and Subjective* in Useful Terms.) If possible, choose some situation that you know from reading or experience.
3. Continue the plot summary of Rettie's movie into the future, showing the consequences of forces at work in the world today. (Will you supply the movie with a happy or an unhappy ending?)
4. Write a fable of your own, setting forth a moral. One familiar method of fable-writing is that of Aesop, who makes animals and inanimate objects talk. If you like, you might instead write a science fictional fable as Rettie does, based on observations of the actual world.

· Herman Melville ·

HERMAN MELVILLE (1819–1891) had the most disappointing career of any major American writer. Made famous by his first book, *Typee* (1846), a romanticized account of life in the South Seas, Melville lived on to be forgotten. As a young man he served aboard whaling vessels and in the maritime fleet; in the Marquesas Islands he jumped ship and lived among friendly cannibals. These experiences nourished *Typee* and its sequel *Omoo* (1847); but his masterpiece *Moby-Dick, or The Whale* (1851) found few readers in its time, and Melville came to feel that his later works were as he put it, "eminently adapted for unpopularity." Despite the brilliance of many of his late poems and his short novel *Billy Budd* (published posthumously), Melville died an obscure customs official in New York. Thirty years later, Raymond Weaver's biography *Herman Melville: Mariner and Mystic* (1921) helped twentieth-century readers to rediscover him.

Fast-Fish and Loose-Fish

Though *Moby-Dick* tells the absorbing story of Captain Ahab's vengeful pursuit of the great white whale who took away his leg, the book is full of leisurely moments. In one of these, Melville gives us a digression on law and marriage, and by means of analogy and metaphor, playfully sets forth a good deal of philosophy. "Fast-Fish and Loose-Fish" is Chapter 89 of *Moby-Dick*.

It frequently happens that when several ships are cruising in company, a whale may be struck by one vessel, then escape, and be finally killed and captured by another vessel; and herein are indirectly comprised many minor contingencies, all partaking of this one grand feature. For example — after a weary and peril-

ous chase and capture of a whale, the body may get loose from
the ship by reason of a violent storm; and drifting far away to
leeward, be retaken by a second whaler, who, in a calm, snugly
tows it alongside, without risk of life or line. Thus the most vexatious and violent disputes would often arise between the fishermen, were there not some written or unwritten, universal, un-
disputed law applicable to all cases.

Perhaps the only formal whaling code authorized by   2
legislative enactment, was that of Holland. It was decreed by the
States-General in A.D. 1695. But though no other nation has
ever had any written whaling law, yet the American fishermen
have been their own legislators and lawyers in this matter. They
have provided a system which for terse comprehensiveness sur-
passes Justinian's Pandects[1] and the By-laws of the Chinese
Society for the Suppression of Meddling with other People's
Business. Yes; these laws might be engraven on a Queen Anne's
farthing or the barb of a harpoon, and worn round the neck, so
small are they.

   1. A Fast-Fish belongs to the party fast to it.   3
   2. A Loose-Fish is fair game for anybody who can soonest   4
catch it.

But what plays the mischief with this masterly code is the   5
admirable brevity of it, which necessitates a vast volume of commentaries to expound it.

First: What is a Fast-Fish? Alive or dead a fish is technically 6
fast, when it is connected with an occupied ship or boat, by any
medium at all controllable by the occupant or occupants — a
mast, an oar, a nine-inch cable, a telegraph wire, or a strand of
cobweb, it is all the same. Likewise a fish is technically fast
when it bears a waif, or any other recognized symbol of possession; so long as the party waifing it plainly evince their ability at
any time to take it alongside, as well as their intention so to do.

These are scientific commentaries; but the commentaries of   7
the whalemen themselves sometimes consist in hard words and

---

[1]A fifty-volume digest of Roman civil law compiled in the sixth century at
the order of the emperor Justinian.

harder knocks — the Coke-upon-Littleton[2] of the fist. True, among the more upright and honorable whalemen allowances are always made for peculiar cases, where it would be an outrageous moral injustice for one party to claim possession of a whale previously chased or killed by another party. But others are by no means so scrupulous.

Some fifty years ago there was a curious case of whale-trover litigated in England, wherein the plaintiffs set forth that after a hard chase of a whale in the northern seas, they (the plaintiffs) had succeeded in harpooning the fish; but at last, through peril of their lives, were obliged to forsake, not only their lines, but their boat itself — Furthermore: ultimately the defendants (the crew of another ship) came up with the whale; struck, killed, seized, and finally appropriated it before the very eyes of the plaintiffs; — Yet again: — and when those defendants were remonstrated with, their captain snapped his fingers in the plaintiffs' teeth, and assured them that by way of doxology to the deed he had done, he would now retain their line, harpoons, and boat, all of which had remained attached to the whale at the time of the seizure. Wherefore, the plaintiffs now sued for the recovery of the value of their whale, line, harpoons, and boat.

Mr. Erskine was counsel for the defendants; Lord Ellenborough was the judge. In the course of the defense, the witty Erskine went on to illustrate his position, by alluding to a recent crim. con. case,[3] wherein a gentleman, after in vain trying to bridle his wife's viciousness, had at last abandoned her upon the seas of life; but in the course of years, repenting of that step, he instituted an action to recover possession of her. He then proceeded to say that, though the gentleman had originally harpooned the lady, and had once had her fast, and only by reason of the great stress of her plunging viciousness, had at last abandoned her; yet abandon her he did, so that she became a loose-

8

9

---

[2]A classic law textbook, in which seventeenth-century English jurist Sir Edward Coke wrote a commentary on an earlier work, Thomas Littleton's study of the laws of property.

[3]A "criminal conversation case," or lawsuit in which one spouse charges the other with adultery.

fish; and therefore when a subsequent gentleman re-harpooned her, the lady then became that subsequent gentleman's property, along with whatever harpoon might have been found sticking in her.

Now in the present case Erskine contended that the examples of the whale and the lady were reciprocally illustrative of each other. 10

These pleadings, and the counter pleadings, being duly heard, the very learned judge in set terms decided, to wit: — That as for the boat, he awarded it to the plaintiffs, because they had merely abandoned it to save their lives; but that with regard to the controverted whale, harpoons, and line, they belonged to the defendants; the whale, because it was a Loose-Fish at the time of the final capture; and the harpoons and line because when the fish made off with them, it (the fish) acquired a property in those articles; and hence anybody who afterwards took the fish had a right to them. Now, the defendants afterwards took the fish; ergo, the aforesaid articles were theirs. 11

A common man looking at this decision of the very learned Judge, might possibly object to it. But ploughed up to the primary rock of the matter, the two great principles laid down in the twin whaling laws previously quoted, and applied and elucidated by Lord Ellenborough in the above cited case; these two laws touching Fast-Fish and Loose-Fish, I say, will, on reflection, be found the fundamentals of all human jurisprudence; for notwithstanding its complicated tracery of sculpture, the Temple of the Law, like the Temple of the Philistines, has but two props to stand on. 12

Is it not a saying in every one's mouth, Possession is half of the law: that is, regardless of how the thing came into possession? But often possession is the whole of the law. What are the sinews and souls of Russian serfs and Republican slaves but Fast-Fish, whereof possession is the whole of the law? What to the rapacious landlord is the widow's last mite but a Fast-Fish? What is yonder undetected villain's marble mansion with a door-plate for a waif; what is that but a Fast-Fish? What is the ruinous discount which Mordecai, the broker, gets from poor Woebegone, the bankrupt, on a loan to keep Woebegone's fam- 13 ily from starvation; what is that ruinous discount but a Fast-Fish? What is the Archbishop of Savesoul's income of £100,000 seized from the scant bread and cheese of hundreds of thousands of broken-backed laborers (all sure of heaven without any Savesoul's help); what is that globular 100,000 but a Fast-Fish? What are the Duke of Dunder's hereditary towns and hamlets but Fast-Fish? What to that doubted harpooneer, John Bull,[4] is poor Ireland, but a Fast-Fish? What to that apostolic lancer, Brother Jonathan,[5] is Texas but a Fast-Fish? And concerning all these, is not Possession the whole of the law?

But if the doctrine of Fast-Fish is pretty generally applicable,   14
the kindred doctrine of Loose-Fish is still more widely so. That is internationally and universally applicable.

What was America in 1492 but a Loose-Fish, in which Co-   15
lumbus struck the Spanish standard by way of waifing it for his royal master and mistress? What was Poland to the Czar? What Greece to the Turk? What India to England? What at last will Mexico be to the United States? All Loose-Fish.

What are the Rights of Man and the Liberties of the World   16
but Loose-Fish? What all men's minds and opinions but Loose-Fish? What is the principle of religious belief in them but a Loose-Fish? What to the ostentatious smuggling verbalists are the thoughts of thinkers but Loose-Fish? What is the great globe itself but a Loose-Fish? And what are you, reader, but a Loose-Fish and a Fast-Fish, too?

• QUESTIONS ON MEANING AND PURPOSE •

1. What is the purpose of Lawyer Erskine's analogy between the lady and the loose-fish? What do you take to be Melville's purpose in citing it?

[4]Personification of England (comparable to Uncle Sam, a personification of the U.S.).

[5]Personification of the United States, said to be derived from George Washington's nickname for Jonathan Trumbull, governor of Connecticut.

2. How does Melville define "fast-fish," "loose-fish," and "waif" in paragraphs 2 through 5? As the essay goes on, does he stick to these definitions or does he amplify them?
3. Do you take the Chinese society mentioned in paragraph 2 to be invented or actual?
4. What do you need to know about history to follow paragraphs 12 through 15? Is it necessary to catch every one of these allusions to catch the writer's meaning?

· QUESTIONS ON WRITING STRATEGY ·

1. How does Melville employ humor? In what passages are you aware of it?
2. What statements seem ironic? (See *Irony* in Useful Terms.) Explain in each statement what seems a discrepancy.
3. Comment on Melville's use of made-up names in paragraph 13. What do they connote (or denote)? (See *Connotation and Denotation* in Useful Terms.)
4. Does the stream of questions at the essay's conclusion set forth one analogy, many analogies, or just a series of metaphors? (See metaphor under *Figures of Speech* in Useful Terms.)
5. How does "Fast-Fish and Loose-Fish" show that it was written for a mid-nineteenth-century audience? What interest can it hold for readers today?

· QUESTIONS ON LANGUAGE ·
· AND VOCABULARY ·

1. What nautical terms does Melville use? Why are they necessary?
2. Explain the allusion to the Philistines in paragraph 12.
3. With the aid of your dictionary, define the following words: comprised, contingencies, leeward, vexatious (paragraph 1); code, legislative, enactment, farthing, barb (2); plays the mischief (5); scrupulous (7); whale-trover, litigated, plaintiffs, remonstrated, doxology (8); reciprocally (10); controverted, ergo (11); jurisprudence, notwithstanding, tracery (12); sinews, serfs, rapacious, globular, hereditary, apostolic (13); kindred (14); ostentatious, verbalists (15).

· SUGGESTIONS FOR WRITING ·

1. Attack Lawyer Erskine as a sexist porker, and propose a different analogy for the lady he likens to a loose-fish.

2. Write an analogy in which you take fishing (or some other sport) either for your subject or for the thing with which your subject is explained. For instance, you might liken the familiar experience of smashing a baseball and pleasing spectators and the possibly less familiar experience of writing a smashing essay and pleasing readers. (Maybe the degree of familiarity, for you, might be the other way around.)

· Marjorie Waters ·

MARJORIE WATERS, born in 1945, is a freelance writer who col-
laborated with James Crockett, the late public television
gardening expert, to produce *Crockett's Flower Garden* (1981).
Besides her books, she has written catalogues and training
materials for the Polaroid Corporation and the Harvard
Graduate School of Design. She is presently at work on *Food
and Emotion*, a study of how diet influences human
psychology.

Coming Home

The decision to begin her essay with the return to a summer
home long closed provides the author with a sensitive approach to her subject. What is it like when mourning finally
comes to an end?

After the cruelest of winters, the house still stood. It was   1
pale, washed clean by elements gone wild, and here and there a
shutter dangled from a broken hinge. But the structure was
sound, the corners had held. I walked around it slowly, studying every detail: the fine edge where window frame met clap-
board, the slice of shadow across the roofline, the old wooden
railing around the porch. When I climbed the stairs toward the
door, I heard the floorboards groan beneath my weight as they
had always done. Hello yourself, old friend, I said.

Inside, I made those rooms my own again, drew the curtains   2
back, threw open the window, pulled the covers from the furniture, slapped all the upholstery with my hands. I could feel
fresh air move in through open windows, replacing a season's
worth of staleness with a smell of moist earth, a hint of flowers.
After all the months of darkness light poured again into the
house, fell in familiar angled patterns across furniture, walls,
and floors. Where light beams passed through moving air, even
the dust seemed alive; I watched it swirl, dance, resettle.

I made myself at home, kicked off my shoes so I could feel ³
the floors beneath my feet again. I tilted my head, read the titles
on the spines of all my books. I played old songs I hadn't heard
in months, felt the summer music move through me as if my
muscles were the strings. It carried me from room to room while
I swept away the mustiness of winter, shook the rugs, cleaned
cobwebs out of corners, hung laundered linens on the line to
whip dry in the outdoor air. I pulled closed boxes out of closets
and unwrapped all my things, slowly, one by one. I held and
turned them in my hands before I put them out again on
shelves, in cupboards and drawers. And when I had each room
all full of me again, I showered and washed away the last of
winter's claims in hot lather and steam.

Night fell and brought a chill to the air outside. I built a fire ⁴
in the stove, drank tea that smelled of oranges and spice. I
warmed my fingers round the cup and thought of how my
house would look to passers-by, drowsy and content, with soft
rectangles of light on the ground below the windows, a breath
of smoke from the chimney. She's come back, they would say as
they walked through the dark night. She's home again.

For me, the end of grief was a homecoming like this one, a ⁵
returning to myself made sweeter by the long separation. I remember well the months that had followed that most unexpected death, when I felt cut loose, caught in my own cold
storm, far away from all that made me feel at home. I wondered
if I would ever again belong to any time or place. People spoke
to me of sadness and loss, as if they were burdens to carry in my
hands. I nodded in agreement, afraid to tell them that I felt no
burdens, only weightlessness. I thought the world had pulled itself away from me, that I would drift, beyond reach, forever.

But winter ends, and grief does pass. As I had reclaimed my ⁶
house and made it my own again, so I slowly reclaimed my life. I
resumed my small daily rituals: a cup of coffee with a friend,
long walks at sunset. I felt like myself again, and when I
laughed, it was my own laugh I heard, rich and full. I had feared
that, in my absence, the space that I had left behind would close
over from disuse, but I returned to find that my house still
stood, even after the cruelest of winters.

• QUESTIONS ON MEANING AND PURPOSE •

1. What parallels does Waters draw between opening a house long empty and arriving at the end of grief?
2. What do you think is the writer's main purpose in this essay?

• QUESTIONS ON WRITING STRATEGY •

1. At what moment in the essay does Waters disclose that she is writing an analogy? Do you think the essay would have been improved had she set forth her analogy clearly in her introduction? Discuss.
2. Study the writer's transition from paragraph 4 to paragraph 5. (See *Transitions* in Useful Terms.) Evaluate her technique in moving from the homecoming to the end of grief.

• QUESTIONS ON LANGUAGE •
• AND VOCABULARY •

1. Compare the writer's use of the phrase "the cruelest of winters" in paragraph 1 with the usage in paragraph 6. Does each usage connote a different meaning? Explain. (See *Connotation and Denotation* in Useful Terms.)
2. What does Waters mean when she says she was "afraid" to tell people that she "felt no burdens, only weightlessness" (paragraph 5)?
3. What risks might there be in writing an analogy in poetic, highly connotative language instead of in terms as concrete as hammers and nails? (See *Connotation and Denotation* in Useful Terms.) Does Waters successfully outrun such risks?

• SUGGESTIONS FOR WRITING •

1. In a paragraph, explain a mood or feeling with the help of an analogy.
2. Explain by an analogy some moment of crisis you have experienced, helping a reader to understand your particular situation.

── POSTSCRIPT ON PROCESS ──

Selecting the Right Language

In writing her analogy, Marjorie Waters carefully chose the kind of language that seemed most appropriate to her subject. Rejecting both connotation-free, nuts-and-bolts language and the language conventionally associated with death, she finally selected words that would apply to both houses and grief.

Most of the work that went into this analogy was in finding the right language. I was, in the early paragraphs, writing about a house, but I was thinking about grief. The question was, how to describe the house in a way that made the two subjects connect. 1

I did not want to use language that was too realistic. I wasn't concerned with what it is actually like to clean out a house, and I didn't want to lose the subject of grief in talk of nuts and bolts and scrubbing floors. If realistic language became one barrier to the analogy, so did language taken directly from grief, though I did spend several drafts experimenting with this approach: I had shrouds over the furniture, a roomful of ghosts, and so on. I rejected this language because it destroyed the integrity of the house as a separate subject. It brought grief and death into the house, and made it seem like a funeral parlor. I came to realize that in order to explore the similarities between these two subjects, I had to respect their differences. 2

I decided finally on an intermediate language, limited to neither the house nor the grief. I looked for terms that could legitimately apply to both. As a rule these were commonplace words, rich with associations in everyday use. Take, for instance, the "dust" in the second paragraph. In a closed house, dust is inevitable. Because it implies that no one is home caring for things, it evokes loneliness and disuse. It has quite a different meaning when the subject is grief, however. It is the end-product of death and decay, and it implies that this process is 3 over. So when the house-dust comes to life, swirls and dances, the message is that the process of grieving is over as well.

This amounts to using one word in the service of two sub-   4
jects, and it can be a tricky business. I found it necessary to play each word over and over, listening for subtle associations. In an analogy, these ordinary words echo back and forth between the two subjects, often borrowing meanings as they do so. Those nuances will be heard, however faintly, and they have to fur-ther the writer's intentions, not interfere with them.

Consider, for instance, the initial phrase of the second   5
sentence: it was pale. What if I had written instead: it needed paint. This might have described the house accurately enough, but that phrase carries meanings and associations that are dam-aging to the analogy. It suggests that the writer is worried about appearances, so worried in fact that it's nearly the first thing she has to say. It implies that she wants to hide, not repair, the ef-fects of the harsh weather. And worst of all, there is even a hint of shame in the comment. In some subconscious way the reader will carry all those implications to the end of the analogy, and feel a hint of shame in the subject of grief.

In my opinion the word "pale" passed this echo test. It's   6
neither judgment nor complaint. Its primary meaning is a loss of color. It brings to mind an image of someone who has suffered with illness or exhaustion, and there's an element of both in grief. If "it needed paint" describes the house as it should be, "it was pale" describes it as it was. There's an implied acceptance that transfers from the house to the subject of grief. In this con-text, pale seems the right word to me. For all its brief simplicity, it speaks less of suffering than of survival.

Develop one of these topics by the method of analogy. (You might consider several of these topics, until one of them blooms into a bright idea for an analogy.)

1. The training of a professional writer.
2. The body's circulatory system.
3. The way a rumor spreads.
4. Succeeding in whatever you do.
5. The way a child learns to walk and talk.
6. What it's like to get behind in your school work.
7. The presence of God in your life.
8. Becoming sure of yourself in a new situation.
9. Trying to understand a difficult concept.
10. Getting the job done through cooperation instead of competition.
11. Teaching worthwhile values to a child.
12. How violent crime intrudes upon our lives.
13. Competition between the sexes.
14. Building character.
15. A crushing failure.
16. The brightest spot in your day.
17. Learning a new skill.
18. How your body fights germs.
19. Being a nonconformist.
20. Trying to "get by" without sufficient preparation.
21. Going into debt.
22. An allergic reaction.
23. The experience of unexpected happiness.

· 8 ·

CAUSE AND EFFECT

Asking Why

· THE METHOD ·

Press the button of a doorbell and, inside the house or apartment, chimes sound. Why? Because the touch of your finger on the button closed an electrical circuit. But why did you ring the doorbell? Because you were sent by your dispatcher: you are a bill-collector calling on a customer whose payments are three months overdue.

The touch of your finger on the button is the *immediate cause* of the chimes: the event that precipitates another. That you were ordered by your dispatcher to go ring the doorbell is a *remote cause*: an underlying, more basic reason for the event, not apparent to an observer. Probably, ringing the doorbell will lead to some results: the door will open, and you may be given a check — or a kick in the teeth. To divide the flow of events into reasons and results is the kind of analysis you make when you write by the method of *cause and effect*: This method answers the question, "Why did something happen?" or the question, "What were the consequences?" Don't confuse cause and effect with the method of process analysis, which addresses the question, "How did something happen?" An essay on the sounding chimes written by process analysis might break the happening into stages: (1) the finger presses the button; (2) the circuit closes; (3) the current travels the wire; (4) the chimes sound. (The essay would probably go into more detail and more stages than that.)

Sometimes it is hard to determine a cause. Events do not always lead as neatly to further events as this rhyme from Mother Goose would have us believe:

> For want of a nail the shoe was lost,
> For want of a shoe the horse was lost,
> For want of a horse the rider was lost,
> For want of a rider the battle was lost,
> For want of a battle the kingdom was lost—
> And all for the want of a nail.

In reality, a battle is lost for more than one reason. Perhaps the enemy not only had fewer men, but had expected reinforcements who stopped for a beer and arrived too late. Yet children, who are fond of this Mother Goose rhyme, often demand clear-cut causal explanations: "Why does the sun shine?" — "Why are there ostriches?" — "Why do things fall down instead of up?" To some of these questions, children expect immediately forthcoming answers, though the questions be unanswerable by the learned and the wise. It must have been a grown-up, however, who coined the Armenian saying, " 'Why' is a question only a fool will ask and a madman answer." The mature mind learns to live with the inexplicable — and with a duller, less inquisitive outlook than a child's. Some mature minds, of course, continue to pose questions that are hard to answer. "How was the earth made?" is worth asking — particularly if the questioner is a scientist or a philosopher.

In a way, like bright-eyed children, writers who seek causes and effects ask searching questions. But, unlike children, they distrust answers too easy to find. Behind a large and world-shaking effect, they expect to meet an abundance of causes. They persist in searching even though the answer to "Why?" does not immediately appear. It took a great scholar, Jacob Burckhardt, much of his life to set forth a few cogent reasons for the occurrence of the Italian Renaissance. History is difficult to interpret, and so are human motives. To decide why an accused murderer acted as he did may take the members of a jury days of deliberation, after listening to weeks of testimony from witnesses, police detectives, and psychiatrists. (Even for years after the verdict, people may go on writing books trying to explain why Jean Harris shot the author of *The Scarsdale Diet*.) To set forth all the effects of such a slaying may be equally difficult. The victim may have left a will making someone rich, or leaving his house to an artists' colony — with later, long-continuing consequences. In prison, the convicted slayer may become a philosopher. Still, to ask "Why?" and "What resulted?" is necessary. To perceive events and phenomena and to look for their causes and effects is a workable method for the mind to make sense of reality.

• THE PROCESS •

In writing an essay that seeks causes or one that seeks effects, first make sure that your subject is manageable. Choose a subject you can get to the bottom of, given the time and information you have. For a 500-word essay due Thursday, the causes of teenage rebellion would be a topic less wieldy than why a certain thirteen-year-old you know ran away from home. Excellent papers may be written on large subjects, and yet excellent papers may be written on smaller, more personal subjects as well. You can ask yourself, for instance, why you behaved in a certain way at a certain moment. You can examine the reasons for your current beliefs and attitudes. Such a paper might be rewarding: you might happen upon a truth you hadn't realized before. In fact, both you and your reader may profit from an essay that seeks causes along the lines of these: "Why I Espouse Nudism," or "Why I Quit College and Why I Returned." Such a paper, of course, takes thought. It isn't easy to research your own motivations. A thoughtful, personal paper that discerns *effects* might follow from a topic such as "Where Nudism Led Me" or "What Happened When I Quit College."

When setting out to find causes, travel back to remote causes only as far as seems necessary. If you were explaining why a small town has fallen upon hard times, you might confine yourself to the immediate cause of the hardship: the closing of a factory. If you had room to explore remote causes, you would probably wish to explain the dispute between union and management that caused the shutdown. If you were writing a book and wished to go back to still more remote causes, you might even trace the dispute back to the Industrial Revolution of the eighteenth century. A manageable short paper showing *effect* might work in the other direction, moving from the factory closing to its consequences in town: people out of work, the closing of stores and a movie house, a mass exodus of the population.

Remember, the causes of an event or phenomenon are often complex, perhaps simultaneous. In seeking to explain a social trend (jogging at lunch time or marrying late) or a vast public event (a strike or a war), you may expect to find an array of causes, perhaps as interrelated as the strands of a spider web. Beware of the logical fallacy "after this, therefore because of this" (in Latin, *post hoc, ergo propter hoc*) — that is, don't expect Event A to be the cause of Event B just because A preceded B in time. This is the familiar error on the part of the superstitious person who decides that he was fired from his job as the direct result of having walked under a ladder, or who, when a black cat crosses his path, expects to be hit by a truck. Another error in looking for causes is oversimplification: to claim, for instance, that an increase in urban crime is simply due to "all these gangster shows on television." Such wrong turns in reasoning may be avoided by careful thought and a painstaking search for evidence. (For a list of them see *Logical Fallacies* in Useful Terms.)

In stating what you believe to be causes and effects, however, don't be afraid now and then to voice a well-considered hunch. Your instructor doesn't expect you to write, in a short time, a *definitive* account of the causes of an event or a belief or a phenomenon — only to write a coherent and reasonable one. To discern all causes — including remote ones — and all effects is beyond the power of any one human mind. Still, admirable and well-informed writers on matters such as politics, economics, and world and national affairs are often canny guessers and brave drawers of inferences. At times, even the most cautious and responsible writer has to leap boldly over a void to strike firm ground on the far side. Consider your evidence. Think about it hard. Look well before leaping. Then take off.

• CAUSE AND EFFECT IN A PARAGRAPH •

Why is it that, despite a growing interest in soccer among American athletes, and despite its ranking as the most popular sport in the world, commercial television ignores it? To see a televised North American Soccer League game, you have to tune at odd hours to public TV. Part of the reason stems from the basic nature of network television, which exists not to inform and entertain but to sell. During most major sporting events on television — football, baseball, basketball, boxing — producers can take advantage of natural interruptions in the action to broadcast sales pitches; or, if the natural breaks occur too infrequently, the producers can contrive time-outs for the sole purpose of airing lucrative commercials. But soccer is played in two solid halves of forty-five minutes each; not even injury to a player is cause for a time-out. How, then, to insert the requisite number of commercial breaks without resorting to false fouls or other questionable tactics? After CBS aired a soccer match on May 27, 1967, players reported, according to Stanley Frank, that before the game the referee had instructed them "to stay down every nine minutes." The resulting hue and cry rose all the way to the House Communications Subcommittee. From that day to this, no one has been able to figure out how to screen advertising jingles during a televised soccer game. The result is that the commercial networks have to treat the North American Soccer League as if it didn't exist.

Comment. In this paragraph, the writer seeks a cause, and in her opening sentence poses the "Why?" question she will answer. The middle portion of the paragraph explains that soccer, unlike other sports, is difficult to adapt to commercial television. In mentioning the famous case reported by Frank, she shows what happened when, for a change, a soccer game was telecast, but was artificially orchestrated so as to allow blank moments for commercials. There is only one cause to be found; and it is stated (together with its effect) in the concluding two sentences. Note how the writer illustrates her generalizations with examples. The only unillustrated one is the statement that network TV exists for the purpose of selling things; and this seems an apparent truth we all know already.

· Gore Vidal ·

GORE VIDAL was born in 1925 at the U.S. Military Academy at West Point, where his father was an instructor. At the age of nineteen, he wrote his first novel, *Williwaw* (1946), while serving as a warrant officer aboard an army supply ship. Among his later (and more popular) novels are *Myra Breckinridge* (1968), *Burr* (1973), *1876* (1976), *Kalki* (1978), and *Creation* (1981). He has also written mysteries under the pen name Edgar Box. As a playwright, he is best known for *Visit to a Small Planet* (1957), which was made into a film. The grandson of Senator T. P. Gore, who represented Oklahoma for thirty years, Vidal himself entered politics in 1960 as a Democratic-Liberal candidate for Congress. A frequent contributor of brilliant, opinionated essays to *The New York Review of Books*, Vidal divides his time between Italy and America.

Drugs

Vidal, whom some critics have called America's finest living essayist, first published "Drugs" on the "op ed" page of the *New York Times* (the page opposite the editorial page, reserved for diverse opinions). Vidal included it in *Homage to Daniel Shays: Collected Essays 1952–1972*. In the essay, he suggests some generally unrecognized causes for the nation's problems with drug addiction, and proposes a radical solution. See if you think it might work.

It is possible to stop most drug addiction in the United States within a very short time. Simply make all drugs available and sell them at cost. Label each drug with a precise description of what effect — good and bad — the drug will have on the taker. This will require heroic honesty. Don't say that marijuana is addictive or dangerous when it is neither, as millions of people know — unlike "speed," which kills most unpleasantly, or heroin, which is addictive and difficult to kick.

For the record, I have tried — once — almost every drug and liked none, disproving the popular Fu Manchu theory that a single whiff of opium will enslave the mind. Nevertheless many drugs are bad for certain people to take and they should be told why in a sensible way.

Along with exhortation and warning, it might be good for   3
our citizens to recall (or learn for the first time) that the United
States was the creation of men who believed that each man has
the right to do what he wants with his own life as long as he
does not interfere with his neighbor's pursuit of happiness (that
his neighbor's idea of happiness is persecuting others does confuse matters a bit).

This is a startling notion to the current generation of Amer-   4
icans. They reflect a system of public education which has made
the Bill of Rights, literally, unacceptable to a majority of high
school graduates (see the annual Purdue reports) who now form
the "silent majority" — a phrase which that underestimated wit
Richard Nixon took from Homer who used it to describe the
dead.

Now one can hear the warning rumble begin: if everyone is   5
allowed to take drugs everyone will and the GNP will decrease,
the Commies will stop us from making everyone free, and we
shall end up a race of zombies, passively murmuring "groovy" to
one another. Alarming thought. Yet it seems most unlikely that
any reasonably sane person will become a drug addict if he
knows in advance what addiction is going to be like.

Is everyone reasonably sane? No. Some people will always   6
become drug addicts just as some people will always become alcoholics, and it is just too bad. Every man, however, has the
power (and should have the legal right) to kill himself if he
chooses. But since most men don't, they won't be mainliners
either. Nevertheless, forbidding people things they like or think
they might enjoy only makes them want those things all the
more. This psychological insight is, for some mysterious reason,
perennially denied our governors.

It is a lucky thing for the Amerian moralist that our country   7
has always existed in a kind of time-vacuum: we have no public
memory of anything that happened before last Tuesday. No one
in Washington today recalls what happened during the years alcohol was forbidden to the people by a Congress that thought it
had a divine mission to stamp out Demon Rum — launching, in
the process, the greatest crime wave in the country's history,

causing thousands of deaths from bad alcohol, and creating a general (and persisting) contempt among the citizenry for the laws of the United States.

The same thing is happening today. But the government has learned nothing from past attempts at prohibition, not to mention repression. 8

Last year when the supply of Mexican marijuana was slightly curtailed by the Feds, the pushers got the kids hooked on heroin and deaths increased dramatically, particularly in New York. Whose fault? Evil men like the Mafiosi? Permissive Dr. Spock? Wild-eyed Dr. Leary? No. 9

The Government of the United States was responsible for those deaths. The bureaucratic machine has a vested interest in playing cops and robbers. Both the Bureau of Narcotics and the Mafia want strong laws against the sale and use of drugs because if drugs are sold at cost there would be no money in it for anyone. 10

If there was no money in it for the Mafia, there would be no friendly playground pushers, and addicts would not commit crimes to pay for the next fix. Finally, if there was no money in it, the Bureau of Narcotics would wither away, something they are not about to do without a struggle. 11

Will anything sensible be done? Of course not. The American people are as devoted to the idea of sin and its punishment as they are to making money — and fighting drugs is nearly as big a business as pushing them. Since the combination of sin and money is irresistible (particularly to the professional politician), the situation will only grow worse. 12

• QUESTIONS ON MEANING AND PURPOSE •

1. How readily do you accept Vidal's implicit assumption that a person with easy access to drugs would be unlikely to "interfere with his neighbor's pursuit of happiness"?
2. Spend enough time in the library to learn more about the era of Prohibition in the United States. To what extent do the facts support Vidal's contention that Prohibition was a bad idea?

3. For what reasons, according to Vidal, is it unlikely that our drug laws will be eased? Can you suggest other possible reasons why the Bureau of Narcotics favors strict drug laws?
4. Vidal's essay was first published in 1970. Do you find the views expressed in it still timely, or hopelessly out-of-date?
5. What do you take to be Vidal's main purpose in writing this essay? How well does he accomplish it?

· QUESTIONS ON WRITING STRATEGY ·

1. How would you characterize Vidal's humor? Find some examples of it.
2. In paragraphs 3 and 4, Vidal summons our founding fathers and the Bill of Rights to his support. Is this tactic fair or unfair? Explain.
3. In paragraph 10, Vidal asserts that the Government of the United States is the cause of heroin deaths among the young in New York. By what steps does he arrive at this conclusion? Is the author guilty of oversimplification? (See the discussion of *oversimplification* on page 330).
4. Where in the essay does Vidal appear to anticipate the response of his audience? How can you tell?
5. What function do the essay's rhetorical questions perform? (See *Rhetorical Question* in Useful Terms.)

· QUESTIONS ON LANGUAGE · · AND VOCABULARY ·

1. Know the definitions of the following terms: exhortation (paragraph 3); GNP (5); mainliners, perennially (6); curtailed (9).
2. How do you interpret Vidal's use of the phrase "underestimated wit" to describe Richard Nixon?

· SUGGESTIONS FOR WRITING ·

1. Write a paragraph in which you try to predict both the good and the ill effects you think might result from following Vidal's advice to "make all drugs available and sell them at cost."
2. In a short essay, evaluate Vidal's suggestion that every drug be labeled with a description of its probable effect on the taker. How likely does it seem to you that the warnings printed on containers of addictive or dangerous drugs would be heeded?

· Lewis Thomas ·

LEWIS THOMAS, born in 1913 in Flushing, New York, received his B.S. degree from Princeton in 1933 and his M.D. from Harvard in 1937. A distinguished physician, researcher, educator, and medical administrator, he has held appointments at many medical schools and research hospitals; and his articles have appeared in scientific journals. In 1971 he began writing "Notes of a Biology Watcher," a regular column for the *New England Journal of Medicine*. Out of his column grew *The Lives of a Cell: Notes of a Biology Watcher* (1974), which won a National Book Award for Arts and Letters in 1975. He is also the author of *The Medusa and the Snail: More Notes of a Biology Watcher* (1979). Since 1973 Thomas has been president and chief executive of the Memorial Sloan-Kettering Cancer Center in New York City.

On Warts

"On Warts" is one of the essays in *The Medusa and the Snail*. In lucid, engaging prose Thomas sets forth what scientists know about warts; and, with even more relish, speculating about both causes and effects, he probes the unsolved mysteries of these odd growths. Warts can be cured, as all physicians know. What no one really understands is exactly how the cure works.

Warts are wonderful structures. They can appear overnight on any part of the skin, like mushrooms on a damp lawn, full grown and splendid in the complexity of their architecture. Viewed in stained sections under a microscope, they are the most specialized of cellular arrangements, constructed as though for a purpose. They sit there like turreted mounds of dense, impenetrable horn, impregnable, designed for defense against the world outside.

In a certain sense, warts are both useful and essential, but not for us. As it turns out, the exuberant cells of a wart are the elaborate reproductive apparatus of a virus.

1

2

You might have thought from the looks of it that the cells   3
infected by the wart virus were using this response as a ponder-
ous way of defending themselves against the virus, maybe even
a way of becoming more distasteful, but it is not so. The wart is
what the virus truly wants; it can flourish only in cells undergo-
ing precisely this kind of overgrowth. It is not a defense at all; it
is an overwhelming welcome, an enthusiastic accommodation
meeting the needs of more and more virus.

The strangest thing about warts is that they tend to go   4
away. Fully grown, nothing in the body has so much the look of
toughness and permanence as a wart, and yet, inexplicably and
often very abruptly, they come to the end of their lives and vanish without a trace.

And they can be made to go away by something that can   5
only be called thinking, or something like thinking. This is a
special property of warts which is absolutely astonishing, more
of a surprise than cloning or recombinant DNA or endorphin
or acupuncture or anything else currently attracting attention
in the press. It is one of the great mystifications of science: warts
can be ordered off the skin by hypnotic suggestion.

Not everyone believes this, but the evidence goes back a   6
long way and is persuasive. Generations of internists and der-
matologists, and their grandmothers for that matter, have
been convinced of the phenomenon. I was once told by a
distinguished old professor of medicine, one of Sir William
Osler's original bright young men, that it was his practice to
paint gentian violet over a wart and then assure the patient
firmly that it would be gone in a week, and he never saw it fail.
There have been several meticulous studies by good clinical
investigators, with proper controls. In one of these, fourteen
patients with seemingly intractable generalized warts on both
sides of the body were hypnotized, and the suggestion was made
that all the warts on one side of the body would begin to go
away. Within several weeks the results were indisputably positive; in nine patients, all or nearly all of the warts on the suggested side had vanished, while the control side had just as many
as ever.

It is interesting that most of the warts vanished precisely as   7
they were instructed, but it is even more fascinating that

mistakes were made. Just as you might expect in other affairs requiring a clear understanding of which is the right and which the left side, one of the subjects got mixed up and destroyed the warts on the wrong side. In a later study by a group at the Massachusetts General Hospital, the warts on both sides were rejected even though the instructions were to pay attention to just one side.

I have been trying to figure out the nature of the instructions issued by the unconscious mind, whatever that is, under hypnosis. It seems to me hardly enough for the mind to say, simply, get off, eliminate yourselves, without providing something in the way of specifications as to how to go about it.

I used to believe, thinking about this experiment when it was just published, that the instructions might be quite simple. Perhaps nothing more detailed than a command to shut down the flow through all the precapillary arterioles in and around the warts to the point of strangulation. Exactly how the mind would accomplish this with precision, cutting off the blood supply to one wart while leaving others intact, I couldn't figure out, but I was satisfied to leave it there anyhow. And I was glad to think that my unconscious mind would have to take the responsibility for this, for if I had been one of the subjects I would never have been able to do it myself.

But now the problem seems much more complicated by the information concerning the viral etiology of warts, and even more so by the currently plausible notion that immunologic mechanisms are very likely implicated in the rejection of warts.

If my unconscious can figure out how to manipulate the mechanisms needed for getting around that virus, and for deploying all the various cells in the correct order for tissue rejection, then all I have to say is that my unconscious is a lot further along than I am. I wish I had a wart right now, just to see if I am that talented.

There ought to be a better word than "Unconscious," even capitalized, for what I have, so to speak, in mind. I was brought up to regard this aspect of thinking as a sort of private sanitarium, walled off somewhere in a suburb of my brain, capable only of producing such garbled information as to keep my mind, my proper Mind, always a little off balance.

But any mental apparatus that can reject a wart is some-   13
thing else again. This is not the sort of confused, disordered
process you'd expect at the hands of the kind of Unconscious
you read about in books, out at the edge of things making up
dreams or getting mixed up on words or having hysterics.
Whatever, or whoever, is responsible for this has the accuracy
and precision of a surgeon. There almost has to be a Person in
charge, running matters of meticulous detail beyond anyone's
comprehension, a skilled engineer and manager, a chief executive officer, the head of the whole place. I never thought
before that I possessed such a tenant. Or perhaps more accurately, such a landlord, since I would be, if this is in fact the
situation, nothing more than a lodger.

Among other accomplishments, he must be a cell biologist   14
of world class, capable of sorting through the various classes of
one's lymphocytes, all with quite different functions which I do
not understand, in order to mobilize the right ones and exclude
the wrong ones for the task of tissue rejection. If it were left to
me, and I were somehow empowered to call up lymphocytes and
direct them to the vicinity of my wart (assuming that I could
learn to do such a thing), mine would come tumbling in all un-
sorted, B cells and T cells, suppressor cells and killer cells, and
no doubt other cells whose names I have not learned, incapable
of getting anything useful done.

Even if immunology is not involved, and all that needs do-   15
ing is to shut off the blood supply locally, I haven't the faintest
notion how to set that up. I assume that the selective turning off
of arterioles can be done by one or another chemical mediator,
and I know the names of some of them, but I wouldn't dare let
things like these loose even if I knew how to do it.

Well, then, who does supervise this kind of operation?   16
Someone's got to, you know. You can't sit there under hypnosis, taking suggestions in and having them acted on with such
accuracy and precision, without assuming the existence of
something very like a controller. It wouldn't do to fob off the
whole intricate business on lower centers without sending along
a quite detailed set of specifications, way over my head.

Some intelligence or other knows how to get rid of warts,   17
and this is a disquieting thought.

It is also a wonderful problem, in need of solving. Just think   18
what we would know, if we had anything like a clear understanding of what goes on when a wart is hypnotized away. We
would know the identity of the cellular and chemical participants in tissue rejection, conceivably with some added information about the ways that viruses create foreignness in
cells. We would know how the traffic of these reactants is directed, and perhaps then be able to understand the nature of
certain diseases in which the traffic is being conducted in wrong
directions, aimed at the wrong cells. Best of all, we would be
finding out about a kind of superintelligence that exists in each
of us, infinitely smarter and possessed of technical know-how
far beyond our present understanding. It would be worth a War
on Warts, a Conquest of Warts, a National Institute of Warts
and All.

• QUESTIONS ON MEANING AND PURPOSE •

1. What causes warts? What is it, according to Lewis Thomas, that
   makes them go away?
2. How do you reconcile the fact that Thomas is a scientist with the
   fact that he puts his faith in such an apparently unscientific cure?
3. What is the main purpose of Thomas's essay? How well is that
   purpose accomplished?

• QUESTIONS ON WRITING STRATEGY •

1. Which of Thomas's statements do you find surprising or
   whimsical? Which seem exaggerated? Do such statements benefit
   or detract from the essay? Explain.
2. What, if anything, does this essay gain from having been written
   in the first person? (See *Person* in Useful Terms.)
3. Does Thomas's essay address his fellow scientists or a more
   general audience? Cite evidence for your answer. (See *Evidence* in
   Useful Terms.)
4. Define Thomas's attitude toward his subject. (See *Tone* in Useful
   Terms.) By what means does he reveal his attitude?

• QUESTIONS ON LANGUAGE •
• AND VOCABULARY •

1. In his first paragraph Thomas says that warts appear on the skin "like mushrooms on a damp lawn." List other figures of speech in the essay and explain what each contributes. (See *Figures of Speech* in Useful Terms.)
2. Be sure you know the meanings of the following words: turreted, horn (paragraph 1); cloning, recombinant DNA, endorphin (5); pre-capillary arterioles (9); etiology (10); meticulous (13); lymphocytes (14).
3. What does the expression "warts and all" usually mean? What other well known, more official phrases are parodied in the last sentence?

• SUGGESTIONS FOR WRITING •

1. In a brief story or anecdote, tell what caused the departure of something that you wanted to get rid of — for instance, a common cold.
2. Draw on your reading or your experience to evaluate, in a brief essay, the role of the power of suggestion in one of the following: a miracle cure or faith-healing; a cure effected by a placebo; a spontaneous remission from an incurable disease.

• Sheila Tobias •

SHEILA TOBIAS, born in 1935, is a Radcliffe graduate and has an M.A. in history from Columbia University. She has been a university teacher and administrator, most recently at Wesleyan University in Connecticut. One of the founding members of the National Organization of Women (NOW) and a "math avoider," she published *Overcoming Math Anxiety* in 1978. Shortly afterward, in Washington, D.C., she and two colleagues founded Overcoming Math Anxiety, a consulting and training service that runs math clinics for adults.

Who's Afraid of Math, and Why?

In "Who's Afraid of Math, and Why?," an excerpt from *Overcoming Math Anxiety*, Sheila Tobias attacks the myth of the "mathematical mind" and examines some of the hang-ups people have about learning math. Math avoiders, it seems, are mostly — but not solely — women. Tobias explains why.

The first thing people remember about failing at math is   1
that it felt like sudden death. Whether the incident occurred while learning "word problems" in sixth grade, coping with equations in high school, or first confronting calculus and statistics in college, failure came suddenly and in a very frightening way. An idea or a new operation was not just difficult, it was impossible! And, instead of asking questions or taking the lesson slowly, most people remember having had the feeling that they would never go any further in mathematics. If we assume that the curriculum was reasonable, and that the new idea was but the next in a series of learnable concepts, the feeling of utter defeat was simply not rational; yet "math anxious" college students and adults have revealed that no matter how much the teacher reassured them, they could not overcome that feeling.

A common myth about the nature of mathematical ability 2
holds that one either has or does not have a mathematical
mind. Mathematical imagination and an intuitive grasp of
mathematical principles may well be needed to do advanced research, but why should people who can do college-level work in
other subjects not be able to do college-level math as well? Rates
of learning may vary. Competency under time pressure may differ. Certainly low self-esteem will get in the way. But where is
the evidence that a student needs a "mathematical mind" in
order to succeed at learning math?

Consider the effects of this mythology. Since only a few peo- 3
ple are supposed to have this mathematical mind, part of what
makes us so passive in the face of our difficulties in learning
mathematics is that we suspect all the while we may not be one
of "them," and we spend our time waiting to find out when our
nonmathematical minds will be exposed. Since our limit will
eventually be reached, we see no point in being methodical or
in attending to detail. We are grateful when we survive frac-
tions, word problems, or geometry. If that certain moment of
failure hasn't struck yet, it is only temporarily postponed.

Parents, especially parents of girls, often expect their 4
children to be nonmathematical. Parents are either poor at
math and had their own sudden-death experiences, or, if math
came easily for them, they do not know how it feels to be slow.
In either case, they unwittingly foster the idea that a mathematical mind is something one either has or does not have.

Mathematics and Sex

Although fear of math is not a purely female phenomenon, 5
girls tend to drop out of math sooner than boys, and adult
women experience an aversion to math and math-related activities that is akin to anxiety. A 1972 survey of the amount of
high school mathematics taken by incoming freshmen at Berkeley revealed that while 57 percent of the boys had taken four
years of high school math, only 8 percent of the girls had had
the same amount of preparation. Without four years of high
school math, students at Berkeley, and at most other colleges
and universities, are ineligible for the calculus sequence, unlike-

ly to attempt chemistry or physics, and inadequately prepared for statistics and economics.

Unable to elect these entry-level courses, the remaining 92 percent of the girls will be limited, presumably, to the career choices that are considered feminine: the humanities, guidance and counseling, elementary school teaching, foreign languages, and the fine arts. 6

Boys and girls may be born alike with respect to math, but certain sex differences in performance emerge early according to several respected studies, and these differences remain through adulthood. They are: 7

1. Girls compute better than boys (elementary school and on).

2. Boys solve word problems better than girls (from age thirteen on).

3. Boys take more math than girls (from age sixteen on).

4. Girls learn to hate math sooner and possibly for different reasons.

Why the differences in performance? One reason is the amount of math learned and used at play. Another may be the difference in male-female maturation. If girls do better than boys at all elementary school tasks, then they may compute better for no other reason than that arithmetic is part of the elementary school curriculum. As boys and girls grow older, girls become, under pressure, academically less competitive. Thus, the falling off of girls' math performance between ages ten and fifteen may be because: 8

1. Math gets harder in each successive year and requires more work and commitment.

2. Both boys and girls are pressured, beginning at age ten, not to excel in areas designated by society to be outside their sex-role domains.

3. Thus girls have a good excuse to avoid the painful struggle with math; boys don't.

Such a model may explain girls' lower achievement in math overall, but why should girls even younger than ten have dif- 9 ficulty in problem-solving? In her review of the research on sex differences, psychologist Eleanor Maccoby noted that girls are generally more conforming, more suggestible, and more dependent upon the opinion of others than boys (all learned, not innate, behaviors). Being so, they may not be as willing to take risks or to think for themselves, two behaviors that are necessary in solving problems. Indeed, in one test of third-graders, girls were found to be not nearly as willing to estimate, to make judgments about "possible right answers," or to work with systems they had never seen before. Their very success at doing what is expected of them up to that time seems to get in the way of their doing something new.

If readiness to do word problems, to take one example, is as   10
much a function of readiness to take risks as it is of "reasoning ability," then mathematics performance certainly requires more than memory, computation, and reasoning. The differences in math performance between boys and girls — no matter how consistently those differences show up — cannot be attributed simply to differences in innate ability.

Still, if one were to ask the victims themselves, they would   11
probably disagree: they would say their problems with math have to do with the way they are "wired." They feel they are somehow missing something — one ability or several — that other people have. Although women want to believe they are not mentally inferior to men, many fear that, where math is concerned, they really are. Thus, we have to consider seriously whether mathematical ability has a biological basis, not only because a number of researchers believe this to be so, but because a number of victims agree with them.

The Arguments from Biology

The search for some biological basis for math ability or   12
disability is fraught with logical and experimental difficulties. Since not all math underachievers are women, and not all women are mathematics-avoidant, poor performance in math is unlikely to be due to some genetic or hormonal difference between the sexes. Moreover, no amount of research so far has unearthed a "mathematical competency" in some tangible, mea-

surable substance in the body. Since "masculinity" cannot be injected into women to test whether or not it improves their mathematics, the theories that attribute such ability to genes or hormones must depend for their proof on circumstantial evidence. So long as about 7 percent of the Ph.D.'s in mathematics are earned by women, we have to conclude either that these women have genes, hormones, and brain organization different from those of the rest of us, or that certain positive experiences in their lives have largely undone the negative fact that they are female, or both.

Genetically, the only difference between males and females (albeit a significant and pervasive one) is the presence of two chromosomes designated X in every female cell. Normal males exhibit an X-Y combination. Because some kinds of mental retardation are associated with sex-chromosomal anomalies, a number of researchers have sought a converse linkage between specific abilities and the presence or absence of the second X. But the linkage between genetics and mathematics is not supported by conclusive evidence. 13

Since intensified hormonal activity commences at adolescence, a time during which girls seem to lose interest in mathematics, much more has been made of the unequal amounts in females and males of the sex-linked hormones androgen and estrogen. Biological researchers have linked estrogen — the female hormone — with "simple repetitive tasks," and androgen — the male hormone — with "complex restructuring tasks." The assumption here is not only that such specific talents are biologically based (probably undemonstrable) but also that one cannot be good at *both* repetitive and restructuring kinds of assignments. 14

Sex Roles and Mathematics Competence

The fact that many girls tend to lose interest in math at the age they reach puberty (junior high school) suggests that puberty might in some sense cause girls to fall behind in math. Several explanations come to mind: the influence of hormones, more intensified sex-role socialization, or some extracurricular learning experience exclusive to boys of that age. 15

One group of seventh-graders in a private school in New   16
England gave a clue as to what children themselves think about
all of this. When asked why girls do as well as boys in math until
the sixth grade, while sixth-grade boys do better from that point
on, the girls responded: "Oh, that's easy. After sixth grade, we
have to do real math." The answer to why "real math" should
be considered to be "for boys" and not "for girls" can be found
not in the realm of biology but only in the realm of ideology of
sex differences.

Parents, peers, and teachers forgive a girl when she does   17
badly in math at school, encouraging her to do well in other
subjects instead. " 'There, there,' my mother used to say when I
failed at math," one woman says. "But I got a talking-to when I
did badly in French." Lynn Fox, who directs a program for
mathematically gifted junior high boys and girls on the campus
of Johns Hopkins University, has trouble recruiting girls and
keeping them in her program. Some parents prevent their
daughters from participating altogether for fear that excellence
in math will make them too different. The girls themselves are
often reluctant to continue with mathematics, Fox reports, because they fear social ostracism.

Where do these associations come from?   18

The association of masculinity with mathematics sometimes   19
extends from the discipline to those who practice it. Students,
asked on a questionnaire what characteristics they associate
with a mathematician (as contrasted with a "writer"), selected
terms such as rational, cautious, wise, and responsible. The
writer, on the other hand, in addition to being seen as individ-
ualistic and independent, was also described as warm, interested
in people, and altogether more compatible with a feminine
ideal.

As a result of this psychological conditioning, a young   20
woman may consider math and math-related fields to be inimical to femininity. In an interesting study of West German
teenagers, Erika Schildkamp-Kuendiger found that girls who
identified themselves with the feminine ideal underachieved in
mathematics, that is, did less well than would have been expected of them based on general intelligence and performance
in other subjects.

Street Mathematics: Things, Motion, Scores

Not all the skills that are necessary for learning mathematics are learned in school. Measuring, computing, and manipulating objects that have dimensions and dynamic properties of their own are part of the everyday life of children. Children who miss out on these experiences may not be well primed for math in school. 21

Feminists have complained for a long time that playing with dolls is one way of convincing impressionable little girls that they may only be mothers or housewives — or, as in the case of the Barbie doll, "pinup girls" — when they grow up. But doll-playing may have even more serious consequences for little girls than that. Do girls find out about gravity and distance and shapes and sizes playing with dolls? Probably not. 22

A curious boy, if his parents are tolerant, will have taken apart a number of household and play objects by the time he is ten, and, if his parents are lucky, he may even have put them back together again. In all of this he is learning things that will be useful in physics and math. Taking parts out that have to go back in requires some examination of form. Building something that stays up or at least stays put for some time involves working with structure. 23

Sports is another source of math-related concepts for children which tends to favor boys. Getting to first base on a not very well hit grounder is a lesson in time, speed, and distance. Intercepting a football thrown through the air requires some rapid intuitive eye calculations based on the ball's direction, speed, and trajectory. Since physics is partly concerned with velocities, trajectories, and collisions of objects, much of the math taught to prepare a student for physics deals with relationships and formulas that can be used to express motion and acceleration. 24

What, then, can we conclude about mathematics and sex? If math anxiety is in part the result of math avoidance, why not require girls to take as much math as they can possibly master? If being the only girl in "trig" is the reason so many women drop math at the end of high school, why not provide psychological counseling and support for those young women who wish to go 25 on? Since ability in mathematics is considered by many to be unfeminine, perhaps fear of success, more than any bodily or mental dysfunction, may interfere with girls' ability to learn math.

· QUESTIONS ON MEANING AND PURPOSE ·

1. According to Tobias, what effect does the myth of the "mathematical mind" have upon the ordinary person's performance in math?
2. To what does the author attribute the fact that girls tend to compute better than boys? How does Tobias account for boys' superior problem-solving ability?
3. Of the probable causes Tobias cites for the fact that girls as they mature generally perform less well in math than boys, which one does the author rule out? On what basis? Are you satisfied that she is justified in doing so?
4. According to the author, what differences exist between the play patterns of little boys and those of little girls? In what way do these differences favor boys and handicap girls in their later efforts to acquire math skills?
5. In what additional ways, according to Tobias, does gender influence math performance? Of these, which does the author rank as the most important?
6. How would you expect a math avoider to react to this essay?

· QUESTIONS ON WRITING STRATEGY ·

1. At what point in her essay does Tobias shift her emphasis from math anxiety in general to math anxiety as a special problem for girls?
2. What do the statistics quoted in paragraphs 5, 6, and 7 contribute to the essay's effect? (See *Effect* in Useful Terms.)
3. What, if anything, does Tobias gain by putting her "arguments from biology" ahead of the other possible causes of poor math performance?
4. Do you think this essay would have been as effective if Tobias had written it as a first-person narrative of her own experiences with math? Why or why not? (See *Person* in Useful Terms.)

· QUESTIONS ON LANGUAGE ·
· AND VOCABULARY ·

1. How would you characterize Tobias's prose: terse, poetic, utilitarian, or persuasive?
2. In paragraph 11, Tobias twice refers to "victims." Comment on her word choice.
3. The title of this essay contains an allusion. What is its source? (See *Allusion* in Useful Terms.)
4. What does Tobias mean by "wired" (paragraph 11)?
5. Be sure you can define the following words: socialization (paragraph 15); ideology (16); ostracism (17); dysfunction (25).

· SUGGESTIONS FOR WRITING ·

1. Write a brief description or narrative in which math panic (or stage fright, or final exam panic) strikes you or someone you know. A little exaggeration, you will find, just might add zest to your account.
2. Identify a few differences between men and women that, like differences in mathematical ability, seem the result not of biology but of cultural conditioning. Then, in a paragraph or two, trace the causes of one such difference. Or attempt to show, as some researchers do, that mathematical ability really is an inborn, sex-linked trait.

· John Houseman ·

JOHN HOUSEMAN was born in Rumania in 1902. Educated in England, he came to the United States in 1925. In addition to producing movies and Broadway plays, he has been a director, actor, teacher, and writer. With Orson Welles, Houseman co-founded the Mercury Theater, which did shows on Broadway and later on CBS radio. In 1974 he won an Academy Award for his role as best supporting actor in the movie *The Paper Chase*; and in 1978 he starred in the television series by the same name. Houseman is the author of a memoir entitled *Run-through* (1972) and of *Front and Center* (1979).

The Night the Martians Landed

By October 1938, the CBS Mercury Theater on the Air was well into its fall radio drama season. Scheduled for the October 30 broadcast was the forty-year-old H. G. Wells novel, *The War of the Worlds*. No one was prepared for the broadcast's astonishing impact on the American populace. Ten years later, probing both cause and effect, Houseman detailed the events of that memorable evening.

On Sunday, October 30, 1938, at 8:00 P.M., E.S.T., in a   1
studio littered with coffee cartons and sandwich paper, Orson Welles swallowed a second container of pineapple juice, put on his earphones, raised his long white fingers and threw the cue for the Mercury theme — the Tchaikovsky Piano Concerto in B Flat Minor #1. After the music dipped, there were routine introductions — then the announcement that a dramatization of H. G. Wells' famous novel, *The War of the Worlds*, was about to be performed. Around 8:01 Orson began to speak, as follows:

Welles

We know now that in the early years of the twentieth century this world was being watched closely by intelligences greater than man's and yet as mortal as his own. We know now that as human beings busied themselves about their various concerns they were scrutinized and studied, perhaps almost as narrowly as a man with a microscope might scrutinize the transient creatures that swarm and multiply in a drop of water. With infinite complacence people went to and fro over the earth about their little affairs, serene in the assurance of their dominion over this small spinning fragment of solar driftwood which by chance or design man has inherited out of the dark mystery of Time and Space. Yet across an immense ethereal gulf minds that are to our minds as ours are to the beasts in the jungle, intellects vast, cool, and unsympathetic regarded this earth with envious eyes and slowly and surely drew their plans against us. In the thirty-ninth year of the twentieth century came the great disillusionment.

It was near the end of October. Business was better. The war scare was over. More men were back at work. Sales were picking up. On this particular evening, October 30, the Crossley service estimated that thirty-two million people were listening in on their radios. . . .

Neatly, without perceptible transition, he was followed on the air by an anonymous announcer caught in a routine bulletin: 2

Announcer

. . . for the next twenty-four hours not much change in temperature. A slight atmospheric disturbance of undetermined origin is reported over Nova Scotia, causing a low pressure area to move down rather rapidly over the northeastern states, bringing a forecast of rain, accompanied by winds of light gale force. Maximum temperature 66; minimum 48. This weather report comes to you from the Government Weather Bureau. . . . We now take you to the Meridian Room in the Hotel Park Plaza in downtown New York, where you will be entertained by the music of Ramon Raquello and his orchestra.

At which cue, Bernard Herrmann led the massed men of the CBS house orchestra in a thunderous rendition of "La Cumparsita." The entire hoax might well have exploded there and then — but for the fact that hardly anyone was listening. They were being entertained by Charlie McCarthy — then at the height of his success. 3

The Crossley census, taken about a week before the broadcast, had given us 3.6 per cent of the listening audience to Edgar Bergen's 34.7 per cent. What the Crossley Institute (that hireling of the advertising agencies) deliberately ignored, was the healthy American habit of dial-twisting. On that particular evening, Edgar Bergen in the person of Charlie McCarthy temporarily left the air about 8:12 P.M., E.S.T., yielding place to a new and not very popular singer. At that point, and during the following minutes, a large number of listeners started twisting their dials in search of other entertainment. Many of them turned to us — and when they did, they stayed put! For by this time the mysterious meteorite had fallen at Grovers Mill in New Jersey, the Martians had begun to show their foul leathery heads above the ground, and the New Jersey State Police were racing to the spot. Within a few minutes people all over the United States were praying, crying, fleeing frantically to escape death from the Martians. Some remembered to rescue loved ones, others telephoned farewells or warnings, hurried to inform neighbors, sought information from newspapers or radio stations, summoned ambulances and police cars.

The reaction was strongest at points nearest the tragedy — in Newark, New Jersey, in a single block, more than twenty families rushed out of their houses with wet handkerchiefs and towels over their faces. Some began moving household furniture. Police switchboards were flooded with calls inquiring, "Shall I close my windows?" "Have the police any extra gas masks?" Police found one family waiting in the yard with wet cloths on faces contorted with hysteria. As one woman reported later:

> I was terribly frightened. I wanted to pack and take my child in my arms, gather up my friends and get in the car and just go north as far as we could. But what I did was just sit by one window, praying, listening, and scared stiff, and my husband by the other sniffling and looking out to see if people were running. . . .

In New York hundreds of people on Riverside Drive left their homes ready for flight. Bus terminals were crowded. A woman calling up the Dixie Bus Terminal for information said impatiently, "Hurry please, the world is coming to an end and I have a lot to do."

In the parlor churches of Harlem evening service became "end of the world" prayer meetings. Many turned to God in that moment:

> I held a crucifix in my hand and prayed while looking out of my open window for falling meteors. . . . When the monsters were wading across the Hudson River and coming into New York, I wanted to run up on my roof to see what they looked like, but I couldn't leave my radio while it was telling me of their whereabouts.
>
> Aunt Grace began to pray with Uncle Henry. Lily got sick to her stomach. I don't know what I did exactly but I know I prayed harder and more earnestly than ever before. Just as soon as we were convinced that this thing was real, how petty all things on this earth seemed; how soon we put our trust in God!

The panic moved upstate. One man called up the Mt. Vernon Police Headquarters to find out "where the forty policemen were killed." Another took time out to philosophize:

> I thought the whole human race was going to be wiped out — that seemed more important than the fact that we were going to die. It seemed awful that everything that had been worked on for years was going to be lost forever.

In Rhode Island weeping and hysterical women swamped the switchboard of the Providence *Journal* for details of the massacre, and officials of the electric light company received a score of calls urging them to turn off all lights so that the city would be safe from the enemy. The Boston *Globe* received a call from one woman "who could see the fire." A man in Pittsburgh hurried home in the midst of the broadcast and found his wife in the bathroom, a bottle of poison in her hand screaming, "I'd rather die this way than that." In Minneapolis a woman ran into church screaming, "New York destroyed this is the end of the world. You might as well go home to die I just heard it on the radio."

7

8

9

The Kansas City Bureau of the AP received inquiries about   10
the "meteors" from Los Angeles; Salt Lake City; Beaumont,
Texas; and St. Joseph, Missouri. In San Francisco the general
impression of listeners seemed to be that an overwhelming force
had invaded the United States from the air — was in process of
destroying New York and threatening to move westward. "My
God," roared an inquirer into a telephone, "where can I volunteer my services, we've got to stop this awful thing!"

As far south as Birmingham, Alabama, people gathered in   11
churches and prayed. On the campus of a Southeastern college —

> The girls in the sorority houses and dormitories huddled
> around their radios trembling and weeping in each other's
> arms. They separated themselves from their friends only to
> take their turn at the telephones to make long distance calls
> to their parents, saying goodbye for what they thought might
> be the last time. . . .

There are hundreds of such bits of testimony, gathered from
coast to coast.

At least one book[1] and quite a pile of sociological literature   12
has appeared on the subject of "The Invasion from Mars."
Many theories have been put forward to explain the "tidal
wave" of panic that swept the nation. I know of two factors that
largely contributed to the broadcast's extraordinarily violent effect. First, its historical timing. It came within thirty-five days of
the Munich crisis. For weeks, the American people had been
hanging on their radios, getting most of their news no longer
from the press, but over the air. A new technique of "on-the-
spot" reporting had been developed and eagerly accepted by an
anxious and news-hungry world. The Mercury Theater on the
Air by faithfully copying every detail of the new technique —
including its imperfections — found an already enervated audience ready to accept its wildest fantasies. The second factor
was the show's sheer technical brilliance. To this day it is impossible to sit in a room and hear the scratched, worn, off-the-
air recording of the broadcast, without feeling in the back of

---

[1]*The Invasion from Mars* by Hadley Cantril, Princeton University Press,
from which many of the above quotations were taken.

your neck some slight draft left over from that great wind of terror that swept the nation. Even with the element of credibility
totally removed it remains a surprisingly frightening show.

Radio drama was taken seriously in the thirties — before the   13
Quiz and the Giveaway became the lords of the air. In the work
of such directors as Reis, Corwin, Fickett, Welles, Robson,
Spier, and Oboler there was an eager, excited drive to get the
most out of this new, all too rapidly freezing medium. But what
happened that Sunday, up on the twentieth floor of the CBS
building, was something quite special. Beginning around two,
when the show started to take shape under Orson's hands, a
strange fever seemed to invade the studio — part childish mischief, part professional zeal.

First to feel it were the actors. I remember Frank Readick   14
(who played the part of Carl Phillips, the network's special reporter) going down to the record library and digging up the
Morrison recording of the explosion of the Hindenburg at Lake-
hurst. This is a classic reportage — one of those wonderful, un-
predictable accidents of eyewitness description. The broadcaster
is casually describing a routine landing of the giant gasbag. Suddenly he sees something. A flash of flame! An instant later the
whole thing explodes. It takes him time — a full second — to
react at all. Then seconds more of sputtering ejaculations before
he can make the adjustment between brain and tongue. He
starts to describe the terrible things he sees — the writhing
human figures twisting and squirming as they fall from the
white burning wreckage. He stops, fumbles, vomits, then quickly continues. Readick played the record to himself, over and
over. Then, recreating the emotion in his own terms, he described the Martian meteorite as he saw it lying inert and harmless in a field at Grovers Mill, lit up by the headlights of a hundred cars — the coppery cylinder suddenly opening, revealing
the leathery tentacles and the terrible pale-eyed faces of the
Martians within. As they begin to emerge he freezes, unable to
translate his vision into words; he fumbles, retches — and then
after a second continues.

A few moments later Carl Phillips lay dead, tumbling over   15
the microphone in his fall — one of the first victims of the Martian Ray. There followed a moment of absolute silence — an

eternity of waiting. Then, without warning, the network's emergency fill-in was heard — somewhere in a quiet studio, a piano, close on mike, playing "Clair de Lune," soft and sweet as honey, for many seconds, while the fate of the universe hung in the balance. Finally it was interrupted by the manly reassuring voice of Brigadier General Montgomery Smith, Commander of the New Jersey State Militia, speaking from Trenton, and placing "the counties of Mercer and Middlesex as far west as Princeton and east to Jamesburg" under Martial Law! Tension — release — then renewed tension. For soon after that came an eyewitness account of the fatal battle of the Watchung Hills; and then, once again, that lone piano was heard — now a symbol of terror, shattering the dead air with its ominous tinkle. As it played, on and on, its effect became increasingly sinister — a thin band of suspense stretched almost beyond endurance.

16   That piano was the neatest trick of the show — a fine specimen of the theatrical "retard," boldly conceived and exploited to the full. It was one of the many devices with which Welles succeeded in compelling, not merely the attention, but also the belief of his invisible audience. *The War of the Worlds* was a magic act, one of the world's greatest, and Orson was just the man to bring it off.

17   For Welles is at heart a magician whose particular talent lies not so much in his creative imagination (which is considerable) as in his proven ability to stretch the familiar elements of theatrical effect far beyond their normal point of tension. For this reason his productions require more elaborate preparation and more perfect execution than most. At that — like all complicated magic tricks — they remain, till the last moment, in a state of precarious balance. When they come off, they give — by virtue of their unusually high intensity — an impression of great brilliance and power; when they fail — when something in their balance goes wrong or the original structure proves to have been unsound — they provoke, among their audience, a particularly violent reaction of unease and revulsion. Welles' flops are louder than other men's. The Mars broadcast was one of his unqualified successes.

18   Among the columnists and public figures who discussed the affair during the next few days (some praising us for the public

service we had rendered, some condemning us as sinister scoundrels) the most general reaction was one of amazement at the "incredible stupidity" and "gullibility" of the American public, who had accepted as real, in this single broadcast, incidents which in actual fact would have taken days or even weeks to occur. "Nothing about the broadcast," wrote Dorothy Thompson[2] with her usual aplomb, "was in the least credible." She was wrong. The first few minutes of our broadcast were, in point of fact, strictly realistic in time and perfectly credible, though somewhat boring, in content. Herein lay the great tensile strength of the show; it was the structural device that made the whole illusion possible. And it could have been carried off in no other medium than radio.

Our actual broadcasting time, from the first mention of the   19
meteorites to the fall of New York City, was less than forty minutes. During that time men traveled long distances, large bodies of troops were mobilized, cabinet meetings were held, savage battles fought on land and in the air. And millions of people accepted it — emotionally if not logically.

There is nothing so very strange about that. Most of us do   20
the same thing, to some degree, most days of our lives — every time we look at a movie or listen to a broadcast. Not even the realistic theater observes the literal unities; motion pictures and, particularly, radio (where neither place nor time exists save in the imagination of the listener) have no difficulty in getting their audiences to accept the telescoped reality of dramatic time. Our special hazard lay in the fact that we purported to be, not a play, but reality. In order to take advantage of the accepted convention, we had to slide swiftly and imperceptibly out of the "real" time of a news report into the "dramatic" time of a fictional broadcast. Once that was achieved — without losing the audience's attention or arousing their skepticism, if they could be sufficiently absorbed and bewitched not to notice the transition — then, we felt, there was no extreme of fantasy through which they would not follow us. We were keenly aware of our problem; we found what we believed was the key to its solution.

[2]A writer and commentator (1894–1961) who in 1938 wrote a syndicated column.

And if, that night, the American public proved "gullible," it was because enormous pains and a great deal of thought had been spent to make it so.

In the script, *The War of the Worlds* started extremely slowly — dull meteorological and astronomical bulletins alternating with musical interludes. These were followed by a colorless scientific interview and still another stretch of dance music. These first few minutes of routine broadcasting "within the existing standards of judgment of the listener" were intended to lull (or maybe bore) the audience into a false security and to furnish a solid base of realistic time from which to accelerate later. Orson, in making over the show, extended this slow movement far beyond our original conception. "La Cumparsita," rendered by "Ramon Raquello, from the Meridian Room of the Hotel Park Plaza in downtown New York," had been thought of as running only a few seconds; "Bobby Millette playing first 'Stardust' from the Hotel Martinet in Brooklyn," even less. At rehearsal Orson stretched both these numbers to what seemed to us, in the control room, an almost unbearable length. We objected. The interview in the Princeton Observatory — the clockwork ticking monotonously overhead, the woolly-minded professor mumbling vague replies to the reporters' uninformed questions — this, too, he dragged out to a point of tedium. Over our protests, lines were restored that had been cut at earlier rehearsals. We cried there would not be a listener left. Welles stretched them out even longer.

He was right. His sense of tempo, that night, was infallible. When the flashed news of the cylinder's landing finally came — almost fifteen minutes after the beginning of a fairly dull show — he was able suddenly to spiral his action to a speed as wild and reckless as its base was solid. The appearance of the Martians; their first treacherous act; the death of Carl Phillips; the arrival of the militia; the battle of the Watchung Hills; the destruction of New Jersey — all these were telescoped into a space of twelve minutes without overstretching the listeners' emotional credulity. The broadcast, by then, had its own reality, the reality of emotionally felt time and space.

At the height of the crisis, around 8:31, the Secretary of the Interior came on the air with an exhortation to the American people. His words, as you read them now, ten years later, have a Voltairean ring.[3] (They were admirably spoken — in a voice just faintly reminiscent of the President's — by a young man named Kenneth Delmar, who has since grown rich and famous as Senator Claghorn.)[4]

The Secretary

Citizens of the nation: I shall not try to conceal the gravity of the situation that confronts the country, nor the concern of your Government in protecting the lives and property of its people. However, I wish to impress upon you — private citizens and public officials, all of you — the urgent need of calm and resourceful action. Fortunately, this formidable enemy is still confined to a comparatively small area, and we may place our faith in the military forces to keep them there. In the meantime placing our trust in God, we must continue the performance of our duties, each and every one of us, so that we may confront this destructive adversary with a nation united, courageous, and consecrated to the preservation of human supremacy on this earth. I thank you.

Toward the end of this speech (*circa* 8:32 E.S.T.), Davidson   24 Taylor, supervisor of the broadcast for the Columbia Broadcasting System, received a phone call in the control room, creased his lips, and hurriedly left the studio. By the time he returned, a few moments later — pale as death — clouds of heavy smoke were rising from Newark, New Jersey, and the Martians, tall as skyscrapers, were astride the Pulaski Highway preparatory to wading the Hudson River. To us in the studio the show seemed to be progressing splendidly — how splendidly Davidson Taylor had just learned outside. For several minutes now, a kind of madness had seemed to be sweeping the continent — somehow connected with our show. The CBS switchboards had been swamped into uselessness but from outside sources vague rumors were coming in of deaths and suicides and panic injuries.

---

[3]An echo of Voltaire, eighteenth-century French writer whose best-known work, *Candide*, makes fun of human pride and pomposity.

[4]Delmar invented Claghorn, a character given to windy oratory. He was a feature of comedian Fred Allen's weekly radio program in the 1940s.

Taylor had requests to interrupt the show immediately with   25
an explanatory station-announcement. By now the Martians
were across the Hudson and gas was blanketing the city. The
end was near. We were less than a minute from the Station
Break. The organ was allowed to swirl out under the slackening
fingers of its failing organist and Ray Collins, superb as the "last
announcer," choked heroically to death on the roof of Broadcasting Building. The boats were all whistling for a while as the
last of the refugees perished in New York Harbor. Finally, as
they died away, an amateur shortwave operator was heard,
from heaven knows where, weakly reaching out for human
companionship across the empty world:

> 2 X 2L Calling CQ
> 2 X 2L Calling CQ
> 2 X 2L Calling CQ
> Isn't there anyone on the air?
> Isn't there anyone?

Five seconds of absolute silence. Then, shattering the reality of
World's End — the Announcer's voice was heard, suave and
bright:

Announcer

You are listening to the CBS presentation of Orson Welles
and the Mercury Theater on the Air in an original dramatization of *The War of the Worlds*, by H. G. Wells. The performance will continue after a brief intermission.

The second part of the show was extremely well written and   26
most sensitively played — but nobody heard it. It recounted the
adventures of a lone survivor, with interesting observations on
the nature of human society; it described the eventual death of
the Martian Invaders, slain — "after all man's defenses had
failed by the humblest thing that God in his wisdom had put
upon this earth" — by bacteriological action; it told of the re-
building of a brave new world. After a stirring musical finale,
Welles, in his own person, delivered a charming informal little
speech about Halloween, which it happened to be.[5]

---

[5]Actually, Halloween was the following day; evidently Welles in his remarks was looking forward to it.

I remember, during the playing of the final theme, the   27
phone starting to ring in the control room and a shrill voice
through the receiver announcing itself as belonging to the
mayor of some Midwestern city, one of the big ones. He is
screaming for Welles. Choking with fury, he reports mobs in
the streets of his city, women and children huddled in the
churches, violence and looting. If, as he now learns, the whole
thing is nothing but a crummy joke — then he, personally, is
coming up to New York to punch the author of it on the nose!
Orson hangs up quickly. For we are off the air now and the
studio door bursts open. The following hours are a nightmare.
The building is suddenly full of people and dark blue uniforms.
We are hurried out of the studio, downstairs, into a back office.
Here we sit incommunicado while network employees are busily
collecting, destroying, or locking up all scripts and records of
the broadcast. Then the press is let loose upon us, ravening for
horror. How many deaths have *we* heard of? (Implying they
know of thousands.) What do *we* know of the fatal stampede in
a Jersey hall? (Implying it is one of many.) What traffic deaths?
(The ditches must be choked with corpses.) The suicides?
(Haven't you heard about the one on Riverside Drive?) It is all
quite vague in my memory and quite terrible.

Hours later, instead of arresting us, they let us out a back   28
way. We scurry down to the theater like hunted animals to their
hole. It is surprising to see life going on as usual in the midnight
streets, cars stopping for traffic, people walking. At the Mercury
the company is . . . stoically rehearsing — falling downstairs
and singing the "Carmagnole." Welles goes up on stage, where
photographers, lying in wait, catch him with his eyes raised up
to heaven, his arms outstretched in an attitude of crucifixion.
Thus he appeared in a tabloid that morning over the caption, "I
Didn't Know What I Was Doing!" The *New York Times* quoted
him as saying, "I don't think we will choose anything like this
again."

We were on the front page for two days. Having had to bow   29
to radio as a news source during the Munich crisis, the press was
now only too eager to expose the perilous irresponsibilities of
the new medium. Orson was their whipping boy. They quizzed
and badgered him. Condemnatory editorials were delivered by

our press-clipping bureau in bushel baskets. There was talk for a while, of criminal action.

Then gradually, after about two weeks, the excitement sub- 30
sided. By then it had been discovered that the casualties were not as numerous or as serious as had at first been supposed. One young woman had fallen and broken her arm running down-stairs. Later the Federal Communications Commission held some hearings and passed some regulations. The Columbia Broadcasting System made a public apology. With that the of-ficial aspects of the incident were closed. . . .

Of the suits that were brought against us — amounting to 31
over three-quarters of a million dollars for damages, injuries, miscarriages, and distresses of various kinds — none was sub-stantiated or legally proved. We did settle one claim, however, against the advice of our lawyers. It was the particularly affect-ing case of a man in Massachusetts, who wrote:

"I thought the best thing to do was to go away. So I took 32
three dollars twenty-five cents out of my savings and bought a ticket. After I had gone sixty miles I knew it was a play. Now I don't have money left for the shoes I was saving up for. Will you please have someone send me a pair of black shoes size 9B!"

We did. 33

• QUESTIONS ON MEANING AND PURPOSE •

1. Why, according to Houseman, were more people than usual listening to the station broadcasting *The War of the Worlds?* Of what importance is it that many of them tuned in late?
2. To what causes does Houseman attribute the scope and intensity of the panic that followed this famous broadcast?
3. How did the medium of radio drama itself contribute to the panic? Can you imagine similar effects ensuing from a *telecast* of such a story?
4. Why, according to Houseman, did no one listen to the second half of the broadcast? What difference might it have made if they had?
5. How does the author explain the "stupidity" and "gullibility" of the American people?

6. What is Houseman's main purpose in "The Night the Martians Landed": to tell an interesting story, to illustrate a point, or to explain why something happened as it did? Does the author accomplish his purpose?

• QUESTIONS ON WRITING STRATEGY •

1. How does Houseman convince you that the version of the events recounted in his essay is a true one?
2. How does the account of the crash of the Hindenburg contribute to Houseman's essay?
3. What, as the author explains it, is the difference between "real" time and "dramatic" time? For what reason does Houseman dwell on the difference?
4. How much knowledge of the Martian fiasco on the part of his audience does the author take for granted in "The Night the Martians Landed"? Does the reader need an acquaintance with the history of the 1930s to appreciate Houseman's essay? What points would the author probably have explained in greater detail had his essay been written in 1982 rather than in 1948?

• QUESTIONS ON LANGUAGE •
• AND VOCABULARY •

1. In paragraph 3, Houseman refers to the Orson Welles broadcast as a hoax. Comment on his word choice. (Consider whether Houseman's essay indicates that those involved in the broadcast intended to deceive their audience.)
2. Be sure you know how to define the following words as the author uses them: transient, complacence, dominion, ethereal (paragraph 1); perceptible (2); enervated (12); ominous, sinister (15); precarious, revulsion (17); aplomb, tensile (18); unities, purported (20); tedium (21); infallible, credulity (22); exhortation, formidable, adversary (23); incommunicado, ravening (27).
3. What attitude does Houseman reveal toward the American habit of dial-twisting when he calls it "healthy" (paragraph 4)?

• SUGGESTIONS FOR WRITING •

1. Write an account of a performance whose audience did not react quite as expected.

2. The death of a prominent citizen is a newsworthy event that sometimes elicits little reaction when it is reported. The public reacts to certain other deaths — those of Presidents Lincoln, Roosevelt, and Kennedy, for instance — with crying in the streets. Analyze the population's reaction to the death of a famous person in terms of cause and effect.

3. On the basis of your experience or your reading, write about another event that demonstrated the public's gullibility. In your essay, analyze causes or illustrate effects.

· Marsha Traugot ·

Born in 1951, MARSHA TRAUGOT received a B.A. in literature
from Reed College in 1972. She has been a lecturer in communications at Northeastern University; and she worked
from 1977 to 1979 for the Children's Protective Services of
the Massachusetts Society for the Prevention of Cruelty to
Children.

The Children Who Wait

In "The Children Who Wait," Marsha Traugot suggests reasons for a new trend in adoption. Now a wider variety of families can open their homes to children who in the past would
have been labeled unadoptable. In setting forth the causes for
this phenomenon, she draws from specific case histories.

"This is Tammy who at 5½ years old is petite with brown   1
eyes, dark, curly hair and a light brown complexion. Tammy
has recently been legally freed for adoption, and this is the first
attempt to find her a permanent family."

Looking at the photograph of a little girl whose gentle half   2
smile combines the mystery of the Mona Lisa with the appeal of
a kitten, one wonders why she is being featured in a special
newspaper column on hard-to-place children. The article goes
on to explain that Tammy suffers from fetal alcohol syndrome,
which could put a stop to her intellectual growth at any time.
Following the description of Tammy's background, personality,
and condition, the article then spells out the characteristics of
an ideal adoptive family for her. Her social worker is looking for
a one- or two-parent, black or biracial family with older siblings.
The family will be expected to go through an extended visiting
period to ease Tammy's transition from her foster home to a
permanent home. Tammy will need a lot of affection from a
family who can view intellectual functioning as only one aspect
of the total child.

Twenty years ago Tammy would have been sentenced on 3
three counts to a life of foster or institutional care. She is not
white. She is beyond infancy. And she is handicapped. Also
twenty years ago no social worker screening prospective parents
would have considered, let alone preferred, a nonwhite family
or a family with older siblings; and single parent adoptions were
unheard of. Until about 1960 middle- or upper-class childless
white couples adopted healthy white infants — and that was it.
Handicapped children were more or less regarded as damaged
goods. A five-year-old child was too old. Minority and mixed-
racial children were virtually ignored. So these children waited.

In the last two decades, however, the field of adoption has 4
undergone radical change. With the aid of novel techniques,
children once labeled unadoptable are being placed with sub-
stantially more types of families. Though no single factor can
account for this transformation, the various civil rights move-
ments, birth control, changing mores, and social science research have all had an impact. And ironically, harsh economic
reality was the caustic that finally stripped the "unadoptable"
label from so many children.

The black civil rights movement had both an immediate 5
and a long-range effect. In an effort to encourage integration,
liberal whites gathered black and mixed-race infants and tod-
dlers into their families. Interracial adoption was not a cure-all
— it has been recently criticized for masking the resources available in the black community — but it did move some children
off institutional shelves and illuminate the plight of others.
More generally, the black civil rights movement raised a standard of human decency and justice that could and would be applied to all children. First, though, women needed their say.

The women's movement coincided with the increasing 6
availability of birth control, with legalized abortion, and with
changes in attitudes toward sexual behavior and marriage. Together, they drastically reduced the number of healthy infants
available for adoption. Not only were fewer unwanted babies
being born, but unwed mothers faced less social stigma when
they decided to keep their babies. Women's rights advocates
pointed out that a mature single woman could care for a child as

well as two parents could. And teenagers, among whom out-of-wedlock births were (and still are) alarmingly frequent, more often opted to keep their babies, either providing care themselves or receiving help from their own families.

The rosy-cheeked cherubs of baby food commercials 7 became so scarce that couples wishing to adopt were told they had to wait five years or more. Many agencies, saying they could do nothing, simply turned the couples away. Newspaper headlines decried black market scandals: doctors arranging to sell the babies of desperate teenage girls to equally desperate childless couples. But this scarcity also turned attention toward the other children, the waiting children.

Child welfare specialists were becoming increasingly con- 8 cerned about these other homeless children. Their numbers were growing — dramatically. Between 1960 and 1978 the number of children in foster care doubled to a shocking half million or more. Surveys revealed that many states had no idea how many children did not live with their biological parents, how long children drifted in foster care, or how many of them could be adopted. Research had long before indicated that children consigned to foster care for more than eighteen months would probably hang in this limbo until they reached maturity. The consequences could be dire: pseudo-mental retardation, learning disabilities, mental illness, delinquency, criminality, sexual perversions. Such severe aberrations can root in the children's personalities, plague their adult lives, and be passed on to their children. The system, gone so terribly awry, victimized the very children it purported to serve.

But knowing the system was failing was not sufficient to 9 bring change. Funding was needed to revamp systems, establish new procedures, set up training programs, reduce social workers' case loads, run pilot projects. And, because children don't vote, funding for children's services has always been scarce. Then astute child welfare specialists had the sense to turn the dollar sign back on the politicians. They pointed out that in 1979 the cost of keeping one child in foster care for one year averaged $3,600 and could run as high as $24,000. The annual price tag for foster care in the United States: a staggering $2

billion. Suddenly it became clear to all that storing children in
foster care was as expensive as it was cruel.

So the system's focus finally changed, and with it the con-   10
ception of the ideal adoptive family. Unlike their predecessors,
today's social workers cannot exclusively seek middle-class,
home-owning, two-parent, one-career families for the children
they want to place. For one thing, the stereotypical family has
all but disappeared. And for another, no single family type is
appropriate for children of widely varying needs. Today's buzz
word is "matching." First the worker evaluates the child's characteristics — not just the handicaps, but personality, cultural
background, existing relationships with biological or foster
family, and emotional state. Based on these factors, the worker
draws up a profile of an appropriate family.

Consider two examples. One is a fifteen-year-old boy with a   11
stormy history of disrupted placements, fighting, and poor
school performance. What he needs most is a strong male who
can allow him reasonable freedom, set some limits, and provide
a stable home. Until about 1975 single-parent adoptions were
unheard of, but the two-parent family is no longer required and
this child might now be placed with a single man. The other
child is an eleven-year-old boy with Down's Syndrome, a heart
defect, and a hearing disability. Adoptable? Yes, the specialists
insist. As with many intellectually limited children, his social
worker suggests a family with older children. Not only can the
other children help care for him and serve as role models, but
the parents will have less ego invested in the adopted child than
a childless couple would. Although the worker would not specify it, a deeply religious, working-class family would be the most
likely candidate. In a case like this, where the medical costs
promise to undermine any family budget, an adoption subsidy
might be allocated.

In seeking to match a child and a family, the social worker   12
must overcome his or her own attitudinal barriers. First, it takes
a certain courage to hold on to the idea that a disturbed or multiply handicapped child is adoptable. Then, visiting a prospective home, the worker may have to revise certain value judgments. The single male may not be much of a decorator or

housekeeper. The working-class family may represent a socioeconomic or ethnic group different from the worker's. It is the worker's job to ignore these factors in favor of an objective evaluation of the man's or the family's ability to provide childcare. Aware of these conflicts, specialists have recently introduced values-clarification workshops for placement workers and their supervisors.

But how do the adoption agencies find these potential adoptive parents at all? Naturally, agencies look first to the families listed with them. If there are no likely candidates, the child is registered with the regional or state adoption exchange, which distributes a photo and description (and perhaps a videotape) of the child to all other agencies. Some exchanges hold monthly meetings where placement workers looking for a match can discuss waiting children or families, and they also sponsor parties where children, workers, and prospective parents meet informally.

And if a match still cannot be made? Exchanges and other child welfare organizations now employ media blitzes as aggressive as those of commercial advertising. Profiles of waiting children, like the one quoted above, appear in newspapers throughout the country, while television is beginning to introduce children to millions of viewers. Although some may see these techniques as maudlin or exploitative, the *Boston Globe*'s "Sunday's Child" is one of the newspaper's most popular columns. The proof? Of approximately 160 children featured, 115 have found homes.

As for Tammy, the search is on. Thanks to two decades of change, her hopes for a warm, supportive family life have not ended with her fifth birthday.

• QUESTIONS ON MEANING AND PURPOSE •

1. According to Traugot, what changes are transforming the American adoption scene? What factors are responsible for the changes?

2. In what paragraph does Traugot state her thesis? (See *Thesis* in Useful Terms.) Sum up the writer's purpose in this essay.

• QUESTIONS ON WRITING STRATEGY •

1. What does Traugot's essay gain from the fact that she begins it with an example? Where else in her account does she use examples? What is the effect of her returning to her original example in the last paragraph?
2. Point out the words, phrases, and sentences in Traugot's essay that serve as transitions from one paragraph to the next. What relationship does each transition make clear? (See *Transitions* in Useful Terms.)

• QUESTIONS ON LANGUAGE •
• AND VOCABULARY •

1. How well is Traugot's vocabulary tailored to the audience she aims to reach with her essay? To what extent, for instance, does she use occupational jargon? Unfamiliar words?
2. What is "fetal alcohol syndrome" (paragraph 2)? What is a "buzz word" (paragraph 10)?

• SUGGESTIONS FOR WRITING •

1. Write a paragraph in which, on the basis of the new trends in adoption that Traugot outlines, you express an opinion about who benefits the most: the agencies, the adoptive parents, or the children.
2. Many changes have buffeted society over the past several years: the increasing popularity of joint custody as a way for divorced parents to provide for their children; the rising number of wives and mothers in the work force; the apparent decline of reading and writing skills among the young; the increasing number of middle-aged people continuing their formal education; the increasing number of unmarried couples living together; the rising number of divorces; the population shift to the Sunbelt. Choose from among these possibilities, or spot a trend, and write an essay tracing the causes of the change.

— POSTSCRIPT ON PROCESS —

Leaving Some Things Out

Sometimes a writer knows more about her subject than she can easily confine within the word limit assigned to her. That's when an outline can be a valuable tool, as Marsha Traugot discovered early in the process of whittling her topic down to size.

I have written public-relations materials about child abuse, foster care, and adoption for about five years, and usually I sit down to write with a very specific point in mind. But when I started this essay, I had only a rather vague subject: recent changes in the methods of adoption agencies. I knew that the essay should demonstrate cause-and-effect analysis as an expository technique (that was my assignment), and I knew that a historical approach would best suit that technique. I also could assume that the students reading the essay would not know much about the subject and probably would not be plannning to adopt a child; thus the treatment should be more general than it would be if the audience were social workers or people considering adoption. But still the subject was wide open. How far back in history should I go? How should I balance causes and effects? How many of the important side-issues should I try to cover?

Since I was unsure of what to include in the essay, I sketched an informal outline before I began writing. In it I listed the main topics I needed to cover — adoption twenty years ago, the intervening social and other changes, their effect on adoption today, and so on. Under each main topic I listed the ideas, examples, and facts I would use to support it.

This preliminary work helped me narrow my focus and avoid digression. For instance, the first child-abuse trial drew on laws protecting animals from abuse because no laws existed to protect children from their own parents. Fascinating — one of my pet facts. But in my outline it was definitely irrelevant and even potentially confusing, so I cut it. I also cut some other information — such as the complexities of interracial adoptions and minority recruitment, and the hot controversy over adoptions by homosexuals — that was important but too tangential for a relatively brief treatment. And as the outline took shape, I saw that space would allow me no more than a mention of deserving topics like how advocacy for the disabled has affected the placement of handicapped children.

I started writing the essay only when I was satisfied that I   4
knew precisely what I would include. Still, some topics that had seemed appropriate in the outline refused to fit into the writing. One idea that distracted me was the relationship between recruiting adoptive parents and marketing children for adoption. You can see suggestions of this idea in the essay; unable to abandon it completely, I compromised by hinting at it.

My essay might have been the same if I had begun writing as   5
soon as I had my subject, my approach, and a conception of my audience. But without a clear focus, without knowing precisely what I wanted to include, I would have stumbled more in writing than I actually did. Preparing an outline beforehand guided me to exactly what I was trying to say, and the material selected itself.

In a short essay, explain *either* the causes *or* the effects of a situation that concerns you. Narrow your topic enough to treat it in some detail, and provide more than a mere list of causes or effects. If seeking causes, you will have to decide carefully how far back to go in your search for remote causes. If stating effects, fill your essay with examples. Here are some topics to consider:

1. The scarcity of jobs for teen-agers.
2. Friction between two roommates, or two friends.
3. The pressure on students to get good grades.
4. The fact that important sports events are often televised on holidays.
5. The persistent drop in S.A.T. scores, starting in 1963.
6. Some quirk in your personality, or a friend's.
7. The increasing need for more than one breadwinner per family.
8. The temptation to do something dishonest to get ahead.
9. The popularity of a particular television program, comic strip, or rock group.
10. The steady increase in college costs.
11. The scarcity of people in training for employment as skilled workers: plumbers, tool and die makers, electricians, masons, carpenters, to name a few.
12. A decision to enter the ministry or a religious order.
13. The fact that cigarette advertising has been banned from television.
14. The installation of seat belts in all new cars.
15. The fact that the average child spends more time in front of a TV screen than in the classroom.
16. The absence of a peacetime draft.
17. The fact that more couples are choosing to have only one child, or none.
18. The growing popularity of private elementary and high schools.
19. The fact that most Americans can communicate in no language other than English.
20. Being "born again."

21. The grim tone of recent novels for young people (such as Robert Cormier's *I Am the Cheese* and other best-selling juvenile fiction dealing with violence, madness, and terror).
22. The fact that women increasingly are training for jobs formerly regarded as for men only.
23. The pressure on young people to conform to the standards of their peers.
24. The emphasis on competitive sports in high school and college.

· 9 ·

DEFINITION

Establishing a Boundary

· THE METHOD ·

As a rule, when we hear the word *definition*, we immediately think of a dictionary. In that helpful storehouse — a writer's best friend — we find the literal and specific meaning (or meanings) of a word. The dictionary supplies this information concisely: in a sentence, in a phrase, or even in a synonym — a single word that means the same thing ("**narrative** [năr ə - tĭv] *n.* **1:** story . . .").

To state such a definition is often an excellent way for the writer of an essay to begin. A short definition may clarify your subject to your reader, and perhaps help you to limit what you have to say. If, for instance, you are going to discuss a demolition derby, explaining such a spectacle to readers who may never have seen one, you might offer at the outset a short definition of *demolition derby*, your subject and your key term.

In constructing a short definition, a usual procedure is this. First, you state the general class to which your subject belongs; then you add any particular features that distinguish it. You could say: "A demolition derby is a contest" — that is its general class — "in which drivers ram old cars into one another until only one car is left running." Short definitions may also be useful at *any* moment in your essay. If you introduce a technical term, you'll want to define it briefly: "As the derby proceeds, there's many a broken manifold — that's the fitting that connects the openings of a car engine's exhaust."

In this chapter, however, we are mainly concerned with another sort of definition. It is *extended definition*, a kind of expository writing that relies on a variety of other methods. Suppose you wanted to write an essay to make clear what *poetry* means. You'd cite poems for examples. You might compare and contrast poetry with prose. You could analyze (or divide) poetry by specifying its elements: rhythm, metaphor and other figures of speech, imagery, and so on. You could distinguish it from prose by setting forth its effects on the reader. (Emily Dickinson, a poet herself, once stated the effect that reading a poem had upon her: "I feel as if the top of my head were taken off.") In fact, extended definition, unlike the methods of writing discussed in this book, is perhaps less a method in itself than the application of a variety of methods to clarify a purpose. Like description, in a way, extended definition tries to *show* a reader its subject. It does so by establishing boundaries, for its writer tries to differentiate a subject from anything that might be confused with it. When Alvin Toffler, in his essay in this chapter, seeks to define a certain trend he has noticed in magazines, newspapers, radio, and television, he describes exactly what he sees happening, so that we, too, will understand that what he calls "the de-massified media" differ from media of the past. In an extended definition, a writer studies the nature of a subject, carefully sums up its chief characteristics, and strives to answer the question, "What is this?" — or "What makes this what it is, not something else?"

An extended definition can *define* (from the Latin, "to set bounds to") a word, or it can define a thing (a laser beam), a concept (male chauvinism), or a general phenomenon (the popularity of the demolition derby). Unlike a sentence definition, or any you would find in a standard dictionary, an extended definition takes room: at least a paragraph, perhaps an entire volume. The subject may be as large as the concepts of *work*, *rights*, and *decency* — as some of the essays in this chapter will indicate.

Outside an English course, how is this method of writing used? In a newspaper feature, a sports writer defines what makes a "great team" great. In a journal article, a physician defines the nature of a previously unknown syndrome or disease. In a written opinion, a judge defines not only a word but a concept. (See, for a legal instance, Alistair Cooke's remarks in this chapter on the difficulty of defining *obscenity*.) In a book review, a critic defines a newly prevalent kind of poem. In a letter to a younger brother or sister contemplating college, a student might define a *gut course* and how to recognize one.

Unlike a definition in a dictionary that sets forth the literal meaning of a word in an unimpassioned manner, some definitions imply biases. In defining *patron* to the Earl of Chesterfield, who had tried to befriend him after ignoring his petitions for aid during his years of grinding poverty, Samuel Johnson wrote scornfully: "Is not a Patron, my Lord, one who looks with unconcern on a man struggling for life in the water, and, when he has reached the ground, encumbers him with help?" Irony, metaphor, and short definition have rarely been wielded with such crushing power. (*Encumbers*, by the way, is a wonderfully physical word in its context: it means "to burden with dead weight.") In his extended definition of *work* (in this chapter), Russell Baker is biased, even jaundiced, in his view of American business life. As Baker's essay also demonstrates, it is possible to define a thing humorously. In having many methods of writing at their disposal, writers of extended definitions have ample freedom and wide latitude.

• THE PROCESS •

Writing an extended definition, you'll want to employ whatever method or methods of writing can best answer the question, "What is the nature of this subject?" You will probably find yourself making use of anything you have earlier learned from this book. If your subject is the phenomenon of the demolition derby, you might wish to begin by giving a short definition, like the definition of *demolition derby* on page 378. Feel no duty, however, to place a dictionaryish definition in the introduction of every essay you write. In explaining a demolition derby, you might decide that your readers already have at least a vague idea of the meaning of the term and that they need no short, formal definition of it. You might open your extended definition with the aid of *narration*. You could relate the events at a typical demolition derby, starting with the line-up of one hundred old, beat-up vehicles. Following the method of *description*, you might begin:

> One hundred worthless cars — everything from a 1940 Cadillac to a Dodge Dart to a recently wrecked Thunderbird — their glass removed, their radiators leaking, assemble on a racetrack or an open field. Their drivers, wearing crash helmets, buckle themselves into their seats, some pulling at beer cans to soften the blows to come.

You might proceed by *example*, listing demolition derbies you have known ("The great destruction of 184 vehicles took place at the Orleans County Fair in Barton, Vermont, in the summer of '81. . . . "). If you had enough examples, you might wish to *classify* them; or perhaps you might *divide* a demolition derby into its components — cars, drivers, judges, first-aid squad, and spectators — discussing each. You could *compare and contrast* a demolition derby with that amusement park ride known as Bumper Cars or Dodge-'ems, in which small cars with rubber bumpers bash one another head-on, but (unlike cars in the derby) harmlessly. A *process analysis* of a demolition derby might help your readers understand the nature of the spectacle: how in round after round cars are eliminated until one remains. You might ask: What causes the owners of old cars to want to smash them? Or perhaps: What causes people to watch the destruction? Or: What are the consequences? To answer such questions in an essay, you would apply the method of *cause and effect*.

Perhaps an *analogy* might occur to you, one that would explain the demolition derby to someone unfamiliar with it: "It is like a birthday party in which every kid strives to have the last un-popped balloon."

In defining something, you need not try to forge a definition so absolute that it will stand till the mountains turn to plains. Indeed, in his essay in this chapter Alistair Cooke suggests that the territory to which most definitions apply is in constant change. Like a map maker, the writer of an extended definition draws approximate boundaries, takes in only some of what lies within them, and ignores what lies outside. The boundaries, of course, may be wide; and for this reason, the writing of an ex-tended definition sometimes tempts a writer to sweep across a continent airily and to soar off into abstract clouds. Like any other method of expository writing, though, definition will work only for the writer who remembers the world of the senses and supports every generalization with concrete evidence. There may be no finer illustration of the perils of definition than, in Charles Dickens's novel *Hard Times*, the scene of the grim schoolroom of a teacher named Gradgrind, who insists on facts but who completely ignores living realities. When a girl whose father is a horse trainer is unable to define a horse, Gradgrind blames her for not knowing what a horse is; and he praises the definition of a horse supplied by a pet pupil:

> "Quadruped. Graminivorous. Forty teeth, namely twen-ty-four grinders, four eye-teeth, and twelve incisive. Sheds coat in the spring; in marshy countries, sheds hoofs, too. Hoofs hard, but requiring to be shod with iron. Age known by marks in mouth."

To anyone who didn't already know what a horse is, this enumeration of statistics would prove of little help. In writing an extended definition, never lose sight of the reality you are at-tempting to bound, even if its frontiers are as inclusive as those of *psychological burn-out* or *human rights*. Give your reader ex-amples, tell an illustrative story, use an analogy, bring in spe-cific description — in whatever method you use, keep coming down to earth. Without your eyes on the world, you will define no reality. You might define *animal husbandry* till the cows come home, and never make clear what it means.

• DEFINITION IN A PARAGRAPH •

In *The Dukes of Hazzard*, who is a villain? What character, saturated with evil, is a true menace? At first, the prime candidate might seem pudgy Jefferson Davis Hogg, political boss of the territory. Two desires smolder in Boss Hogg's heart: to make money, and to jail Bo and Luke Duke, the show's young Galahads. Hogg lies, cheats, deceives, steals, forges signatures — even rewrites the law. Yet he stops short of wholehearted villainy. He will not kill. Being a native of Hazzard County, he can't quite escape the goodness that springs from its soil. And so he runs the Boar's Head Tavern like a jolly master of revels, affording Daisy, cousin of the Duke boys, the job of dispensing tap beer. His blithering henchman, Sheriff Roscoe P. Coltraine, who can't even set up a roadblock without ramming his own cruiser into it, is hardly a villain, either. Each week Hogg and his stooge are outclassed by sharks more deadly and purposeful: racketeers, dealers in poisonous moonshine, widow-swindlers, kidnappers, counterfeiters, escaped public enemies. Unlike the locals, these grim professionals are eager to kill. We sense that Hazzard County stands alone against the world, its natives surrounded by a sea of inscrutable evil whose waves keep breaking against the county line. Once in a while an outsider who isn't a villain strays into Hazzard, but such harmless visitors are never total strangers. They're bluegrass music stars whose faces and songs every soul in the county knows. On *The Dukes*, the nature of villainy is simple. A villain is any new face in town.

Comment. In this one-paragraph essay, the writer begins with a short definition of a villain: a character saturated with evil; a true menace. This short definition given, the writer's next step is to demonstrate (by the method of description) that it doesn't apply to Boss Hogg. On *The Dukes of Hazzard*, there are characters more sinister, and the writer discerns their traits: (1) they are killers; and (2) they are outsiders. Still another method of exposition may be seen in the paragraph: example.

Hogg's likable traits are illustrated; and we are given examples, too, of the various, more sinister enemies the Dukes must face (racketeers, and so on). Although the paragraph doesn't fully compare and contrast Hazzard County natives with outsiders, its final statement makes clear that such a distinction can be drawn. The TV show, implies the writer, gives us a crudely simplified world.

· Russell Baker ·

RUSSELL BAKER was born in Virginia in 1925 and earned his B.A. from Johns Hopkins University. A contributor to a number of magazines, including the *Ladies' Home Journal*, *McCall's*, *Sports Illustrated*, *Saturday Evening Post*, and *The New York Times Magazine*, he worked as a reporter for the Baltimore *Sun* from 1947 to 1954 and as a member of the Washington Bureau of the *New York Times* from 1954 to 1962, covering the White House. Since then he has written a widely syndicated column, "The Observer," in which humor and social criticism are blended. In 1979 he won the Pulitzer Prize for distinguished commentary. His most recent books are *The Upside Down Man* (1977) and *So This Is Depravity* (1980).

Work in Corporate America

Russell Baker included "Work in Corporate America" (editors' title) in *Poor Russell's Almanac* (1972). In the essay, with tongue firmly in cheek, he defines the nature of work by demonstrating why the jobs white-collar workers do are impossible for children to visualize. What *does* go on in all those offices?

It is not surprising that modern children tend to look blank and dispirited when informed that they will someday have to "go to work and make a living." The problem is that they cannot visualize what work is in corporate America.

Not so long ago, when a parent said he was off to work, the child knew very well what was about to happen. His parent was going to make something or fix something. The parent could take his offspring to his place of business and let him watch while he repaired a buggy or built a table.

When a child asked, "What kind of work do you do, Daddy?" his father could answer in terms that a child could come to grips with. "I fix steam engines." "I make horse collars."

Well, a few fathers still fix steam engines and build tables, 4
but most do not. Nowadays, most fathers sit in glass buildings
doing things that are absolutely incomprehensible to children.
The answers they give when asked, "What kind of work do you
do, Daddy?" are likely to be utterly mystifying to a child.

"I sell space." "I do market research." "I am a data pro- 5
cessor." "I am in public relations." "I am a systems analyst."
Such explanations must seem nonsense to a child. How can he
possibly envision anyone analyzing a system or researching a
market?

Even grown men who do market research have trouble 6
visualizing what a public relations man does with his day, and it
is a safe bet that the average systems analyst is as baffled about
what a space salesman does at the shop as the average space
salesman is about the tools needed to analyze a system.

In the common everyday job, nothing is made any more. 7
Things are now made by machines. Very little is repaired. The
machines that make things make them in such a fashion that
they will quickly fall apart in such a way that repairs will be pro-
hibitively expensive. Thus the buyer is encouraged to throw the
thing away and buy a new one. In effect, the machines are making junk.

The handful of people remotely associated with these 8
machines can, of course, tell their inquisitive children "Daddy
makes junk." Most of the work force, however, is too remote
from junk production to sense any contribution to the industry.
What do these people do?

Consider the typical twelve-story glass building in the 9
typical American city. Nothing is being made in this building
and nothing is being repaired, including the building itself.
Constructed as a piece of junk, the building will be discarded
when it wears out, and another piece of junk will be set in its
place.

Still, the building is filled with people who think of 10
themselves as working. At any given moment during the day
perhaps one-third of them will be talking into telephones. Most
of these conversations will be about paper, for paper is what oc-
cupies nearly everyone in this building.

Some jobs in the building require men to fill paper with 11
words. There are persons who type neatly on paper and persons
who read paper and jot notes in the margins. Some persons
make copies of paper and other persons deliver paper. There are
persons who file paper and persons who unfile paper.

Some persons mail paper. Some persons telephone other 12
persons and ask that paper be sent to them. Others telephone to
ascertain the whereabouts of paper. Some persons confer about
paper. In the grandest offices, men approve of some paper and
disapprove of other paper.

The elevators are filled throughout the day with young men 13
carrying paper from floor to floor and with vital men carrying
paper to be discussed with other vital men.

What is a child to make of all this? His father may be so emi- 14
nent that he lunches with other men about paper. Suppose he
brings his son to work to give the boy some idea of what work is
all about. What does the boy see happening?

His father calls for paper. He reads paper. Perhaps he scowls 15
at paper. Perhaps he makes an angry red mark on paper. He telephones another man and says they had better lunch over
paper.

At lunch they talk about paper. Back at the office, the 16
father orders the paper retyped and reproduced in quintupli-
cate, and then sent to another man for comparison with paper
that was reproduced in triplicate last year.

Imagine his poor son afterwards mulling over the mysteries 17
of work with a friend, who asks him, "What's your father do?"
What can the boy reply? "It beats me," perhaps, if he is not very
observant. Or if he is, "Something that has to do with making
junk, I think. Same as everybody else."

· QUESTIONS ON MEANING AND PURPOSE ·

1. For what reasons, according to Baker, is it difficult for children to
   understand the work their fathers do?

2. How accurate is Baker's description of work in corporate America? What elements are missing from his definition?
3. Is Baker's primary intention to hand us a laugh at the expense of office workers, or do you think the essay contains a more serious purpose? If so, how would you state it?

• QUESTIONS ON WRITING STRATEGY •

1. Define Baker's attitude toward work in corporate America. How does his repeated use of the word *paper* contribute to the tone of his essay? (See *Tone* in Useful Terms.)
2. What role does exaggeration play in Baker's essay?
3. What does the child's point of view (in the last four paragraphs) contribute to Baker's definition?
4. This essay was originally a newspaper column. What segment of Baker's audience would you expect to enjoy it most?

• QUESTIONS ON LANGUAGE •
• AND VOCABULARY •

1. What exactly does Baker mean by *corporate America*?
2. Why does Baker use the general word *paper* instead of more specific terms such as *reports, memoranda,* or *letters*? (See *General and Specific* in Useful Terms.)
3. Comment on Baker's choice of the word *grandest*: "In the grandest offices, men approve of some paper and disapprove of other paper" (paragraph 12).

• SUGGESTIONS FOR WRITING •

1. Write an essay in which a child instead of asking "What kind of work do you do, Daddy?" asks a similar question of his mother. She may be a housewife or a corporate executive, or she may be otherwise employed.
2. Write an essay defining work in an American college, or, if you prefer, in a typical fast-food restaurant.
3. Write an angry retort to Baker in the character of a corporate executive. You may be either a narrow company worker who fails to perceive Baker's humor, or a reasonable and intelligent executive who sets forth a defense — arguing, perhaps, that handling paper is only part of what a corporate employee does.

· Harold J. Morowitz ·

HAROLD JOSEPH MOROWITZ, born in Poughkeepsie, N.Y., in 1927, pursues three careers simultaneously: as scientist, teacher, and author. Since 1955 he has taught at Yale, where he is now Professor of Molecular Biophysics and Biochemistry and (according to his own report) "covered with ivy up to the sternum." Besides textbooks in the physical sciences and biology, Dr. Morowitz has written a popular collection, *The Wine of Life and Other Essays on Societies, Energy, and Living Things* (1979), whose contents originally appeared in *Hospital Practice*, a magazine for medical professionals.

The Six Million Dollar Man

Like Lewis Thomas, whose essay "On Warts" appears in Chapter 8, Harold J. Morowitz makes specialized knowledge clear and engaging to nonspecialists. You have probably heard the famous statistic that the chemical value of the human body is only a few cents. In the following memorable essay from *The Wine of Life*, the author examines this statement by setting forth a definition of the value of the human body. "The Six Million Dollar Man" has enjoyed wide popularity. Photocopied frequently, it has been circulated from hand to hand, and sermons have been preached on it.

Another annual cycle inevitably passed and the pain was 1
eased by a humorous birthday card from my daughter and son-in-law. The front bore the caption "According to BIOCHEM-ISTS the materials that make up the HUMAN BODY are only worth 97¢" (Hallmark 25B 121-8, 1975). Before I could get to the birthday greeting I began to think that if the materials are only worth ninety-seven cents, my colleagues and I are really being taken by the biochemical supply companies. Lest the granting agencies were to find out first, I decided to make a thorough study of the entire matter.

I started by sitting down with my catalogue from the (name 2
deleted) Biochemical Co. and began to list the ingredients. He-

moglobin was $2.95 a gram, purified trypsin was $36 a gram, and crystalline insulin was $47.50 a gram. I began to look at slightly less common constituents such as acetate kinase at $8,860 a gram, alkaline phosphatase at $225 a gram, and NADP at $245 a gram. Hyaluronic acid was $175 a gram, while bilirubin was a bargain at $12 a gram. Human DNA was $798 a gram, while collagen was as little as $15 a gram. Human albumin was down at $3 a gram, whereas bradykinin was $12,000 for a gram. The real shocker came when I got to follicle-stimulating hormone at $4,800,000 a gram — clearly outside the reach of anything that Tiffany's could offer. I'm going to suggest it as a gift for people who have everything. For the really wealthy, there is prolactin at $175,500,000 a gram, street price.

Not content with a brief glance at the catalogue, I averaged all the constituents over the best estimate of the percent composition of the human body and arrived at $245.54 as the average value of a gram dry weight of human being. With that fact burning in my head I rushed over to the gymnasium and jumped on the scale. There it was, 168 pounds, or, after a quick go-round with my pocket calculator, 76,364 grams. Remembering that I was 68% water, I calculated my dry weight to be 24,436 grams. The next computation was done with a great sense of excitement. I had to multiply $245.54 per gram dry weight by 24,436 grams. The number literally jumped out at me — $6,000,015.44. I was a Six Million Dollar Man — no doubt about it — and really an enormous upgrade to my ego after the ninety-seven cent evaluation!

Assuming that the profits of the biochemical companies are considerably less than the 618,558.239% indicated above, we must still strike a balance between the ninety-seven cent figure and the six million dollar figure. The answer is at the same time very simple and very profound: information is much more expensive than matter. In the six million dollar figure I was paying for my atoms in the highest informational state in which they are commercially available, while in the ninety-seven cent figure, I was paying for the informationally poorest form of coal, air, water, lime, bulk iron, etc.

This argument can be developed in terms of proteins as an example. The macromolecules of amino acid subunits cost somewhere between $3 and $20,000 a gram in purified form, yet the simpler, information-poorer amino acids sell for about twenty-five cents a gram. The proteins are linear arrays of the amino acids that must be assembled and folded. Thus we see the reason for the expense. The components such as coal, air, water, limestone and iron nails are, of course, simple and correspondingly cheap. The small molecular weight monomers are much more complex and correspondingly more expensive, and so on for larger molecules.

This means that my six million dollar estimate is much too 6 low. The biochemical companies can sell me their wares for a mere six million because they isolate them from natural products. Doubtless, if they had to synthesize them from ninety-seven cents worth of material they would have to charge me six hundred million or perhaps six billion dollars. We have, to date, synthesized only insulin and ribonuclease. Larger proteins would be even more difficult.

A moment's reflection shows that even if I bought all the 7 macromolecular components, I would not have purchased a human being. A freezer full of unstable molecules at $-70°$ C does not qualify to vote or for certain other inalienable rights. At six billion it would certainly qualify for concern over my $-70°$ deep freezer, which is always breaking down.

The next step is to assemble the molecules into organelles. 8 Here the success of modern science is limited as we are in a totally new area of research. A functionally active subunit of ribosomes has been assembled from the protein and RNA constituents. Doubtlessly other cellular structures will similarly yield to intensive efforts. The ribosome is perhaps the simplest organelle, so that considerably more experimental sophistication will be required to get at the larger cell components. One imagines that if I wanted to price the human body in terms of synthesized cellular substructures, I would have to think in terms of six hundred billion or perhaps six trillion dollars. Lest my university begin to salivate about all the overhead they would get on these purchases, let me point out that this is only a thought exercise, and I have no plans to submit a grant request in this area.

Continuing the argument to its penultimate conclusion, we   9
must face the fact that my dry-ice chest full of organelles (I have
given up the freezer, at six trillion it simply can't be trusted) cannot make love, complain, and do all those other things that
constitute our humanity. Dr. Frankenstein was a fraud. The
task is far more difficult than he ever realized. Next, the
organelles must be assembled into cells. Here we are out on a
limb estimating the cost, but I cannot imagine that it can be
done for less than six thousand trillion dollars. Do you hear me,
Mr. Treasury Secretary, Mr. Federal Reserve Chairman? Are
these thoughts taking a radical turn?

A final step is necessary in our biochemical view of man.   10
An incubator of 76,364 grams of cell culture at 37°C still does
not measure up, even in the crassest material terms, to what we
consider a human being. How would we assemble the cells into
tissues, tissues into organs, and organs into a person? The very
task staggers the imagination. Our ability to ask the question in
dollars and cents has immediately disappeared. We suddenly
and sharply face the realization that each human being is priceless. We are led cent by dollar from a lowly pile of common
materials to a grand philosophical conclusion — the infinite
preciousness of each person. The scientific reasons are clear. We
are, at the molecular level, the most information-dense structures around, surpassing by many orders of magnitude the best
that computer engineers can design or even contemplate by
miniaturization. The result must, however, go beyond science
and color our view of the world. It might even lead us to Alfred
North Whitehead's conclusion that "the human body is an instrument for the production of art in the life of the human
soul."

· QUESTIONS ON MEANING AND PURPOSE ·

1. From your knowledge of television, explain the title of this essay
   and the author's joy in discovering that he is a Six Million Dollar
   Man.

2. What definition of the human body is implied in the statement on the greeting card? Why does Morowitz question it?
3. At what strikingly different definition does the author finally arrive?
4. In his conclusion, Morowitz declares that how we think about humans must color our view of the world. Define the world view of someone who answers the question "What is a human?" with the greeting card assumption: "A human is 97¢ worth of chemicals."

• QUESTIONS ON WRITING STRATEGY •

1. What accounts for the fact that this essay, originally written for medical professionals, appeals as well to a wider audience?
2. Does the author take the greeting card in complete seriousness? What is the tone of his essay (until the last paragraph)? How is it indicated? (See *Tone* in Useful Terms.)
3. Why is the last sentence of paragraph 9 a vital transition? What ideas does it serve to bridge? What "radical turn" in the writer's thought does it announce? (See *Transitions* in Useful Terms.)
4. "Morowitz shifts his subject. He starts out talking about the human body and ends up talking about the human being." Do you agree, or do you think the author's subject remains the same all the way through?

• QUESTIONS ON LANGUAGE •
• AND VOCABULARY •

1. In reading the list of chemicals in paragraph 2, why isn't it necessary to look up every unfamiliar term in a dictionary? Why don't their *denotations* matter greatly? (See *Connotation and Denotation* in Useful Terms.)
2. What do the allusions to Tiffany's (paragraph 2) and to Dr. Frankenstein (9) add to the essay? (See *Allusion* in Useful Terms.) Explain them.
3. Look up, if need be, the following terms: biochemist (paragraph 1); gram, DNA (2); macromolecules, linear, monomers (5); synthesized, insulin (6); inalienable (7); organelles, RNA, cellular, salivate (8); penultimate (9); magnitude, miniaturization (10).
4. What does the author mean by *information*? Define *informational state* (paragraph 4) and *information-dense* (10).

• SUGGESTIONS FOR WRITING •

1. Begin an essay with a rough definition of one of the following: a man, a woman, a child, a senior citizen, a black, a Hispanic, a Jew, a Fundamentalist (or some other general term for one of many people). Spend your essay in refining and improving the definition you began with, and try to arrive at a more accurate definition at the end.

2. In a brief essay, define a branch of science, technology, or medicine (such as bionics, astrophysics, computer programming, or first aid), using examples to make your definition clear.

· Alistair Cooke ·

ALFRED ALISTAIR COOKE, well-known host of public television's *Masterpiece Theater*, was born in Manchester, England, in 1908. He became a U. S. citizen in 1941. A feature writer for the *London Daily Herald* and a correspondent for the *London Times* and the *Manchester Guardian*, he also served as host for another widely acclaimed television series, *Omnibus*, from 1952 to 1961. In 1972 and 1973 he wrote and narrated the television series *America*. Among his books are *Talk About America* (1968), *Alistair Cooke's America* (1968), *Six Men* (1977), and a recent bestseller, *The Americans* (1979).

Justice Holmes and the Doffed Bikini

In this essay Alistair Cooke brings together a naked sunbather and a noted Supreme Court justice from a former era. As the author reasons along in leisurely fashion, he arrives at a fresh view of the grand-jury system in the United States and draws forth two workable definitions — of "rights" and of "decency." Cooke addresses his observations to a British audience. Like other essays in *The Americans*, "Justice Holmes and the Doffed Bikini" was originally delivered as a radio talk for the British Broadcasting Corporation.

One day last summer a young woman sunning on a public   1
beach decided to take off her bikini and lie naked on the sand.
Pretty soon the families lolling nearby came awake. Husbands
began to dive for their cameras and in no time wives were diving
for their husbands. One husband, at the instigation of his wife,
called the police. The young woman was arrested and last week
she appeared before a judge.

That's all. Or that *would* have been all a few years ago. But   2
the young woman was furious over her arrest. She is a product
of the 1970s. She is therefore not a law-breaker but an

evangelist. She maintained, as a daring and original proposition, that the naked human body is decent and that she was causing no harm, only going about her decent business of sunning in the nude.

Her lawyer asked to have the case dismissed on the legal   3
ground that she had a constitutional right to go naked, the implication being that her arrest violated the First Amendment to the Constitution, which says, among other things, that Congress shall make no law — nor by extension shall the states — "abridging the freedom of speech or the right of the people peaceably to assemble." The judge asked her a rhetorical question to which no answer was reported. What would she think if people chose to go naked in the subway?

There will be many people, in countries that don't have a   4
written Bill of Rights and so cannot keep pointing to their private interpretation of what the original authors made public — there must be many of you who find this case hard to credit. But the burden of it is almost as constant as a ballad refrain, in the public outcries of radicals and even of liberals who ought to know better. It's the fairly new assertion that anything you feel like doing in public, short of assault or robbery, is an actual right of citizenship.

When the first play was shown in New York in which the   5
characters mimicked sexual intercourse, the defense maintained that their performance was a form of free speech sanctioned by the Constitution. Possibly the thought of James Madison and John Jay and George Mason and Jefferson and the rest whirling in their graves with disbelief was too much for the court. Anyway, the claim of free speech was not allowed, and the play had to close. The verdict sparked a manifesto from a group of playwrights who leaped to the barricades to defend a fellow worker without ever defining what they were supposed to be defending: namely, how limited is the right of free speech? (By the way, since then New York, San Francisco, and other cities have sprouted a rash of little theater and back-alley "massage" parlors that advertise "live sex" and perform it and go untroubled by the courts, which apparently have given up on the whole question.)

The courts have found obscenity impossible to pin down as   6
a punishable offense and have turned in great relief to asking
how free can speech get before it threatens society by inciting to
riot? They have a pat and famous answer already at hand, in
Justice Oliver Wendell Holmes's assertion that there is no right
to shout "Fire!" in a crowded theater unless there is a fire.

I have just come on a passage from the same great judge   7
which he delivered to the New York State Bar Association
seventy-three years ago. And I think — to coin a well-worn
word — it is "relevant" today. He's talking about how much
strain you can put on the word "right" when you say that
you're exercising one.

For those who never had the pleasure of knowing the ma-   8
jestic old Yankee, one of the two or three greatest jurists of his
time, let me say that he was not so wedded to the sacredness of
precedent as some of his English colleagues. In fact, he often
scolded them for citing a precedent and saying, "Well, that's the
law," and then delivering a final judgment, however greatly or
subtly the social conditions of the time had changed.

Talking about the jury system, for example, Holmes says: "I   9
have not found juries specially inspired for the discovery of
truth. I have not found them freer from prejudice than an ordinary judge would be." But in certain cases he believed in juries "because of one of their gravest defects from the point of
view of their theoretical function, namely that they will introduce into their verdict a certain amount, a very large amount
as far as I have observed, of popular prejudice and thus keep the
administration of the law in accord with the wishes and feelings
of the community."

Well, it may be, in the matter of the young woman doffing   10
her bikini, that the wishes and feelings of the community will
come to be on her side in some early future, and that public
nakedness will be legally okay. But when people assert a right,
they have to watch out that they don't do what Justice Holmes
described as "letting the word stand for some great external
principle. Right itself," he says, "is a vague generalization. Different rights are of different extent, and have different histories,
and it does not follow that because one right is absolute, another is." He then picks out a couple of rights that we might think,

even today, are absolute: the right to sell your own property, and the right to make out a character reference for somebody who's about to employ a person who has worked for you.

Says Holmes: "Under the statutes, the right to sell property is about as absolute as any I can think of." But suppose your intention is to get the jump on your creditors. Would the right not be modified by "the motive of deceit"? 11

And about vouching for somebody's character, he says, "A man may write down actual untruths in a character reference volunteered in good faith out of love." But would the same "right" extend to "statements volunteered simply out of hate for the man"? 12

In recent years no part of the First Amendment has been more frequently claimed as an absolute protection of free speech than that which gives the people the right "peaceably to assemble." It has been triumphantly claimed by street marchers taunting the police and fighting them, by students storming and breaking up university offices, even by random mobs setting fire to things. In all the subsequent court hearings that I have followed, the magistrate or the judge never seems to remember the qualifying adverb that the Founding Fathers, after a long debate, were careful to put in: "peaceably" — the right "peaceably to assemble." Of course, there were in the 1960s, and are still today, outrageous cases of court injunctions and police prohibitions of parades and protests *before* the event, before they'd assembled either peaceably or unpeaceably. 13

But now listen to this tricky test of free speech. In upstate New York a judge has asked a sitting grand jury to investigate a book of nursery rhymes, or rather a book of satirical, mock nursery rhymes. The judge did this on quite positive grounds. He said, "This book of so-called nursery rhymes advocates the commission of certain crimes." And he read aloud one of them. This is it: 14

> Jack be nimble,
> Jack be quick,
> Snap the blade
> And give it a flick,
> Grab the purse,
> It's easily done,

Then just for kicks,
Just for fun,
Plunge the knife,
And cut and run.

It may seem that the judge was pre-judging the case by tell-   15
ing the jury what to find. But I ought to stress that this was not
a trial but a hearing before a grand jury, whose job is no more
and no less than that of a magistrates' hearing: to decide if
there's a case, if the charges brought before the grand jury warrant a trial. It's important to say this especially for countries,
like Britain, which abolished the grand-jury system. It started,
by the way, in England, in the Middle Ages, when there were
few settled courts. So that judges rode off on circuit to hear
cases in towns with which they were unfamiliar. They called in,
so to speak, the neighbors — sixteen people who might know
the defendant and could say, from their knowledge of him and
the place he lived in, whether the charge was ridiculous or
plausible. Sometime in the 1910s Lord Birkenhead, later the
Lord Chancellor of Great Britain, wrote a scathing and charac-
teristically ironical piece about the likelihood of sixteen people
drawn from a city with a population of seven million knowing
more about a defendant than the ordinary competent magistrate. The grand-jury system was already declining, and in 1933
it was formally abolished. It continues in the United States with
great vigor, and if it has a fault — two faults — they are: that too
often the grand jury becomes the creature of the prosecutor;
and that the press, champing under the restraint of not being
able to report what is a secret hearing, explodes at the end,
whenever an indictment is handed down, with a streaming
headline: "George Spelvin indicted!" I'm sorry to say that, from
the results of a recent galloping poll of my own, most Americans
tend to confuse the word "indictment" with the word "conviction." And when the indicted man comes to trial, too many
Americans think of him as a guilty man who is going to have to
prove his innocence.

Well, back to the mock nursery rhymes. All is not lost for   16
the saucy author. But the judge did declare as a peril what Jus-

tice Holmes might have introduced as a warning. The book is called *The Inner City Mother Goose*. It was written by the author of thirty-five straightforward children's books, and it seems that this one was written as a bitter warning to parents. Unfortunately, it's in school libraries. And whereas adults may take it as a satire on the problems of the cities, it's possible that some children may take it as a book of recipes.

I'd like to add a final note to the ringing announcement of the bikini-doffer that the naked human body is decent. The word "decent" is another victim of the habit, common both to politicians and to their enemies, of using noble or impressive words not for thinking with but for raising, like those boards they hold up before television audiences, as invitations to applaud. Vice President Spiro Agnew simply proclaims that something is indecent, and the cheers ring out on the Right. A girl takes her clothes off and says the human body is decent, and there is an ovation from the Left. The word "decent" means "becoming," and the question surely is: becoming to whom and in what place? It was Bernard Shaw, I think, who defined evil as "matter out of place."

Anyway, the plea of the actors prosecuted for mimicking sexual intercourse was that it was natural. So, of course is diarrhea. But on the stage, is it becoming? My own view is that of the late Mrs. Patrick Campbell, who didn't mind what people did in private "so long as they don't do it in the streets and frighten the horses." At any rate, I think the judges could make a sensible clearing through the verbal undergrowth of such words as "rights" and "decency" if they went back and considered the original meaning of the word "indecency" as whatever is unbecoming in a certain person, place, or time.

17

18

• QUESTIONS ON MEANING AND PURPOSE •

1. How does Cooke define (with the aid of Justice Holmes) a *right*?
2. How does the author define *decent*? How would he qualify the one-word definition he uses?

3. What connection does Cooke make between *rights* and *decency*?
4. What is the difference between a trial and a grand-jury hearing? How does the author make the difference clear?
5. What further purpose, beyond defining two difficult concepts, do you find in Cooke's essay?

• QUESTIONS ON WRITING STRATEGY •

1. What is the tone of Cooke's essay? (See *Tone* in Useful Terms.)
2. In paragraphs 3, 11, 12, and 18 the author includes rhetorical questions. (See *Rhetorical Question* in Useful Terms.) In each case, what seems to be the answer expected? Does Cooke state or imply answers?
3. Where in his essay does Cooke display a sense of humor?
4. How do paragraphs 14, 15, and 16 relate to the rest of the essay?
5. What evidence do you find that this essay originally was directed to British listeners?

• QUESTIONS ON LANGUAGE •
• AND VOCABULARY •

1. Consult your dictionary if you need help defining the following words: instigation (paragraph 1); evangelist (2); sanctioned, manifesto (5); precedent (8); subsequent, injunctions (13); plausible, competent, champing (15).
2. Explain Cooke's labeling *relevant* a "well-worn word" (paragraph 7).
3. Explain the pun in paragraph 15.
4. What does Cooke mean when he says, "But the judge did declare as a peril what Justice Holmes might have introduced as a warning" (paragraph 16)?

• SUGGESTIONS FOR WRITING •

1. Find Eve Merriam's satiric *Inner City Mother Goose* in your library and read a few of its verses. Then, in a brief essay, either defend the book from charges that it incites children to dangerous behavior, or attack it as a dangerous influence. (See *Satire* in Useful Terms.)
2. In two paragraphs, show how the same idea or term may be defined from opposing points of view. For example, you might

define *a woman's place* first as a feminist and then as a male chauvinist, or define *Federal government* first as a liberal and then as a conservative.

3. Using examples, write an essay in which you define an abstract concept: freedom, success, justice, love, honor, patriotism, fame, or one of your choice. (See *Abstract* in Useful Terms.)

· Alvin Toffler ·

ALVIN TOFFLER was born in New York City in 1928. He received an A. B. degree from New York University in 1949. A Washington correspondent for various newspapers and magazines in 1957–58, he has also been associate editor of *Fortune*, a member of the faculty at the New School for Social Research, and a visiting professor at Cornell University. Of his books, perhaps the most famous are two best-sellers: *Future Shock* (1970) and *The Third Wave* (1980).

The De-Massified Media

Alvin Toffler in *The Third Wave* visualizes all of human history in three rolling waves of change. The First Wave brought agriculture and a new way of life to nomadic hunters, herders, and fishermen. The Second Wave of change rolled in with the Industrial Revolution at the end of the seventeenth century. Today, Toffler says, the force of the First Wave has been largely spent. In many parts of the world, the Second Wave continues, and even gains momentum. But about 1955, a Third Wave began moving across the United States. "The De-Massified Media" defines one manifestation of this Third Wave of change.

Today a startling change is taking place. As the Third Wave thunders in, the mass media, far from expanding their influence, are suddenly being forced to share it. They are being beaten back on many fronts at once by what I call the "de-massified media." 1

Newspapers provide the first example. The oldest of the Second Wave mass media, newspapers are losing their readers. By 1973 U.S. newspapers had reached a combined aggregate circulation of 63 million copies daily. Since 1973, however, instead of adding circulation, they have begun to lose it. By 1978 the total had declined to 62 million and worse was in store. The percentage of Americans who read a paper every day also fell, from 2

69 percent in 1972 to 62 percent in 1977, and some of the nation's most important papers were the hardest hit. In New York, between 1970 and 1976, the three major dailies combined lost 550,000 readers. The *Los Angeles Times*, having peaked in 1973, went on to lose 80,000 readers by 1976. The two big Philadelphia papers dropped 150,000 readers, the two big Cleveland papers 90,000 and the two San Francisco papers more than 80,000. While numerous smaller papers cropped up in many parts of the country, major U.S. dailies like the *Cleveland News*, the *Hartford Times*, the *Detroit Times*, *Chicago Today*, or the *Long Island Press* all fell by the wayside. A similar pattern appeared in Britain where, between 1965 and 1975, the national dailies lost fully 8 percent of their circulation.

Nor were such losses due merely to the rise of television. Each of today's mass-circulation dailies now faces increasing competition from a burgeoning flock of mini-circulation weeklies, biweeklies, and so-called "shoppers" that serve not the metropolitan mass market but specific neighborhoods and communities within it, providing far more localized advertising and news. Having reached saturation, the big-city mass-circulation daily is in deep trouble. De-massified media are snapping at its heels.[1]

Mass magazines offer a second example. From the mid-1950s on, hardly a year has passed without the death in the United States of a major magazine. *Life*, *Look*, the *Saturday Evening Post* — each went to its grave, later to undergo resurrection as a small-circulation ghost of its former self.

Between 1970 and 1977, despite a 14 million rise in U.S. population, the combined aggregate circulation of the remaining top twenty-five magazines dropped by 4 million.

[1]Some publishers do not consider newspapers to be mass media because many have small circulations and serve small communities. But most papers, at least in the United States, are filled with nationally produced "boilerplate" — news from the AP and UPI wires, comic strips, crosswords, fashions, feature articles — which are largely the same from one city to the next. To compete with the smaller, more localized media the larger papers are increasing local coverage and adding a variety of special-interest sections. The surviving dailies of the 1980s and 1990s will be drastically changed by the segmentation of the reading public.

Simultaneously, the United States experienced a population   6
explosion of mini-magazines — thousands of brand new magazines aimed at small, special-interest, regional, or even local
markets. Pilots and aviation buffs today can choose among
literally scores of periodicals edited just for them. Teen-agers,
scuba divers, retired people, women athletes, collectors of antique cameras, tennis nuts, skiers, and skateboarders each have
their own press. Regional magazines like *New York, New West,
D* in Dallas, or *Pittsburgher*, are all multiplying. Some slice the
market up even more finely by both region and special interest
— the *Kentucky Business Ledger*, for example, or *Western Farmer*.

With new, fast, cheap short-run printing presses, every   7
organization, community group, political or religious cult and
cultlet today can afford to print its own publication. Even
smaller groups churn out periodicals on the copying machines
that have become ubiquitous in American offices. The mass
magazine has lost its once powerful influence in national life.
The de-massified magazine — the mini-magazine — is rapidly
taking its place.

But the impact of the Third Wave in communications is not   8
confined to the print media. Between 1950 and 1970 the number of radio stations in the United States climbed from 2,336 to
5,359. In a period when population rose only 35 percent, radio
stations increased by 129 percent. This means that instead of
one station for every 65,000 Americans, there is now one for
every 38,000, and it means the average listener has more programs to choose from. The mass audience is cut up among more
stations.

The diversity of offerings has also sharply increased, with   9
different stations appealing to specialized audience segments instead of to the hitherto undifferentiated mass audience. All-
news stations aim at educated middle-class adults. Hard rock,
soft rock, punk rock, country rock, and folk rock stations each
aim at a different sector of the youth audience. Soul music stations aim at Black Americans. Classical music stations cater to
upper-income adults, foreign language stations to different ethnic groups, from the Portuguese in New England to Italians,
Hispanics, Japanese, and Jews. Writes political columnist

Richard Reeves, "In Newport, R.I., I checked the AM radio dial and found 38 stations, three of them religious, two programmed for blacks and one broadcasting in Portuguese."

Relentlessly, newer forms of audio communication chip   10
away at what remains of the mass audience. During the 1960s tiny, cheap tape recorders and cassette players spread like prairie fire among the young. Despite popular misconceptions to the contrary, today's teen-agers spend *less*, not more, time with their ears glued to the radio than was the case in the sixties. From an average of 4.8 hours a day in 1967, the amount of radio listening time plummeted to 2.8 hours in 1977.

Then came citizens band radio. Unlike broadcast radio,   11
which is strictly one-way (the listener cannot talk back to the programmer), CB radios in cars make it possible for drivers within a five- to fifteen-mile radius to communicate with each other.

Between 1959 and 1974, only one million CB sets came into   12
use in America. Then, in the words of an astounded official of the Federal Communications Commission, "It took eight months [for us] to get the second million and three months to get the third." CB blasted off. By 1977 some 25 million CB sets were in use, and the airwaves were filled with colorful chatter — from warnings that "smokies" (police) were setting speed traps, to prayers and prostitutes' solicitations. The fad is now over, but its effects are not.

Radio broadcasters, nervous about their advertising   13
revenues, vigorously deny that CB has cut into radio listenership. But the ad agencies are not so sure. One of them, Marsteller, Inc., conducted a survey in New York and found that 45 percent of CB users report a 10 to 15 percent drop in listening to their regular car radios. More significantly, the survey found that over half the CB users listened to both their car radios *and* their CBs simultaneously.

In any case, the shift toward diversity in print is paralleled   14
in radio. The soundscape is being de-massified along with the printscape.

Not until 1977, however, did the Second Wave media suffer   15
their most startling and significant defeat. For a generation the most powerful and the most "massifying" of the media has, of

course, been television. In 1977 the picture tube began to flicker. Wrote *Time* magazine, "All fall, broadcast and ad executives nervously peeked at the figures . . . they could not believe what they were seeing. . . . For the first time in history, television viewing declined."

"Nobody," mumbled one astonished ad man, "*ever* assumed that viewership would go down." 16

Even now explanations abound. We are told the shows are even more miserable than in the past. That there is too much of this and not enough of that. Executive heads have rolled down the network corridors. We have been promised this or that new type of show. But the deeper truth is only beginning to emerge from the clouds of tele-hype. The day of the all-powerful centralized network that controls image production is waning. Indeed, a former president of NBC, charging the three main U.S. television networks with strategic "stupidity," has predicted their share of the prime-time viewing public would drop to 50 percent by the late 1980s. For the Third Wave communications media are subverting the dominance of the Second Wave media lords on a broad front. 17

Cable television today already reaches into 14.5 million American homes and is likely to spread with hurricane force in the early 1980s. Industry experts expect 20 to 26 million cable subscribers by the end of 1981, with cabling available to fully 50 percent of U.S. households. Things will move even faster once the shift is made from copper wires to cheap fiber optic systems that send light pulsing through hair-thin fibers. And like short-run printing presses or Xerox copiers, cable de-massifies the audience, carving it into multiple mini-publics. Moreover, cable systems can be designed for two-way communication so that subscribers may not merely watch programs but actively call various services. 18

In Japan, by the early 1980s entire towns will be linked to light-wave cable, enabling users to dial requests not only for programs but for still photographs, data, theater reservations, or displays of newspaper and magazine material. Burglar and fire alarms will work through the same system. 19

In Ikoma, a bedroom suburb of Osaka, I was interviewed on a TV show on the experimental Hi-Ovis system, which places a 20 microphone and television camera on top of the TV set in the home of every subscriber, so that viewers can become senders as well. As I was being interviewed by the program host, a Mrs. Sakamoto, viewing the program from her own living room, switched in and began chatting with us in broken English. I and the viewing pubic saw her on the screen and watched her little boy romping around the room as she welcomed me to Ikoma.

Hi-Ovis also keeps a bank of video cassettes on everything from music to cooking to education. Viewers can punch in a code number and request the computer to play a particular cassette for them on their screen at whatever hour they wish to see it. 21

Though it involves only about 160 homes, the Hi-Ovis experiment is backed by the Japanese government and contributions from such corporations as Fujitsu, Sumitomo Electric, Matsushita, and Kinetsu. It is extremely advanced and already based on fiber optics technology. 22

In Columbus, Ohio, a week earlier, I had visited Warner Cable Corporation's Qube system. Qube provides the subscriber with thirty TV channels (as against four regular broadcast stations) and presents specialized shows for everyone from preschoolers to doctors, lawyers, or the "adults only" audience. Qube is the most well-developed, commercially effective two-way cable system in the world. Providing each subscriber with what looks like a hand-held calculator, it permits him or her to communicate with the station by push button. A viewer using the so-called "hot buttons" can communicate with the Qube studio and its computer. *Time,* in describing the system, waxes positively rhapsodic, noting that the subscriber can "voice his opinions in local political debates, conduct garage sales and bid for *objets d'art* in a charity auction. . . . By pressing a button, Joe or Jane Columbus can quiz a politician, or turn electronic thumbs down or up on a local amateur talent program." Consumers can "comparison-shop the local supermarkets" or book a table at an Oriental restaurant. 23

Cable, however, is not the only worry facing the networks. 24

Video games have become a "hot item" in the stores. Millions of Americans have discovered a passion for gadgets that convert a TV screen into a Ping-Pong table, hockey rink, or ten- 25 nis court. This development may seem trivial or irrelevant to orthodox political or social analysts. Yet it represents a wave of social learning, a premonitory training, as it were, for life in the electronic environment of tomorrow. Not only do video games further de-massify the audience and cut into the numbers who are watching the programs broadcast at any given moment, but through such seemingly innocent devices millions of people are learning to play with the television set, to talk back to it, and to interact with it. In the process they are changing from passive receivers to message senders as well. They are manipulating the set rather than merely letting the set manipulate them.

Information services, fed through the TV screen, are now 26 already available in Britain where a viewer with an adapter unit can push a button and select which of a dozen or so different data services he or she wants — news, weather, financial, sports, and so forth. This data then moves across the TV screen as though on ticker tape. Before long users will no doubt be able to plug a hard-copier into the TV to capture on paper any images they wish to retain. Once again there is wide choice where little existed before.

Video cassette players and recorders are spreading rapidly as 27 well. Marketers expect to see a million units in use in the United States by 1981. These not only allow viewers to tape Monday's football match for replay on, say, Saturday (thus demolishing the synchronization of imagery that the networks promote), but lay the basis for the sale of films and sports events on tape. (The Arabs are not asleep at the proverbial switch: the movie *The Messenger*, about the life of Muhammad, is available in boxed cassettes with gilt Arabic lettering on the outside.) Video recorders and players also make possible the sale of highly specialized cartridges containing, for example, medical instructional material for hospital staff, or tapes that show consumers how to assemble knockdown furniture or rewire a toaster. More fundamentally, video recorders make it possible for any *consumer* to become, in addition, a *producer* of his or her own imagery. Once again the audience is de-massified.

Domestic satellites, finally, make it possible for individual 28 television stations to form temporary mini-networks for special-

ized programming by bouncing signals from anywhere to anywhere else at minimal cost, thus end-running the existing networks. By the end of 1980 cable-TV operators will have one
thousand earth stations in place to pick up satellite signals. "At
that point," says *Television/Radio Age,* "a program distributor
need only buy time on a satellite, presto, he has a nationwide
cable TV network . . . he can selectively feed any group of systems he chooses." The satellite, declares William J. Donnelly,
vice-president for electronic media at the giant Young &
Rubicam advertising agency, "means smaller audiences and a
greater multiplicity of nationally distributed programs."

All these different developments have one thing in com- 29
mon: they slice the mass television public into segments, and
each slice not only increases our cultural diversity, it cuts deeply
into the power of the networks that have until now so completely dominated our imagery. John O'Connor, the perceptive critic
of *The New York Times,* sums it up simply. "One thing is certain," he writes. "Commercial television will no longer be able
to dictate either what is watched or when it is watched."

What appears on the surface to be a set of unrelated events 30
turns out to be a wave of closely interrelated changes sweeping
across the media horizon from newspapers and radio at one end
to magazines and television at the other. The mass media are
under attack. New, de-massified media are proliferating, challenging — and sometimes even replacing — the mass media that
were so dominant in all Second Wave societies.

The Third Wave thus begins a truly new era — the age of 31
the de-massified media. A new info-sphere is emerging alongside
the new techno-sphere.[2] And this will have a far-reaching impact on the most important sphere of all, the one inside our
skulls. For taken together, these changes revolutionize our images of the world and our ability to make sense of it.

---

[2]Terms coined by the author. An info-sphere is any system for sending
messages across time and space. A techno-sphere is defined earlier in Toffler's
book as follows: "All societies — primitive, agricultural, or industrial — use
energy; they make things; they distribute things. In all societies the energy
system, the production system, and the distribution system are interrelated
parts of something larger. This larger system is the techno-sphere." — Editors.

• QUESTIONS ON MEANING AND PURPOSE •

1. What reasons does Toffler cite for the fact that big-city news-papers and mass magazines are losing their readers? What has happened to radio programming since 1950?
2. What is the most important reason, according to Toffler, for the decline in the popularity of network television broadcasts since 1977?
3. When Toffler says, "In 1977 the picture tube began to flicker" (paragraph 15), whose picture tube does he mean?
4. What connection does the author discern between video games and the trend toward media de-massification?
5. What is Toffler's thesis? (See *Thesis* in Useful Terms.) Where in his essay does he state it?
6. What is the author's definition of the de-massified media?
7. Assuming that the movement toward media de-massification in our country will continue unabated, what possible effects on the American populace can you foresee?

• QUESTIONS ON WRITING STRATEGY •

1. By what method does Toffler define the de-massified media? Are you satisfied that he offers a good definition of a real phenom-enon?
2. Is it easier, do you think, to define a phrase you invent yourself, or to write a definition of a word or phrase already in existence? Give reasons for your answer.
3. What does the author's use of statistical evidence contribute to the impact of his ideas? (See *Evidence* in Useful Terms.)
4. How can you tell that "The De-Massified Media" is a section from a larger work?
5. What sentences or passages effectively serve as transitions? (See *Transitions* in Useful Terms.)

• QUESTIONS ON LANGUAGE •
• AND VOCABULARY •

1. Consult your dictionary if you do not know the meanings of the following words: aggregate (paragraph 2); burgeoning, saturation (3); ubiqitous (7); diversity, undifferentiated (9); subverting (17);

premonitory (25); synchronization (27); multiplicity (28); proliferating (30).

2. What is a *cultlet* (paragraph 7)? What other familiar word does it recall? In the preceding paragraph (6), and the following paragraph (8), what hints do you find that *cultlet* is a pun?

3. Evidently, Toffler is fond of coined words. Besides *cultlet* he invents *info-sphere* and *techno-sphere* (paragraph 31, defined in the editors' note), *soundscape* (14), and *tele-hype* (17). From their context in the essay, how would you define these last two words?

• SUGGESTIONS FOR WRITING •

1. In an essay, discuss either the advantages or the disadvantages that might result from living in a society where media de-massification has taken place.

2. Spot a new phenomenon in contemporary society and invent a name for it. Then, using plenty of examples, write a definition that will give your reader a clear understanding of the phenomenon you have named. (You might, for instance, name and define some trend you observe in television programs of today, in music, in fashion, or in eating habits.)

· Gary Goshgarian ·

GARY GOSHGARIAN was born in 1942. For several years a physicist, he is now an associate professor of English at Northeastern University, where his immensely popular science fiction course, one of the first to be offered in the nation, is also, after twelve years, one of the longest running. Goshgarian is the editor of *Exploring Language* (1977; second edition, 1980). He has also published a suspense-adventure novel, *Atlantis Fire* (1980).

Zeroing in
on Science Fiction

Not every paperback on the bookstore's science fiction rack belongs there. How are you to know which books do and which do not? Well, first you need a good working definition of science fiction.

For the sake of argument, let's say you don't know a thing 1 about science fiction but want to. It makes sense to begin your research at your local bookstore. Toward the rear of the store, just past a sign saying WESTERNS and pressed between sections labeled MYSTERIES and THE OCCULT you find a collection of titles labeled SCIENCE FICTION. You're standing before a rack six rows high and twenty feet long — a small galaxy of paperback SF books from A to Z. You randomly select a few and read the publishers' blurbs hoping to get some idea of what SF is all about, hoping to see what all these books have in common. And that's where your troubles begin.

At one end you find Isaac Asimov's *Caves of Steel*, which is 2 about a man and a robot who in some distant future solve a murder; at the other end is Roger Zelazny's *Lord of Light*, in which Hindu deities are reincarnated as people. A little confused, you pull out *Frankenstein*, a classic SF tale about a scientist who creates a human monster in his laboratory, then *Rosemary's Baby*, a recent best-seller about a woman who gives birth to a little devil. Even more confused, you begin yanking books off the shelves wondering if you're going to discern a common denominator, or at least some clear categories. *A Clockwork Orange*: a gang of ultra-violent youths who rule the night streets of an iron-gray society. *The Fires of Azeroth*: the people of three planets experience an Armageddon. *Starship Troopers*: a young soldier of the twenty-second century discovers courage in interplanetary battles. *War of the Worlds*: beings from Mars invade the earth. *Clash of the Titans*: Perseus, son of Zeus, slays Medusa and saves Andromeda. They can't all be "science fiction," can they? Some sound rational and scientific, while others sound magical and mystical. Some seem to describe worlds and events that are probable, while others clearly deal with matters impossible. Some appear to have messages, while others appear to be pure escapism.

What you need, of course, is a reasonable definition of science fiction, one that distinguishes it from the non-SF sometimes mistakenly shelved with it. The best place to begin defining is with the name, *science fiction*. The second word first. *Fiction* signals a kind of literature. In form, then, SF should have the basic fictional ingredients of a story — plot, character, setting, action, point of view. In function, SF, like all forms of literature, should tell us something about the human experience. Now to the second word, the qualifier, *science*. This crucial word separates SF from other fiction genres like fantasy, westerns, and the occult. What makes SF is the science, real or imaginary; without it there is no science fiction. Putting the two halves together produces a general formula that should subsume most SF material — "most" because no literary definition is totally inclusive or exclusive. *Science fiction is the branch of literature that imaginatively speculates on the consequences of living in a scientific or technological world.*

A closer look at the definition will help outline some SF prerequisites. The word *speculates* implies the future. Therefore, a writer who "imaginatively speculates" is one who creates experiences and conditions that have not yet occurred in the real world. Certainly humans have experienced love, hate, and fear before, and any nonhistorical fiction may presume some general future time. But — and this is where SF differs from non-SF — the future experiences and conditions in science fiction are categorically scientific or technological. In other words, SF is about being human in some imagined technological future. The definition does not specify locale, so SF stories can be set on earth, in space, or on worlds galaxies away. Nor does the definition specify *whose* technology. In *War of the Worlds*, by H. G. Wells, the know-how of bug-eyed Martians transports them millions of miles to earth and then nearly devastates the planet with deadly gases and heat rays.

It is the science and scientific rationale of SF that separate it   5
from fantasy, with which it is often confused. The SF author explains even the most fantastic events with science or pseudoscience to make the improbable seem plausible. A fantasy writer, on the other hand, breaks the laws of nature by crediting fantastic events to magic or supernatural powers. The world of SF is a world that could be; the world of fantasy is a world that could never be. Two rival classics, one SF and one fantasy, underscore the distinction. Perhaps the first SF novel was Mary Shelley's *Frankenstein*, published in 1819 at the beginning of the modern scientific age. As everyone knows, it is the tale of a young scientist named Frankenstein who discovers a means of animating a composite corpse. Once alive, the monstrous creation responds to its creator's rejection by destroying Frankenstein's friends and relatives. Nearly eighty years after the publication of *Frankenstein*, Bram Stoker wrote *Dracula* about a 400-year-old vampire who thrives on the blood of innocents. Both novels center on human monsters, both contain scientists, both are steeped in brooding Gothic atmosphere. So why is *Frankenstein* SF and *Dracula* fantasy? It is a matter of strategies. Frankenstein's monster is born of scientific experimentation in a laboratory, the product of some future breakthrough in biology and chemistry that seemed plausible at the time Shelley wrote. Dracula, however, is a creature from outside the natural order; neither his existence nor his ability to take the form of bats and wolves could be or can be explained scientifically.

Distinct as they are, fantasy and science fiction sometimes 6 overlap in a hybrid category called *fantasy science fiction*. Here an odd juxtaposition of impossibility and plausibility, the magical and the scientific, flying unicorns and atomic-powered space ships, creates a tension that highlights the limitations of both human sciences and human perceptions of nature. A whole body of fantasy SF known as *sword and sorcery* deals with the high adventures of superhumans who are pitted against fiendish warlords in some faraway world. Two of the most famous writers of such space opera are Fritz Leiber, known for his famous Gray Mouser series, and Edgar Rice Burroughs, who wrote a dozen Martian adventure novels. (Burroughs, of course, is also the creator of Tarzan.) What qualifies their stories as fantasy SF is the scientific hardware, the machinery that transports characters to Burroughs's Barsoom or Leiber's Lankhmar, where the extraordinary events occur.

Just as science and logic distinguish SF from fantasy, so the 7 degree of scientific emphasis distinguishes *hard science fiction* from *soft science fiction*. Hard SF, which flourished in the 1930s and 1940s, stresses scientific knowledge and gadgetry. To create the illusion of a scientifically credible future, hard SF writers draw on known principles and innovations to stock their stories with hard details and jargon. Their protagonists, usually scientists and engineers, romp among the stars seeking a logical solution to some problem. In a sense, the true heroes of hard SF are Yankee ingenuity and modern science. A prime example is Asimov's *Caves of Steel* — a detective story celebrating the cooperation of humans and machines. The book's positive attitude toward the scientific pursuit of truth and invention is characteristic of the form.

Soft SF focuses not so much on the benefits of scientific advancement as on its social and moral consequences. Drawing on sociology, psychology, philosophy, archaeology, and political science, soft SF dramatizes how a technological culture may change the quality of human life, altering morality, evolution, and the environment. Though a soft SF story is always set in the future, its writer draws on some current trend or innovation, thus gaining the opportunity for social commentary and criticism. Such is the case with Anthony Burgess's *A Clockwork Orange*, in which Alex, a juvenile thug, is conditioned by experimental psychologists to become incapable of violence. Science succeeds in rendering Alex nonviolent, but it does not make him morally good. In fact, it dehumanizes him because he can no longer defend himself against the hostile world he inhabits. In the end, the government is forced to recondition Alex back to his old anti-social self, just as the harsh, loveless state conditioned him to violence from his birth. And Burgess thus poses the question of whether humans are creatures of free will or just mechanically conditioned organisms, clockwork oranges. The special advantage of soft SF is that it can raise such moral questions out of the context of daily existence. How will humans live in a world that is run by machines? That is grossly overpopulated? That is polluted by chemicals? That is out of fuel? That is a radioactive wasteland? That has lost its ancient gods?

In attempting to understand what SF is all about, you   9
should not get too caught up in classing a story as fantasy SF or hard SF or soft SF. The categories are just not that neat, and elements of each will share the same page. What is true of SF — and of no other kind of fiction — is that it deals with unfamiliar situations brought about by science. But it is important to recognize that, like all literature, science fiction is about humanity — not robots, Martians, and star ships. Such marvels may cram the pages, but they are there only to test the limits of human experience.

· QUESTIONS ON MEANING AND PURPOSE ·

1. How does Goshgarian distinguish science fiction from other kinds of fiction?
2. What important point does the writer stress in his conclusion? (See *Conclusion* in Useful Terms.)

· QUESTIONS ON WRITING STRATEGY ·

1. What does the comparison and contrast in paragraph 5 contribute to Goshgarian's definition?
2. What purpose is served by the distinction Goshgarian draws between hard science fiction and soft science fiction?

· QUESTIONS ON LANGUAGE ·
· AND VOCABULARY ·

1. Find the metaphor in the first paragraph. (See *Figures of Speech* in Useful Terms.) What makes it appropriate?
2. Is "a little devil" a metaphor (paragraph 2)? In the same paragraph, what word is echoed in "ultra-violent"?

· SUGGESTIONS FOR WRITING ·

1. Choose a comic strip that features a superhero and, on the basis of Goshgarian's definition, demonstrate in a paragraph or two whether it is or is not science fiction.
2. Using examples from your own reading, write a definition of any of the following: a fairy tale, a young adult novel, a potboiler, a Gothic tale, a picaresque novel. Or, using examples from television, define any of the following: a soap opera, a sitcom, a made-for-TV movie, a game show.

Getting Started

Sometimes, as Gary Goshgarian dramatically illustrates, the hardest thing about writing an essay is putting down the first sentence. Refusing to settle for any but a catchy and useful opening, the writer of "Zeroing in on Science Fiction" had to spend a day trying a few different outlets before the right light flashed in his brain.

When I was first asked to write "Zeroing in on Science Fiction" I thought it would be a snap. I had been teaching the material for twelve years, I knew the field pretty well, and I knew what to say about it in a short essay. So on scratch paper I made a scanty outline of what I would cover: first, a broad definition of science fiction followed by some discussion; then an illustration of how that definition distinguished SF from other fiction, particularly fantasy, with which it is often confused; and, finally, an explanation of the genre's subcategories — hard SF, soft SF, and fantasy SF — with specific examples to demonstrate diversity. I was well aware of the three kinds of people in my audience: those very familiar with SF, junkies who had been reading the stuff since they were kids; those whose only exposure to SF was *Star Trek* reruns and the beasties that stalk late-night television; and those who were totally alien to the SF world.

When I sat down at my typewriter at 9:00 A.M., I expected to buzz right through the piece in a couple of hours. I rolled in a blank, inviting sheet of paper and began: "Science fiction is like pornography: it's easy to recognize but hard to define." Catchy and clever, the single-sentence paragraph looked good on the page. My fingers hummed on the keys. Ten minutes later they were still humming, but not typing. It was a great opener, a provocative comparison, but I was running the risk of making the reader more interested in smut than in science fiction. I could

talk about the Supreme Court's difficulties in defining pornography and liken that dilemma to my own, but I foresaw a
distracting and lengthy tangent that wasn't worth the effort. Besides, I'd never get to what SF was all about.

Another cup of coffee and Sheet Number 2. A few minutes   3
later, a cartoon light bulb clicked on, and my fingers tapped
away: "Trying to define science fiction is like trying to photograph the Grand Canyon." Though perhaps not as provocative
as Opener Number 1, this one was still sharp and catchy. A sip
of coffee.

> The subject matter is too immense, the point of view too
> varied. A narrow formula, like a close-up lens, will render fine
> details but will fail to capture the awesome scope and poten-
> tial. Too broad a definition, like a wide-angle lens, will render
> the subject vague, flat, and ultimately meaningless.

But I had constructed another elaborate trap, for the
photography simile was entangling me in a treatise on focal
points and lenses. Hum, hum, then tilt. Sheet Number 2 joined
its predecessor in the wastebasket.

I was beginning to sweat. Already it was past 10:00 A.M.,   4
and I was wondering if I could come up with a decent opening
by sunset. I resolved to forego comparisons since they only side-
tracked me and ate up space; but Sheet Number 3 refused to
suggest anything else. Then another but a dimmer light bulb
went on: How about starting with a no-nonsense definition that
got right to the heart of the matter? "Science fiction is the
branch of literature that imaginatively speculates on the consequences of living in a technological world." But how bald. How
dull. Who would want to read on?

My wastebasket was beginning to fill up with balls of paper,   5
my stomach was a cauldron of acid, and the sun was tilting toward the west. Time for a walk to air things out. I thought
about what I had learned from writing a novel. I needed a good
opening scene, not an antiseptic definition or some cute simile. I
needed something to illustrate why SF is hard to define, why it
is often confused with other kinds of fiction, and just how diver-
sified the field is. My walk took me to the campus bookstore and

right to the section of paperbacks labeled SCIENCE FICTION — a typical jumble of science fiction, horror stories, Gothic tales, sword and sorcery tales, fantasies, and straight novels. While I scanned the books, a bright bulb suddenly blazed on in my head: A novice tries to determine what SF is all about while standing before such a bookstore rack.

I knew in an instant this scene was my opener. I could illustrate the problem of diversity and confusion and at the same time introduce specific titles. I could also use the scene to launch the definition of SF, and that, in turn, would be a springboard to detailing the qualities that distinguish SF from other genres. Then I could work in the three subcategories and, to tighten the discussion, introduce representatives of each one from the titles mentioned in the opener. Thematically and structurally, the bookstore scene made good sense. I headed back to the office and wrote the first draft, undistracted by the sound of the night crew's vacuum cleaners. 6

So what does my experience illustrate? Perhaps that starting friction is greater than stopping friction. This may not be a universal law of physics, but it is a law of writing. And the lesson it teaches is to plan carefully, not to jump right into the essay with just any bright idea. That may mean, as it did for me, starting again and again in search of something catchy, efficient, thematically appropriate, and rhetorically useful — that is, something you can return to in the essay and perhaps even round off the piece with. Finding the right opener is not easy, but no writing is. As Thomas Edison said of genius, it's 1 percent inspiration and 99 percent perspiration. 7

· ADDITIONAL WRITING TOPICS ·
DEFINITION

Write an essay in which you define an institution, a trend, a phenomenon, or an abstraction. Following are some suggestions designed to stimulate ideas. Before you begin, limit your subject as far as possible; and illustrate your essay with specific examples.

1. Education.
2. Male chauvinism.
3. Progress.
4. Advertising.
5. Happiness.
6. Overpopulation.
7. Personality.
8. Fads.
9. Women's liberation.
10. Reaganomics.
11. Marriage.
12. A "free spirit."
13. A Fascist.
14. Sportsmanship.
15. Politics.
16. Leadership.
17. Leisure.
18. Originality.
19. "Burn-out."
20. Character.
21. Friendship.
22. Imagination.
23. Democracy.
24. "Soul" (referring to black music or culture).
25. A smile.
26. A classic (of music, literature, art, or film).
27. "Mellow."
28. Dieting.
29. Meditation.

· 10 ·

ARGUMENT AND PERSUASION

Appealing to Reason and Emotion

· THE METHOD ·

Some people love to argue for the joy of doing so, the way some people love to take part in a brawl. The knock-down, drag-out kind of argument, however, is not the kind we are concerned with. In this chapter we will be dealing with a form of expression that, in ancient Athens, could be heard in speeches in a public forum. Today we find it in excellent newspaper editorials, thoughtful magazine articles, and other effective statements of a writer's view.

Argument is one of the four varieties of prose writing — along with narration, description, and exposition — already familiar to you. (Exposition is that sort of writing whose several methods have been set forth in Chapters 3 through 9.) The method of argument is to make an appeal to reason or feelings (or both).

The end of argument is *persuasion*: to move readers to accept the writer's view — even to act on it.

Without being aware that we follow any special method, we try daily to persuade our listeners — including ourselves. We talk ourselves into doing something ("Time for that visit to the dentist. Don't want to get cavities, right?"); we try to convince mate or roommate to buy a new rug ("Look at this dump!"). A lawyer presents one side of a case; a marketing executive urges the launching of a new product; a candidate appeals to voters to go to the polls. Advertisers bombard us with their urgings. Ministers, priests, and rabbis implore us to lead better lives. Small wonder, then, that to learn how to persuade — and when necessary, how to resist persuasion — may be among the most useful skills you can acquire.

How do you write an argument? You set forth an assertion (sometimes called a *proposition*): a statement of what you believe, and sometimes, too, a course of action you recommend. Usually, but not always, you make such an assertion at the beginning of your essay: "Welfare funds need to be trimmed from our state budget," or, "To cut back welfare funds now would be a mistake."

In argument, you will probably draw on the methods of writing you have previously learned. You might give *examples* of wasteful welfare spending, or of areas where welfare funds are needed. You might foresee the probable *effects* of cutting welfare programs or retaining them. You might *compare and contrast* one course of action with the other. You might use *narration* to tell a pointed anecdote; you might *describe* (whether you are for or against the funding) certain welfare recipients and their lives. You might employ several methods in one argument.

When we say that an argument appeals to the reason *or* to the emotions of a reader, we make only a rough distinction between the two. In fact, no argument is ever purely reasonable or purely emotional, for people can't be divided neatly into thinking parts and feeling parts. A kind of argument that *seems* almost wholly rational — certainly it tries hard to be — is a newspaper column of advice to investors. On the basis of evidence and reasoning, the columnist urges the purchase of stocks and commodities; but probably investors and their advisors are, like everyone else, subject to excitement and given to fear and greed. Perhaps the nearest thing to purely emotional argument is found in advertising that seeks to arouse our desires to buy a new car or a roll-on deodorant — not to awaken our minds. But generally, the arguments we read will mingle thought and feelings, in greater or lesser proportion. The most forcefully written appeal to reason is the one that supports an assertion the writer deeply cares about; and in the most effective appeal to emotion the writer doesn't just froth wildly and passionately, but makes sense and considers evidence. Though H. L. Mencken's "The Penalty of Death" (in this chapter) is written with feeling and touches the feelings of an audience, it is mainly a reasoned argument. In Martin Luther King's inspiring "I Have a Dream" (also in this chapter), the heart of the hearer matters more than the mind.

Sometimes the writer of an appeal to reason will follow a formal method of *logic*: the science of orderly thinking. We find such a method in a *syllogism*, a three-step form of reasoning:

> All men are mortal.
> Socrates is a man.
> Therefore, Socrates is mortal.

The first statement is the *major premise*, the second the *minor premise*, and the third the *conclusion*. Few people today argue in this strict, three-part form; yet many writers argue by using the thinking behind the syllogism — *deductive reasoning*. Beginning with a statement of truth, this kind of logic moves to a statement of truth about an individual or particular. If you observe that conservative Republicans desire less government regulation of business, that William F. Buckley is a conservative Republican, and conclude that Buckley may be expected to desire less government regulation of business, then you employ deductive reasoning. If, on the other hand, you were to interview Buckley and a hundred other conservative Republicans, find that they were unanimous in their views, and then conclude that conservative Republicans favor less government regulation of business, you would be using the opposite method: *inductive reason-*

ing. Inductive reasoning is essential to the method of scientists, who collect many observations of individuals and then venture a general statement that applies to them all. Writing in *Zen and the Art of Motorcycle Maintenance*, Robert M. Pirsig gives examples of deductive and inductive reasoning:

> If the cycle goes over a bump and the engine misfires, and then goes over another bump and the engine misfires, and then goes over another bump and the engine misfires, and then goes over a long smooth stretch of road and there is no misfiring, and then goes over a fourth bump and the engine misfires again, one can logically conclude that the misfiring is caused by the bumps. That is induction: reasoning from particular experiences to general truths.
>
> Deductive inferences do the reverse. They start with general knowledge and predict a specific observation. For example if, from reading the hierarchy of facts about the machine, the mechanic knows the horn of the cycle is powered exclusively by electricity from the battery, then he can logically infer that if the battery is dead the horn will not work. That is deduction.[1]

Either method of reasoning is only as accurate as the observations on which it is based. In arguments we read or hear, we often meet logical fallacies, or errors of reasoning that lead to the wrong conclusions. (Some of these are listed and explained in the back of this book; see *Logical Fallacies* in Useful Terms.)

Often, in appealing to reason, a writer brings readers new facts. In appealing to emotion, however, the writer sometimes just restates what the readers already know well. Editorials in publications for special audiences (members of ethnic groups or religious denominations, also people whose political views are far to the left or right), tend to contain few factual surprises for their subscribers, who presumably read to be reassured or reinspired. In spoken discourse, this kind of appeal to emotion may be heard in the commencement day speech or the Fourth of July oration; or, to give an impressive example, in Dr. King's speech "I Have a Dream." This speech does not tell its audience

---

[1] *Zen and the Art of Motorcycle Maintenance* (New York: William Morrow, 1974), p. 107.

anything new to them, for the listeners were mostly blacks disappointed in the American dream. Dr. King appeals not primarily to reason, but to emotions — and to the willingness of his audience to be inspired.

Emotional argument can, of course, be cynical manipulation. It can entail selling a sucker a bill of shoddy goods by appealing to pride ("Don't you want the best for your children?") in the fashion of unscrupulous advertisers, con artists, and hard-sell pushers. But argument can stir readers to constructive action by fair means, recognizing that we are not intellectual robots, but creatures with feelings, and that our feelings matter. Indeed, sometimes the readers' feelings must be engaged, or they may reply to an argument, "True, but who cares?" Argument, when it is effective, makes us feel that the writer's views must also be our own.

An appeal to emotion makes its case in definite, concrete, and memorable terms. It may proceed by using clear and colorful examples, description, metaphor and analogy, narrative. Concreteness of diction, including figures of speech, marks the writing of Revolutionary War patriot Thomas Paine. Attempting to persuade his countrymen to rise against the King, Paine begins his pamphlet *The Crisis*:

> These are the times that try men's souls. The summer
> soldier and the sunshine patriot will, in this crisis, shrink
> from the service of their countrymen. . . . Tyranny, like Hell,
> is not easily conquered.

Paine's phrase "the summer soldier and the sunshine patriot" is something more than mere name-calling. By splendid metaphors the pamphleteer points to a recognizable form of hypocrisy: some soldiers and patriots are faithful to their cause only when the cause is easy to uphold. Paine selects words that carry powerful suggestions: *tyranny, Hell*. Writers whose purpose is to sway an audience are fond of such language. To take an example of a different kind, a writer of advertising for a restaurant, in trying to describe the Wednesday night special so that the reader's mouth waters, may write — choosing words rich in favorable connotations — "Sizzling prime cut of charcoal-broiled sirloin garnished with fresh sautéed mushrooms." (A flat, objective description might instead read: "U.S. choice grade sirloin steak with fried mushrooms.") At the other extreme, a different writer, perhaps arguing in favor of vegetarianism, might describe the same meal as "hot slab of dead steer buried under fungus." (That description, however, might seem to the reader a little too heavily biased.)

Recklessly employed, such strongly connotative words may only thwart the writer's appeal. *Name-calling* (or *mud-slinging*) is often self-defeating. In this sort of verbal abuse, one's opponents become "mere pantywaist liberals and stooges of Moscow," or "rabid gold bugs and royalists-come-lately" (to give examples of unfair names for political thinkers on the left and on the right). Any cause the writer opposes is defined in emotionally loaded terms. Prison reform becomes "the mollycoddling of cutthroats and child-molesters," and proposed equal rights legislation "the flinging open of ladies' rest rooms to Peeping Toms." But the reader who hasn't completely dispensed with reason will not be swayed.

The responsible writer, to be sure, will gladly argue with the aid of richly connotative words. Consider the varied (and variously useful) meanings, for instance, of the words *idea, concept,* and *notion*. A writer might choose any one of them to refer to a thought, but the thought would sound more impressive if called an idea. Calling it a concept would glorify it: a concept, according to William Safire, "is an idea with big ideas." To downgrade the thought, the writer might call it a notion — a word conveying suggestions of bargain stores with "notions counters." Different words can't help having sharply different connotations, as every sensitive writer is aware.

Still another resource in argument is *ethical appeal*: impressing your reader that you are a well-informed person of good will, good sense, and good moral character — therefore, to be believed. You make such an appeal mainly by reasoning carefully, collecting ample evidence, and writing well. You can also cite or quote respected authorities.

In argument, you do not prove your assertion in the same irrefutable way that a chemist can prove that hydrogen will burn. If you assert, "The cost of living index should be recalculated because it now gives disproportionate weight to housing costs," that is not the kind of assertion that is either true or false. Argument exists precisely because it deals with matters about which more than one opinion is possible. When you write an argument, you try to help your reader behold and understand just one open-eyed and open-minded view of reality.

• THE PROCESS •

In writing an argument, your main concern is to maintain an assertion you believe. You may find such an assertion by thinking and feeling, by scanning a newspaper, by listening to a discussion of some problem or controversy.

State clearly, if possible at the beginning of your essay, the assertion you intend to defend. If you like, you can explain why it is worth upholding, showing, perhaps, that it concerns many of your readers, perhaps the whole country. (You may wish to set forth at the start of your paper some solution or course of action; or you may prefer to save this element for your conclusion.)

Introduce your least important point first and build in a crescendo to the strongest point you have. This structure will lend emphasis to your essay, and perhaps make your chain of ideas more persuasive as the reader continues to follow it.

For every point, give evidence: facts, figures, or observations. If you introduce statistics, make sure that they are up-to-date and fairly represented. In an essay advocating a law against smoking, it would be unfair to declare that "In Pottsville, Illinois, last year, 50 percent of all deaths were caused by lung cancer," if only two people died in Pottsville last year — one of them struck by a car.

Provided you can face potential criticisms fairly, and give your critics due credit, you might want to recognize the objections you expect your assertion will meet. This is the strategy H. L. Mencken uses in "The Penalty of Death," and he introduces it in his essay near the beginning.

In your conclusion, briefly restate your basic assertion, if possible in a fresh, pointed way. (For examples, see the concluding sentences in the essays in this chapter by Ellen Goodman and William F. Buckley.) In emotionally persuasive writing, you will probably want to end in one final, strong appeal. (See "I Have a Dream.")

Finally, don't forget the power of humor in argument. You don't have to crack gratuitous jokes, but there is often an advantage in having a reader or listener who laughs on your side. When Abraham Lincoln debated Stephen Douglas, he triumphed in his reply to Douglas's snide remark that Lincoln had once been a bartender. "I have long since quit my side of the bar," Lincoln declared, "while Mr. Douglas clings to his as tenaciously as ever."

Here are two short examples of argument and persuasion. In the first paragraph, the writer tries mainly to appeal to your reason, and in the second, to your feelings. Does he at all succeed?

· ARGUMENT AND PERSUASION ·
· IN TWO PARAGRAPHS ·

In the offices of public television these days, nervousness prevails. Congress has slashed by twenty percent the 1983 budget for the Public Broadcasting System; Exxon and other once-generous corporations have pared down their gift lists; and now the very audience on whom the 277 PBS stations depend for contributions — educated people with high incomes — is being courted by cable television with promises of Broadway plays and live ballet. Should PBS expire, some believe, the nation will suffer no great loss. Won't commercial networks pick up *Nova, Great Performances,* and other relatively popular public television programs? Let those who don't like commercials subscribe to pay TV. In defense of PBS, we might argue that a *Sesame Street* packed with cereal commercials would be a less effective teaching instrument. Besides, for millions of Americans, cable TV is priced out of reach. In most areas, installation costs currently run from $30 to $60, followed by monthly viewing charges. But, skeptics retort, if low-income viewers must keep watching commercial television, what will change? PBS is elitist. Its audience contains less than two percent of the populace. Although it may be elitist to claim that no taxi driver watches opera or Shake-spearean plays on PBS, public television is strongly oriented toward affluent upper middlebrows. Yet, that this orientation need be permanent is questionable.

If public television is to serve in the future those whom it now serves only in token fashion — working people, the old, adolescents, inner-city black and Hispanic adults — it will need to increase both the variety and the quantity of its offer-ings. How? ask the skeptics. By pumping in more government money? The result will be pork barreling. Give PBS producers fatter funding and soon their office rugs will be as deep as those in the executive suites of ABC, NBC, and CBS. This objection, however, seems trivial. So little government money is spent on any of the arts today that it seems miserly to deny PBS a slightly increased measure of support. The power of the cathode tube to nourish or starve the mind is undeniable. Let PBS be subsidized as generously as museums and parks, public schools, state colleges. Let it be supported even more generously, for most of us spend more hours with television. If the cost seems high, we have only to ponder the alternative. It is to sentence lower-income viewers to keep watching whatever will pry their slim paychecks away from them. Should public television fold, it is safe to predict, then spot commercials, bandit chases, and witless situation com-edies will smother to intellectual death an audience unable to escape from them.

Comment. The first of these paragraphs (the one that primarily appeals to reason) is relatively calm and objective. It gives a few general facts about the current plight of public televi-sion; cites arguments against worrying over this plight; and of-fers arguments in rebuttal. In the second paragraph (the one that primarily appeals to feelings), the tone becomes more emo-tional — both in the skeptics' charges (including words loaded with unfavorable connotations — *pork barreling, fatter* —and the reference to deep office rugs, suggesting lavish spending) and in the counterarguments. The rhetorical device of parallelism is invoked in the two sentences that begin "Let . . . ," and the conclusion pulls out the emotional restraints — especially with the phrase "smother to intellectual death." The writer tries to arouse the sympathies of the reader toward the underprivileged, who (he argues) will be the greatest losers if public television expires. The writer might have introduced more facts in his second paragraph. The contention that few government funds are spent on the arts, for instance, could have been bolstered with the report that about one-fortieth of one percent of the previous federal budget was devoted to the arts. But the main purpose of the second paragraph is to arouse an emotional response. The paragraph is reasonable, but not (like paragraph one) a factual, reasoned argument.

· Ellen Goodman ·

ELLEN GOODMAN was born in Brookline, Massachusetts, in 1941. After her graduation from Radcliffe in 1963, she worked as a reporter-researcher for *Newsweek*; and from 1965 to 1971 she was a reporter for the Detroit *Free Press*. She joined the Boston *Globe* as a full-time columnist in 1971, and since 1976 her column has been syndicated to more than 200 newspapers across the country. Goodman has earned many honors, among them the 1980 Pulitzer Prize for distinguished commentary. She is the author of *Turning Points* (1979), a study of life changes culled from interviews with over a hundred and fifty people. She has collected her essays in *Close to Home* (1979) and *At Large* (1981).

Steering Clear of the One True Course

"Steering Clear of the One True Course" is an essay from *Close to Home*. In it, with her usual good sense, Ellen Goodman takes a look at the kind of education whose sole purpose is to guide students into safe, big-money careers. Taking time to smell the flowers along the way, she argues, is not only enjoyable but, in the end, practical.

1   This is the time of year when 2.7 million young Americans can be found chewing anxiously on crocuses while waiting for proof of their acceptability to come fluttering through the mails from some university or other.

2   Yes, it's college acceptance season, a time to stir the hearts of all those parents contemplating remortgaging their homes, and all those children figuring out a package of loans and scholarships that will introduce them to the glories of deficit financing from now until 1992.

3   But while they are all riveted on getting in, what are they getting into?

The late philosopher, Alan Watts — a man far too sane to   4
be considered anything but silly — once suggested a new college
entrance exam. Instead of multiple-choice questions on the difference between synonyms and antonyms, he thought the applicants should write a twenty-page paper on "What They
Want." What they want from college. What they want from life.
These essays, he suggested, should be turned over to a tutor. He
would examine the applicants closely. Do they know the side effects, the costs, the ramifications of "it"?

At no time would this "test" be more useful than now, with   5
the crop of college students who are in the main so "practical,"
so sensible, so downright flat-footed about the whole thing.

What so many students today "want" out of college is   6
graduate school. Or, alternatively, a Good Job. Most of them
seem to be majoring in initials — embarked on a lock-step
course to gain an M.D., a Ph.D., or a V.P.

This is what is called being "hardheaded about life," looking   7
at the "bottom line" and making sure that college is "cost-
effective." In accounting terms, they say, a liberal arts degree
and 25 cents will get you a cup of coffee.

I have nothing against earning a living, but using college as   8
an employment agency seems like the ultimate extravagance to
me. Rather than being "sensible," this notion is motivated by
fear — fear of the future — and by a profound misconception
that the best armament against uncertainty is a life plan that
reads like a Piece of the Rock.

Colleges are urged to "get on with the business of life," as if   9
life were a business, and thousands of families will break the
bank in order to prepare their children for a future that is
myopically limited to the day after graduation. It's short-term
insurance of the most expensive kind.

If I were one of Alan Watts's tutors (and I am eminently   10
qualified, having planned my future once and for all half a
dozen times), I'd point out that majoring in what Gail Sheehy
labeled "The One True Course" will lead inexorably to a crash.

They can get there by following in the footsteps of pro-   11
fessors who are in one stage or other of the midlife crisis, or of
parents who are currently feeling locked in. They are being ex-

pensively prepared for their own middle-aged discontent, and may end up as the next generation of consumers for self-help books, divorce lawyers and employment agencies specializing in second careers.

The only adults I know who are still merrily marching along 12 their one true course are boring, insensitive or lucky. The rest of us are survivors, survivors of crises, reverses, life changes. What you need to survive is a sense of humor, some joy, flexibility and a philosophy to hang your hat on.

In that case, isn't it at least as practical a thing to teach 13 twenty-year-olds the management of personal transitions as to teach them the management of a department store? Doesn't liberal arts go well with a cup of coffee?

Why not something as sensible as electives in Flexibility 14 209, Coping 14B (given alternately with Crisis Survival 14A) and Change 143?

They might be antidotes to the sort of practicality that 15 threatens to turn us all into hardheads like the father in *Goodbye Columbus*. He's the one, you may remember, who shrieked at his son, "What's the matter with you? Four years of college and you can't load a truck!"

• QUESTIONS ON MEANING AND PURPOSE •

1. Against what is Ellen Goodman arguing? What course does she favor instead?
2. Consider the merits of the college entrance examination proposed by Alan Watts (paragraph 4). Would it be practicable?
3. How seriously are we to take Goodman's suggestions in paragraph 14? Give reasons for your answer.
4. What reasons does Goodman give for the beliefs she holds? In supporting her assertions with very few facts, to what extent does she weaken her position? In what areas might she have strengthened it with more evidence? (See *Evidence* in Useful Terms.)
5. Which of the points she raises do you find most persuasive? By what exactly are you persuaded? Reasoning? Evidence?

· QUESTIONS ON WRITING STRATEGY ·

1. Are the majority of Ellen Goodman's points in favor of something or against something? What is the overall effect of her essay? (See *Effect* in Useful Terms.)
2. When trying to appeal to emotion, what advantages are there in writing in the first person? (See *Person* in Useful Terms.)
3. "Steering Clear of the One True Course" was originally written as a newspaper column. What constraints or limitations does such a form impose upon a writer? How well has Goodman triumphed over them?

· QUESTIONS ON LANGUAGE ·
· AND VOCABULARY ·

1. What does the phrase "chewing anxiously on crocuses" (paragraph 1) contribute to Goodman's beginning?
2. What is *deficit financing* (paragraph 2)?
3. Be sure you know the meanings of these words: ramifications (paragraph 4); myopically (9); inexorably (10).
4. What does Goodman mean by "a Piece of the Rock" (paragraph 8)?
5. In view of the fact that Goodman wrote this selection as a newspaper column, how appropriate is her diction? (See *Diction* in Useful Terms.)

· SUGGESTIONS FOR WRITING ·

1. Write an essay in which you play devil's advocate to Ellen Goodman and argue in favor of career training in college, as opposed to a broader education.
2. Write a brief argument in favor of some educational choice you have made. Set forth, as persuasively as you can, your reasons for making it.

· H. L. Mencken ·

HENRY LOUIS MENCKEN (1880–1956) was a native of Baltimore, where for four decades he worked as newspaper reporter, editor, and columnist. In the 1920s, his boisterous, cynical observations on American life, appearing regularly in *The Smart Set* and later in *The American Mercury* (which he founded and edited), made him probably the most widely quoted writer in the country. Mencken leveled blasts at pomp, hypocrisy, and the middle classes (whom he labeled "the booboisie"). As editor and literary critic, he championed Sinclair Lewis, Theodore Dreiser, and other realistic writers. In 1933, when Mencken's attempts to laugh off the Depression began to ring hollow, his magazine died. He then devoted himself to revising and supplementing *The American Language* (fourth edition, 1948), a learned and highly entertaining survey of a nation's speech habits and vocabulary. Two dozen of Mencken's books are now in print, including *A Mencken Chrestomathy* (1949), a representative selection of his best writings of various kinds; and *A Choice of Days* (1980), a selection from his memoirs.

The Penalty of Death

Above all, Mencken is a humorist whose thought has a serious core. He argues by first making the reader's jaw drop, then inducing a laugh, and finally causing the reader to ponder, "Hmmmm — what if he's right?" The following still-controversial essay, from *Prejudices, Fifth Series* (1926), shows Mencken the persuader in top form. His work is enjoying a revival of attention nowadays — not so much for his ideas as for his style. No writer is better at swinging from ornate and abstract words to salty and concrete ones, at tossing a metaphor that makes you smile even as it kicks in your teeth.

Of the arguments against capital punishment that issue   1
from uplifters, two are commonly heard most often, to wit:

1. That hanging a man (or frying him or gassing him) is a dreadful business, degrading to those who have to do it and revolting to those who have to witness it.
2. That it is useless, for it does not deter others from the same crime.

The first of these arguments, it seems to me, is plainly too weak to need serious refutation. All it says, in brief, is that the work of the hangman is unpleasant. Granted. But suppose it is? It may be quite necessary to society for all that. There are, indeed, many other jobs that are unpleasant, and yet no one thinks of abolishing them — that of the plumber, that of the soldier, that of the garbage-man, that of the priest hearing confessions, that of the sand-hog, and so on. Moreover, what evidence is there that any actual hangman complains of his work? I have heard none. On the contrary, I have known many who delighted in their ancient art, and practiced it proudly.

In the second argument of the abolitionists there is rather more force, but even here, I believe, the ground under them is shaky. Their fundamental error consists in assuming that the whole aim of punishing criminals is to deter other (potential) criminals — that we hang or electrocute A simply in order to so alarm B that he will not kill C. This, I believe, is an assumption which confuses a part with the whole. Deterrence, obviously, is *one* of the aims of punishment, but it is surely not the only one. On the contrary, there are at least a half dozen, and some are probably quite as important. At least one of them, practically considered, is *more* important. Commonly, it is described as revenge, but revenge is really not the word for it. I borrow a better term from the late Aristotle: *katharsis*. *Katharsis*, so used, means a salubrious discharge of emotions, a healthy letting off of steam. A school-boy, disliking his teacher, deposits a tack upon the pedagogical chair; the teacher jumps and the boy laughs. This is *katharsis*. What I contend is that one of the prime objects of all judicial punishments is to afford the same grateful relief (*a*) to the immediate victims of the criminal punished, and (*b*) to the general body of moral and timorous men.

These persons, and particularly the first group, are concerned only indirectly with deterring other criminals. The thing they crave primarily is the satisfaction of seeing the criminal actually before them suffer as he made them suffer. What they want is the peace of mind that goes with the feeling that accounts are squared. Until they get that satisfaction they are in a state of emotional tension, and hence unhappy. The instant they get it they are comfortable. I do not argue that this yearning is noble; I simply argue that it is almost universal among human beings. In the face of injuries that are unimportant and can be borne without damage it may yield to higher impulses; that is to say, it may yield to what is called Christian charity. But when the injury is serious Christianity is adjourned, and even saints reach for their sidearms. It is plainly asking too much of human nature to expect it to conquer so natural an impulse. A keeps a store and has a bookkeeper, B. B steals $700, employs it in playing at dice or bingo, and is cleaned out. What is A to do? Let B go? If he does so he will be unable to sleep at night. The sense of injury, of injustice, of frustration will haunt him like pruritus. So he turns B over to the police, and they hustle B to prison. Thereafter A can sleep. More, he has pleasant dreams. He pictures B chained to the wall of a dungeon a hundred feet underground, devoured by rats and scorpions. It is so agreeable that it makes him forget his $700. He has got his *katharsis*.

The same thing precisely takes place on a larger scale when there is a crime which destroys a whole community's sense of security. Every law-abiding citizen feels menaced and frustrated until the criminals have been struck down — until the communal capacity to get even with them, and more than even, has been dramatically demonstrated. Here, manifestly, the business of deterring others is no more than an afterthought. The main thing is to destroy the concrete scoundrels whose act has alarmed everyone, and thus made everyone unhappy. Until they are brought to book that unhappiness continues; when the law has been executed upon them there is a sigh of relief. In other words, there is *katharsis*.

I know of no public demand for the death penalty for ordinary crimes, even for ordinary homicides. Its infliction would shock all men of normal decency of feeling. But for crimes involving the deliberate and inexcusable taking of human life, by men openly defiant of all civilized order — for such crimes it seems, to nine men out of ten, a just and proper punishment. Any lesser penalty leaves them feeling that the criminal has got the better of society — that he is free to add insult to injury by laughing. That feeling can be dissipated only by a recourse to *katharsis*, the invention of the aforesaid Aristotle. It is more effectively and economically achieved, as human nature now is, by wafting the criminal to realms of bliss.

The real objection to capital punishment doesn't lie against   7
the actual extermination of the condemned, but against our brutal American habit of putting it off so long. After all, every one of us must die soon or late, and a murderer, it must be assumed, is one who makes that sad fact the cornerstone of his metaphysic. But it is one thing to die, and quite another thing to lie for long months and even years under the shadow of death. No sane man would choose such a finish. All of us, despite the Prayer Book, long for a swift and unexpected end. Unhappily, a murderer, under the irrational American system, is tortured for what, to him, must seem a whole series of eternities. For months on end he sits in prison while his lawyers carry on their idiotic buffoonery with writs, injunctions, mandamuses, and appeals. In order to get his money (or that of his friends) they have to feed him with hope. Now and then, by the imbecility of a judge or some trick of juridic science, they actually justify it. But let us say that, his money all gone, they finally throw up their hands. Their client is now ready for the rope or the chair. But he must still wait for months before it fetches him.

That wait, I believe, is horribly cruel. I have seen more than '   8
one man sitting in the death-house, and I don't want to see any more. Worse, it is wholly useless. Why should he wait at all? Why not hang him the day after the last court dissipates his last hope? Why torture him as not even cannibals would torture their victims? The common answer is that he must have time to make his peace with God. But how long does that take? It may be accomplished, I believe, in two hours quite as comfortably as in two years. There are, indeed, no temporal limitations upon God. He could forgive a whole herd of murderers in a millionth of a second. More, it has been done.

• QUESTIONS ON MEANING AND PURPOSE •

1. Identify Mencken's three reasons for his support of capital punishment. Do all three seem to you equally strong?
2. In paragraph 3, Mencken asserts that there are at least half a dozen reasons for punishing offenders. In his essay, he mentions two, deterrence and revenge. What others can you supply?
3. For which class of offenders does Mencken advocate the death penalty?
4. How do you react to Mencken's final statement? What does it contribute to his purpose?

• QUESTIONS ON WRITING STRATEGY •

1. How would you characterize Mencken's humor? Point to examples of it. In the light of his grim subject, do you find it funny?
2. In his first paragraph, Mencken pares his subject down to manageable size. What techniques does he employ for this purpose?
3. In paragraph 2, Mencken draws an analogy between the executioner's job and other jobs that are "unpleasant." How effective is this device? What flaw do you see in Mencken's argument by analogy? (See *Logical Fallacies* in Useful Terms.)
4. At the start of paragraph 7, Mencken shifts his stance from concern for the victims of crime to concern for the victims of life imprisonment. Does the shift help or weaken the effectiveness of his earlier justification for capital punishment?
5. Do you think the author expects his audience to agree with him? At what points does he seem to recognize the fact that some readers may see things differently?

• QUESTIONS ON LANGUAGE •
• AND VOCABULARY •

1. Mencken opens his argument by referring to those who reject capital punishment as "uplifters." What connotations does that word have for you? (See *Connotation and Denotation* in Useful Terms.) Does the use of this "loaded" word strengthen or weaken Mencken's position? Explain.
2. Be sure you know the meanings of the following words: refutation, sand-hog (paragraph 2); salubrious, pedagogical, timorous (3); pruritus (4); wafting (6); mandamuses, juridic (7).

3. What emotional overtones can you detect in Mencken's reference to the hangman's job as an "ancient art" (paragraph 2)?
4. What does Mencken's argument gain from his substitution of the word "katharsis" for "revenge"?

• SUGGESTIONS FOR WRITING •

1. Write a paper in which you suggest one reform in current methods of apprehending, trying, and sentencing criminals. Supply evidence to persuade a reader that your idea would improve the system.
2. Write an essay in which you refute Mencken's argument; or, take Mencken's side but use different arguments to support your point of view. Be sure to defend your stance, point by point.

· William F. Buckley, Jr. ·

WILLIAM FRANK BUCKLEY, JR., was born in 1925, the son of a millionaire. Soon after his graduation from Yale he wrote *God and Man at Yale* (1951), a memoir with a bias in conservative political values and traditional Christian principles. With the publication of *McCarthy and His Enemies* (1954), a defense of the late Senator Joseph McCarthy and his crusade against communists, Buckley and his co-author L. Brent Bozell infuriated liberals. He has continued to outrage them ever since, in many other books (including *Up from Liberalism*, 1959), in a syndicated newspaper column, and in the conservatively oriented magazine he founded and still edits, *The National Review.* A man of a certain wry charm, Buckley has been a successful television talk-show host on the program *Firing Line.* In 1965 he ran for mayor of New York as a candidate of the Conservative Party. Lately he has taken to writing novels of espionage and adventure, including *Stained Glass* (1978).

Why Don't We Complain?

Most people, riding in an overheated commuter train, would perspire quietly. For Buckley, this excess of warmth sparks an indignant essay in which he takes to task both himself and his fellow Americans. Does the essay appeal mainly to reason or to emotion? And what would happen if everyone were to do as Buckley urges?

It was the very last coach and the only empty seat on the entire train, so there was no turning back. The problem was to breathe. Outside, the temperature was below freezing. Inside the railroad car the temperature must have been about 85 degrees. I took off my overcoat, and a few minutes later my jacket, and noticed that the car was flecked with the white shirts of the passengers. I soon found my hand moving to loosen my tie. From one end of the car to the other, as we rattled through Westchester County, we sweated; but we did not moan.

I watched the train conductor appear at the head of the   2
car. "Tickets, all tickets, please!" In a more virile age, I thought,
the passengers would seize the conductor and strap him down
on a seat over the radiator to share the fate of his patrons. He
shuffled down the aisle, picking up tickets, punching commuta-
tion cards. *No one addressed a word to him.* He approached my
seat, and I drew a deep breath of resolution. "Conductor," I began with a considerable edge to my voice. . . . Instantly the
doleful eyes of my seatmate turned tiredly from his newspaper
to fix me with a resentful stare: what question could be so important as to justify my sibilant intrusion into his stupor? I was
shaken by those eyes. I am incapable of making a discreet fuss,
so I mumbled a question about what time were we due in Stam-
ford (I didn't even ask whether it would be before or after dehy-
dration could be expected to set in), got my reply, and went
back to my newspaper and to wiping my brow.

The conductor had nonchalantly walked down the gauntlet   3
of eighty sweating American freemen, and not one of them had
asked him to explain why the passengers in that car had been
consigned to suffer. There is nothing to be done when the temperature *outdoors* is 85 degrees, and indoors the air conditioner
has broken down; obviously when that happens there is nothing to do, except perhaps curse the day that one was born. But
when the temperature outdoors is below freezing, it takes a positive act of will on somebody's part to set the temperature *indoors* at 85. Somewhere a valve was turned too far, a furnace
overstocked, a thermostat maladjusted: something that could
easily be remedied by turning off the heat and allowing the
great outdoors to come indoors. All this is so obvious. What is
not obvious is what has happened to the American people.

It isn't just the commuters, whom we have come to visualize   4
as a supine breed who have got on to the trick of suspending
their sensory faculties twice a day while they submit to the
creeping dissolution of the railroad industry. It isn't just they
who have given up trying to rectify irrational vexations. It is the
American people everywhere.

A few weeks ago at a large movie theatre I turned to my wife   5
and said, "The picture is out of focus." "Be quiet," she
answered. I obeyed. But a few minutes later I raised the point

again, with mounting impatience. "It will be all right in a minute," she said apprehensively. (She would rather lose her eyesight than be around when I make one of my infrequent scenes.) I waited. It was *just* out of focus — not glaringly out, but out. My vision is 20-20, and I assume that is the vision, adjusted, of most people in the movie house. So, after hectoring my wife throughout the first reel, I finally prevailed upon her to admit that it *was* off, and very annoying. We then settled down, coming to rest on the presumption that: a) someone connected with the management of the theatre must soon notice the blur and make the correction; or b) that someone seated near the rear of the house would make the complaint in behalf of those of us up front; or c) that — any minute now — the entire house would explode into catcalls and foot stamping, calling dramatic attention to the irksome distortion.

What happened was nothing. The movie ended, as it had begun *just* out of focus, and as we trooped out, we stretched our faces in a variety of contortions to accustom the eye to the shock of normal focus.

I think it is safe to say that everybody suffered on that occasion. And I think it is safe to assume that everyone was expecting someone else to take the initiative in going back to speak to the manager. And it is probably true even that if we had supposed the movie would run right through the blurred image, someone surely would have summoned up the purposive indignation to get up out of his seat and file his complaint.

But notice that no one did. And the reason no one did is because we are all increasingly anxious in America to be unobtrusive, we are reluctant to make our voices heard, hesitant about claiming our rights; we are afraid that our cause is unjust, or that if it is not unjust, that it is ambiguous; or if not even that, that it is too trivial to justify the horrors of a confrontation with Authority; we will sit in an oven or endure a racking headache before undertaking a head-on, I'm-here-to-tell-you complaint. That tendency to passive compliance, to a heedless endurance, is something to keep one's eyes on — in sharp focus.

I myself can occasionally summon the courage to complain, but I cannot, as I have intimated, complain softly. My own instinct is so strong to let the thing ride, to forget about it — to

6

7

8

9

expect that someone will take the matter up, when the grievance is collective, in my behalf — that it is only when the provocation is at a very special key, whose vibrations touch
simultaneously a complexus of nerves, allergies, and passions,
that I catch fire and find the reserves of courage and assertiveness to speak up. When that happens, I get quite carried
away. My blood gets hot, my brow wet, I become unbearably
and unconscionably sarcastic and bellicose; I am girded for a
total showdown.

Why should that be? Why could not I (or anyone else) on   10
that railroad coach have said simply to the conductor, "Sir" — I
take that back: that sounds sarcastic — "Conductor, would you
be good enough to turn down the heat? I am extremely hot. In
fact, I tend to get hot every time the temperature reaches 85
degr — " Strike that last sentence. Just end it with the simple
statement that you are extremely hot, and let the conductor infer the cause.

Every New Year's Eve I resolve to do something about the   11
Milquetoast in me and vow to speak up, calmly, for my rights,
and for the betterment of our society, on every appropriate occasion. Entering last New Year's Eve I was fortified in my
resolve because that morning at breakfast I had had to ask the
waitress three times for a glass of milk. She finally brought it —
after I had finished my eggs, which is when I don't want it any
more. I did not have the manliness to order her to take the milk
back, but settled instead for a cowardly sulk, and ostentatiously
refused to drink the milk — though I later paid for it — rather
than state plainly to the hostess, as I should have, why I had not
drunk it, and would not pay for it.

So by the time the New Year ushered out the Old, riding in   12
on my morning's indignation and stimulated by the gastric
juices of resolution that flow so faithfully on New Year's Eve, I
rendered my vow. Henceforward I would conquer my shyness,
my despicable disposition to supineness. I would speak out like a
man against the unnecessary annoyances of our time.

Forty-eight hours later, I was standing in line at the ski   13
repair store in Pico Peak, Vermont. All I needed, to get on with
my skiing, was the loan, for one minute, of a small screwdriver,

to tighten a loose binding. Behind the counter in the workshop were two men. One was industriously engaged in servicing the complicated requirements of a young lady at the head of the line, and obviously he would be tied up for quite a while. The other — "Jiggs," his workmate called him — was a middle-aged man, who sat in a chair puffing a pipe, exchanging small talk with his working partner. My pulse began its telltale acceleration. The minutes ticked on. I stared at the idle shopkeeper, hoping to shame him into action, but he was impervious to my telepathic reproof and continued his small talk with his friend, brazenly insensitive to the nervous demands of six good men who were raring to ski.

Suddenly my New Year's Eve resolution struck me. It was 14
now or never. I broke from my place in line and marched to the counter. I was going to control myself. I dug my nails into my palms. My effort was only partially successful.

"If you are not too busy," I said icily, "would you mind 15
handing me a screwdriver?"

Work stopped and everyone turned his eyes on me, and I 16
experienced that mortification I always feel when I am the center of centripetal shafts of curiosity, resentment, perplexity.

But the worst was yet to come. "I am sorry, sir," said Jiggs 17
deferentially, moving the pipe from his mouth. "I am not supposed to move. I have just had a heart attack." That was the signal for a great whirring noise that descended from heaven. We looked, stricken, out the window, and it appeared as though a cyclone had suddenly focused on the snowy courtyard between the shop and the ski lift. Suddenly a gigantic army helicopter materialized, and hovered down to a landing. Two men jumped out of the plane carrying a stretcher, tore into the ski shop, and lifted the shopkeeper onto the stretcher. Jiggs bade his companion goodby, was whisked out the door, into the plane, up to the heavens, down — we learned — to a near-by army hospital. I looked up manfully — into a score of man-eating eyes. I put the experience down as a reversal.

As I write this, on an airplane, I have run out of paper and 18
need to reach into my briefcase under my legs for more. I cannot do this until my empty lunch tray is removed from my lap. I

arrested the stewardess as she passed empty-handed down the aisle on the way to the kitchen to fetch the lunch trays for the passengers up forward who haven't been served yet. "Would you please take my tray?" "Just a *moment*, sir!" she said, and marched on sternly. Shall I tell her that since she is headed for the kitchen *anyway*, it could not delay the feeding of the other passengers by more than two seconds necessary to stash away my empty tray? Or remind her that not fifteen minutes ago she spoke unctuously into the loudspeaker the words undoubtedly devised by the airline's highly paid public relations counselor: "If there is anything I or Miss French can do for you to make your trip more enjoyable, *please* let us — " I have run out of paper.

I think the observable reluctance of the majority of Americans to assert themselves in minor matters is related to our increased sense of helplessness in an age of technology and centralized political and economic power. For generations, Americans who were too hot, or too cold, got up and did something about it. Now we call the plumber, or the electrician, or the furnace man. The habit of looking after our own needs obviously had something to do with the assertiveness that characterized the American family familiar to readers of American literature. With the technification of life goes our direct responsibility for our material environment, and we are conditioned to adopt a position of helplessness not only as regards the broken air conditioner, but as regards the overheated train. It takes an expert to fix the former, but not the latter; yet these distinctions, as we withdraw into helplessness, tend to fade away. 19

Our notorious political apathy is a related phenomenon. Every year, whether the Republican or the Democratic Party is in office, more and more power drains away from the individual to feed vast reservoirs in far-off places; and we have less and less say about the shape of events which shape our future. From this alienation of personal power comes the sense of resignation with which we accept the political dispensations of a powerful government whose hold upon us continues to increase. 20

An editor of a national weekly news magazine told me a few years ago that as few as a dozen letters of protest against an 21 editorial stance of his magazine was enough to convene a pleni-potentiary meeting of the board of editors to review policy. "So few people complain, or make their voices heard," he explained to me, "that we assume a dozen letters represent the inar-ticulated views of thousands of readers." In the past ten years, he said, the volume of mail has noticeably decreased, even though the circulation of his magazine has risen.

When our voices are finally mute, when we have finally sup-pressed the natural instinct to complain, whether the vexation is trivial or grave, we shall have become automatons, incapable of feeling. When Premier Khrushchev first came to this country late in 1959 he was primed, we are informed, to experience the bitter resentment of the American people against his tyranny, against his persecutions, against the movement which is respon-sible for the great number of American deaths in Korea, for bil-lions in taxes every year, and for life everlasting on the brink of disaster; but Khrushchev was pleasantly surprised, and reported back to the Russian people that he had been met with over-whelming cordiality (read: apathy), except, to be sure, for "a few fascists who followed me around with their wretched posters, and should be horsewhipped."   22

I may be crazy, but I say there would have been lots more posters in a society where train temperatures in the dead of winter are not allowed to climb to 85 degrees without com-plaint.   23

• QUESTIONS ON MEANING AND PURPOSE •

1. How does Buckley account for his failure to complain to the train conductor? What reasons does he give for not taking action when he notices that the movie he is watching is out of focus?
2. Where does Buckley finally place the blame for the average American's reluctance to try to "rectify irrational vexations"?
3. By what means does the author bring his argument around to the subject of political apathy?
4. What thesis does Buckley attempt to support? Where in the essay does he state it? (See *Thesis* in Useful Terms.)

• QUESTIONS ON WRITING STRATEGY •

1. Buckley includes five stories in his essay, four of them taken from personal experience. Which support his thesis? (See *Thesis* in Useful Terms.)
2. In taking to task not only his fellow Americans but also himself, does Buckley strengthen or weaken his charge that, as a people, Americans do not complain enough?
3. Judging from the vocabulary displayed in this essay, would you say that Buckley is writing for a highly specialized audience, an educated but nonspecialized audience, or an uneducated general audience such as most newspaper readers?
4. As a whole, is Buckley's essay an example of appeal to emotion or of reasoned argument? Give evidence for your answer.

• QUESTIONS ON LANGUAGE •
• AND VOCABULARY •

1. Define the following words: virile, doleful, sibilant (paragraph 2); supine (4); hectoring (5); unobtrusive, ambiguous (8); intimated, unconscionably, bellicose (9); ostentatiously (11); despicable (12); impervious (13); mortification, centripetal (16); deferentially (17); unctuously (18); notorious, dispensations (20); plenipotentiary, inarticulated (21); automatons (22).
2. What does Buckley's use of the capital *A* in *Authority* (paragraph 8) contribute to the sentence in which he uses it?
3. What is Buckley talking about when he alludes to "the Milquetoast in me" (paragraph 11)? (Notice how well the name fits into the paragraph, with its emphasis on breakfast and a glass of milk.) (See *Allusion* in Useful Terms.)

• SUGGESTIONS FOR WRITING •

1. Write about an occasion when you should have registered a complaint and did not; or, recount what happened when you did in fact protest against one of "the unnecessary annoyances of our time."
2. Write a paper in which you take issue with any one of Buckley's ideas. Argue that he is wrong and you are right.
3. Think of some disturbing incident you have witnessed, or some annoying treatment you have received in a store or other public place, and write a letter of complaint to whoever you believe responsible. Be specific in your evidence, be temperate in your language, and be sure to put your letter in the mail.

· Martin Luther King, Jr. ·

MARTIN LUTHER KING, JR. (1929–1968) was born in Atlanta, the son of a Baptist minister, and was himself ordained in the same denomination. Stepping to the forefront of the civil rights movement in 1955, King led blacks in a boycott of segregated city buses in Montgomery, Alabama; became first president of the Southern Christian Leadership Conference; and staged sit-ins and mass marches that helped bring about the Civil Rights Act passed by Congress in 1964 and the Voting Rights Act of 1965. He received the Nobel Peace Prize in 1964. In view of the fact that King preached "nonviolent resistance," it is particularly ironic that he was himself the target of violence. He was stabbed in New York, pelted with stones in Chicago; his home in Montgomery was bombed; and at last in Memphis he was assassinated by a hidden sniper. On his tombstone near Atlanta's Ebenezer Baptist Church are these words from the spiritual he quotes at the conclusion of "I Have a Dream": "Free at last, free at last, thank God Almighty, I'm free at last." In nine states and the District of Columbia, Martin Luther King's birthday, January 15, is now an official holiday.

I Have a Dream

In Washington, D.C., on August 28, 1963, King's campaign of nonviolent resistance reached its historic climax. On that date, commemorating the centennial of Lincoln's Emancipation Proclamation freeing the slaves, King led the march of 200,000 persons, black and white, from the Washington Monument to the Lincoln Memorial. Before this throng, and to millions who watched on television, he delivered this unforgettable speech.

Five score years ago, a great American, in whose symbolic 1 shadow we stand, signed the Emancipation Proclamation. This momentous decree came as a great beacon light of hope to millions of Negro slaves who had been seared in the flames of withering injustice. It came as a joyous daybreak to end the long night of captivity.

But one hundred years later, we must face the tragic fact that the Negro is still not free. One hundred years later, the life of the Negro is still sadly crippled by the manacles of segregation and the chains of discrimination. One hundred years later, the Negro lives on a lonely island of poverty in the midst of a vast ocean of material prosperity. One hundred years later, the Negro is still languishing in the corners of American society and finds himself an exile in his own land. So we have come here today to dramatize an appalling condition.

In a sense we have come to our nation's capital to cash a check. When the architects of our republic wrote the magnificent words of the Constitution and the Declaration of Independence, they were signing a promissory note to which every American was to fall heir. This note was a promise that all men would be guaranteed the unalienable rights of life, liberty, and the pursuit of happiness.

It is obvious today that America has defaulted on this promissory note insofar as her citizens of color are concerned. Instead of honoring this sacred obligation, America has given the Negro people a bad check; a check which has come back marked "insufficient funds." But we refuse to believe that the bank of justice is bankrupt. We refuse to believe that there are insufficient funds in the great vaults of opportunity of this nation. So we have come to cash this check — a check that will give us upon demand the riches of freedom and the security of justice. We have also come to this hallowed spot to remind America of the fierce urgency of *now*. This is no time to engage in the luxury of cooling off or to take the tranquilizing drugs of gradualism. *Now* is the time to make real the promises of Democracy. *Now* is the time to rise from the dark and desolate valley of segregation to the sunlit path of racial justice. *Now* is the time to open the doors of opportunity to all of God's children. *Now* is the time to lift our nation from the quicksands of racial injustice to the solid rock of brotherhood.

It would be fatal for the nation to overlook the urgency of the moment and to underestimate the determination of the Negro. This sweltering summer of the Negro's legitimate discontent will not pass until there is an invigorating autumn of freedom and equality. 1963 is not an end, but a beginning. Those who hope that the Negro needed to blow off steam and will now be content will have a rude awakening if the nation returns to business as usual. There will be neither rest nor tranquillity in America until the Negro is granted his citizenship rights. The whirlwinds of revolt will continue to shake the foundations of our nation until the bright day of justice emerges.

But there is something that I must say to my people who 6 stand on the warm threshold which leads into the palace of justice. In the process of gaining our rightful place we must not be guilty of wrongful deeds. Let us not seek to satisfy our thirst for freedom by drinking from the cup of bitterness and hatred. We must forever conduct our struggle on the high plane of dignity and discipline. We must not allow our creative protest to degenerate into physical violence. Again and again we must rise to the majestic heights of meeting physical force with soul force. The marvelous new militancy which has engulfed the Negro community must not lead us to a distrust of all white people, for many of our white brothers, as evidenced by their presence here today, have come to realize that their destiny is tied up with our destiny and their freedom is inextricably bound to our freedom. We cannot walk alone.

And as we walk, we must make the pledge that we shall 7 march ahead. We cannot turn back. There are those who are asking the devotees of civil rights, "When will you be satisfied?" We can never be satisfied as long as the Negro is the victim of the unspeakable horrors of police brutality. We can never be satisfied as long as our bodies, heavy with the fatigue of travel, cannot gain lodging in the motels of the highways and the hotels of the cities. We cannot be satisfied as long as the Negro's basic mobility is from a smaller ghetto to a larger one. We can never be satisfied as long as a Negro in Mississippi cannot vote and a Negro in New York believes he has nothing for which to vote. No, no, we are not satisfied, and we will not be satisfied until justice rolls down like waters and righteousness like a mighty stream.

I am not unmindful that some of you have come here out of 8 great trials and tribulations. Some of you have come fresh from narrow jail cells. Some of you have come from areas where your quest for freedom left you battered by the storms of persecution and staggered by the winds of police brutality. You have been the veterans of creative suffering. Continue to work with the faith that unearned suffering is redemptive.

Go back to Mississippi, go back to Alabama, go back to South Carolina, go back to Georgia, go back to Louisiana, go back to the slums and ghettos of our northern cities, knowing that somehow this situation can and will be changed. Let us not wallow in the valley of despair. 9

I say to you today, my friends, that in spite of the difficulties and frustrations of the moment I still have a dream. It is a dream deeply rooted in the American dream. 10

I have a dream that one day this nation will rise up and live out the true meaning of its creed: "We hold these truths to be self-evident; that all men are created equal." 11

I have a dream that one day on the red hills of Georgia the sons of former slaves and the sons of former slaveowners will be able to sit down together at the table of brotherhood. 12

I have a dream that one day even the state of Mississippi, a desert state sweltering with the heat of injustice and oppression, will be transformed into an oasis of freedom and justice. 13

I have a dream that my four little children will one day live in a nation where they will not be judged by the color of their skin but by the content of their character. 14

I have a dream today. 15

I have a dream that one day the state of Alabama, whose governor's lips are presently dripping with the words of interposition and nullification, will be transformed into a situation where little black boys and black girls will be able to join hands with little white boys and white girls and walk together as sisters and brothers. 16

I have a dream today. 17

I have a dream that one day every valley shall be exalted, every hill and mountain shall be made low, the rough places will be made plain, and the crooked places will be made straight, and the glory of the Lord shall be revealed, and all flesh shall see it together. 18

This is our hope. This is the faith with which I return to the 19
South. With this faith we will be able to hew out of the mountain of despair a stone of hope. With this faith we will be able to transform the jangling discords of our nation into a beautiful symphony of brotherhood. With this faith we will be able to work together, to pray together, to struggle together, to go to jail together, to stand up for freedom together, knowing that we will be free one day.

This will be the day when all of God's children will be able 20
to sing with new meaning

> My country, 'tis of thee,
> Sweet land of liberty,
>   Of thee I sing:
> Land where my fathers died,
> Land of the pilgrims' pride,
> From every mountain-side
>   Let freedom ring.

And if America is to be a great nation this must become 21
true. So let freedom ring from the prodigious hilltops of New Hampshire. Let freedom ring from the mighty mountains of New York. Let freedom ring from the heightening Alleghenies of Pennsylvania!

Let freedom ring from the snowcapped Rockies of Colorado! 22

Let freedom ring from the curvaceous peaks of California! 23

But not only that; let freedom ring from Stone Mountain of 24
Georgia!

Let freedom ring from Lookout Mountain of Tennessee! 25

Let freedom ring from every hill and molehill of Mississippi. 26
From every mountainside, let freedom ring.

When we let freedom ring, when we let it ring from every 27
village and every hamlet, from every state and every city, we will be able to speed up that day when all of God's children, black men and white men, Jews and Gentiles, Protestants and Catholics, will be able to join hands and sing in the words of the old Negro spiritual, "Free at last! free at last! thank God almighty, we are free at last!"

• QUESTIONS ON MEANING AND PURPOSE •

1. What is the apparent purpose of this speech?
2. What thesis does King develop in his first four paragraphs? (See *Thesis* in Useful Terms.)
3. What does King mean by the "marvelous new militancy which has engulfed the Negro community" (paragraph 6)? Does this contradict King's nonviolent philosophy?
4. In what passages of his speech does King notice events of history? Where does he acknowledge the historic occasion on which he is speaking?
5. To what extent does King's personal authority lend power to his words?

• QUESTIONS ON WRITING STRATEGY •

1. What examples of particular injustices does King offer in paragraph 7? In his speech as a whole, do his observations tend to be general or specific? (See *General and Specific* in Useful Terms.)
2. Explain King's analogy of the bad check (paragraphs 3 and 4). What similarity do you find between it and any of the parables of Luke in Chapter 7?
3. What other analogy does King later develop?
4. What indicates that King's words were meant primarily for an audience of listeners, and only secondarily for a reading audience? To hear these indications, try reading the speech aloud. What use of parallelism do you notice? (See *Parallelism* in Useful Terms.)
5. Where in the speech does he acknowledge that not all of his listeners are black?
6. How much emphasis does King place on the past? On the future? (See *Emphasis* in Useful Terms.)

• QUESTIONS ON LANGUAGE •
• AND VOCABULARY •

1. In general, is the language of King's speech abstract or concrete? (See *Abstract and Concrete* in Useful Terms.) How is this level appropriate to the speaker's message and to the span of history with which he deals?

2. Point to memorable figures of speech. (See *Figures of Speech* in Useful Terms.)
3. Define momentous (paragraph 1); manacles, languished (2); promissory note (3); defaulted, hallowed, gradualism (4); inextricably (6); mobility, ghetto (7); tribulations, redemptive (8); interposition, nullification (16); prodigious (21); curvaceous (23); hamlet (27).

• SUGGESTIONS FOR WRITING •

1. Has America (or your locality) today moved closer in any respects to the fulfillment of King's dream? Discuss this question in an essay, giving specific examples.
2. Argue in favor of some course of action in a situation that you consider an injustice. Racial injustice is one possible area, or unfairness to any minority, or to women, children, the old, exconvicts, the handicapped, the poor. If possible, narrow your subject to a particular incident or a local situation on which you can write knowledgeably.

· John Lempesis ·

JOHN LEMPESIS was born in 1949. In 1972 he received a B.A. in political science from Jacksonville University in Florida. A newspaper reporter and feature writer in Waltham, Massachusetts, he has also written feature articles for the Boston *Globe*.

Murder in a Bottle

In his essay, Lempesis examines our drunken driving laws and finds them wanting. He suggests improvements that could, he argues, stem the alarming loss of life on our nation's roads.

Gail Tietjin was eighteen when the accident happened. Her 1
nineteen-year-old boyfriend was driving her home from a dinner party. He was drunk. About 1:30 A.M. that July morning in 1972, he drove the car around a curve and into a tree. It was two hours before the crash was discovered. Police thought Gail was dead until they heard a gurgle in her throat.

Gail regained consciousness after two weeks, but she had 2
suffered brain damage. This young woman who had earned two university scholarships now began learning how to use eating utensils, a comb, and the toilet. She did not know her family and was unable to remember her home when she finally returned there. For fourteen long months after the accident, she worked to relearn everything she could. When she had finally progressed enough to enter Stanford University, she had to forego the science courses she had always excelled in and settle instead for a less demanding major. In her first year she failed almost every course, but university officials allowed her to remain when they learned of the accident. She worked hard and graduated in June 1978. She got a job as an office secretary, though she had to struggle to keep it. Six years after Gail had suffered her injuries, it was still doubtful whether she could live independently.

Gail's boyfriend, meanwhile, had fully recovered from his   3
accident injuries and had paid his court-ordered punishment for
a misdemeanor — a $500 fine.[1]

Cari Lightner's story is briefer than Gail's. The thirteen-   4
year-old was killed by a hit-and-run drunken driver in May
1980 as she was walking home. The driver had been arrested
three times in four years for driving under the influence of alcohol. Just two days before he killed Cari, he had been released on
bail after another drunken-driving, hit-and-run accident. But
he still had his license to drive.

Drunken drivers are the primary cause of automobile ac-   5
cidents. Six of every ten people killed in single-car crashes are
drunk. Each year drunken drivers kill 25,000 men, women, and
children; and they seriously injure another 125,000. Each year
40,000 people aged sixteen to twenty-four suffer permanent injuries from drunken-driving accidents. And for all people under
forty years old drunken driving is the leading cause of death.

What can be done to reduce this terrible toll? First, change   6
the laws to reduce the amount a driver may legally drink, to discourage the average person from driving drunk, and to deal
more effectively with problem drunken drivers. Second, moti-
vate and train police to spot and arrest intoxicated motorists.
And, finally, on an individual level, change attitudes that permit if not encourage drunken driving.

The primary determinant of drunkenness is blood alcohol   7
content (BAC), the percentage of alcohol in a person's blood. In
forty-eight states a motorist with a BAC of or higher than .10
(that is, ten one-hundredths of a percent) can be arrested for
driving under the influence of alcohol. (The exceptions, Utah
and Idaho, allow arrest for a BAC of .08 or more.) But how
many drinks must be consumed to produce a .10 BAC? For the
average person the number depends on body weight, how fast
the alcohol is consumed and whether the stomach contains
food. It also depends on the drink: A 12-ounce beer, 3½ ounces
of wine, and an ounce of 100-proof liquor have about the same

---

[1]The story of Gail Tietjin adapted with permission from "They've Killed
My Daughter Twice" by Joseph Blank, *Readers Digest*, January 1981.

alcohol content. In general, a 120-pound person reaches a .10 BAC after imbibing 3½ of any of these drinks within an hour; a 160-pound person reaches a .10 BAC after 4½ drinks; and a 200-pound person reaches it after 5½ drinks.

Alcohol puts the brain to sleep, starting with the most 8 sophisticated part and continuing to the most primitive. A BAC of .05 reduces inhibitions and ability to concentrate, increases reaction time, and impairs judgment, reason, and memory. A driver with a .05 is two times more likely to have an accident than one who has drunk no alcoholic beverages. At .08 BAC, driving ability deteriorates dramatically. At .10 BAC, a person's vision and hearing diminish, movement becomes uncoordinated, and judgment, memory, and inhibitions decrease even further. A driver with a .10 BAC increases the chance of accident seven times; to medical authorities, he or she is incapable of driving safely. When BAC reaches .15, all physical and mental functions suffer major impairment: motion, distance and dimension perception, memory, judgment, reaction time. A driver's chance of having an accident becomes twenty-five times higher than normal. At .15 BAC, one probation officer remarked, "you shouldn't even be walking." Yet the average person arrested for drunken driving has a BAC of .18.

Clearly, the laws governing the alcohol permissible in a 9 driver's blood are not stringent enough. The blood alcohol content at which a person can be arrested for drunken driving should be reduced from .10 or .08 to .05, the point at which the average person's functions are just becoming impaired.

Besides reducing the permissible level of blood alcohol, new 10 laws should also be enacted to keep the drunken driver off the road. A loss of license should be mandatory — not optional — on the first conviction for drunken driving. So should an education program that teaches offenders the effects of alcohol and forces them to examine their drinking patterns. Driving drunk is often an early sign of a developing problem with alcohol, and many first-time offenders have learned in alcohol-education workshops that their drinking is propelling them toward trouble. According to the five-year statistics kept by the administrators of one such program, the majority of social drinkers who participated in the program were not arrested again for drunken driving.

Problem drinkers — about two-thirds of all drunken 11 drivers — are more difficult to reform. To get at them, penalties for repeat offenses should be more severe than those for first offenses. Mandatory loss of license should be extended to at least two years for a second drunken driving conviction and to five years for a succeeding conviction. Multiple offenders should be required to enter an alcohol treatment program or seek other counseling to control their drinking. And second and subsequent offenses should in some cases be punishable by brief imprisonment, the term perhaps servable on weekends, or by public service work. The motorist who cannot or will not stop driving drunk, even in the face of these penalties, should be barred from driving for life. The hardship thus inflicted is small compared to the harm the drinker might cause.

Many states already hold alcohol-education workshops for 12 convicted drunken drivers, though few of the programs are mandatory. And while several states, including Maine, Maryland, Oregon, and Wisconsin, allow judges the option of suspending offenders' licenses, only a few states require mandatory license suspensions. In Georgia, for instance, a first conviction for drunken driving means loss of license for a year, a second conviction within ten years brings a three-year suspension, and a third conviction within ten years means permanent loss of license.

But mandatory education and license suspension cannot 13 solve the problem alone, for about 65 percent of persons whose licenses are suspended continue to drive drunk and without a license. Those who are caught should receive a one-year jail sentence, but the real problem is catching them. Only one of every two thousand drunken drivers is apprehended, a discouraging record that can be improved only by better police training. When Oregon's state police, using federal money, first received training in recognizing and arresting drunken drivers, and then concentrated their patrols where alcohol-related accidents were frequent, the arrests for driving while intoxicated increased 300 percent in just six years. A similar program for the police of

Phoenix, Arizona, also federally funded, increased the annual drunken driving arrests from 6,500 to 12,000.

When the law is enforced and penalties are certain, people 14 change their habits. In Sweden, where people can be arrested for drunken driving if they have a BAC of .05 or more, police set up roadblocks to test drivers for drunkenness. A driver who is over the limit receives a mandatory jail sentence. Even a member of Sweden's royal family, sentenced for drunken driving several years ago, could not escape the required penalty. And the result of such rigid enforcement? The Swedes, who drink as much as Americans do, determine at the start of their parties who may drink freely and who must stay sober. Then they form carpools or take taxis so nobody has to drive drunk.

What can you do? Don't drive drunk. Discourage your 15 family and friends from driving drunk. At your own parties or those you attend, don't force drinks on people. Invite drunken guests to spend the night at your home. If they insist on driving, make them wait until they're sober. Cold water, hot coffee, or exercise won't sober up a drunk person; only time — about 1½ hours for every drink taken — will do the trick. And if drunken guests refuse to wait, ask sober friends to drive them, drive them yourself (if you're sober), or hire a taxi for them. The inconvenience or few dollars these precautions cost you may save someone else from experiencing the agonies of Gail Tietjin and her family.

After she landed her office job in 1978, Gail found she 16 worked much more slowly than the other secretaries, but she was determined to succeed. As she worked through her lunch periods, studied secretarial skills after hours, and read extensively, her mind quickened and her skills improved. She knew she would be able to support herself. "I'm probably stronger now because of what I went through," she said. "I'm happy the way I am."

In December 1979 Gail was killed in a head-on collision 17 with a car going the wrong way on a highway exit ramp. The driver of the car was drunk. Three years earlier the same woman had been convicted of drunken driving and fined $190.

Gail's case is unusual but her death was not. The day she 18 died sixty-seven other people in the United States were killed by drunken drivers. In the last twenty-four hours, sixty-eight more people have been killed. In the next twenty-four hours, another sixty-eight will die. Tragedies like these will not be stopped without strict laws, stiff mandatory penalties, better education of both the public and the police, and our own intervention.

• QUESTIONS ON MEANING AND PURPOSE •

1. How does Gail Tietjin's story help to fulfill the author's purpose in this essay?
2. In which paragraphs does the author appeal mainly to reason? Which appeal mainly to our feelings?

• QUESTIONS ON WRITING STRATEGY •

1. How effective is the author's device of interrupting Gail's story after paragraph 3 and returning to it in paragraph 16?
2. Where in the essay does Lempesis address the reader directly? What does he achieve by doing so?

• QUESTIONS ON LANGUAGE •
• AND VOCABULARY •

1. What evidence do you find in "Murder in a Bottle" that Lempesis chose his words with his audience in mind?
2. How would you characterize the author's vocabulary: poetic, utilitarian, colloquial, formal? Is his language appropriate to his subject?

• SUGGESTIONS FOR WRITING •

1. In a paragraph, evaluate the Swedish methods of dealing with drunken driving and decide whether or not you think they would work in this country. Give reasons for your conclusion.
2. Using examples and evidence, write a brief essay in which you argue that a law needs to be enforced, or changed.

Hunting for Evidence

Having decided he wanted to write about deaths caused by drunken driving, John Lempesis discovered that the task required legwork. In his postscript, he discloses where his search for material led him, what he found out, and how new information shaped his final draft.

To write an argumentative essay, I needed a topic that I   1
already held strong views about. Memory led me quickly to my
friend Bob Gillis, a casual, fun-loving man with a keen, dry wit
and an infectious, toothy grin. One misty September night, Bob
was killed by a drunken driver. After Bob's senseless death,
drunken driving became an important concern to me. Writing
an essay on how to prevent more deaths like his would give me
a chance to express that concern. I knew before I even started
that the essay would be dominated by dry facts and data, so
while I conducted my research I kept an eye out for dramatic examples of deaths caused by drunken driving that would make
the problem more immediate. I didn't hope for an example as
gripping and sad as that of Gail Tietjin.

I had a topic but no thesis other than a general argument   2
that drunken driving should be stopped. But how? Before I began research, I jotted down what I thought would discourage
drunken driving: punishment — fines, jail sentences, and license suspensions. This working thesis helped me think about
what I needed to include in the essay (for example, what is the
legal limit on blood alcohol level for a driver?), and I might have
both started and finished with library research into the penalties in different states and countries and their relative effectiveness. But I decided to interview experts as well, to get their
opinions of the magnitude of the problem and how to solve it.

The interviews were an eye-opener. I started with police of-   3
ficers because they have the first contact with drunken drivers.
Though some of the officers agreed with me that harsher pun-

ishments would dissuade many people from driving drunk, others weren't so sure. They talked of their difficulties in apprehending drunken drivers. And they noted that if the penalties were too stiff, authorities would be reluctant to enforce them. So already my thesis needed changing. Harsher punishment had to be accompanied by improved enforcement and prosecution. The police need training.

I next interviewed probation officers who supervise people 4 convicted of drunken driving and the instructors who run a state alcohol-education workshop for first-time offenders. These people provided yet another slant, for they pointed out that fines and short jail sentences — two-thirds of my original solution — do little to stop drunken driving by the problem drinkers who are two of every three violators. Clearly, this group requires different treatment — perhaps mandatory alcohol treatment, a preventive measure I had not considered before. For a while I toyed with the idea of including a section on alcohol abuse in the essay, but it would have been a digression from my developing thesis and I decided against it. Besides, I hadn't yet tapped all the available sources on deterrents.

My final research was done at the local office of the National Highway Traffic Safety Administration (NHTSA). The 5 agency provided a national overview of the problem and the data I needed to fill out the essay and support my main points. But here, too, the data did not tell all. In interviews with NHTSA specialists, I learned that judges are sometimes reluctant to impose sentences on convicted drunken drivers and instead suspend them. Thus many of the penalties should be mandatory. The NHTSA people also told me that suspension of driving licenses is a more effective weapon against drunken driving than any other penalty. The remaining problem, then, was what to recommend for offenders who are caught driving drunk while their licenses are suspended. Sadly, the only deterrent for these people seems to be a stiff jail sentence.

In the end my thesis was quite a bit broader and more complicated than it had been at the beginning. But it also better 6 reflected the facts and the opinions of experts. Changing my approach was essential to developing an accurate, effective argument.

· ADDITIONAL WRITING TOPICS ·
ARGUMENT AND PERSUASION

1. Write a persuasive essay in which you appeal primarily to either reason or emotion. In it, address a particular person or audience. For instance, you might direct your essay:

   To a friend unwilling to attend a ballet performance (or a wrestling match) with you on the grounds that such an event is for the birds.

   To a teacher who asserts that more term papers, and longer ones, are necessary.

   To a state trooper who intends to give you a ticket for speeding.

   To a male employer skeptical of hiring women.

   To a developer who plans to tear down a historic house.

   To someone who sees no purpose in studying a foreign language.

   To someone you are trying to persuade to sign a petition.

   To a high school class whose members don't want to go to college.

   To an older generation skeptical of the value of "all that noise" (meaning current popular music).

   To an atheist who asserts that religion is a lot of pie-in-the-sky.

   To the members of a library board who want to ban a certain book.

2. Write a letter to your campus newspaper, or to a city newspaper, in which you argue for or against a certain cause or view. Perhaps you may wish to object to a particular feature, column, or editorial in the paper. Send your letter and see if it is published.

3. Write a short letter to your congressional or state representative, arguing in favor (or against) the passage of some pending legislation. See a news magazine or a newspaper for a worthwhile bill to champion. Or else write in favor of some continuing cause: for instance, saving whales, reducing (or increasing) armaments, or providing more aid to the arts.

FOR
FURTHER READING

· Jonathan Swift ·

JONATHAN SWIFT (1667–1745), the son of English parents who had settled in Ireland, divided his energies among literature, politics, and the Church of England. Dissatisfied with the quiet life of an Anglican parish priest, Swift spent much of his time in London hobnobbing with men of letters and writing pamphlets in support of the Tory Party. In 1713 Queen Anne rewarded his political services with an assignment the London-loving Swift didn't want: to supervise St. Patrick's Cathedral in Dublin. There, as Dean Swift, he ended his days — beloved by the Irish, whose interests he defended against the English government.

Although Swift's chief works include the remarkable satires *The Battle of the Books* and *A Tale of a Tub* (both 1704) and scores of fine poems, he is best remembered for *Gulliver's Travels* (1726), an account of four imaginary voyages. This classic is always abridged when it is given to children because of its frank descriptions of human filth and viciousness. In *Gulliver's Travels* Swift pays tribute to the reasoning portion of "that animal called man," and delivers a stinging rebuke to the rest of him.

A Modest Proposal

For Preventing the Children of Poor People in Ireland from Being a Burden to Their Parents or Country, and for Making Them Beneficial to the Public

Three consecutive years of drought and sparse crops had worked hardship upon the Irish when Swift wrote this ferocious essay in the summer of 1729. At the time, there were said to be 35,000 wandering beggars in the country: whole families had quit their farms and had taken to the roads. Large landowners, of English ancestry, preferred to ignore their tenants' sufferings and lived abroad to dodge taxes and payment of church duties. Swift writes out of indignation and out of impatience with the many proposals to help the Irish offered in England without result.

Although printed as a pamphlet in Dublin, Swift's essay is clearly meant for English readers as well as Irish ones. When circulated, the pamphlet caused a sensation in both Ireland and England and had to be reprinted seven times in the same year. Swift is a master of plain, vigorous English prose and "A Modest Proposal" is a masterpiece of irony. (If you are uncertain what Swift argues for, see the discussion of *Irony* in Useful Terms.) The Dean of St. Patrick's had no special fondness for the Irish, but he hated the inhumanity he witnessed.

It is a melancholy object to those who walk through this great town[1] or travel in the country, when they see the streets, the roads, and cabin doors, crowded with beggars of the female sex, followed by three, four, or six children, all in rags and importuning every passenger for an alms. These mothers, instead of being able to work for their honest livelihood, are forced to employ all their time in strolling to beg sustenance for their helpless infants, who, as they grow up, either turn thieves for want of work, or leave their dear native country to fight for the Pretender in Spain, or sell themselves to the Barbados.[2]

I think it is agreed by all parties that this prodigious number of children in the arms, or on the backs, or at the heels of their mothers, and frequently of their fathers, is in the present deplorable state of the kingdom a very great additional grievance; and therefore whoever could find out a fair, cheap, and easy method of making these children sound, useful members of the commonwealth would deserve so well of the public as to have his statue set up for a preserver of the nation.

But my intention is very far from being confined to provide only for the children of professed beggars; it is of a much greater extent, and shall take in the whole number of infants at a cer-

[1]Dublin.

[2]The Pretender was James Stuart, exiled in Spain; in 1718 many Irishmen had joined an army seeking to restore him to the English throne. Others wishing to emigrate had signed papers as indentured servants, agreeing to work for a number of years in the Barbados or other British colonies in exchange for their ocean passage.

tain age who are born of parents in effect as little able to support them as those who demand our charity in the streets.

As to my own part, having turned my thoughts for many years upon this important subject, and maturely weighed the several schemes of other projectors,[3] I have always found them grossly mistaken in their computation. It is true, a child just dropped from its dam may be supported by her milk for a solar year, with little other nourishment; at most not above the value of two shillings, which the mother may certainly get, or the value in scraps, by her lawful occupation of begging; and it is exactly at one year that I propose to provide for them in such a manner as instead of being a charge upon their parents or the parish, or wanting food and raiment for the rest of their lives, they shall on the contrary contribute to the feeding, and partly to the clothing, of many thousands.

There is likewise another great advantage in my scheme, that it will prevent those voluntary abortions, and that horrid practice of women murdering their bastard children, alas, too frequent among us, sacrificing the poor innocent babes, I doubt, more to avoid the expense than the shame, which would move tears and pity in the most savage and inhuman breast.

The number of souls in this kingdom being usually reckoned one million and a half, of these I calculate there may be about two hundred thousand couples whose wives are breeders; from which number I subtract thirty thousand couples who are able to maintain their own children, although I apprehend there cannot be so many under the present distress of the kingdom; but this being granted, there will remain an hundred and seventy thousand breeders. I again subtract fifty thousand for those women who miscarry, or whose children die by accident or disease within the year. There only remain an hundred and twenty thousand children of poor parents annually born. The question therefore is, how this number shall be reared and provided for, which, as I have already said, under the present situation of affairs, is utterly impossible by all the methods hitherto proposed. For we can neither employ them in handicraft or agriculture; we neither build houses (I mean in the country) nor

[3]Planners.

cultivate land. They can very seldom pick up a livelihood by stealing till they arrive at six years old, except where they are of towardly parts;[4] although I confess they learn the rudiments much earlier, during which time they can however be looked upon only as probationers, as I have been informed by a principal gentleman in the country of Cavan, who protested to me that he never knew above one or two instances under the age of six, even in a part of the kingdom so renowned for the quickest proficiency in that art.

I am assured by our merchants that a boy or a girl before   7
twelve years old is no salable commodity; and even when they come to this age they will not yield above three pounds, or three pounds and half a crown at most on the Exchange; which cannot turn to account either to the parents or the kingdom, the charge of nutriment and rags having been at least four times that value.

I shall now therefore humbly propose my own thoughts,   8
which I hope will not be liable to the least objection.

I have been assured by a very knowing American of my ac-   9
quaintance in London, that a young healthy child well nursed is at a year old a most delicious, nourishing, and wholesome food, whether stewed, roasted, baked, or boiled; and I make no doubt that it will equally serve in a fricassee or a ragout.[5]

I do therefore humbly offer it to public consideration that of   10
the hundred and twenty thousand children, already computed, twenty thousand may be reserved for breed, whereof only one fourth part to be males, which is more than we allow to sheep, black cattle, or swine; and my reason is that these children are seldom the fruits of marriage, a circumstance not much regarded by our savages, therefore one male will be sufficient to serve four females. That the remaining hundred thousand may at a year old be offered in sale to the persons of quality and fortune through the kingdom, always advising the mother to let them suck plentifully in the last month, so as to render them plump and fat for a good table. A child will make two dishes at an entertainment for friends; and when the family dines alone, the fore or hind quarter will make a reasonable dish, and

---

[4]Teachable wits, innate abilities.
[5]Stew.

seasoned with a little pepper or salt will be very good boiled on the fourth day, especially in winter.

11   I have reckoned upon a medium that a child just born will weigh twelve pounds, and in a solar year if tolerably nursed increaseth to twenty-eight pounds.

12   I grant this food will be somewhat dear, and therefore very proper for landlords, who, as they have already devoured most of the parents, seem to have the best title to the children.

13   Infant's flesh will be in season throughout the year, but more plentiful in March, and a little before and after. For we are told by a grave author, an eminent French physician,[6] that fish being a prolific diet, there are more children born in Roman Catholic countries about nine months after Lent than at any other season; therefore, reckoning a year after Lent, the markets will be more glutted than usual, because the number of popish infants is at least three to one in this kingdom; and therefore it will have one other collateral advantage, by lessening the number of Papists among us.

14   I have already computed the charge of nursing a beggar's child (in which list I reckon all cottagers, laborers, and four-fifths of the farmers) to be about two shillings per annum, rags included; and I believe no gentleman would repine to give ten shillings for the carcass of a good fat child, which, as I have said, will make four dishes of excellent nutritive meat, when he hath only some particular friend or his own family to dine with him. Thus the squire will learn to be a good landlord, and grow popular among the tenants; the mother will have eight shillings net profit, and be fit for work till she produces another child.

15   Those who are more thrifty (as I must confess the times require) may flay the carcass; the skin of which artificially[7] dressed will make admirable gloves for ladies, and summer boots for fine gentlemen.

16   As to our city of Dublin, shambles[8] may be appointed for this purpose in the most convenient parts of it, and butchers we may be assured will not be wanting; although I rather recom-

---

[6]Swift's favorite French writer, François Rabelais, sixteenth-century author not "grave" at all, but a broad humorist.
[7]With art or craft.
[8]Butcher shops or slaughterhouses.

mend buying the children alive, and dressing them hot from the knife as we do roasting pigs.

A very worthy person, a true lover of his country, and   17 whose virtues I highly esteem, was lately pleased in discoursing on this matter to offer a refinement upon my scheme. He said that many gentlemen of his kingdom, having of late destroyed their deer, he conceived that the want of venison might be well supplied by the bodies of young lads and maidens, not exceeding fourteen years of age nor under twelve, so great a number of both sexes in every county being now ready to starve for want of work and service; and these to be disposed of by their parents, if alive, or otherwise by their nearest relations. But with due deference to so excellent a friend and so deserving a patriot, I cannot be altogether in his sentiments; for as to the males, my American acquaintance assured me from frequent experience that their flesh was generally tough and lean, like that of our schoolboys, by continual exercise, and their taste disagreeable; and to fatten them would not answer the charge. Then as to the females, it would, I think with humble submission, be a loss to the public, because they soon would become breeders themselves; and besides, it is not improbable that some scrupulous people might be apt to censure such a practice (although indeed very unjustly) as a little bordering upon cruelty; which, I confess, hath always been with me the strongest objection against any project, how well soever intended.

But in order to justify my friend, he confessed that this ex-   18 pedient was put into his head by the famous Psalmanazar,[9] a native of the island Formosa, who came from thence to London above twenty years ago, and in conversation told my friend that in his country when any young person happened to be put to death, the executioner sold the carcass to persons of quality as a prime dainty; and that in his time the body of a plump girl of fifteen, who was crucified for an attempt to poison the emperor, was sold to his Imperial Majesty's prime minister of state, and other great mandarins of the court, in joints from the

[9]Georges Psalmanazar, a Frenchman who pretended to be Japanese, author of a completely imaginary *Description of the Isle Formosa* (1705), had become a well-known figure in gullible London society.

gibbet, at four hundred crowns. Neither indeed can I deny that if the same use were made of several plump young girls in this town, who without one single groat to their fortunes cannot stir abroad without a chair, and appear at the playhouse and assemblies in foreign fineries which they never will pay for, the kingdom would not be the worse.

Some persons of a desponding spirit are in great concern 19 about that vast number of poor people who are aged, diseased, or maimed, and I have been desired to employ my thoughts what course may be taken to ease the nation of so grievous an encumbrance. But I am not in the least pain upon that matter, because it is very well known that they are every day dying and rotting by cold and famine, and filth and vermin, as fast as can be reasonably expected. And as to the younger laborers, they are now in almost as hopeful a condition. They cannot get work, and consequently pine away for want of nourishment to a degree that if any time they are accidentally hired to common labor, they have not strength to perform it; and thus the country and themselves are happily delivered from the evils to come.

I have too long digressed, and therefore shall return to my 20 subject. I think the advantages by the proposal which I have made are obvious and many, as well as of the highest importance.

For first, as I have already observed, it would greatly lessen 21 the number of Papists, with whom we are yearly overrun, being the principal breeders of the nation as well as our most dangerous enemies; and who stay at home on purpose to deliver the kingdom to the Pretender, hoping to take their advantage by the absence of so many good Protestants, who have chosen rather to leave their country than to stay at home and pay tithes against their conscience to an Episcopal curate.

Secondly, the poorer tenants will have something valuable 22 of their own, which by law may be made liable to distress,[10] and help to pay their landlord's rent, their corn and cattle being already seized and money a thing unknown.

Thirdly, whereas the maintenance of an hundred thousand 23 children, from two years old and upwards, cannot be computed

[10]Subject to seizure by creditors.

at less than ten shillings a piece per annum, the nation's stock will be thereby increased fifty thousand pounds per annum, besides the profit of a new dish introduced to the tables of all gentlemen of fortune in the kingdom who have any refinement in taste. And the money will circulate among ourselves, the goods being entirely of our own growth and manufacture.

Fourthly, the constant breeders, besides the gain of eight shillings sterling per annum by the sale of their children, will be rid of the charge of maintaining them after the first year.   24

Fifthly, this food would likewise bring great custom to taverns, where the vintners will certainly be so prudent as to procure the best receipts for dressing it to perfection, and consequently have their houses frequented by all the fine gentlemen, who justly value themselves upon their knowledge in good eating; and a skillful cook, who understands how to oblige his guests, will contrive to make it as expensive as they please.   25

Sixthly, this would be a great inducement to marriage, which all wise nations have either encouraged by rewards or enforced by laws and penalties. It would increase the care and tenderness of mothers toward their children, when they were sure of a settlement for life to the poor babes, provided in some sort by the public, to their annual profit instead of expense. We should see an honest emulation among the married women, which of them could bring the fattest child to the market. Men would become as fond of their wives during the time of their pregnancy as they are now of their mares in foal, their cows in calf, or sows when they are ready to farrow; nor offer to beat or kick them (as is too frequent a practice) for fear of a miscarriage.   26

Many other advantages might be enumerated. For instance, the addition of some thousand carcasses in our exportation of barreled beef, the propagation of swine's flesh, and improvements in the art of making good bacon, so much wanted among us by the great destruction of pigs, too frequent at our tables, which are no way comparable in taste or magnificence to a well-grown, fat, yearling child, which roasted whole will make a considerable figure at a lord mayor's feast or any other public entertainment. But this and many others I omit, being studious of brevity.   27

Supposing that one thousand families in this city would be 28
constant customers for infants' flesh, besides others who might
have it at merry meetings, particularly weddings and christenings, I compute that Dublin would take off annually about
twenty thousand carcasses, and the rest of the kingdom (where
probably they will be sold somewhat cheaper) the remaining
eighty thousand.

I can think of no one objection that will possibly be raised 29
against this proposal, unless it should be urged that the number
of people will be thereby much lessened in the kingdom. This I
freely own, and it was indeed one principal design in offering it
to the world. I desire the reader will observe, that I calculate my
remedy for this one individual kingdom of Ireland and for no
other that ever was, is, or I think ever can be upon earth. Therefore let no man talk to me of other expedients: of taxing our
absentees at five shillings a pound: of using neither clothes nor
household furniture except what is of our own growth and manufacture: of utterly rejecting the materials and instruments that
promote foreign luxury: of curing the expensiveness of pride,
vanity, idleness, and gaming in our women: of introducing a
vein of parsimony, prudence, and temperance: of learning to
love our country, in the want of which we differ even from
Laplanders and the inhabitants of Topinamboo:[11] of quitting
our animosities and factions, nor acting any longer like the
Jews, who were murdering one another at the very moment
their city was taken:[12] of being a little cautious not to sell our
country and conscience for nothing: of teaching landlords to
have at least one degree of mercy toward their tenants: lastly, of
putting a spirit of honesty, industry, and skill into our shop-
keepers; who, if a resolution could now be taken to buy only
our native goods, would immediately unite to cheat and exact
upon us in the price, the measure, and the goodness, nor could
ever yet be brought to make one fair proposal of just dealing,
though often and earnestly invited to it.

---

[11]District of Brazil inhabited by primitive tribes.

[12]During the Roman siege of Jerusalem (70 A.D.), prominent Jews were executed on the charge of being in league with the enemy.

Therefore I repeat, let no man talk to me of these and the   30
like expedients, till he hath at least some glimpse of hope that
there will ever be some hearty and sincere attempt to put them
in practice.

But as to myself, having been wearied out for many years   31
with offering vain, idle, visionary thoughts, and at length utterly despairing of success, I fortunately fell upon this proposal,
which, as it is wholly new, so it hath something solid and real,
of no expense and little trouble, full in our own power, and
whereby we can incur no danger in disobliging England. For
this kind of commodity will not bear exportation, the flesh being of too tender a consistence to admit a long continuance in
salt, although perhaps I could name a country which would be
glad to eat up our whole nation without it.

After all, I am not so violently bent upon my own opinion   32
as to reject any offer proposed by wise men, which shall be
found equally innocent, cheap, easy, and effectual. But before
something of that kind shall be advanced in contradiction to
my scheme, and offering a better, I desire the author or authors
will be pleased maturely to consider two points. First, as things
now stand, how they will be able to find food and raiment for
an hundred thousand useless mouths and backs. And secondly,
there being a round million of creatures in human figure
throughout this kingdom, whose sole subsistence put into a
common stock would leave them in debt two millions of pounds
sterling, adding those who are beggars by profession to the bulk
of farmers, cottagers, and laborers, with their wives and children who are beggars in effect; I desire those politicians who
dislike my overture, and may perhaps be so bold to attempt an
answer, that they will first ask the parents of these mortals
whether they would not at this day think it a great happiness to
have been sold for food at a year old in this manner I prescribe,
and thereby have avoided such a perpetual scene of misfortunes
as they have since gone through by the oppression of landlords,
the impossibility of paying rent without money or trade, the
want of common sustenance, with neither house nor clothes to
cover them from the inclemencies of the weather, and the most

inevitable prospect of entailing the like or greater miseries upon their breed forever.

I profess, in the sincerity of my heart, that I have not the least personal interest in endeavoring to promote this necessary work, having no other motive than the public good of my country, by advancing our trade, providing for infants, relieving the poor, and giving some pleasure to the rich. I have no children by which I can propose to get a single penny; the youngest being nine years old, and my wife past childbearing. 33

· Henry David Thoreau ·

HENRY DAVID THOREAU (1817–1862) was born in Concord, Massachusetts, where, except for short excursions, he remained. After his graduation from Harvard College, he taught school briefly, worked sometimes as surveyor and house-painter, and for a time worked in his father's pencil factory (and greatly improved the product). The small sales of his first, self-published book, *A Week on the Concord and Merrimac Rivers* (1849) led him to remark, "I have now a library of nearly nine hundred volumes, over seven hundred of which I wrote myself."

The philosopher Ralph Waldo Emerson befriended his neighbor Thoreau; but although the two agreed that a unity exists between man and nature, they did not always see eye to eye on matters of politics. Unlike Emerson, Thoreau was an activist. He helped escaped slaves flee to Canada; he went to jail rather than pay his poll tax to a government that made war against Mexico. He recounts this brush with the law in his essay "Civil Disobedience" (1849), in which later readers (including Mahatma Gandhi of India and Martin Luther King, Jr.) have found encouragement for their own nonviolent resistance. One other book appeared in Thoreau's lifetime: *Walden* (1854), a searching account of his life in (and around, and beyond) the one-room cabin he built for himself at Walden Pond near Concord. When Thoreau lay dying, an aunt asked whether he had made his peace with God. "I did not know we had quarreled," he replied.

Getting a Living

"What may a man do and not be ashamed of it?" the young Thoreau asked himself in his journal for March, 1838, during a period of reluctant employment in the family pencil business. It was a question that would preoccupy him all the years of his maturity. "As long as possible live free and uncommitted," he urges his readers in *Walden*. "It makes but little difference whether you are committed to a farm or the county jail."

At Walden Pond, Thoreau lived on few dollars, simplifying his needs mercilessly, and demonstrated to his own satisfaction that he could raise beans, write, read Plato, observe the natural world, and be practically self-sustaining. In the following portion of a lecture, "Life Without Principle" (1861), Thoreau sums up his thinking on the subject of gainful work. Originally, the lecture was called "Getting a Living," which seems to apply only to this opening section of it. Not only Thoreau's thought but his prose style continues to engage us. He wrote with care, like a craftsman lovingly joining together fine wood to make a cabinet. To revise *Walden*, a relatively short book, took him seven years. Thoreau's is a style marked by a distinctly New England Yankee tightness of lip — for there are no needless words — and an amazing way with a metaphor.

Let us consider the way in which we spend our lives.   1

This world is a place of business. What an infinite bustle! I   2
am awaked almost every night by the panting of the locomotive. It interrupts my dreams. There is no sabbath. It would be glorious to see mankind at leisure for once. It is nothing but work, work, work. I cannot easily buy a blank-book to write thoughts in; they are commonly ruled for dollars and cents. An Irishman, seeing me making a minute in the fields, took it for granted that I was calculating my wages. If a man was tossed out of a window when an infant, and so made a cripple for life, or scared out of his wits by the Indians, it is regretted chiefly because he was thus incapacitated for — business! I think that there is nothing, not even crime, more opposed to poetry, to philosophy, ay, to life itself, than this incessant business.

There is a coarse and boisterous money-making fellow in   3
the outskirts of our town, who is going to build a bank-wall under the hill along the edge of his meadow. The powers have put this into his head to keep him out of mischief, and he wishes me to spend three weeks digging there with him. The result will be that he will perhaps get some more money to hoard, and leave for his heirs to spend foolishly. If I do this, most will commend me as an industrious and hard-working man; but if I choose to devote myself to certain labors which yield more real profit, though but little money, they may be inclined to look on me as an idler. Nevertheless, as I do not need the police of meaningless labor to regulate me, and do not see anything ab-

solutely praiseworthy in this fellow's undertaking, any more than in many an enterprise of our own or foreign governments, however amusing it may be to him or them, I prefer to finish my education at a different school.

If a man walk in the woods for love of them half of each day,   4
he is in danger of being regarded as a loafer; but if he spends his whole day as a speculator, shearing off those woods and making earth bald before her time, he is esteemed an industrious and enterprising citizen. As if a town had no interest in its forests but to cut them down!

Most men would feel insulted, if it were proposed to employ   5
them in throwing stones over a wall, and then in throwing them back, merely that they might earn their wages. But many are no more worthily employed now. For instance: just after sunrise, one summer morning, I noticed one of my neighbors walking beside his team, which was slowly drawing a heavy hewn stone swung under the axle, surrounded by an atmosphere of industry — his day's work begun, — his brow commenced to sweat — a reproach to all sluggards and idlers — pausing abreast the shoulders of his oxen, and half turning round with a flourish of his merciful whip, while they gained their length on him. And I thought, Such is the labor which the American Congress exists to protect — honest, manly toil, — honest as the day is long — that makes his bread taste sweet, and keeps society sweet — which all men respect and have consecrated: one of the sacred band, doing the needful, but irksome drudgery. Indeed, I felt a slight reproach, because I observed this from the window, and was not abroad and stirring about a similar business. The day went by, and at evening I passed the yard of another neighbor, who keeps many servants, and spends much money foolishly, while he adds nothing to the common stock, and there I saw the stone of the morning lying beside a whimsical structure intended to adorn this Lord Timothy Dexter's premises,[1] and the dignity forthwith departed from the teamster's labor, in my eyes. In my opinion, the sun was made

---

[1]A wealthy and eccentric merchant who styled himself a lord, Timothy Dexter had built a mansion in Newburyport, Massachusetts, decorated with statues of Greek gods, of George Washington, and of himself.

to light worthier toil than this. I may add, that his employer has since run off, in debt to a good part of the town, and, after passing through Chancery,[2] has settled somewhere else, there to become once more a patron of the arts.

The ways by which you may get money almost without exception lead downward. To have done anything by which you earned money *merely* is to have been truly idle or worse. If the laborer gets no more than the wages which his employer pays him, he is cheated, he cheats himself. If you would get money as a writer or lecturer, you must be popular, which is to go down perpendicularly. Those services which the community will most readily pay for it is most disagreeable to render. You are paid for being something less than a man. The State does not commonly reward a genius any more wisely. Even the poet-laureate would rather not have to celebrate the accidents of royalty. He must be bribed with a pipe of wine; and perhaps another poet is called away from his muse to gauge that very pipe. As for my own business, even that kind of surveying which I could do with most satisfaction my employers do not want. They would prefer that I should do my work coarsely and not too well, ay, not well enough. When I observe that there are different ways of surveying, my employer commonly asks which will give him the most land, not which is most correct. I once invented a rule for measuring cord-wood, and tried to introduce it in Boston; but the measurer there told me that the sellers did not wish to have their wood measured correctly — that he was already too accurate for them, and therefore they commonly got their wood measured in Charlestown before crossing the bridge.

The aim of the laborer should be, not to get his living, to get "a good job," but to perform well a certain work; and, even in a pecuniary sense, it would be economy for a town to pay its laborers so well that they would not feel that they were working for low ends, as for a livelihood merely, but for scientific, or even moral ends. Do not hire a man who does your work for money, but him who does it for love of it.

It is remarkable that there are few men so well employed, so much to their minds, but that a little money or fame would

6

7

8

---

[2]A court of equity that settles the claims of creditors.

commonly buy them off from their present pursuit. I see advertisements for *active* young men, as if activity were the whole of a
young man's capital. Yet I have been surprised when one has
with confidence proposed to me, a grown man, to embark in
some enterprise of his, as if I had absolutely nothing to do, my
life having been a complete failure hitherto. What a doubtful
compliment this is to pay me! As if he had met me half-way
across the ocean beating up against the wind, but bound nowhere, and proposed to me to go along with him! If I did, what
do you think the underwriters would say? No, no! I am not
without employment at this stage of the voyage. To tell the
truth, I saw an advertisement for able-bodied seamen, when I
was a boy, sauntering in my native port, and as soon as I came
of age I embarked.

The community has no bribe that will tempt a wise man.   9
You may raise money enough to tunnel a mountain, but you
cannot raise money enough to hire a man who is minding *his
own* business. An efficient and valuable man does what he can,
whether the community pay him for it or not. The inefficient
offer their inefficiency to the highest bidder, and are forever expecting to be put into office. One would suppose that they were
rarely disappointed.

Perhaps I am more than usually jealous with respect to my   10
freedom. I feel that my connection with and obligation to society are still very slight and transient. Those slight labors which
afford me a livelihood, and by which it is allowed that I am to
some extent serviceable to my contemporaries, are as yet commonly a pleasure to me, and I am not often reminded that they
are a necessity. So far I am successful. But I foresee, that, if my
wants should be much increased, the labor required to supply
them would become a drudgery. If I should sell both my fore-
noons and afternoons to society, as most appear to do, I am
sure, that, for me, there would be nothing left worth living for. I
trust that I shall never thus sell my birthright for a mess of pottage.[3] I wish to suggest that a man may be very industrious, and

---

[3]How Esau foolishly sold his birthright to his brother Jacob for a mess of
pottage, or thick soup, is told in Genesis 25:30–34.

yet not spend his time well. There is no more fatal blunderer than he who consumes the greater part of his life getting his living. All great enterprises are self-supporting. The poet, for instance, must sustain his body by his poetry, as a steam planing-mill feeds its boilers with the shavings it makes. You must get your living by loving. But as it is said of the merchants that ninety-seven in a hundred fail, so the life of men generally, tried by this standard, is a failure, and bankruptcy may be surely prophesied.

Merely to come into the world the heir of a fortune is not to be born, but to be still-born, rather. To be supported by the charity of friends, or a government-pension — provided you continue to breathe — by whatever fine synonyms you describe these relations, is to go into the almshouse. On Sundays the poor debtor goes to church to take an account of stock, and finds, of course, that his outgoes have been greater than his income. In the Catholic Church, especially, they go into Chancery, make a clean confession, give up all, and think to start again. Thus men will lie on their backs, talking about the fall of man, and never make an effort to get up. 11

As for the comparative demand which men make on life, it is an important difference between two, that the one is satisfied with a level success, that his marks can all be hit by point-blank shots, but the other, however low and unsuccessful his life may be, constantly elevates his aim, though at a very slight angle to the horizon. I should much rather be the last man, — though, as the Orientals say, "Greatness doth not approach him who is forever looking down; and all those who are looking high are growing poor." 12

It is remarkable that there is little or nothing to be remembered written on the subject of getting a living: how to make getting a living not merely honest and honorable, but altogether inviting and glorious; for if *getting* a living is not so, then living is not. One would think, from looking at literature, that this question had never disturbed a solitary individual's musings. Is it that men are too much disgusted with their experience to speak of it? The lesson of value which money teaches, which the Author of the Universe has taken so much 13 pains to teach us, we are inclined to skip altogether. As for the means of living, it is wonderful how indifferent men of all classes are about it, even reformers, so called — whether they inherit, or earn, or steal it. I think that society has done nothing for us in this respect, or at least has undone what she has done. Cold and hunger seem more friendly to my nature than those methods which men have adopted and advise to ward them off.

The title *wise* is, for the most part, falsely applied. How can   14
one be a wise man, if he does not know any better how to live than other men? — if he is only more cunning and intellectually subtle? Does Wisdom work in a tread-mill? or does she teach how to succeed *by her example?* Is there any such thing as wisdom not applied to life? Is she merely the miller who grinds the finest logic? It is pertinent to ask if Plato got his *living* in a better way or more successfully than his contemporaries — or did he succumb to the difficulties of life like other men? Did he seem to prevail over some of them merely by indifference, or by assuming grand airs? or find it easier to live, because his aunt remembered him in her will? The ways in which most men get their living, that is, live, are mere make-shifts, and a shirking of the real business of life, — chiefly because they do not know, but partly because they do not mean, any better.

The rush to California,[4] for instance, and the attitude, not   15
merely of merchants, but of philosophers and prophets, so called, in relation to it, reflect the greatest disgrace on mankind. That so many are ready to live by luck, and so get the means of commanding the labor of others less lucky, without contributing any value to society! And that is called enterprise! I know of no more startling development of the immorality of trade, and all the common modes of getting a living. The philosophy and poetry and religion of such a mankind are not worth the dust of a puff-ball. The hog that gets his living by rooting, stirring up the soil so, would be ashamed of such company. If I could command the wealth of all the worlds by lifting my finger, I would not pay *such* a price for it. Even Mahomet knew that God did not make this world in jest. It makes God to be a moneyed

---

[4]The California Gold Rush of 1849.

gentleman who scatters a handful of pennies in order to see mankind scramble for them. The world's raffle! A subsistence in the domains of Nature a thing to be raffled for! What a comment, what a satire on our institutions! The conclusion will be, that mankind will hang itself upon a tree. And have all the precepts in all the Bibles taught men only this? and is the last and most admirable invention of the human race only an improved muck-rake? Is this the ground on which Orientals and Occidentals meet? Did God direct us so to get our living, digging where we never planted — and He would, perchance, reward us with lumps of gold?

God gave the righteous man a certificate entitling him to food and raiment, but the unrighteous man found a *facsimile* of the same in God's coffers, and appropriated it, and obtained food and raiment like the former. It is one of the most extensive systems of counterfeiting that the world has seen. I did not know that mankind were suffering for want of gold. I have seen a little of it. I know that it is very malleable, but not so malleable as wit. A grain of gold will gild a great surface, but not so much as a grain of wisdom.

The gold-digger in the ravines of the mountains is as much a gambler as his fellow in the saloons of San Francisco. What difference does it make, whether you shake dirt or shake dice? If you win, society is the loser. The gold-digger is the enemy of the honest laborer, whatever checks and compensations there may be. It is not enough to tell me that you worked hard to get your gold. So does the Devil work hard. The way of transgressors may be hard in many respects. The humblest observer who goes to the mines sees and says that gold-digging is of the character of a lottery; the gold thus obtained is not the same thing with the wages of honest toil. But, practically, he forgets what he has seen, for he has seen only the fact, not the principle, and goes into trade there, that is, buys a ticket in what commonly proves another lottery, where the fact is not so obvious.

After reading Howitt's account of the Australian gold-diggings one evening, I had in my mind's eye, all night, the numerous valleys, with their streams, all cut up with foul pits, from ten to one hundred feet deep, and half a dozen feet across, as close as they can be dug, and partly filled with water — the locality to which men furiously rush to probe for their fortunes — uncertain where they shall break ground — not knowing but the gold is under their camp itself — sometimes digging one hundred and sixty feet before they strike the vein, or then missing it by a foot — turned into demons, and regardless of each other's rights, in their thirst for riches — whole valleys, for thirty miles, suddenly honey-combed by the pits of the miners, so that even hundreds are drowned in them — standing in water, and covered with mud and clay, they work night and day, dying of exposure and disease. Having read this, and partly forgotten it, I was thinking, accidentally, of my own unsatisfactory life, doing as others do; and with that vision of the diggings still before me, I asked myself, why I might not be washing some gold daily, though it were only the finest particles — why I might not sink a shaft down to the gold within me, and work that mine. *There* is a Ballarat, a Bendigo for you — what though it were a Sulky Gully?[5] At any rate, I might pursue some path, however solitary and narrow and crooked, in which I could walk with love and reverence. Wherever a man separates from the multitude, and goes his own way in this mood, there indeed is a fork in the road, though ordinary travellers may see only a gap in the paling. His solitary path across-lots will turn out the *higher way* of the two.

Men rush to California and Australia as if the true gold   19 were to be found in that direction; but that is to go to the very opposite extreme to where it lies. They go prospecting farther and farther away from the true lead, and are most unfortunate when they think themselves most successful. Is not our *native* soil auriferous?[6] Does not a stream from the golden mountains flow through our native valley? and has not this for more than geologic ages been bringing down the shining particles and forming the nuggets for us? Yet, strange to tell, if a digger steal

---

[5]Ballarat and Bendigo, in Victoria, Australia, were sites of famous gold strikes in 1851; Sulky Gully is just a humble, unglamorous American place name.

[6]Yielding gold.

away, prospecting for this true gold, into the unexplored sol-
itudes around us, there is no danger that any will dog his steps,
and endeavor to supplant him. He may claim and undermine
the whole valley even, both the cultivated and the uncultivated
portions, his whole life long in peace, for no one will ever dispute his claim. They will not mind his cradles or his toms.[7] He is
not confined to a claim twelve feet square, as at Ballarat, but
may mine anywhere, and wash the whole wide world in his
tom.

[7]Cradles are box-like devices set on rockers; toms, large shallow pans —
both used by miners for washing ore out of sand.

· George Orwell ·

GEORGE ORWELL was the pen name of Eric Blair (1903–1950), born in Bengal, India, the son of an English civil servant. After attending Eton on a scholarship, he joined the British police in Burma, where he acquired a distrust for the methods of the Empire. Then followed years of tramping, odd jobs, and near-starvation — recalled in *Down and Out in Paris and London* (1933). From living on the fringe of society and from his reportorial writing about English miners and factory workers, Orwell deepened his sympathy with underdogs.

Severely wounded while fighting in the Spanish Civil War, he wrote a memoir, *Homage to Catalonia* (1938), voicing disillusionment with Loyalists who, he claimed, sought not to free Spain but to exterminate their political enemies. A socialist by conviction, Orwell kept pointing to the dangers of a collective state run by totalitarians. In *Animal Farm* (1945), he satirizes Soviet bureaucracy; and in his famous novel *1984* (1949) he foresees a regimented England whose government perverts truth and spies on citizens by two-way television. (The motto of the state and its leader: "BIG BROTHER IS WATCHING YOU.")

Politics and
the English Language

In *1984*, a dictatorship tries to replace both spoken and written English with Newspeak, an official language that limits thought by reducing the size of its users' vocabulary. (The words *light* and *bad*, for instance, are suppressed in favor of *unlight* and *unbad*.) This concern with language and with its importance to society is constant in George Orwell's writings. "Looking back through my work," he declares in an essay ("Why I Write"), "I see that it is invariably where I lacked a *political* purpose that I wrote lifeless books and was betrayed into purple passages, sentences without meaning, decorative adjectives, and humbug generally."

No English writer of the twentieth century wrote humbug more rarely than did Orwell. First published in 1946, "Politics and the English Language" still stands as one of the most devastating attacks on muddy writing and thinking ever penned. To illustrate his argument Orwell carefully classifies examples of clichés, vague and pretentious diction, and meaningless words. His six short rules for writing responsible prose are well worth remembering.

Most people who bother with the matter at all would admit that the English language is in a bad way, but it is generally assumed that we cannot by conscious action do anything about it. Our civilization is decadent and our language — so the argument runs — must inevitably share in the general collapse. It follows that any struggle against the abuse of language is a sentimental archaism, like preferring candles to electric light or hansom cabs to aeroplanes. Underneath this lies the half-conscious belief that language is a natural growth and not an instrument which we shape for our own purposes.

Now, it is clear that the decline of a language must ultimately have political and economic causes: it is not due simply to the bad influence of this or that individual writer. But an effect can become a cause, reinforcing the original cause and producing the same effect in an intensified form, and so on indefinitely. A man may take to drink because he feels himself to be a failure, and then fail all the more completely because he drinks. It is rather the same thing that is happening to the English language. It becomes ugly and inaccurate because our thoughts are foolish, but the slovenliness of our language makes it easier for us to have foolish thoughts. The point is that the process is reversible. Modern English, especially written English, is full of bad habits which spread by imitation and which can be avoided if one is willing to take the necessary trouble. If one gets rid of these habits one can think more clearly, and to think clearly is a necessary first step towards political regeneration: so that the fight against bad English is not frivolous and is not the exclusive concern of professional writers. I will come back to this presently, and I hope that by that time the meaning of what I have said here will have become clearer. Meanwhile, here are five specimens of the English language as it is now habitually written.

These five passages have not been picked out because they ³
are especially bad — I could have quoted far worse if I had
chosen — but because they illustrate various of the mental vices
from which we now suffer. They are a little below the average,
but are fairly representative samples. I number them so that I
can refer back to them when necessary:

(1) I am not, indeed, sure whether it is not true to say that
the Milton who once seemed not unlike a seventeenth-century Shelley had not become, out of an experience ever more
bitter in each year, more alien[*sic*] to the founder of that Jesuit
sect which nothing could induce him to tolerate.
                Professor Harold Laski (Essay in *Freedom of Expression*).

(2) Above all, we cannot play ducks and drakes with a
native battery of idioms which prescribes such egregious col-
locations of vocables as the Basic *put up with* for *tolerate* or *put
at a loss* for *bewilder*.
                Professor Lancelot Hogben (*Interglossa*).

(3) On the one side we have the free personality: by definition it is not neurotic, for it has neither conflict nor dream.
Its desires, such as they are, are transparent, for they are just
what institutional approval keeps in the forefront of consciousness; another institutional pattern would alter their
number and intensity; there is little in them that is natural, ir-
reducible, or culturally dangerous. But *on the other side*, the
social bond itself is nothing but the mutual reflection of these
self-secure integrities. Recall the definition of love. Is not this
the very picture of a small academic? Where is there a place in
this hall of mirrors for either personality or fraternity?
                Essay on psychology in *Politics* (New York).

(4) All the "best people" from the gentlemen's clubs, and
all the frantic fascist captains, united in common hatred of
Socialism and bestial horror of the rising tide of the mass revolutionary movement, have turned to acts of provocation, to
foul incendiarism, to medieval legends of poisoned wells, to
legalize their own destruction of proletarian organizations,
and rouse the agitated petty-bourgeoisie to chauvinistic fervor
on behalf of the fight against the revolutionary way out of the
crisis.
                Communist pamphlet.

(5) If a new spirit *is* to be infused into this old country,
there is one thorny and contentious reform which must be

tackled, and that is the humanization and galvanization of the B.B.C. Timidity here will bespeak cancer and atrophy of the soul. The heart of Britain may be sound and of strong beat, for instance, but the British lion's roar at present is like that of Bottom in Shakespeare's *Midsummer Night's Dream* — as gentle as any sucking dove. A virile new Britain cannot continue indefinitely to be traduced in the eyes or rather ears, of the world by the effete languors of Langham Place, brazenly masquerading as "standard English." When the Voice of Britain is heard at nine o'clock, better far and infinitely less ludicrous to hear aitches honestly dropped than the present priggish, inflated, inhibited, school-ma 'amish arch braying of blameless bashful mewing maidens!

Letter in *Tribune.*

Each of these passages has faults of its own, but, quite apart   4
from avoidable ugliness, two qualities are common to all of them. The first is staleness of imagery: the other is lack of precision. The writer either has a meaning and cannot express it, or he inadvertently says something else, or he is almost indifferent as to whether his words mean anything or not. The mixture of vagueness and sheer incompetence is the most marked characteristic of modern English prose, and especially of any kind of political writing. As soon as certain topics are raised, the concrete melts into the abstract and no one seems to think of turns of speech that are not hackneyed: prose consists less and less of *words* chosen for the sake of their meaning, and more and more of *phrases* tacked together like the sections of a prefabricated hen-house. I list below, with notes and examples, various of the tricks by means of which the work of prose-construction is habitually dodged:

Dying Metaphors

A newly invented metaphor assists thought by evoking a   5
visual image, while on the other hand a metaphor which is technically "dead" (e.g., *iron resolution*) has in effect reverted to being an ordinary word and can generally be used without loss of vividness. But in between these two classes there is a huge dump of worn-out metaphors which have lost all evocative power and

are merely used because they save people the trouble of inventing phrases for themselves. Examples are: *Ring the changes on, take up the cudgels for, toe the line, ride roughshod over, stand shoulder to shoulder with, play into the hands of, no axe to grind, grist to the mill, fishing in troubled waters, on the order of the day, Achilles' heel, swan song, hotbed.* Many of these are used without knowledge of their meaning (what is a "rift," for instance?), and incompatible metaphors are frequently mixed, a sure sign that the writer is not interested in what he is saying. Some metaphors now current have been twisted out of their original meaning without those who use them even being aware of the fact. For example, *toe the line* is sometimes written *tow the line.* Another example is *the hammer and the anvil*, now always used with the implication that the anvil gets the worst of it. In real life it is always the anvil that breaks the hammer, never the other way about: a writer who stopped to think what he was saying would be aware of this, and would avoid perverting the original phrase.

Operators or Verbal False Limbs

These save the trouble of picking out appropriate verbs and nouns, and at the same time pad each sentence with extra syllables which give it an appearance of symmetry. Characteristic phrases are: *render inoperative, militate against, make contact with, be subjected to, give rise to, give grounds for, have the effect of, play a leading part (role) in, make itself felt, take effect, exhibit a tendency to, serve the purpose of, etc., etc.* The keynote is the elimination of simple verbs. Instead of being a single word, such as *break, stop, spoil, mend, kill*, a verb becomes a *phrase*, made up of a noun or adjective tacked on to some general-purpose verb such as *prove, serve, form, play, render.* In addition, the passive voice is wherever possible used in preference to the active, and noun constructions are used instead of gerunds (*by examination of* instead of *by examining*). The range of verbs is further cut down by means of the *-ize* and *de-* formation, and the banal statements are given an appearance of profundity by means of the *not un-* formation. Simple conjunctions and prepositions are replaced by such phrases as *with respect to, having regard to, the fact that, by dint of, in view of, in the interests of, on the hypothesis that*; and the ends of sentences are saved from anticlimax by such resounding commonplaces as *greatly to be desired, cannot be left out of account, a development to be expected in the near future, deserving of serious consideration, brought to a satisfactory conclusion*, and so on and so forth.

Pretentious Diction

Words like *phenomenon, element, individual* (as noun), *objective, categorical, effective, virtual, basic, primary, promote, constitute, exhibit, exploit, utilize, eliminate, liquidate*, are used to dress up simple statements and give an air of scientific impartiality to biased judgments. Adjectives like *epoch-making, epic, historic, unforgettable, triumphant, age-old, inevitable, inexorable, veritable*, are used to dignify the sordid processes of international politics, while writing that aims at glorifying war usually takes on an archaic color, its characteristic words being: *realm, throne, chariot, mailed fist, trident, sword, shield, buckler, banner, jackboot, clarion*. Foreign words and expressions such as *cul de sac, ancien régime, deus ex machina, mutatis mutandis, status quo, gleichshaltung, weltanschauung*, are used to give an air of culture and elegance. Except for the useful abbreviations *i.e., e.g.*, and *etc.*, there is no real need for any of the hundreds of foreign phrases now current in English. Bad writers, and especially scientific, political and sociological writers, are nearly always haunted by the notion that Latin or Greek words are grander than Saxon ones, and unnecessary words like *expedite, ameliorate, predict, extraneous, deracinated, clandestine, subaqueous* and hundreds of others constantly gain ground from their Anglo-Saxon opposite numbers.[1] The jargon peculiar to Marx-

[1]An interesting illustration of this is the way in which the English flower names which were in use till very recently are being ousted by Greek ones, *snapdragon* becoming *antirrhinum, forget-me-not* becoming *myosotis*, etc. It is hard to see any practical reason for this change of fashion: it is probably due to an instinctive turning-away from the more homely word and a vague feeling that the Greek word is scientific.

ist writing (*hyena, hangman, cannibal, petty bourgeois, these gentry, lackey, flunkey, mad dog, White Guard,* etc.) consists largely of words and phrases translated from Russian, German or French; but the normal way of coining a new word is to use a Latin or Greek root with the appropriate affix and, where necessary, the *-ize* formation. It is often easier to make up words of this kind (*deregionalize, impermissible, extramarital, nonfragmentatory* and so forth) than to think up the English words that will cover one's meaning. The result, in general, is an increase in slovenliness and vagueness.

Meaningless Words

In certain kinds of writing, particularly in art criticism and literary criticism, it is normal to come across long passages which are almost completely lacking in meaning.[2] Words like *romantic, plastic, values, human, dead, sentimental, natural, vitality,* as used in art criticism, are strictly meaningless in the sense that they not only do not point to any discoverable object, but are hardly ever expected to do so by the reader. When one critic writes, "The outstanding feature of Mr. X's work is its living quality," while another writes, "The immediately striking thing about Mr. X's work is its peculiar deadness," the reader accepts this as a simple difference of opinion. If words like *black* and *white* were involved, instead of the jargon words *dead* and *living,* he would see at once that language was being used in an improper way. Many political words are similarly abused. The word *Fascism* has now no meaning except in so far as it signifies "something not desirable." The words *democracy, socialism, freedom, patriotic, realistic, justice,* have each of them several different meanings which cannot be reconciled with one another.

8

---

[2]Example: "Comfort's catholicity of perception and image, strangely Whitmanesque in range, almost the exact opposite in aesthetic compulsion, continues to evoke that trembling atmospheric accumulative hinting at a cruel, an inexorably serene timelessness . . . Wrey Gardiner scores by aiming at simple bull's-eyes with precision. Only they are not so simple, and through this contented sadness runs more than the surface bitter-sweet of resignation." (*Poetry Quarterly.*)

In the case of a word like *democracy*, not only is there no agreed definition, but the attempt to make one is resisted from all sides. It is almost universally felt that when we call a country democratic we are praising it: consequently the defenders of every kind of regime claim that it is a democracy, and fear that they might have to stop using the word if it were tied down to any one meaning. Words of this kind are often used in a consciously dishonest way. That is, the person who uses them has his own private definition, but allows his hearer to think he means something quite different. Statements like *Marshal Pétain was a true patriot, The Soviet Press is the freest in the world, The Catholic Church is opposed to persecution,* are almost always made with intent to deceive. Other words used in variable meanings, in most cases more or less dishonestly, are: *class, totalitarian, science, progressive, reactionary, bourgeois, equality.*

Now that I have made this catalogue of swindles and perversions, let me give another example of the kind of writing that they lead to. This time it must of its nature be an imaginary one. I am going to translate a passage of good English into modern English of the worst sort. Here is a well-known verse from *Ecclesiastes:*   9

> I returned and saw under the sun, that the race is not to the swift, nor the battle to the strong, neither yet bread to the wise, nor yet riches to men of understanding, nor yet favor to men of skill; but time and chance happeneth to them all.

Here it is in modern English:

> Objective consideration of contemporary phenomena compels the conclusion that success or failure in competitive activities exhibits no tendency to be commensurate with innate capacity, but that a considerable element of the unpredictable must invariably be taken into account.

This is a parody, but not a very gross one. Exhibit (3),   10 above, for instance, contains several patches of the same kind of English. It will be seen that I have not made a full translation. The beginning and ending of the sentence follow the original meaning fairly closely, but in the middle the concrete illustrations — race, battle, bread — dissolve into the vague phrase "success or failure in competitive activities." This had to be so, because no modern writer of the kind I am discussing — no one capable of using phrases like "objective consideration of contemporary phenomena" — would ever tabulate his thoughts in that precise and detailed way. The whole tendency of modern prose is away from concreteness. Now analyze these two sentences a little more closely. The first contains forty-nine words but only sixty syllables, and all its words are those of everyday life. The second contains thirty-eight words of ninety syllables: eighteen of its words are from Latin roots, and one from Greek. The first sentence contains six vivid images, and only one phrase ("time and chance") that could be called vague. The second contains not a single fresh, arresting phrase, and in spite of its ninety syllables it gives only a shortened version of the meaning contained in the first. Yet without a doubt it is the second kind of sentence that is gaining ground in modern English. I do not want to exaggerate. This kind of writing is not yet universal, and outcrops of simplicity will occur here and there in the worst-written page. Still, if you or I were told to write a few lines on the uncertainty of human fortunes, we should probably come much nearer to my imaginary sentence than to the one from *Ecclesiastes*.

As I have tried to show, modern writing at its worst does   11
not consist in picking out words for the sake of their meaning and inventing images in order to make the meaning clearer. It consists in gumming together long strips of words which have already been set in order by someone else, and making the results presentable by sheer humbug. The attraction of this way of writing is that it is easy. It is easier — even quicker once you have the habit — to say *In my opinion it is a not unjustifiable assumption that* than to say *I think*. If you use ready-made phrases, you not only don't have to hunt about for words; you also don't have to bother with the rhythms of your sentences, since these phrases are generally so arranged as to be more or less euphonious. When you are composing in a hurry — when you are dictating to a stenographer, for instance, or making a public speech — it is natural to fall into a pretentious, Latinized

style. Tags like *a consideration which we should do well to bear in mind* or *a conclusion to which all of us would readily assent* will save many a sentence from coming down with a bump. By using stale metaphors, similes and idioms, you save much mental effort, at the cost of leaving your meaning vague, not only for your reader but for yourself. This is the significance of mixed metaphors. The sole aim of a metaphor is to call up a visual image. When these images clash — as in *The Fascist octopus has sung its swan song, the jackboot is thrown into the melting pot* — it can be taken as certain that the writer is not seeing a mental image of the objects he is naming; in other words he is not really thinking. Look again at the examples I gave at the beginning of this essay. Professor Laski (1) uses five negatives in fifty-three words. One of these is superfluous, making nonsense of the whole passage, and in addition there is the slip *alien* for akin, making further nonsense, and several avoidable pieces of clumsiness which increase the general vagueness. Professor Hogben (2) plays ducks and drakes with a battery which is able to write prescriptions, and, while disapproving of the every-day phrase *put up with*, is unwilling to look *egregious* up in the dictionary and see what it means. (3), if one takes an uncharitable attitude towards it, is simply meaningless: probably one could work out its intended meaning by reading the whole of the article in which it occurs. In (4), the writer knows more or less what he wants to say, but an accumulation of stale phrases chokes him like tea leaves blocking a sink. In (5), words and meaning have almost parted company. People who write in this manner usually have a general emotional meaning — they dislike one thing and want to express solidarity with another — but they are not interested in the detail of what they are saying. A scrupulous writer, in every sentence that he writes, will ask himself at least four questions, thus: What am I trying to say? What words will express it? What image or idiom will make it clearer? Is this image fresh enough to have an effect? And he will probably ask himself two more: Could I put it more shortly? Have I said anything that is avoidably ugly? But you are not obliged to go to all this trouble. You can shirk it by simply throwing your mind open and letting the ready-made phrases come crowding in. They will construct your sentences for you — even think your thoughts for you, to a certain extent — and at need they will perform the important service of partially concealing your meaning even from yourself. It is at this point that the special connection between politics and the debasement of language becomes clear.

In our time it is broadly true that political writing is bad 12 writing. Where it is not true, it will generally be found that the writer is some kind of rebel, expressing his private opinions and not a "party line." Orthodoxy, of whatever color, seems to demand a lifeless, imitative style. The political dialects to be found in pamphlets, leading articles, manifestos, White Papers and the speeches of under-secretaries do, of course, vary from party to party, but they are all alike in that one almost never finds in them a fresh, vivid, home-made turn of speech. When one watches some tired hack on the platform mechanically repeating the familiar phrases — *bestial atrocities, iron heel, bloodstained tyranny, free peoples of the world, stand shoulder to shoulder* — one often has a curious feeling that one is not watching a live human being but some kind of dummy; a feeling which suddenly becomes stronger at moments when the light catches the speaker's spectacles and turns them into blank discs which seem to have no eyes behind them. And this is not altogether fanciful. A speaker who uses that kind of phraseology has gone some distance towards turning himself into a machine. The appropriate noises are coming out of his larynx, but his brain is not involved as it would be if he were choosing his words for himself. If the speech he is making is one that he is accustomed to make over and over again, he may be almost unconscious of what he is saying, as one is when one utters the responses in church. And this reduced state of consciousness, if not indispensable, is at any rate favorable to political conformity.

In our time, political speech and writing are largely the 13 defense of the indefensible. Things like the continuance of British rule in India, the Russian purges and deportations, the dropping of the atom bombs on Japan, can indeed be defended, but only by arguments which are too brutal for most people to face, and which do not square with the professed aims of political parties. Thus political language has to consist largely of euphemism, question-begging and sheer cloudy vagueness. Defenseless villages are bombarded from the air, the inhabitants driven out into the countryside, the cattle machine-gunned, the huts set on fire with incendiary bullets: this is called *pacification.* Millions of peasants are robbed of their farms and sent trudging along the roads with no more than they can carry: this is called *transfer of population* or *rectification of frontiers.* People are imprisoned for years without trial, or shot in the back of the neck or sent to die of scurvy in Arctic lumber camps: this is called *elimination of unreliable elements.* Such phraseology is needed if one wants to name things without calling up mental pictures of them. Consider for instance some comfortable English professor defending Russian totalitarianism. He cannot say outright, "I believe in killing off your opponents when you can get good results by doing so." Probably, therefore, he will say something like this:

"While freely conceding that the Soviet régime exhibits certain features which the humanitarian may be inclined to deplore, we must, I think, agree that a certain curtailment of the right to political opposition is an unavoidable concomitant of transitional periods, and that the rigors which the Russian people have been called upon to undergo have been amply justified in the sphere of concrete achievement." 14

The inflated style is itself a kind of euphemism. A mass of Latin words fall upon the facts like soft snow, blurring the outlines and covering up all the details. The great enemy of clear language is insincerity. When there is a gap between one's real and one's declared aims, one turns as it were instinctively to long words and exhausted idioms, like a cuttlefish squirting out ink. In our age there is no such thing as "keeping out of politics." All issues are political issues, and politics itself is a mass of lies, evasions, folly, hatred and schizophrenia. When the general atmosphere is bad, language must suffer. I should expect to find — this is a guess which I have not sufficient 15 knowledge to verify — that the German, Russian and Italian languages have all deteriorated in the last ten or fifteen years, as a result of dictatorship.

But if thought corrupts language, language can also corrupt thought. A bad usage can spread by tradition and imitation, even among people who should and do know better. The debased language that I have been discussing is in some ways very convenient. Phrases like *a not unjustifiable assumption, leaves much to be desired, would serve no good purpose, a consideration which we should do well to bear in mind*, are a continuous temptation, a packet of aspirins always at one's elbow. Look back through this essay, and for certain you will find that I have again and again committed the very faults I am protesting against. By this morning's post I have received a pamphlet dealing with conditions in Germany. The author tells me that he "felt impelled" to write it. I open it at random, and here is almost the first sentence that I see: "(The Allies) have an opportunity not only of achieving a radical transformation of Germany's social and political structure in such a way as to avoid a nationalistic reaction in Germany itself, but at the same time of laying the foundations of a co-operative and unified Europe." You see, he "feels impelled" to write — feels, presumably, that he has something new to say — and yet his words, like cavalry horses answering the bugle, group themselves automatically into the familiar dreary pattern. This invasion of one's mind by ready-made phrases (*lay the foundations, achieve a radical transformation*) can only be prevented if one is constantly on guard against them, and every such phrase anaesthetizes a portion of one's brain.

I said earlier that the decadence of our language is probably curable. Those who deny this would argue, if they produced an argument at all, that language merely reflects existing social conditions, and that we cannot influence its development by any direct tinkering with words and constructions. So far as the general tone or spirit of a language goes, this may be true, but it is not true in detail. Silly words and expressions have often disappeared, not through any evolutionary process but owing to the conscious action of a minority. Two recent examples were *explore every avenue* and *leave no stone unturned*, which were killed by the jeers of a few journalists. There is a long list of flyblown metaphors which could similarly be got rid of if enough people would interest themselves in the job; and it should also be possible to laugh the *not un-* formation out of existence,[3] to reduce the amount of Latin and Greek in the average sentence, to drive out foreign phrases and strayed scientific words, and, in general, to make pretentiousness unfashionable. But all these are minor points. The defense of the English language implies more than this, and perhaps it is best to start by saying what it does *not* imply.

To begin with it has nothing to do with archaism, with the salvaging of obsolete words and turns of speech, or with the setting up of a "standard English" which must never be departed from. On the contrary, it is especially concerned with the scrapping of every word or idiom which has outworn its usefulness. It has nothing to do with correct grammar and syntax, which are of no importance so long as one makes one's meaning clear, or with the avoidance of Americanisms, or with having what is called a "good prose style." On the other hand it is not concerned with fake simplicity and the attempt to make written English colloquial. Nor does it even imply in every case preferring the Saxon word to the Latin one, though it does imply using the fewest and shortest words that will cover one's meaning. What is above all needed is to let the meaning choose the word, and not the other way about. In prose, the worst thing one can do with words is to surrender to them. When you think of a concrete object, you think wordlessly, and then, if you want to describe the thing you have been visualizing you probably hunt about till you find the exact words that seem to fit. When you think of something abstract you are more inclined to use words from the start, and unless you make a conscious effort to prevent it, the existing dialect will come rushing in and do the job for you, at the expense of blurring or even changing your mean- 18

---

[3]One can cure oneself of the *not un-* formation by memorizing this sentence: *A not unblack dog was chasing a not unsmall rabbit across a not ungreen field.*

ing. Probably it is better to put off using words as long as possible and get one's meaning as clear as one can through pictures or sensations. Afterwards one can choose — not simply *accept* — the phrases that will best cover the meaning, and then switch round and decide what impression one's words are likely to make on another person. This last effort of the mind cuts out all stale or mixed images, all prefabricated phrases, needless repetitions, and humbug and vagueness generally. But one can often be in doubt about the effect of a word or a phrase, and one needs rules that one can rely on when instinct fails. I think the following rules will cover most cases:

(i) Never use a metaphor, simile or other figure of speech which you are used to seeing in print.

(ii) Never use a long word where a short one will do.

(iii) If it is possible to cut a word out, always cut it out.

(iv) Never use the passive where you can use the active.

(v) Never use a foreign phrase, a scientific word or a jargon word if you can think of an everyday English equivalent.

(vi) Break any of these rules sooner than say anything outright barbarous.

These rules sound elementary, and so they are, but they demand a deep change in attitude in anyone who has grown used to writing in the style now fashionable. One could keep all of them and still write bad English, but one could not write the kind of stuff that I quoted in those five specimens at the beginning of this article.

I have not here been considering the literary use of language, but merely language as an instrument for expressing and not for concealing or preventing thought. Stuart Chase and others have come near to claiming that all abstract words are meaningless, and have used this as a pretext for advocating a kind of political quietism. Since you don't know what Fascism is, how can you struggle against Fascism? One need not swallow such absurdities as this, but one ought to recognize that the present political chaos is connected with the decay of language, and that one can probably bring about some improvement by starting at the verbal end. If you simplify your English, you are freed from the worst follies of orthodoxy. You cannot speak any of the necessary dialects, and when you make a stupid remark its stupidity will be obvious, even to yourself. Political language — and with variations this is true of all political parties, from Conservatives to Anarchists — is designed to make lies sound truthful and murder respectable, and to give an appearance of solidity to pure wind. One cannot change this all in a moment, but one can at least change one's own habits, and from time to time one can even, if one jeers loudly enough, send some worn-out and useless phrase — some *jackboot, Achilles' heel, hotbed, melting pot, acid test, veritable inferno* or other lump of verbal refuse — into the dustbin where it belongs.

• A NOTE ON POLITICS •
• AND THE ENGLISH LANGUAGE •

George Orwell's complaint that political language has to consist of "sheer cloudy vagueness" seems still to apply in our day. In February 1981, shortly after President Reagan's appointee as Secretary of State appeared before Congress to be confirmed, *The Guardian*, an English newspaper, printed the following editorial, "Nuancing in the Dark." In the writer's opinion, Mr. Haig's diction and syntax deserve parody. By the pun *Clausewitz*, the editorial suggests that a holocaust like that of Auschwitz has been visited upon the English language.

> General Alexander Haig has contexted the Polish watchpot somewhat nuancely. How, though, if the situation decontrols, can he stoppage it mountingly conflagrating?
> Haig, in Congressional hearings before his confirmatory, paradoxed his auditioners by abnormalling his responds so that verbs were nouned, nouns verbed, and adjectives adverbized. He techniqued a new way to vocabulary his thoughts so as to informationally uncertain anybody listening about what he had actually implicationed.
> At first it seemed that the general was impenetrabling what at basic was clear. This, it was suppositioned, was a new linguistic harbingered by NATO during the time he bellwethered it. But close observers have alternatived that idea. What

Haig is doing, they concept, is to decouple the Russians from everything they are moded to. An example was to obstacle Soviet Ambassador Dobrynin from personalizing the private elevator at Foggy Bottom. Now he has to communal like everybody else.

Experts in the Kremlin thought they could recognition the word-forms of American diplomacy. Now they have to afreshly language themselves up before suddenly told to knight their bishops and rook their pawns.

If that is how General Haig wants to nervous breakdown the Russian leadership he may be shrewding his way to the biggest diplomatic invent since Clausewitz. Unless, that is, he schizophrenes his allies first.

Evidently the parodist is recalling Mr. Haig's use of words and phrases such as "epistemologicallywise," "nuanced departures," "caveat my response," and "saddle myself with a statistical fence." For such dustbin language, the 1981 convention of the National Council of Teachers of English paid Mr. Haig the ironic tribute of their "Doublespeak Award" (an unwanted honor whose title recalls Orwell's Newspeak and Doublethink), citing him as "the most confusing, evasive, and contradictory public speaker of the year."

· Susan Allen Toth ·

SUSAN ALLEN TOTH was born in 1940 and grew up, unhurriedly, in Ames, Iowa. A Phi Beta Kappa graduate of Smith College, she earned her Ph.D. at the University of Minnesota. Her critical and scholarly articles have appeared in the *New England Quarterly*, *Studies in Short Fiction*, and *The American Scholar*. She has also written articles and fiction for *Redbook*, *Harper's*, and *Ms*. Toth teaches modern fiction, creative writing, and the novel at Macalester College. *Blooming* (1981) is her first book.

Nothing Happened

The first chapter of *Blooming*, "Nothing Happened" is the author's probing, funny, and touching examination of her 1950s adolescence in a midwestern college town. The essay's extended examples underscore her youthful innocence concerning death, divorce, sex, and suicide: matters discussed then in whispers, if at all. Yet, though seemingly uneventful, Toth's growing-up years provided her with what some teenagers today might envy: a chance to mature at her own pace.

We huddled together in the cool spring night, whispering in hoarse voices, thrumming with the excitement that vibrated through the crowd gathering in the parking lot outside the Ames train station. All the way home from Des Moines we had hugged each other, laughed, cried, and hugged each other again. When we passed through the small farming towns between Des Moines and Ames, we rolled down the windows of the Harbingers' station wagon and shouted down the quiet streets, "We beat Marshalltown in seven overtimes! We beat Marshalltown in seven overtimes!" It had a rhythmic beat, a chant we repeated to each other in unbelieving ecstasy. We beat Marshalltown in seven overtimes! For the first time in ten years, Ames High School had won the state basketball championship.

1

507

Most of us sophomores felt nothing so important could ever happen to us again.

As a string of cars began threading off the highway, filling up the lot, someone turned the lights along Main Street on full. It was close to midnight, but families were pouring down the street toward the station as though it held a George Washington's Birthday sale. We were all waiting for the team. The mayor had ordered out the two fire engines, which were waiting too, bright red and gleaming under the lights. When the bus finally came around the corner, a cheering erupted from the crowd that didn't stop until the boys had walked down the steps, grinning a little sheepishly, and climbed onto the engines. The coach rode on one, the mayor on another. Following our cheerleaders, voices gone but valiantly shrieking, who were leading the way in their whirling orange pleated skirts and black sweaters, we snake-danced down Main Street behind blowing sirens and paraded to the high-school auditorium. There we listened to speeches from the mayor, the principal, the coach, and the team captain. We would have no school tomorrow, the principal told us (we cheered again), just a pep assembly, then dismissal. Then Mr. J. J. Girton, who owned all three movie theaters in Ames, came to the mike and said that in honor of the occasion he would show a free movie at the New Ames tomorrow at two P.M. We cheered, but this time not as loudly. We knew whenever Mr. Girton showed free movies, he always picked the oldest Looney Tunes and a dull Western. The coach thanked everyone and sat down quickly; he looked tired. But when he introduced the team captain, who made his teammates rise, we jumped to our feet and clapped and stomped.

I was filled with love and admiration for all of them, for stocky little Tom Fisher, who had made a critical free throw; for tall, gangly Charlie Stokowski, who had racked up thirty points; for George Davis, who usually stood most of the game in front of the bench with his mouth hanging open, but who tonight in the midst of the team looked like a hero. Next to me Patsy Jones, George's girlfriend, looked smug and proud. We knew she was planning to meet him backstage for a few moments after the assembly. When our new celebrities filed off the

2

3

stage, our parents, who had been sitting together in the last rows, took us home. Next morning at breakfast we could read all about ourselves, with headlines and pictures, in the Des Moines *Register*. Though we knew other stories would topple ours after a few days, it didn't matter.

Perhaps I remember that night so vividly because it stands out like a high hill in the flat, uneventful landscape that was both the physical and emotional setting for our town. Our lives were not dull, oh, no; but our adolescence bubbled and fermented in a kind of vacuum. In Ames, in the 1950s, as far as we were concerned, nothing happened. 4

Ames had once had a murder. It had happened a few years before we were in junior high, to someone we didn't know, a man who hadn't lived in Ames long. He had somehow accumulated gambling debts, probably on his travels out West, and one night he was found shot to death at the Round-up Motel. No one ever found a weapon or the murderers. After a few blurred photographs in the Ames Daily *Tribune* and interviews with the cleaning woman who'd found him, the motel owner, the county sheriff and local police, even the newspaper abandoned the story. But for many years afterward, when we drove with strangers past the Round-up, we would point it out in reverential tones. It might look just like a tidy modern bungalow, stretched out into longer wings than usual, but we knew it was a bloody place. 5

Other than our murder, we had little experience with violence. Sometimes there were accidents. One of my girlfriends had a brother who had lost an eye when another boy had aimed badly with a bow and arrow. We stared surreptitiously at his glass eye, which was bigger and shinier than it ought to be. Someone else's sister, much younger, had toddled in front of a truck on the highway and been killed. Her picture, done in careful pastels by an artist from Des Moines, hung over the sofa in her parents' living room. When they spoke of her, I tried not to look at the picture, which made me feel uncomfortable. 6

When death came to Ames, it seldom took anyone we knew. We were all shocked when one morning we saw our high-school teachers whispering together in the halls, a few of them 7 weeping openly, over the history teacher's four-year-old daughter, who had been rushed the previous night to the hospital and who had died almost immediately of heart failure. Visitation was to be that night at the Jefferson Funeral Parlor. Those of us who felt close to Mr. Sansome wanted to go to "pay our respects," a phrase someone had heard from another teacher. We discussed solemnly what to wear, what to do, what to say. When two girlfriends came to pick me up, I was nervous, with a sinking feeling in my stomach because I did not know what to expect. I had never seen a dead person before.

We didn't stay at the funeral parlor long. The room was   8
crowded with friends of the Sansomes. Mrs. Sansome wasn't there — home, in bed, someone said sympathetically — and Mr. Sansome stood with a glazed expression on his face, shaking hands, muttering politeness, to everyone who came up to him. We shook his hand and moved on to the coffin. Mary Sansome looked just as she always did, dressed perhaps more neatly in a Sunday dress with bright pink bows tied onto her long pigtails. As we leaned closer, I thought her skin looked rubbery and waxen, like a doll I had once had. Her eyes were shut, but she looked as though she might wake up any minute, disturbed by the murmured talk around her. I looked over at Mr. Sansome, usually a gesturing, dramatic man, standing woodenly a few feet away, staring straight ahead of him. The feeling in my stomach got worse. I wanted to cry, but I couldn't. Soon my friends and I went silently home.

The few deaths we knew in those years seemed rare and ac-   9
cidental. Once Mrs. Miller, an elderly neighbor, came fluttering to our house in high excitement. She didn't want my sister and me to hear what she had to tell my mother, but we hovered quietly in our room with the door open a crack and listened intently. Behind Mrs. Miller lived Sam and Martha Doyle, five children, a collie, and a tiger cat. It was a large, noisy, happy family. Mr. Doyle was like any other father, kindly, offhand, seldom home. But for some reason no one understood, not even patiently inquisitive Mrs. Miller, Mr. Doyle had tried to kill himself that morning. "I heard screams," she said breathlessly to my mother, "and when I ran to the back door, there was

Martha Doyle standing in the driveway trying to open the garage door. I guess it must have stuck. Right behind her was Sam, with some kitchen towels wrapped around his wrists all covered with blood. Then she got the door open, they both got in the car and drove off."

We never heard what happened after the Doyles got to the hospital, but everything was quickly hushed up. Soon afterward the whole family moved away. I thought about Mr. Doyle for a long time. What could ever be so bad you would want to hurt yourself, make yourself bleed like that? Tragedy, as far as we knew it existed in adult lives, merely extended to freakish twists of fate, like the death of little Mary Sansome. Most of us were convinced that life was going to be wonderful.

As far as we knew, people in Ames didn't get divorced. But one woman did. Sallie Houlton, the divorcee, looked like any other grown-up. In her late twenties, she had an average figure, nondescript brown hair, a pleasant but undistinguished face. Sallie lived sometimes with her arthritic aunt, Miss Houlton, on the far side of town. Mother knew them both because an aunt of mine had taught with Miss Houlton years ago in Minnesota. Sometimes Sallie disappeared for temporary employment in other cities. She was a dietitian, Mother said, and ran hospital kitchens. All I really knew about Sallie Houlton was that she had been divorced. No one would say why, but once Mrs. Miller had been talking about Sallie to Mother and I heard her say, with disapproving fervor, "And on top of all that, he *drank*." I was very curious to know what "all that" was. Mother, usually fairly straightforward in her replies to my questions, hedged this one; she said it was very complicated, hard to explain. Many years later, when for some ignoble reason I was still curious about "all that," Mother said simply, "He was impotent." Oh, I said. Her answer was something of a letdown.

It was almost as difficult to understand what could happen to a husband and wife so terrible that they would want a divorce as it was to understand what had driven Mr. Doyle to cut his wrists. As I grew older and moved through high school, I began to have occasional focus, as though a blurred picture had suddenly sharpened, on a few of the marriages I had taken so far for granted. My first illumination took place outside our house one hot summer night, when my mother had given one of her four-to-six sherry parties. Her friends, all married couples, came to sip a little Taylor's Cocktail Sherry or ginger ale, smoke, talk, sip some more and go home at a decent hour. But at this party, four of the guests stayed until past ten. Two were Australians, a visiting professor of agricultural economics and his pale blonde wife, who was a part-time secretary in the foreign students' office; the others were my mother's old friends Mike and Helen Snyder, who had lived next door to her before I was born. The Snyders were probably in their forties then, the Australians in their twenties. Mike always liked to stay late at parties, and he and Helen had begun to snipe at each other about whether it was time to leave. I had heard their rapid fire before, seen Helen's mouth tighten at the corners, watched Mike defiantly pour more sherry into his glass; neither I nor anyone else ever took their bickering seriously. Mike was a sharp-tongued mathematician, and his cutting edge seemed almost professional. Tonight Mike kept his back turned to Helen as much as possible and talked vehemently to the Australian wife. Sometimes when he got particularly excited he picked up her hand and held it for a while. Finally the Australian economist got up. His wife rose obediently, and Mother, who was looking tired, rose too to walk them to their car. I tagged along, bored with the party, and, surprisingly, found that Mike Snyder was walking beside me.

"So how's your summer going?" he asked me absentminded- 13 ly, but he was watching the light-haired woman in front of him. He swayed, bumped into me, and straightened up again. At the car, after her husband got in, he reached through the front window and patted her on the shoulder. "Lucy, Lucy, Lucy," he said in a kind of singsong. The car pulled quickly away from the curb. Mike turned to my mother. With astonishment, I could see that he had tears in his eyes. "What am I going to do, Hazel?" he said in a voice in which anguish had conquered the alcohol. "I love her so damn much. What am I going to do?" Mother put her arm around Mike and began to guide him back to the house. "It's going to be all right, Mike," I heard her say comfortingly, just as she did to me when I was overcome with despair. "It's all right. You know they're leaving soon. It's going to be all right."

Maybe for a while it *was* all right. The summer passed. The Australian visitors went back to Melbourne, and the Snyders continued to come to Mother's sherry parties. I tried not to talk to them much. I had been both confused and embarrassed by what I had seen. Four or five years later, when I was in college, one of the bits of news that Mother had for me at Christmas vacation was that the Snyders were getting a divorce. It was not the shock it would once have been. I asked Mother about the Australian woman, but Mother looked surprised. That was a long time ago, she said, and had nothing to do with it anyway.

If I knew little about love, I knew nothing about sex. The closest thing Ames had to offer as sex education was the Hudson station, a rickety gas outlet beyond the city limits that sold rubbers in a coin-operated machine in its men's room, or so we girls were told. A girl's reputation could be ruined if her date stopped for gas at the Hudson station. A lot of us had to ask more knowing friends what a rubber was. That piece of information was conveyed to me in patronizing tones by a fellow sixth-grader, Joyce Schwartz, who motioned me upstairs one day to her parents' bedroom when they were out. She carefully opened her father's top drawer, lifted up a pile of neatly folded handkerchiefs, and showed me a small cardboard box. "Those are rubbers," she said wisely. She let me open the top of the box but didn't want me to take anything out. I couldn't make much of what I saw anyway.

Not long after that, another friend, Emily Harris, also mature beyond my years, took me for a walk behind her house to an old deserted greenhouse that had once belonged to the college. There couples came sometimes at night and did things, she said. "Sometimes I find rubbers here in the grass," she added, staring intently around her feet, and I stared at my feet too, though I wasn't sure what I was looking for. I only saw bits of broken glass from long-gone windows, bottle caps, and used Kleenex. Suddenly Emily shouted, "There's one!" She looked around quickly for a stick, and then fished in the grass until she

managed to hoist aloft a squishy shapeless piece of latex. It was
the fleshlike color that seemed obscene to me. "Don't touch it,"
Emily warned. "You can get awful diseases from these things." I
thought you could also get awfully cold out here at night. What
could drive anyone to such an uncomfortable spot to do something with that icky piece of rubber?

Besides having had a murder and a divorce, Ames had a   17
prostitute. Her name was Nancy, and all the boys in high
school joked about her. She lived near the college, but I never
saw her until one dark rainy night when I was a senior in high
school, almost ready to graduate. It was late in May, the kind of
balmy weather that opened up the promise of a long drowsy
summer ahead. My friend Charlie, who had dropped over on a
dull evening just to talk awhile, agreed to walk with me in the
rain all the way to Campustown, the tiny shopping district
about a mile distant.

When we were dressed for outdoors, we looked like brothers   18
in our wrinkled trenchcoats, the Penney's double-breasted
poplin style that was practically unisex even in those days. I bor-
rowed Charlie's shapeless old hat and jammed it down over my
short hair. You couldn't see much of me except my nose,
though I would lift my face up from time to time to catch the
fresh feel of the rain. It was a lovely walk, as we sloshed through
puddles, stared at the bright glowing lights in all the darkened
houses, reveled in the quiet of the deserted streets. It seemed to
me as if we were all alone in the world, wet and happy, with
only the faint whooshing of tree branches and the occasional
splash of passing cars to interrupt our intent conversation.
When we got to Campustown, it too was deserted, the stores
shuttered tight, a few small neon signs flashing in dark windows, "Cat's Paw," "Pop's Grill," "Cigars." Tonight we seemed
to own this little main street, which echoed to our steps and low
voices.

Striding along, matching Charlie's pace as best I could, I   19
soon saw someone approaching from the other direction. I
didn't bother to notice who it was until she drew abreast of us,
paused for a moment, and said quickly but distinctly, "Want to
fuck?" I looked up in disbelief. I caught a glimpse of a lined face,

bright yellow stringy hair, garish lips, and then it was gone.
Charlie, though startled, was beginning to laugh. "Did she say
what I thought she said?" I asked anxiously. "Yup," he said,
now laughing openly. "That was Nancy. She probably thought
you were a boy. She must've been really startled when she saw
you up close." I turned and looked behind me, but Nancy was
gone. Charlie, who kept chuckling for a long while, couldn't
understand why I seemed upset; I wasn't sure myself. But it
seemed as though the interruption had broken something
fragile, as evanescent as the rainbow oil slick in the gutter at our
feet.

If I was vouchsafed some faint but definite glimmerings   20
about sex in Ames, I saw little else troubling that small society.
One reason I was so blind to common attitudes toward blacks
was that Ames didn't have any. Or rather, like everything else,
Ames had only one. For most of the years I was growing up,
there was a single family in town who were black, or, to be precise, an unassuming shade of brown. The Elliotts, quiet and
hardworking, lived far from the college campus in an unfashionable section where small businesses, warehouses and run-
down older houses crowded together. It wasn't exactly a slum,
but it wasn't a place where anyone I knew lived either. Alexander Elliott was in my class, his younger sister two classes
behind me. They too were hardworking and quiet, always neatly dressed, pleasant expressions on their faces, ready to respond
politely. What went on behind those carefully composed smiles
no one then ever wondered.

We thought the Elliott kids were nice enough, we ex-   21
changed casual greetings with them, but Alexander was never
invited to any parties. He did not belong to any social groups. I
do not remember seeing him anywhere, except in a crowd
cheering at a football game or sitting a little apart in school assembly. Once or twice I think I remember Alexander's bringing
a date, also black — though "Negro" was what we called them,
enunciating the word carefully — to the Junior-Senior Prom.
Wherever she was from, it wasn't Ames. They danced by
themselves all evening. Yet none of us thought we were
prejudiced about Alex, and almost every year we elected him to

some class office. The year Alex became student-body president, our principal pointed to Ames High proudly as an example of the way democracy really worked.

If I was unaware that Ames was prejudiced toward blacks, I [22] could not miss the town's feelings about Catholics. I myself was fascinated by the glamour that beckoned at the door of St. Cecilia's, the imposing brick church defiantly planted right on the main road through town. Every Christmas St. Cecilia's erected a life-size nativity scene on its lawn, floodlit, Mary in blue velvet, glowing halos, real straw in the wooden manger. None of the Methodists, Lutherans, Baptists or Presbyterians did anything quite so showy. I always begged Mother to slow down as we drove by so I could admire it. Sometimes I could see one of the nuns from the small convent behind the church billowing in her black robes down the street. If I was with my friend Peggy O'Reilly, who was Catholic, she would stop and greet the nun respectfully. She knew each one by name, though they all looked alike to me.

Peggy told me bits and pieces about Catholic doctrine, [23] which was so different from the vague advice I was gathering haphazardly in my own Presbyterian Sunday School that I didn't know what to make of it. Catholics had exotic secrets. One of the saints — was it Bernadette? — had been given the exact date of the end of the world, Peggy said, and she on her death had bequeathed it to the Pope. Every Pope kept this secret locked in a special case, and when he was about to die, he opened it, read the date, and expired — probably, I thought, out of shock. Why didn't the Popes share this wonderful knowledge with the world, so we could all get ready for the end? I asked Peggy. Peggy couldn't say.

Even if we hadn't known from friends like Peggy that [24] Catholics were different, our parents would have told us. One of the few rigid rules enforced on many of us was the impossibility of "getting serious" about a Catholic boy. For a Protestant to marry a Catholic in Ames produced a major social upheaval, involving parental conferences, conversions, and general disapproval on both sides. Even our liberal minister, who encouraged his Presbyterian parishioners to call him "Doctor Bob" because he didn't want to appear uppish about his advanced degree, came to our high-school fellowship group one night to lecture on Catholicism. He probably knew that one of his deacons' daughters was going very steadily with a Catholic boy. Warning us about the autocratic nature of the Catholic Church, its iron hand, its idolatry, and most of all the way it could snatch our very children from us and bring them up in the manacles of a strange faith, Doctor Bob heated with the warmth of his topic until his cheeks glowed as he clenched and unclenched his fists.

Since I never fell in love with one of the few Catholic boys in our class, I never faced such direct fire. But my friend Peggy did. Much to her parents' disapproval, she began going steadily with Alvin Barnes, a Methodist boy who had never dated at all before he discovered Peggy. He was a quiet, withdrawn boy who seldom talked about anything, let alone his feelings, but we could all tell by the way he looked at Peggy that he loved her with a single-minded devotion. Her parents tolerated the romance for a year, though we knew they often had long talks with Peggy about it. But during their senior year, when Peggy and Alvin were still holding hands in daylight, Peggy's family decided that enough was enough. They gave Peggy an ultimatum, which she repeated to us, sobbing, one night when we girls had gathered together at someone's house for popcorn and gossip. She was distraught, but she had no thought of disobeying them; she was going to tell Alvin they must break it off. We were indignant, sympathetic, but helpless; the price Peggy's parents were willing to pay was a year away at college, and no one thought Peggy could give that up instead.

A few days later Alvin was absent from school, and the whispers were alarming. After hearing Peggy's news, he had come to her house to try to argue with her parents. They had refused to let him in, had told him to go home and not to bother their daughter again. When he called their house, they wouldn't let Peggy come to the phone. So later that night, he had returned. There in the sloping driveway he had lain down behind the rear wheels of the O'Reilly family car. All night he lay there, waiting for the still-dark morning when Mr. O'Reilly would come out, start the engine, and back the car down the driveway on his way to work.

Of course, when morning finally came, Mr. O'Reilly saw   27
Alvin at once. Horrified, he called Alvin's parents. They came and took Alvin away, and he did not come back to school until close to the end of the semester. Then he kept aloof, refusing to talk about what had happened, and hovered silently at the edges of our games and parties. Soon we all graduated, Alvin left town, and we lost track of him entirely. But I felt as though he had somehow been sacrificed, offered up to the fierce religious hatred I had seen gleaming in Doctor Bob's eyes. For several years, until even more bitter images etched over this one, I thought of the effects of prejudice as embodied in Alvin's quiet figure, lying patiently and hopelessly in the chilly darkness behind the wheels of the O'Reilly car.

Such drama, however, was rare. It was a quiet town and a   28
quiet time. That may be why I can still hear the whispers of notebooks slapping shut and a pencil-sharpener grinding in the high-school study hall; the scratchy strains of "Blue Tango" on an overamplified record-player at the Friday dance; the persistent throb of grasshoppers in a rustling cornfield on a summer night when my boyfriend Peter parked his old Ford on a country road. In a world where nothing seemed to happen, small sounds were amplified so clearly that they still echo in my mind. So now on a hot summer night, when I sit by myself on my city steps, trying to block out nearby traffic and concentrating instead on the slightest rustle of leaves in the warm breeze, I remember the years of my growing up in Ames. Against that background of quiet, a girl could listen to her heart beating.

During the summer the long hot weekend days seemed to   29
stretch out like the endless asphalt ribbons of highway winding into the country. We never had quite enough to do, especially on Saturday mornings. So we often drifted in and out of Olson's Bowling Alley, just a few lanes, hand-set pins, a quarter a line. Tucked on the second floor above a Spiegel catalogue

order house at the end of Main Street, it was a most unlikely location for a bowling alley. Although the nearby high school hired it for occasional gym classes, I doubt that it ever paid its way. Sometimes we arrived at Olson's Alley early, by nine o'clock, when the downtown stores were opening their doors and hosing down their sidewalks. The heat was beginning to pour in the open windows, streaking sunshine across the dirty wooden floor and the three brightly gleaming lanes. We settled haphazardly into a game. Before long our hands were sweaty; we'd wipe them on our shorts, hoping the crispness of our carefully ironed blouses wouldn't wilt too much before the boys came.

Some boys always did drift through Olson's on those long hazy mornings, as aimlessly as the dusty sunshine. They banged noisily up the stairs, yelling to each other, and clambered over the church-pew benches to hoot at our self-conscious strides as we struggled to aim our bowling balls straight. The girl whose turn it was to be pin-setter, huddled behind the racks at the end of the long alley, looked through the intricate metal network at the faraway girls laughing and flirting with the boys. Even a boy who liked you was too embarrassed to walk all the way to the back of the lanes when everyone could see where he was going. 30

Though it seems odd to think of a bowling alley as a quiet place, Olson's was. Though we girls giggled and gossiped, the only other sounds beyond those occasional noisy interruptions of the boys were the heavy thud of the bowling balls, the clang of the pin-setting rack, and the flap of the torn shade at the open window. The morning seemed to stretch on forever. When we'd used up our quarters and given up on seeing any more boys, we'd tuck in our blouses, comb our hair, and emerge from the oppressive sweaty room into the blinding full-noon sun. Down Main Street we'd hurry to the Rainbow Cafe, newly air-conditioned, and treat ourselves to icy root-beer floats before taking the bus home. 31

When I plunge back into those uneventful Saturday mornings, I am once more lapped around by waves of time, repetitious, comforting, like the gentle undulations of Blaine's Pool when the late-afternoon breezes blew over its empty blue-green 32 water. We all felt as though summer would go on forever. I would go to Olson's, or not; I would bowl a little, or not; I would see the boy I cared about, or I wouldn't. Other Saturday mornings stretched ahead like oases in the shimmering sun.

As I grew older, I began to realize that this quiet was not go-   33
ing to last. Time was speeding up; at some sharply definable point I would grow up and leave Ames. At odd moments in those last years I would be surprised by sadness, a strange feeling that perhaps I had missed something, that maybe life was going to pass me by. At the same time I nestled securely in the familiar landscape of streets whose every bump and jog I knew, of people who smiled and greeted me by name wherever I went, of friends who appeared at every movie, store, or swimming pool.

Nowhere did I feel this conflicting sense of security and   34
impending loss as sharply as I did at the train station. Ames lay on some important transcontinental routes, and trains passed through daily on their way from Chicago to Portland, San Francisco, Los Angeles. I had ridden on trains for short trips, but I had never been on one overnight and I was too young to remember clearly what the country was like west of Ames when the prairies stopped and the mountains began. From a long auto trip when I was eight, I only remembered endless spaces punctuated by the Grand Canyon. So for me the crack passenger trains, the *City of San Francisco*, the *City of Denver*, the *City of Los Angeles*, had titles that rang in my imagination like the purest romance. Big cities, the golden West, life beckoned to me from every flashing train window.

On slow spring or summer nights, I would often ask my   35
friend Charlie to take me down to the station to watch the trains come in. The *City of San Francisco* was due to pass through at ten o'clock, the *City of Denver* at eleven. Down at the deserted station we sat on an abandoned luggage cart near the tracks, staring into the darkness, listening for the first tell-tale hoot of a faraway whistle. The night was so quiet we whispered, hearing above our voices the grasshoppers, a squeal of brakes three blocks away at the beer parlor, the loud click of the station clock. The trains were always late, but we were in no hurry.

Eventually we'd hear a rumble on the tracks and then see a ³⁵ searching eye of light bearing down on us. Quickly we'd leap to our feet and get as close to the tracks as we dared, plugging our ears as the train ground to a stop in front of us, its metallic clamor deafening, its cars looming in the night like visitors from another world. As we stood there, we could see people moving back and forth inside the lighted windows. If we were outside a Pullman car, we might catch a glimpse of someone seated next to the window staring wordlessly back at us. I wondered why everyone wasn't asleep. A frowsy-haired woman with a brown felt hat pinned to her graying curls looked like someone I might know but didn't. Two young boys, jumping on their seats and pounding silently on the glass, could have been the Evans kids down the street, but weren't. They were strangers, separated from us not only by thick glass but by chance, being whisked away from their old lives to new ones. I felt the pull of the future, of adventure, waiting for them and someday for me.

After a few moments, an exchange of luggage flung by the ³⁷ stationmaster, who had suddenly emerged from inside the darkened hut, a few shouts, the train began to grind again. As we winced with the jarring sound of metal against metal, it picked up speed. I tried to watch the car with the frowsy-haired woman and the two jumping boys, but it was soon lost in a blur of streaming silver metal. A last long low shriek, and the train was gone, off to Denver or San Francisco.

I always felt let down when Charlie and I walked back to his ³⁸ car. I comforted myself with thinking that someday I too would be traveling on one of those trains, leaving Ames for college someplace far away, maybe even Denver or San Francisco. When I got on that train, I would head into a new and wonderful life. It never occurred to me that I would be taking my old self, and Ames, with me.

· Richard Rodriguez ·

RICHARD RODRIGUEZ was born in 1944 in San Francisco, the son of Spanish-speaking Mexican-Americans. In the memoir that follows Rodriguez chronicles his early struggles to speak English and reluctance to depart from Spanish. After doing graduate work at Columbia University, the Warburg Institute, London, and the University of California, Berkeley, he remained at Berkeley as a teacher. His essays have appeared in *The American Scholar, Change,* and *Saturday Review*; and he is working on a book of essays in autobiography to be called *Hunger of Memory* (scheduled for publication in 1982).

Aria: A Memoir of
a Bilingual Childhood

"Aria: A Memoir of a Bilingual Childhood," first published in *The American Scholar* in 1981, contains both poignant memoir and persuasive argument. Setting forth his views of bilingual education, the author measures the gains and losses that resulted when English gradually replaced the Spanish spoken in his childhood home. To the child Rodriguez, Spanish was a private language, English a public one. But intimacy, he learns at last, depends not on words but on people.

I remember, to start with, that day in Sacramento, in a   1
California now nearly thirty years past, when I first entered a classroom — able to understand about fifty stray English words. The third of four children, I had been preceded by my older brother and sister to a neighborhood Roman Catholic school. But neither of them had revealed very much about their classroom experiences. They left each morning and returned each afternoon, always together, speaking Spanish as they climbed the five steps to the porch. And their mysterious books, wrapped in brown shopping-bag paper, remained on the table next to the door, closed firmly behind them.

An accident of geography sent me to a school where all my classmates were white and many were the children of doctors and lawyers and business executives. On that first day of school, my classmates must certainly have been uneasy to find themselves apart from their families, in the first institution of their lives. But I was astonished. I was fated to be the "problem student" in class.

The nun said, in a friendly but oddly impersonal voice: "Boys and girls, this is Richard Rodriguez." (I heard her sound it out: *Rich-heard Road-ree-guess.*) It was the first time I had heard anyone say my name in English. "Richard," the nun repeated more slowly, writing my name down in her book. Quickly I turned to see my mother's face dissolve in a watery blur behind the pebbled-glass door.

Now, many years later, I hear of something called "bilingual education" — a scheme proposed in the late 1960s by Hispanic-American social activists, later endorsed by a congressional vote. It is a program that seeks to permit non-English-speaking children (many from lower class homes) to use their "family language" as the language of school. Such, at least, is the aim its supporters announce. I hear them, and am forced to say no: It is not possible for a child, any child, ever to use his family's language in school. Not to understand this is to misunderstand the public uses of schooling and to trivialize the nature of intimate life.

Memory teaches me what I know of these matters. The boy reminds the adult. I was a bilingual child, but of a certain kind: "socially disadvantaged," the son of working-class parents, both Mexican immigrants.

In the early years of my boyhood, my parents coped very well in America. My father had steady work. My mother managed at home. They were nobody's victims. When we moved to a house many blocks from the Mexican-American section of town, they were not intimidated by those two or three neighbors who initially tried to make us unwelcome. ("Keep your brats away from my sidewalk!") But despite all they achieved, or perhaps because they had so much to achieve, they lacked any deep feeling of ease, of belonging in public. They regarded the people at work or in crowds as being very distant from us. Those were the others, *los gringos*. That term was interchangeable in their speech with another, even more telling: *los americanos*.

I grew up in a house where the only regular guests were my relations. On a certain day, enormous families of relatives would visit us, and there would be so many people that the noise and the bodies would spill out to the backyard and onto the front porch. Then for weeks no one would come. (If the doorbell rang, it was usually a salesman.) Our house stood apart — gaudy yellow in a row of white bungalows. We were the people with the noisy dog, the people who raised chickens. We were the foreigners on the block. A few neighbors would smile and wave at us. We waved back. But until I was seven years old, I did not know the name of the old couple living next door or the names of the kids living across the street.

In public, my father and mother spoke a hesitant, accented, and not always grammatical English. And then they would have to strain, their bodies tense, to catch the sense of what was rapidly said by *los gringos*. At home, they returned to Spanish. The language of their Mexican past sounded in counterpoint to the English spoken in public. The words would come quickly, with ease. Conveyed through those sounds was the pleasing, soothing, consoling reminder that one was at home.

During those years when I was first learning to speak, my mother and father addressed me only in Spanish; in Spanish I learned to reply. By contrast, English (*inglés*) was the language I came to associate with gringos, rarely heard in the house. I learned my first words of English overhearing my parents speaking to strangers. At six years of age, I knew just enough words for my mother to trust me on errands to stores one block away — but no more.

I was then a listening child, careful to hear the very different sounds of Spanish and English. Wide-eyed with hearing, I'd listen to sounds more than to words. First, there were English (gringo) sounds. So many words still were unknown to me that when the butcher or the lady at the drugstore said something,

7

8

9

10

exotic polysyllabic sounds would bloom in the midst of their sentences. Often the speech of people in public seemed to me very loud, booming with confidence. The man behind the counter would literally ask, "What can I do for you?" But by being so firm and clear, the sound of his voice said that he was a gringo; he belonged in public society. There were also the high, nasal notes of middle-class American speech — which I rarely am conscious of hearing today because I hear them so often, but could not stop hearing when I was a boy. Crowds at Safeway or at bus stops were noisy with the birdlike sounds of *los gringos*. I'd move away from them all — all the chirping chatter above me.

My own sounds I was unable to hear, but I knew that I 11 spoke English poorly. My words could not extend to form complete thoughts. And the words I did speak I didn't know well enough to make distinct sounds. (Listeners would usually lower their heads to hear better what I was trying to say.) But it was one thing for *me* to speak English with difficulty; it was more troubling to hear my parents speaking in public: their high-whining vowels and guttural consonants; their sentences that got stuck with "eh" and "ah" sounds; the confused syntax; the hesitant rhythm of sounds so different from the way gringos spoke. I'd notice, moreover, that my parents' voices were softer than those of gringos we would meet.

I am tempted to say now that none of this mattered. (In 12 adulthood I am embarrassed by childhood fears.) And, in a way, it didn't matter very much that my parents could not speak English with ease. Their linguistic difficulties had no serious consequences. My mother and father made themselves understood at the county hospital clinic and at government offices. And yet, in another way, it mattered very much. It was unsettling to hear my parents struggle with English. Hearing them, I'd grow nervous, and my clutching trust in their protection and power would be weakened.

There were many times like the night at a brightly lit 13 gasoline station (a blaring white memory) when I stood uneasily hearing my father talk to a teenage attendant. I do not recall what they were saying, but I cannot forget the sounds my father made as he spoke. At one point his words slid together to form one long word — sounds as confused as the threads of blue and green oil in the puddle next to my shoes. His voice rushed through what he had left to say. Toward the end, he reached falsetto notes, appealing to his listener's understanding. I looked away at the lights of passing automobiles. I tried not to hear any more. But I heard only too well the attendant's reply, his calm, easy tones. Shortly afterward, headed for home, I shivered when my father put his hand on my shoulder. The very first chance that I got, I evaded his grasp and ran on ahead into the dark, skipping with feigned boyish exuberance.

But then there was Spanish: *español*, the language rarely 14 heard away from the house; *español*, the language which seemed to me therefore a private language, my family's language. To hear its sounds was to feel myself specially recognized as one of the family, apart from *los otros*. A simple remark, an inconsequential comment could convey that assurance. My parents would say something to me and I would feel embraced by the sounds of their words. Those sounds said: *I am speaking with ease in Spanish. I am addressing you in words I never use with los gringos. I recognize you as someone special, close, like no one outside. You belong with us. In the family. Ricardo.*

At the age of six, well past the time when most middle-class 15 children no longer notice the difference between sounds uttered at home and words spoken in public, I had a different experience. I lived in a world compounded of sounds. I was a child longer than most. I lived in a magical world, surrounded by sounds both pleasing and fearful. I shared with my family a language enchantingly private — different from that used in the city around us.

Just opening or closing the screen door behind me was an 16 important experience. I'd rarely leave home all alone or without feeling reluctance. Walking down the sidewalk, under the canopy of tall trees, I'd warily notice the (suddenly) silent neighborhood kids who stood warily watching me. Nervously, I'd arrive at the grocery store to hear there the sounds of the gringo, reminding me that in this so-big world I was a foreigner. But if leaving home was never routine, neither was coming back. Walking toward our house, climbing the steps from the sidewalk, in summer when the front door was open, I'd hear voices beyond the screen door talking in Spanish. For a second or two I'd stay, linger there listening. Smiling, I'd hear my mother call out, saying in Spanish, "Is that you, Richard?" Those were her words, but all the while her sounds would assure me: *You are home now. Come closer inside. With us.* "*Sí,*" I'd reply.

Once more inside the house, I would resume my place in the family. The sounds would grow harder to hear. Once more at home, I would grow less conscious of them. It required, however, no more than the blurt of the doorbell to alert me all over again to listen to sounds. The house would turn instantly quiet while my mother went to the door. I'd hear her hard English sounds. I'd wait to hear her voice turn to soft-sounding Spanish, which assured me, as surely as did the clicking tongue of the lock on the door, that the stranger was gone.

Plainly it is not healthy to hear such sounds so often. It is not healthy to distinguish public from private sounds so easily. I remained cloistered by sounds, timid and shy in public, too dependent on the voices at home. And yet I was a very happy child when I was at home. I remember many nights when my father would come back from work, and I'd hear him call out to my mother in Spanish, sounding relieved. In Spanish, his voice would sound the light and free notes that he never could manage in English. Some nights I'd jump up just hearing his voice. My brother and I would come running into the room where he was with our mother. Our laughing (so deep was the pleasure!) became screaming. Like others who feel the pain of public alienation, we transformed the knowledge of our public separateness into a consoling reminder of our intimacy. Excited, our voices joined in a celebration of sounds. *We are speaking now the way we never speak out in public — we are together*, the sounds told me. Some nights no one seemed willing to loosen the hold that sounds had on us. At dinner we invented new words that sounded Spanish, but made sense only to us. We pieced together new words by taking, say, an English verb and giving it Spanish endings. My mother's instructions at bedtime would be lacquered with mock-urgent tones. Or a word like *sí*, sounded in several notes, would convey added measures of feeling. Tongues

17

18

lingered around the edges of words, especially fat vowels: And we happily sounded that military drum roll, the twirling roar of the Spanish *r*. Family language, my family's sounds: the voices of my parents and sisters and brother. Their voices insisting: *You belong here. We are family members. Related. Special to one another. Listen!* Voices singing and sighing, rising and straining, then surging, teeming with pleasure which burst syllables into fragments of laughter. At times it seemed there was steady quiet only when, from another room, the rustling whispers of my parents faded and I edged closer to sleep.

Supporters of bilingual education imply today that students like me miss a great deal by not being taught in their family's language. What they seem not to recognize is that, as a socially disadvantaged child, I regarded Spanish as a private language. It was a ghetto language that deepened and strengthened my feeling of public separateness. What I needed to learn in school was that I had the right, and the obligation, to speak the public language. The odd truth is that my first-grade classmates could have become bilingual, in the conventional sense of the word, more easily than I. Had they been taught early (as upper middle-class children often are taught) a "second language" like Spanish or French, they could have regarded it simply as another public language. In my case, such bilingualism could not have been so quickly achieved. What I did not believe was that I could speak a single public language.   19

Without question, it would have pleased me to have heard my teachers address me in Spanish when I entered the classroom. I would have felt much less afraid. I would have imagined that my instructors were somehow "related" to me; I would indeed have heard their Spanish as my family's language. I would have trusted them and responded with ease. But I would have delayed — postponed for how long? — having to learn the language of public society. I would have evaded — and for how long? — learning the great lesson of school: that I had a public identity.   20

Fortunately, my teachers were unsentimental about their responsibility. What they understood was that I needed to speak   21 public English. So their voices would search me out, asking me questions. Each time I heard them I'd look up in surprise to see a nun's face frowning at me. I'd mumble, not really meaning to answer. The nun would persist. "Richard, stand up. Don't look at the floor. Speak up. Speak to the entire class, not just to me!" But I couldn't believe English could be my language to use. (In part, I did not want to believe it.) I continued to mumble. I resisted the teacher's demands. (Did I somehow suspect that once I learned this public language my family life would be changed?) Silent, waiting for the bell to sound, I remained dazed, diffident, afraid.

Because I wrongly imagined that English was intrinsically a public language and Spanish was intrinsically private, I easily noted the difference between classroom language and the language at home. At school, words were directed to a general audience of listeners. ("Boys and girls . . . ") Words were meaningfully ordered. And the point was not self-expression alone, but to make oneself understood by many others. The teacher quizzed: "Boys and girls, why do we use that word in this sentence? Could we think of a better word to use there? Would the sentence change its meaning if the words were differently arranged? Isn't there a better way of saying much the same thing?" (I couldn't say. I wouldn't try to say.) 22

Three months passed. Five. A half year. Unsmiling, ever watchful, my teachers noted my silence. They began to connect my behavior with the slow progress my brother and sisters were making. Until, one Saturday morning, three nuns arrived at the house to talk to our parents. Stiffly they sat on the blue living-room sofa. From the doorway of another room, spying on the visitors, I noted the incongruity, the clash of two worlds, the faces and voices of school intruding upon the familiar setting of home. I overheard one voice gently wondering, "Do your children speak only Spanish at home, Mrs. Rodriguez?" While another voice added, "That Richard especially seems so timid and shy." 23

That Rich-heard! 24

With great tact, the visitors continued, "Is it possible for you and your husband to encourage your children to practice 25 their English when they are home?" Of course my parents complied. What would they not do for their children's well-being? And how could they question the Church's authority which those women represented? In an instant they agreed to give up the language (the sounds) which had revealed and accentuated our family's closeness. The moment after the visitors left, the change was observed. *"Ahora,* speak to us only *en inglés,"* my father and mother told us.

At first, it seemed a kind of game. After dinner each night, 26 the family gathered together to practice "our" English. It was still then *inglés,* a language foreign to us, so we felt drawn to it as strangers. Laughing, we would try to define words we could not pronounce. We played with strange English sounds, often over-anglicizing our pronunciations. And we filled the smiling gaps of our sentences with familiar Spanish sounds. But that was cheating, somebody shouted, and everyone laughed.

In school, meanwhile, like my brother and sisters, I was re- 27 quired to attend a daily tutoring session. I needed a full year of this special work. I also needed my teachers to keep my attention from straying in class by calling out, *"Rich-heard"* — their English voices slowly loosening the ties to my other name, with its three notes, *Ri-car-do.* Most of all, I needed to hear my mother and father speak to me in a moment of seriousness in "broken" — suddenly heartbreaking — English. This scene was inevitable. One Saturday morning I entered the kitchen where my parents were talking, but I did not realize that they were talking in Spanish until, the moment they saw me, their voices changed and they began speaking English. The gringo sounds they uttered startled me. Pushed me away. In that moment of trivial misunderstanding and profound insight, I felt my throat twisted by unsounded grief. I simply turned and left the room. But I had no place to escape to where I could grieve in Spanish. My brother and sisters were speaking English in another part of the house.

Again and again in the days following, as I grew increasing- 28 ly angry, I was obliged to hear my mother and father encouraging me: "Speak to us *en inglés."* Only then did I determine to learn classroom English. Thus, sometime afterward it happened: one day in school, I raised my hand to volunteer an answer to a question. I spoke out in a loud voice and I did not think it remarkable when the entire class understood. That day I moved very far from being the disadvantaged child I had been only days earlier. Taken hold at last was the belief, the calming assurance, that I *belonged* in public.

Shortly after, I stopped hearing the high, troubling sounds of *los gringos*. A more and more confident speaker of English, I didn't listen to how strangers sounded when they talked to me. With so many English-speaking people around me, I no longer heard American accents. Conversations quickened. Listening to persons whose voices sounded eccentrically pitched, I might note their sounds for a few seconds, but then I'd concentrate on what they were saying. Now when I heard someone's tone of voice — angry or questioning or sarcastic or happy or sad — I didn't distinguish it from the words it expressed. Sound and word were thus tightly wedded. At the end of each day I was often bemused, and always relieved, to realize how "soundless," though crowded with words, my day in public had been. An eight-year-old boy, I finally came to accept what had been technically true since my birth: I was an American citizen.

But diminished by then was the special feeling of closeness at home. Gone was the desperate, urgent, intense feeling of being at home among those with whom I felt intimate. Our family remained a loving family, but one greatly changed. We were no longer so close, no longer bound tightly together by the knowledge of our separateness from *los gringos*. Neither my older brother nor my sisters rushed home after school any more. Nor did I. When I arrived home, often there would be neighborhood kids in the house. Or the house would be empty of sounds.

Following the dramatic Americanization of their children, even my parents grew more publicly confident — especially my mother. First she learned the names of all the people on the block. Then she decided we needed to have a telephone in our house. My father, for his part, continued to use the word gringo, but it was no longer charged with bitterness or distrust. Stripped of any emotional content, the word simply became a name for those Americans not of Hispanic descent. Hearing him, sometimes, I wasn't sure if he was pronouncing the Spanish word *gringo*, or saying gringo in English.

There was a new silence at home. As we children learned   32
more and more English, we shared fewer and fewer words with
our parents. Sentences needed to be spoken slowly when one of
us addressed our mother or father. Often the parent wouldn't
understand. The child would need to repeat himself. Still the
parent misunderstood. The young voice, frustrated, would end
up saying, "Never mind" — the subject was closed. Dinners
would be noisy with the clinking of knives and forks against
dishes. My mother would smile softly between her remarks; my
father, at the other end of the table, would chew and chew his
food while he stared over the heads of his children.

My mother! My father! After English became my primary   33
language, I no longer knew what words to use in addressing my
parents. The old Spanish words (those tender accents of sound)
I had earlier used — *mamá* and *papá* — I couldn't use any more.
They would have been all-too-painful reminders of how much
had changed in my life. On the other hand, the words I heard
neighborhood kids call their parents seemed equally unsatisfactory. "Mother" and "father," "ma," "papa," "pa," "dad," "pop"
(how I hated the all-American sound of that last word) — all
these I felt were unsuitable terms of address for *my* parents. As a
result, I never used them at home. Whenever I'd speak to my
parents, I would try to get their attention by looking at them. In
public conversations, I'd refer to them as my "parents" or my
"mother" and "father."

My mother and father, for their part, responded differently,   34
as their children spoke to them less. My mother grew restless,
seemed troubled and anxious at the scarceness of words exchanged in the house. She would question me about my day
when I came home from school. She smiled at my small talk.
She pried at the edges of my sentences to get me to say something more. ("What . . . ?") She'd join conversations she overheard, but her intrusions often stopped her children's talking.
By contrast, my father seemed to grow reconciled to the new
quiet. Though his English somewhat improved, he tended more
and more to retire into silence. At dinner he spoke very little.
One night his children and even his wife helplessly giggled at his

garbled English pronunciation of the Catholic "Grace Before Meals." Thereafter he made his wife recite the prayer at the start of each meal, even on formal occasions when there were guests in the house.

Hers became the public voice of the family. On official business it was she, not my father, who would usually talk to strangers on the phone or in stores. We children grew so accustomed to his silence that years later we would routinely refer to his "shyness." (My mother often tried to explain: both of his parents died when he was eight. He was raised by an uncle who treated him as little more than a menial servant. He was never encouraged to speak. He grew up alone — a man of few words.) But I realized my father was not shy whenever I'd watch him speaking Spanish with relatives. Using Spanish, he was quickly effusive. Especially when talking with other men, his voice would spark, flicker, flare alive with varied sounds. In Spanish he expressed ideas and feelings he rarely revealed when speaking English. With firm Spanish sounds he conveyed a confidence and authority that English would never allow him.

The silence at home, however, was not simply the result of fewer words passing between parents and children. More profound for me was the silence created by my inattention to sounds. At about the time I no longer bothered to listen with care to the sounds of English in public, I grew careless about listening to the sounds made by the family when they spoke. Most of the time I would hear someone speaking at home and didn't distinguish his sounds from the words people uttered in public. I didn't even pay much attention to my parents' accented and ungrammatical speech — at least not at home. Only when I was with them in public would I become alert to their accents. But even then their sounds caused me less and less concern. For I was growing increasingly confident of my own public identity.

I would have been happier about my public success had I not recalled, sometimes, what it had been like earlier, when my family conveyed its intimacy through a set of conveniently private sounds. Sometimes in public, hearing a stranger, I'd hark back to my lost past. A Mexican farm worker approached me one day downtown. He wanted directions to some place.

"Hijito, . . . " he said. And his voice stirred old longings. Another time I was standing beside my mother in the visiting room of a Carmelite convent, before the dense screen which rendered the nuns shadowy figures. I heard several of them speaking Spanish in their busy, singsong, overlapping voices, assuring my mother that, yes, yes, we were remembered, all our family was remembered, in their prayers. Those voices echoed faraway family sounds. Another day a dark-faced old woman touched my shoulder lightly to steady herself as she boarded a bus. She murmured something to me I couldn't quite comprehend. Her Spanish voice came near, like the face of a never-before-seen relative in the instant before I was kissed. That voice, like so many of the Spanish voices I'd hear in public, recalled the golden age of my childhood.

Bilingual educators say today that children lose a degree of "individuality" by becoming assimilated into public society. (Bilingual schooling is a program popularized in the seventies, that decade when middle-class "ethnics" began to resist the process of assimilation — the "American melting pot.") But the bilingualists oversimplify when they scorn the value and necessity of assimilation. They do not seem to realize that a person is individualized in two ways. So they do not realize that, while one suffers a diminished sense of *private* individuality by being assimilated into public society, such assimilation makes possible the achievement of *public* individuality.   38

Simplistically again, the bilingualists insist that a student should be reminded of his difference from others in mass society, of his "heritage." But they equate mere separateness with individuality. The fact is that only in private — with intimates — is separateness from the crowd a prerequisite for individuality; an intimate "tells" me that I am unique, unlike all others, apart from the crowd. In public, by contrast, full individuality is achieved, paradoxically, by those who are able to consider themselves members of the crowd. Thus it happened for me. Only when I was able to think of myself as an American, no longer an alien in gringo society, could I seek the rights and opportunities necessary for full public individuality. The social and political advantages I enjoy as a man began on the day I   39 came to believe that my name is indeed *Rich-heard Road-ree-guess*. It is true that my public society today is often impersonal; in fact, my public society is usually mass society. But despite the anonymity of the crowd, and despite the fact that the individuality I achieve in public is often tenuous — because it depends on my being one in a crowd — I celebrate the day I acquired my new name. Those middle-class ethnics who scorn assimilation seem to me filled with decadent self-pity, obsessed by the burden of public life. Dangerously, they romanticize public separateness and trivialize the dilemma of those who are truly socially disadvantaged.

If I rehearse here the changes in my private life after my Americanization, it is finally to emphasize a public gain. The loss implies the gain. The house I returned to each afternoon was quiet. Intimate sounds no longer greeted me at the door. Inside there were other noises. The telephone rang. Neighborhood kids ran past the door of the bedroom where I was reading my schoolbooks — covered with brown shopping-bag paper. Once I learned the public language, it would never again be easy for me to hear intimate family voices. More and more of my day was spent hearing words, not sounds. But that may only be a way of saying that on the day I raised my hand in class and spoke loudly to an entire roomful of faces, my childhood started to end.

I grew up the victim of a disconcerting confusion. As I became fluent in English, I could no longer speak Spanish with confidence. I continued to understand spoken Spanish, and in high school I learned how to read and write Spanish. But for many years I could not pronounce it. A powerful guilt blocked my spoken words; an essential glue was missing whenever I would try to connect words to form sentences. I would be unable to break a barrier of sound, to speak freely. I would speak, or try to speak, Spanish, and I would manage to utter halting, hiccupping sounds which betrayed my unease. (Even today I speak Spanish very slowly, at best.)

When relatives and Spanish-speaking friends of my parents came to the house, my brother and sisters would usually manage to say a few words before being excused. I never managed so gracefully. Each time I'd hear myself addressed in Spanish, I couldn't respond with any success. I'd know the words I wanted to say, but I couldn't say them. I would try to speak, but everything I said seemed to me horribly anglicized. My mouth wouldn't form the sounds right. My jaw would tremble. After a phrase or two, I'd stutter, cough up a warm, silvery sound, and stop.

My listeners were surprised to hear me. They'd lower their heads to grasp better what I was trying to say. They would repeat their questions in gentle, affectionate voices. But then I would answer in English. No, no, they would say, we want you to speak to us in Spanish (*"en español"*). But I couldn't do it. Then they would call me *Pocho*. Sometimes playfully, teasing, using the tender diminutive — *mi pochito*. Sometimes not so playfully but mockingly, *pocho*. (A Spanish dictionary defines that word as an adjective meaning "colorless" or "bland." But I heard it as a noun, naming the Mexican-American who, in becoming an American, forgets his native society.) "¡Pocho!" my mother's best friend muttered, shaking her head. And my mother laughed, somewhere behind me. She said that her children didn't want to practice "our Spanish" after they started going to school. My mother's smiling voice made me suspect that the lady who faced me was not really angry at me. But searching her face, I couldn't find the hint of a smile.

Embarrassed, my parents would often need to explain their children's inability to speak fluent Spanish during those years. My mother encountered the wrath of her brother, her only brother, when he came up from Mexico one summer with his family and saw his nieces and nephews for the very first time. After listening to me, he looked away and said what a disgrace it was that my siblings and I couldn't speak Spanish, *"su propria idioma."* He made that remark to my mother, but I noticed that he stared at my father.

One other visitor from those years I clearly remember: a long-time friend of my father from San Francisco who came to stay with us for several days in late August. He took great interest in me after he realized that I couldn't answer his questions in Spanish. He would grab me, as I started to leave the kitchen.

43

44

45

He would ask me something. Usually he wouldn't bother to wait for my mumbled response. Knowingly, he'd murmur, "*¿Ay pocho, pocho, donde vas?*" And he would press his thumbs into the upper part of my arms, making me squirm with pain. Dumbly I'd stand there, waiting for his wife to notice us and call him off with a benign smile. I'd giggle, hoping to deflate the tension between us, pretending that I hadn't seen the glittering scorn in his glance.

I recount such incidents only because they suggest the fierce   46
power that Spanish had over many people I met at home, how strongly Spanish was associated with closeness. Most of those people who called me a *pocho* could have spoken English to me, but many wouldn't. They seemed to think that Spanish was the only language we could use among ourselves, that Spanish alone permitted our association. (Such persons are always vulnerable to the ghetto merchant and the politician who have learned the value of speaking their clients' "family language" so as to gain immediate trust.) For my part, I felt that by learning English I had somehow committed a sin of betrayal. But betrayal against whom? Not exactly against the visitors to the house. Rather, I felt I had betrayed my immediate family. I knew that my parents had encouraged me to learn English. I knew that I had turned to English with angry reluctance. But once I spoke English with ease, I came to feel guilty. I sensed that I had broken the spell of intimacy which had once held the family so close together. It was this original sin against my family that I recalled whenever anyone addressed me in Spanish and I responded, confounded.

Yet even during those years of guilt, I was coming to grasp   47
certain consoling truths about language and intimacy — truths that I learned gradually. Once, I remember playing with a friend in the backyard when my grandmother appeared at the window. Her face was stern with suspicion when she saw the boy (the *gringo* boy) I was with. She called out to me in Spanish, sounding the whistle of her ancient breath. My companion looked up and watched her intently as she lowered the window and moved (still visible) behind the light curtain, watching us both. He wanted to know what she had said. I started to tell

him, to translate her Spanish words into English. The problem was, however, that though I knew how to translate exactly what she had told me, I realized that any translation would distort the deepest meaning of her message: it had been directed only to me. This message of intimacy could never be translated because it did not lie in the actual words she had used but passed through them. So any translation would have seemed wrong; the words would have been stripped of an essential meaning. Finally I decided not to tell my friend anything — just that I didn't hear all she had said.

This insight was unfolded in time. As I made more and   48
more friends outside my house, I began to recognize intimate messages spoken in English in a close friend's confidential tone or secretive whisper. Even more remarkable were those instances when, apparently for no special reason, I'd become conscious of the fact that my companion was speaking *only to me*. I'd marvel then, just hearing his voice. It was a stunning event to be able to break through the barrier of public silence, to be able to hear the voice of the other, to realize that it was directed just to me. After such moments of intimacy outside the house, I began to trust what I heard intimately conveyed through my family's English. Voices at home at last punctured sad confusion. I'd hear myself addressed as an intimate — in English. Such moments were never as raucous with sound as in past times, when we had used our "private" Spanish. (Our English-sounding house was never to be as noisy as our Spanish-sounding house had been.) Intimate moments were usually moments of soft sound. My mother would be ironing in the dining room while I did my homework nearby. She would look over at me, smile, and her voice sounded to tell me that I was her son. *Richard.*

Intimacy thus continued at home; intimacy was not stilled   49
by English. Though there were fewer occasions for it — a change in my life that I would never forget — there were also times when I sensed the deep truth about language and intimacy: *Intimacy is not created by a particular language; it is created by intimates.* Thus the great change in my life was not linguistic but social. If, after becoming a successful student, I no longer heard

intimate voices as often as I had earlier, it was not because I spoke English instead of Spanish. It was because I spoke public language for most of my day. I moved easily at last, a citizen in a crowded city of words.

As a man I spend most of my day in public, in a world large- 50 ly devoid of speech sounds. So I am quickly attracted by the glamorous quality of certain alien voices. I still am gripped with excitement when someone passes me on the street, speaking in Spanish. I have not moved beyond the range of the nostalgic pull of those sounds. And there is something very compelling about the sounds of lower-class blacks. Of all the accented versions of English that I hear in public, I hear theirs most intently. The Japanese tourist stops me downtown to ask me a question and I inch my way past his accent to concentrate on what he is saying. The eastern European immigrant in the neighborhood delicatessen speaks to me and, again, I do not pay much attention to his sounds, nor to the Texas accent of one of my neighbors or the Chicago accent of the woman who lives in the apartment below me. But when the ghetto black teenagers get on the city bus, I hear them. Their sounds in my society are the sounds of the outsider. Their voices annoy me for being so loud — so self-sufficient and unconcerned by my presence, but for the same reason they are glamorous: a romantic gesture against public acceptance. And as I listen to their shouted laughter, I realize my own quietness. I feel envious of them — envious of their brazen intimacy.

I warn myself away from such envy, however. Overhearing 51 those teenagers, I think of the black political activists who lately have argued in favor of using black English in public schools — an argument that varies only slightly from that of foreign-language bilingualists. I have heard "radical" linguists make the point that black English is a complex and intricate version of English. And I do not doubt it. But neither do I think that black English should be a language of public instruction. What makes it inappropriate in classrooms is not something in the language itself but, rather, what lower-class speakers make of it. Just as Spanish would have been a dangerous language for me to have used at the start of my education, so black English would be a dangerous language to use in the schooling of teenagers for whom it reinforces feelings of public separateness.

This seems to me an obvious point to make, and yet it must   52
be said. In recent years there have been many attempts to make the language of the alien a public language. "Bilingual education, two ways to understand . . . " television and radio commercials glibly announce. Proponents of bilingual education are careful to say that above all they want every student to acquire a good education. Their argument goes something like this: Children permitted to use their family language will not be so alienated and will be better able to match the progress of English-speaking students in the crucial first months of schooling. Increasingly confident of their ability, such children will be more inclined to apply themselves to their studies in the future. But then the bilingualists also claim another very different goal. They say that children who use their family language in school will retain a sense of their ethnic heritage and their family ties. Thus the supporters of bilingual education want it both ways. They propose bilingual schooling as a way of helping students acquire the classroom skills crucial for public success. But they likewise insist that bilingual instruction will give students a sense of their identity apart from the English-speaking public.

Behind this scheme gleams a bright promise for the alien   53
child: one can become a public person while still remaining a private person. Who would not want to believe such an appealing idea? Who can be surprised that the scheme has the support of so many middle-class ethnic Americans? If the barrio or ghetto child can retain his separateness even while being publicly educated, then it is almost possible to believe that no private cost need be paid for public success. This is the consolation offered by any of the number of current bilingual programs. Consider, for example, the bilingual voter's ballot. In some American cities one can cast a ballot printed in several languages. Such a document implies that it is possible for one to exercise that most public of rights — the right to vote — while still keeping oneself apart, unassimilated in public life.

It is not enough to say that such schemes are foolish and   54
certainly doomed. Middle-class supporters of public bilin-

gualism toy with the confusion of those Americans who cannot speak standard English as well as they do. Moreover, bilingual enthusiasts sin against intimacy. A Hispanic-American tells me, "I will never give up my family language," and he clutches a group of words as though they were the source of his family ties. He credits to language what he should credit to family members. This is a convenient mistake, for as long as he holds on to certain familiar words, he can ignore how much else has actually changed in his life.

It has happened before. In earlier decades, persons ambitious for social mobility, and newly successful, similarly seized upon certain "family words." Workingmen attempting to gain political power, for example, took to calling one another "brother." The word as they used it, however, could never resemble the word (the sound) "brother" exchanged by two people in intimate greeting. The context of its public delivery made it at best a metaphor; with repetition it was only a vague echo of the intimate sound. Context forced the change. Context could not be overruled. Context will always protect the realm of the intimate from public misuse. Today middle-class white Americans continue to prove the importance of context as they try to ignore it. They seize upon idioms of the black ghetto, but their attempt to appropriate such expressions invariably changes the meaning. As it becomes a public expression, the ghetto idiom loses its sound, its message of public separateness and strident intimacy. With public repetition it becomes a series of words, increasingly lifeless.

The mystery of intimate utterance remains. The communication of intimacy passes through the word and enlivens its sound, but it cannot be held by the word. It cannot be retained or ever quoted because it is too fluid. It depends not on words but on persons.

My grandmother! She stood among my other relations mocking me when I no longer spoke Spanish. *Pocho*, she said. but then it made no difference. She'd laugh, and our relationship continued because language was never its source. She was a woman in her eighties during the first decade of my life — a mysterious woman to me, my only living grandparent, a woman of Mexico in a long black dress that reached down to her shoes.

She was the one relative of mine who spoke no word of English. She had no interest in gringo society and remained completely aloof from the public. She was protected by her daughters, protected even by me when we went to Safeway together and I needed to act as her translator. An eccentric woman. Hard. Soft.

When my family visited my aunt's house in San Francisco, 58 my grandmother would search for me among my many cousins. When she found me, she'd chase them away. Pinching her granddaughters, she would warn them away from me. Then she'd take me to her room, where she had prepared for my coming. There would be a chair next to the bed, a dusty-jellied candy nearby, and a copy of *Life en Español* for me to examine. "There," she'd say. And I'd sit content, a boy of eight. *Pocho*, her favorite. I'd sift through the pictures of earthquake-destroyed Latin-American cities and blonde-wigged Mexican movie stars. And all the while I'd listen to the sound of my grandmother's voice. She'd pace around the room, telling me stories of her life. Her past. They were stories so familiar that I couldn't remember when I'd heard them for the first time. I'd look up sometimes to listen. Other times she'd look over at me, but she never expected a response. Sometimes I'd smile or nod. (I understood exactly what she was saying.) But it never seemed to matter to her one way or the other. It was enough that I was there. The words she spoke were almost irrelevant to that fact. We were content. And the great mystery remained: intimate utterance.

I learn nothing about language and intimacy listening to 59 those social activists who propose using one's family language in public life. I learn much more simply by listening to songs on a radio, or hearing a great voice at the opera, or overhearing the woman downstairs at an open window singing to herself. Singers celebrate the human voice. Their lyrics are words, but, animated by voice, those words are subsumed into sounds. (This suggests a central truth about language: all words are capable of becoming sounds as we fill them with the "music" of our life.) With excitement I hear the words yielding their enormous power to sound, even though their meaning is never totally obliterated. In most songs, the drama or tension results from the way that the singer moves between words (sense) and notes (song). At one moment the song simply "says" something; at another moment the voice stretches out the words and moves to the realm of pure sound. Most songs are about love: lost love, celebrations of loving, pleas. By simply being occasions when sounds soar through words, however, songs put me in mind of the most intimate moments of life.

Finally, among all types of music, I find songs created by   60
lyric poets most compelling. On no other public occasion is sound so important for me. Written poems on a page seem at first glance a mere collection of words. And yet, without musical accompaniment, the poet leads me to hear the sounds of the words that I read. As song, a poem moves between the levels of sound and sense, never limited to one realm or the other. As a public artifact, the poem can never offer truly intimate sound, but it helps me to recall the intimate times of my life. As I read in my room, I grow deeply conscious of being alone, sounding my voice in search of another. The poem serves, then, as a memory device; it forces remembrance. And it refreshes; it reminds me of the possibility of escaping public words, the possibility that awaits me in intimate meetings.

The child reminds the adult: to seek intimate sounds is to   61
seek the company of intimates. I do not expect to hear those sounds in public. I would dishonor those I have loved, and those I love now, to claim anything else. I would dishonor our intimacy by holding on to a particular language and calling it my family language. Intimacy cannot be trapped within words; it passes through words. It passes. Intimates leave the room. Doors close. Faces move away from the window. Time passes, and voices recede into the dark. Death finally quiets the voice. There is no way to deny it, no way to stand in the crowd claiming to utter one's family language.

The last time I saw my grandmother I was nine years old. I   62
can tell you some of the things she said to me as I stood by her bed, but I cannot quote the message of intimacy she conveyed with her voice. She laughed, holding my hand. Her voice il-

lumined disjointed memories as it passed them again. She remembered her husband — his green eyes, his magic name of Narcissio, his early death. She remembered the farm in Mexico, the eucalyptus trees nearby (their scent, she remembered, like incense). She remembered the family cow, the bell around its neck heard miles away. A dog. She remembered working as a seamstress, how she'd leave her daughters and son for long hours to go into Guadalajara to work. And how my mother would come running toward her in the sun — in her bright yellow dress — on her return. "MMMMAAAAMMMMÁÁÁÁ," the old lady mimicked her daughter (my mother) to her daughter's son. She laughed. There was the snap of a cough. An aunt came into the room and told me it was time I should leave. "You can see her tomorrow," she promised. So I kissed my grandmother's cracked face. And the last thing I saw was her thin, oddly youthful thigh, as my aunt rearranged the sheet on the bed.

At the funeral parlor a few days after, I remember kneeling   63 with my relatives during the rosary. Among their voices I traced, then lost, the sounds of individual aunts in the surge of the common prayer. And I heard at that moment what since I have heard very often — the sound the women in my family make when they are praying in sadness. When I went up to look at my grandmother, I saw her through the haze of a veil draped over the open lid of the casket. Her face looked calm — but distant and unyielding to love. It was not the face I remembered seeing most often. It was the face she made in public when the clerk at Safeway asked her some question and I would need to respond. It was her public face that the mortician had designed with his dubious art.

· Barbara W. Tuchman ·

BARBARA WERTHEIM TUCHMAN was born in 1912 in New York City. After her graduation from Radcliffe, she became an editorial assistant for *The Nation*, and in 1937 was assigned to Madrid as the magazine's observer of the Spanish Civil War. Later she worked as American correspondent for the *New Statesman and Nation* of London, and during World War II, as an editor of Far East news for the Office of War Information.

It is as a historian that Tuchman has achieved her widest audience. Two of her eight studies in history have been Pulitzer Prize winners: *The Guns of August* (1962), an account of the outbreak of World War I, and *Stilwell and the American Experience in China* (1971). More recently she has published *A Distant Mirror: The Calamitous 14th Century* (1978) and her selected essays, *Practicing History* (1981). A writer who brings to history a journalist's willingness to do "legwork," Tuchman believes in visiting historic sites before describing them. Before she wrote *The Guns of August* she walked across battlefields in France and Belgium; and in doing research for *A Distant Mirror*, she retraced the steps of the fourteenth-century Crusaders. Like James Anthony Froude, she thinks history has to be readable. "There should be," she declares, "a beginning, a middle, and an end, plus an element of suspense to keep a reader turning the pages."

An Inquiry into the Persistence of Unwisdom in Government

What did George III, Napoleon, Kaiser Wilhelm, Chiang Kai-shek, and countless other world leaders have in common? According to Barbara W. Tuchman, it was wooden-headedness: a refusal to face facts and to learn from experience. In "An Inquiry into the Persistence of Unwisdom in Government," first published in *Esquire* (May 1980), Tuchman ranges through history and finds abundant evidence to support her stern opinion that, from earliest times, wisdom has rarely prevailed among those who govern — even those who in recent years have governed the United States. Whether or not you agree with the author, you will find this contemporary essay intelligent, frank, and thought-provoking.

A problem that strikes one in the study of history, 1 regardless of period, is why man makes a poorer performance of government than of almost any other human activity. In this sphere, wisdom — meaning judgment acting on experience, common sense, available knowledge, and a decent appreciation of probability — is less operative and more frustrated than it should be. Why do men in high office so often act contrary to the way that reason points and enlightened self-interest suggests? Why does intelligent mental process so often seem to be paralyzed?

Why, to begin at the beginning, did the Trojan authorities 2 drag that suspicious-looking wooden horse inside their gates? Why did successive ministries of George III — that "bundle of imbecility," as Dr. Johnson called them collectively — insist on coercing rather than conciliating the Colonies though strongly advised otherwise by many counselors? Why did Napoleon and Hitler invade Russia? Why did the kaiser's[1] government resume unrestricted submarine warfare in 1917 although explicitly warned that this would bring in the United States and that American belligerency would mean Germany's defeat? Why did Chiang Kai-shek[2] refuse to heed any voice of reform or alarm until he woke up to find that his country had slid from under him? Why did Lyndon Johnson, seconded by the best and the brightest, progressively involve this nation in a war both ruinous and halfhearted and from which nothing but bad for our side resulted? Why does the present Administration continue to avoid introducing effective measures to reduce the wasteful consumption of oil while members of OPEC follow a

[1]Kaiser Wilhelm (1859–1941), grandson of Queen Victoria and emperor of Germany, in part responsible for the outbreak of World War I.

[2]Chinese general and statesman (1887–1975). President of China, 1948–49, and of Taiwan, 1950–75.

price policy that must bankrupt their customers? How is it possible that the Central Intelligence Agency, whose function it is to provide, at taxpayers' expense, the information necessary to conduct a realistic foreign policy, could remain unaware that discontent in a country crucial to our interests was boiling up to the point of insurrection and overthrow of the ruler upon whom our policy rested? It has been reported that the CIA was ordered *not* to investigate the opposition to the shah of Iran in order to spare him any indication that we took it seriously, but since this sounds more like the theater of the absurd than like responsible government, I cannot bring myself to believe it.

There was a king of Spain once, Philip III, who is said to 3
have died of a fever he contracted from sitting too long near a hot brazier, helplessly overheating himself because the functionary whose duty it was to remove the brazier when summoned could not be found. In the late twentieth century, it begins to appear as if mankind may be approaching a similar stage of suicidal incompetence. The Italians have been sitting in Philip III's hot seat for some time. The British trade unions, in a lunatic spectacle, seem periodically bent on dragging their country toward paralysis, apparently under the impression that they are separate from the whole. Taiwan was thrown into a state of shock by the United States' recognition of the People's Republic of China because, according to one report, in the seven years since the Shanghai Communiqué, the Kuomintang rulers of Taiwan had "refused to accept the new trend as a reality."

Wooden-headedness is a factor that plays a remarkably 4
large role in government. Wooden-headedness consists of assessing a situation in terms of preconceived, fixed notions while ignoring or rejecting any contrary signs. It is acting according to wish while not allowing oneself to be confused by the facts.

A classic case was the French war plan of 1914, which con- 5
centrated everything on a French offensive to the Rhine, leaving the French left flank from Belgium to the Channel virtually unguarded. This strategy was based on the belief that the Germans would not use reserves in the front line and, without them, could not deploy enough manpower to extend their invasion through the French left. Reports by intelligence agents in 1913 to the effect that the Germans were indeed preparing their

reserves for the front line in case of war were resolutely ignored because the governing spirits in France, dreaming only of their own offensive, did not want to believe in any signals that would require them to strengthen their left at the expense of their march to the Rhine. In the event, the Germans could and did extend themselves around the French left with results that determined a long war and its fearful consequences for our century.

Wooden-headedness is also the refusal to learn from experience, a form in which fourteenth-century rulers were supreme. No matter how often and obviously devaluation of the currency disrupted the economy and angered the people, French monarchs continued to resort to it whenever they were desperate for cash until they provoked insurrection among the bourgeoisie. No matter how often a campaign that depended on living off a hostile country ran into want and even starvation, campaigns for which this fate was inevitable were regularly undertaken.   6

Still another form is identification of self with the state, as currently exhibited by the ayatollah Khomeini. No wooden-headedness is so impenetrable as that of a religious zealot. Because he is connected with a private wire to the Almighty, no idea coming in on a lesser channel can reach him, which leaves him ill equipped to guide his country in its own best interests.   7

Philosophers of government ever since Plato have devoted their thinking to the major issues of ethics, sovereignty, the social contract, the rights of man, the corruption of power, the balance between freedom and order. Few — except Machiavelli,[3] who was concerned with government as it is, not as it should be — bothered with mere folly, although this has been a chronic and pervasive problem. "Know, my son," said a dying Swedish statesman in the seventeenth century, "with how little wisdom the world is governed." More recently, Woodrow Wilson warned, "In public affairs, stupidity is more dangerous than knavery."   8

[3]Italian statesman and political philosopher (1469–1527). Author of *The Prince.*

Stupidity is not related to type of regime; monarchy, oligar-   9
chy, and democracy produce it equally. Nor is it peculiar to nation or class. The working class as represented by the Communist governments functions no more rationally or effectively
in power than the aristocracy or the bourgeoisie, as has notably
been demonstrated in recent history. Mao Tse-tung may be admired for many things, but the Great Leap Forward, with a steel
plant in every backyard, and the Cultural Revolution were exercises in unwisdom that greatly damaged China's progress and
stability, not to mention the chairman's reputation. The record
of the Russian proletariat in power can hardly be called enlightened, although after sixty years of control it must be ac-
corded a kind of brutal success. If the majority of Russians are
better off now than before, the cost in cruelty and tyranny has
been no less and probably greater than under the czars.

After the French Revolution, the new order was rescued   10
only by Bonaparte's military campaigns, which brought the
spoils of foreign wars to fill the treasury, and subsequently by
his competence as an executive. He chose officials not on the
basis of origin or ideology but on the principle of "*la carrière
ouverte aux talents*"[4] — the said talents being intelligence, energy,
industry, and obedience. That worked until the day of his own
fatal mistake.

I do not wish to give the impression that men in office are   11
incapable of governing wisely and well. Occasionally, the exception appears, rising in heroic size above the rest, a tower visible
down the centuries. Greece had her Pericles, who ruled with
authority, moderation, sound judgment, and a certain nobility
that imposes natural dominion over others. Rome had Caesar,
a man of remarkable governing talents, although it must be said
that a ruler who arouses opponents to resort to assassination is
probably not as smart as he ought to be. Later, under Marcus
Aurelius and the other Antonines,[5] Roman citizens enjoyed
good government, prosperity, and respect for about a century.
Charlemagne was able to impose order upon a mass of contend-

---

[4]A French saying: "tools to those who can handle them."
[5]Name for several second-century Roman emperors, including Antoninus
Pius, Marcus Aurelius, and Commodus.

ing elements, to foster the arts of civilization no less than those of war, and to earn a prestige supreme in the Middle Ages — probably not equaled in the eyes of contemporaries until the appearance of George Washington.

Possessor of an inner strength and perseverance that enabled him to prevail over a sea of obstacles, Washington was one of those critical figures but for whom history might well have taken a different course. He made possible the physical victory of American independence, while around him, in extraordinary fertility, political talent bloomed as if touched by some tropical sun. For all their flaws and quarrels, the Founding Fathers, who established our form of government, were, in the words of Arthur Schlesinger, Sr., "the most remarkable generation of public men in the history of the United States or perhaps of any other nation." It is worth noting the qualities Schlesinger ascribes to them: They were fearless, high-principled, deeply versed in ancient and modern political thought, astute and pragmatic, unafraid of experiment, and — this is significant — "convinced of man's power to improve his condition through the use of intelligence." That was the mark of the Age of Reason that formed them, and though the eighteenth century had a tendency to regard men as more rational than they in fact were, it evoked the best in government from these men.

For our purposes, it would be invaluable if we could know what produced this burst of talent from a base of only two million inhabitants. Schlesinger suggests some contributing factors: wide diffusion of education, challenging economic opportunities, social mobility, training in self-government — all these encouraged citizens to cultivate their political aptitudes to the utmost. Also, he adds, with the Church declining in prestige and with business, science, and art not yet offering competing fields of endeavor, statecraft remained almost the only outlet for men of energy and purpose. Perhaps the need of the moment — the opportunity to create a new political system — is what brought out the best.

Not before or since, I believe, has so much careful and reasonable thinking been invested in the creation of a new political system. In the French, Russian, and Chinese revolutions, too much class hatred and bloodshed were involved to allow for fair results or permanent constitutions. The American experience was unique, and the system so far has always managed to right itself under pressure. In spite of accelerating incompetence, it still works better than most. We haven't had to discard the system and try another after every crisis, as have Italy and Germany, Spain and France. The founders of the United States are a phenomenon to keep in mind to encourage our estimate of human possibilities, but their example, as a political scientist has pointed out, is "too infrequent to be taken as a basis for normal expectations."

The English are considered to have enjoyed reasonably benign government during the eighteenth and nineteenth centuries, except for their Irish subjects, debtors, child laborers, and other unfortunates in various pockets of oppression. The folly that lost the American colonies reappeared now and then, notably in the treatment of the Irish and the Boers,[6] but a social system can survive a good deal of folly when circumstances are historically favorable or when it is cushioned by large resources, as in the heyday of the British Empire, or absorbed by sheer size, as in this country during our period of expansion. Today there are no more cushions, which makes folly less affordable.

Elsewhere than in government, man has accomplished marvels: invented the means in our time to leave the world and voyage to the moon; in the past, harnessed wind and electricity, raised earthbound stone into soaring cathedrals, woven silk brocades out of the spinnings of a worm, composed the music of Mozart and the dramas of Shakespeare, classified the forms of nature, penetrated the mysteries of genetics. Why is he so much less accomplished in government? What frustrates, in that sphere, the operation of the intellect? Isaac Bashevis Singer,[7] discoursing as a Nobel laureate on mankind, offers the opinion

---

[6]South Africans of Dutch extraction.

[7]Author of novels and stories in Yiddish (b. 1904), now an American citizen and winner of the Nobel Prize for Literature.

that God had been frugal in bestowing intellect but lavish with passions and emotions. "He gave us," Singer says, "so many emotions and such strong ones that every human being, even if he is an idiot, is a millionaire in emotions."

I think Singer has made a point that applies to our inquiry. 17 What frustrates the workings of intellect is the passions and the emotions: ambition, greed, fear, face-saving, the instinct to dominate, the needs of the ego, the whole bundle of personal vanities and anxieties.

Reason is crushed by these forces. If the Athenians out of 18 pride and overconfidence had not set out to crush Sparta for good but had been content with moderate victory, their ultimate fall might have been averted. If fourteenth-century knights had not been obsessed by the idea of glory and personal prowess, they might have defeated the Turks at Nicopolis with incalculable consequence for all of Eastern Europe. If the English, 200 years ago, had heeded Chatham's[8] knocking on the door of what he called "this sleeping and confounded Ministry" and his urgent advice to repeal the Coercive Acts[9] and withdraw the troops before the "inexpiable drop of blood is shed in an impious war with a people contending in the great cause of publick liberty" or, given a last chance, if they had heeded Edmund Burke's[10] celebrated plea for conciliation and his warning that it would prove impossible to coerce a "fierce people" of their own pedigree, we might still be a united people bridging the Atlantic, with incalculable consequence for the history of the West. It did not happen that way, because king and Parliament felt it imperative to affirm sovereignty over arrogant colonials. The alternative choice, as in Athens and medieval Europe, was close to psychologically impossible.

In the case we know best — the American engagement in 19 Vietnam — fixed notions, preconceptions, wooden-headed

---

[8]William Pitt, Earl of Chatham (1708–1788), British statesman who denounced his country's harsh measures against the American colonies.

[9]A series of British laws, passed in 1774 in reaction to the Boston Tea Party, designed to close the port of Boston to commerce.

[10]Burke (1729–1797) was a British statesman and orator.

thinking, and emotions accumulated into a monumental mistake and classic humiliation. The original idea was that the lesson of the failure to halt fascist aggression during the appeasement era dictated the necessity of halting the so-called aggression by North Vietnam, conceived to be the spearhead of international communism. This was applying the wrong model to the wrong facts, which would have been obvious if our policy makers had taken into consideration the history of the people on the spot instead of charging forward wearing the blinkers of the cold war.

The reality of Vietnamese nationalism, of which Ho Chi Minh had been the standard-bearer since long before the war, was certainly no secret. Indeed, Franklin Roosevelt had insisted that the French should not be allowed to return after the war, a policy that we instantly abandoned the moment the Japanese were out. Ignoring the Vietnamese demand for self-government, we first assisted the return of the French, and then, when, incredibly, they had been put to rout by the native forces, we took their place, as if Dien Bien Phu had no significance whatever. Policy founded upon error multiplies, never retreats. The pretense that North versus South Vietnam represented foreign aggression was intensified. If Asian specialists with knowledge of the situation suggested a reassessment, they were not persuasive. As a Communist aggressor, Hanoi was presumed to be a threat to the United States, yet the vital national interest at stake, which alone may have justified belligerency, was never clear enough to sustain a declaration of war. 20

A further, more fundamental error confounded our policy. This was the nature of the client. In war, as any military treatise or any soldier who has seen active service will tell you, it is essential to know the nature — that is, the capabilities *and* intentions — of the enemy and no less so of an ally who is the primary belligerent. We fatally underestimated the one and foolishly overestimated the other. Placing reliance on, or hope in, South Vietnam was an advanced case of wooden-headedness. Improving on the Bourbons,[11] who forgot nothing and learned 21

[11]Last house of the royal family of France.

nothing, our policy makers forgot everything and learned nothing. The oldest lesson in history is the futility and, often, fatality of foreign interference to maintain in power a government unwanted or hated at home. As far back as 500 B.C., Confucius stated, "Without the confidence of the people, no government can stand," and political philosophers have echoed him down through the ages. What else was the lesson of our vain support of Chiang Kai-shek, within such recent experience? A corrupt or oppressive government may be maintained by despotic means but not for long, as the English occupiers of France learned in the fifteenth century. The human spirit protests and generates a Joan of Arc, for people will not passively endure a government that is in fact unendurable.

The deeper we became involved in Vietnam during the 22 Johnson era, the greater grew the self-deception, the lies, the false body counts, the cheating on Tonkin Gulf, the military mess, domestic dissent, and all those defensive emotions in which, as a result, our leaders became fixed. Their concern for personal ego, public image, and government status determined policy. Johnson was not going to be the first President to preside over defeat; generals could not admit failure nor civilian advisers risk their jobs by giving unpalatable advice.

Males, who so far in history have managed government, are 23 obsessed with potency, which is the reason, I suspect, why it is difficult for them to admit error. I have rarely known a man who, with a smile and a shrug, could easily acknowledge being wrong. Why not? *I* can, without any damage to self-respect. I can only suppose the difference is that deep in their psyches, men somehow equate being wrong with being impotent. For a Chief of State, it is almost out of the question, and especially so for Johnson and Nixon, who both seem to me to have had shaky self-images. Johnson's showed in his deliberate coarseness and compulsion to humiliate others in crude physical ways. No self-confident man would have needed to do that. Nixon was a bundle of inferiorities and sense of persecution. I do not pretend to be a psychohistorian, but in pursuit of this inquiry, the psychological factors must be taken into account. Having no special knowledge of Johnson and Nixon, I will not pursue the question other than to say that it was our misfortune during the Vietnam period to have had two Presidents who lacked the self-confidence for a change of course, much less for a grand withdrawal. "Magnanimity in politics," said Edmund Burke, "is not seldom the truest wisdom, and a great Empire and little minds go ill together."

An essential component of that "truest wisdom" is the self-confidence to reassess. Congressman Morris Udall made this point in the first few days after the nuclear accident at Three Mile Island. Cautioning against a hasty decision on the future of nuclear power, he said, "We have to go back and reassess. There is nothing wrong about being optimistic or making a mistake. The thing that is wrong, as in Vietnam, is *persisting* in a mistake when you see you are going down the wrong road and are caught in a bad situation."   24

The test comes in recognizing when persistence has become a fatal error. A prince, says Machiavelli, ought always to be a great asker and a patient hearer of truth about those things of which he has inquired, and he should be angry if he finds that anyone has scruples about telling him the truth. Johnson and Nixon, as far as an outsider can tell, were not great askers; they did not want to hear the truth or to face it. Chiang Kai-shek knew virtually nothing of real conditions in his domain because he lived a headquarters life amid an entourage all of whom were afraid to be messengers of ill report. When, in World War I, a general of the headquarters staff visited for the first time the ghastly landscape of the Somme, he broke into tears, saying, "If I had known we sent men to fight in that, I could not have done it." Evidently he was no great asker either.   25

Neither, we now know, was the shah of Iran. Like Chiang Kai-shek, he was isolated from actual conditions. He was educated abroad, took his vacations abroad, and toured his country, if at all, by helicopter.   26

Why is it that the major clients of the United States, a country founded on the principle that government derives its just powers from the consent of the governed, tend to be unpopular autocrats? A certain schizophrenia between our philos-   27 ophy and our practice afflicts American policy, and this split will always make the policy based on it fall apart. On the day the shah left Iran, an article summarizing his reign said that "except for the generals, he has few friends or allies at home." How useful to us is a ruler without friends or allies at home? He is a kind of luftmensch, no matter how rich or how golden a customer for American business. To attach American foreign policy to a ruler who does not have the acceptance of his countrymen is hardly intelligent. By now, it seems to me, we might have learned that. We must understand conditions — and by conditions, I mean people and history — on the spot. Wise policy can only be made on the basis of *informed*, not automatic, judgments.

When it has become evident to those associated with it that   28
a course of policy is pointed toward disaster, why does no one resign in protest or at least for the peace of his own soul? They never do. In 1917, the German chancellor Bethmann Hollweg pleaded desperately against the proposed resumption of unrestricted submarine warfare, since, by bringing in the United States, it would revive the Allies' resources, their confidence in victory, and their will to endure. When he was overruled by the military, he told a friend who found him sunk in despair that the decision meant "*finis Germaniae.*" When the friend said simply, "You should resign," Bethman said he could not, for that would sow dissension at home and let the world know he believed Germany would fail.

This is always the refuge. The officeholder tells himself he   29
can do more from within and that he must not reveal division at the top to the public. In fact if there is to be any hope of change in a democratic society, that is exactly what he must do. No one of major influence in Johnson's circle resigned over our Vietnam policy, although several, hoping to play it both ways, hinted their disagreement. Humphrey, waiting for the nod, never challenged the President's policy, although he campaigned afterward as an opponent of the war. Since then, I've always thought the adulation given to him misplaced.

Basically, what keeps officeholders attached to a policy they   30
believe to be wrong is nothing more nor less, I believe, than the

lure of office, or Potomac fever. It is the same whether the locus
is the Thames or the Rhine or, no doubt, the Nile. When Herbert Lehman ran for a second term as senator from New York
after previously serving four terms as governor, his brother
asked him why on earth he wanted it. "Arthur," replied the
senator, "after you have once ridden behind a motorcycle
escort, you are never the same again."

Here is a clue to the question of why our performance in   31
government is worse than in other activities: because government offers power, excites that lust for power, which is subject
to emotional drives — to narcissism, fantasies of omnipotence,
and other sources of folly. The lust for power, according to
Tacitus,[12] "is the most flagrant of all the passions" and cannot
really be satisfied except by power over others. Business offers a
kind of power but only to the very successful at the very top,
and even they, in our day, have to play it down. Fords and Du
Ponts, Hearsts and Pulitzers nowadays are subdued, and the
Rockefeller who most conspicuously wanted power sought it in
government. Other activities — in sports, science, the professions, and the creative and performing arts — offer various satisfactions but not the opportunity for power. They may appeal to
status seeking and, in the form of celebrity, offer crowd worship
and limousines and recognition by headwaiters, but these are
the trappings of power, not the essence. Of course, mistakes and
stupidities occur in nongovernmental activities too, but since
these affect fewer people, they are less noticeable than they are
in public affairs. Government remains the paramount field of
unwisdom because it is there that men seek power over others —
and lose it over themselves.

There are, of course, other factors that lower competence in   32
public affairs, among them the pressure of overwork and over-
scheduling; bureaucracy, especially big bureaucracy; the contest
for votes that gives exaggerated influence to special interests and
an absurd tyranny to public opinion polls. Any hope of intelligent government would require that the persons entrusted

[12]Roman historian (A.D. 55?–after 117).

with high office should formulate and execute policy according to their best judgment and the best knowledge available, not according to every breeze of public opinion. But reelection is on their minds, and that becomes the criterion. Moreover, given schedules broken down into fifteen-minute appointments and staffs numbering in the hundreds and briefing memos of never less than thirty pages, policy makers never have time to *think*. This leaves a rather important vacuum. Meanwhile, bureaucracy rolls on, impervious to any individual or cry for change, like some vast computer that when once penetrated by error goes on pumping it out forever.

Under the circumstances, what are the chances of improving the conduct of government? The idea of a class of professionals trained for the task has been around ever since Plato's *Republic*. Something of the sort animates, I imagine, the new Kennedy School of Government at Harvard. According to Plato, the ruling class in a just society should be men apprenticed to the art of ruling, drawn from the rational and the wise. Since he acknowledged that in natural distribution these are few, he believed they would have to be eugenically bred and nurtured. Government, he said, was a special art in which competence, as in any other profession, could be acquired only by study of the discipline and could not be acquired otherwise. 33

Without reference to Plato, the Mandarins of China were trained, if not bred, for the governing function. They had to pass through years of study and apprenticeship and weeding out by successive examinations, but they do not seem to have developed a form of government much superior to any other, and in the end, they petered out in decadence and incompetence. 34

In seventeenth-century Europe, after the devastation of the Thirty Years' War, the electors of Brandenburg, soon to be combined with Prussia, determined to create a strong state by means of a disciplined army and a trained civil service. Applicants for the civil positions, drawn from commoners in order to offset the nobles' control of the military, had to complete a course of study covering political theory, law and legal philosophy, economics, history, penology, and statutes. Only after 35 passing through various stages of examination and probationary terms of office did they receive definitive appointments and tenure and opportunity for advancement. The higher civil service was a separate branch, not open to promotion from the middle and lower levels.

The Prussian system proved so effective that the state was able to survive both military defeat by Napoleon in 1807 and the revolutionary surge of 1848. By then it had begun to congeal, losing many of its most progressive citizens in emigration to America; nevertheless, Prussian energies succeeded in 1871 in uniting the German states in an empire under Prussian hegemony. Its very success contained the seed of ruin, for it nourished the arrogance and power hunger that from 1914 through was to bring it down. 36

In England, instead of responding in reactionary panic to the thunders from the Continent in 1848, as might have been expected, the authorities, with commendable enterprise, ordered an investigation of their own government practices, which were then the virtually private preserve of the propertied class. The result was a report on the need for a permanent civil service to be based on training and specialized skills and designed to provide continuity and maintenance of the long view as against transient issues and political passions. Though heavily resisted, the system was adopted in 1870. It has produced distinguished civil servants but also Burgess, Maclean, Philby, and the fourth man.[13] The history of British government in the last 100 years suggests that factors other than the quality of its civil service determine a country's fate. 37

In the United States, civil service was established chiefly as a barrier to patronage and the pork barrel rather than in search of excellence. By 1937, a presidential commission, finding the system inadequate, urged the development of a "real career service . . . requiring personnel of the highest order, competent, highly trained, loyal, skilled in their duties by reason of long experience, and assured of continuity." After much effort and 38

[13]British civil servants who in the 1970s were exposed as Russian spies.

some progress, that goal is still not reached, but even if it were, it would not take care of elected officials and high appointments — that is, of government at the top.

I do not know if the prognosis is hopeful or, given the [39] underlying emotional drives, whether professionalism is the cure. In the Age of Enlightenment, John Locke[14] thought the emotions should be controlled by intellectual judgment and that it was the distinction and glory of man to be able to control them. As witnesses of the twentieth century's record, comparable to the worst in history, we have less confidence in our species. Although professionalism can help, I tend to think that fitness of character is what government chiefly requires. How that can be discovered, encouraged, and brought into office is the problem that besets us.

No society has yet managed to implement Plato's design. [40] Now, with money and image-making manipulating our elective process, the chances are reduced. We are asked to choose by the packaging, yet the candidate seen in a studio-filmed spot, sincerely voicing lines from the TelePrompTer, is not the person who will have to meet the unrelenting problems and crucial decisions of the Oval Office. It might be a good idea if, without violating the First Amendment, we could ban all paid political commercials and require candidates (who accept federal subsidy for their campaigns) to be televised live only.

That is only a start. More profound change must come if we [41] are to bring into office the kind of person our form of government needs if it is to survive the challenges of this era. Perhaps rather than educating officials according to Plato's design, we should concentrate on educating the electorate — that is, ourselves — to look for, recognize, and reward character in our representatives and to reject the ersatz.

[14]English philosopher (1632–1704).

USEFUL TERMS

Abstract and **Concrete** are names for two kinds of language. Abstract words refer to ideas, conditions, and qualities we cannot directly perceive: *truth, love, courage, evil, wealth, poverty, progressive, reactionary.* Concrete words indicate things we can know with our senses: *tree, chair, bird, pen, motorcycle, perfume, thunderclap, cheeseburger.* The use of concrete words lends vigor and clarity to writing, for such words help a reader to picture things. See *Image*.

Writers of expository essays tend to shift back and forth from one kind of language to the other. They often begin a paragraph with a general statement full of abstract words ("There is *hope* for the *future* of *motoring*"). Then they usually go on to give examples and present evidence in sentences full of concrete words ("Inventor *Jones* claims his *car* will go from *Fresno* to *Los Angeles* on a *gallon* of *peanut oil*"). Beginning writers often use too many abstract words and not enough concrete ones.

Allusion refers a reader to any person, place, or thing in fact, fiction, or legend that the writer believes is common knowledge. An allusion (a single reference) may point to a famous event, a familiar saying, a noted personality, a well-known story or song. Usually brief, an allusion is a space-saving way to convey much meaning. For example, the statement that "The game was Coach Johnson's Waterloo" informs the reader that, like Napoleon meeting defeat in a celebrated battle, the coach led a confrontation that resulted in his downfall and that of his team. If the writer is also showing Johnson's character, the allusion might also tell us that the coach is a man of Napoleonic ambition and pride. To observe "He is our town's J. R. Ewing" concisely says several things: that a leading citizen is unscrupulous, deceptive, merciless, rich, and eager to become richer — perhaps superficially charming and promiscuous as well. To make an effective allusion, you have to be aware of your audience. If your readers are not likely to recognize the allusion, it will only confuse. Not everyone, for example, would understand you if you alluded to a neighbor, to a seventeenth-century Russian harpsichordist, or to a little-known stock car driver.

Analogy is a form of exposition that uses an extended comparison based on the like features of two unlike things: one familiar or easily understood, the other unfamiliar, abstract, or complicated. See Chapter 7. For *Argument by Analogy* see *Logical Fallacies*.

Argument is one of the four principal modes of writing, whose function is to convince readers. See Chapter 10.

Audience, for a writer, means readers. Having in mind a particular audience helps the writer in choosing strategies. Imagine, for instance, that you are writing two reviews of the movie *Raiders of the Lost Ark*: one for the students who read the campus newspaper, the other for amateur and professional film-makers who read *Millimeter*. Writing for the first audience, you might write about the actors, the plot, and especially dramatic scenes. You might judge the picture and urge your readers to see it — or to avoid it. Writing for *Millimeter*, you might discuss special effects, shooting techniques, problems in editing and in mixing picture and sound. In this review, you might use more specialized and technical terms. Obviously an awareness of the interests and knowledge of your readers, in each case, would help you decide how to write. If you told readers of the campus paper too much about filming techniques, you would lose most of them. If you told *Millimeter*'s readers the plot of the film in detail and how you liked its humor, probably you would put them to sleep.

You can increase your awareness of your audience by asking yourself a few questions before you begin to write. Who are to be your readers? What is their age level? Background? Education? Where do they live? What are their beliefs and attitudes? What interests them? What, if anything, sets them apart from most people? How familiar are they with your subject? Knowing your audience can help you write so that your readers will not only understand you better, but more deeply care about what you say.

Cause and Effect is a form of exposition in which a writer analyzes reasons for an action, event, or decision, or analyzes its consequences. See Chapter 8.

Classification is a form of exposition in which a writer sorts out plural things (contact sports, college students, kinds of music) into categories. See Chapter 6.

Cliché (French for *stereotype*) is a name for any worn-out, trite expression that a writer employs thoughtlessly. Although at one time the expression may have been colorful, from heavy use it has lost its luster. It is now "old as the hills." In conversation, most of us sometimes use clichés, but in writing they "stick out like sore thumbs." Alert writers, when they revise, replace a cliché with a fresh, concrete expression. Writers who have trouble recognizing clichés generally need to read more widely than they do. Their problem is that, so many expressions being new to them, they do not know which ones are full of moths.

Coherence is the clear connection of the parts in a piece of effective writing. This quality exists when the reader can easily follow the flow of ideas between sentences, paragraphs, and larger divisions, and can see how they relate successively to one another.

In making your essay coherent, you may find certain devices useful. Transitions, for instance, can bridge ideas. Reminders of points you have stated earlier are helpful to a reader who may have forgotten them — as readers tend to do sometimes, particularly if your essay is long. However, a coherent essay is not one merely pasted together with transitions and reminders. It derives its coherence from the clear relationship between its thesis (or central idea) and all of its parts.

Colloquial Expressions are those which occur primarily in speech and informal writing that seeks a relaxed, conversational tone. "My favorite chow is a burger and a shake" or "This math exam has me climbing the walls" may be acceptable in talking to a roommate, in corresponding with a friend, or in writing a humorous essay for general readers. Such a choice of words, however, would be out of place in formal writing — in, say, a laboratory report or a letter to your Senator. Contractions (*let's, don't, we'll*) and abbreviated words (*photo, sales rep, TV*) are the shorthand of spoken language. Good writers use such expressions with an awareness that they produce an effect of casualness.

Comparison and Contrast, two writing strategies, are usually found together. They are a form of exposition in which a writer examines the similarities and differences between two things in order to reveal their natures. See Chapter 4.

Conclusions are those sentences or paragraphs that bring an essay to a satisfying and logical end. They are purposefully crafted to give a sense of unity and completeness to the whole essay. The best conclusions evolve naturally out of what has gone before and convince the reader that the essay is indeed at an end, not that the writer has run out of steam.

Conclusions vary in type and length depending on the nature and scope of the essay. A long research paper may require several paragraphs of summary to review and emphasize the main points. A short essay, however, may benefit from a few brief closing sentences.

In concluding an essay, beware of diminishing the impact of your writing by finishing on a weak note. Don't apologize for what you have or have not written, or cram in a final detail that would have been better placed elsewhere.

Although there are no set formulas for closing, the following list presents several options:

1. Restate the thesis of your essay, and perhaps your main points.

2. Mention the broader implications or significance of your topic.

3. Give a final example that pulls all the parts of your discussion together.

4. Offer a prediction.

5. End with the most important point as the culmination of your essay's development.

6. Suggest how the reader can apply the information you have just imparted.

7. End with a bit of drama or flourish. Tell an anecdote, offer an appropriate quotation, ask a question, make a final insightful remark. Keep in mind, however, that an ending shouldn't sound false and gimmicky. It truly has to sum up and conclude.

Concrete: See *Abstract and Concrete*.

Connotation and **Denotation** are names for the two types of meanings most words have. Denotation is the explicit, literal, dictionary definition of a word. Connotation refers to the implied meaning, resonant with associations, of a word. The denotation of *blood* is "the fluid that circulates in the vascular system." The word's connotations range from *life force* to *gore* to *family bond*. A doctor might use the word *blood* for its denotation, and a mystery writer might rely on the rich connotations of the word to heighten a scene.

Because people have different experiences, they bring to the same word different associations. A conservative Republican's emotional response to the word *welfare* is not likely to be the same as a liberal Democrat's response to the word. And referring to your senator as a statesman evokes a different response, from him and from others, than if you were to call him a baby-kisser, or even a politician. The effective use of words involves knowing both what they mean literally and what they are likely to suggest.

Deduction is the method of reasoning from general to specific. See page 425.

Definition may refer to a statement of the literal and specific meaning or meanings of a word (*short definition*), or to a form of expository writing (*extended definition*). In the latter, the writer usually explains the nature of a word, a thing, a concept, or a phenomenon; in doing so the writer may employ narration, description, or any of the expository methods. See Chapter 9.

Denotation: See *Connotation and Denotation*.

Description is a mode of writing that conveys sensory evidence. See Chapter 2.

Diction is a choice of words. Every written or spoken statement contains diction of some kind. To describe certain aspects of diction, the following terms may be useful:

Standard English: words and grammatical forms that native speakers of the language use in formal writing.

Nonstandard English: words and grammatical forms such as "theirselves" and "ain't" that occur mainly in the speech of people of a particular social background.

Slang: certain words in highly informal speech or writing.

Colloquial Expressions: words and phrases from conversation. See *Colloquial Expressions* for examples.

Regional terms: words heard in a certain locality, such as *spritzing* for raining in Pennsylvania Dutch country.

Dialect: a variety of English based on differences in geography, education, or social background. Dialect is usually spoken, but may be written. Two essays in Chapter 1 transcribe the words of dialect speakers: Maya Angelou's people waiting for the fight broadcast ("He gone whip him till that white boy call him Momma") and James Herriot's Yorkshire farmers ("Does 'e live about 'ere?").

Technical terms: words and phrases that form the vocabulary of a particular discipline (*monocotyledon* from botany), occupation (*drawplate* from die-making), or avocation (*interval training* from running).

Archaisms: old-fashioned expressions, once common but now used to suggest an earlier style, such as *ere*, *yon*, and *forsooth*. (Actually, *yon* is still current in the expression *hither and yon*; but if you say "Behold yon glass of beer!" it is an archaism.)

Obsolete diction: words that have passed out of use (such as the verb *werien*, to protect or defend, and the noun *isetnesses*, agreements). *Obsolete* may also refer to certain meanings of words no longer current (*fond* for foolish, *clipping* for hugging or embracing).

Pretentious diction: use of words more numerous and elaborate than necessary, such as *institution of higher learning* for college, and *partake of solid nourishment* for eat.

To be sure, archaisms and pretentious diction have no place in good writing unless a writer deliberately uses them for ironic or humorous effect: H. L. Mencken has delighted in the hifalutin use of *tonsorial studio* instead of barber shop. Still, any diction may be the right diction for a certain occasion: the choice of words depends on a writer's purpose and audience.

Division is a form of expository writing in which the writer separates a single subject into its parts. See Chapter 6.

Effect, the result of an event or action, is usually considered together with *cause* as a form of exposition. See the discussion of cause and effect in Chapter 8. The term *effect* may also refer to the impression a word, sentence, paragraph, or entire work makes upon its audience.

Emphasis is stress or special importance given to a certain point or element to make it stand out. A skillful writer draws attention to what is most important in a sentence, paragraph, or essay by controlling emphasis in any of the following ways:

Proportion: Important ideas are given greater coverage than minor points.

Position: The beginning and end of sentences, paragraphs, and larger divisions are the strongest positions. Placing key ideas in these spots helps draw attention to their importance. The end is the stronger position, for what stands last stands out. A sentence in which less important details precede the main point is called a *periodic sentence*: "Having disguised himself as a guard and walked through the courtyard to the side gate, the prisoner made his escape." A sentence in which the main point precedes less important details is a *loose sentence*: "Autumn is orange: gourds in baskets at roadside stands, the harvest moon hanging like a pumpkin, and oak and beech leaves flashing like goldfish."

Repetition: Careful repetition of key words or phrases can give them greater importance. (Careless repetition, however, can cause boredom.)

Mechanical devices: Italics (underlining), capital letters, and exclamation points can make words or sentences stand out. Writers sometimes fall back on these devices, however, after failing to show significance by other means. Italics and exclamation points can be useful in reporting speech, but excessive use sounds exaggerated or bombastic.

Essay refers to a short nonfiction composition on one central theme or subject in which the writer sometimes offers personal views. Essays are sometimes classified as either formal or informal. In general, a *formal essay* is one whose diction is that of the written language (not colloquial speech), serious in tone, and usually focused on a subject the writer believes is important. (For example, see Barbara W. Tuchman's "An Inquiry into the Persistence of Unwisdom in Government.") An *informal essay*, in contrast, is more likely to admit colloquial expressions; the writer's tone tends to be lighter, perhaps humorous, and the subject is likely to be personal, sometimes even trivial. (See James Thurber's "University Days," Jim Villas's "Fried Chicken," and Brendan Boyd's "Packaged News.") These distinctions, however, are rough ones: an essay such as Judy Syfers' "I Want a Wife" may use colloquial language and speak of personal experience, though it is serious in tone and has an undeniably important subject.

Evaluation is judging merits. In evaluating a work of writing, you suspend personal preference and judge its success in fulfilling the writer's apparent purpose. For instance, if an essay tells how to tune up a car and you have no interest in engines, you nevertheless decide how clearly and effectively the writer explains the process to you.

Evidence is the factual basis for an argument or an explanation. In a courtroom, an attorney's case is only as good as the evidence marshalled to support it. In an essay, a writer's opinions and generalizations also must rest upon evidence, usually given in the form of facts and examples.

Example, also called exemplification, is a form of exposition in which the writer illustrates a general idea. See Chapter 3. An example is a verbal illustration.

Exposition is the mode of prose writing that explains a subject. Its function is to inform, to instruct, or to set forth ideas. Exposition may call various methods to its service: example, comparison and contrast, process analysis, division, classification, analogy, cause and effect. Expository writing exposes information: the major trade routes in the Middle East, how to make a dulcimer, why the United States consumes more energy than it needs. Most college writing is exposition, and most of the essays in this book (those in Chapters 3 through 9) are expository.

Figures of Speech occur whenever a writer, for the sake of emphasis or vividness, departs from the literal meanings (or denotations) of words. To say "She's a jewel" doesn't mean that the subject of praise is literally a kind of shining stone; the statement makes sense because its connotations come to mind: rare, priceless, worth cherishing. Some figures of speech involve comparisons of two objects apparently unlike. A *simile* (from the Latin, "likeness") states the comparison directly, usually connecting the two things using "like," "as," or "than": "The moon is like a snowball," "He's lazy as a cat full of cream," "My feet are flatter than flyswatters." A *metaphor* (from the Greek, "transfer") declares one thing *to be* another: "A mighty fortress is our God," "The sheep were bolls of cotton on the hill." (A *dead metaphor* is a word or phrase that, originally a figure of speech, has come to be literal through common usage: "the *hands* of a clock.") *Personification* is a simile or metaphor that assigns human traits to inanimate objects or abstractions: "A stoopshouldered refrigerator hummed quietly to itself," "All of a sudden the solution to the math problem sat there winking at me."

Other figures of speech consist of deliberate misrepresentations. *Hyperbole* (from the Greek, "throwing beyond") is a conscious exaggeration: "I'm so hungry I could eat a horse and saddle," "I'd wait for you a thousand years." Its opposite, *understatement*, creates an ironic or humorous effect: "I accepted the ride. At the moment, I didn't much feel like walking across the Mojave Desert." A *paradox* is a seemingly self-contradictory statement that, on reflection, makes sense: "Children are the poor man's wealth." (Wealth can be monetary, or it can be spiritual.)

Focus is the narrowing of a subject to make it manageable. Beginning with a general subject, you concentrate on a certain aspect of that subject. For instance, you may select crafts as a general subject, then decide your main interest lies in weaving. You could focus your essay still further by narrowing it to operating a hand loom. You can also focus your writing according to who will read it (*Audience*) or what you want it to achieve (*Purpose*).

General and **Specific** refer to words and describe their relative degrees of abstractness. General words name a group or class (*flowers*); specific words limit the class by naming its individual members (*rose, violet, dahlia, marigold*). Words may be arranged in a series from general to specific: *clothes, pants, jeans, Levis.* The word *cat* is more specific than *animal*, but less specific than *tiger cat*, or *Garfield*. See also *Abstract and Concrete.*

Generalization refers to a statement about a class based on an examination of some of its members: "Lions are fierce." The more members examined and the more representative they are of the class, the sturdier the generalization. Insufficient or nonrepresentative evidence often leads to a hasty generalization. The statement "Solar heat saves homeowners money" would be challenged by homeowners who have yet to recover their installation costs. "Solar heat can save homeowners money in the long run" would be a sounder generalization. Words such as *all, every, only,* and *always* have to be used with care. "Some artists are alcoholics" is more credible than "Artists are always alcoholics." Making a trustworthy generalization involves the use of *inductive reasoning* (discussed on pages 425–426).

Illustration is another name for the expository method of giving examples. See Chapter 3.

Image refers to a word or word sequence that evokes a sensory experience. Whether literal ("We picked two red apples") or figurative ("His cheeks looked like two red apples, buffed and shining"), an image appeals to the reader's memory of seeing, hearing, smelling, touching, or tasting. Images add concreteness to fiction: "The farm looked as tiny and still as a seashell, with the little knob of a house surrounded by its curved furrows of tomato plants" (Eudora Welty in a short story, "The Whistle") — and are an important element in poetry. But writers of essays, too, find images valuable in giving examples, in describing, in comparing and contrasting, and in drawing analogies.

Induction is the process of reasoning to a conclusion about an entire class by examining some of its members. See pages 425–426.

Introductions are the openings of written works. Often they state the writer's subject, narrow it, and communicate an attitude toward it (*Tone*). Introductions vary in length, depending on their purposes. A research paper may need several paragraphs to set forth its central idea and its plan of organization; on the other hand, a brief, informal essay may need only a sentence or two for an introduction. Whether long or short, effective introductions tell us no more than we need to know when we begin reading. Here are a few possible ways to open an essay effectively:

1. State your central idea, perhaps showing why you care about it.

2. Present startling facts about your subject.

3. Tell an illustrative anecdote.

4. Give background information that will help your reader understand your subject, or see why it is important.

5. Begin with an arresting quotation.

6. Ask a challenging question. (In your essay, you'll go on to answer it.)

Irony is a manner of speaking or writing that does not directly state a discrepancy, but implies one. *Verbal irony* is the intentional use of words to suggest a meaning other than literal: "What a mansion!" (said of a shack); "There's nothing like sunshine" (said on a foggy morning). If irony is delivered contemptuously with intent to hurt, we call it *sarcasm:* "Oh, you're a real friend!" (said to someone who refuses to lend the speaker a dime to make a phone call). Certain situations also can be ironic, when we sense in them some incongruity, some result contrary to expectation, or some twist of fate: Juliet regains consciousness only to find that Romeo, believing her dead, has stabbed himself.

Jargon, strictly speaking, is the special vocabulary of a trade or profession; but the term has also come to mean inflated, vague, meaningless language of any kind. It is characterized by wordiness, abstractions galore, pretentious diction, and needlessly complicated word order. Whenever you meet a sentence that obviously could express its idea in fewer words and shorter ones, chances are that it is jargon. For instance: "The motivating force compelling her to opt continually for the most labor-intensive mode of operation in performing her functions was consistently observed to be the single constant and regular factor in her behavior patterns." Translation: "She did everything the hard way." For more specimens of jargon, see the examples George Orwell gives in "Politics and the English Language" (Essays for Further Reading).

Logical Fallacies are errors in reasoning, sometimes found in argument. To help you to recognize them and to guard against them in your own writing, here is a list of a few common ones:

Non sequitur (from the Latin, "it does not follow"): stating a conclusion that doesn't follow from the first premise or premises.

"I've lived in this town a long time — why, my grandfather was the first mayor — so I'm against putting fluoride in the drinking water."

Oversimplification: supplying neat and easy explanations for large and complicated phenomena. "These scientists are always messing around with the moon and the planets; that's why the climate is changing nowadays." Oversimplified solutions are also popular: "All these teenage kids that get in trouble with the law — why, they ought to ship 'em over to Russia. That would straighten 'em out!"

Either/or reasoning: assuming that a reality may be divided into only two parts or extremes; assuming that a given problem has only one of two possible solutions. "What do we do about these sheiks who keep jacking up oil prices? Either we kowtow to 'em, or we bomb 'em off the face of the earth, right?" Obviously, either/or reasoning is another kind of extreme oversimplification.

Argument from doubtful or unidentified authority: "Certainly we ought to castrate all sex-offenders; Steve Martin says we should." Or: "According to reliable sources, my opponent is lying."

Argumentum ad hominem (from the Latin, "argument to the man"): attacking a man's views by attacking his character. "Mayor Burns was seen with a prostitute on Taylor Street. How can we listen to his plea for a city nursing home?"

Begging the question: taking for granted from the start what you set out to demonstrate. When you reason in a *logical* way, you state that because something is true, then, as a result, some other truth follows. When you beg the question, however, you repeat that what is true is true. If you argue, for instance, that dogs are a menace to people because they are dangerous, you don't prove a thing, since the idea that dogs are dangerous is already assumed in the statement that they are a menace. Beggers of questions often just repeat what they already believe, only in different words. This fallacy sometimes takes the form of *arguing in a circle*, or demonstrating a premise by a conclusion and a conclusion by a premise: "I should go to college because that is the right thing to do. Going to college is the right thing to do because it is expected of me."

Post hoc, ergo propter hoc (from the Latin, "after this, therefore because of this"): confusing cause and effect. See page 330.

Argument from analogy: using an extended metaphor (discussed in Chapter 7) as though it offers evidence. Pierre Berton, a Canadian journalist, once wrote a clever article "Is There a Teacher in the House?" satirizing opponents of public health care. In it Berton writes in the voice of an after-dinner speaker alarmed by the idea of establishing a public school system — which in fact, of course, already exists:

> Under this foreign system each one of us would be forced by government edict, and under penalty of imprisonment, to send our children to school until each reaches the age of sixteen — whether we wish to or not. . . . Ask yourself, gentlemen, if it is economically sane to hand a free education, no strings attached, to everybody in the nation between the ages of six and sixteen!

Berton's speaker doesn't even mention free public health care, but he echoes accusations made familiar by its opponents. He calls the whole idea "foreign" and too costly; he complains that its advocates are "pie-in-the-sky idealists." We realize that we have heard these accusations before, but directed against another idea. Free clinics, Berton suggests, are just like free schools — a system we all take for granted. By this analogy, Berton implies that because public health care and public education are similar, they are equally practicable and desirable. If Berton were writing a serious, reasoned argument, then an opponent might protest that clinics and schools aren't quite alike and that Berton omits all their important differences. This is the central weakness in most arguments by analogy. Dwelling only on similarities, a writer doesn't consider *dissimilarities* — since to admit them might weaken the analogy.

Metaphor: See *Figures of Speech*.

Narration is the mode of writing that tells a story. See Chapter 1.

Objective and **Subjective** are names for kinds of writing that differ in emphasis. In objective writing, the emphasis falls on the topic; in subjective writing, it falls on the writer's view of the topic. Objective writing occurs in factual reporting, certain kinds of process analysis (such as recipes, directions, and instructions), and logical arguments in which the writer attempts to omit personal feelings and opinions. Subjective writing sets forth the writer's feelings, opinions, and interpretations. It occurs in friendly letters, journals, editorials, by-lined feature stories and columns in newspapers, personal essays, and arguments that appeal to emotion. Very few essays, however, contain one kind of writing exclusive of the other.

Paradox: See *Figures of Speech*.

Paragraph refers to a group of closely related sentences that develop a central idea. In an essay, a paragraph is the most important unit of thought because it is both self-contained and part of the larger whole. Paragraphs separate long and involved ideas into smaller parts that are more manageable for the writer and easier for the reader to take in. Good paragraphs, like good essays, possess unity and coherence. The central idea is usually stated in the topic sentence, often found at the beginning of the paragraph. All other sentences in the paragraph relate to this topic sentence, defining it, explaining it, illustrating it, providing it with evidence and support. Sometimes you will meet a unified and coherent paragraph that has no topic sentence. It usually contains a central idea that no sentence in it explicitly states, but that every sentence in it clearly implies.

Parallelism, or **parallel structure**, is a name for a habit of good writers: keeping ideas of equal importance in similar grammatical form. A writer may place nouns side by side ("*Time* and *tide* wait for no man") or in a series ("Give me *wind, sea,* and *stars*"). Phrases, too, may be arranged in parallel structure ("*Out of my bed, into my shoes, up to my classroom* — that's my life"); or clauses ("Ask not what your country can do for you; ask what you can do for your country").

Parallelism may be found not only in single sentences, but in larger units as well. A paragraph might read: "Rhythm is everywhere. It throbs in the rain forests of Brazil. It vibrates ballroom floors in Vienna. It snaps its fingers on street corners in Chicago." In a whole essay, parallelism may be the principle used to arrange ideas in a balanced or harmonious structure. See, for instance, James C. Rettie's essay " 'But a Watch in the Night,' " in which paragraphs 5 through 14 begin with transitions indicating when certain events took place. See the famous speech given by Martin Luther King, Jr. (Chapter 10), in which each paragraph in a series (paragraphs 11 through 18) begins with the words "I have a dream" and goes on to describe an imagined future. Not only does such a parallel structure organize ideas, but it also lends them force.

Paraphrase is putting another writer's thoughts into your own words. In writing a research paper or an essay containing evidence gathered from your reading, you will find it necessary to paraphrase — unless you are using another writer's very words with quotation marks around them. In paraphrasing, you rethink what the other writer has said, decide what is essential, and determine how you would say it otherwise. (Of course, you still acknowledge your source.) The purpose of paraphrasing is not merely to avoid copying word for word, but to adapt material to the needs of your own paper.

Although a paraphrase sometimes makes material briefer, it does not always do so; in principle, it rewrites and restates, sometimes in the same number of words, if not more. A condensation of longer material that renders it more concise is called a *summary*: for instance, a statement of the plot of a whole novel in a few sentences.

Person is a grammatical distinction made between the speaker, the one spoken to, and the one spoken about. In the first person (*I*, *we*), the subject is speaking; in the second person (*you*), the subject is being spoken to; in the third person (*he*, *she*, *it*), the subject is being spoken about. The *point of view* of an essay or work of fiction is often specified according to person: "This short story is told from a first person point of view." See *Point of View*.

Personification: See *Figures of Speech*.

Persuasion is a function of argument. See Chapter 10.

Point of View, in an essay, is the physical position or the mental angle from which a writer beholds a subject. Assuming the subject is starlings, the following three writers have different points of view. An ornithologist might write about the introduction of these birds into North America. A farmer might advise other farmers how to prevent the birds from eating seed. A bird-watcher might describe a first glad sighting of an unusual species. Furthermore, the *person* of each essay would probably differ. The scientist might present a scholarly paper in the third person; the farmer might offer advice in the second; the bird-watcher might recount the experience in the first. See *Person*.

Premise is a name for a proposition that supports a conclusion. In a *syllogism* we reason deductively from the major and minor premises to the conclusion that necessarily follows. See *Deduction*. In expository writing, premises are the assumptions on which an author bases an argument.

Prewriting generally refers to that stage or stages in the process of composition before words start to flow. It is the activity of the mind before setting pen or typewriter keys to paper, and may include evoking ideas, deciding on a topic, narrowing the topic, doing factual reading and research, defining your audience, planning and arranging material. An important stage of prewriting usually comes first: *invention*, the creation or discovery of ideas. Invention may follow from daydreaming or meditation, reading, keeping a journal, or perhaps carefully ransacking your memory.

As composition theorist D. Gordon Rohman has observed, prewriting may be defined as "the stage of discovery in the writing process when a person assimilates his subject to himself." In practice, the prewriting stage sometimes doesn't neatly end with the picking up of paper; reading, research, taking into account your audience, and further discovery may take place even while you write.

Process Analysis is a form of exposition that most often explains step by step how something is done or how to do something. See Chapter 5.

Purpose is a writer's reason for writing; it is whatever the writer of any work tries to achieve. To achieve unity and coherence, a writer identifies a purpose before beginning to write. The more clearly defined the purpose, the better the writer can concentrate on achieving it. In his essay "Fried Chicken" (Chapter 5), Jim Villas's general purpose is to analyze a process, and his particular purpose is to show the reader how to make what he considers the real thing.

In trying to define the purpose of an essay you read, ask yourself, "Why did the writer write this?" or "What was this writer trying to achieve?" Even though you cannot know the writer's intentions with absolute certainty, an effective essay always makes some purpose clear.

Rhetoric is the study (and the art) of using language effectively. Often the modes of prose discourse (narration, description, exposition, and argument) and the various methods of exposition (exemplification, comparison and contrast, and the others) are called rhetorical forms.

Rhetorical Question indicates a question posed for effect, one that requires no answer. Instead, it often provokes thought, lends emphasis to a point, asserts or denies something without making a direct statement, launches further discussion, introduces an opinion, or leads the reader where the writer intends. Sometimes a writer throws one in to introduce variety in a paragraph full of declarative sentences. The following questions are rhetorical: "When will the United States learn that sending men to the moon does not feed them on earth?" — "Shall I compare thee to a summer's day?" — "What shall it profit a man to gain the whole world if he lose his immortal soul?" Both reader and writer know what the answers are supposed to be. (1. Someday, if the United States ever wises up; 2. Yes; 3. Nothing.) For examples of rhetorical questions used well, see Malcolm Cowley's essay "Vices and Pleasures: The View from 80."

Satire is a form of writing that employs wit to attack folly. Unlike most comedy, the purpose of satire is not merely to entertain, but to bring about enlightenment — even reform. Frequently, satire will employ irony — as in Jonathan Swift's "A Modest Proposal." For other illustrations of this form see the essays by Brendan Boyd (Chapter 6) and Russell Baker (Chapter 9).

Sentimentality is a quality sometimes found in writing that fails to communicate. Such writing calls for an extreme emotional response on the part of an audience, although its writer fails to supply adequate reason for any such reaction. A sentimental writer delights in waxing teary over certain objects: great-grandmother's portrait, the first stick of chewing gum baby chewed (now a shapeless wad), an empty popcorn box saved from the World Series of 1952. Sentimental writing usually results when writers shut their eyes to the actual world, preferring to snuffle the sweet scents of remembrance.

Simile: See *Figures of Speech.*

Slang: See *Diction.*

Strategy refers to whatever means a writer employs to write effectively. The methods set forth in each chapter of this book are strategies; but so are narrowing a subject, organizing ideas clearly, using transitions, writing with an awareness of your reader, and other effective writing practices.

Style is the distinctive manner in which a writer writes; it may be seen especially in the writer's choice of words and sentence structure. Two writers may write on the same subject, even express similar ideas, but it is style that gives each writer's work a personality.

Suspense is often an element in narration: the pleasurable expectation or anxiety we feel that keeps us reading a story. In an exciting mystery story, suspense is constant: how will it all turn out? — Will the detective get to the scene in time to prevent another murder? But there can be suspense in less melodramatic accounts as well. In reading Larry L. King's "Shoot-out with Amarillo Slim," we probably suspect early in the essay that Slim will defeat the author; the suspense lies in our desire to see exactly how this defeat will come about.

Syllogism: is a name for a three-step form of reasoning that employs deduction. See page 425 for an illustration.

Symbol is a name for a visible object or action that suggests some further meaning. The flag suggests country, the crown suggests royalty — these are conventional symbols familiar to us. Life abounds in such relatively clear-cut symbols. Football teams use dolphins and rams for easy identification; married couples symbolize their union with a ring.

In writing, symbols usually do not have such a one-to-one correspondence, but evoke a whole constellation of associations. In Herman Melville's *Moby-Dick*, the whale suggests more than the large mammal it is. It hints at evil, obsession, and the untamable forces of nature. Such a symbol carries meanings too complex or elusive to be neatly defined.

More common in fiction and poetry than in expository writing, symbols can be used to good purpose in exposition because they often communicate an idea in a compact and concrete way. In Mark Twain's essay (Chapter 2) the steamboat suggests more to the Hannibal boys than just a means of transportation. It conveys glamour, excitement, wealth, commerce, far-off cities, and much more.

Thesis is the central idea in a work of writing, to which everything else in the work refers. In some way, each sentence and each paragraph in an effective essay serves to support the thesis and to make it clear and explicit to an audience. Good writers, before they begin to write, often set down a *thesis sentence* or *thesis statement* to help them define their purpose. This thesis sentence, for instance, might have served Andrew Ward in writing his essay in Chapter 3: "The miserable old neighborhood gas station was preferable to the self-service station of today."

Tone refers to the way a writer regards subject, audience, or self. It is the writer's attitude, and sets the prevailing spirit of whatever he or she writes. Tone in writing varies as greatly as tone of voice varies in conversation. It can be serious, distant, flippant, angry, enthusiastic, sincere, or sympathetic. Whatever tone a writer chooses, usually it informs an entire essay and helps a reader decide how to respond.

Topic sentence is a name for the statement of the central idea in a paragraph. Often it will appear at (or near) the beginning of the paragraph, announcing the idea and beginning its development. Because all other sentences in the paragraph explain and support this central idea, the topic sentence is a way to create unity.

Transitions are words, phrases, sentences, or even paragraphs that relate ideas. In moving from on topic to the next, a writer has to bring the reader along by showing how the ideas are developing, what bearing a new thought or detail has on an earlier discussion, or why a new topic is being introduced. A clear purpose, strong ideas, and logical development certainly aid coherence, but to ensure that the reader is following along, good writers provide signals, or transitions.

To bridge paragraphs and to point out relationships within them, you can use some of the following devices of transition:

1. Repeat words or phrases to produce an echo in the reader's mind.

2. Use parallel structures to produce a rhythm that moves the reader forward.

3. Use pronouns to refer back to nouns in earlier passages.

4. Use transitional words and phrases. These may indicate a relationship of time (*right away, later, soon, meanwhile, in a few minutes, that night*), of proximity (*beside, close to, distant from, nearby, facing*), effect (*therefore, for this reason, as a result, consequently*), comparison (*similarly, in the same way, likewise*), contrast (*yet, but, nevertheless, however, despite*). Some words and phrases of transition simply add on: *besides, too, also, moreover, in addition to, second, last, in the end.*

Understatement: See *Figures of Speech.*

Unity is the quality of good writing in which all parts relate to the thesis. (See *Thesis.*) In a unified essay, all words, sentences, and paragraphs support the single central idea. Your first step in achieving unity is to state your thesis; your next step is to organize your thoughts so that they make your thesis clear.

ESSAYS ARRANGED
BY SUBJECT

CHILDREN AND FAMILY

THE CONDUCT OF LIFE

CONTEMPORARY ISSUES

HISTORY

HUMOR AND SATIRE

LAW

WRITING AND LANGUAGE

Joan Didion, "In Bed." From *The White Album* by Joan Didion. Copyright © 1979 by Joan Didion. Reprinted by permission of Simon & Schuster, a Division of Gulf & Western Corporation.

J. Frank Dobie, "My Horse Buck." From *The Mustangs* by J. Frank Dobie. Copyright 1934, 1951, 1952 by The Curtis Publishing Company. Copyright 1936, 1949, 1950, 1951, 1952 by J. Frank Dobie.

Ellen Goodman, "Steering Clear of the One True Course." From *Close to Home* by Ellen Goodman. Copyright © 1979 by The Washington Post Company. Reprinted by permission of Simon & Schuster, a Division of Gulf & Western Corporation.

Jeff Greenfield, "The Black and White Truth about Basketball." Reprinted by permission of The Sterling Lord Agency, Inc. Copyright © 1980 by Jeff Greenfield as first appeared in *Esquire*.

James Herriot, "Just Like Bernard Shaw." From *The Lord God Made Them All* by James Herriot, published by St. Martin's Press, Inc., Macmillan & Co., Ltd. Reprinted by permission.

John Houseman, "The Night the Martians Landed." From "The Men from Mars," by John Houseman. Reprinted from *Harper's*, December 1948, by permission of the author.

Dina Ingber, "Computer Addicts." Reprinted from *Science Digest*, July 1981 by permission of the author.

Larry L. King, "Shoot-out with Amarillo Slim." From *Of Outlaws, Conmen, Whores, Politicians and Other Artists* by Larry King. Copyright © 1978 by Larry King. Reprinted by permission of Viking Penguin Inc.

Martin Luther King, Jr., "I Have a Dream." Reprinted by permission of Joan Daves. Copyright © 1963 by Martin Luther King, Jr.

H. L. Mencken, "The Penalty of Death." From *A Mencken Chrestomathy*, by H. L. Mencken. Copyright 1926 by Alfred A. Knopf, Inc. and renewed 1954 by H. L. Mencken. Reprinted by permission of Alfred A. Knopf, Inc.

Don Ethan Miller, "How the Bare Hand Passes Through the Bricks." Reprinted by permission of Candida Donadio & Associates, Inc. Copyright © 1980 by Don Ethan Miller. Originally appeared in *The Atlantic Monthly*, September 1980.

Jessica Mitford, "Behind the Formaldehyde Curtain." From *The American Way of Death* by Jessica Mitford. Copyright © 1963, 1978 by Jessica Mitford. Reprinted by permission of Simon & Schuster, a Division of Gulf & Western Corporation.

Harold J. Morowitz, "The Six Million Dollar Man." From *The Wine of Life and Other Essays on Societies, Energy and Living Things* by Harold J. Morowitz, published by St. Martin's Press, Inc., Macmillan & Co., Ltd. Reprinted by permission of the publisher.

Desmond Morris, "Salutation Displays." Excerpted from *Manwatching: A Field Guide to Human Behavior* by Desmond Morris. Text © 1977 by Desmond Morris. Published by Harry N. Abrams, Inc. Reprinted by permission of the publisher.

George Orwell, "Politics and the English Language." Copyright 1946, 1974 by Sonia Orwell. Reprinted from *Shooting an Elephant and Other Essays* by George Orwell by permission of Harcourt Brace Jovanovich, Inc.; the estate of the late George Orwell; and Martin Secker & Warburg.

William Ouchi, "Japanese and American Workers: Two Casts of Mind." Reprinted from *Theory Z: How American Business Can Meet the Japanese Challenge* by William G. Ouchi. Copyright © 1981, by permission of Addison-Wesley Publishing Co., Reading, MA.

Ruth B. Purtilo and Christine K. Cassel, "Hateful Patients: The Gomer, the Gork, and the Crock." Reprinted from *Ethical Dimensions in the Health Professions* (Philadelphia; W. B. Saunders, 1981). Used with permission.

James C. Rettie, " 'But a Watch in the Night': A Scientific Fable." From *Forever the Land* edited by Russell and Kate Lord. Copyright 1950 by Harper & Row, Publishers, Inc. Reprinted by permission of Harper & Row, Publishers, Inc.

Richard Rodriguez, "Aria: A Memoir of a Bilingual Childhood." First published in *The American Scholar*. Copyright © 1980, by Richard Rodriguez. Reprinted by permission of Brandt & Brandt Literary Agents Inc.

Roger Rosenblatt, "Oops! How's That Again?" Copyright 1981 Time Inc. All rights reserved. Reprinted by permission from *Time*.

A. M. Rosenthal, "No News from Auschwitz." © 1958 by The New York Times Company. Reprinted by permission.

Gail Sheehy, "Predictable Crises of Adulthood." Adapted from *Passages: Predictable Crises of Adult Life* by Gail Sheehy. Copyright © 1974, 1976 by Gail Sheehy. Reprinted by permission of the publisher, E. P. Dutton.

Judy Syfers, "I Want a Wife." Originally appeared in MS., December 31, 1971. Reprinted by permission of the author.

Lewis Thomas, "On Warts." From *The Medusa and the Snail* by Lewis Thomas. Copyright © 1979 by Lewis Thomas. Reprinted by permission of Viking Penguin Inc.

James Thurber, "University Days." Copyright © 1933, 1961, James Thurber. From *My Life and Hard Times*, published by Harper & Row.

Sheila Tobias, "Who's Afraid of Math, and Why?" Reprinted from *Overcoming Math Anxiety* by Sheila Tobias, with the permission of W. W. Norton & Company, Inc. Copyright © 1978 by Sheila Tobias.

Alvin Toffler, "The De-Massified Media." From *The Third Wave* by Alvin Toffler. Copyright © 1980 by Alvin Toffler. By permission of William Morrow & Company.

Susan Allen Toth, "Nothing Happened." From *Blooming: A Small-Town Girlhood* by Susan Allen Toth. © 1981 by Susan Allen Toth. By permission of Little, Brown and Company.

Barbara W. Tuchman, "An Inquiry into the Persistence of Unwisdom in Government." Reprinted by permission of Russell & Volkening, as agents for the author. Copyright © 1980, by Barbara W. Tuchman. First appeared in *Esquire*.

Gore Vidal, "Drugs." From *Homage to Daniel Shays: Collected Essays 1952–1972*, by Gore Vidal. Copyright © 1972 by Gore Vidal. Reprinted by permission of Random House, Inc.

Jim Villas, "Fried Chicken." From *Esquire* (December 1975). Copyright © 1975 by Esquire Publishing Inc. Used by permission.

Andrew Ward, "They Also Wait Who Stand and Serve Themselves." Copyright © 1979, by the Atlantic Monthly Company, Boston, Massachusetts. Reprinted with permission.

Marjorie Waters, "Coming Home" and "Selecting the Right Language." Copyright © 1982 by Marjorie Waters.

E. B. White, "Once More to the Lake." From *Essays of E. B. White* by E. B. White. Copyright 1941 by E. B. White. Reprinted by permission of Harper & Row, Publishers, Inc.

To the Student

We regularly revise the books we publish in order to make them better. To do this well we need to know what instructors and students think of the previous edition. At some point your instructor will be asked to comment on *The Bedford Reader*; now we would like to hear from you.

Please take a few minutes to complete this questionnaire and send it to Bedford Books of St. Martin's Press, 165 Marlborough Street, Boston, Massachusetts 02116. We promise to listen to what you have to say. Thanks.

School _____

School location (city, state) _____

Course title _____

Instructor's name _____

Please rate the selections.

	Liked a lot	Okay	Didn't like	Didn't read
Angelou, *Champion of the World*	___	___	___	___
Herriot, *Just Like Bernard Shaw*	___	___	___	___
Thurber, *University Days*	___	___	___	___
Froude, *The Execution of Queen Mary*	___	___	___	___
Didion, *In Bed*	___	___	___	___
Dobie, *My Horse Buck*	___	___	___	___
Twain, *S-t-e-a-m-boat a-comin!*	___	___	___	___
White, *Once More to the Lake*	___	___	___	___
Rosenblatt, *Oops! How's That Again?*	___	___	___	___
Ward, *They Also Wait Who Only Stand and Serve Themselves*	___	___	___	___
Ingber, *Computer Addicts*	___	___	___	___

	Liked a lot	Okay	Didn't like	Didn't read
Cowley, *Vices and Pleasures: The View from 80*	——	——	——	——
Kantrov, *Women's Business*	——	——	——	——
Postscript on Process	——	——	——	——
Greenfield, *The Black and White Truth About Basketball*	——	——	——	——
Ouchi, *Japanese and American Workers: Two Casts of Mind*	——	——	——	——
Catton, *Grant and Lee: A Study in Contrasts*	——	——	——	——
Rosenthal, *No News from Auschwitz*	——	——	——	——
Goodman, *Shouts and Whispers: Academic Life in the Sixties and Seventies*	——	——	——	——
Postscript on Process	——	——	——	——
Villas, *Fried Chicken*	——	——	——	——
King, *Shoot-out with Amarillo Slim*	——	——	——	——
Mitford, *Behind the Formaldehyde Curtain*	——	——	——	——
Miller, *How the Bare Hand Passes Through the Bricks*	——	——	——	——
Boyer, *How to Hype Hot Dogs*	——	——	——	——
Postscript on Process	——	——	——	——
Syfers, *I Want a Wife*	——	——	——	——
Purtilo and Cassel, *Hateful Patients: The Gomer, the Gork and the Crock*	——	——	——	——
Sheehy, *Predictable Crises of Adulthood*	——	——	——	——
Morris, *Salutation Displays*	——	——	——	——

	Liked a lot	Okay	Didn't like	Didn't read
Boyd, *Packaged News*	___	___	___	
Postscript on Process	___	___	___	___
Luke, *Three Parables*	___	___	___	___
Crompton, *The Magnitude of the Spider's Task*	___	___	___	___
Rettie, *"But a Watch in the Night": A Scientific Fable*	___	___	___	___
Melville, *Fast-Fish and Loose-Fish*	___	___	___	___
Waters, *Coming Home*	___	___	___	___
Postscript on Process	___	___	___	___
Vidal, *Drugs*	___	___	___	___
Thomas, *On Warts*	___	___	___	___
Tobias, *Who's Afraid of Math, and Why?*	___	___	___	___
Houseman, *The Night the Martians Landed*	___	___	___	___
Traugot, *The Children Who Wait*	___	___	___	___
Postscript on Process	___	___	___	___
Baker, *Work in Corporate America*	___	___	___	___
Morowitz, *The Six Million Dollar Man*	___	___	___	___
Cooke, *Justice Holmes and the Doffed Bikini*	___	___	___	___
Toffler, *The De-Massified Media*	___	___	___	___
Goshgarian, *Zeroing in on Science Fiction*	___	___	___	___
Postscript on Process	___	___	___	___
Goodman, *Steering Clear of the One True Course*	___	___	___	___

	Liked a lot	Okay	Didn't like	Didn't read
Mencken, *The Penalty of Death*	___	___	___	___
Buckley, *Why Don't We Complain?*	___	___	___	___
King, *I Have a Dream*	___	___	___	___
Lempesis, *Murder in a Bottle*	___	___	___	___
Postscript on Process	___	___	___	___
Swift, *A Modest Proposal*	___	___	___	___
Thoreau, *Getting a Living*	___	___	___	___
Orwell, *Politics and the English Language*	___	___	___	___
Toth, *Nothing Happened*	___	___	___	___
Rodriguez, *Aria: A Memoir of a Bilingual Childhood*	___	___	___	___
Tuchman, *An Inquiry into the Persistence of Unwisdom in Government*	___	___	___	___

Are there any writers not included you would like to see added?

_____

_____

Any general comments or suggestions? _____

_____

_____

Name _____

Mailing Address _____

Date_____